NO PEACE

The dog following the children in the bayou began barking. That surprised one of the children who had been reaching for the side of the boat. The small figure toppled over in the water and disappeared beneath its surface with a gurgling shriek of surprise and panic.

Larry was running toward the weed-choked banks before he was conscious of having risen to his feet. And in between strides, the full mosaic of unfolding disaster became clear.

The barking dog had only been part of the reason the child had stumbled and was now in over its head. The more urgent fact was that the last coil of the mooring line had obviously been lazily laid and, with the persistent, gentle motion of the water, had slipped free. That extra play in the mooring line had allowed the boat to drift three or four feet farther from the shore, where the shelflike apron of mud and sand gave way to a steeper drop-off into five feet of water.

But the dog's bark had not been a warning of deeper water ahead, but rather, predators inbound. As his long strides carried Larry closer to the edge of the bayou, they also put more of the tunnel of tree canopy behind him. The increased periphery of sightlines showed him what the dog was barking at: a pair of mostly sunken narrow logs drifting downstream in the direction of the children.

Except those were not logs.

They were alligators.

THE RING OF FIRE SERIES

To purchase any of these titles in e-book form, please go to www.baen.com.

1637
NO PEACE
BEYOND THE LINE

ERIC FLINT
CHARLES E. GANNON

1637: No Peace Beyond the Line

This is a work of fiction. All the characters and events portrayed in this book are fictional, and any resemblance to real people or incidents is purely coincidental.

A Baen Books Original

Baen Publishing Enterprises
P.O. Box 1403
Riverdale, NY 10471
www.baen.com

ISBN: 978-1-9821-2574-5

Cover art by Tom Kidd
Maps by Michael Knopp

First printing, November 2020
First mass market printing, November 2021

Distributed by Simon & Schuster
1230 Avenue of the Americas
New York, NY 10020

Library of Congress Control Number: 2020031321

Pages by Joy Freeman (www.pagesbyjoy.com)
Printed in the United States of America

10 9 8 7 6 5 4 3 2 1

To My Wife,
Andrea Trisciuzzi,
with love and deep, deep gratitude.
She made this career possible,
and this book even more so.

If it was not for her and her sacrifices
to ensure that I had the time to
complete it when necessary, you would
not have this in your hands now.

—Charles E. Gannon

To my grandchildren, Lucy and Zachary

—Eric Flint

Contents

The Caribbean
as of Jan. 1636

Anguilla
St Maarten
St Barthelemy
Saba
St. Eustatia
St. Christopher
Nevis
Montserrat

Anegada Passage

Vieques
St. Croix

Bermuda

Atlantic Ocean

The Bahamas

Tortuga
Luperón

Havana

Greater Antilles

Hispaniola

Santo Domingo
Isla Saona

Mona Passage

San Juan

Puerto Rico

Anegada Passage

Leeward Islands

Antigua

Guadeloupe

Dominica

Martinique

Windward Islands

Barbados

Grenada

Caribbean Sea

Leeward Antilles

Aruba
Curaçao
Bonaire

Puerto Cabello

Tobago

Trinidad

Gulf of
Paria

Tierra Firme

Cartagena

Michael Knopp

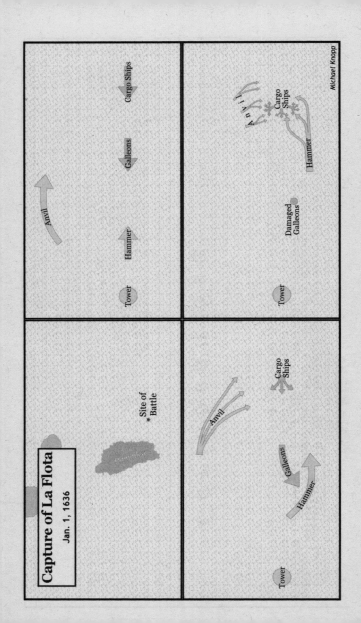

Capture of La Flota
Jan. 1, 1636

Dominica

Site of Battle

Anvil

Cargo Ships

Galleons

Hammer

Tower

Anvil

Cargo Ships

Galleons

Hammer

Tower

Damaged Galleons

Anvil

Cargo Ships

Hammer

Tower

Michael Knopp

Trinidad
as of Jan. 1636

Dragon's Mouth

Port of Spain

San José de Oruña

Gulf of Paria

Fort St. Patrick

Pitch Lake

Point Fortin

Michael Knopp

Battle of Pitch Lake
as of Jan. 1636

Tropic Surveyor & Jachts

Rear Echelon

Spanish Fleet

Spanish Infantry Landing Point

Landing

Echelon 1

Fort St. Patrick

Pitch Lake

Cornelisz.'s of Ships

Fluyts Hiding Behind Pt. Fortin

Michael Knopp

| 0 | 500 | 1,000 | 1,500 | 2,000 m |

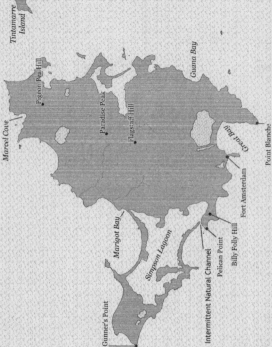

St. Maarten
as of Jan. 1636

Tintamarre Island

Marcel Cove

Pigeon Pea Hill

Paradise Peak

Flagstaff Hill

Guana Bay

Marigot Bay

Gunner's Point

Simpson Lagoon

Intermittent Natural Channel

Pelican Point

Billy Folly Hill

Fort Amsterdam

Great Bay

Point Blanche

Michael Knopp

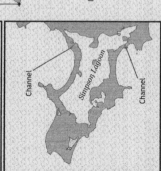

Simpson Lagoon
as shown on Up-Time Maps

Channel

Simpson Lagoon

Channel

Part One

April–May 1636

Pale ravener of horrible meat
—Herman Melville,
"The Maldive Shark"

Chapter 1

East of the island of Dominica

Commodore Eddie Cantrell looked past the bowsprit of the USE steam cruiser *Intrepid* into the nautical twilight brightening the eastern horizon. The stars above it were fading slowly, the predawn glow washing out what had been their laser-sharp brilliance of only a few minutes before. But on those days when his time on deck started along with the morning watch, he had learned that this was not just a time for novel sights.

Eddie closed his eyes and listened: wind, sails slapping lightly, the slow hobnail-on-wood tread of the closest of the four crew walking watch on the main deck. On a ship in the seventeenth century, that was as hushed and quiet a moment as one ever experienced.

He opened his eyes as he turned and looked west. The stars were still bright there, but an irregular dark hump of blackness blotted them out at the center of the horizon: Dominica. More or less at the center of the eastward bowing arc of the Lesser Antilles, the island was known for terrain and inhabitants that were equally unforgiving. No colony had ever been successfully planted upon it. And if Eddie and his bosses had their way, none ever would be.

A faint, lazy hiss of rubber on hemp, a sound out of place on most ships of this era, drew his attention upward. Rising from a vertical guide tube laid along the mainmast, a thin strand of blackness disappeared into the gloom overhead. At first glance, it was as if a solitary hair of a dark-maned goddess had sprung loose from her tresses and fallen to brush along the surface of the mortal earth.

But staring overhead dispelled the illusion: it was a tarred rope and a naturally black telegrapher's wire, loosely twinned as they rose and disappeared into the night sky—or rather, into a small circle of absolute darkness that blotted out the stars behind it. That was the silhouette of *Intrepid*'s observation balloon, almost seven hundred and thirty feet above the deck. Although it had ascended to that new height while training for this operation, this was the highest ceiling it had ever made during an active mission.

Happily, there hadn't been any surprises since they'd commenced filling the balloon's envelope with hot air, just before six bells of the middle watch. But that was less a matter of luck than preparation. As Eddie's commanding officer and stern (albeit increasingly paternal) mentor Admiral Simpson had taught him, training for actual operations is effective only so far as it is faithful to real conditions. And they had certainly applied that in regard to this ascent.

The challenge to increase the balloon's maximum operating ceiling had required a consideration of diverse factors. Rate of fuel consumption determined the average temperature of the air in the envelope which also determined rate of ascent. But going higher meant more rope to tether the balloon to its platform (in this case, *Intrepid*), and more of the perpetually scarce telegraph cable. That additional weight meant it was necessary to generate more lift, lighten the operational weight of the vehicle, or both.

With considerable mental and physical effort, that had been achieved over the winter, but the solutions had consequences and complications of their own. Reduced duration required a more disciplined schedule of activities while aloft and greater attention to the meteorological signs of optimum flying weather. Those new demands combined to impose additional criteria upon the selection process for new observers: lighter physical bodies and greater educational prerequisites. Less operational time meant that more work had to be conducted with greater accuracy in fewer minutes, including swift and near-flawless signaling of observations back down to the wire.

But the difficulties and the costs had now proved their worth, as Eddie had insisted they would. Before, the balloons that served the naval amalgam of both United States of Europe and Dutch warships had been lucky to see a vessel at thirty-three nautical miles. Now, they had proven that they could spot a galleon's topsails at better than thirty-eight miles. Practically speaking, even if an oncoming ship was making four knots, that gave an hour and fifteen minutes of additional warning. That much more time to slip away unseen, or to set a wide-ranging ambush from which the spotted ship would have no escape.

But at this particular point in the Atlantic Ocean, just six and a half nautical miles due east of Baraisiri Pointe on Dominica's wave-whitened windward side,

those five extra miles of range became ten extra miles
of observational diameter. Consequently, the observer
in the balloon would not only detect ships approaching directly, but also, any that made for either of
the channels that bracketed the island behind them:
the Dominica Passage, which separated it from Guadeloupe to the north; and the Martinique Passage,
which separated it from the island of the same name
to the south. In short, *Intrepid*'s airborne eyes covered
a seventy-six-mile-wide expanse that no sizeable ship
could cross without her being aware. Which was the
entire strategic and tactical reason for *Intrepid* to be
waiting at this precise latitude and longitude.

Eddie stifled a yawn. If only they had had equally
precise data for determining the day that they had to
begin waiting there. And in point of fact, they had not
been one hundred percent certain that their current
position was casting a wide enough net to catch the
fish ... well, the whale ... they were after. All the intel
from the USE and its closest allies pointed toward
the week *Intrepid* should be on station, but even that
was only an estimate.

Boots behind; a slower tread, not hobnailed. "Report
as you requested, Commodore Cantrell."

Eddie turned, nodded at his tall, lanky executive
officer. "A smile, Svantner? Some unusually good news
to report?"

The Swede shook his head. "No, sir. Frankly, I
don't know how the news could get any better than
it already is. This is just a confirmation that their
formation is still on the same heading. That's almost
an hour now. Unlikely they would adjust course before
clapping eyes on Dominica, sir."

"Very good, Svantner, but still: why the grin?"

"Well, damned if they aren't right where you said they would be, Commodore." He aimed his prominent nose forward, as if to compete with the prow. "Radios and telegraphs and steamships don't answer to all of it. Nor even luck." He shook his head. "Seems to me that God loves each of you up-timers so much that he doesn't just put a sage's library between your ears. He whispers into them about time, tides, and fortunes, too."

Eddie merely nodded. Months ago, his first impulse would have been to attempt to explain that while fortune was certainly not working against them, this morning's success owed little to chance. But time and acquaintance had taught him that Svantner's mind, while quick to learn and well ordered, was of neither a figurative nor philosophical bent. If anything, it was *too* well ordered, inclined to perceive the world as an improbably tidy and well-defined place. For the tall Swede, whatever contemporary knowledge did not explain was attributable to the works of a just yet unknowable God. That he also implicitly believed that the same God possessed an innate preference for Western perspectives, values, and outcomes evidently did not strike him as being inconsistent with a deity characterized by mysteries of both intent and method.

Svantner's voice was like a vocal jog at the elbow of Eddie's awareness. "Orders, sir?"

Eddie nodded. "Radio check. And summon the flight master to the winches. We'll soon need his gang up here for reeling her in. Also, pass this word along to the comms master's mate: send code Delta Five Charlie."

The Swede frowned. "Sir? I do not believe I have been apprised of an internal communication with that designation—"

Eddie waved a stilling hand at Svantner. "Last-minute change, Arne. That code is for relay to the observer in the balloon. No way to know we'd spot the bad guys this far off, but it's dark and they're running stern lights." *Because why should they anticipate that anyone could spot them at this hour and so far out?* "So they won't see anything when our observer uses the Aldis lamp at cherubs five."

"So: descent to five hundred and hold to signal. Very good, Commodore. Will you be wanting to raise steam?"

Eddie met Svantner's frank, dutiful eyes for a moment before smiling and shaking his head. "No, XO. If the wind holds, we can save the fuel and move to Objective Bravo by canvas alone. Send the word."

A crisp "Aye, sir!" accompanied Arne's equally crisp salute, which was followed by a sharp step toward the speaking tube down to the intraship comms cubby, just beneath *Intrepid*'s flying bridge.

Eddie watched and listened to Svantner pass the orders smoothly, efficiently, smartly down to the master's mate, then respond to an unheard question from the comms master in the radio room. Svantner was a solid officer, a good sailor, enjoyed the respect of the crew, knew *Intrepid* in all her particulars. He even understood how they functioned in relation to each other: no small feat, given the complexities of a ship which incorporated steam, a new hull type with new sailing characteristics, and several electronic systems. He was an eminently capable tactical XO, and had even displayed good-natured flexibility when that designation officially replaced the title that he, like his colleagues, had grown to manhood coveting: first mate. He might even make a fine post captain one day, but he would never truly grasp that the new technologies did not merely improve performance statistics, but signified a complete transformation in the calculus of how war at sea would now be conducted.

This had nothing to do with any intellectual want on Svantner's part, but what the machinery and its application implied about the increasing reliance upon intelligence reports. And of course, research. Often mind-numbingly meticulous research, such as the kind that Eddie had conducted for the mission to the New World under the direction of Admiral John Simpson.

Long before today's operation could have even been envisioned, it was understood that even with balloons and radios and the improved signaling of Aldis lamps, the USE's formations would be at pains to gather a timely and expansive knowledge of their battlespace. Fortunately, Simpson had known there was another advantage the up-timers could count on, at least for a while: precision charts. Compared to the mostly approximated shapes and distances on down-time maps, up-time cartography was nothing short of miraculous in its precision and quality of render. What that meant to a commander in terms of projecting travel times, rendezvous points, or—in the current case—patrol areas was difficult to overstate.

Eddie smiled and glanced south. Out there, well over the horizon, was a small, swift Dutch jacht. And beyond her view of the southern horizon was yet another, similar ship. And another beyond that, and so forth. To the north, a similar but shorter daisy chain of fore-and-aft-rigged pickets waited at the same intervals. And because they were able to maintain relatively constant positions by periodically triangulating on the landmarks behind them, the actual interception net that Eddie's recon mission had cast was almost three times the width of the observation diameter from the balloon. Or in other words, slightly more than two hundred miles. Because if their target had approached from further to the north or the south, the captains of those jachts were prepared to fire long-barreled launchers that would send magnesium-tipped flares high into the night sky. Flares which the adjacent picket ships were sure to see and relay, since—again because of the precision charts—they knew exactly what part of the sky they had to keep under constant observation.

Eddie felt his smile grow rueful as he recalled the monotonous labor which had led to the creation of those charts. After recovering from the loss of his left foot and ankle and arriving at his new naval posting in Magdeburg, he was made Simpson's aide and line-officer-in-training. And creating the precision navigational charts he was now relying upon had been his first job. And the only way to accomplish it was to pull the needed information from materials that had come along for the ride when the Ring of Fire swept them from twentieth-century West Virginia to seventeenth-century Germany.

The first step was to explore and catalog every relevant source in Grantville, a tedious task compared to the one he would have much rather been embarked upon: exploring and cataloging all the characteristics of his beautiful new wife's mind and body. Albeit not always in that order.

However, one visit to Grantville revealed that the high school was not going to be the convenient mother lode for this particular data mining operation. It had plenty of maps of every region of the globe, but they were the kind with which you teach geography, rather than navigate. Instead, upon going to the house of a recently deceased up-time boater, Eddie discovered where he would find the actual treasure trove of nautical maps: in the personal collections of naval buffs.

What followed next was a little detective work and a lot of socializing. Specifically, finding out which of Grantville's citizens had known about the community's other devotees of all things maritime, and then getting cooperation from those individuals—or, in almost half of the cases, their heirs. It seemed that a yen for the tales and technologies of the high seas was heavily correlated with older folks—not because of their advanced years, Eddie realized, but because of the topics that had inspired and sparked young imaginations back when they had been kids.

He sent a preliminary report of his findings to Simpson. It produced two results: a request to Ed Piazza for a half-dozen individuals—drawn from the State of Thuringia and Franconia's bureaucracy, if need be—to search for useful documents and images in the houses of those who had agreed to cooperate. Secondly, the admiral ordered Eddie to return to Magdeburg at once with the greatest treasures he had unearthed so far: books that provided not only details, but diagrams of the construction of various Civil War-era vessels. Most notably, both the Union

ships *Hartford* and *Kearsarge*: the vessels that the
USE's steam cruisers and steam destroyers had been
patterned upon, respectively. Eddie had telegraphed
back: what was he to do about the growing pile of
maps? Simpson's response came back so quickly it was
a wonder that the electrons had been able to keep
up with it: "Transshipment to Magdeburg not your
concern. Process as they arrive HQ."

And so Eddie did. Crate upon crate of personal
collections that had belonged to people who'd been
fascinated by all things nautical. However, the books
did not actually make the most decisive contributions to Eddie's cartographic quest. Rather, it was
what had been found slipped in amidst them, at the
back of bookcases, lurking even in the pages of well-
worn manuals: maps and navigation charts of places
to which their starry-eyed owners would never go.
Happily, the Caribbean and the Gulf of Mexico had
been their preferred stuff of dreams, perhaps because
their comparative proximity made those regions seem
more accessible, more easy to imagine going to one
distant day.

A would-be mariner's mind is a strange thing, Eddie
had decided as he catalogued countless charts that
had never been used. Indeed, actual boaters would
not have had use for the majority of them unless they
had made a project of sailing to the most obscure
ports of the Greater and Lesser Antilles. And yet
those charts had been pored over. Their edges were
crinkled and yellowed from the lustful touch of those
whose longing to set the sails and man the wheels of
tall ships had never gone beyond sitting hunched on
the thwart of a square-bowed skiff, motionless upon

an inland Appalachian lake, fishing rod in hand and high seas in their minds' eyes.

Sorting through the water-stained cardboard boxes was often complicated by the age of the would-be captains, the sad chaos of encroaching dementia wreaking havoc among what were already erratic filing systems. But by the time he finished categorizing and collating and assembling, Eddie had compiled an extraordinarily detailed picture of most of the Caribbean and much of the Gulf of Mexico: the area to which he and his flotilla—Task Force X-Ray—had been dispatched not quite a year earlier.

The ship's bell rang once. Eddie didn't listen for the other two he knew were coming. It was 0530. The watching and waiting was over.

Now it was time to move.

Chapter 2

East of Dominica

"Mr. Svantner!" Eddie cried, stepping forward on his ergonomically designed prosthesis.

"Sir!" the Swede shouted in the reply, approaching at the double-quick.

"Are all sections in readiness for next evolution?"

"They are, sir!"

"Very good. Pilot?"

"Sir!" came the response from the opened steel shutters of the flying bridge.

"We will be proceeding under sail only."

"Aye, sir!"

"Flight master?"

"Here, sir!"

"Reel platform down to five hundred feet." Eddie leaned toward the speaking tube. "Comms mate, send Delta Alpha Charlie to the observer."

"Signaling directions, sir?"

"Observer already has them, down to the degree. He'll want this, though: send code India Echo Zero Delta."

Svantner frowned. "Aye-ee-zero-dee, sir?"

14

"'Intercept envelope is zero deviation' from plan, Svantner. As you said, they're right where we hoped they'd be."

He nodded. "So the pickets will start closing search net around them?"

"That our opponents won't fully see for another five hours." Eddie noticed that Svantner was looking back toward Dominica, or rather, through it. "Concerns, Arne?"

"Sir," the Swede murmured, keeping his voice low, "I'm still...unsettled about the lack of a rearguard, sir."

Eddie appreciated his XO's attempt at discretion; ratings were already running past them, having been brought up by three bells. *Intrepid*'s crew was readying her for the next evolution. He leaned closer to his subordinate. "Svantner, I appreciate the reservations you had about having so many jachts on picket duty and none watching the waters behind us. But firstly, we didn't have enough jachts on hand to do both jobs, and secondly, we wanted to see what would happen if we turned our backs."

Svantner frowned. "Sir? I don't follow."

Eddie sighed. "I know. And I regret that we couldn't include you in the brief. But when we outlined this plan to the civilian council back at Oranjestad two weeks ago, we didn't do that to keep them apprised. We did it to see if there were intel leaks."

Svantner blinked. "Sir?"

Eddie shrugged. "It was a test, to see if any of them were either knowing or unwitting intel sources for our enemies."

Svantner's eyes widened. "So if there had been any ships behind us now..."

". . . it would strongly suggest that the Spanish, or more likely their pirate lackeys, had gotten word and come out here to make some mischief."

"And did you actually reveal our objective to them?"

Eddie shrugged. "We had to give them some warning regarding the amount of work that will be returning back to home port with us, if we are successful. So we gave them the bare-bone basics."

Arne's frown was back. "But we still can't be sure that there aren't ships lying in wait further behind us."

Eddie smiled. "Well, they'd have appeared behind Admiral Tromp. Granted, he's been underway since we first telegraphed our sighting of the enemy an hour and a half ago. But he did leave one jacht behind, tucked near Dominica's southern headland to watch for any unwelcome company. But frankly, we already had a dedicated force patrolling to leeward of these islands."

Svantner didn't even try to conceal his perplexity. "And what force would that be, sir?"

"Our own, well, 'pirates.'"

The Swede's face rapidly transformed into an ugly combination of surprise and disgust. "Our pirates? So we are resorting to the same tactics as the Spanish?"

Eddie frowned. "Watch your tone—and your volume—XO. Our pirates remain so because we don't have authority to give most of them letters of marque. Most are affiliated with Moses Cohen Henriques Eanes, who's been coordinating with Cornelis Jol for years now."

The confusion had left Svantner's face, but the disapproval remained, darker than before. "As you said, sir: our own pirates."

"Mr. Svantner, if you cannot set aside your compunctions enough to remain fully committed to the operation and respectful to your superiors, then you may consider yourself relieved for the duration of this operation."

The dark expression—and all color—bled out of the Swede's face. "I simply regret that we are compelled to employ such . . . expedients, sir. It caught me by surprise."

Of course it did. Another reason why you'll never make more than post captain. "I understand, Arne. But they were the perfect rear pickets in that even our adversaries would not suspect them of helping us that way. And oddly, they were far less likely to be a source of intelligence leaks. Moses and Jol were contacted over a month ago and have been cruising these waters since, watching for intruders and without putting into port. All coordinated through scheduled meetings at uninhabited locales. And the one or two times pirates thought they'd have a go at our convoys to and from Trinidad, they broke off as soon as they saw the escorts coming after them."

"And so Jol and Moses have not reported any contacts?"

"None, although if they had an encounter in the past two days, we might not have heard about it, yet. They operate independently and they are outside the intelligence loop on this operation."

Svantner lowered his head, frowning. "I see, sir."

Eddie thought it possible that he did, in fact. "As soon as the comms mate reports that the observer has finished signaling to the pickets, complete recovery of the balloon."

The Swede nodded sharply at someone well beyond Eddie's shoulder. "Those orders are being executed now, Commodore. Anything else?"

"It's time to send our final message to Tromp."

He nodded. "I'll send up the runner, sir." Svantner saluted and darted away, seeming a bit relieved to go.

His departure gave Eddie an unobstructed view over the taffrail, where the outline of Dominica was growing clearer against the brightening sky. Although the sun was only half an hour away from rising above the opposite horizon, the stars were still faintly visible over the dark landmass astern. He recognized the early-morning constellations—and suddenly found himself recollecting a similar sky he'd seen on an early-morning astronomy outing for his senior year science class. That had been six years ago—or, from another perspective, three hundred sixty-four years in the future. A future that could now never occur, given all the changes wrought by the appearance of Grantville and its inhabitants.

"Commodore Cantrell, sir?" asked a young voice at his elbow. Eddie's runner—a skinny eleven-year-old with a stubbornly unruly thatch of dirty blond hair—was waiting with pad in hand. Eddie smiled. "Ready, Cas?"

"As always, sir!"

"Okay. From E. Cantrell, CO *Intrepid* to M. Tromp, aboard *Resolve*, D. Simonszoon CO. Message follows.

"Confirming all prior reports. Stop. Detected OPFOR lights 0400, appx thirty-seven NM due east Baraisiri Pointe, Dominica. Stop. Heading was west southwest, making four knots with stern wind and following seas. Stop. Observations at 0430 and 0500 show course and speed unchanged. Stop. As per OPORD, am commencing evolution Bravo. Stop. Balloon secured and *Intrepid* under sail to Guadeloupe, Petit Cul-de-Sac Marin. Stop. Wind over starboard quarter. Stop. ETA 1300. Stop."

Eddie considered a moment. He was averse to speculation, but he should convey some impression of the enemy's numbers. He added:

"OPFOR estimated at fifty primary hulls. Stop. Two to four smaller craft, probably packets. Stop. Formation consistent with descriptions of OPFOR's prior Dominica landfalls. Stop. Message ends." He nodded at Cas. "Read it back, please."

Cas did so, ending with: "Revisions or additions, sir?"

Eddie shook his head. "No. Send it and advise when receipt is confirmed."

"Aye, sir," and Cas was off with a light-footed scampering.

As that sound faded, the creaking of the balloon's lines became louder and sharper as it neared the poop deck, the mizzen boom having been cleared to provide enough room for its operations off the quarterdeck.

"XO!" Eddie shouted.

Svantner appeared as swiftly as a summoned spirit. "Yes, sir?"

Cantrell nodded toward the just-landed balloon, bulging and swaying like a distressed gaseous amoeba. "As soon as the envelope is clear, bring the boom inboard, and smartly. Sail handlers to stand ready."

"They'll be hopping to the task, sir. Wouldn't do to be around when La Flota arrives and finds Admiral Tromp waiting for them, would it, sir?"

"No," Eddie affirmed, glancing east to where this year's treasure fleet from Spain was approaching in the distant dark. "It wouldn't do at all."

Chapter 3

East of Dominica

Admiral Maarten Tromp lowered the spyglass, which he still preferred to the binoculars being made in Amsterdam. "The leading galleons are within two nautical miles." He leaned toward the runner. "Tell the captain that he will want to beat to quart—" He checked himself with a small smile. "He will want to sound general quarters."

He gestured for the waiting signalman. "Send the word to the fleet: prepare to engage the enemy." As the comms rating disappeared down the companionway to the various control compartments under the cruiser's armored pilothouse, drums and coronets arose in contending staccato alerts. Deckhands began clearing for action. The weather shrouds were lifted and borne away from both the fore and aft eight-inch wire-wrapped breechloaders.

The sea was just choppy enough that its sibilant rise and rush drowned out most of the similar flourishes and tattoos that followed a moment later on the two closest ships: *Salamander* and Tromp's own fifty-four-gun *Amelia*.

Except that today, it was not *his* ship. In keeping with one of the few parallels between both seventeenth-century and up-time naval practice, admirals were not also the captains of their own vessel. Managing an entire battle while simultaneously directing the operations of a warship were deemed beyond the ability of any human to perform without severely undercutting both. Each role involved too many wholly disparate activities, all of which were infamous for how quickly they could go wrong without warning—and potentially, at the same time. In short, Maarten Tromp acknowledged that there was good reason not to be the captain of a ship today.

But that didn't mean he was comfortable with it. He glanced over at *Amelia*, three hundred yards to starboard, and thought he saw a single curt hand wave from the back near the stern. Probably not the current captain, but his own first mate—*no, "executive officer"*—who he had left behind there: Adriaen Banckert. Almost as accomplished a mariner as his father the admiral, the twenty-year-old had not taken it as a slight, but rather, as a point of pride that Tromp had left him on *Amelia*: as the admiral had explained, aside from himself, no one knew the ship better than young Banckert.

Well, Tromp reflected, perhaps *Amelia*'s prior XO, Cornelis "Kees" Evertsen, could lay claim to equal knowledge. But young Kees had one of the most rare and important aptitudes among all the Dutch officers: an innate knack for working with both the complexities and strange synergies of the up-time technologies that predominated upon *Resolve*. Because of that, Tromp had apologetically called him away from his first independent command, the swift thirty-eight-gun *Wappen van Rotterdam*, to serve as his personal aide and staff officer while aboard the USE steam cruiser. An admiral's assistant has to be at least as conversant with the new realities of the war as the commander himself, and Kees was one of the few who met that criterion.

Tromp glanced to port, over the lively dark blue waters, in-running crests stippled bright white in the late-morning sun. He could just pick out *Wappen van Rotterdam*, the northern- and easternmost hull of the squadron that Maarten had dubbed his fleet's "Anvil." A fine, smooth sailer, she looked eager to run against the Spanish, like a sprinter leaning forward eagerly, anticipating the thrill of the trials to come.

Tromp not only heard someone approach his other side, but could sense it in the way the wind, channeled between two adjacent bodies, began to buffet his sleeve on that side.

"Inspecting the *Wappen*, Admiral?" It was Kees' voice.

Tromp squinted against a gust and the brightness of the sun. "I was. To the extent that unaided eyes may. And you? Eyes or thoughts upon your ship, just now?"

Evertsen took a half step forward. "Yes, but she's not *my* ship, today." He smiled sideways at his commanding officer. "I saw your attention was upon *Amelia*, a few moments ago. Thinking similar thoughts, perhaps?"

Tromp smiled back. "Perhaps."

A brusque, darker voice put an abrupt end to whatever reveries might have followed. "And how does it feel, letting the Spanish have the weather gauge, Admiral?"

Tromp smiled, turned slightly more to his left. Dirck Simonszoon, captain of *Resolve*, came up on the admiral's other side. By general acclaim, Simonszoon was the best mariner—and most laconically taciturn— among the Dutch captains. He nodded out beyond the bowsprit; it edged a bit toward the sky before drifting back down to point at the approaching galleons. "I'm sure they're not complaining about having the advantage, today."

Tromp nodded. "I'm sure they're not. And I share your unease, Dirck. This is an unnerving position, when our whole lives have been spent making sure we have the wind coming over our quarter and the enemy on our bow."

"And here we are, doing the opposite."

Tromp heard Simonszoon's unvoiced addition: *"And on your orders, no less."*

From a few feet further aft, a younger voice offered a counterpoint, not just higher in pitch, but spirits: "Ah, but you must concede, Captain Simonszoon, that this is an excellent opportunity to put our new technical training to the only test that matters: against an enemy on the open sea."

Dirck turned a baleful glare upon his young Norwegian XO, Henrik Bjelke, whose effortless and thorough understanding of the steamships seemed akin to an up-timer's. "Remind me, Rik: I used a word to describe you last week. But it's slipped my mind. It was a word I had been looking for since you became my 'executive officer' half a year ago. But I've forgotten the term. I've even forgotten how I stumbled upon it."

Rik's cheeks reddened a bit; Tromp was quite sure it was not from the occasionally gusting wind. "I suspect it may have slipped your mind because you were in a state of...of singular inspiration, sir."

Dirck's answering frown was histrionic. "Eh? 'Singular inspiration'?"

Tromp smiled. Kees was trying very hard not to.

Lieutenant Bjelke stood straight. "At the tavern, sir. A month ago, actually, not a week. Just before we weighed anchor for this mission."

Dirck rolled his eyes. "You are altogether too well mannered, Rik. If I was bleary-eyed in my cups, just say so. But take care to start that assassination of my character with the honorific 'sir,' or I'll have you flogged and keelhauled. At the same time."

A suffocated laugh burst beyond Kees' tightly clenched lips: Simonszoon's surreal suggestion of inflicting these punishments simultaneously was a droll capstone to his other absurdities.

Dirck pretended not to notice Kees' chortle. "Blast you, Bjelke, you near-polar Norwegian pup; don't make me ask again. What was the word I used to describe you?"

"I believe it was 'indefatigable.' Sir."

Dirck nodded vigorously. "Yes, that's it! And you are! Indefatigably cheery! A walking, talking, smiling cross to be borne by realists such as me. And the Admiral." Simonszoon squinted at Tromp. "Except when he gets that pleased little smile on his face— like that one—his eyes get that insufferable 'Father Christmas' twinkle." At which point, the tall, dark Dutchman's sour expression buckled into a grin at his own therapeutic nonsense.

Tromp chuckled. "You never change, Dirck. Always bizarre fancies before a battle."

"Well, less cost to one's pocket and wits than gin, hey?" He grew slightly more serious. "Although I do miss the gin. There's another ritual consigned to the bottomless depths of the past." He turned toward Bjelke. "I'm all for learning these new ships—and these new ways and titles—by feel as well as thought. But it's likely easier for those who haven't grown up before the mast." He nodded meaningfully at the Norwegian, whose first assignment had been to Task Force X-Ray a year ago.

Bjelke nodded back. "I suppose it must be akin to breaking an ingrained habit."

Simonszoon scoffed lightly, stared at the Spanish ships coming toward them. "Harder. Because these habits kept us alive. Since we were boys. It's more like trying to resist an instinct. Or better still, like trying to prevent your eye from shutting—quicker than thought—when something comes flashing toward it."

Cornelis Evertsen nodded at Bjelke, then toward the oncoming Spanish van. "And stationkeeping like this, as the war galleons bear down?" He shook his head. "It goes against what every lesson and every battle teaches: having weather gauge at sea is even more crucial than having the high ground on land."

Tromp realized he was no longer smiling, but staring, like the others, at the oncoming fleet. He pointed. "Look out there, Lieutenant Bjelke. That is what an admiral sees in his nightmares. One's sworn enemies closing from windward while you are caught motionless before them. No way to win the battle. No way to save your ships and your men." He sighed, rubbed his face; the fine, infrequent spray kept it moist, despite the sun. "Yet here we wait, like lightly armored skirmishers standing before a charge of black-hulled knights which outnumber us almost two to one. And outweigh us, both in tonnage and broadside shot, by three to one. Easily."

"Which proves," Simonszoon grunted, "that I'm the greater fool than Bjelke." He turned on his heel.

Rik sputtered, "H-how's that then, sir?"

Dirck turned back. "Because, as the realist, I should be steaming—or if need be, swimming—away from those Iberian leviathans. Yet here I remain." He paused at the stairs that mounted the side of the pilothouse to the flying bridge, squinted to starboard. "Bjelke, that Bermudan sloop has finally caught up to us. Have a detail see that her master's brought aboard. And smartly; we don't have much time left for chatting."

Tromp turned to Evertsen. "I'll want that master's report directly."

"Yes, sir."

"And Kees, get Sehested."

Evertsen paused, glanced to the east. "Sir, granted that we have at least three quarters of an hour yet, but is it prudent that we—?"

"Kees. This is why Sehested came along. If we can risk our lives for our sovereigns, he can do the same."

"I'll have him called above, Admiral."

Tromp simply nodded and gestured Evertsen on his way. He considered the slowly growing vanguard of the Spanish fleet: eleven galleons. The three out in front were specially built for combat, decks reinforced to enable them to carry upwards of forty guns, each. Most of those pieces were likely to be thirty-two-pounders—demi-cannons, as many still called them. But almost as many were likely to be the monstrous forty-two-pound full cannons which were restricted to the lower decks, lest the ship become so top-heavy that it sailed crank or even rolled. They were all comparatively inaccurate guns, short-ranged, and often took several minutes to reload.

Having faced them before, Maarten Tromp knew their limitations. He also knew the strength of *Resolve*'s hull, its speed, and had seen her shrug off hits from just such guns. But she had never sailed against so many, and never from what amounted to a standing start. If anything went wrong with *Resolve*'s engines now . . . He put that thought out of his head, and formulated yet another set of contingencies should his men's new apex of trust in up-time technology prove to be a precipitous height from which their fortunes would fall.

The black ships seemed to have grown slightly larger in the last several seconds.

Chapter 4

East of Dominica

Hannibal Sehested scrambled up *Resolve*'s almost vertical "stairs" from his berth beneath the quarterdeck. As his head cleared the top of the companionway, a gust from the bow sped past his nose, pulling his forelock after it.

Cornelis Evertsen was smiling at him from the rail. "Not a morning for wigs, eh, Lord Sehested?"

"Evidently not," the Norwegian replied as he came on deck, unsure whether Evertsen's jocular tone was simply an extension of his general good spirits or a veiled snicker at the noble's incongruous presence aboard the warship. "You summoned me to meet a representative of the English? Here?"

"Nothing quite so grand as that, sir," Evertsen said with the same smile. "Merely the master of a Bermudan sloop. But Admiral Tromp thought it prudent to summon you."

Sehested nodded, resisting the urge to bat away the locks now flying about his face like angry, diaphanous birds. "Thank you, Lieutenant. Please lead on."

Evertsen made a small bow and led aft.

Sehested trailed behind, reflecting that, possibly for the first time since arriving in the New World, he might look every bit as ridiculous as he felt. Particularly when people addressed him as "Lord" Sehested.

Oh, he had always aspired to that. Certainly that had been the point of all his expensive schooling and travel in Denmark, France, Germany, and Holland: to enable him to make the leap from aristocrat to bona fide nobility. But then the up-timers had arrived in their mysterious Ring of Fire and, within a year, he was being summoned to the court of King Christian IV in Copenhagen. Why? Because of the attainments and abilities of his older self in that other history.

He soon noted a similar predilection growing among the rulers of his era. A surprising number of even the most enlightened monarchs had rushed to consult the histories of that world which would now never be as a means of identifying promising young assistants and protégés based on the exploits of their other selves. The logical and philosophical bases of such a course of action seemed dubious at best, to young Hannibal, but as their beneficiary, he was not disposed to make those opinions public.

So Christian IV had made him a noble a full five years before he had been so elevated in the "other" world, an act that was, to Sehested's mind, a rather stunning display of his sovereign's tendency toward both blind egoism and uncritical teleology. Ever since then, Hannibal had operated under a self-imposed pressure that few other humans had ever known: the need to meet the expectations spawned by the deeds of an alter ego who had never existed.

He watched Evertsen reach the stern of *Resolve*, extend a hand over the side to assist someone coming up the Jacob's ladder that was hanging down over the transom. The Dutchman was probably just a good-natured fellow, the kind who greeted others with a smile as a matter of habit, but Hannibal could no longer see such things clearly. His unwonted ascendance had spawned enough veiled dismay and amusement in Christian's court, and in other places of prestige and power, that he no longer trusted those instincts.

Evertsen was surprisingly strong for his long, lean build; he practically hauled a diminutive individual over the stern of *Resolve* with a single hand. The masthead of a Bermuda-rigged sloop bobbed into and out of sight beyond the taffrail.

The small man—his skin weathered and tanned to the texture and color of a walnut—stared from Kees to Hannibal. "Ye're neither of ye Tromp hisself, I wager?"

Kees smiled broadly. "You would win that bet, Captain—?"

"Stirke. Master Timothy Stirke. I've got news for yer admiral." He grimaced apologetically. "Only fer him, I'm afraid."

"I understand," Evertsen said calmly. "But before we join the admiral, my I present Lord Hannibal Sehested from the court of His Majesty King Christian IV of Denmark?"

Stirke considered Hannibal. "Denmark, it is? That's news to these ears. What's yer interest in these waters, then?"

Sehested was oddly relieved by the small man's absolute lack of social courtesies. "As part of the Union of Kalmar, Denmark is pleased to assist King

Gustav of Sweden and the nations of the United States of Europe over which he presides, in clearing these waters of Spanish influence and righting the many wrongs they have wrought."

Stirke squinted at Sehested. "You've rehearsed that? Fer me?" He shook his head. "A turr'ble waste of time, that. I'm naught but a ship's master who freights from the Indies what I can sell in Somers Isles and the Bahamas."

Sehested smiled. "You are right; I practiced it. And had it memorized long before I came to the Lesser Antilles, now almost a year ago."

Stirke's smile was easier, amused. "'Ad much use fer it, have ye?"

"Only a little. But that is still too much."

Stirke's laughter was like a barking cough. "Ah, 'an ye ain't so much of a dandy as I took 'e for. Ye're all right, Hannibal Sehested. Now, since I've no cannon nor belly for a fight this day, I'd as soon deliver me messages and be off."

As they made their way to the pilothouse, the little Bermudan stared around at the unfamiliar cannons and gear that was being worked and tended on *Resolve*'s weather deck. "'An sure that it's a New Age in the New World. I've no idea what half this ironmongery might be, but I ken it set those Spanish dogs back on their haunches last year, hey?"

"There's probably some truth to that," Evertsen admitted as a German soldier indicated that they had to wait a moment before proceeding up the stairs to the flying bridge.

Timothy took no note of the delay. "Hsst," he sneered at Cornelis' understatement. "This winter past, there was little talk of aught else. At least on the islands I sail 'tween. For near on two years, there wasn't a ship from Europe that didn't fly the yellow and red. But now, others be showin' up again. And the food we freight from Kitts and your home port on Statia? Might've saved us all, I wager. As I hear it, your lot weren't much better off."

In the space of two seconds, Cornelis Evertsen went from being the marginally laconic executive officer of the *Resolve* to an animated storyteller. Sehested chided himself for having missed the subtle signs that such a transformation might be possible—very probably because he himself had been too preoccupied attempting to discern if the young officer's demeanor had been genuine or carefully veiled mockery. But as his story of the Dutch travails of the past two years unfolded, the source of his sudden garrulousness was clear: an enthusiastic and outgoing person by nature, Evertsen had learned to keep that in check. Certainly, part of that was due to the reserve expected of leaders in combat. But it was also a likely adaptation to being the right hand of an admiral who was not only an introvert but who would otherwise have been routinely outshined by his staff officer's brighter and more engaging personality.

But now, warming to his topic and freed of all those constraints, Evertsen commenced to unfold his tale with energy and conviction. And detail. Lots and lots of detail. Indeed, Hannibal had the distinct impression that his retelling of the events was as every bit as therapeutic for him as it was informative for Stirke.

A rising tide of anxiety had surged into Dutch-held Recife along with Tromp's badly damaged ships in 1633. That Christmas had been a dismal one: not only did the colonists learn that the majority of their nation's fleet was now resting in pieces on the seabed off Dunkirk, but word arrived on a jacht from newly settled St. Eustatia that the Dutch colony on St. Martin had fallen to the Spanish in June.

After considerable initial debate, most of Recife's councilors conceded that their position was untenable. What Dutch ships remained were either trapped in Amsterdam, or out of touch in the East Indies. It was only a matter of time before Spanish and Portuguese forces pressed their advantage, knowing that no further succor was coming to the New Holland colony in Brazil.

So, after first setting the Portuguese back on their heels with a sharp offensive that had them suing for a truce, Tromp immediately set in motion subtle plans that put the colony in a position to evacuate swiftly. Which they had done in May of 1634, to the utter amazement of the Portuguese.

But safe distance from their Iberian antagonists had been purchased at the expense of a year of extreme privation. Over ten times the number of colonists already on St. Eustatia, the refugees from Recife hadn't the tools, skills, or time to raise an adequate crop before their supplies ran out. Rationing was adopted. Fresh water was scarce. Life in tents invited illnesses that thrice threatened to become epidemics. And with men outnumbering women almost ten to one, tensions remained perpetually poised to explode into violence.

A year later, the first rays of hope arrived along with the first crop from leased lands on St. Kitts. But it was not quite three months later that full, bright deliverance arrived in the form of the USE and Danish flotilla known as Task Force X-Ray.

As Cornelis related that happy ending, he gestured toward Hannibal—who was glad that neither the storyteller nor his listener could see what was in his own mind: the squalid tent city that had been Oranjestad; the stick-thin colonists with sunken and desperate eyes; the stink of more wastes than could be readily removed from those dusty streets; and the perpetual moaning of the old who were sick and the children who were hungry. And he, Hannibal Sehested, was ashamed to remember and relive his reaction: horror, revulsion, and a genuine desire to turn immediately about and return to Europe.

His mind's eye shut, and he was abruptly back in the present, Stirke staring at him intently. Had the little sunbaked Englishman seen him reexperiencing that disgust, that vile failure of courage, morality, and empathy which had been his first reaction to the plight of the Dutch?

Stirke squinted. "Not often a man knows he's able to do so much for so many of his fellow men, eh, Hannibal Sehested?"

"Sadly," Hannibal forced out of a dry throat, "that epiphany is even rarer than you think."

"So you must share it widely, then!"

Hannibal swallowed a sudden spurt of bile. "I am not worthy to do so. Of that I solemnly assure you. But I can testify to this: you are right when you aver that Lieutenant Evertsen, and his comrades—both Dutch and those of our other nations—have put the Spanish back on their heels. And that is why it is important that we have met." Sehested lowered his voice to a murmur. "For only by combining efforts, will we be able to prevent Spain from reasserting her stranglehold upon all our communities."

Stirke glanced sideways at him as the German guard stepped aside and Evertsen motioned him toward the steps. "Ah, now I see why your king has a man here, Hannibal Sehested. To gather us 'round a flag." He started up. "Well, we might be willing, but Bermuda and her boats are but so much flotsam and jetsam in the currents of great nations and kings."

"Wars are not always won by the heaviest broadside alone, Timothy. Sometimes, the keenest eyes and the fastest ships are just as important."

Stirke stopped with one foot on the flying bridge, looked back at Sehested. "Aye, an' that's true enough. True enough that it bears more speech, I'm thinking." He smiled and mounted the last step—and stopped as if he'd been clapped in irons.

Sehested, hurrying to join Stirke, discovered what had stopped the small Bermudan in his tracks: his surprise encounter with a spectacle from another world:

A telegrapher hammering away at a device that was all levers and wires. Instructions being shouted down speaking tubes. An auxiliary binnacle with down-time copies of up-time barometric instruments. A tactical plot table with a glass—or was that "plastic"?—weather cover, grease-pencil markings showing the positions and headings of both allied and enemy ships. A compass-like instrument showing the firing arc of the *Resolve*'s two naval rifles. Runners scribbling furiously, emerging from and disappearing down the stairs affixed to the other side of the pilothouse. German guards with long rifles that had percussion nipples in place of frizzens and pans.

For a master of an inter-island sloop barely half the dimensions of the smallest Dutch jacht, it hardly looked like a conn at all. Nor did it sound or feel like it. Despite the constant chatter and activity, most of the exchanges sounded like chanted rituals, with subordinates often repeating their superiors' instructions even as they began to act upon them.

Sehested set Stirke back into motion with a gentle palm that guided his elbow. "I know," the Norwegian murmured. "I felt it too, at first. It's not like any vessel I have traveled upon before."

Stirke rounded on him with wide eyes, crow's feet momentarily vanishing. "'Sooth, but it's not like a ship at all." He struggled for words as Evertsen joined them. "It—it's as if a man be standing in the guts of both a windmill and a . . . a orrery, is it? . . . with naught but gears and wheels turning about 'is head. Doing work, aye—but to what end?"

As Evertsen neared the group at the tactical plot, he was beset by runners eager to make report. He motioned for the boys to follow just as Bjelke leaned over the map-backed transparency to study the close intervals between the marks that charted the progress of the enemy ships. He looked up at the mast-mounted anenometer and then the telltales on the sails. "Given that they've a brisk wind astern and following seas, the Flota should be approaching more swiftly. Yet, the war galleons have reefed their topsails and topgallants." He frowned. "Might they be more concerned with maintaining formation than maximum speed?"

When the two older men glanced at him without a word, he shrugged and explained his reasoning. "The intelligence indicates that when Spain's two treasure fleets make the Atlantic crossing together, they take great pains to arrive off Dominica in good order so they may rapidly divide into the respective parts: La Flota de Nueva España, and La Flota de Tierra Firme."

Simonszoon shook his head. "Look through your glass again, Bjelke. And not at those seagoing fortresses leading the van, but the ships further back, the ones the war galleons cut in front of when they spotted us."

Bjelke brought up his binoculars; Stirke squinted quizzically at the device. After a moment, the XO muttered. "The freeboard of the cargo ships is . . . surprisingly low."

Simonszoon nodded. "Now look at their aft draft."

Bjelke did. "They're out of trim, sitting back on their rudders."

Simonszoon's brief look of approval vanished before it had finished settling upon his face. "That's a sure sign they're all overloaded. Not a surprise; prior to first landfall, the cargo galleons usually are. So they'll not sail well under full canvas. They're too heavy to respond to a strong following wind. That's why the Spaniards are letting their sails luff so. If they were rigged to catch all of this breeze, they'd be torn to strips and streamers."

"So: although the Spanish have the weather gauge, they dare not take full advantage of it."

Simonszoon made a sour face. "Not all of them, at any rate. But mind, the less laden hulls can make more use than the others. So we'd best assume that when the war galleons come within half a league, they'll crowd sail for the last rush to close with us. Their canvas will hold that long. Of course, when they do that, they'll pull further away from their cargo ships."

He grinned darkly in Tromp's direction. "Which is all part of the greater plan, if memory serves."

The admiral nodded. "Yes, but the weather is not optimal for us, either, Dirck. This seaway is livelier than is typical for this time of year, more than we would like for our eight-inch rifles." He nodded toward the two long guns, both pointing toward the Spanish, their crews loose-limbed but at their action stations. "All things being equal, I'd rather their ships had more speed and that we had more calm." He half-turned toward Cornelis Evertsen. "Conditions, Kees?"

"No change, Admiral. Fast, low wavelets, mostly, but there are occasional swells large enough to force our gunners to reacquire their targets. Once we're underway, *Resolve* will cut a more level track; there should be no surges large enough to affect our aim."

Tromp tilted his head upward, as if he meant to catch the sun more fully upon his face, but his eyes were closed and his features were taut, as if he was contemplating, or sensing. "We'd lessen the surges if we turn a point off the in-running current. We've no reason to keep the galleons dead ahead."

Dirck leaned his elbows on the plot. "No, but the more we swing away from the current, the more roll we'll have."

"We'll also be bearing away from the wind," Rik added.

Simonszoon nodded. "Our fellows aloft will have a lively dance, trying to keep the canvas in the right trim. None of which is the best conditions for our gunnery."

Tromp opened his eyes and nodded. "Yes, but I will take the roll from a current on our port bow, rather than the pitch when our bowsprit is set dead into its surgest. The roll is more constant but less marked. And less sudden. And the more we stand athwart the current, the better our gunners can read the swells, time their discharges."

Bjelke canted his head forward. "Admiral, these conditions are less conducive to accuracy than when we met the Spanish galleons head-on in the Grenada Passage, last year. There, at least, we had two cruisers—*Resolve* and *Intrepid*—to take them under fire. And we had the weather gauge."

Tromp nodded. "Worthy points, Rik, but I am decided: we shall swing two points to starboard. If we are to be sure of making full use of the guns we have, we must be sure that neither the forward mount nor the funnel blocks the aft, and by turning away from the current, we give the gunners the best possible view of swells. It also puts our bow directly on our next course heading, and so we shall come to flank speed without unnecessary delay."

He glanced at the young Norwegian. "However, your counsel makes me wonder if we should reconsider the range at which we will commence the engagement."

At the words "commence the engagement," Stirke began shuffling his feet anxiously. The group around the plot turned in his direction.

Sehested smiled, inclined his head. "Admiral, I have the honor of presenting Master Stirke of the Somers Islands. He comes with news for you. He also reports that his colony has had much word of your actions against the Spanish last year." Sehested paused to give his last words subtle emphasis. "That may be a subject worth touching upon—if only for a minute, under these hurried conditions."

Chapter 5

East of Dominica

Tromp involuntarily raised his left eyebrow in response to Sehested's subtle prompt. "I see. Well, Master Stirke, I presume you come with news from leeward?"

"Bless me if there's any news worth sayin', sahr. Nary a ship with uncertain intents. Hardly a ship at all."

"Any hulls at all around Guadeloupe?"

"Excepting your own jachts, bow into the wind and waiting, nothing."

"And did you meet as agreed with Admiral Jol?"

"I did, sahr. Not two days ago. He'd little more to report than I 'ave. Says he sank a pair of piraguas five days back. Would have taken them as prizes but the Spanish were not about to give over without a scuffle."

Simonszoon's amusement was saturnine. "Piraguas? Against a Jol's ship and the two jachts attached to him?"

"Aye. Though they were too tired to row and the wind against them." Stirke's head bobbed like that of a pecking bird. "Peg Le—er, Admiral Jol says they turned about, full of fight and with naught but two *petereroes* between 'em. He was hoping to take them as prizes, but two touches of shot and they were in pieces. Men and boats, alike." He shrugged. "So naught but open seas behind yer fleet, sahr."

Simonszoon rolled his eyes; if Sehested hadn't known to look for it, he wouldn't have detected the faint hint of a grin. "Well, the news comes later than we hoped...but better late than never."

Stirke looked stricken. "We crowded sail and tacked as sharp and quick as the wind allowed, sahr! Maybe too much so. Nearly went turtle twice. But by the time we rounded the Cachacrou headland—your captains call it Scott's Pointe—the aftermost of yer ships were already on the horizon. And well ye know that there's no free runnin' from there to here: your bow'd be right in the eye of the wind if you tried. We came on as fast as we could but it was dreadful long tacks just to keep speed enough, if't please yer."

Simonszoon smiled, trying to show the Englishman—*well, Bermudan, now,* Sehested supposed—that he'd meant no harm by his comment.

But whether it was Dirck's long, somber face or looming height, the fellow turned toward Tromp in a desperate appeal. "You were powerful hard to catch, as God's me witness, sahr. We didn't lollygag, me word on it! S'blood, it was as if ye were trying to flee us!"

Tromp smiled faintly. "Not at all, but we could not tarry. Once our ship watching the eastern approaches signaled that she had spotted the Spanish, we had to weigh anchor immediately. Though we were beyond the windward mouth of the passage and had the wind in a broad reach, getting distance from Dominica meant beating and often tacking, too. And right across the current. Still, we made seven nautical miles by dawn."

Stirke frowned, glanced at the oncoming galleons, seemed to do some mental math. "Sahr, forgive me asking, but how's it that they're still so far a-sea? Even if your picket ship saw their lights at four, that's what? Twenty or twenty-two miles, at best? But they've had six and a half hours with the wind abaft. Even 'twere they making a whisker under three knots, they'd ha' been at broadsides with you half an hour ago! But there they are, still shaping for battle, as if they've had but half that time. Which makes even less sense, since it were full dawn by six. So how'd they fail to spot ye and adjust? Crow's nest to crow's nest on your great ships, ye'd sure see each other at eighteen miles, seventeen at the least."

Tromp shrugged. "We had Dominica behind us, and our topsails and gallants were reefed. At even fifteen miles, it's work for an eagle's eye to pick out thin, dark mastheads above a black horizon and against an island's black outline."

"Ah! So you were slowed, yourselves, then."

"That was the price of remaining unseen," Simonszoon drawled. "But until they saw us, they came on with both the wind and the sun behind them, so—with their sails as wide and white as a gull's wings—we had the measure of them at fifteen miles.

"It was near unto eight o'clock when the Spanish sent out a pair of pataches to check the waters and ways around Dominica. Slightly before eight-thirty, they must have caught sight of us. They heeled over, beating for all they were worth—and those pataches are right-rigged for that kind of work."

"And since then?"

"Since then," Tromp answered, "La Flota slowed

considerably. Most of their fighting ships—we count eleven galleons specifically constructed for combat—swung ahead into the van from their original screening formation on the north. But that evolution slowed the fleet. The cargo ships—about forty galleons and naos—had to give their protectors enough time to get well out in front."

Stirke nodded at all the explanations, but maintained a side-glancing skepticism throughout. There was still something off about the numbers and causes he'd been given.

"You still seem puzzled," Tromp commented, looking over his shoulder at the approaching galleons.

Stirke's gaze went there as well, then connected with his. "Well, just—just why here, Admiral?"

Tromp made sure his smile, if small, was kind. "You have a better location in mind?"

"Not as such, sir. I mean, one place on the globe is as good—or bad—as another fer men to make mince of their fellow men. But men usually 'ave something to gain by fighting where they do, if you follow me. Such as yer own Piet Hein, sahr. Back in '28, at the Battle of Manzantas Bay. Defeated La Flota, he did, just like you mean to do today.

"But Hein were there to take hold of a true treasure fleet, Admiral—so loaded with silver that the ships were near unto sinking without his help, as they tell it." Stirke shifted his feet, sent his arm in a wide motion that took in the bright sky, sun, and sea. "Meanin' no disrespect, sahr, but what's the point o' being *here*, where there's no silver to be had at all?"

Tromp smiled. "And that is precisely what the Spanish have thought as well, every year before their ships weigh anchor for the New World. That they are not only invulnerable because of their strength and numbers, but because they carry nothing to stir interest, much less avarice. A habit of thought which has now worked to our advantage."

Stirke scratched his head. "Well, I see how they'd be surprised. But—"

"But you think we are—what is that English word?—'daft' for attacking a fleet without treasure. Yes?"

"Well . . . apologies, but yes, Admiral. Utterly daft, if I mus' say."

Tromp's smile became a bit feral. "And what if I was to tell you that the Flota out there, racing toward us, is in fact *filled* with treasure? So loaded with valuables that even from here, you can see how low their naos ride in the water?"

"I'd say that's not because they are loaded with silver, sahr, but because they're freighting no end of goods from Spain—all heavy, too. Tools and nails and cannons and shot and every 'tuther needful thing that Spaniards don't make for themselves here in the New World."

"Yes," Tromp murmured. "All priceless treasure. Every bit of it." He nodded as Stirke's responding frown began to clear like clouds giving way to sunlight. "You see, now."

"Aye, an' it's genius, it is!" He nodded as he unfolded the logic for himself. "For more'n two years, none of us have had ships from home. Us because King Charles forsook every one of his subjects here in the Caribbean, and you because the Spaniards sunk your great fleet off Dunkirk and then blockaded ever' one of yer ports. And so we've made do with what we had on hand where we could and did without where we couldn't. And it's showed: in our ships, our shops, our houses. And everything so dear that nary a one of us could buy any of it."

Tromp nodded once in return. "As it has been in Oranjestad, and all the other English and Dutch colonies. Merchants are almost without stock and yet have no use for coin. Barter for goods or services kept us all alive, but did not answer the crucial shortages for finished goods. Now: see those ships?" He pointed back at the broad array of small dark blots upon the water, topped by cream-white wings. "They are the answer to those troubles. As you yourself said, Master Stirke, they are brim-full with *needful* things. And the men on those ships are confident—as only a century and a half of unexceptioned experience can make them—that we not only lack the capacity to stand in a full-blown battle, but haven't the belly for it, either. Because, after all, they have nothing that we would truly want, let alone need." He stood straight.

"And they are so terribly wrong." He looked out over *Resolve* and the ships to either side of her. "About both our need and our capacity to win this battle."

He took a step closer to the small man, pointed behind at a small cluster of ships only a mile off Dominica's eastern coast, the ones he had detailed to maintain observation during the coming battle. "You are welcome to remain with those ships, especially the one now lofting a balloon. For reasons I no longer have time to explain, that ship will come to no harm and cannot be caught. If, however, you still feel threatened, you will be able to leave at any time. Of this I assure you."

Stirke turned his hat slowly in his hands; one full, fretful revolution. "With all respect, Admiral, it's hard to put faith in so sweeping an oath as that. It's the kind that only God Hisself could make."

Tromp's eyes were calm, almost detached. "Reason with me, Master Stirke. Why would I mislead you regarding your safety? For what possible reason, malign or malfeasant, would I want your destruction?"

"None. Unless you fear you'll lose this battle. Then ye might want to keep me from spreading word of such a defeat."

Tromp's eyebrow raised. "I had not considered that." He smiled. "I am doubly glad to have you here, then."

"But . . . why, M'lord?"

"I am not your lord. I hold a rank I earned, not a title I was born to. It should be thus with all men, I think. But, to resolve this matter: I am especially glad for your presence because you think quickly and accurately. And I will want that quality in one who makes report to Bermuda and the Bahamas."

"What is it you wish me to report, then, sir?"

"Everything you shall presently observe in the coming battle, so that you may relate it to your people, your community, your leaders."

"With all due respect, we've heard tell of the fine qualities of these ships of yours, Admiral."

"Yes. You've heard about outcomes. Fine outcomes. Improbable outcomes, actually . . . unless you see these ships in action. Then you will not only be able to tell the story of this battle, but it will become clear, in hindsight, just how all the others were won so decisively.

"You must see this so that your people understand. In the New World, we are not and never will be so numerous as the Spanish. They hold much territory and we hold little. They have many ships; we have few.

"But their size has made them both complacent and reluctant to change, whereas we are bold and innovative. Today, you shall have a chance to observe Spain's quantities confronted by our qualities. Knowing not just the outcome, but how it was attained, assures that your leaders will be better able to decide if it is truly in their best interests to remain evasive when it comes to making firm agreements and even alliances with us here in the Leeward Islands."

Stirke crumpled his hat in his hands. "Admiral, I'm a mastern of a ship, 'at's true enough. But it's a little ship and, as captains go, I'm littler still. As even a blind man can see." He cracked a smile. "But little or no, I've a wife and children to feed. So if I fail to leave this place now, and so, never do, it's them that would be suffering, not me. And it's that suffering which is on me mind, what with a great battle looming before me eyes."

Tromp softened his tone. "I'm sorry not to have asked after your circumstances, Captain. You must do as you think right. However, I must also point out that, by staying safe in the shadows of greater ships, quite distant from where the guns will thunder, you may also discover the means to accrue great wealth this day. Wealth so great that you and your family will never know want again."

The man's eyes lit as if kindled. Tromp was glad to see the fear in them replaced by eagerness, but that did not make Stirke's suddenly predatory expression pleasant to see. "I beg your pardon, Admiral?"

Tromp gestured toward the east. "Today's battle will

have more ships in it than any since Dunkirk, three and a half years ago. I was the loser that day. If I am right, we shall not lose today. Indeed, I suspect there will be so many spoils that my forces shall not be able to secure them all." He regarded the man levelly. "And there is no reason to abandon to the deep that which men might salvage for their benefit."

"And we'd have yer leave to take what you haven't the time or burthen to carry off?"

"To know I made my allies that much stronger would be a comfort to me and a blessing to our common cause. I bid you 'fare well'—whatever you choose to do in the coming hours." He glanced over the Bermudan's shoulder and his eyes twinkled. "Oh, and by the way, that's how we knew the Spanish were coming so many hours before they arrived." He pointed back over the stern. Stirke turned to look.

The great ball of an observation balloon rose slowly up from the deck of a large ship, well abaft *Resolve* and the other warships waiting in two groups: one large and to the north, the other small and to the south. Stirke's mouth was as round as the sphere, but reshaped into a half-toothed grin as he turned back toward Tromp. "So it's true! Ye've flying machines! Ye smite them from the air like God's own angels!"

Simonszoon rolled his eyes, but before the captain's trademark sardonicism could rattle the Bermudan again, Sehested leaned forward. "Master Stirke, this balloon serves as an eye, not a weapon. The observer in it can tell us, almost instantly, the location of all our enemies, their respective courses, and their current conditions."

Stirke nodded, turned haltingly back toward Tromp. "I can't say until I speak to me lads, but, if 't still please yeh, sahr, I think we might tarry to witness your great battle."

Tromp nodded, allowed a faint smile to bend his lips before turning back to the binnacle.

Once he heard Stirke heading down the stairs, the admiral leaned toward Evertsen. "Send word back to Tower: the observer is to use the gas burner to reach two hundred feet with all speed."

"Tower?" Sehested repeated uncertainly, frowning.

Tromp, still facing the plot instead of the Dane, indulged in a brief rueful smile. On the one hand, it was an annoyance having a civilian official—and a diplomat, no less!—on his bridge. On the other hand, Sehested was the direct conduit back to King Christian IV, who followed their progress in the New World with unusual avidity. So keeping Sehested well informed—and impressed—was worth the minor nuisance of explaining the occasional operational detail to him. Although it didn't particularly feel that way right now, with the Spanish ships so close.

Tromp gestured behind at the balloon and then to the western edge of the tactical plot. "We have designated the balloon and the ships dedicated to its operation 'Tower.' For obvious reasons, I trust."

Sehested nodded, pointed at the two groups of blue marks that were arrayed between it and the oncoming red icons of the Spanish. "And they are?"

"The larger, northern squadron is 'Anvil.' We are in this much smaller southern group 'Hammer.' Again, I presume those labels are also self-defining."

"Within certain broad margins of meaning, yes. I see that Hammer's complement—this ship, *Amelia*, *Salamander*, *Prins Hendrik*, and *Crown of Waves*—is comprised of unusually fine sailers. Although I do not recognize this craft: *SP One*?"

"One of our steam pinnaces," Kees explained. "For towing. There to ensure that *Prins Hendrik* keeps up with the others."

"And now, Lord Sehested," said Tromp, turning to face the Dane, "I must turn my full attention to the matter at hand. You are welcome, however, to stay and observe."

Sehested inclined his head, took a step back, did not make for the stairs.

He is brave, curious, or both, Tromp decided as he compared the plot with the unfolding scene upon the sea.

Before he could even ask for the latest range estimate to the closest war galleon, Bjelke delivered it as he lowered his telescope. "The Spanish vanguard is nearing fourteen hundred yards."

When Tromp did not speak immediately, Simonszoon glanced at him. "Maarten, are we still following Plan Alpha?"

Tromp, studying the sea, hardly heard the question. "We are."

Simonszoon turned toward Bjelke and nodded.

Rik leaned toward his speaking tubes. "Engineering, raise steam. Master Gunner, prepare to acquire targets and—"

"Belay those orders," Tromp instructed quietly.

"Sir?" Bjelke asked, confused.

"New orders, Rik."

"Maarten—" began Simonszoon.

"Yes, Dirck, I know the clock. The war galleons will be at fair range for ten minutes, alongside in eleven."

"Not a lot of time to shift to a different plan."

"We're not doing so. I'm making just one adjustment: we shall no longer commence firing at thirteen hundred fifty yards."

"What's the new range, then?"

"One thousand yards. Lieutenant Bjelke, raise steam."

Simonszoon sidled closer. His voice had none of its usual dark jocularity. "Maarten, reducing the range to one thousand yards means we'll have them under our guns for only seven and a half minutes, not eleven. We won't even put two thirds of the rounds we planned on into the Spanish."

"Actually, barely half, since I am no longer presuming forty seconds between each pull of the lanyard but forty-five." Seeing that Simonszoon was about to object yet again, he cut to the heart of the matter: "Captain, the sea is slightly choppy and we shall be firing into the wind. In these conditions, we will be fortunate to hit the enemy ten percent of the time at thirteen hundred fifty yards. At one thousand, we will surely miss, too, but we shall correct more quickly and with less wasted ammunition. And if you have been counting the rounds left in your magazine, you will surely understand why that concerns me. Particularly now."

He pointed at the Spanish. "We know there are at least fifty galleons and naos in this treasure fleet. Probably more, given reports from some of our other ships. That means we will be relying on these two naval rifles more than we planned. More than we ever imagined."

"We needn't take them *all*, sir," Bjelke murmured.

"Probably not, but we are going to try, Lieutenant. That is how we're going to send the Spanish a message that they cannot fail to understand."

"And that is?" Simonszoon asked through a sigh.

"That their dominance in the New World is at an end."

Dirck's smile was part dark mirth and part rue. "And maybe that Maarten Tromp is returning the favor for Dunkirk?"

Tromp looked past his old friend and straight at Bjelke. "Send to the Master Gunner: commence acquiring targets. Prepare to open fire at one thousand yards. Mr. Evertsen, pass the word to the fleet: follow orders for engagement plan Alpha at the sound of our guns. And God be with us all."

Chapter 6

East of Dominica

"Captain Simonszoon," Rik Bjelke said sharply, "lead war galleon now approaching one thousand yards."

"Forward mount reconfirm: target acquired and tracking?"

A pause as the signal went down the wires to the turrets and the reply sped back. "Aye, and aye, sir."

Simonszoon glanced at Tromp.

Maarten relented and this time raised the binoculars to his eyes. "At your leisure, Capt—"

"Watch the rise and fire!" Simonszoon shouted, so loud that the forward mount heard him.

The master gunner, seated in what looked like an armor-plated pulpit mounted on the side of the eight-incher's gunshield, hunched over the inclinometer that tracked the pitch and the yaw of the hull, a position that also gave him a good view of the water. A tense moment elapsed—

The naval rifle sounded like a lightning-throated lion: a report that was both a roar and a sharp crack. Tromp felt as much as heard the weapon slam back in its recoil carriage. A blink later, a tall jet of water appeared twenty yards abeam the lead galleon's waist.

At a nod from Dirck, Bjelke sent the planned order to Mount One. "Load, adjust, fire when ready." As the weapon drifted back from its recoil and the crew began unspinning the breech, the intraship signalman howled up through the tube from the pilothouse: "Mount Two confirms target acquired, but could lose it behind the funnel."

"*Duivels kont!*" Simonszoon snapped, turned to his runner: "Send word: trim the main, and let 'er drift a point to starboard." Back down the tube: "Mount Two, reacquire."

Bjelke, in addition to everything else, was watching a timepiece. Sehested made to ask him what he was doing, but Kees leaned over. "He's timing the rounds."

The Dane frowned. "You mean, how fast they are reloading?" He gestured beyond the mainmast. Half-concealed by the low ring-shaped wall, or "tub," that screened them from small arms and splinters, the crew of Mount One was swabbing the open breech as four men approached with the next round. Almost thirty-two inches long and weighing over one hundred fifty pounds, the perversely delicate job of manhandling such shells into the weapon was not a job for scrawny men.

But Kees was shaking his head. "*Nee*, he is timing how fast they are firing."

Sehested's glance seemed to take in the oncoming ships, the water, the slight bob of the bowsprit all at once. "But given the conditions, how can one accurately predict those intervals?"

"How, indeed?" Simonszoon muttered. "We planned

on firing twenty rounds per gun. Now, we'll be lucky to get off ten before they come alongsi—"

Bjelke's shout ended his sentence. "Mount Two reports target acquired and—"

Simonszoon chopped his hand downward.

"Fire!" Bjelke howled to the rear as he made a matching hand signal to the comms rating in the pilothouse.

As the breech of Mount One was being spun tight, Mount Two flung thunder downrange, the trailing jet of smoke slowing as it stretched toward the northernmost of the three galleons. Water gouted fifteen yards off the Spaniards' port bow.

"Is this . . . typical?" Sehested asked in a low voice.

Tromp was about to reply—uncharitably—when Mount One fired again. Only when the round went through the rigging and put a hole in the mainsail did he realize that he had been holding his breath. "Typical for this weather, yes," he murmured.

"Time?" Simonszoon asked, not taking his eyes away from his telescope.

"Forty-three seconds," Bjelke answered. "Nine of which were for aiming," he added as Simonszoon prepared to ask another question.

Simonszoon smiled at the young Norwegian's anticipation of his request. No wonder Eddie was so disappointed to lose him as his executive officer, Tromp thought, and not for the first time.

"Closing on eight hundred yards," Kees said calmly—right before both guns tore at their ears in back-to-back discharges that sent a tremor under their feet.

Mount One had evidently been a bit eager; its round was not quite so high, but did little more than punch a gap into the galleon's starboard gunwale.

But Mount Two's shot raised a spurt of dust, planks, and rigging from its target. When the cloud of debris cleared, the Spaniard's waist had a chunk torn out of its weather deck and nearby bulwark, the mainsail's starboard shrouds swinging free and ratlines shredded.

Some cheers started in the two mounts, but each gun crew's chief barked ferociously to still it: merely getting on target was not a cause for celebration.

As reloading commenced, Tromp glanced toward Rik, wondering if the young Norwegian had any revised gunnery estimates, yet . . .

Simonszoon's XO was not just highly intelligent and swift with numbers, but apparently read minds, as well. "We are sustaining the projected rate of fire. Barely. The aiming interval will probably diminish as the range closes and target profile grows." He glanced at Tromp and Simonszoon. "It is my duty to point out that, if we were to shift to explosive shell, we would inflict heavier damage and hasten our defeat of these first three ships."

Tromp felt as much as saw Simonszoon's quick sideways glance; *Resolve* was his ship, but the outcome of this first engagement would ultimately determine when and where the whole fleet began to move, and so, determine the course of the battle. Tromp shook his head. "One more round of solid shot. Have them load explosive after. Kees, distance to the rest of the Spanish van?"

"The closest of the eight following war galleons is five hundred yards behind these three, which look to be the largest of their kind. The rearmost is at seven hundred yards."

Tromp nodded. "We continue with Plan Alpha:

cripple these three if possible, and be sure to make one an example to the rest."

Simonszoon curled an eyebrow. "Maarten, at four knots, that second pack of Spanish wolfhounds will be on us in eleven minutes. Maybe ten, since they've started crowding sail, now."

Tromp nodded. "By which time we will be moving faster than they could reasonably expect. And if they decide to veer after us, as they must if they wish to keep us from getting among their cargo-carrying sheep, they'll be turning out of the wind and the current."

"Very well, so they'll be at three knots then. Still, that's only thirteen minutes."

Tromp inspected the northernmost galleon; although the damage had looked superficial, she was listing. The eight-inch shells penetrated deep into ships; sometimes, they came out the other side. "Captain, let us assume the gods of the sea are blowing in our enemies' sails to get them here in twelve minutes. Even then, we can still travel more than three times as far as they, a bit more with sail." He allowed a small smile to emerge. "Assuming your engineers have not broken our engines."

Simonszoon rolled his eyes but also returned the smile. "I'll check."

The next two discharges from *Resolve*'s naval rifles came about four seconds apart; the forward mount had taken a few seconds longer to aim, this time.

Dust and debris vomited up from both galleons. The one that had already been hit showed a slight list. Tromp pointed at her. "Captain Simonszoon, I believe the next round is likely to put that Spaniard out of the fight. If it does, the aft mount is to acquire the third target."

Simonszoon was already shouting those orders as Tromp lifted his glasses again. The second hit on the northernmost galleon had struck her low in the bows, near the stem of the prow, but her list was to the other, starboard side. *Probably went through down near the waterline*, he surmised. It was a wound she could probably control, given calm and time. But she would have neither.

He shifted his view to the other, central ship. It was not clear where Mount One's shell had struck her, but there was frenzied activity amidships, and a small, persistent telltale of smoke. No decrease in speed, no sign of major structural damage. She might take more than one explosive shell to finish off: she was the leviathan of the fleet, with over fifty guns. *Resolve* was still almost twice as long as she was, and sturdier, but the Spaniard was heavy-timbered and built to absorb punishment. Against Tromp's own largest ships, and with the weather gauge, she would have been an extremely dangerous opponent.

Tromp stole a moment to check after the northern squadron of his "largest ships," sweeping the binoculars around to port. The bulk of his fleet swam into view: the northern part his plan designated as the "Anvil."

With its lighter hulls in the lead, those thirteen warships were moving northeast as briskly as a close reach would allow. They were significantly better at sailing close to the wind than their Spanish adversaries, but under these conditions, their movement could not be described as swift. However, it was also clearly unanticipated. The Spanish would logically have expected them to engage or flee, but their current course suggested neither. If the eleven war galleons that had formed up as La Flota's van were perturbed by this development, they gave no sign of it. Indeed, it was quite probable that many of them were still not aware: unlike Tromp's ships, which had all been retrofitted with the clever up-time innovation known as Aldis lamps, the Spanish ability to send signals to each other was slow and uncertain.

The three Dutch men-of-war with forty or more guns—*Prins Willem*, *Amsterdam*, and *Gelderland*— were actually keeping pace with the smaller, faster hulls, thanks to the three small steam tugs, powered by down-time-manufactured steam plants from Germany. Not particularly powerful, they still provided an extra knot or so of speed no matter the wind or seas, which was enabling Tromp's Anvil to maneuver steadily north of La Flota's main body.

Tromp lowered the glasses as cries from both gun mounts announced that the loaders were finished and clear.

Sehested sounded like a man forcing himself to maintain an admirably calm demeanor while only seven hundred yards from three of the most dreaded ships upon the waves of any sea. "Lieutenant Bjelke, is there still time to—succeed?"

"Lord Sehested, I—"

"This is the last explanation you shall provide to Lord Sehested," Tromp interrupted. "I mean no disrespect to our visitor, but until we resolve matters with the enemy's van, I will not tolerate further digressions from the task at hand."

Bjelke nodded, might have looked relieved. "Lord Sehested, our revised estimates are that, at the worst, we should strike our enemies with seven of the twenty rounds we fire. Nine is a more likely number, given the decreasing range."

"And is that enough to disable ... no, er ... what is that up-time term ... ?"

"To achieve three 'mission kills'?"

Sehested nodded uncertainly. "Yes: that."

"It is possible. We can increase the odds if—"

"Don't get lost in your math, schoolboy," Simonszoon muttered as he watched the gunners hunch over their sights. "If we've hit them twice by the time they come within two hundred and fifty yards the carronades of the first portside battery will be able to bear. That's about two more minutes, and three more rounds each time they fire."

Tromp tried to keep his tone level. "And three more rounds we will not have for later in this engagement."

Kees nodded. "If necessary, you could order *Salamander* and *Amelia* to—"

"No, it is imperative that they remain unengaged, lest we become embroiled here. We must retain freedom of movement. Our entire battle plan depends upon it."

Dirck smiled darkly. "Which is to say, our entire battle plan depends upon this hull."

Tromp shrugged. "As if that was ever in question," he said—just before the two naval rifles fired, nearly in unison.

The effect upon the already-listing galleon was so obvious that Tromp did not need his binoculars. The shell struck the ship just aft of its waist and the resulting explosion vomited out strakes, bulkheads, guns, and men.

The larger one was also hit, but in something of a freak of gunnery, the shell impacted the foremast dead center, just beneath the foreyard. Whereas most crippled masts tip and fall, this one, being bisected by the explosion, half jumped out of its stays and crashed forward in a rush. The men on the foc'sle who had not been riven by splinters or other fragments from the blast disappeared under the ruin of wood and rigging, the twisting canvas pulled after like a phantom being sucked down to hell.

Sehested cut off his satisfied grunt when he realized he was the only one enthused by the result.

Simonszoon growled in Bjelke's direction. "Tell Mount One to lower its aim or I will lower the rank of every man on that crew." He glanced at Tromp. "Admiral—"

"I know, Dirck. They will still be able to fight that hull."

"Can't catch us, though," Kees offered.

"No, but..." Tromp turned to look aft, measuring the distance between *Resolve* and the ships of the balloon detachment he'd labeled "Tower." Three and a half nautical miles astern, and the only actual warship was the one being used as the balloon's platform: *Provintie van Utrecht.* Besides a jacht and a steam pinnace that was lashed to her to provide extra speed and maneuverability, the only other ships were two fluyts and the USE cargo ship *Serendipity.* He frowned.

Simonszoon's voice echoed his thoughts from over his shoulder. "*Ja*, when that Spanish leviathan realizes she can't catch us, she'll go after those pigeons. Won't catch 'em, but that's because they'll have to run or be torn to matchsticks. And when they do, there goes our 'Tower.'"

Tromp nodded. "Mr. Bjelke," he said loudly.

"Admiral?"

"Instruct Mount One to use explosive shells until its target is destroyed."

"Destroyed, sir? Or do you mean disab—?"

"I said, and mean, destroyed." He turned back forward as Simonzsoon was instructing Mount Two to shift to the third war galleon, now barely six hundred yards away and still untouched. It turned out they were already tracking it.

Kees mumbled. "So the biggest ship is going to be made the example for the rest of La Flota. Expensive, but probably worth the rounds."

Tromp shook his head bitterly. "*Nee*, it's a waste. But we've no choice, after that shot. We have to stop her, and she's taken no significant hull damage that we know of. We have to assume she could absorb at least two explosive shells before she begins to burn badly enough that they cannot save her."

The rifles fired again. Predictably, Mount Two missed her new target, but only by ten yards in front of her bowsprit. However, Mount One's fourth round finally found its proper mark: the starboard waist, down on the lowest gundeck. The explosion seemed to go off from within the ship; possibly the shell had gone through a gunport. Although it did not leave a vast hole in the leviathan's hull, the blast propelled two guns halfway through their ports, flames licking the rims, and black smoke leaking out.

Tromp leaned toward Kees. "Alert the other ships of 'Hammer': raise anchors all haste. Course and instructions as per Plan Alpha on our signal. Mr. Bjelke, inform engineering and deck crew: prepare to get underway."

The two young officers sent the orders, which raised urgent shouts and replies from the bowels, and along the length, of *Resolve*.

The after mount fired again. The solid shell hit the third galleon, sent timbers spinning out from its hull and leaving a ragged scar just behind her foc'sle. But Tromp's focus returned immediately to the largest of the three. He raised his binoculars—

—just in time to hear and feel the faint backdraft from Mount One's fifth shot.

Maarten knew, an instant before the shell exploded, where it was ultimately going to hit; for no apparent reason, half of the big galleon's mainsail's starboard ratlines flew asunder in a confused spasm of rope and rigging, like a nest of furious, beheaded snakes. The shell had torn through the shrouds just before it plunged into the lower margin of where the quarterdeck rose up from the maindeck.

An explosion shook the stern of the ship, followed quickly by an even more ferocious and fiery detonation which blew open almost every hatch, door, and gunport lid abaft the beam. Black smoke began pouring out of half of them. Flames were visible in several. She veered away from her course, but not dramatically.

"Steering ropes are gone," Simonszoon speculated as a tongue of flame licked up along the mizzenmast, just high enough to be seen above the gunwale. "She's done."

Tromp spoke from instinct as much as experience. "She's more than done. Ahead one half, and give her a wide berth."

"At last," the captain grumbled. "Port Battery One! Prepare to acquire target: third galleon!"

Resolve began creeping forward...but suddenly, was not creeping at all. Her speed built so rapidly that it still surprised Tromp. "Kees," he muttered, "have your lads update the tactical plot. From here on, our primary focus is on moving, not shooting."

"Aye, sir."

As Simonszoon kept a firm leash on the overeager gun crews of Port Battery One, Bjelke was already calling new targets for Mounts One and Two: the closest of the next eight war galleons. Telegraph chatter from the Tower drove Kees' instructions for drawing updates on the tactical plot's clear, gridded overlay. And the chief engineer's voice was a dim, hoarse shout emerging from the dedicated speaking tube; the boilers were at temperature. He could give full steam.

Tromp let out the breath he hadn't realized he'd been holding. Finally, they were no longer measuring seconds and yards and rounds, no longer acting like bookkeepers rather than naval officers. Finally, they were doing what every fleet and every admiral since the beginning of time had been built and bred to do:

To close with the enemy and defeat him.

Chapter 7

East of Dominica

"Do we need to hit her again, Captain?" Rik Bjelke asked, looking at the smoke rising up from the side of the third war galleon.

Simonszoon squinted at the devastation wrought by the two hits that had been scored by the three guns in Port Battery One as they had crossed her bows. "*Nee*, she's fighting a fire even as she's taking water. And that mainmast won't bear the pull of canvas in a strong wind anymore. It will be hours before she's underway, and she'd be lucky to make two knots. We'll be back before she gets as far as Dominica."

Tromp nodded. "Time to lead the rest of their van on a short chase. Engine to three quarters, please, Captain. Time to catch up with the rest of Hammer."

"At three quarters, we'll be past them in eight minutes."

Tromp put his nose into the wind. "Ten. The wind has shifted a point. They'll have it full over their beam as they head southeast. But we'll be turning again before then." He pointed to the eight remaining war galleons, which were less heavily built than the first three: fitted for war, but not built specifically for it. Like most galleons.

Kees followed Tromp's finger and smiled. "Already steering more southward to come after us. They're confident, I will give them that."

"And brave," Maarten added without any enthusiasm or rancor. "They're falling under three knots as the wind starts coming more over their beam than their stern, and they are falling out of the current in the barga—"

A bright flash, followed by a biblical-scale thunderclap, silenced Tromp mid-word. Simonszoon was the only one who did not start, did not even bother to look around. "And there's the example you wanted to make, Maarten."

Tromp turned, scanning for the large war galleon they had last seen drifting, its crew fighting fires breaking out at numerous points abaft her waist. In that location there was now a still-expanding ash-gray cloud, planks and spars beginning into a down-arc as the debris that had once been the immense galleon started falling, some of it stippling the water four hundred yards from the site of its self-annihilation.

"Fire reached the magazine," Kees whispered. "Did she put down any boats, beforehand?"

Sehested's voice was sober. "I did not see any. And I was watching."

Tromp shrugged. It was a terrible loss of life and a terrible waste of a ship that would have proven very useful. But he had seen the same happen to his own ships at the hands of his current opponents.

In the pilothouse below, there was a staccato rush

of chattering from the higher-pitched telegraph clapper dedicated to relaying the balloon reports being radioed by *Provintie van Utrecht*. The precise coordinates, speeds, and bearings for the remaining war galleons matched what Tromp's long-practiced eye had already discerned. Rather than wheeling as a whole formation, they were all turning individually. In short, their uneven line was rapidly becoming a still more uneven column.

"How long do we lead the bull by the nose?" Dirck asked.

Tromp checked the changes being made to the tactical plot, the anemometer, the compass, the speed at which they were cutting through the water. "Fifteen minutes. They'll be heading due south by then. The wind and current will be fully on their beam, rather than astern."

"And then?" Sehested asked quietly.

"And then," Tromp answered, assessing the line of luffing enemy sails that started one thousand yards away and stretched to almost two thousand five hundred, "we shall turn north to intercept and teach them the consequences of their current actions."

This time, Sehested watched the tactics unfold quietly. Possibly because he had begun to understand the profound differences between *Resolve* and her opponents, or possibly because these maneuvers seemed even more bold.

By the time *Resolve* heeled hard to port to head north toward her foes, their speed had dropped under two knots. Spanish galleons were ill-designed and ill-rigged to make use of a reaching wind coming straight over their beam. Worse still, Tromp's course made it clear that he meant to approach them along their eastern side: the same side as the wind was coming from. So to block him meant turning even more into the wind, and ultimately, would put their prows staring straight into the eye of it.

They responded as would any competent captain: to luff up and trim the mainsails to reduce drag and catch the breeze with any canvas that could use a reaching wind to advantage. Their intent was obvious: to maneuver so as to make a close pass on *Resolve*'s western side, staying on a southerly heading and thereby avoid putting their bows into the wind.

A reasonable plan, Tromp allowed, if they'd had the speed to carry it out. But with *Resolve* moving almost six times as fast as the galleons, that was simply not possible. It might have been, had they been in a well-distributed pack, closing in from all sides as the steam cruiser approached them. But having turned so as to form a column, it was *Resolve* versus each galleon individually. Time and conditions had made their maneuver inevitable, and they had no doubt seen a benefit to it: as *Resolve* passed along each one, that side's batteries would have the opportunity to fire a broadside at the infernal warship.

The first of the galleons discovered the outcome of that stratagem only ten minutes after Tromp turned to the north to engage. With his screws turning slowly, just enough to give him added ability to outmaneuver and frustrate his opponents, he unveiled his plans only five hundred yards away from the target: he bore suddenly away from it, turning two points to starboard.

Resolve's speed dropped a bit and the canvas luffed

fitfully. But in order to keep alive any hope of eventually unleashing a broadside at the steamship, the galleon now had to turn toward her. If the Spaniard did not do so, the *Resolve* would race past by moving outside the range of the broadside which had seemed imminent given the convergence of their courses. But of course, as the galleon made that turn, she put herself in a close reach and her speed dropped further.

At which point, Tromp, now possessing the weather gauge, swung back to port, and closed to cross her bows. At two hundred yards, several of the Spaniard's forward broadside guns spoke, but the shells landed almost a hundred yards short and even further behind *Resolve*. The Spaniard's guns could neither be turned far enough to bear and the range was too great; half a pistol shot—or one hundred yards—was deemed the outer limit of a conventional cannon's effective range at sea. Firing at two hundred yards was a sign of complete incompetence, wild optimism, or utter desperation—the latter being the case on this occasion.

Conversely, *Resolve*'s speed now had her cutting through the low swells that had made aiming problematical when she had been station keeping. The vastly reduced chop meant she was now a far more stable platform, and her side batteries, now trained upon targets at less than three hundred yards range, boasted impressive first-shot accuracy.

Still, Simonszoon waited until *Resolve* was at a hundred fifty yards range and with a sixty-degree angle of approach to the galleon before he signaled for Bjelke to call down to Port Battery One to confirm it had sufficient elevation. When the answer came back in the affirmative, Simonszoon gave the order for its guns to fire when ready. The three carronades—short-barreled guns which had shorter range, but also shorter recoil and heavier projectiles than regular cannons—were still for a few long moments, and then barked in a ragged chorus.

But instead of three balls arcing toward the war galleon, three full sabots flew forth. Their casing fell apart and chain shot uncoiled into a wind-cutting moan. Although slow enough to track with the eye, the whirling lengths arced high and two of the three cut a path through the stays, shrouds, and sails of the fore- and mainmast both. The enemy's already poor speed dropped precipitously and the foretopmast appeared to be tilting from the point where one of the chain ends—a subcaliber ball—had cracked into it.

Bjelke turned to Simonszoon. "Captain, Battery Two is asking: chain again, or ball?"

Simonszoon glared at the Spaniard, as if willing its foremast to collapse. "Both," he sighed.

Tromp smiled at his reluctance to use chain shot, regardless of design, in the carronades. "The cases don't harm the rifling of the barrels. That's been proven."

Dirck mumbled darkly about the inherent untrustworthiness of mathematicians and engineers, just before all four guns of Port Battery Two discharged in an uneven ripple as the ship crossed the bow of the galleon.

One of the chain rounds went wide, but the other tore straight through the foretopsail and went on to splinter the mainyard behind it. The first ball sent up a white frothy divot just three yards to the port bow, but the other landed square on the foc'sle's weather deck with a burst of dust, planks, and splinters.

Bjelke looked to Simonszoon, who glanced over at Tromp. "Mount One says target is acquired. They are loaded with explosive round."

Tromp regretted every one he used, but they had been intended for the war galleons, so . . . "At the captain's discretion."

Simonszoon's grin was feral. "Mount One: fire!"

The weapon roared, and, as if in reply, the quarterdeck of the galleon blasted outward almost instantly, with two smaller explosions following immediately afterward.

"We hit a thirty-two-pounder dead-on, or I'm a goose," Kees muttered.

Tromp nodded at Kees' comment, then toward to Simonszoon, who while watching the admiral, was already giving helm directions for turning two points to starboard, thereby keeping *Resolve* out of the arc of the stricken galleon's batteries. "On to the next?"

Tromp nodded. "As soon as we get an update from Tower. Let's see what plan they're trying to come up with so that we can ruin it."

Simonszoon smiled and started giving the pilot instructions for approaching the next galleon in line.

With the balloon's constant updates on the enemy's positions and courses, *Resolve*'s only surprises came from her own side. The other ships in Tromp's Hammer element occasionally had to be brought back in line, like bloodhounds eagerly pulling at the leash to run after and bring down wounded prey: in this case, the galleons that *Resolve* had already crippled. The worst was *Salamander*, a particularly swift ship with a new captain who was eager to prove himself. The other three hulls—*Amelia*, *Prins Hendrik*, and *Crown of Waves*—were better behaved, if no less impatient to join the battle. But for now, their job was crucial (if dull) and twofold: to present a terrifying and swift wedge of ships ready to pounce upon the unprotected cargo galleons of the main body to the north; and as a reaction force in the event that one of the damaged war galleons managed to get sorted out well enough to pose a risk to *Resolve* or the progress of the battle.

But as Tromp worked down the line of eight galleons, and the "cased chain shot" proved itself during its first use in combat, he took more time with each Spaniard, closing a little more as he crossed the bows and using shot instead of ball. Less damage to the ships, yes, but the losses to their crew and troops were profound, not to say ghastly. Also, with each successive engagement, it was becoming more certain that he would not need to use a second explosive shell to incapacitate any of these hulls. In consequence, he became less concerned with trying to save as many of those precious rounds as possible. In most cases, between the losses to crew, rigging, and sails, and the fires that usually sprouted in the wake of the explosive shell, it was dubious that many of these ships would be underway before the sun sank behind Dominica.

Another surprise occurred when the balloon had to return to the *Provintie van Utrecht* earlier than anticipated: the batteries for the radio in the balloon had either leaked or discharged more rapidly than anticipated. So when *Resolve* reached the fifth galleon in line, it was necessary to engage without benefit of updates. However, in some respects, it was a welcome break to fight a ship the way men had always fought them up to now: by eye, and experience, and instincts born of long hours at sea. The outcome of the engagement with the fifth Spaniard was, for all intents and purposes, identical, and the sixth was different only insofar as the marksmanship of both *Resolve*'s side batteries and deck mounts had improved so markedly that the explosive round might not have been necessary. Indeed, judging from the fires which began raging along its length, Tromp realized that it might eventually prove to have been an unintentional coup de grâce.

As *Resolve* began sweeping toward the seventh galleon, the main barrelman—the lookout in the mainmast's crow's nest—cried that the last two war galleons were putting their bows over to starboard to get the breeze and current behind them once again. But having steered so near to the eye of the wind, they were slow in turning.

Simonszoon leaned back just as, miles to the west, the balloon surged aloft again, and the higher-pitched clicks and clacks of its dedicated receiver recommenced with a vigor. "Now, it's just a chase."

Bjelke nodded. "We'll be on that next galleon before she'll feel any wind upon her stern."

"Which we shall cross at fifty yards and rake with shot. Never mind the stern cannons, either. They're such small bore that they will barely dent the pitch on our strakes."

Tromp did not add that if a full battery of carronades loaded with canister swept a galleon from the stern, there was a better than even chance that her rear-aiming guns would not be able to retaliate. "It won't be much different with the last of the Spaniards.

We'll close the distance to her in five minutes, assuming she's already making two knots in that time. Like the other, she has to show us her stern in order to run, and that will be the end of the combat. And finally, after we've finished with her, we can get to work."

Sehested sputtered in amused surprise, held up hands when critical eyes turned his way. "Gentlemen, please understand: I am not laughing. I am simply amazed that all of what has transpired is somehow *not* work."

"Well," Simonszoon offered in a surprisingly thoughtful tone, "I cannot disagree with that. But, this has all been the work we are hungry for—the work we dream about. What comes next, is, well—"

"Dull?" Sehested interrupted. "Boring?"

Tromp saw that his surprise at Sehested's confident tone was reprised in the faces of the other officers on the flying bridge.

The Danish diplomat waved a hand. "Gentlemen, I may not be a naval officer, but I like to think that I learn relatively quickly. I have seen, all day, in your eyes, that the risks, the challenge, of this battle are what you live for. It is why you became and remain naval officers. And as much as you worried and argued about the risks, that is all part of what excites you.

"You remained still to draw their warships closer to you and away from the main body. That audacity went against all naval wisdom, which is why you alternated between complaining about it and being alert and eager. And then, when it worked, you still had to turn the tables upon them. Which you have done, by using this ship and that balloon and even those steam tugs in ways that the Spanish could not hope to understand."

He saw Kees' quizzical look. "Yes, I understand the point of the steam tugs, Lieutenant. It was not enough that the Spanish war galleons sped ahead of their main body and then could not maneuver back to engage you without turning into the wind and the current." He smiled. "You had to begin the engagement motionless. That way, it wasn't just the war galleons that kept coming on, but the cargo ships of La Flota as well. In order to get Anvil—the largest part of your fleet—to the north of their main body, the tugs had to move the largest ships at the same rate as the smaller, swifter ones. And because of that, they now are just where you need them: opposite your Hammer and with the Spanish merchantmen between."

He smiled back at the slow appreciative smiles arising around him. "Come now, gentlemen, even a child would understand that if the northern squadron is called Anvil, then we can predict the role of this small but incredibly powerful Hammer." He gestured to *Resolve* and her escorts. "Now, with the Spanish warships almost all accounted for, you are just south of La Flota's main body, and ready to strike. Dominica blocks them to the west, and the currents and the wind from the east keep them from making way in that direction. Their only choice is to flee north: toward the Anvil as the Hammer pressed hard after them." His smile faded slightly. "But, I must ask: can you actually hope to destroy so many ships?"

"Maybe, thanks to our admiral's inherent stinginess," Simonszoon grinned. "By making their warships come to us, we also conserved a great deal of fuel and ammunition. Most of which we're going to need in this last phase."

"I am not stingy; I am thrifty," Tromp amended while maintaining a straight face. "But to answer your question, Lord Sehested, we do not intend to destroy all those ships. We mean to capture them. Or at least as many as we can."

Sehested stared. "How can you hope to achieve that? You haven't enough boarding parties. And even if you did, there are so many galleons and naos before us that you would be fighting for days."

Simonszoon pointed astern, first at the flaming fragments that had once been the mightiest war galleon in La Flota, and then at the one that they had more recently set aflame from stem to stern. "All the wallowing cargo haulers have seen how that happened, and know it could happen to them, too. With just a few rounds. No broadsides required."

"And do you have so many of the explosive rounds that you can fire one at every ship which decides to challenge you, despite those fears?"

"Not for our rifles, no"—Tromp suppressed a grin—"but the Spanish don't know that. Once we finish crippling these last two war galleons, we shall steam straight into the midst of the main body. They have seen that we are too fast for them to elude, and that also, from beyond the maximum range of their guns, we can inflict crippling damage with but a few shells. Just as we did to their war galleons. Given their slow and uncertain signaling, they will not be able to coordinate movements and so will almost certainly scatter in all directions. Some are already discovering that in order to maneuver—either to escape south through us or north through our Anvil—they are having to gather in their mainsails and make what way they can.

"At that point, the other ships of our flotilla are simply there to prevent them from escaping; like sheepdogs working with frightened ewes. One by one our warships shall approach the Spanish merchantmen. If any galleon or nao so much as fires a warning shot, we put a shell into it from one of our naval rifles. A few such demonstrations and I predict that most of them will strike colors as soon as one of our other ships comes alongside."

Simonszoon shrugged. "Me? I suspect most of them will still need to have the personal experience of at least one nonexplosive round before they'll comply. But since we will be sailing and moving at our leisure, beyond the range of their guns, and putting crushing damage upon them while rarely missing, I am hopeful that a good number of the others will realize the futility of fighting us at all."

Sehested nodded, understanding. "That is why you have cargo ships back with the Tower; to offload the Spanish goods."

Trompe scratched his ear. "Well, in part . . . but mostly, those ships with Tower are carrying prize crews. We don't mean to just take the Spanish goods; we mean to take their ships."

Sehested shook his head. "Admiral, to attempt all by depending upon the performance of this one ship goes beyond mere audacity. It is—is breathtaking."

"Yes." Simonszoon's grin would have looked atypically fierce on a wolf. "Isn't it, though?"

"But . . . but was it really necessary?" Sehested persisted. "After all, Commodore Cantrell's *Intrepid* was present, as well. He could certainly have loitered nearby, entered the battle at any time. And two hulls instead of one would certainly have made gathering this unruly flock of Spanish merchantmen much easier."

"Yes, it would have," Tromp agreed. "But that was exactly why we did not do so."

"I beg your pardon?"

Tromp turned to face him directly. "Lord Sehested, this war we are fighting beyond the Tordesillas Line— for let us not delude ourselves; we are at war with Spain, here—is unique in two ways. Firstly, neither one of us knows the full disposition of the other's forces. Such uncertainty applies to all military campaigns to some degree, but it is several orders of magnitude greater, here. Secondly, one of the combatants—us— possesses a variety of capabilities that are not merely unavailable to, but are incompletely comprehended by, our opponent. Now consider how both of these factors influence our decision to carry out this entire operation with—apparently—only *Resolve*.

"The Spanish—and now the Bermudans—will know and report that only *one* of our cruisers was here. Consider what they will be told by witnesses: that all the losses inflicted upon them were orchestrated and enabled by a single steam warship. There can be no greater display of how powerful they are individually.

"But secondly, knowing that we have two such ships, it also tells them that our threat to them is actually twice that of what we demonstrated today. Or, to put it in terms of a defender's worst nightmare, it means that we can exercise this power at two different locations in the Caribbean at the same time. This will at least double the apprehension of the Spanish, as well as the amount of assets they will deem necessary for defense." Tromp shrugged. "Besides, two ships would have been overkill."

"Would have been what?" Sehested asked.

Tromp managed to suppress a pleased smile. Some up-time terms seemed intrinsically rich with echoes of lethality and dark panache. "Overkill," Tromp repeated. "More force than is needed to complete a task." He glanced north. "Besides, *Intrepid* was needed elsewhere."

Sehested nodded. "Guadeloupe?"

Of course he would have heard. Tromp nodded back. "It is essential that we secure certain arrangements and come to certain agreements with the Kalinago of that island."

"Well," drawled Simonszoon, as the gun crews started readying for action against the seventh galleon, "*Intrepid* is quite a show of force. Quite enough to shock the natives into meek complacency, I suspect."

"I hope so," Tromp answered. His eyes were not on the enemy ship; they were still fixed on the northern horizon. "I truly hope so."

Chapter 8

Petit Cul-de-Sac Marin, Guadeloupe

"Starboard Battery Two, A gun, reports ready, Commodore!" Svantner cried over the flap of *Intrepid*'s sails.

"Fire at the crew chief's discretion, Lieutenant!" Eddie shouted back, albeit with none of his XO's animation.

That permission, shouted down a speaking tube to the cruiser's gun deck, brought no immediate response from the weapon. *Take your time*, thought Eddie, raising his binoculars to examine the state of their target.

The French bark, only two hundred thirty yards away, was in difficult straits—literally and figuratively. Barely more than a third the length or freeboard of the *Intrepid*, she had been at anchor in Guadeloupe's large southern bay, the Petit Cul-de-Sac Marin, when the larger ship appeared with the Dutch jachts *Zuidsterre* and *Fortuin*.

These escorts, lately attached after completing their duties as the northern arms of the detection net spread before La Flota, harried the larger bark, dancing away from her guns, but cutting off any escape out into open water. Eddie had kept *Intrepid* slightly back from those maneuvers, watching the Frenchman for signs of where she felt it safe to go and where not. Had he been conning the bark, his goal would have been to entice the impossibly large steam cruiser to follow him into shallows and there either run aground, or be in enough danger of doing so that she would abandon pursuit in favor of carefully navigating back to safe waters.

That did indeed seem to be what the Frenchman had been hoping to achieve. After the first quarter hour, when it was clear that the cruiser was not taking that bait, he made one run to escape, hard along the eastern shore. He had not counted on the range of *Intrepid*'s carronades. Starboard Battery One had discharged all three guns. The result was one embarrassingly wide miss, a very near one, and a solid hit amidships. The power of that sixty-eight-pound ball at such close range sent strakes, planks, and a deck gun flying up and the Frenchman flying back the way he had come.

As the bark heeled over to beat that retreat, Eddie would almost certainly have scored at least one more hit by coming a point to port, thereby giving Battery Two a ready target. But by chasing the enemy hull back into the Petit Cul-de-Sac Marin, he hoped its captain would see and submit to the hopelessness of his situation, and thereby surrender his ship to ensure the survival of his crew.

Either the captain was made of sterner stuff or was simply stubborn. For the next half hour, he attempted to entice *Intrepid* into chasing him, ultimately tucking tightly around the western end of one of the bay's small islands—Îlet Cochon—and making for the glorified sandbar named Îlet Boissard. It was an act of desperation, in that no mariner worth their salt would have followed him there, not even the shallow-drafted jachts. But the French captain had little choice; he was now operating in a patch of water so small, and so uneven in the rise and drop of its sandy bed, that his only remaining hope was for his enemies to make a foolish mistake or intercession by force majeure. Which on a day as clear as this one, Eddie reflected with a rueful smile, would mean the freakish appearance of either a water funnel or a hoary-hided kraken.

Neither appeared, and his opponent's desperation took its toll: it was the Frenchman that ultimately found itself brushing the bottom in a touch-and-go dance with running aground. Instead of *Intrepid*, it was the bark that had to slow and, using sails ill suited for the purpose, reverse her course out of the labyrinth of silt and sand at the foot of the bay. And at the present moment, that meant showing her stern to *Intrepid*.

And still, Eddie realized, Starboard Two's A gun had yet to fire. He was about to make a loud suggestion that sooner would be better than later when the gun released its raucous blast along with a plume of white smoke. An eyeblink later, its ball punched down upon the amidship deck planks of the bark, just aft of the mainmast. Its angle of impact—extremely acute—had the effect of almost skipping the shot back up, but it was blocked by two very solid objects: the mainmast and its deck collar.

The impact generated a crack like a wood-splitting

lightning strike, and the surrounding planks buckled or sheared, broken ends sticking up like sawed-off toe tips. The chaotic spray of wood dropped several deckhands and those who remained fought to keep the mast up. Either orders or a greater understanding of the damage reversed those labors; now they were trying to ensure that its fall would not bring down the foremast.

They managed that, but settling back into the divot dug by the carronade's ball, the mainmast tilted and then rushed down sternward, stripping the gaff clean off the mizzen as swiftly and surely as an axe trimming a dried branch.

"She's done!" Svantner said enthusiastically, loudly. "They'll strike colors any second, now."

Eddie crossed his arms and frowned. This captain had persisted when most others would have accepted the inevitable. "We'll see," was all he said.

Three minutes later, the Frenchman's starboard stern cannon roared defiance at her three opponents; the six-pound ball missed *Zuidsterre* by thirty yards. Not bad shooting, given the range of two hundred fifty yards. On the shattered deck, men were moving with purpose: making repairs, passing out muskets, adjusting the foresail to renew their attempts to escape the twisting shallow, and tossing the dead over the side.

Eddie shook his head; just what he'd feared.

Svantner was outraged. "What instructions for the Master Gunner, sir?" he almost shouted, although the cannons were still that moment.

Eddie sighed. "Starboard Battery One is to load with canister."

"To bring down their foresail, sir?"

"Svantner, it's not their foresail that keeps them fighting." Eddie sighed more deeply. "Aim low. Sweep the length of the deck. Stop when she strikes her colors."

"And if she doesn't?"

"Then keep firing until there's no one left to shoot back."

As his longboat's prow touched the sand with a grating hiss, Eddie glanced past the white flag fluttering over its transom: *Intrepid* looked deceptively small at this distance. It was the first time since coming to the New World that he'd been in potentially enemy territory while outside of her protective umbrella and stout hull. It was not, he decided, a particularly enjoyable sensation.

He rose from the seat as the team of Marines in the bow—armed with percussion cap rifles and revolvers—jumped into the knee-deep water on either side and made their way out of the lazy surf. There was no indication that anyone in the small encampment a hundred yards east and just beyond the margin of the beach had noticed their arrival. Nor was there a Kalinago war party waiting for them, either. About which he had to wonder: was that a good sign or the calm before a storm?

Since being lowered down from *Intrepid*'s aft davits, Eddie had thought more than once that maybe Svantner had been right: mount the outboard motor for this mission. Probably wouldn't be needed, but if it was, there was nothing like a thirty-horse-power engine to ensure a quick getaway. But mounting it and testing it would have meant a delay, and following up the decisive defeat of the French bark with a prompt, confident visit under a flag of truce was the best way to keep the initiative.

Which, Eddie acknowledged with a sigh, would not be achieved by remaining on *Intrepid*'s skiff. As he made ready to stand—not easy with a prosthetic foot and ankle, even one of up-time design and manufacture—Lieutenant Gallagher jumped out and pulled the boat a foot or two further up the strand. The young Irishman—one of the Wild Geese mercenaries—smiled back at him. "Mind, there's a wee undertow, Commodore."

Eddie nodded, pushed down two resentments. First, that he didn't have two feet of his own any longer. And second, that he'd agreed to having the commander of his elite troops accompany him as a personal guard, the notion of which fit Eddie's view of himself and the world about as well as kneepads fit a chicken. But Svantner's objections had bordered on insubordination: it was his role to make landfall instead of his CO. And, under other circumstances, he would have been right.

But these circumstances were not typical, and required a diplomatic touch that Svantner sorely lacked. So Eddie had suggested that one of the Wild Geese could look after his safety. Even that failed to mollify Svantner until Gallagher overheard the debate and promptly volunteered himself for the duty.

Which left Eddie with three choices. Decide against a guard from the Wild Geese (no good; it had been his idea); insist upon another of the mercenaries (a slap to Gallagher's face), or reverse his order and refuse any guard at all (probably stupid and a CO can't even *appear* to waffle).

With a nod to the two ship's troops who were remaining behind to guard the skiff and maintain visual contact with Svantner (who was probably about to have kittens), Eddie threw his good leg over the side, waited for the slack in the space between the tide's ebb and flow, got his prosthetic solidly on the sand, and marched toward the tents to the east.

Eddie had anticipated many possibilities when he had seen the cluster of tents and lean-tos from the deck of *Intrepid*. It could have been the starving survivors of a failed colony; a camp of invalids, weakened by malnutrition and struck down by a local disease; cripples who, after fleeing from retribution after their failed attack on St. Eustatia, had lost their health along with the limbs taken by a combination of gangrene and the surgeon's saw. The only thing that seemed certain was that its inhabitants were neither numerous nor vigorous; forty-five minutes of observation through a spyglass had yielded only a few signs of brief, labored movement.

But none of that prepared him for what he discovered as he approached the tents. For the first few moments, he couldn't even come up with a mental label for it. But then one emerged: The Colony of Lost Women. Almost all of whom were malnourished, sickly, or both.

At the center, one thin, well-featured man—pale, dark-haired, bearded—was sitting on the remains of a sun-bleached crate. He stood unsteadily and said, "I am Jacques Dyel du Parque. Nephew of Pierre d'Esnambuc, late the governor of the French colony on St. Christopher, whose ship and life you have just erased from this world." His smile was both sardonic and rueful. "I suspect you wish our surrender."

Chapter 9

Petit Cul-de-Sac Marin, Guadeloupe

Even after the French survivors had all been removed to *Intrepid*, the Kalinago didn't emerge from the forest until she lowered a longboat carrying the warriors they'd left behind when fleeing St. Eustatia.

Two of them rose into view and approached at a brisk walk. As Eddie and Gallagher went to meet them, the Kalinago seemed to take notice of the unevenness of Eddie's gait; he noticed that they were both missing an eye. They stopped when they were ten feet away.

The taller, and considerably older one—still impressively muscled and with the chiseled features of a movie star—pointed at the longboat and unleashed a stream of French.

Which Eddie had been expecting, and for which he had studied, but which now flew out of his head under the pressure of the situation. "*P-pardon,*" he stammered—*great strong start, Eddie*—"*mais je ne parle pas français.*"

The two Kalinago glanced at each other. The

87

smaller one jerked his head at Eddie and whispered, "*Mais il le fait!*"

Uh, what? Eddie was conscious of the seconds ticking past as he struggled to remember words which resembled those. It didn't help when Gallagher whispered, "Y'don't *parlez vous*, Commodore?"

"Geez, Gallagher, does it *sound* like I can?" *Wait.* "Do you?"

"I've been known to aggravate a few Flemish gentlemen by doing business with them in that language they love so well."

"So...what'd he say?"

"Ah. So, when you said, 'Pardon, I don't speak French' that confused 'em, and the little one said, 'But 'e does!'"

Under other circumstances, Eddie might have laughed, but the look in the remaining eyes of the two Kalinago made him suspect that it could be perceived as a grave insult. With the emphasis on grave.

The taller of the two Kalinago pointed at the oncoming longboat. "Our mans."

Wait. "You speak English?"

"Small of it." He jabbed his finger at the boat again. "Our mans. You keep *otage*?"

"Gallagher...?"

"Asks if they're being held hostage by you. Shall I make introductions, sir?"

"You go right ahead with that, Gallagher. You are now our designated interpreter."

Gallagher presented Eddie and learned that the tall one was the cacique Touman, and the smaller his nephew Youacou. The tarnish of disuse rapidly fell away from the Kalinagos' surprisingly good English.

"We were taught by Tegreman, the last cacique of Liamuiga," Touman explained.

"Who your people killed," Youacou added.

"Whoa!" Eddie objected, hands raised. "I didn't kill anybody! And I'm here to make sure that none of our people ever kill each other again. So, let's start with this: the men on the boat just coming ashore are not hostages. They were wounded warriors left behind when you fled St. Eustatia—uh, Aloi."

The first of them were already leaping over the bows of the longboat and racing toward their cacique. Touman held up a palm against their rush: they stopped as if they'd struck a wall. He looked at Eddie. "My people—they are free? Without, eh, conditions?"

"Free, yes. No conditions."

Touman waved sharply at the forest behind him; the twelve Kalinago prisoners sprinted for the trees. His one eye narrowed as he reconsidered Eddie. "You have not come from Liamuiga—St. Christopher—just to return these men."

"No, but I would have, had that been my only business with you."

Touman looked unconvinced but also seemed willing to listen. "Speak your other business."

Eddie nodded. "Firstly, we appreciate that you allowed the French innocents to live here until someone came to remove them from Guadelou—eh, um, Karukera."

Touman's eye softened for the briefest instant when Eddie used the Kalinago name for Guadeloupe. "They are the last of the French who came here. After our attack on Aloi, the ship of d'Esnambuc, one of their leaders, was pushed away by storms. When he returned, we met him before he came ashore and told him that the other French chief, du Plessis, had fled. He said he shared our anger."

Touman shrugged. "We knew that d'Esnambuc might be lying. But we also knew that he truly loved his nephew, he whom you met at the camp. So we told d'Esnambuc he would be welcome to come ashore again if he returned with the coward du Plessis. He sailed away to find him.

"Many months passed. The other Frenchmen tried to steal food from us. Du Parque, the man you met, was good and honest but could not control them, so they were killed. We brought the others—the women and the children—to this shore." Touman sighed. "Many became sick and died. We do not know why.

"Two days ago, d'Esnambuc returned, but he had not found du Plessis. Still, he wanted to take away his nephew and the other survivors. We were considering this when your ship arrived and destroyed his. Now, all matters are settled."

He fixed his one eye upon Eddie. "You say you came to make sure that no more Kalinago would die fighting your people. Are you a cacique, that you can make such a promise?"

Eddie shook his head. "I am not. However, my leaders have made it a law not to harm your people, and they will punish any who do so."

"And this applies just to the Kalinago of Karukera, or to all the Kalinago?"

Eddie nodded. "All the Kalinago. And not just them. All the peoples of all these islands and the lands beyond."

Touman narrowed his eye again. "In the places

where both our peoples live, your people take land and then refuse to share it or even let us walk upon it. How then will there not be war?"

"Actually," Eddie said uncomfortably, "after we remove the last few French remaining on Martinique, there will be no islands where both your people and those of us from over the sea have communities. We have searched carefully and found no more Kalinago on any of what we call the Leeward Islands."

Touman shrugged and nodded. "That seems true, yet you do not speak of leaving those islands so that we may return."

Eddie had known this moment would come, but had not expected it to arrive so quickly. "Cacique Touman, just as no leader has the power to undo what has been done, those people no longer have homes to which they may return. Here is what we propose: unless we are invited, we shall not visit the lands where your people still live, the ones we call the Windward Islands. My people shall live only on those lands where your people no longer dwell: the Leeward Islands."

Eddie leaned back. *So now, Touman, it's raise, call, fold—or kill me where I sit.*

When Touman did not answer immediately, Youacou glared at him. "You cannot—"

"I am cacique. I 'can' whatever I wish," Touman interrupted quietly.

Youacou's lips sealed into a rigid horizontal line.

Touman's one eye had not left Eddie's two. "What you say is not pleasant to hear. That is why I am inclined you mean what you have said, and that you are an honest man. But there is another matter: our ancestors."

Eddie nodded. "Cacique, we know that many of your people trace their roots to Tegreman's tribe on Liamuiga. We shall set aside a haven for them on the windward side of the island, which they may visit at any time, and from there, travel to all other parts of the island."

Touman could not keep his face completely free of the telltale hints of surprise.

Eddie wasn't done. "We also know that you have burial sites among the Leeward Islands, where you go to honor your ancestors—"

Touman leaned forward sharply. "And you mean to allow us to return to those places?"

"As often as you like."

"And we would be the only ones allowed to go there?"

"We presumed anything else would desecra—er, destroy their holiness."

"And when we go to such sites, none will intrude upon us?"

Eddie hadn't even thought of that. "No."

Touman looked suddenly, even ferociously, suspicious. "Then how may you be sure that we will not use such places and permissions to gather a force and attack one of your nearby settlements?"

Eddie shrugged. "Because it wouldn't achieve anything, Cacique Touman." He gestured toward *Intrepid*. "You are a wise man. You understand the significance of the changes you see around you. That is why you were willing to help the French attack the radio on St. Eustat—uh, Aloi.

"So you must also know that sneak attacks such as you describe would only bring retributions and hardship. There are those among my people who might then be able to convince my leaders that you cannot be trusted and so, should not be allowed to live on any of these islands. Or anywhere else."

Touman nodded soberly, stood, and faced back where his invisible entourage was waiting. After a moment, they rose. He pointed at Eddie and started speaking loudly in French.

Gallagher whispered the translation over Eddie's shoulder. "This pale man from over the sea has come with words and proposals of peace and respect"—and he rattled off what Eddie had proposed.

At the end of that list, he paused for a moment to let the gathered warriors reflect on it. "He is the first pale man who has even tried to understand the ways in which we honor our ancestors in their old places. I have looked into his eyes as he said these things. He respects our ways, and as a war leader of his people, has come to seek an agreement that shall not only end the wars between us, but keep new ones from arising."

Touman's tone became slightly more grave. "He knows that what he offers cannot right all the wrongs that have been suffered. But if his leaders honor his words, then we shall regain through peace what we can no longer reclaim by war. Our numbers are too small, and their weapons are too powerful. Two of you: send word. Despite the cannons we heard today, we have peace."

He sat and then smiled at Eddie. "And now you will tell me what your leaders want, Edd-ee Kant-rell."

"It's that obvious?" Eddie said miserably.

"I am a cacique. I know leaders *always* want something. What is it that yours want?"

Trying to feel like he wasn't in kindergarten, Eddie

shrugged. "At this moment, a great fleet of ours is in battle with the great fleet that the Spanish send every year."

"Ah-mm," Touman said with a nod. "La Flota."

Eddie wondered just how many languages Touman spoke. He also wondered how the Europeans had even thought to label indigenous peoples as "ignorant." "Yes. Messages through our smaller radios tell me that we shall win. However, the victory will be so great that we will have more prisoners than we can care for. Far too many."

Touman looked perplexed. "How is this a difficulty? They are your enemies."

And here comes the cultural disconnect. Eddie pointed to the longboat that had brought the former Kalinago prisoners. "When we take prisoners, we do not kill them later. There is a word—a French word, I think—that explains this rule of war among us: parole."

Touman nodded. "Yes. We know this word. But among us, this honor is only given to those of the same people. Otherwise, prisoners live only if a cacique wishes it."

Eddie nodded. "I understand. Among us, if one side signals that it wishes to surrender, the leaders of both armies meet and, if they can agree to terms, those losers become the prisoners of the winners. Or they are given parole."

Youacou's voice was careful. "From what I have heard and seen, many of your leaders kill those who attempt to surrender."

Eddie nodded. "I cannot deny that is often true. So yes, Youacou: there are many faults with this." He returned his attention to Touman. "Cacique, we have no way to keep all those who surrender after the sea battle as our prisoners. So we must leave them in a place where they may survive long enough to build boats and sail to a Spanish colony."

Touman nodded. "Au-hmm. Now I see what your leaders wish of us: to leave the prisoners here."

"Well, not here on Guad...uh, Karukera itself. We were thinking of one of the smaller islands not too far away. They will be left with the means to depart, but no weapons."

Touman frowned. "Will there be wounded? Women, children?"

Eddie shrugged; more questions he hadn't anticipated. "Wounded, surely. Probably some women: wives and passengers. Children? Maybe, but only a few."

"Then those persons shall wait on Karukera, beside us. Let the Spanish see what it is to have the Kalinago as friends, and regret that they shall never know us as such."

Oh, boy: how to handle this *one?* "Cacique Touman, that is a great kindness you offer, but even if you only take the ones who seem least dangerous among you, they might find a way to pass information to the men we have marooned, who might then try to come ashore by stealth and take what they want rather than build their ships."

Touman's expression was one of disappointment, possibly disgust. "They might be so bad as that?"

"Would it be so surprising if they *were* that bad, given what men from over the sea have already done to you and your people?"

Touman nodded. "It requires a strong heart to speak a truth that shames one's own people."

Eddie's spine had gone ramrod straight before he was aware of it. "Cacique, these prisoners might look like me, but they are *not* my people."

Touman frowned and nodded. "That is fairly said. But it will be a happy surprise if I meet more men who look like you who also speak truth like you. For now, bring the Spanish, but not to Karukera itself."

Eddie nodded. "Thank you, Cacique Touman. With your permission, we shall maroon them on the small, linked islands to the southeast. We call them by one name: Petite-Terre."

Touman's eye widened slightly; if he noticed the grim satisfaction on his nephew's face, he gave no sign of it. "Men cannot live there for long."

"Which is precisely why it suits, Cacique Touman. The Spanish will understand that they must work quickly to depart or they will perish. But be careful if you must visit them; having tools, they may be able to fashion crude spears."

"We have experience of the Spanish," Touman assured him with a nod.

Okay, segue time. "In the event that they become worrisome to you, we could leave you the means to contact us."

Touman looked wary but also intrigued. "And how might we do that?"

Well, here goes nothin'... "You have seen us signal with lights?"

Touman nodded. "Flashes that are a code for making words."

"Yes."

"And this is also how your radio communicates, yes?"

He's more interested than wary, now. "Yes. You

understand it perfectly."

"Are you offering us the means of such communications?"

Uh-oh, didn't see him jumping to that. *Time to manage heightened expectations.* "Teaching you how to send light signals with what we call a heliograph is fairly quick and simple. Radios are much more difficult. However, before you can use either in your own language, you must have, um, codes for each word you want to send. We could only teach you the codes in one of our languages, one that you know how to read. French, perhaps?"

Touman was evidently considering other complexities as well. "First you promise we shall have complete privacy on our islands. Now you hold out the temptation of communication." The eyebrow over Touman's empty socket raised, pulling the scarred flesh into an ugly cluster of wrinkles and folds. "These are your leaders speaking through you, once again."

Eddie cocked his head. "Actually, the communication was my idea. And I believe it will help us both. But if you are not comfortable having it, I will not mention it again."

Touman seemed even more intrigued by that response. "Tell me how it would help us both."

Eddie shrugged. "From the top of the Leeward Islands to the end of the Windward Islands, the greatest gap between any two sequential islands is between here and Antigua. Even that is well within heliograph range."

Touman nodded. "So messages could travel from mountain top to mountain top."

"Yes, Cacique. All the way up and down the Lesser Antilles. Complex messages take a long time to send.

But there are also short codes—alerts—that can be sent and spread quickly."

"Such as if a fleet of your enemy's ships is sighted," Touman offered knowingly.

Eddie nodded. "Or ships bringing invaders back to your shores."

Youacou's tone was suspicious, but measured. "I like this not, my cacique. Why would these men be so concerned for our welfare? This is for their benefit alone."

Touman shook his head, then nodded toward Eddie. "He thinks like a chief. He knows that if his enemies return to attack us, then our problems shall become his problems quickly enough." He lifted his chin. "How many of your people would it take to operate these 'heliographs'?"

"It could be done with five men. And you would be free to enter their station any time you wish." He shrugged. "It is your land."

Touman smiled sideways at his nephew without taking his eyes off the up-timer. "And now you see how he shows that his intent is genuine: he gives us hostages." He nodded at Eddie and stood. "We shall do well together, Edd-ee Kant-rell. Come: let us eat."

Chapter 10

East of Dominica

Maarten Tromp empathized with the Spanish, even if he felt less than an iota of sympathy for them.

If they had had a balloon of their own, they could have foreseen each step of the disaster that had unfolded in the seaway before Dominica. And if they had had a radio, the cargo galleons might have fashioned an organized response to *Resolve*'s dash into their midst at flank speed: a wolf plunging into a flock of sheep. For instance, they might have attempted to box in the USE warship from all points of the compass. However, even had they been able to coordinate, they were also massively undergunned and the wind and current was now against the majority of them. So such an undertaking would have been risky and quite perilous. At best.

Instead, *Resolve* had struck terror into her foes, both near and far. Her carronades—split into forward and after batteries of three guns and two four-gun waist batteries, one afore the beam, one abaft—had engaged any target within four hundred yards or less.

The percentage of hits was only moderate, but the impact upon Spanish morale was severe. The wallowing galleons veered away from the steam cruiser without any thought to wind or current. Their understandable instinct was to diminish their target profile in the face of gunnery that struck its targets with one out of four balls it fired, and in which every hit penetrated the stoutest hull and wreaked unprecedented havoc.

Those few captains who did attempt to close with *Resolve*, either from an excess of martial spirit or dearth of tactical intelligence, found their boldness rewarded with catastrophe. Even two who had been able to find enough wind and current to make three knots toward the cruiser discovered that, in the three minutes it took to close from four hundred yards to one hundred, *Resolve*'s rate of fire and murderous close-range accuracy reduced them to drifting hulks before they could turn and deliver a broadside. Even if two such galleons had chanced to close simultaneously from opposite sides of *Resolve*'s compass rose, she would simply have added a bit of steam or set her sails to catch a little more wind until the range had opened once again. In the event that both ships had not been thoroughly brutalized, the survivor would then have had to choose between trying cases with her once again or to sheer off from another exercise in naval futility.

After having roughed up, or outright mauled, half a dozen merchantmen in this fashion, the Dutch spyglasses saw what the reports from Tower were confirming: that the Spanish were now pressing north. Not in response to any orders—they were maneuvering so frantically that signals were all but useless—but simply because it was the only direction which offered any chance of survival. That the thirteen waiting ships of Tromp's Anvil had more guns and were better rigged for reaching winds did not seem to deter them.

At about that time, sails appeared behind the Spanish on the far northeastern and southeastern horizons: the nearest jachts of the net that Eddie had used to detect La Flota had now reached it, like the ends of a seine pulling close to seal behind a great school of trapped fish.

Kees adjusted the plot, swallowed a cup of water handed to him by one of the runners. Although the breeze kept them cool and the awning over the flying bridge helped, they'd all been in and out of the tropical sun throughout the day, and it was nearing two in the afternoon. "Some of the galleons closest to us are coming about, Admiral."

Tromp nodded. "Like a school of fleeing fish, each is hoping it will be one of the lucky ones to slip past."

"Widen the head of our Hammer, sir?"

"Yes. That time has come."

Kees sent a runner with a message. Within minutes, *Resolve*'s four escorts sheered away from the cruiser, which they had been paralleling closely. No further instructions were needed. This was the next part of Plan Alpha: to obstruct, and if necessary cripple, the ships. Under normal circumstances, achieving that would have been far more difficult than it sounded. But with the Spaniards fleeing and unable to outsail the Dutch warships, they could not maneuver to deliver a broadside, nor could they deny their adversaries the opportunity to cross their stern and lay into them with broadsides of shot and chain. The first two that tried to slip past *Resolve* in this fashion were soon nearly dead in the water, one with flames springing up at various points. Tromp tried to see that as a victory, but he could only see it as one less ship and cargo with which to strengthen his fleet and its home port.

A very similar situation was playing out in the north. Although the Spanish outnumbered the Dutch ships of Tromp's Anvil better than two to one, they were coming as scattered, desperate hulls, not a formation. Again, Tromp's ships simply followed Plan Alpha, with occasional tweaks and adjustments made possible by the Tower's observations. And with *Resolve* heading into the rear of that diffuse collection of galleons, Anvil would not need to take on all of them alone.

Tromp decided to come quite close to the rearmost of the fleeing merchantmen—five hundred yards—before ordering a standard round fired for ranging purposes. Ironically, it hit the afterdeck and the Spaniards' progress became unsteady: damage to the tiller ropes, probably. He steamed past, changing his tactics as he went. Plan Alpha called for controlled, high-accuracy fire into the galleons, starting by hitting the rearmost until she burned high and fast. Then *Resolve* would work methodically forward through the other shaken Spaniards.

But the Spanish were now so panicked that Maarten feared such a spectacle of destruction abaft would only resolve them to more desperate measures. Better to make the path ahead more fearsome, and so, propel them into a state of indecision. Once in that state of mind, the notion of surrender might have enough time to push up through their panic as a reasonable option.

Tromp called for the range to the galleon closest to Anvil.

Bjelke was about twenty seconds in getting the measurement. "Twenty-two hundred yards, sir."

Tromp glanced at Dirck, whose gesture was one of invitation and his permission; the admiral was cleared to give direct orders to *Resolve*.

"Engineer, full speed."

"Full speed, aye."

"Helm, give me a course toward that lead galleon, but adjust for the current and the swells. I need low chop rather than maximum speed."

"Understood, Admiral."

"Mounts One and Two, can you both bear on lead ship?" Affirmatives came in. "Commence tracking. Load standard round. You will commence fire at fifteen hundred yards, pending my orders."

More affirmatives as the full measure of steam reached the propellers and *Resolve* surged forward.

Galleons struggled away from the cruiser's path like lead-coated pigeons. There was little conversation on the flying bridge; the day had been long and this was not the thrill of the hunt, so much as it was ending a battle that was already decided.

At fifteen hundred yards, Tromp called for speed to reduce to one half, and, as soon as *Resolve* had settled into what felt like an almost frictionless glide, he gave the order for both mounts to fire. As expected, both mounts missed, but only by thirty yards or so. Forty seconds later, the mounts reported ready and the range had dropped to just over twelve hundred. Both mounts fired, both missed again, but the forward mount's round was so close that as it passed harmlessly through the rigging, the sheets and ratlines swayed in its wake. Another forty seconds: nine hundred yards, two more rounds, and this time, two hits. Pieces and dust flew up from both the stern and foc'sle of the galleon. The other Spanish ships that *Resolve* had sped past were sheering off from her line of advance. Their northward rush was rapidly becoming a roiling, multidirectional chaos that Tower was updating every minute. Tromp ordered the rifles loaded with explosive round. He had about a dozen left for them: the last in the New World except what remained in *Intrepid*'s magazine.

At seven hundred yards, Mounts One and Two fired.

In a day that had been difficult for gunnery to begin with, and with marginally substandard accuracy, the gun crews of *Resolve*'s naval rifles redeemed themselves in that moment: one round went in amidships, the other into the starboard quarter. The explosions were akin to flame demons bursting out through its sides, multiple secondary explosions cracking and blasting in their wake. Smoke poured out of her. The sea around her was thick with smoking debris.

Rik looked over at Tromp. "Sir, what orders for the rifles?"

Tromp took a quick look around; at least half of the galleons were still trying to flee north, but they had all sheered away from *Resolve* and her victim. Maarten had seen captains in a fleet lose their nerve before—and it looked just like this.

"Mounts One and Two: load explosive shell."

Dirck Simonszoon raised an eyebrow but said nothing.

The cries of the forward guncrew announced the start of the reloading process which had taken on the sound of a familiar ritual, one that might be practiced in the temple of a dispassionate god of war. Tromp looked up—

—just in time to see the stricken galleon vanish in a furious flash, followed closely by a deafening— literally deafening—roar. From almost a third of a mile, a sudden puff of wind marked the power of the explosion as smoke jetted out in every direction. The top half of the foremast flew upward even faster, a malformed and broken javelin.

Dirck made a teeth-sucking sound. "Well, that's two rounds saved."

Tromp muttered to Rik. "Mounts One and Two, secure from battery. Prepare to reload with standard. Await instructions."

Then he sighed and tried not to think of all the human souls he had just sent to their Maker in parts too small for even God Himself to recognize.

The standard rounds that were readied for loading never went into the breeches of their respective rifles. The Spanish had had enough. However, it took a while for all of them to actually realize that they were out of options.

One or two still tried running north. The smaller and faster of the Dutch ships gave chase, crossing the Spaniards' sterns at will, peppering them shot and chain until the much bigger galleons struck their colors. So heavily laden that they were low in the water and sluggish, they could barely run at all, and fighting the speedy and maneuverable jachts while doing so was out of the question. And then there was the concern that doing so might attract the attention and displeasure of the satanic steam cruiser that could run down and destroy any ship at will. Indeed, it moved and inflicted so much damage so quickly, that the primal logic of what Tromp had mentally labeled the "fleeing sheep reflex"—scattering with the knowledge that a single predator could not bring down more than one or two prey—no longer obtained. *Resolve* had demonstrated why that desperate logic no longer applied: she was a wolf so swift and so deadly that she could lay waste to the whole flock—or certainly, any sheep that called attention to themselves by daring to kick at the lesser wolves in the pack.

Similar outcomes prevailed in the seaway that had been the site of most of the day's action. But here, a few galleons—possibly taking confidence from being in an area still thick with their own numbers—actually fired defiant shots at the larger Dutch vessels. Which, although not as swiftly as jachts, were easily able to gain the wind gauge and cross either the bows or sterns of their adversaries with horrific effect. And when one such pass failed to compel a Spanish captain to strike his colors, a quick set of signals by flag, Aldis, or both brought *Resolve* around, heading for the recalcitrant galleon. Which hastily relented and suffered to be taken. So *Resolve* spent the better part of the following hour moving toward one troublesome Spaniard after another, her dire intent working in place of her guns.

Even when all the jachts of Tromp's detection net arrived, the number of hulls in his fleet still did not equal the number of galleons that were undamaged or only moderately so. The enemy ships were all ordered to fix each gun's tompion in its muzzle, lower their anchors, reef their sails, and have their full crews gather on deck. Compliance with the latter was no doubt woefully incomplete, but with so many men staring into shot-loaded guns less than fifty yards away, they well understood the gruesome execution that would follow the slightest sign of defiance. On those galleons where Dutch captains detected suspiciously restive or lethargic reactions to their orders, they loudly added that they were already sorely tempted to show the same kind of "mercy" that the Spanish had shown the Dutch at Dunkirk, two and a half years ago. That did not fail to produce swift if bitter compliance.

However, when the Spanish sullenly asked if the formal surrender was to be effected aboard the galleon or the Dutch hull that was its warder, they were told to hold fast. Philip the IV's captains were baffled: did the Dutch not mean to take the ship, to board it? In our good time, was the only answer they got. In the meantime, each prize hull was visited by one of the Dutch steam tugs, which remained long enough to affix a crude spar torpedo directly to the stern, close on to the rudder. Once the tug moved on, a skiff from the Dutch warder put down and its well-armored team fastened its painter to the rudder itself. If the crews of those captive galleons had begun to entertain thought of treachery, of turning on their captors either now or when they attempted to board, it was now entirely defused. Clearly, the first response of the Dutch would be to sweep their decks, followed shortly by lighting the fuse of the explosive and so, destroy their rudder and probably breach the hull.

As if to establish these outcomes as a rule, there were several exceptions where a junior officer or a deckhand was resolved to die for the glory (or more dubiously, the honor) of Spain. Their actions varied: a ragged broadside that surprised the Dutch because of its utter hopelessness; a cannon discharged moments after a captain had struck his colors; an attempt to surprise the enemy with a flurry of fire from hidden muskets. Tromp had known from the outset that there was no such thing as a perfect outcome. If battles were replete with dead and mangled bodies, they evinced an unthinkable superabundance of mishaps, mistakes, misunderstandings, and what Eddie called Murphy's Law. In sum, and in short, anything that could go wrong would, at some point and time in any given engagement.

The resulting consequences to the Dutch were minimal; some damage was done, some lives were lost. The consequences to the Spanish were severe but, contraintuitively, were worst in the case where the Spanish captain who struck his colors at the mere approach of an enemy warship was killed by his own men. They turned their guns toward the approaching *Omlandia*, perhaps emboldened by its modest gun decks. However, their attack was made in haste, no doubt to commit any uncertain crewmembers to an unalterable course of action. In consequence, only one of her twelve portside guns hit home at one hundred yards range. *Omlandia* was still under enough sail to come sharply about and cross the Spaniards' stern, raking it with shot. Whether from lack of control, heat of battle, or both, the galleon's crew did not rethink their course of action, but turned toward *Omlandia* as she passed, thereby giving her starboard batteries a shot as well. The results were inconclusive and within a few minutes, the speedy *Wappen van Rotterdam* arrived and brought her thirty-eight guns into play. The result: *Omlandia* would require some minor repairs and would have to consign several of her crew to the deeps, whereas the Spaniard was sprouting fires both on and below the weather deck while lacking the crew or organization to control them promptly.

And so, Tromp thought as he felt the onset of regret and anticlimax that followed every battle he had ever won, *La Flota of 1636 is no more.*

Chapter 11

East of Dominica

Tromp was still watching black smoke rise, unabated, from the merchantman that *Omlandia* and *Wappen van Rotterdam* had battered into submission when drums and a coronet announced the approach of a small craft. The steam pinnace that had originally been detailed to assist *Prins Hendrik* was in the process of coming alongside. Her pilot called across that she was ready to ferry *Resolve*'s boarding-party "experts" to the various sites where they were needed. At a nod from Tromp, Kees passed the necessary orders and then informed the pilot of the pinnace to stand by.

"So, Maarten," Dirck Simonszoon smirked, "I told you this would all go perfectly."

Tromp stifled a guffaw; Dirck had been the extremely useful voice of gloom, doom, and dire predictions throughout the long planning stage for intercepting La Flota. "How could I ever have doubted you?" Tromp murmured.

"I don't know, but I do know this: we need to decide how to get the Spanish commander here to formally surrender his fleet to you."

Rik frowned. "We have been presuming that their captain-general was lost along with the largest of their war galleons, have we not?"

Kees nodded. "I didn't see a command ensign, but that might have been intentional. Not as if we'd have guessed he was on any other ship."

Tromp frowned. "I agree, which means we are seeking their admiral. They, too, are usually on a war galleon, but they might also be on an unusually large merchantman, if she has more than thirty guns and is of great burthen. Rik, has Tower had anything to say on that matter?"

"No, sir. Shall I ask?"

Tromp frowned: balloon observers were picked for their eyes, their ability to relay information rapidly with a handheld telegraph, and manipulate the balloon's devices. Reading the subtle nuances of initial ship position and subsequent maneuver that might suggest which vessel was carrying La Flota's second-in-command was not part of their skill set. And since the Spanish admiral was often chosen because of his birth rather than naval experience, his reaction to a crisis such as the one that had led to their undoing might not have been any more well reasoned or evenhanded than the most junior captain in the fleet. Still . . . "Have the observer ignore all the naos. Ignore any galleon with less than twenty guns. Consider the rest in terms of their maneuver up until now and seek this pattern: look for a number of ships that kept traveling together, possibly even picking up additional hulls as they went. Have the observer report such past or present activity to me."

"But can you not see this already by looking at

the courses you have marked on the tactical plot?" asked Sehested. Muffled coronets blared beneath the deck as he finished.

Tromp sighed. "We did not mark the time of each plotting, so I cannot be sure if what looks like group movement was merely ships that passed through the same grid coordinates at different times." It annoyed him that he could not remember those details. Then again, he *had* been rather busy. "Besides, I am looking for a report that describes ships shaping their courses to match a leader. In the face of today's chaos, if a captain is within sight of one of the fleet's flagships, he will follow that in the absence of signals to the contrary. It was the only shred of organization they had left, once we finished off the balance of their warships."

The hatches to the amidship companionways were thrown back and troops started emerging. They wore buff coats, sabres and dirks on opposite hips, carried pepperbox revolvers and a few musketoons. Their faces were all obscured by helmets of the barbuta style. *Resolve*'s full contingent of Wild Geese was turning out.

Sehested frowned. "Surely, there are not enough of them to board all the Spanish ships."

"You are correct," Tromp agreed. "They are advisors and assistants, one to each of our ships' own boarding team."

Sehested's frown deepened. But before he could ask the question Tromp expected—what benefit a single man could be to a boarding team—it was answered in practice by the arrival of yet another Dutchman on the mostly German-crewed *Resolve*. Emerging from the port companionway beneath the pilothouse, he came up shouting in a language that still sounded wholly alien to Maarten. Sehested's frown turned to surprised confusion.

Dirck Simonszoon leaned over the removable railing of the flying bridge (itself removable, at need) and called down to the dark-haired officer. "Michiel, what the devil are you telling those bog-hoppers?"

The fellow turned, nodded to the officers gathered above him as if on a balcony. "That they are soon to board the Spanish ships and are not to put heavy hands to their weapons, nor light fingers to anything they might find aboard."

Simonszoon grinned darkly. "Thieves, are they?"

Michiel's smile was small. "Children of want, sir." Behind him, some of the Wild Geese were muttering with exaggerated rolls of their eyes and barely suppressed chuckles. He rounded on them, and started an equally histrionic beration in a mix of Dutch and Gaelic. Several of the men laughed.

Sehested looked from face to face on the flying bridge. "And that language is—?"

"Irish Gaelic," answered Kees. "My chum down there, Adriaenszoon—no relation to the Banckerts—worked in their country as a factor for a Dutch merchant house. Learned their speech."

Sehested shook his head as if the unfamiliar cadences and diphthongs were stuck in his ears and had to be dislodged. "I see. And why is it that they are the expert boarders?"

Rik nodded respectfully at his countryman. "Because they were—and remain—in the service of the Lowlands. Specifically, the Spanish Lowlands."

Sehested smiled. "Why I did not recall that, I do not know. Early dotage, I fear."

Tromp smiled. "A long, tense day will have that effect, Lord Sehested. Trust me; I know."

Michiel, who the Irish were addressing as de Ruyter, was now speaking mostly in Dutch. "No, you will *not* board with weapons in hand."

"Makes it a lot harder to kill t'other fellas," one drawled. Although Tromp could not see much of that one's mouth through the barbuta's limited facial opening, he could hear the grin.

"Ye eedjit," another yelled at the back of the first one's armored head, "did yeh not hear the man? Yer not to be killin' the Spanish at'all!"

"In point o' fact, Reilly," the first one retorted without turning, "'is precise words were, 'not to kill *indiscriminately.*'"

Michiel paced slowly toward the mercenary, smiling. "Yes, although that was qualified by: 'even in the event some Spanish *resist.*' Or did you forget that part?"

"Well, now—I might've."

Michiel's smile widened and he clapped a hand down hard on the Irishman's shoulder. "Thomas Terrell, must you always question orders?"

Terrell tilted his head as if considering. "Not *always.*" There was general laughter.

De Ruyter shook his head, smiled, stepped back. "Ah, well, I shouldn't have asked. In my time with you Irish, I have learned that there is constant trait among you."

"That we're great fighters?"

"That we all have a bit o' the silver-tongued bard in us?"

"That we've always room for one more dram of poteen?"

Michiel laughed at the last, shook his head. "No: that you are an excessively democratic gaggle of geese when you begin to gabble. Like now." He folded his hands behind his back, and his voice became serious. "But I am no Irishman, and these are your orders. You will obey them, yes?"

The responses—"aye"; "yes"; "of course!"—were offered in tones of almost offended surprise, as if the matter and their answer had never been in question.

And indeed, Tromp reflected, perhaps it hadn't been. But, as de Ruyter had implied, the gregarious nature of the Wild Geese could readily become disputatious. Not because they were inherently contrarian—that quirk was more frequently encountered on the continent, Maarten had discerned—but rather because they always wanted to know *why* they were being given the orders they received.

However, those inquiries weren't necessarily rooted in practical curiosity. Rather, they seemed to arise more as a means of reminding their leaders that they did not follow out of obligation, but choice. By asking for explanations, they were in fact underscoring that their opinions, and lives, were not beneath regard. A leader whom they knew and respected could defer answering such questions until after the impending action. An officer who had not yet earned their trust often had to answer in advance, lest he march forward with a surly, even unreliable, lot at his back.

As the forty-odd Wild Geese followed Michiel aft toward the steam pinnace, Tromp realized why they had adopted the Dutchman so easily, so readily. He not only understood their behavior, but what it both predicted and explained about their reputation: that their regard for faceless authority was as dismal as their respect for a proven leader was legendary.

Tromp watched them line up to make their way over the sides using retired cargo nets, and reflected that their independent streak was a good trait for small groups of men in trying situations far away from help and home. But that same trait, and the temperament that went with it, would never build an empire. Then again, while the Irish were fiercely patriotic, they were largely indifferent—and often averse—to sweeping ambitions of national destiny and supremacy. Perhaps that was one of the reasons they had been unable to unite their own fractious island.

"Have you decided, Maarten?"

Tromp turned.

Dirck was staring at him, bemused. "Maybe there is something to what you were saying about dotage, *ja*? So, now: assuming we find the Spanish admiral and bring him here for—"

Tromp shook his head. "We are not taking his surrender on *Resolve*, Captain."

Bjelke started, then straightened. "Yes, Admiral. I understand."

"Then perhaps you will explain it to *me*," Dirck sighed. "Maarten, if you want to put the fear of God—theirs, ours, anyone's—into the Spanish, then compel them to surrender on the machine which single-handedly defeated them. They'll be so terrified that they won't be able to think straight."

Tromp folded his hands. "Let us say you are correct, Dirck. Let us say that all but one of the Spanish who come aboard are too terrified to even observe their surroundings. But what of that one who can? What would you, or I, make of this?" He gestured to the various—and well-labeled—comms gear, the chart, the overlay. "A naval officer with a clear mind will see these as pieces of a puzzle that he won't be long in solving. And he will realize, and explain to his superiors, that *this* is how we beat them. Not our guns or engines. Yes, they made the job easier, less costly, more decisive. But knowing where your opponents are, in what force, and traveling on what heading, allows you to manage the battle, not discover it as it unfolds before you. The key weapons in this engagement were the balloon and our radios. And those are easier and less expensive to build than *Resolve*'s engine and guns."

"And you think they won't figure that out soon enough, Maarten?"

Sehested cleared his throat. "If I may interject," he said, ignoring the looks that clearly indicated that the others very much wished he would not, "a matter of statecraft illustrates the admiral's point. Specifically, spycraft. Let us say that we have one confidential agent who is able to collect a dozen accounts of how an enemy state is preparing for war: their troop movements, their border probes, their supply readiness, their procurement of mounts and ostlers, and a thousand other details. Through those, we might come up with a hypothesis of what that enemy is planning. We might even be correct.

"But instead, our spy vouchsafes a map of their plans. At that point, all those other details become unnecessary. We no longer need to hope to use disparate pieces of information to build what *might* be an accurate picture of their intents. A map not only gives us a *precise* picture, but also a trustworthy basis for extrapolating our foe's further intents."

Sehested pointed not just at the much-marked overlay but all the equipment surrounding it. "However, this plot is a map to something much larger and more complicated than the stretch of sea and islands it depicts. The data upon it is clearly derived from all the devices which are clustered at hand. Take a step back and the entire design of this flying bridge is akin to a light, illuminating the path to how all these technologies not only create a precise picture of the battlefield, but allow us to respond almost instantly to any move our adversary might make."

He shrugged. "Before today, I was familiar with all of these machines. I have even had some of you, and Commodore Cantrell, explain their operation. But what I could not appreciate, could not truly understand until witnessing the events of the past three hours, was how they would all work together. As I said earlier but without full cognizance, the integration of these machines is a whole that is much, much greater than the sum of its parts. *This* is the future of war. And the later our adversaries come to that realization, the longer we shall dominate them and the battlefields upon which our fates are decided."

He leaned toward Simonszoon. "So, as the only representative of the nations that built and operate this vessel, I implore you: do not give our enemy the map to understand how we blend these systems and achieve seemingly impossible outcomes. Such as today's."

Simonszoon's eyes were no longer hooded and cautious, but attentive, maybe even admiring. "Lord Sehested, I will be frank: when this day started, I could not for the life of me foresee what purpose it might serve to have you along." He straightened up from the tactical plot. "Now I know. Thank you for pulling me back to see a picture that I have been examining in such close detail that I could no longer see the whole of it." He turned to Tromp. "What hull should we use to receive these Spanish dogs?"

Before Tromp could speak, Kees was mumbling. "It would be poetic justice for them to surrender aboard the very flagship of the fleet—and the nation—they thought they had destroyed. The one on which a Dutch admiral decided that his remaining ships had to flee, that they might live to fight another day." He looked at Tromp. "This day."

Maarten smiled at Evertsen. "It is decided."

Chapter 12

East of Dominica

Shortly after a skiff delivered Tromp to the *Amelia*, the first preliminary report of the engagement was handed to him.

La Flota, as hoped and anticipated, had elected not to split into its two primary parts before making landfall in the New World. That was why it was still so large. The bigger of the two parts, the Tierra Firme fleet, existed to collect the goods waiting along the Spanish Main, from Santa Margarita Island all the way to Cartagena. The route of the Nueva Espana fleet varied, but always crossed the Gulf of Mexico and wound up at Vera Cruz, where riches from most of New Spain accumulated.

This year, the Tierra Firme fleet had been comprised of eight war galleons and twenty-one merchantmen: enough to send smaller detachments to various ports of call, each with their own security contingent. The Nueva Espana fleet had numbered seventeen merchantmen and only three war galleons; not many pirates ventured into the open waters of the Gulf, where the currents were unhelpful or weak and the wind was scarce and fickle. So in total, Tromp had intercepted no fewer than thirty-eight merchantmen and eleven war galleons. There had been either three or four pataches as well, but they had slipped away during the battle.

So too had six of the rearmost naos, which were not dual-purpose ships like galleons. Built strictly for commerce, they had burthens of five hundred *toneladas* or more and rode out storms as well or better than galleons. However, they were even slower and so, were always kept at the rear of La Flota, where they were easiest to protect and least likely to be the first to encounter a threat.

On this day, however, that rearmost position had enabled six of the naos' captains to decide that discretion was the better part of valor. Three must have done so within the first quarter hour of sighting the allied fleet. Despite unpromising winds, they went south as close-hauled as their rigging allowed, frantically dumping their cargo as they went. That was known only because the jacht which briefly gave chase fished out some light crates that were still floating in their vanished wake.

The other three naos fled somewhat later. Judging from what Tower observed, their decision to do so occurred shortly after the thirteen ships of Anvil began maneuvering to cut off any chance of escape to the north. Perhaps one or more of the nao's maintopmen had also caught sight of the jachts flying in from their picket positions as part of the detection net. That would have been more than enough evidence to convince any nao's captain that the attackers meant to surround the entirety of La Flota. One of the merchantmen had fled southeast, another northeast, another perversely turned about and began the risky job of beating hard into what had been their strong eastern tailwind.

In the end, that dubious plan of escape proved to be no worse than the others. Tromp still had a super-abundance of enemy ships to commandeer or scuttle, as well as Spanish seamen and troops to transfer to temporary mass prisons in same holds that had carried the seamen who would now sail the many prize hulls back to St. Eustatia. As it was, he could barely spare the jacht he did send in pursuit, which left so late that he had every expectation that she'd lose the nao in the dark. As she did.

The greater disappointment of the day was the need to scuttle six of the Spaniards. But first, the carpenters and bosuns among his boarding teams had to determine which ships were likely to remain afloat for at least a day or two, or had to be unloaded immediately.

That presented a slew of immediate challenges. Firstly, the four ships which were safe enough to unload had to have their complements gotten off before they could be searched and adequately assessed. Only then could a salvage team be put aboard. Meanwhile, the Spanish crew had to be transferred under guard to the overcrowded holds of Tromp's fluyts and the capacious USE merchantman *Serendipity*. But that could not be effected until these temporary prison ships came alongside the smoking hulks, assisted by overtaxed steam tugs during their final approaches. Meanwhile, courier skiffs were racing to and fro between the mostly radio-less Dutch ships, whose Aldis lamps were still being reserved for combat and emergency signals. All the movement and hurry made the battle seem serene, by comparison.

Had the Dutch not had the unemployed manpower and months of training to prepare, it could not have been accomplished. And had the weather been poor or the seas too rough, all the preparation would have been for naught; salvage operations in those conditions were not merely difficult but terribly dangerous, particularly those involving cannon.

There had been considerable debate whether the Spanish guns could even be claimed from those ships which ultimately required scuttling. The Dutch did have the portable tackle required; they'd brought some from Recife and had constructed more since. Additional operators had been trained in the prior months, and they now went about their business with singular fervor. In addition to their wages, each cannon carried a bonus which went up along with its weight of throw. Besides, the mere idea of turning so many Spanish guns back upon their makers had the special savor of revenge seasoned by irony.

Even after being grounded near Dominica's windward coast, the four ships that could be safely unloaded proved particularly treacherous when it came to disassembling and moving the largest guns, which were of course in the lower batteries. A quick consideration of the manpower available and time required decided Tromp; he would remain on *Amelia* and lead the rest of the fleet to rendezvous with Eddie off Guadeloupe. Meanwhile, *Resolve* and the remainder of Hammer would remain with the salvage teams as they undertook the careful extraction of the guns. The other stores and supplies of the four grounded hulks would be removed first and transferred to the rest of the fleet, however. Because, if the weather turned and the waves grew, the stricken ships might be floated off the bottom and driven onto rocks, or crushed down by high waves that could either roll them or break them up.

The last two of the six ships to be scuttled were two war galleons that were so badly damaged, with so many lingering fires, and such full magazines, that salvage operations would have been suicidal. So, as soon as their crews had been ordered to put down their boats and abandon their ship, the Dutch went aboard with axes and hammers to work away at the hull, and left behind long-fused and carefully tamped powder charges.

As the second scuttling charge went off with a dull crump, Tromp was watching the other one begin its death-roll. Two hours earlier it had been a scourge of the seas; now it was being taken to the benthic bosom of that same element. He sighed and glanced at the tally sheets that summarized what remained of La Flota, and hence, what his fleet had taken this day.

Of eleven war galleons, three had been sunk, two scuttled by charges immediately, and two would meet a similar fate when salvage was complete. That left four as prizes, two of which were so badly damaged that it would be months before Oranjestad's shipwrights made them seaworthy. The pair that would be ready for service sooner were the two survivors of the trio that had sped toward *Resolve* at the start of the battle. They were by far the most handsome prizes in terms of military use, but only modestly so in terms of cargo. Of course, they shouldn't have had any cargo at all, since the warships of La Flota were officially restricted to carrying naval stores. However, as with so many other rules imposed by the Escorial, circumvention was routinely achieved via nepotism, bribes, and/or chicanery. So the war galleons' cargos, while modest, were also choice.

Of the seventeen galleons that had been merchantmen, two had been sunk outright and two more would be scuttled as soon as their off-loading was completed. Of the thirteen that remained, five would require extensive repairs but eight were fit for immediate service.

The twenty-one naos, an unusually high number for any Spanish fleet, had seen the least combat. Six had escaped. Three more had tried to flee but had been brought to heel by several punishing broadsides. Twelve had been taken intact.

Tromp held the sheet further away from his eyes, tried to take in the full implications all at once. Thirty-two ships taken out of forty-nine total. The cargos of an additional four would be salvaged before they were scuttled. About a third would need major repairs before they could be put into service.

Dirck Simonszoon's voice, just behind his shoulder, startled him. "Maarten, you look like Midas counting his gold. By the way, they found the Spanish admiral. He'll be aboard soon."

"Good. One more thing we can get out of the way. Are the boardings complete?"

Simonszoon stared sidelong at him. "That is yet another comment that makes me wonder about 'impending dotage.'"

"Captain, you are impudent."

"No, Admiral: you are delusional. There are thirty-two

prizes that must have their crews transferred to our prison ships, another four made safe for salvage teams prior to scuttling, and two more that had to be evacuated immediately. We've taken care of the ones that were sinking and that we're scuttling. We've sorted out about half of the others, starting with the least damaged. It stands to reason they'd be the first to start thinking about trying to run."

Tromp nodded. "Still, we will not be done by dark."

"Maarten, we will be fortunate to be done by midnight. Or have you forgotten that we have to put our prize crew aboard the ones we're taking?"

"I have forgotten nothing." And indeed, Tromp recalled the matter of the prize crews in great detail, simply because it had been one of the most hotly contested parts of their plan. They had counted on taking, maybe, thirty ships maximum. Unfortunately, the Spanish did not make ships that were labor efficient. Even for the short cruise back to St. Eustatia, each hull should have had thirty-man prize crews, which meant they needed nine hundred such men.

They had maybe a third that number of persons who had maritime skills and were not fully employed. Besides, as Tromp's fleet had no way of being sure when La Flota would arrive, they had to turn the holds of the fluyts and *Serendipity* into cramped quarters as the whole fleet waited on station. Even by putting four hundred men into those holds, and by distributing more into whatever berths remained on the warships, Tromp and Simonszoon were barely able to scrape together and sustain six hundred to serve as prize crews.

But with today's results, that meant they had less

than twenty men per prize hull. Tromp had been thinking about possible solutions to the unanticipated problems of too much success, and did not like the one he decided upon. Unfortunately the rest were even worse. "We will need five Spaniards to remain on each ship. Sail handlers and deckhands, only. No officers, gunners—"

"Yes, Maarten; I see where you are steering." Dirck's grin became sly. "I don't suppose it would interest you to know that several of the ships had a smattering of slaves on board. Not field hands: craftsmen. Well, *mostly* men. Some women, too."

Tromp was staring at Dirck by the time he finished. "Free them! At once! And put them in charge of the Spaniards!"

Dirck actually chuckled. "I was waiting for you to say that. It shall be done. Has Eddie sent word, yet?"

Tromp frowned. "No. But whatever the outcome of his mission, we have no choice but to deposit the prisoners on Petite-Terre. If only for a few days while we make other arrangements."

"You don't mean to bring them to Oranjestad!"

"Of course not!"

"But then where—?"

"Dirck, we have our hands quite full now. Let us cross further bridges when and if we come to them." Coronets pealed. "The Spanish admiral, no doubt."

Simonszoon craned his neck. "Seems to be." He cocked an eyebrow at Tromp. "You ordered formal flourishes for a Spanish dog?"

Tromp straightened. "Captain, I shall not judge the character of an officer I have not met, any more than I shall judge the soul of a man I do not know."

Simonszoon shrugged. "Well, you're a more generous fellow than I am, Deacon Tromp. But we knew that already." He nodded toward Adriaen Banckert, XO of *Amelia*, who was leading the admiral and two other Spanish officers up the stairs to the poop deck. "You don't want to do this in the great cabin?"

"No need. While I mean to be civil, I have no desire to suggest to our visitor that we intend to entertain him."

Simonszoon patted his shoulder and stood beside him. "There's the steely Tromp I know!"

Young Banckert gestured for the guards to keep the fierce-looking *hidalgo* back a step. "Admiral, the Spanish commander, Almirante Antonio de Curco y San Joan de Olacabal has come to surrender his sword and his fleet."

There was some distempered grumbling behind Banckert.

"What was that?" Tromp asked, raising one eyebrow.

"My Spanish is rusty, Admiral, but I believe the Spanish admiral was correcting my assertion that this was *his* fleet. He seems to feel the capitan-general in command, now presumed dead, should keep that title since it was his incompetence that led to their defeat. Or words to that effect."

As Adriaen finished, Simonszoon was grinning. "Your Spanish is just fine, Banckert."

Tromp nodded. "Ask the admiral to join us."

De Curco y San Joan did so, sword proffered across both palms, one of which showed the remains of dried blood. Whether the admiral's or someone else's, Tromp could not tell. "I do not require your sword, Admiral, any more than I wish to diminish the honor it signifies."

If anything, that seemed to make the Spanish admiral even more quietly furious, as though he would have preferred Tromp to be a gloating ogre. "You are most kind," he muttered in a tone that said, "I would happily eat your liver." He rebuckled the sword, straightened his neck. "I, Almirante Antonio de Curco y San Joan de Olacabal, surrender the remains of His Majesty Philip IV's fleet to the New World to you, and ask for Christian restraint and care in addressing the fate of its survivors."

"I accept your surrender," Tromp replied, "as well as responsibility for the restraint and care you request and which we fully intend to observe. Do you have other requests?"

De Curco y San Joan's frustrated fury barely allowed him to shake his head in the negative. Then, as if that had exhausted the last measure of his self-control, he almost spat, "I suppose you think this a great triumph. But it will be the end of you, Tromp. Yes, I know who you are. And you had best enjoy your . . . your 'New World Dunkirk' while you can. Philip will ensure that it is the last victory you ever know."

Tromp folded his hands, considered. "'The New World Dunkirk.'" He smiled. "I like that. I would not have thought of it, myself. I'm afraid I do not possess an Iberian flair for the dramatic. However, I am satisfied that we Dutch possessed whatever qualities helped us prevail, this day."

The Spaniard raised the point of his finely groomed beard. "That was luck . . . and the Lord's sharp reminder to any overly proud Spaniard that it is through Him, and Him alone, that we may be victorious and reign supreme."

"Yes, I'm sure . . . although there is something to be said for the axiom that God helps those who help themselves. At least, that is what is preached in *my* church. Now, let us discuss the matter of your parole."

De Curco y San Joan started as if struck. "P-parole? You are freeing us?"

"In a manner of speaking. Forty miles north of here, just south of Guadeloupe, are a pair of small islands known as Petite-Terre. At least that is how they appear on up-time charts. Are you familiar with them?"

"Vaguely." It was obvious he had never heard of them.

"They are sufficient for a short stay," Tromp assured him. "Certainly long enough to allow you to fashion craft from what remains of those of your ships that will sail that far . . . before they are scuttled in the shallows around those islands."

"You are marooning us?"

"If that word has the same meaning for us as it has for you, then we are not marooning you. We are explicitly leaving you with the means and tools to fashion smaller ships with which you may return to your lands."

"But I have seen your salvagers at work; you are taking all the spare canvas!"

"There will still be smaller spans of cloth that you may secure from the riven sails that we leave behind."

"And what shall we eat?"

"There are fish aplenty in the surrounding waters, and you shall have the long boats from the decks of the galleons. We shall also leave a supply of your own biscuits."

"Which are inedible!"

"Which," Simonszoon sneered, "is in no way a fault of ours, wouldn't you agree?"

Tromp waved him to silence. "Admiral, the Spanish pride themselves on their history of overcoming great obstacles. This is hardly the greatest you have had to face."

"Perhaps not, but we have women and children with us."

Tromp nodded. "If the conditions on the islands are too harsh, I shall bring them to Montserrat."

"And what is on Montserrat, other than more Protestants who will revile and abuse them?"

"In point of fact, Montserrat is now overwhelmingly populated by Irish Catholics, refugees who will certainly sympathize with the plight of your women and children. They have known similar travails, and will no doubt treat your dependents kindly until they may find their ways home."

De Curco had to cast around a moment to find yet another objection to fling at Tromp. "And the fathers of those women and children?"

"From what we have been able to tell so far, there are but a few families on your ships. And frankly, given that the King of Spain does not trouble himself to assign tasks that allow fathers to remain with their families, the separation experienced by those wives and children will not be so very different than they would have suffered when they reached their destinations here in the New World. Indeed, they might be better off." He lowered his brow. "And it will be infinitely better than the treatment you would have given our people, were our situations reversed."

"I do not know what you mean," de Curco claimed defiantly.

"Indeed? So Olivares did not send his message

to your fleet? Even though it pertained to the New World?"

"I tell you: I do not know this message of which you speak."

"Truly? About no longer taking any Dutch prisoners?" Tromp lowered his voice. "Deny that, if you can. On peril of your immortal soul."

The admiral looked away.

"Ah. So it is your forthrightness, not Olivares' correspondence, that is wanting." Tromp raised his chin. "I trust that you have no other fears regarding our presumed 'inhuman' treatment of your passengers and crew? Good." He started away, then turned back. "I suppose I should remark that there are those among my fleet who feel that my terms of treatment are, in fact, too generous." He paused, let both his tone and his brow drop again. "Entirely too generous. Now, I bid you safe travels from this place, Admiral de Curco y San Joan."

The Spaniard did not meet Tromp's eyes before turning on his heel and striding away and down the quarterdeck's stairs.

Adriaen Banckert waved the senior trooper to see the admiral and his officers back to the skiff that had brought them. The young XO looked after the Spaniards. "There's a part of me that feels it would be better to have simply killed them. Well, the men, I mean." When he saw Tromp's look, he hastily added, "If they live, they will simply try to kill us again, you know."

Tromp shook his head. "If one behaves like one's enemies, one becomes them. Besides, survivors are a benefit to us."

"How?"

"We have left them most of their small boats. Some will try their luck in those. If they are good and careful sailors, they will survive. They will follow north along the Lesser Antilles, then skip from Saba to St. Croix and so reach Puerto Rico without hazarding the Anegada Passage.

"If they are not fortunate or are too impatient, then their end will have been of their own choosing. And, even though they are arch-papists, I still commend their souls not only to the deep, but to the grace of God. But be assured, *some* survivors will arrive in Puerto Rico, and from thence, their report will be conveyed to Cuba and Spain."

"And so our enemies will have intelligence on us!"

"Yes, to the extent that the survivors have reported accurately. And you may rest assured that, between the terror of this day and their desire to be held blameless for having failed against a numerically inferior opponent, they will exaggerate our capabilities and numbers. And so the Escorial will pause and debate, and worry will ensue. In the meantime, one fact will resonate."

"Which is?"

"Which is that the silver and gold that their forces gathered all over the New World last year cannot be collected, now. Not in time to prop up Madrid's failing economy at the very moment when it most needs its next injection of specie. Olivares will be fortunate indeed if he can scratch together another fleet to fetch it before September."

Simonszoon smiled, amplified: "And even if Olivares hastened such a last-minute Flota into the dark waves of the late-year Atlantic to arrive here before winter, that is still too late. By the time it could collect and then return with the silver, that treasure would arrive ten months later than promised. But be assured, Adriaen Banckert, the real trouble for us will start the moment news of this day reaches Spain, whose ruler will be most discomfited."

Adriaen sounded far more worried than edified. "Who will see to it that we are most assiduously sought and pursued."

Tromp shrugged. "Undoubtedly so. But that was an inevitability. Now it might simply occur sooner rather than later." He nodded toward the wheel. "Tell the pilot that when we get underway, I want to keep on as broad a reach as we can. We must adjust our sailing to these Spanish scows, so we'll need to put every gust that we can in their sails. Otherwise, we shall not make Guadeloupe by noon tomorrow."

He turned toward the bows, felt the wind on his right cheek, then glanced left at the setting sun. It was limning Dominica's high, dark profile in burnished gold. The perfect end for a day that just might find its way into history books...

The senior telegrapher came up to the weather deck two steps at a time. "Report from *Intrepid*, Admiral. Shall I read it?"

"A summary would be preferable, Jost."

"Very well, sir. Commodore Cantrell reports that his contact with the indigenous peoples of Guadeloupe went better than hoped, and that Petite-Terre is cleared for disembarking our prisoners." *Amelia*'s comms mate looked up from the sheet. "Wonderful news, *ja*, sir?"

"Yes, Jost." But with that worry resolved, another

leaped up to take its place: "Any signal from Major Quinn or *Courser*, yet?"

"Still nothing, sir."

"Well," Tromp sighed, "let us hope that his attempt to befriend the native peoples of the mainland goes half so well as Eddie's on Guadeloupe."

Chapter 13

Upper Mermentau River, Louisiana

Major Larry Quinn rested an index finger on young Karl Klemm's right shoulder as they moved out of the stronger current of the upper Mermentau River. "A little less speed, a little more to starboard."

The young Bavarian eased back the throttle of the bright red 180 Sportsman motorboat, turned the steering wheel slightly to the right. He glanced across the river to where a tree had collapsed far out beyond its banks. Judging from the lack of mold on the trunk, it couldn't have been down for more than a few weeks. "Was I not giving it enough clearance, Major? When I read the operation manual for this boat, the section concerning areas of uncertain navigation recommended—"

Larry exerted a little more pressure to the shoulder under his index finger. "Trust me. Look at the bole of that fallen tree, and the shallow angle at which it enters the water. And how close the stump is to the bank."

Karl frowned as they drew abreast of it at a distance

of fifteen yards. "And what do you deduce from these observations, Major?"

It was Kleinbaum who answered. "The trunk is wide. Which means it is a big tree, and so, tall. And it was not deadfall; see how green the stump is? How clean the bole? And mind the angle. Add it together, *junge*, and it is quite possible that the top of it is beneath us, even here. The closer we passed, the more likely that some branch we cannot see beneath this filth"—he eyed the green-brown Mermentau warily—"will tear our bottom out. And that would be the end of us in this godforsaken place."

Karl's frown deepened. "I see. But as regards our survival: are you so very certain? The handbook on the Louisiana bayou region specifically stated that—"

Larry turned his finger on Karl's scapula into a pat on the shoulder. "Whether we live or die, it certainly would be the end of our mission. Although I am sure that the handbook had some useful advice if we were to wreck the boat and be forced to fend for ourselves. And I will count upon you to share that information, should we need it." And Larry knew that Karl would not only have that full store of information ready between his ears, but it would come out of his mouth damn near the way it had been written in the handbook. The young Bavarian was not merely extremely, even terrifyingly, smart, but had what some people called a photographic memory. Which he had demonstrated more than once. And which had saved their bacon when everything went to hell, three months ago.

It had started well before that, with the hurricane. After splitting off from Task Force X-Ray, they had made their way across the Gulf on sail alone, both to conserve the coal in *Courser*'s bunkers and to reduce the possibility of other ships sighting them. And *Courser*, having a hull and rigging layout that was modeled after the USS *Kearsarge* of Civil War fame, had far superior sailing characteristics to any ship of this age—even the Quality-class cruisers, *Intrepid* and *Resolve*.

However, because her guns were on a covered gun deck, not the weather deck, and because that meant her freeboard was increased, she wasn't as sleek as the steam sloop which had inspired her. She had a faint tumblehome and that cut some speed and maneuverability. Also, her engines were of down-time manufacture. The very finest quality possible, of course, and carried out under Admiral Simpson's unstinting—not to say hypercritical—supervision, but still, they were only going to get so close to the performance specs that had been achievable with the technology and alloys of the 1860s.

Long story made short, she wasn't as fast as the ships that inspired her, was heavier, and that all worked against a rapid crossing of an unusually windless Gulf of Mexico. And when they were finally getting close to their destination—Louisiana—they saw a storm mounting high and dark coming in from the southeast.

It was a problem with that part of the Gulf Coast, in the undeveloped, undredged world of 1635: there wasn't anything vaguely resembling a safe anchorage until you got to Galveston. Which they could probably reach in time—if they were willing to burn coal to do it.

Larry, the master of the ship, and Olle Haraldsen, its commander, only had to confab for seven seconds:

better a ship with low or no coal than a ship in pieces at the bottom of the Gulf. So they called for full steam and ran like hell before the storm. And worst of all, there was no one on board who would have understood any of the puns Larry had in mind regarding the Doors song of almost the same name.

They got to Galveston in time—just—but after the hurricane, its migratory sandbars had rearranged themselves even more than usual. So the channel they'd sounded on the way in was gone. And while it would have been nice to send a message to Eddie and their pals back on Statia to call for help or just send an update, their radio didn't have the range. At least they kept hearing The Quill's daily squelch breaks: those short, contentless transmissions that rose just above the background noise. But it had been known from the outset that once *Courser* got beyond the range where she could ping back, there was no way to let anyone else know that she was still afloat, much less what was happening to her.

After waiting a while to see if the natural action of the tide would help clear the bay, it was obvious that while the process was occurring, it was doing so at a pace that would have made molasses in winter look like a downhill racer. That was the point at which Larry and Captain Haraldsen had another confab, this one much lengthier and more heated than the first.

The mission was to get to Mermentau River, then the Nezpique Bayou and navigate up toward the closest known coordinates of the Jennings oil field. While not as deep and wide as its Texas cousins, Jennings was ultimately easier to reach, produced sweeter crude, and was much closer to the surface. Larry's contention was that with the Sportsman and all its gasoline, he and a handful of others could continue that mission. They'd follow the Gulf Coast east, get to the entry into the Mermentau Basin—for lack of a better umbrella term—and wind their way up to the objective.

Haraldsen countered with far less involved arguments. They boiled down to this: the Sportsman would not survive any major storm. If anything went wrong and they could not proceed, the boat could not hold much in the way of spares or supplies. If they encountered indigenous peoples, even their lever-action rifles would not keep so few of them from being overrun. And most importantly, Larry was clearly clinically insane for proposing such a mission.

Larry's definitive reply was twofold. Firstly, contacting the indigenous people was a crucial part of the mission because Grantville had made its cooperation with oil extraction contingent upon recognizing the innate and inalienable rights of the peoples who were native to those lands. Secondly, Larry was in charge and had the letter—with Gustav's seal—to prove it.

Captain Haraldsen ceded to that authority with about as much grace as could be expected; in other words, some anger but not everlasting hatred. And so the mission to coast-follow along to the mouth of the Mermentau was cobbled together as the crew of *Courser* began realizing that if they wanted to be sure of eating until the tide moved the sandbars out of the way, they'd better get hunting and start rationing carbohydrates. That last operational caveat came from Larry, who had been given the Army's full spiel on how protein isn't enough; that would put you in full ketosis in a few weeks and render the affected person at least temporarily useless.

So with her almost nonexistent draft, the 180 Sportsman was able to cruise back out and follow along the coast, hopping from bay to inlet. They made fine progress for the first two days. In retrospect, Larry damned himself for not having seen that fine weather as a dire harbinger of things to come. After all, he'd been in the military and had learned as only soldiers can that when everything is going according to plan, that means it's just about to come apart. Spectacularly.

And so it did. A storm that must have been following in the wake of the hurricane came up out of the southeast really quickly the day they put in at the Calcasieu River, which in this time, was not a reliable inlet to the large inland lake of the same name. The storm was certainly not a large one, but it was enough to do to Larry's mission what the hurricane had done to *Courser*: it deposited silt in the narrow inlet. Enough to lock them into the Calcasieu Lake area the same way that *Courser* was still stuck in Galveston.

They took shelter on Monkey Island, the only high ground nearby and from which they could watch for signs that the silt was washing away—if you could call a meter above the water "high ground." But that was higher than anywhere else. At least it wasn't summer, so the bugs were bearable. Barely.

The team's frustration with their circumstances was aggravated by the fact that it was just sixty-five nautical miles back to Galveston Bay and comparative safety. But it might as well have been Pluto. At least the commercial radio on the Sportsman had enough range to trade squelch breaks, albeit barely.

Fortunately, the raised waters had also removed their potentially greatest problem: a camp of indigenous peoples on the other side of the Calc (as they came to call it), near the mouth of the river on the north end of the bay. And since the best information they had from Grantville was that the only tribe they were likely to encounter here was the Atakapa, that would have meant having cannibals for neighbors. Almost as bad as college kids who were all-night partiers, as far as Larry was concerned.

The real and unrelenting problems were food and firewood. The water a mile upstream the Calcasieu River was okay for drinking, but where it entered the northern end of the lake, the flow was too sluggish for Quinn's comfort: bacteria just loved warm, slow-moving water. So getting water meant rowing upstream (thank God Quinn had insisted on retrofitting oarlocks) which in turn meant risking a chance encounter with—whatever. Bears, snakes, natives, boar, and probably a dozen other things that could and would kill them deader than Elvis. So keeping the risk of such an encounter—and therefore, discovery—low meant minimizing the number of trips they took for water. That was further problematized by the limited number of containers they had. All in all, retrofitted oarlocks notwithstanding, Larry Quinn was less than impressed with his own mission preparations.

One of the Hibernians, Winkelman, was so dissatisfied with his water ration that he decided to try the water from where the Calcasieu entered the lake of the same name. Seventy-two hours of misery later, he repented his decision—and was the object of considerable resentment: rehydrating him cut deeply into their supplies. Of course, they could have boiled the local water, but then there was that pesky firewood problem. So in order to ensure his recovery, they'd had to lean heavily into their only reserve of truly palatable water, that which they'd taken with them from *Courser*. It still tasted of the purification tanks, but now, they barely noticed it.

Fortunately, there was another source of truly clean water: rain. And it just so happened that, according to the almost encyclopedic references that had been compiled for the mission, the Calcasieu-Sabine area was the eighth rainiest region in the continental US. It had precipitation one hundred and four days out of the year, with an average total of about fifty inches. And as luck would have it, January was the rainiest month of its year.

Except, this time, it seemed that the hurricane and the storm behind it had exhausted the rain until February. They also had the additional problem of how to catch it. And that just happened to coincide with the most ominous sign of all: *Courser* went off the air. No more daily squelch breaks. For Larry, the steam destroyer was no longer as far off as Pluto; it was well past Alpha Centauri.

Fortunately, no one speculated on the cause of the sudden silence because, as far as Larry could tell, they were all experienced or insightful enough to realize that if they started down that path, they'd go mad with it. Despondency would follow when they realized that there was no reassurance to be gained in that pointless exercise. Not the path you want to be on since it was when things got the worst that you needed morale at its best.

Thankfully, fate seemed willing to repay them for that minimum wisdom and unflagging determination to survive and believe that all was not lost. Shortly after *Courser* went dark, their fishing skills began to improve, as did their experiments in sun-drying and salting any excess catch. A week after that, the rains finally arrived, better late than never. And, after a silence of more than a month, *Courser* resumed her daily squelch breaks.

Once the emergency codes for breaking radio discipline were exchanged, Larry discovered that although Galveston's sandbars were beginning to shift and recede, they still had *Courser* locked in. Fuel to keep the condensers running and radio's batteries charged had run low, so Captain Haraldsen took the necessary step of sending out foraging parties. They found food and water occasionally, but never more wood than what they needed to cook the game they managed to bring down.

Once they reached the ten-percent mark in the fuel bunkers, Captain Haraldsen made the hard but inevitable decision to keep the burner cold until they were ready to attempt to navigate out of Galveston Bay. And since fully draining the charge in their primitive chemical batteries was inadvisable, he made the hardest decision of all: to suspend all radio use until he had enough wood to run the engines, and thereby generate power for the batteries and the squelch breaks.

In hindsight, he might have been able to make it out of Galveston Bay under sail alone, but in the event that the wind became fickle at just the moment she was running a gauntlet between two close sandbars, Haraldsen had wisely decided that it was essential to reserve a measure of coal to ensure reaching open water. Once there, the wind would allow them to make way, even if *Courser*'s bunkers were empty. As it was, yesterday's signal reported that they had indeed used more than half of their remaining fuel to finally exit the bay, and while they did, to provide power to the condensers to make much-needed fresh water for the boilers.

With the wind remaining uncooperative, Haraldsen's last message was that he could not be sure when they would reach Calcasieu. Between dried driftwood and coal, they had barely enough fuel for another thirty minutes of steam and there was no reason to suspect that the weather was done making their lives miserable. Larry told them to bypass Calcasieu, promising that he would meet them near the equally narrow and unreliable mouth of the Mermentau.

What he didn't tell them was that he couldn't remain in the Calcasieu. The chances of sufficient fish were decreasing and of returning natives were increasing, so Larry and his team would very likely be dead by the time *Courser* arrived. They had to leave while the channel was still open and they had enough food and water to reach the Mermentau, get inland, and maybe bring down some game.

The Calcasieu was only thirteen miles from the inlet of the Mermentau, so they made it in one day. But once they found the inlet, and then followed its winding inland course through the Mud Lakes, Grand Lake, and Lake Arthur, the dense bayou foliage did not reveal any game. Even the alligators—if they had been willing to chance taking on one of those leftover wannabe dinosaurs—were few and far between. So as night fell, and with the bugs clearly trying to convince them to return to Texas, they consumed their meager rations of fish and water, crowded together while rank with the chemical stink of ketosis, and slept in the boat.

Or tried to. Because tomorrow they would enter the

Mermentau, where they would either find sustenance or die in the attempt.

Larry Quinn smiled ruefully at the memory of last night's sleep-stealing anxiety over dying from hunger or dehydration. Because almost as soon as they had entered the Mermentau this morning, it became evident that they had stealthy company observing their progress. So it turned out Larry and his team had been worrying about the wrong things. It wasn't starvation that was proving to be their likeliest cause of death: it was an arrow between the eyes.

"They're watching us from the thickets on the right," Vogel muttered. Maneuvering around the fallen tree had brought them closer to that bank.

Larry simply nodded and put a hand on Karl Klemm's tense arm. "Ease off the engine. Let us coast."

"Why?" muttered Kleinbaum from his perch back on the barrels carrying the last of their gasoline. "To make us easier targets?"

Quinn turned and bestowed his "dead-fish eyes" stare upon the woodsman and tracker, who looked away, grumbling inaudibly. If the small, wiry fellow hadn't come so highly recommended for his work with the Dutch in the jungles of the Pernambuco and the attempted relief of Bahia, Larry would have sent him packing. What Kleinbaum lacked in size he made up for in mouth, and Quinn had already had one sharp, private conversation with him during their sojourn beside Lake Calcasieu. Another frank exchange of views might be necessary, if they lived to have it.

Karl had brought the throttle back slowly, smoothly, reducing the engine sounds to a dyspeptic mutter.

Eckdahl, the Swedish leadsman who'd eased them into Galveston Bay, peered over the bright red nose of the motorboat and commented, "We're drifting toward weeds, sir. Water lilies of some kind. Could snare the propeller if we drift in too far."

"Use the gaff to push us back off. Slowly, gently," Quinn ordered with a faint nod.

Eckdahl picked up the pole, lowered it into the water and leaned into it. The Sportsman's bow veered back toward the center of the Mermentau River. As the boat slowed and Quinn felt the sluggish current begin to push them back toward the Gulf that was now almost fifty miles of meandering river and muddy lakes behind them, he casually asked, "Vogel? Any reaction from our watching friends?"

"No," the hunter's son from Rothenburg ob der Tauber drawled. "They left."

"Do you think they even knew we saw them?" Winkelman wondered.

Vogel shrugged. "Well, one of them nodded at me."

"Nodded at you?" echoed Kleinbaum.

"Yes. You know, it was one of those 'I can see that you are watching me watching you' kind of nods. The one that scouts use to acknowledge the nonsense of having to play hide-and-seek like so many children. But with real weapons."

"I mean no disrespect, Herr Vogel," Karl commented, "but can you be so sure that what a nod means in Europe is what it means here?"

Vogel smiled; it was not unkind, just mildly amused. "You were the son of a townsman, and then, lived in cities, yes, Herr Klemm?"

Quinn saw the back of Karl's neck redden. "That is so."

"Then allow me to assure you of this: hunters are hunters the world over, just as scouts are scouts. And from one to another, you have ways to acknowledge the skill of the other. Signs of professional respect, if you will. That nod, and the leaf he turned back that he did not have to, were such signs."

"Well," sighed Larry, "let's hope that mutual respect means they're interested in meeting us." With any luck, raising that possibility would keep Karl from wigging out.

Vogel cleared his throat. "Er, Major, not all scouts who exchange such compliments are friendly. In fact, most often, they are your enemy. That is why you are hiding from each other, to begin with."

Larry nodded, but stared hard at Vogel: *you just* had *to say that, didn't you?* But what he said was, "I am aware of that," as Karl swallowed loudly. "Well, let's hope for a different situation here. Karl, we should be coming up on a tributary to the left. There, beyond that stand of willows. That's the Nezpique Bayou."

Karl stared at what looked like a thirty-foot-wide tunnel that vanished into the black shadows of the overhanging trees and Spanish moss. "We are to go in there?" he asked hoarsely.

"We are. That's the way to the Jennings oil field. And, hopefully, a meeting with the Atakapas."

Karl nodded again and eased the nose of the Sportsman over toward the Stygian hole in the foliage. Standing behind the young German, Larry noticed that Klemm's embarrassed flush was quite gone. Instead, the back of his neck had acquired a pallor, despite the mild case of sunburn he'd picked up on their coast-hugging trip along the Gulf coast.

Chapter 14

Nezpique Bayou, Louisiana

After motoring two and a half miles along the winding Nezpique Bayou, Templeton pointed up through a gap in the canopy. "There. Smoke. Up ahead."

"Smoke?" Eckdahl echoed. "A camp?"

Quinn shook his head. "More like an invitation, I think. Karl, nice and slow now. Winkelman, you keep that lever gun lower and relax."

"Sir," said the big soldier from Jena, "will they even know what this weapon is, since they have not—?"

"Winkelman, firstly, they may not know what a lever-action rifle is, but you can be damned sure they know it's a gun of some kind. And secondly, your primary job, even before using that rifle, is to know how to take orders. Particularly ones that you might not agree with or might make you anxious. I thought you had learned that lesson back on the Calc. Have you forgotten that, or do you remain capable of carrying out your orders?"

Winkelman nodded tightly. "Yes, Herr Major. My apologies."

"You keep calm and everything is going to be fine. They wouldn't start a fire unless they were looking to meet us. And they wouldn't want to meet us unless they were at least curious, and possibly friendly."

Karl canted his voice so the others in the boat couldn't hear it, not even keen-eared Wright. "Or maybe the fire is to draw us to a place where we may be most conveniently ambushed?"

"Karl," Quinn muttered, "just drive the boat. And use that big brain of yours for another minute. Why is that fear pretty much nonsense?"

The young man from Ingolstadt grew still, then nodded. "They know this bayou so well that they must have dozens of points along the shore from which they could ambush us. It has been as narrow as twenty feet across, in some stretches. So it is extremely unlikely that they would need to lure us to a single spot, and thereby, alert us to their presence. As they have done now."

"There you go. See? Nothing to be afraid of," Larry said with a smile as he congratulated himself for keeping his teeth from chattering. Because although everything he said was logical, they were still pushing into unknown waters to meet an unknown tribe with unknown intentions toward visitors—or trespassers— upon their lands. Suddenly, he heard the line from a movie he hadn't seen in years—*Apocalypse Now*—in which another commander had guided a small boat through a jungle-walled maze of muddy, serpentine waterways. But that major had offered very different counsel to his men: "Don't get out of the boat."

As the 180 Sportsman rounded a bend, the dense foliage seemed to slouch aside to reveal a long, straight stretch in the Nezpique Bayou. A hundred yards ahead, the trees fell back from the right bank, where a small fire was burning and two figures were waiting beside it. It was fronted by a sandy skirt of shoreline that slipped into the water at a gentle angle. With the dark-shadowed woods hemming it in behind, and the beachlike landing disappearing into muddy, weed-choked shallows beyond, it momentarily struck Larry as a kind of natural bandshell scalloped out of the dark waters and jungle. "Show time," he murmured.

"Not a very big cast, though," observed Templeton.

"Not that we can *see*," emphasized his countryman Wright.

Quinn nodded. "Okay. Karl, you come with me. Stay right by my side. Vogel,"—who was calm, quick, and was not prone to question orders—"you follow us, two paces behind. No sudden motions. And no guns. Wright,"—who combined levelheadedness with a quiet ability to take charge—"you're in command. And you already know there's more than meets the eye in the current surroundings."

"Most assuredly, sir. Motor running, or off?"

"That's a good question." Larry mulled over the possible ramifications. "Leave it turning over, as low as she can go. They've never heard it off, so they probably won't think much of it on low rpms."

"And if our hosts turn out to be, er, less motivated by curiosity than we hope?"

Wright smiled. Even in the 1600s, he found occasion to admire the singular British gift for understatement and irony that often masqueraded as excessive tactfulness. "I won't shackle you with a list of do's and don'ts. If you think you can get us out of there and not start a wholesale massacre, do so. If not, or if there is any reasonable possibility that you are misreading native actions as aggressive, then wait an extra moment. Like the Englishman sang, 'give peace a chance.'"

Wright's lean face contracted into a maze of perplexed creases and wrinkles. "Which Englishman was that, sir?"

"One who hasn't been born. And now, never will be. Wish us luck."

With the silt hissing along the keel, Larry hopped out, steadied himself and the boat, made sure that it rested only lightly on the bank. Karl slid over the side, the water not quite up to the crotch of his breeches. Larry waited until Vogel had joined them, and with a nod, led them toward the shore.

The two figures by the fire stood, dressed sparingly, as seemed common among the subtropical Amerinds. Both were men, one fairly advanced in years, the other about Larry's age, maybe a little bit older. Probably a former chief or counselor and the current chief, respectively. Or maybe the chief's lieutenant, Quinn corrected. It was only sensible that the contact with unknown visitors be made by persons who were, fundamentally, expendable. After all, that was why he, Larry Quinn, was here, not Mike Stearns or Gustav Adolf, or any of the other big shots back home. If Larry Quinn died here, well, there might be some moist eyes in Grantville, but no policy or war or social program would miss a beat. He was, ultimately, just a very small cog in a very big machine.

Quinn stopped at a distance of about ten feet, spread his fingers, held up his hands, showed them to be empty, showed their backs.

The older of the two men nodded, and copied the motions, tried a few words in a language that Larry didn't recognize. "Did you catch that?" he murmured sideways at Karl.

"No, sir. But I don't think it was a local Amerind language. It sounded more akin to a pidgin dialect of some kind. Maybe of—French?"

Well, that could be. Semipermanent French tent towns of buccaneers and native traders were known to be sprinkled in the Florida Keys, but would any have come this far? Or would these natives have traveled so far to trade? *Well, one way to find out.* "Help me, here, Karl. My French is going to run out after about two seconds. *Allo! Parlez vous Français?*"

The two natives exchanged glances, shrugged, turned back to their guests and shook their heads.

"Would you like me to try the Natchez words we have, Major?" Karl wondered.

"Hell, can't hurt," Larry said with a sigh. Personally, he had wondered if all the research it had taken to find the few words of Gulf Coast Native American languages buried in the books and journals of the Grantville library had been worth it. But Admiral Simpson had insisted on it, pointing out that if the contact team understood just one word in common with the natives, that could make the difference between striking up a relationship, or parting with a sense of permanent futility.

Klemm held up a hand, kept his fingers closed. "*I'c*," he articulated slowly.

The two natives stared for a moment, and then the older one's eyes widened. "*I'c!*" he repeated. "*I'c!*" He held up his own hand. "*Woc! Woc!*" he exclaimed.

"*Woc*," Klemm repeated, nodding. "*Woc*." Then, sideways to Larry: "Not Natchez, Major, but he recognized it." Karl nodded at the natives again, waited a moment, and presented his hand anew. "Hand," he emphasized, "hand."

The natives understood immediately, repeated the word with fair accuracy and growing smiles. Nodding, they gestured to mats arrayed near the fire, and seated themselves on the two furthest away from the shore.

Larry patted Klemm on the shoulder. "An invitation to sit means we're halfway there, Karl. Keep going."

The attempt at establishing common language hit a snag almost immediately thereafter. Karl, ever the logician, tried moving on to numbers, starting, sensibly enough, with "one," which he signified by raising his finger. They offered their word—*nāk*—and waited. Karl raised another digit, his index finger, for which they produced a clearly related word: *woknāk*. But when Karl raised a third finger, confusion ensued. The natives doubled back to *nāk*, then variations on it, and shook their heads in frustration when Karl unhelpfully held up a fourth finger.

It took a few minutes of careful reconstruction to discover what would have probably seemed quite obvious, had everyone not had so much at stake in making sure that clear communications were established. While Karl was trying to work on translating numbers, the natives had quite logically presumed he was continuing with a list of body parts, and thus answered with their word for finger, and then "index finger" when he held up a second digit.

But with that confusion out of the way, the numbers came along quickly. They then turned to the naming of body parts, then yes versus no, common objects such as man, woman, and finally personal names. The younger man was named Katkoshyok and the older one Tulak, who eagerly learned the names of their visitors and nodded approvingly. So, things were going pretty well, after all. Time to find out if they were, indeed, speaking with the Atakapa. "Karl, tell me, have you learned their word for 'big,' yet?"

"I have."

"And family?"

"I—I think so."

"Ask them if they are of the big, big family Atakapa." Karl did so.

The younger of the two natives rose slowly, his smile having undergone a rapid conversion to confusion tending toward rage. The older man remained seated, also looked annoyed, but was more a study in perplexity. He shook his head. "Atakapa no," he insisted. "Ata kapa," he articulated the words more separately. "Man food," and shook his head in something like disgust and contempt.

"Man food?" echoed Larry, glancing at Karl.

Klemm was frowning, tried the word he had learned in their language that meant "no," followed it with "atta kappa." Then he stopped, murmured the two sounds several times, and his eyes opened wide. "*Gott in himmel!*" he hissed to himself. Going back over the words he had learned from the two natives, he confirmed the word for food, then mimed eating. The response from the old man that identified the act of eating food sounded like a garbled, shortened version of Atakapa.

"Karl?" asked Quinn, starting to wonder if the

younger native would ever sit down again or stop frowning. "What's going on?"

"Our word for their tribe is wrong."

"Atakapa?"

"Yes. It's not their name for themselves. It's what they were called by others. It must be a slur, maybe by the Spanish."

"So Atakapa doesn't mean 'man food'?"

"Not quite. It means, 'eaters of men.'"

Oh. Well, yes, that might be a pretty upsetting mistranslation. On the other hand, it means that they either weren't cannibals, as most of the Grantville sources had claimed, or at least, did so as a matter of special ritual, not a means of getting routine nourishment. Which was good news. As long as the linguistic blunder by which they'd learned it didn't get them killed. Or, yeah: eaten.

Klemm seemed to be working on preventing exactly that outcome. "You great family no Atakapa. Our great family no Atakapa. Our great family"—he gestured toward all the Europeans—"People of Far Boats."

The younger fellow looked a little less angry, but also a little more confused. However, the older man nodded vigorously. "Our great family"—and he gestured toward himself, his companion, and the jungle around them—"are Sunrise People." Which sounded a great deal like *ee-shak*.

Klemm struck his head with his palm. "*Ishak*. They are the Ishak. The tribe was mentioned in one list that I saw, a list which did not include the name Atakapa. So, yes: Atakapa is not their name for themselves. They are the Ishak." And he smiled, triumphantly, at the older man.

Who nodded back happily, touched his own head and pointed to Klemm's, and then nodded again. The younger fellow's confusion was already fading when the older man directed a long stream of the liquid Ishak language at him, interspersed with a few chuckles, one of which elicited a full-throated laugh from the other. Then he waved at the woods, as if summoning the trees to come toward him.

Instead, similarly dressed persons emerged from deep in the shadows, the men approaching cautiously, the women somewhat hesitantly, the children eagerly— so eager that they raced straight past the newcomers. Stunned, Larry turned to follow their progress and learned what rated more interest than a group of strangely equipped, strangely speaking pale men who had come from afar.

It was the bright red boat that drew them like summer bugs to an unshaded lightbulb. They did slow as they drew closer to the water's edge, but their pointing fingers and unmistakable tones of whispered yet giddy speculation reminded Larry of the first vintage car show he'd ever gone to. His eyes had been every bit as big as theirs, his hands itching to touch the shiny, sleek vehicles as if, somehow, that would make them more real, would allow him to take some microscopic part of their essence away with him.

Larry turned to the two Ishak who had been selected, obviously for their intelligence and bravery, to contact the pale-skinned newcomers. He jerked his head at the excited children with a smile. "Kids," he said with a slight shake of his head.

"*Nomc,*" Klemm translated, along with the same smile that was all at once rueful and indulgent.

The older Ishak returned the same smile and nodded. "Yes," he answered with a laugh. "Kids."

And Quinn realized: *We're going to be okay. All of us. See, Larry? Not so hard, after all!*

But that glib self-assurance flew in the face of the risks he'd rightly anticipated upon contacting native peoples whose only prior experience of Europeans was likely to involve deceit, theft, rapine, and pillage.

Larry Quinn glanced south, hoping that the most uncertain of the fleet's various indigenous contact missions worked out as well as his had today.

And if not, that they got away alive.

Chapter 15

Port-of-Spain, Trinidad

Morning started for Hugh O'Donnell with the face of his aide and old friend Aodh O'Rourke scowling down at him. "A fine example to your men, sleeping away half the morning," was how the veteran aide-de-camp said "good morning," before howling for drums and coronets to awaken the Wild Geese mercenaries that were traveling with them. In actuality, the middle watch had not ended long before, but the east was already gray and Port-of-Spain would soon be aware of the presence of the ship that had carried them there: the Dutch jacht *Eendracht*.

When Hugh arrived on deck, he saw that the second, promised ship had joined them during the night. This was the comparatively high-sided *Hollandische Tuijn*, which sported the same number of guns as the *Eendracht*—thirty-eight—but was equipped with twenty-two-pounders. Any knowledgeable person ashore, equipped with a spyglass, would know instantly what those big brass and iron muzzles portended: a truly ruinous bombardment.

Evidently, some such knowledgeable observer had been present—either that or Port-of-Spain simply had no belly for a fight. Which was not too surprising: the Spanish had a history of none-too-benign neglect of this outpost which was routinely bypassed when each year's Flota invariably made its first landfall further along the Main. After all, neither silver nor spices made their way to this easternmost point on Tierra Firme, so what was the profit in stopping there?

In consequence, the harbor's modest defenses were dilapidated, as Hugh could plainly see while he and ten of his Wild Geese made their way to shore in a pair of Dutch skiffs. He was met by the Spanish equivalent of a sergeant who reeked of wine and whose belly suggested it was a common indulgence. The fellow was startled at Hugh's polished Spanish, expressed further confusion that Irish mercenaries were landing from Dutch ships, and then became speechlessly compliant when Hugh informed him that Port-of-Spain was now under the control of the Dutch and the USE. And the Union of Kalmar.

The Spaniard had blinked, sputtered once, and then gestured mutely toward the approximate center of the town—well, village—that serviced the harbor. Whether or not Hugh's proclaimed source of authority mattered to the sergeant, the many ominous muzzles bristling from the side of two ships and pointed in his direction evidently conferred a sufficient measure of political legitimacy.

Next to a small central church was an equally small garrison that was responsible for manning the four-gun battery which overlooked the harbor. Only two guns had ready powder and shot and there was only one guard present—who had to be awakened by the Wild Geese when they approached him. Just inside, the "governor" of the tiny town also had to be roused and seemed relieved to surrender it to Hugh. Or anyone else who wanted to take responsibility for it.

The transfer of power having been effected, O'Rourke had left the next senior of the Wild Geese, O'Bannon, in charge of rounding up weapons and securing the paroles of the Spanish militia and any locals who had been inveigled to offer services in support of it. Hugh, in the meantime, had asked to be shown the officer's paddock. There he found a reasonable gelding, a rather sweet-natured old mare, and a third ill-kept creature that was bound for the stew-pot if its care did not improve immediately and dramatically.

Giving orders for that care to be furnished, he and O'Rourke mounted and rode to the eastern margins of Port-of-Spain where they found, as they had been told to expect, two Nepoia guides waiting in concealment. Exchanging nods, the two Irishmen followed the natives.

However, before O'Donnell and O'Rourke felt comfortable enough to distract themselves with conversation, more Nepoia emerged from fields and forests until their escort numbered upwards of twenty. Hugh had the strong impression that perhaps a dozen more shadowed their flanks just beyond the edges of the tree lines that hemmed in the small farm plots on either side of the cart track. This cautious security force, and the absence of farmers working the fields or moving their livestock, confirmed what Hugh had instinctively felt when he had walked through the few, dusty lanes of Port-of-Spain: this was a land poised in the midst of a war. And presently there was, so to speak, another shoe waiting to fall.

The anticipation of which had been what led to his being here in the first place...

Hugh had been to Spain while in the service of Philip IV's vassal—and aunt—Archduchess Isabella of the Spanish Lowlands, but even there, February was noticeably chilly. But here on St. Eustatia? It was as balmy as ever. Whereas last year at this time, he and his tercio of Wild Geese had been in Brussels, shivering in freezing rain and bitter winds every time they poked a nose outside.

He turned away from the view out the window and let his eyes readjust to the comparative gloom of the second-floor council chamber of Fort Oranje. Mike McCarthy, the up-timer who'd brought him into the scheme to secure Trinidad's oil, was standing in front of a phenomenally detailed and accurate map of that same island. He was pointing to the strongpoint Hugh had constructed, Fort St. Patrick, and assuring Eddie Cantrell that the neighboring Arawaks represented a minimal threat, at most.

"They're not much to worry about," he was saying, "not when you've got a well-armed force in a prepared position like this one."

Eddie shook his head. "I'm not worried about them attacking, Mike. I'm worried about them telling the Spanish where they can find us."

The older up-timer rubbed his chin. "Well, I don't like it, but we should be able to keep the Arawak busy enough that they don't have the time to go wandering over to Pitch Lake, which is further west than they usually range."

Eddie leaned forward. "And how do we do that?"

Mike sighed. "By heating up the war they're waging against the Nepoias."

"Last I heard, the Nepoia cacique Hyarima had stopped asking to meet Hugh and started asking for more guns. He's barely holding his own."

Hugh nodded. "Right before setting sail to join you here, he sent an emissary to make that same request. The Nepoia are badly outnumbered."

Mike stared at his feet. "Then we send them more guns. Not like we don't have hundreds of outdated pieces left over from last year's attack on Oranjestad and The Quill." He sounded like he might spit.

Eddie was frowning. "So, we fuel a brush war to keep the Arawak too busy to think about going to Pitch Lake or, if they do, telling the Spanish about what they found there?" When there was no answer, he pressed, "Mike, is that wise? Is it *right*?"

Mike shrugged. "Is it wise? Sure, because it will work. Is it right?" He scratched his cheek. "Look, Eddie, about five minutes after I started hatching this wild-ass Trinidad scheme, I realized why I never should have started in: because the choices aren't between what's right and what's wrong, or what's good and what's bad. Here, the choices are always between what's bad—and what's worse.

"So, is supplying the Nepoia with enough guns so that they can take the war to the Arawaks 'right'? I don't know. All I know for sure is that we've got to keep all the Spanish eyes in the Caribbean focused on Trinidad for as long as we can. So yeah, if making sure that the war with the Nepoias gets hot enough to pull the Arawak lookouts away from Pitch Lake and the oil rig, then that's the right thing to do." He did not look up as he spoke.

Eddie was running a hand through his hair. "I dunno, Mike. I don't think that's enough. I think we need to actively coordinate with the Nepoia."

"Coordinate? How?"

"Well, when our contacts bring them that load of guns you're talking about, they also bring a message."

Mike looked up. "This oughta be good."

Eddie nodded. "We let them know that the Spanish won't be able to supply the Arawak anymore. Because we won't let them."

Mike stared, laughed mirthlessly. "Yeah, good luck with that." He sighed. "As best as we know, the Arawaks are still crawling all over the majority of the island's landmass in the east. That's a lot of supply line to sever."

Eddie shook his head. "We're not thinking about that whole area, Mike. In fact, the last thing we want and the last thing we can afford is to put a lot of troops into an unfamiliar jungle region. We know how that works out. Besides, it's our intention to stay out of the way, to let the native groups settle their own affairs, as much as possible."

"That will be a nice trick, since both sides are now providing them with guns."

"I agree it won't be easy, might not even be possible. But if we can cut off the Arawaks' Spanish supply of guns and powder, don't join any fights, and stay the hell off of ninety-eight percent of their land, hopefully the Arawaks will feel safe making peace with the Nepoia. Maybe they'd even come around to accepting our presence at Pitch Lake, too."

"And in the meantime? Could be a lot of body counts and massacres until that happy time when we're all passing the jug and singing kumbaya, Eddie."

Eddie nodded, but Hugh was no stranger to councils of war and state. The look in the young up-timer's eyes was exceedingly patient as was his tone as he answered: he was placating as much as he was agreeing. "No argument. For now, however, let me be more specific about how we can cut off the Spanish supply to the Arawak: we isolate the inland capital of San José de Oruña by taking the small harbor town that connects it to the wider world, Port-of-Spain."

Mike leaned forward. "I'm listening."

"The last known governor there is Cristoval de Aranda, who has a pitifully small garrison. He has so little Spanish help or local control that he has to allow the island's tobacco farmers to freight smoke on any ship that happens by. Now, in our timeline, those were almost all French, English, or Dutch. But in this timeline, that means he's even in worse straits: the Dutch are hiding, the only English left can't even freight their own tobacco, and before summer comes, we'll have eliminated the last French colonies in the Caribbean.

"But, so long as San José de Oruña and Port-of-Spain are in Spanish hands, they can use it to anchor ships, land troops, store or gather food, and most important, send guns to the Arawaks. Fortunately, given our forces in that region, we can visit Port-of-Spain with such a profoundly superior show of force that we should be able to take the place without having to fire a shot. Literally."

Mike studied Eddie. "I know that smile of yours; there's a kicker."

"A what?" asked Hugh.

"A final card he can play to ensure that this plan actually works."

Eddie's smile broadened. "Sure there's a kicker, Mike. We make sure Hyarima knows when it's going to happen, so he can make whatever plans he considers best. And we also let him know who he can thank for taking Port-of-Spain and thereby, cutting off his enemies' access to weapons and powder."

Hugh smiled. "You needn't glance at me next, Eddie. I know what you're thinking and why you're thinking it."

Mike frowned. "Well . . . I don't. So, you wanna tell me?"

Hugh smiled at his friend. "O'Rourke was part of the original party that met with Hyarima's representatives to trade guns for food last year. Also, given the Wild Geese's share in the oil profits, we have a personal investment in ensuring an outcome on Trinidad that makes the Nepoia our happy and willing friends. And finally, most of us are all too well acquainted with both the Spanish language and the empire's bureaucracy.

"So," Hugh finished, looking back at Eddie, "if anyone is able to compel this fellow Aranda to relent without a fight, I suspect it would be us. And the 'kicker' is that by sending me, Hyarima gets the meeting he's been asking for."

Eddie nodded, his eyes bright and appreciative. "That was my thinking precisely, Hugh."

Chapter 16

Just outside San José de Oruña, Trinidad

So far, everything had gone as the three of them had planned. Which many men might have found reassuring, but over the course of his life, Hugh O'Donnell had been orphaned, adopted, knighted, and decreed a traitor, and at each step, fate had not merely taken a hand, but had turned his world upside down. Demonstrating that, just when you think events are unfolding according to plan, you may rest assured that you'll be proven wrong in a trice.

It also meant there was no use worrying over it, because fate was as capricious as it was contrary, so it would not obey any human expectation or anticipation, whether malign or benign. So Hugh, glad to be back in the saddle for the first time in months, enjoyed the surety and strength of the gelding he'd taken from the small officer's paddock at Port-of-Spain and spurred it as they approached an incline.

The horse trotted up and over the crest of a slight ridge. The ground leveled off, revealing small farms marking a winding path toward a town in the distance:

San José de Oruña. The Nepoia scouts ahead of him maintained their jog, waving curious warriors of their tribe back from the narrow cart track. A few of the houses up ahead were marked by faint strings of dirty smoke that rose almost straight up until they reached the level of the hills sheltering the valley and there leaned over westward, following the breeze. The only thing missing was—

"Aodh O'Rourke? Tell me now; are you riding or napping back there?"

Behind, Hugh heard a muffled curse. O'Rourke, sitting an old nag that moved as gracelessly as he rode, was attempting to catch up to him and not succeeding. Hugh smiled, put faint backward pressure on his reins. As his forward progress slowed, he realized that this would be the first time in almost a day that he and O'Rourke would be beyond the earshot of anyone who spoke English or Gaelic or better-than-rudimentary Spanish.

Once alongside Hugh, O'Rourke started with a comment that picked up eerily on his commander's own train of thought. "I wonder what they're waiting for," he said, drawing abreast of Hugh. "Seems like the Nepoia have the situation here in hand already."

"Seems so," Hugh nodded. "But it's interesting that none of the warriors we've seen so far are armed with trade muskets."

O'Rourke huffed. "Probably better to use 'em as clubs. It was mostly old Spanish matchlocks and arquebuses that we gave 'em."

"Yes, but according to Michael, there were some current weapons as well. But whatever pieces they've been furnished with, the Nepoia are clearly masters of this ground. Enough so that they haven't even bothered to sack or encircle Port-of-Spain."

"Sacking a village is hardly a 'bother,' Hugh. I'd have expected it to be the first thing they'd do, given the chance."

Hugh nodded. "But they haven't. I suppose we'll find out why when we reach Hyarima."

O'Rourke looked about. The inscrutable, silent Nepoia hemmed them in all around. "I'll be happy enough when we've finished that task, my earl."

Hugh was surprised by O'Rourke's wariness and suddenly serious and formal form of address. "'My earl'?"

O'Rourke looked over at Hugh. "Yes, 'my earl.' And I'm a fool for agreeing to this meeting without a guard detachment."

Hugh looked over his shoulder. "We seem very well guarded, O'Rourke."

"With respect, we are very well 'escorted.' Not the same thing. If it was our own men, *then* you'd be under guard. As you always should be, now."

Hugh nodded, understanding. "It's the news we got about O'Neill. But that was months ago. What's put you on edge, now? This nonsense about me being the last earl of Ireland, last heir to—"

O'Rourke's voice was sharp. "My earl, at the risk of offending, I must assert that it is not nonsense. And you seem to think too much of yourself, in it."

Hugh almost stopped the gelding in his surprise. "I beg your pardon?"

"My earl, I apologize, but we have always had frank speech between us, and I'd have just a bit more now. You may think that the greatest import in the news of

John O'Neill's death is how it affects you, as the last earl of Ireland. But if you think that, you are wrong: dead wrong. The fate most changed by the death of the Earl of Tyrone is that of the Irish people—*your* people, my earl."

"O'Rourke, what's gotten into you?"

"Nothing that shouldn't have been in me all along. And I've been wrong not to see it, wrong ever since I failed to set aside our familiarity when you came of age. I own it was natural enough to let those brotherly ways continue, being as how I was the first one to teach you how to hold a sword and watch your own back. But when you received a command of your own so young, and we rolled right along as we'd always been, I didn't stop to think how things should change, mostly because we worked so well together, and so easily.

"And that camaraderie made the lads in the tercio feel like they were being welcomed straight into a ready family, like they were safe in a little bit of *Eireann*, and the unit was truly their home. And that's an important thing for exiled *cultchies* who're taking coin to serve a foreign banner in a foreign land."

Hugh stared at O'Rourke—garrulous, flippant, fiercely loyal O'Rourke—wondering at the seriousness of his tone, his face. "Aodh O'Rourke, why worry about this? Have things really changed so much because there's one less landless, impoverished Irish earl in this world?"

"With respect, things *have* changed, but only because last fall's news that John O'Neill was killed in Rome has been slowly awakening me, has shown me what I've been slumbering through: that you are a prince and must be treated as one."

Hugh laughed. "Treated as a prince?"

But Aodh O'Rourke was deadly serious. "Aye, as a prince. And because you didn't put on airs about your title like John O'Neill—God rest his quarrelsome soul—it was easy enough to put aside. Your men love you because—just like the better, older kings of Ireland—you do not separate yourself from them behind the high walls of titles and curtsies, insisting on bent knees and lowered heads. And because that brought such loyalty, such dedication, on battlefields, I never stopped to think: 'and is this powerful familiarity any wiser than John O'Neill's mighty arrogance?'"

Hugh shook his head. "I'll tell you why you didn't think that: because there was no reason to, O'Rourke. Our tercio has—"

"No, m'lord: there *is* reason to think it. And to think it through carefully. Which is what I've been doing, these months. It's a fine thing that you are not a prideful man, Hugh O'Donnell. That bodes well for all that might come. But you must think on this: your pride is not just your own. It never was, wholly, but now it is not so at all."

"O'Rourke, stop talking in riddles. For once, it is *I* that cannot understand *you.*"

O'Rourke did not take the dangled bait of a friendly gibe. "You cannot understand me because I am speaking a language you've long refrained from speaking, m'lord: the language of courts and thrones and kings. A sovereign's pride is not simply his own, Lord O'Donnell. And you know that right enough. An insult to a crown is not just an insult to the man who wears it, but to the kingdom which it represents."

"I wear no crown, old friend."

O'Rourke fixed him with a peculiarly intense gaze. "Not yet, m'lord. But I've been considering how last fall, we didn't just hear the news of O'Neill's death. We were also notified that, thanks to Don Michael's sly provisos regarding oil taken from this place, the last surviving earl will now have access to independent sources of income that will make for—forgive me—a princely sum, indeed. And we learned that King Fernando's war against the Dutch could not continue without both sides committing mutual financial suicide. And we learned that Don Michael McCarthy's actions are not simply a matter of his individual interest in Eireann's fate, but were planned and blessed by some of the highest powers in the United States of Europe.

"My lord, in the space of that one day, we went from being penniless, desperate, ill-fed exiles, to a moneyed group of armed expatriates with powerful allies. And in that same day, Ireland's future went from a dismal certainty of endless servitude and oppression to a glimmer of hope for new and better possibilities. And those hopes center on you, m'lord, which is why we should not be ambling through the weeds without our own bodyguard, at least twenty strong. And we shall never do so again."

Hugh was silent for several seconds. He prided himself on having a relatively good measure of all the men around him, but he hadn't seen the faintest hint of this change growing in O'Rourke. "Even if everything you say were true—which I contest—I could still not do as you suggest. We have much work to do, and I cannot do my part in it from behind a phalanx of guards."

O'Rourke nodded grimly. "A truth that will no doubt

rob me of much sleep in the months to come. Would that we had one of the other colonels here—Preston, or Owen Roe O'Neill, even—to assume the risks of—"

"Aodh O'Rourke, I'll not be hiding behind the swords of brave men in order to play at statecraft. You might recall that the greatest kings of Ireland were also fighting kings, kings who led from the front, not the rear, of their hosts. And they did not stand on ceremony or titles."

Again, O'Rourke nodded. "Aye, you've the right of all that." His voice became dark and regretful. "But those past days of Ireland are not these days. And kings now must tread a different, more careful, path. In those elder days, to lead and to govern was much the same thing. Those ancient kings knew almost every chieftain and person of note in their realm. But now"—the gruff Irishman shrugged—"a king cannot know but a handful of the most powerful persons in his kingdom. And if he falls on a battlefield, chaos follows. So if he is to govern long and well and consistently, he must not risk himself by leading on a battlefield. And that means he lives—unavoidably—at greater remove from the people of his land."

"Yes, his 'subjects,'" O'Donnell almost spat. "What a hateful word. To be 'subject' to another person is too close to being their 'thrall,' if you ask me. And as for a modern king governing from a palace but not leading on a battlefield—well, it seems that Gustav of Sweden's successes in both domains give the lie to that theory."

"Do they?" O'Rourke shook his head. "How many times have his larks, leading charges and gallivanting about in disguise, almost killed him? Mark my word, his fine personal courage will be his undoing. But it will be the countries of which he is the sovereign that will pay the price in confusion and contention among a sudden spate of successors. No, Lord O'Donnell, in this age, kings should not die quickly on the battlefield, but slowly, in their own beds, with their chosen successor close at hand. They owe their nations no less."

Hugh shrugged. "I'll not say your words are unwise, O'Rourke, but I'm also not sure the wisdom they hold is the only kind that matters. Perhaps a measure of both, as in so many things, is the best approach. But I'll not suffer to be held at remove from my men."

"No one's asking you to, though the Lord above knows well how much I'd like to. But He's fond of His mysterious ways, He is. Even when it comes to dealings with our newest friends."

"The up-timers?"

"Aye, and the Dutch. They're cagey and thick as thieves, if you've not been paying adequate attention, m'lord. As clear as avarice gleams in a tinker's eye, it's been plain from the moment our paths crossed and aligned with Tromp and Cantrell that we're not to be confidants in *all* their plans."

"You mean the scuttlebutt that one of the up-timer's ships went its own way just before the flotilla arrived in the Caribbees?"

"That's the one. And still no word of it, you'll note. Neither of its whereabouts or its business."

Hugh smiled. "Any guesses, O'Rourke?"

"Not a one, except that it's something that neither the up-timers nor the Dutch want us to know about."

Hugh glanced up at the green slopes rising steeply to their left: the foothills of the mountains that marked the northern extents of Trinidad. "I'm not sure that they don't want *us* to know about it. It may be that they don't want *anyone* else to know about it."

"And that's supposed to make us feel better, that we can't be trusted to keep a secret?"

"I don't think we should feel one way or the other about it, myself. If they want to make sure the Spanish don't hear about it, the best way is to let as few people know as possible, *whoever* those people might happen to be."

"Aye, there's sense enough in that. But what would be so secret that it shouldn't be shared? Maybe the up-timers know where the fountain of youth—or El Dorado—really is?"

Hugh grinned at the waggish speculation. "I'm thinking the matter may be a bit more earthy than those fantasies. Indeed, it may be about something in the earth, itself."

"As usual, m'lord, you've lost me. Nice to see we're back to the regular state of affairs between us, with you confusing me and not t' other way 'round."

"And with you being perpetually insolent. At any rate, while I was in Grantville, I had the opportunity to read fairly widely. And when I didn't have my nose in their damned small-typeset books, much of our talk concerned the up-time world and their New World homeland, America. Seems that country had a great deal of oil in it."

O'Rourke glanced sideways at Hugh. "Did it, now?"

"Oh, yes. And most of these immense deposits are located near the Gulf of Mexico. Which was the general direction in which it was said the other steamship, the *Courser*, was heading."

O'Rourke nodded thoughtfully. "Fair enough. But if that's what the up-timers are playing at, why keep it a secret from us?"

"As I said, they may simply be worried about someone telling the Spanish, which would be particularly ticklish, since their silver fleet sails past the Gulf Coast on its way to Havana and then on to Seville."

O'Rourke's nod was vigorous this time. "So if the Spanish were to find out, it would be two stallions in one paddock. But if they can be kept in the dark, then the up-timers can go after the oil there without having to worry about any unwelcome visitors."

"And to make their presence in the paddock known at a time and place of their own choosing. Of course, the up-timers would have to confide in the Dutch, with whom they seem to be coordinating almost all their naval movements. If I was Admiral Tromp and learned that there's another one of those steamships somewhere about, I know *I'd* insist on knowing why it wasn't available to help the larger, allied fleet."

As they neared the top of yet another gentle slope, the senior of their Nepoia guides/protectors held up one long-fingered hand and ventured over the crest.

"Smell that?" O'Rourke asked, leaning toward Hugh.

O'Donnell nodded. "Not a cooking fire." Burning houses always sent up a mix of odors, many unctuous, that were heavier than the scents produced by wood alone.

The Nepoia leader reappeared at the top of the slope and nodded. The scouts behind them flared out to either side, crouching a little as they walked.

"I'm thinking—" O'Rourke started.

"—that it is time to dismount," Hugh finished for

him. They did so and led their horses over the lip of
the rise before them.

About four hundred yards ahead, a low, sprawling
town emerged from the flatland at the bottom of a
lopsided valley. A sparsely wooded southern ridge
rose slowly to the right. Thickly forested mountain
sides soared on the left. Several houses close to the
town were throwing up fresh smoke plumes, flickers
at their base indicating that the structures were not
yet fully gutted. Perhaps midway to the town, Hugh
could make out a rough ring of natives, many of whom
were carrying firearms. However, there was no sound
of gunfire, and no sign of bodies.

It appeared that the Nepoia had decided to exert
their own force against the Spanish colony on the same
day their friends' ships did the same from the sea.

Following the leader of the escort, Hugh and
O'Rourke led their mounts away from the cart track
and closer to the northern slopes, keeping buildings
between themselves and the town as much as possible. Just because there was no shooting going on
presently, and the range was very long, there was
also no reason to tempt fate.

Within a minute, they were approaching what first
struck Hugh as a shabby, open-air pavilion, but then
he recognized it—by sight and smell both—for what it
was: a sorting and pre-drying shed for tobacco. Seated
in the shade of the spatulate leaves which were its
roof, and surrounded by a group of younger, musket-
armed warriors, was a well-muscled, squarish man of
medium height and youthful middle age. The leader
of the escort went ahead and spoke to him, nodding
respect when he started his report.

The older man returned the nod gravely, and although he did not move his head, Hugh saw that his eyes shifted to O'Rourke and himself. After a moment's consideration, he signed assent, and gestured for them to approach. Then he rose to his feet.

This simple act clearly caught his warriors off guard. They scrambled to follow their leader's example, exchanging surprised looks. Hugh nodded his thanks to the leader of his escort, who returned that gesture deeply before taking his leave. *Well, if this isn't Hyarima, he's doing a most convincing job of acting the part.*

When Hugh approached to within ten feet, the older native stepped forward briskly and proffered his right hand. It was an awkward, slightly stiff gesture, but unmistakable. Hugh shook the wide brown hand. It was calloused and very hard. He inclined his head slightly in respect, was gratified to see the nod returned. Just as Hugh wondered whether to start introducing himself in Dutch or Spanish, and unsure of the fellow's facility in either, the choice became moot.

"I am Hyarima, cacique of the Nepoia," the older native said in almost completely unaccented Spanish. "If you are O'Donnell, cacique of your people, I have been told you speak Spanish. That is good, for our speaking must be quick. If my warriors do not attack soon, we will not have killed all the Spanish by nightfall."

Chapter 17

Just outside San José de Oruña, Trinidad

"I am O'Donnell," replied Hugh, "and I do speak Spanish, as does my second-in-command, Aodh O'Rourke. We thank you for honoring us with an invitation to speak to you in your war camp."

Hyarima acknowledged the thanks, looked around at his warriors, who seemed to be more surprised than ever. "You do us honor to come. The Dutchmen have spoken of you. They said you were a war captain and leader of your people. They also told us that you are, as they say, a 'man of your word.' We welcome this. Not all of the men who come from over the sea keep their word. No matter what language they speak."

O'Donnell nodded. "I understand. I am grateful you do not assume I am like them."

Hyarima almost smiled as he gestured that they should sit. "I already know you are not like them."

Hugh raised an eyebrow. "How do you know this?"

Hyarima nodded. "You have manners. You act like a Person. You treat me as a Person. O'Rourke and his friend Calabar did no less when they met my cousin

179

Sukumar last year. They too, acted as Persons. All this is well."

From the emphasis Hyarima put on the word "Person," Hugh gathered it meant something akin to a "civilized person." "How else would one act?" he wondered aloud.

Hyarima's face became less expressive. "Men from your lands over the sea are often aloof at first, as a cacique might be with the youngest of his tribe. But then, if they need something from us, they change. They bring gifts and speak as does a captured warrior to the chief of his enemies, wringing hands, promising to do things that have not even been asked of them. But then, after we help them and they become strong again, they return to treating us as children. Bad children.

"Only a few ever do what you have done: to greet us as a Person greets a Person, with respect and expecting the same in return. This is a good sign. I am glad we meet. Now let us discuss the matters that concern us both. I regret I offer no food or drink or even much time, but battlefields are not good places for talking."

No, indeed. But Hugh said aloud, "I agree, Hyarima. I am told you have asked the Dutch that, henceforth, you and I shall sit to discuss and arrange the affairs between our peoples."

"This is so. You are a man who understands my role here."

Hugh heard strong emphasis on the last part of Hyarima's reply. "Hyarima, what do you mean by your 'role here'? And why would I understand it more than other men?"

Hyarima swept his arm at the war-poised tableau behind him. "I fight the Spanish to retake my homeland. This land was Nepoia land before the Spanish came and took it for themselves and their Arawak allies. You, the Dutch tell me, know how this feels. You would be a great cacique in your homeland, but you may not return there. Enemies keep that land by helping rival clans against your own, much as the Spanish have held my homeland. Your enemies, like mine, are given better weapons, and your people— again, like mine—became work-slaves."

Hyarima looked around the valley. "Seven years ago, I was a slave in these fields, before escaping and returning to my people near the place you call Punta de Galera. And I swore our land would be ours again." His eyes came to rest on Hugh's. "And I see in your eyes, and in his"—he gestured at O'Rourke—"that you know this feeling. I think, maybe, the Dutch knew this feeling once, but now, their words and eyes are always filled with gold and silver. And having once been slaves to the Spanish has not made them refuse to keep slaves of their own. But I think it may be different with you."

Hugh nodded. "I know what it is like to lose one's country. Completely, and for a very long time."

Hyarima nodded and his eyes became shiny. "When the Spanish settled, in my grandfather's time, there were forty thousands of us on this island. Now, there are but four thousands. If we would survive as a people, and on the land of our grandmothers and grandfathers, we must free ourselves now."

Hugh looked over Hyarima's shoulder at the ramshackle roofscape of San José de Oruña. "And yet you show great restraint in doing so."

Hyarima's shrug was so slight as to be almost imperceptible. "With the new guns and powder and shot just brought by the Dutchmen, we have been able to defeat many of the Arawak. For many months, we could not fight them well; we had little powder left. They became lazy. So with the new powder, we attacked all at once and without stopping. They were defeated more by their surprise than by us.

"They have abandoned most of the villages they took in my father's time and abandoned the Spanish as well. There are so few of the Spanish and their mixed offspring, that we need not be hasty in finishing our war. Instead, it seemed wise to meet you first."

"Meet me—us?"

"Yes, O'Donnell. We are told that you, or your allies, may wish to live on our island. As friends, who will not grow beyond the limits we grant. There, you will wish to live in your own ways. We understand this. You will want farms such as the Spanish have, buildings such as the Spanish have, wells such as the Spanish have. Once we have killed their owners, we would make a gift of these to you and your people, if you wish them."

The cacique's calm eyes promised genocide as if it were a trifling gift, a small token of respect between friends. Hugh shook his head. "Hyarima, I do not ask or hope you to stain your hands with their blood, just so you may give their buildings to us."

Hyarima shrugged. "That is not why we are killing them. We must eliminate our enemies, but their farms and buildings are of no use to us. I reasoned your people might feel otherwise."

Great God, how do I explain the need for mercy and not sound like I am taking the side of the Spanish against the Nepoias? "If any man, if any people, may claim the right of vengeance, none has better claim than Hyarima and the Nepoia. But I must ask: is there no way to show mercy to those who help end the war by surrendering? I might be able to convince—"

Hyarima was shaking his head. "The blood-debt is too great, O'Donnell. Perhaps it would not be, if the Spanish did not follow a god who speaks of mercy while encouraging murder."

Hugh blinked in surprise. "I do not understand."

"Can you not?" Hyarima's face lost much of its expression. "The Spanish god instructs the Spanish priests to promise mercy and kindness, but does not punish the Spanish soldiers who enslaved and killed my people while wearing the god's cross-symbol around their necks. They even called upon this god to help them as they slaughtered us in our villages. Not just our warriors, but our women and our children." Hyarima's eyes were unblinking and hard. "We have remained peaceful too often, spared the lives of murderers, because of the fine-sounding lies of this god's teachings. No more."

Hugh saw the still-intact town of San José de Oruña over Hyarima's shoulder, felt fresh sweat break along his brow. *If I can't think of a different appeal in the next minute, all those townspeople are as good as dead.* O'Donnell played the last card he held: an appeal to honor. "I understand. The blood of one's own slain innocents calls loudly to any cacique. It shall to me, also, which is why we may not then live in the places you offer to me."

Now it was Hyarima who blinked. "Why should our deeds compel you to reject their houses and fields? Today's blood is not upon your hands, O'Donnell."

Hugh shook his head. "But I cannot stand to gain by that blood, either, Hyarima. How may I invite my people to live in this place, knowing the houses in which they dwell, the fields in which they work, were made ready for them by being washed with the blood of women and children? It may not have been my hand that did the work, but I cannot knowingly gain from your vengeance without becoming party to it."

Hyarima frowned, but Hugh had the distinct impression it was not prompted by his rejection of the cacique's "gift," but at the honor-conundrum behind the rejection. "I understand your words and your concerns, O'Donnell. And they move me. But even if I was to stay my hand against the innocents of these places, one day, the sons of the slain fathers would come for my blood to answer their loss. Or, what is worse, would come for the blood of my sons and grandsons. And daughters and granddaughters, since the Spanish make war upon everyone."

Hugh shrugged. "They would not know so well who slew their fathers if they grew up in a different land."

Hyarima's frown faded. His eyes narrowed. "What do you propose, O'Donnell?"

"The women and children of the Spanish could be moved." *Tromp will want to put my head in a noose when he hears what I've promised. And Cantrell might want to help him.* O'Donnell affected a casual shrug as he felt O'Rourke growing rigid beside him. "The Spanish came by boat. Those you spare could leave by boat."

Hyarima's eyes remained narrow. "You *are* a cacique, O'Donnell. But I was told that the boats are not yours to command. Did the Dutchmen lie to me?"

Hugh shook his head. "They did not lie. But I have many fine soldiers. The Dutch will need those men alongside them, to fight the Spanish, before this year is past." He paused. "The Dutch will grant me this boon."

Hyarima's eyes opened slightly. "You would indebt yourself for the Spanish? I have heard whispers, though I cannot be sure of their truth, that the Spanish have lied to you as well, have used you and your men poorly in many wars."

Hugh shrugged. "Those words are true. But we were not used poorly by their women and children, Hyarima. So I would not make those innocents pay for the misdeeds of men who should have kept their word."

Hyarima's eyes opened wider. Then he nodded. "So be it. The Spanish women and children shall not be killed or harmed. They shall be removed, according to your word. But if your allies will not cooperate as you assure me—" The unfinished statement was terribly eloquent.

Hugh nodded. "I understand that you cannot allow the Spanish to stay on your land. The danger, and the insult to your dead, are both too great."

"It is well you understand this, and it promises a good friendship between us."

"Hyarima, our friendship is so important that I would suggest a further means of ensuring its health." The Nepoia cacique's nod invited explication. "I propose that if I or my allies are attacked *solely* by other men from beyond the sea, that we shall not seek your aid against them. Similarly, if you are attacked solely by the other caciques and tribes of these lands, we shall not become involved."

Hyarima frowned. "This is a strange alliance, O'Donnell."

Hugh smiled ruefully. "It might seem so, but my homeland is also an island of tightly interwoven families and clans. And so I have learned this: never become involved in the family feuds of your neighbors. Too often the stories tell us of how a much-loved visitor interceded in another family's feud, and slew one of their distant relatives to save them from harm. But in the years that follow, that family's gratitude too often becomes rotten with regret and secret resentment." Hugh shrugged. "The host may have thanked the guest for slaying the dangerous relative on the day he was saved, but might, unreasonably, hate the guest a year later for the very same act. I perceive the people of these lands are akin to one great family. So are we from over the sea. And family feuds must remain within the families they pertain to, for this reason."

Hyarima nodded, and although he did not smile, he looked pleased, both with the agreement and Hugh. "You are wise for your years, O'Donnell. Your people are lucky to have such a cacique."

Hugh was preparing to wave off the compliment when O'Rourke interrupted. "We are. Our Lord O'Donnell is too modest to claim it."

"Of course," Hyarima answered calmly. "That is why he has you say it for him. This talk has been good. Next time, we shall have time for food and smoke." He stood, nodded, and left.

After which O'Rourke rounded on his earl. "Damn it, Hugh: you were set to shrug off your title again, if I hadn't jumped in. Whatever happened to the cocky little rascal you started out?"

"What happened, O'Rourke, was that I grew not

only in size but in sense. Which included an accurate measure of my small place in the world, I might add."

"Well, perhaps it is time to remeasure that place, my earl. Besides, the sin o' pride notwithstanding, too much humility is just not how things are done here. And you're the one who was always reminding me, 'when in Rome, do like the Romans.' Or don't you think these fellows are the local Romans?"

Hugh looked into the slight parting of fronds that marked where Hyarima had disappeared into the green wall that skirted the base of the steep northern slopes. "Oh no, O'Rourke. They're the Romans all right, no doubt about it. We exist here at their pleasure. And I hope it shall ever be thus."

The two men were silent as their guide returned and led them back to their horses. Behind, muskets began to sputter fitfully from atop the rude palisade around San José de Oruña.

O'Rourke cocked an ear in that direction. "You took quite a chance back there, m'lord. Regarding the fate of the Spanish, that is."

Hugh mounted the gelding in one fluid, annoyed motion. "Yes, for all the good it did."

"Seemed to have done a world of good for the women and children of this blasted island. And as for their men—well, I can't wonder but that they haven't richly earned what's about to befall 'em. 'Eye for an eye,' as the saying has it."

"'Let he amongst you who is without sin cast the first stone,'" Hugh retorted bitterly. "I won't be consoling myself over the rightness of a massacre, O'Rourke. Even if it's restricted to males old enough to at least have some fuzz on their chin."

"Aye, but it's not as though you've much cause for remorse, either. Let alone time in which to feel it. We're to be underway for St. Eustatia as soon as we can."

Hugh grimaced. "Where, I suspect, Tromp will rake me over the coals for promising to evacuate almost two hundred civilians from Port-of-Spain and San José de Oruña. And Cantrell might help him singe my toes."

"Ah, well, I'm not so sure of that," temporized O'Rourke. "Tromp is a pretty decent sort of fellow. Decent for a heathen Dutchman, that is." O'Rourke grinned. "And Cantrell—well, if memory serves, m'lord, it was you who remarked that most of the up-timers feel a great regret over what their ancestors did to the natives of the New World. I'd think that your making a pact with the Nepoia that saved lives, rather than took 'em, might be pleasing to our young up-time friend."

Hugh shrugged. "It would be a blessing if you're right, O'Rourke." O'Donnell spurred his horse lightly. "Let's make sure we're aboard to catch the evening breeze," he urged.

And let's get out of here before the massacre begins.

Part Two

June–July 1636

From his saw-pit of mouth,
from his charnel of maw
—Herman Melville,
"The Maldive Shark"

Chapter 18

Oranjestad, St. Eustatia

Eddie Cantrell closed the door softly behind him, padded to the stairs, took the first few steps down before sitting and pulling his boots on. Land boots, which you'd think would be more comfortable, but weren't. Probably because—as had been his unvoiced observation since his teens—there was usually an inverse relationship between utility and fashion. The more stylish a thing was, the less comfortable and/ or reliable it proved to be. Yet Anne Cathrine had insisted, within days of his returning at the head of The Prize Fleet, that he had to have fine boots for when he went out in an official capacity. Which was, now, pretty much every time he went out.

He finished trying—unsuccessfully—to wriggle and squirm his feet into a more comfortable position within the attractive torture devices that his wife had acquired for him from God knows who and for God knows how much. He'd thought about putting his foot down (so to speak) and refusing to wear the doggone things. Yeah, he really gave that some heavy-duty, serious thought—until he saw the way Anne was looking at him the first time he wore them. And then, well, then he got ... kinda distracted. Until sometime late the next morning. And now he was wearing the boots.

And had been almost every day since he'd been back. And he'd left their new fortress/house late every day, too. Anne Cathrine had been, from the start, everything a twenty-three-year-old man could want in a bedroom playmate: coy, seductive, aggressive, inventive—oh, so inventive! But now she had added "insatiable" to her repertoire. Not that Eddie was complaining—oh, *hell* no!—but every once in a while, a senior officer really did need to show up on time. Which was to say, thirty minutes early. As it was, he'd be lucky if he just barely made his meeting on time. Again.

Still, when he reached the bottom of the stairs and went briskly out his front door with a nod to the guard, there was a spring in his step. And it wasn't because of the recoil/return plate that Grantville's medical technicians had built into his prosthesis.

Eddie had to push up hard against the wall of Fort Oranje in order to get through the crowd, but that was just as well. Being off to the side of the main road that ran out to St. Eustatia's new dock kept him away from the promenaders who dominated its center: the wealthy, the influential, and no small number of Dutch officers from both the fleet and fort. Eddie, tucked against the closely fitted stones of the fort, made much better time. In large part, it was because he would not have to stop a dozen times to return salutes, which the Dutch were now adopting with the fervor of a new fad.

Until recently, the Dutch military had been fairly typical of the others of its time: wide variations in training and discipline, little standardization, and nothing like a uniform, except for a few elite formations which usually answered to and guarded a monarch. In the New World, the "irregular" nature of military life and action had been even more pronounced. The Dutch navy, if you could even call it such, had arisen from the need to build a self-sustaining force to strike at the shipping of their Spanish oppressors. Half a century later, the men on its warships, regardless of rank, had still been motivated more by profit than patriotism.

But over the past year in the New World, that had begun to change. And then Tromp's extraordinary "Dunkirk at Dominica" had accelerated that transmogrification. What had begun as a loose amalgam of ships and a confederation of clever raiders was rapidly evolving into a military force, its esprit de corps growing in tandem with its successively greater accomplishments. Although, there was, admittedly, another factor at work.

Eddie's glance grazed across that factor as he came to the end of the street: the steam cruisers *Intrepid* and *Resolve*, out beyond the extraordinary clutter of ships lying in the broad anchorage that lay before Oranjestad. It wasn't the ships themselves that had changed attitudes, but what they signified. The new technologies, the crisply efficient crews, the new strategy and tactics: all that resonated with the Dutch, yes, but there was something even beyond that:

They embodied the triumph of method and competence by having proved in battle the merits of the perception and confidence that had created them: that despite war's inherent chaos, the human mind could identify and exploit patterns within it. Science and analysis had successfully revolutionized not just the tools but the conduct of war, with a surety and decisiveness that had not been seen since the Romans. And the Dutch realized that they were more than just the beneficiaries of that growing trend; they themselves had begun to amplify and perfect it.

And today was the day that the broad benefits of those new capabilities and competencies would over-flow into the streets of Oranjestad, almost all at once. That timing was part happy coincidence, part careful coordination, and all about creating a pervasive sense of prosperity and plenty. Which was quite a trick, since neither of those things had actually arrived, just yet.

But to look out in that anchorage, you would never have guessed it. Eddie had to hand it to Jan van Walbeeck, the Dutch governor of St. Eustatia, for having orchestrated the convergence of all this traffic and trade in a most impressive fashion. The intercontinental radio on the island's southern volcanic mountain—The Quill—had made it possible to estimate, to within a few days, when the first major convoy from Europe would finally arrive. For security reasons, direct references to it in the telegraph traffic had to be coded and sparse, but as it coalesced back in the Netherlands and the USE, van Walbeeck was able to track its growing readiness, then its departure date, and then a last confirmation from it when underway.

It was not just the first true resupply mission to St. Eustatia, and through it, the other Dutch colonies in the Caribbean. It was also the first formation of ships to leave the Netherlands since its ports had been blockaded by the Spanish after the Battle of Dunkirk. With eleven well-loaded fluyts at its core, its defense accompaniment had been even more impressive. In addition to a pair of men-of-war that had been in process of construction when Fernando surrounded Amsterdam, it also boasted the first true frigate designs to arrive in the New World. Lower and longer than prior warships, and with almost nonexistent foc'sles and quarterdecks, the four ships—one Swedish, one Danish, and two Dutch—were proudly billed as the first of their class. Which, Eddie knew, was a nice way of saying, "these were prototypes made to assess performance and discover design flaws." Which they had, and which had been corrected to the extent possible. Still, it was like hand-me-down clothes presented as a new outfit.

The same was true with the two new USE steam-ships that accompanied them. One was the sole sister ship of *Courser*, the *Harrier*. Although successful, that first class of steam destroyer—the Speed class—had taught Simpson and his designers many lessons, both during their construction and first half year of operation. The result was to discontinue production of that model and introduce a revised version, the Speed Two. Superficially, it seemed the same except for their naming convention, but it had significant differences in terms of hull strengthening, steam plant and pro-peller design, and electrical wiring and redundancy. The first of that class, the untested *Relentless*, had been deployed to the New World as her shakedown cruise, as had *Courser* before her. Again, a much-touted arrival that was actually added to the allied fleet to see if and when and how it would break.

Those nineteen ships of the convoy that had collected in and sailed from Amsterdam were mostly moored in the northern extents of the anchorage after unloading. The larger ships had been serviced there by lighters, but the fluyts had shallow enough drafts to spend a few days bellied up to the new wooden pier that extended into the bay.

That still-fresh structure was currently swarmed by those same lighters, but they were now off-loading the last general cargos of the prizes Tromp's fleet had taken off Dominica. Although still referred to by some as the New World Dunkirk, the seamen who'd been there had, with the sardonic wit of their tribe, shortened it to the Battle of Dominikirk. Which, although pooh-poohed by officers and gentlefolk alike as undignified, was rapidly becoming the engagement's de facto label. Because, hell, it wasn't a mouthful like the stuffy official-sounding names, none of which seemed to stick.

The dark-hulled Spanish ships were clustered in the southern extents of the anchorage, their battle damage still plain to see. There were, in fact, two less than had sailed away from the seaways where they'd been seized. After putting the Spanish prisoners ashore at Petite-Terre and scuttling the mortally wounded ships in the shallows, Tromp's fleet and the prize hulls had reconsolidated in Guadeloupe's Petit Cul-de-Sac Marin. Once sorted out, they had sailed to leeward, rounding the island's western lobe, known as Basse-Terre, and setting course for St. Eustatia.

However, the brisk eastern winds that had continued to grow since the battle proved to be the harbinger of a storm. It ran in just after the ponderous collection of almost seventy ships made a few miles across the Guadeloupe passage toward Montserrat. Seeing its approach, Tromp and the other captains who'd spent their earliest years at sea assessed the situation and came to unanimous conclusions: the storm would be upon them before they made Montserrat, and it might prove too fierce to ride out.

So Tromp came about and made for the northern bay of Guadeloupe, the Grand Cul-de-Sac Marin. Which sounded a lot more simple than it was, since the shallows of that refuge extended irregularly into its expanse. And without any bar pilots to show the way, it became a matter of ships playing follow-the-leader behind those few hulls which had been furnished with up-time depth charts—such as they were.

Since the wind was still abeam, the Dutch ships made the bay in plenty of time and in good order. The Spanish hulls, on the other hand, once again demonstrated their far more limited ability to use a reaching wind and were badly buffeted by the first savage squall that preceded the actual storm front. Most made it past the northern headland of Grand-Terre, but half a dozen were caught in the open.

One of the badly damaged and more lightly built war galleons had her jury-rigged rudder go loose under the constant pounding, and her under-experienced and overanxious prize pilot never got the feel for correcting her aggravated tendency to yaw. Between the two, she wound up on the rocks. Her keel cracked and hull began buckling beneath the waterline as the high swells pounded her down into the volcanic molars lining that part of Guadeloupe's shore. The one redeeming consequence was that she was also stuck fast and was sturdy enough to hold together throughout the remainder of the storm.

The other casualty was one of the oldest naos. She had been sailing crank when she was taken, despite taking only modest damage during the engagement. But as if warning of hidden infirmities, she groaned piteously whenever the seas were high or contrary. When the teeth of the storm set into her, she shuddered, lost way, struggled to regain it. That was when her foremast went, taking many of the main's spars and shrouds with it. Not surprisingly, the prize pilot lost control of her, and the current and wind pushed her bow around until they were directly upon her beam. As if waiting for that moment, the greatest wave of the squall mounted up and crashed down upon the nao's listing deck. Her planks and frame cracked so loudly that, for a moment, nearby crews thought that the storm had brought thunder with it, as well. As the rain and spray all but hid her, there came a sound like a full forest of trees being ripped asunder. The watery veils of rain and spray parted long enough to show the decrepit nao breaking in two, the water rushing in and taking her down in less than ten seconds.

Most of her crew, seeing land so close, had taken their chances in the waves. Half of them made it to shore, a handful of others washed up lifeless the next day. The rest, and all who had still been aboard, were swallowed by the sea without a trace. And although the other ships had reached safe harbor, two more days were spent kedging *Prins Hendrik* and three of the prize hulls off the sandy shoals of the Grand Cul-de-Sac Marin.

Now, with all the ships of that fleet in Oranjestad Bay and the sea and skies so bright and clear, it was difficult to believe that the weather had ever been otherwise. But the storm made a deep impression upon Eddie. He had often sailed through high risers and rainstorms, but never a squall so wild and fierce. Now he was part of that ancient fraternity of mariners who had seen the face of the sea and knew, or at least suspected, that its patron deity was either monstrously capricious or cruelly malign.

He arrived dockside just as the day's bartering and bickering were gathering momentum. Thirteen small ships from St. Christopher's, escorted by the French brig taken last year at Bloody Point, had made their way across the channel early in the morning and were now unloading their wares and passengers. Mostly pinnaces and pinks, half of which were Bermudan-built, their crews were busy setting up stalls from which to sell what they'd freighted over: soursop, squashes, papaya, coconuts, bananas, wood for sturdy spars and, of course, goats. Eddie caught a glimpse of that island's two most important personages, Governor Thomas Warner and Lieutenant Governor Jeafferson debarking with their retinue. Footmen were present to lead them to Oranjestad's newest construction: the Admiral's Repose, a sprawling complex that included rooms, a large tavern, apartments, and even stables. As such, it was more like a caravansary than a typical seaside inn, and this, its first major event, had filled it to capacity.

Eddie had explored the possibility of extending invitations to some of St. Christopher's much-diminished French community, including Jacques Dyel du Parque.

It was neither wise nor safe to allow appearances to lead anyone, most importantly the French themselves, to conclude that they were permanent pariahs. But although Eddie's friend and governor of Oranjestad, Jan van Walbeeck, agreed with him, he had also pointed out that the people of both islands—and most especially, Governor Warren—would certainly look askance at it. Although none of the French who had taken part in last November's attack remained on St. Christopher's, du Parque's uncle, Pierre Bélain d'Esnambuc, had been the architect of all that death, misery, and destruction. The likelihood that his guilt would rub off on his countrymen, and especially his nephew, was high and so, no invitation had been made.

As Eddie slipped sideways into the narrower lane that paralleled the western, sea-facing wall of the fortress, he watched flat-bottomed lighters hurriedly beaching on the strand yards away. They were bringing in goods from yesterday's arrivals: the returned ships of Admiral Joost Banckert's visit to Bermuda. He slowed as he saw the others waiting for him just ahead, remembered the last time he had walked this narrow, packed-sand lane: following behind the crudely made casket of the original Danish admiral of Task Force X-Ray, Pros Mund. One of the relatively few allied dead at last year's Battle of Grenada, he had been a casualty of his overconfident handling of *Resolve* and an intent desire to please his sovereign. The latter was a pressure that Eddie understood all too well, since that same ambitious and larger-than-life king was also Eddie's father-in-law: King Christian IV of Denmark.

As Eddie drew near the two men he was meeting, the one with a flushed face and broad smile waved toward the bay. "Enjoying that fine view, Commodore Cantrell?"

Eddie smiled back, adopted the same mock formality. "It's passable, Governor van Walbeeck."

The other man—composed and quiet, with broad shoulders but small features—smiled faintly at van Walbeeck. "It seems that Eddie will not be so easily baited to gush over your achievement, Jan."

"Ah, Maarten Tromp, you are delighting in his torment of me," van Walbeeck lamented histrionically. "Soldiers, particularly *jongeren* like this Cantrell fellow, have little appreciation of the trials and tribulations that an administrator must endure to produce such a grand spectacle." He waved a hand at the ship-crowded harbor. "Why, there must be well over one hundred ships, out there!"

"Only if you count the boats from St. Kitts," Eddie needled, barely able to repress a smile.

"I do count them!" van Walbeeck exclaimed. "Why should I not?"

"Well...they're small. And they're loaded with goats."

"Exactly why they figure in my totals, you young ingrate! Those goats are the future of this island."

"Well," Tromp temporized, "their temperaments do resemble those of some of your councilors, Jan."

Who feigned horror. "*My* councilors? Bite your tongue, Admiral! I inherited half of them—and would have been glad to be denied that inheritance. And as far as their resemblance to goats, it might go beyond temperament. Musen, for instance—"

Eddie gulped back a guffaw; Hans Musen did resemble a goat. Sort of. His face was certainly narrow and expressionless.

His incompletely stifled laugh broke the parody of pomposity; the two older men chuckled as well. Even Tromp, whose smile persisted faintly.

Eddie matched it with one of his own. "You seem pretty cheery, Admiral."

Tromp shrugged, nodded toward the ships. "There are enough guns afloat out there to fight off any Spanish fleet that might happen to sail at us from over the horizon today. We haven't been able to say that since coming to the New World. So today—and just today—I shall breathe easy."

Jan van Walbeeck nodded. The three spent a few moments watching as lighters ran in, and others struggled out against the wind for their next load, relying on the slow process of back and fill to push beyond the breakers. No less than a dozen skiffs and skerries were making courier runs between ships, then ship to shore and back again. On the horizon, the cerulean sky met the sapphire sea and above the sun shined and smiled upon the busy labors of both seamen and landsmen as they brought their wares together. "It's like a spring fair," Eddie murmured.

"It is," van Walbeeck nodded in agreement. "And a market day, the first of the season. The first anyone has seen since leaving Recife. Or home."

"Yeah," Eddie agreed, "It's kinda hard to believe."

The other two looked at him.

"All the changes, I mean." He swept a hand toward the bright new roofs of Oranjestad. "Maybe you gu— fellows don't see it as clearly because you've been here, watching it grow through all its stages. But when I got here last year..." Eddie shook his head. "It was a tent city with a few buildings and a fort. One store, no trade, water rationing, barely enough food to survive. And you were burning dung instead of wood for everything except cooking. And now look at it."

They did. Two church steeples, one in the last phases of completion, were tall above dozens of wood-frame homes. Privies had replaced rudimentary waste disposal, a great deal of which had involved using the bay and other beaches as the primary means of public sanitation. The people in the streets were no longer pale or burned, but copper-bronze and, while lean, were no longer gaunt. Children had the energy to play again. Laughing, they were weaving in and out of the stalls where the adults, who had clustered together to sell and buy, sent imprecations and shaken fists in their chaotic wake.

It was tiny and plain, compared to the great Spanish cities of the New World—Havana, Cartagena, Santo Domingo, Vera Cruz—but conversely, it had none of their oppressive edifices and immense populations of impoverished, despised, and resentful mestizo and zambo shack dwellers. Instead, this day had brought out its growing pulse of optimism and energy, of new possibilities and expansion.

"It's been transformed," Eddie said, turning back to face the two Dutchmen. Who were smiling at him. "What?" he asked.

"Oranjestad isn't the only thing that's been transformed," van Walbeeck observed with a wink. "It often happens to happy husbands, I've been told."

"I don't know what you're talking about," Eddie said. His denial didn't sound convincing, not even to himself.

Tromp studied the edge of the shade in which

they all stood. "While not as precise as your up-time wristwatches, my years at sea have given me much occasion to refine my ability to tell the time by the angle of the sun's rays. Consider the crisp shadows of the battlements projected just beyond our feet. I am quite certain that it shows me the time to within ten minutes of what I would see on the face of a clock. And that is close enough to know that you, Commodore Cantrell, were five minutes late. At least. And that is certainly a transformation."

"Oh, indeed!" van Walbeeck added, eyes sparkling. "I remember a time—perhaps as little as a year ago?—when Eddie was never tardy for *any*thing, for *any* reason! And when we asked him about that almost painful punctuality, Maarten, he said . . . Now, what did he say, again?"

Now Maarten *was* smiling. "I believe it was a phrase he had picked up from his commander, the redoubtable Admiral Simpson, who advised him to make it the basis of his life in the Navy. Specifically, that being on time means arriving 'thirty minutes *before* thirty minutes before' the appointed time. And so the commodore was. Unfailingly. It was most impressive."

"Insufferable, even," interjected van Walbeeck.

"But now?" concluded Tromp. "Five minutes late. At least. And no longer an entirely uncommon occurrence. As I said, a transformation."

"But—" Eddie tried to object.

"Now what could cause such a transformation, Maarten?"

"I cannot imagine."

"Well, let's see: it might be a life of boredom. But trifling recent events such as surviving battles and tempests seem to belie that hypothesis. Reduced responsibilities? Heavens, no: anything but that, as I'm sure the commodore himself would be the first to confirm. The ocean air? But from what I can discern, the surroundings and climate seem to invigorate our young friend, rather than inducing torpor. For do we not often see him bathing in the ocean, Maarten?"

"I go swimming. *Swimming*," Eddie objected. To no effect.

"Maybe," van Walbeeck pseudo-mused, "it is because he rarely bathes alone. Inconceivably, he usually takes his wife with him. Or so I'm told. Is that true, Maarten?"

Tromp shrugged. "I have heard it mentioned. But only when he goes to one of the northern beaches. For modesty's sake, I imagine."

"Oh, for modesty's sake, yes. Certainly," van Walbeeck nodded vigorously. "But he always seems particularly susceptible to tardiness after those outings. Probably from the exertion of swimming in the windward surf." Van Walbeeck's impish grin looked incongruous on a man of his considerable proportions. "Because I'm certain it would not have anything to do with his wife, now, would it? Not then...or now?"

Tromp glanced over at his young friend. "Commodore, either you are getting sunburned standing in the shade, or you are flushed."

Eddie held up his hands. "All right, all right. Target practice is over. Yes, I'm a young husband. Yes, I have a beautiful wife. Yes, she's smart, and funny, and kind, and..."

Van Walbeeck put his hand on Eddie's shoulder. "And she has deep and powerful feelings." His voice had grown suddenly and genuinely serious. "I have seen her helping Dr. Brandão with his youngest patients. I saw her fighting in the trenches last year, as much a leader to the women as O'Rourke and Michael McCarthy were to the men. She is a wonderful, splendid being: an improbable combination of angel and Valkyrie. So you must forgive the teasing of two older men who can only look on in admiration, wonder, and perhaps some small measure of envy. Because we know why you are late in the mornings," he smiled, almost fatherly, "and we would be baffled if you were *not*."

Tromp, laconic as usual, merely nodded. "It is a *good* transformation, Eddie. Now, here comes Jol, so let's to business, shall we?"

Chapter 19

Oranjestad, St. Eustatia

Cornelis Jol began stumping along rapidly on his peg leg when he caught sight of the three of them in the far shadows of Fort Oranjestad's seaward wall. He waved to two others behind him, who had become ensnared in the growing tumult of trade and acquaintance-making in the street.

"Keep up, you malingerers!" he shouted over his shoulder. "I've a wooden leg and I move twice as fast as you do!" He grinned at van Walbeeck, clapped a hand down on Tromp's shoulder, and exhaled a rum-scented greeting toward Eddie. "Of course," he muttered conspiratorially, "I had to be sure to push off so that the striplings I have in tow would have a chance with all the young ladies back there. Wouldn't do to have a fine, mature specimen of a man like myself attracting all the female attention and interest, now would it?" He smiled in amusement, thereby revealing that he retained approximately half his very stained teeth. The crow's lines that extended far from his eyes blended with and helped hide the various scars that almost two decades of privateering had left on his well-weathered face. Houtebeen, or "Peg Leg," Jol was at least as famous for his self-deprecating wit as his devilish skill at raiding.

"And do you have any of your equally prepossessing piratical friends in tow?" asked Tromp, folding his hands like a mild-mannered school master.

"Sadly, no," Jol answered. "Moses went his own way again, right after he came to report what he'd encountered in the seas around Dominica just before you clipped Philip's beard, there. He and Calabar are still raiding down along the Main, and they were eager to get back to it. The others?" Jol flipped a palm at the cloudless sky. "Reliability is not what freebooters are known for, as I'm sure you know."

"I'm sure I do," Tromp said, "since I know you."

"Maarten Tromp, I'm a privateer. Why do you lump me in with those bandits?"

"As I said, because I know you. And because if you weren't halfway to living the life they do, they'd never meet with you except over crossed cutlasses."

Jol scratched his furry ear. "Well, I suppose there's some truth to that."

A new voice: "Well, here's a conspiratorial trio if I've ever laid eyes on one!"

Eddie knew the source, was smiling before he turned. "Hugh O'Donnell, it's good to see you again."

"You as well, Eddie." The Irish earl nodded all around as his aide-de-camp Aodh O'Rourke slipped up behind him. "Governor, Admiral. 'Tis a fine show you're putting on here, today."

Tromp looked meaningfully at van Walbeeck, who asked the Irish earl, "Is it truly that obvious, Lord O'Donnell?"

Hugh squinted, assessing the ware-lined roads that ran away from the head of the dock. "Depends upon the eye of the beholder, I'm thinking. For the people who've not been working toward this end, either as confidencers or soldiers, it's merely an overdue turn o' the wheel. Fortune has been frowning, but now fortune smiles again: the seasons of fate, you might say. But for those of us who have been seizing islands for oil, making alliances with England's abandoned colonies, or most recently, making off with the entirety of this year's Flota...well, I've come to wonder: does anything look like happenstance to us anymore?"

Van Walbeeck smiled. "I doubt it. A fair answer for a fair day."

"Aye, and it's a fair all right," added O'Rourke from over Hugh's shoulder. "Maybe not as big as the May market in Brussels or Antwerp, but it's none the less 't any other. It'll bring fair coin to Montserrat, right enough."

Van Walbeeck glanced eagerly at Jol. "So, you ported there on your way up from Trinidad?"

"We did. As luck had it, we saw that nasty squall that caught you as we were crossing the stretch between Carriacou and Union Island. We crowded sail and got into the lee of the southern bay there, just in time to watch the storm slow and move northward. If we'd gone on, we might have lost all the bitumen we're carrying, and the oil itself. Although there's much less of that."

"How much of each?" Eddie asked.

Jol shook his head. "Your up-time friend, Mistress Koudsi, will be able to tell you that when we are all...er, gathered. When we got underway again, we were low on water and decided that was a fine excuse to make port at Montserrat, which was what Lord O'Donnell had been angling for since the beginning."

"New recruits for the Wild Geese," Hugh explained as eyes turned to him. "Also, some hands for the *Eire*, the French bark we took off Bloody Point. And the island needs the trade, so a few of them came along to sell their vegetables, fruit, chickens, and goats."

"More goats?" Eddie asked.

Jol laughed. "These are the Caribbees, Commodore. There are *always* more goats."

O'Rourke, who had not moved forward into the conversational ring, muttered something about how long they'd been tarrying in the shadows and that others were waiting on them. Van Walbeeck spotted Joost Banckert making his way up the dock to the shore, suggested they all join the general movement in that direction: after all, he and Tromp had to put in at least a brief appearance in the thick of the activity.

As the six of them began heading back along the narrow track while staying in the shadow of the fort's wall, Eddie found himself distracted from the frenetic market activity by something that had changed in Aodh O'Rourke's posture since last he'd seen him. The senior sergeant of the Wild Geese glimpsed his attention, nodded and flashed a smile. *And he saw my attention because he's always looking around*, Eddie realized.

He hadn't seen O'Rourke since late January, when the Irish veteran had preceded the still-recuperating Hugh back to Trinidad. "Just to mind the shop," as he put it with the other most senior of the Irish mercenaries, Kevin O'Bannon. When Hugh had returned there, he'd announced the need for more officers. There were more Wild Geese coming over aboard the first convoy—the one in port now—and coin-strapped men from Montserrat had been sending him entreaties that he consider their pleas to join the unit. O'Bannon was glad for the promotion to major, but O'Rourke staunchly and repeatedly refused to become an officer.

The reason had never been made clear to Eddie; it was a private matter without appreciable operational consequences, so inquiries would have been essentially nosiness, not need-to-know. But whatever his reasons, O'Rourke showed neither animus nor resentment toward those who were promoted over him, several of whom were more than a decade his junior. Rather, as senior sergeant and aide-de-camp, he helped the other sergeants who could read and do sums to prepare for life as officers. At the same time, he cheerfully brutalized and buoyed up (in that order) new potential to ready them for the demands of that job. Rumor had it that he wanted nothing to do with the life and society of officers, preferring the gritty tasks and earthy pleasures of his long-held rank.

But in becoming the Wild Geese's de facto head of training, he also seemed to have slowly and subtly moved away from the day-to-day field operations of the Wild Geese. It was unclear to Eddie if he even remained in the unit's table of organization, or if he'd been shifted sideways into something more akin to a staff assistant to O'Donnell.

But even that didn't quite explain the changes. The number of Irish who'd been educated at Leuven meant that Hugh also had a growing cluster of staff officers or "ensigns" who'd also proven themselves in the field. O'Rourke did not have their technical skills and so, was clearly not being retained for that purpose.

Eddie frowned, watching the Irish veteran's behavior as they passed the beach where the lighters were still coming and going so rapidly that near-collisions seemed to be the rule rather than the exception. O'Rourke was looking everywhere and at everything *except* at his commander. It tweaked at a dim memory, at similar behavior that Eddie had noticed before but couldn't remember where or when. But given the way that O'Rourke always had his "head on a swivel," to use Larry Quinn's expression, made Eddie feel that the bluff sergeant should have been wearing sunglasses and an earpiece.

Eddie almost snapped his fingers: the Secret Service! *That's* what O'Rourke's attentive hover looked like. Eddie paused, reflected. *Of course, maybe it looks like that because that's exactly what it is.*

But that wasn't the way bodyguards typically worked in this day and age. They came as a large group, often in formation, and with bright uniforms that sent a clear message to all who saw: "Get too close, and you'll get run through." But maybe it was different with Hugh. After all, even though he was the last prince of Ireland—a quixotic concept if there had ever been one—he certainly didn't *act* like it.

Eddie felt his frown come back. Okay, so Hugh's demeanor and interactions didn't resemble those of an heir apparent to a throne that the English would never let him have. That didn't make it any less likely that any number of English—or other—leaders might want him dead. And maybe now more than ever.

Hugh had grown up in the down-time equivalent of the English crown's crosshairs, as had the only other Irish earl, the late John O'Neill. But now that there was only one left, it was probably more tempting than ever to reduce that number to zero, thereby eliminating the only figurehead around which a rebellion might readily coalesce. That was why Hugh had been subtly maneuvered into his New World sojourn by his aunt, the Archduchess Isabella of the Spanish Lowlands: to put distance between her nephew and potential assassins. But that was at best a temporary expedient, which Aodh O'Rourke had apparently realized.

As they reached the head of the dock, Hugh scanned the street leading into the center of Oranjestad. "And there are our new recruits, looking more like lost sheep than men-at-arms." He turned, smiled. "Maarten, Eddie, I want to thank you for making good on the promise I made to Hyarima. I'd not have made it alone, but lives were in the balance."

The admiral inclined his head. "It was the right decision, morally and strategically." Eddie just grinned and nodded.

Smiling, Hugh shook their hands and then made to step away. "After our new boyos have their heads on straight, I've a promise to keep: that this mortal wound shall be tended to one more time." He held up and wiggled his left small finger. What was left of it was well bandaged.

Van Walbeeck leaned in, concern spiking in his tone. "Is it not healing?"

Hugh laughed. "Quite the contrary; nary a problem, now. Why so concerned, Governor?"

Van Walbeeck was frowning, staring at the mauled pinky as if it might leap free of the earl's hand and begin attacking them. "My first employ was with the Dutch East India Company. In those jungles, an almost-mended wound may yet fester and take not just a limb, but a life."

Hugh nodded. "I appreciate your concern, but no open flesh remains. The scar tissue is complete and no longer tender."

Van Walbeeck's frown changed to one of mere puzzlement. "Then I find it hard to understand why Dr. Brandão would wish you to return."

Hugh chuckled. "Oh, it is not Dr. Brandão that I must see. It did not warrant his expertise. I am under the care of one of his volunteers."

Van Walbeeck's frown was replaced by a round-mouthed, "Ohhh. Yes. I see now." As the earl nodded his farewell and turned to leave, Jan sent an assurance after him: "I'm sure you are in excellent hands." If Hugh heard van Walbeeck's shift to a mischievous drawl, he gave no sign of it. After a moment, van Walbeeck and Jol exchanged winks and grins. Tromp sighed but couldn't hold back a small smile when Peg Leg added, "I am told that Lady Sophie Rantzau was his dedicated nurse. Excellent hands, indeed!"

Eddie stared at the three of them. For one bizarre moment, he felt like he was eight again, watching the old ladies who sat around after Sunday service, furtively inspecting the "young people" and scheming to make matches between their preferred pairings. Which they never did.

And damn it if the three redoubtable Dutch sea captains weren't standing at the intersection of the dock and the main street, staring about them with the same insufferable self-satisfied smiles on their faces. But maybe, Eddie relented, there was cause for that. Spirits were high and competition over merely speaking to a young woman no longer threatened to devolve into rutting combats that he mostly associated

with National Geographic documentaries. Between the
young ladies who'd come by boat from St. Christopher's
and the mass of colonists which had arrived with the
convoy, the ratio was no longer dangerously lopsided.

"Would you say that the timing of tomorrow night's
dance was also another stroke of extraordinary 'luck'?"
van Walbeeck asked over Eddie's shoulder. "Look at
them, men and women alike, running their fingers
over those fine fabrics. The best Seville had to offer.
All 'diverted' here at the most propitious moment!"
Eddie managed not to roll his eyes. "Why," concluded
van Walbeeck, "it's as if someone had planned it all!"

Tromp sighed. "Careful, Jan. You might break your
arm, trying to pat yourself on the back." Jol chuckled.

Van Walbeeck effected umbrage. "Laugh if you
must, but ask yourselves: why is this glorious bedlam
occurring now? Ships have been off-loading for a week."
He shook his finger at them. "Because the colony's
government prohibited open sales until this day. To
ensure a fair opportunity for all potential customers
to inspect all the goods, all at once. And so, all the
merchants would have equal access to the equally full
purses of their clientele." He had to pause his self-praise
for a moment; musicians strolled past, lutes, record-
ers, and mandolas weaving melodies and harmonies
together like closely stitched seams that parted again.

"So," he resumed, "with buyers and sellers all
champing at the bit, we have maximum bartering"—he
gestured outward with both arms—"which drives up
the amount of trade, which drives up tariffs on the
sales. However, steps were taken to offset that bite
from everyone's purse."

Eddie nodded, frowning: he'd been too busy with

strategic and technology matters to follow the market arrangements. "That's why you waived customs and port taxes for this week: that way, anyone selling is only paying what we used to call sales tax. Which they must declare as such to their customers."

Jol frowned. "All very well, but then what keeps the vendors from increasing the sales tax and gouging the customers?"

"Nothing," replied van Walbeeck with a beatific smile.

"But then how can these people afford those prices?"

"Because we, the government of St. Eustatia, are paying their sales taxes for them, this week."

Eddie felt like the lobes of his brain had just hit each other in a high-speed collision. "Wait. But that's a loop. You would have received the taxes from the people. But now you're paying it for them. To yourselves? So...are you writing it off?"

"Not at all, because it is not quite a loop, my innocent young friend. You see, we *are* repaying ourselves... from the most useful items taken from La Flota."

Jol sputtered before he could get out any words. "And you call me cunning and a pirate! So while you've used one hand to wave away the taxes and make everybody happy, you've used the other to dip into all the gold, silver, gems, and coin from La Flota to 'repay' the government for the taxes it agreed to pay for the purchases made this week."

Van Walbeeck grinned. "As I said, it is as if someone had been planning it all from the beginning."

"Planning what from the beginning?" The new voice from behind sounded suspicious. "When van Walbeeck is muttering about careful planning, I clap my hand over my purse."

Chapter 20

Oranjestad, St. Eustatia

Eddie turned, discovered the source of the tongue-in-cheek comments: Joost Banckert. The vice admiral had finally made his way up the dock to them, but the man who'd been walking with him earlier was still on the dock, haggling with a ship's master over an untapped tun of wine.

"I have a similar reaction to Jan's 'careful planning,' Joost," Tromp said mildly. "Welcome home."

"Good to be here," Banckert replied, glancing over their heads at Oranjestad's roofs. "Eight weeks and I hardly recognize this place. And barely enough room in the bay to fit my ships back in."

Van Walbeeck nodded down the dock, toward the man who'd debarked with him. "Did he come aboard your ship or—?"

"No, but he sailed along with us, though. And on the biggest Bermudan sloop I've ever seen. When I told them about this market day, everyone in Somers Isles started falling over each other, trying to get their cargos taken on consignment. Fish in Bahamian salt, cedar, pitch, and pork—both smoked and live. Those pigs made an unholy mess and stink when we had to take them below decks during the high weather just past." He glanced back at his guest. "He's a good fellow, but shrewd. Hard-nosed. If it wasn't for that thick accent of his, he could have been a Dutchman."

"Oh, and where's he from?"

"Scotland."

Eddie almost laughed out loud. If any other group was in a position to teach the Dutch about being hard-nosed and shrewd businessmen, it was probably the Scots.

Banckert was studying the Dutch hulls in the anchorage. "So I am wondering why the standards of each ship's province no longer have the pride of place at the stern. And they're not flying the Company's pennant at all. On the other hand, I see more of the 'national' colors. A great deal more." He smiled, but it was not all mirth. "So, are we all sailing under your flag now, eh, Maarten?"

Tromp shook his head slightly. "Never mine. The banner of Hendrik of the Netherlands."

Banckert smiled. "I see. So has he even bought up the husk of the Companies, then? Has so much changed since I sailed to the Somers Isles?"

Van Walbeeck smiled, but shook his head more vigorously than Tromp had. "You will not bait us with your grinning nonsense, Joost—though it is good to see you, regardless of your so-called sense of humor. In answer: to the best of my knowledge, the Prince of Orange has not changed his position in regard to the Companies. But they are broken, my friend, not just in the Caribbean and the East Indies. Almost all their possessions, at least here in the West Indies—we've had no news from the East Indies in quite some time—are in Spanish or native hands, now. So whose flag should we fly? Ours is better than Spain's, *ja?*"

Banckert smiled back. "Now, Jan: if I couldn't bait my colleagues, where would be the joy in this life? In the main I agree with what I've heard of the changes. But how do we make profit now, hey? Our way has always been to fight for shares, with our own ships and crews, and full freedom in how we went about our missions. Now, we have become like the Spanish, all saluting one flag, all taking orders from one man."

Tromp had less patience for the friendly jousting than van Walbeeck. "Joost, you know perfectly well that the Companies always acted with oversight from the government."

"Some, yes, but they always had a great deal of freedom. They—and we—did better when both the *Raad* and the Stadtholder watched from afar and interfered infrequently."

The Bermudan, his negotiations over, had approached as Banckert completed his riposte. Tromp held up a hand to pause the discussion, turned to the newcomer, led the others in that fusion of bow and shallow nod that was the common greeting among those making a first acquaintance. "Sir, do I have the honor of addressing Councilor Patrick Coapland of the Somers Isles?"

The Bermudan returned the gesture, did a fair job at masking surprise. "I am he, but you have me at a disadvantage, sir. How is that you know who I am?"

"Well, there *is* a radio aboard my ship," Banckert said with a smile.

"Your ship has one of these devices? And you did

not tell me?" Coapland's aggrieved tone was only half playacting.

Banckert's smile widened. "You did not ask."

Van Walbeeck reached out to shake the Bermudan's hand. "I am Governor van Walbeeck, Councilor Coapland. It is my pleasure to welcome you to Oranjestad and to insist that you address me as Jan." He turned to Banckert. "And as far our arrangements with home are concerned, Joost, well, at an earlier time, that would have made for an interesting debate. But now, the matter is already settled. Prince Hendrik remains the Stadtholder. And, as a wise ruler, he well understands that commerce succeeds most when government intrudes least. But right now, we are at war."

"With whom?" Banckert shot back. "With the Spanish dandy who now calls himself King in the Lowlands and to whom we have agreed to bow? I presume not." He smiled wolfishly. "Or has civil war been declared while I was gone?"

Tromp sighed, folded his hands. "Joost, let us put this to rest. The Netherlands is now reunited, but Fredrik Hendrik and the Dutch provinces have full autonomy over their internal affairs. King Fernando controls foreign policy but, just like the Stadtholder, he is given to allow commercial enterprises here in the New World to run themselves as they see fit. So no state of war exists between the Netherlands and Spain. However, this island is far beyond the Tordesillas meridian which Pope Julius II affirmed as the starting point of Spain's New World dominion. And as Madrid has asserted, there is no peace beyond that line. Ever.

"But whereas ten years ago, our business in the New World was mostly as raiders and opportunistic colonizers, we have become a decided presence, along with allies"—he glanced at Eddie—"who share the enmity of Spain. So yes, there is a war on, here. And there will be for some time. And if we were to remain a loose rabble of raiders, we would surely be swept away."

"Perhaps that is only because we have become a permanent and growing irritant to the Spanish," Banckert countered.

Before Eddie could stop himself, he shook his head.

Coapland's eyes cut in his direction. "You believe differently, sir?" His gaze traveled over Eddie's clothes, then studied the boot over his prosthetic. "Ah! As I surmised. You are the young up-time admiral, then!" He bowed.

"Merely a commodore," Eddie corrected.

The Bermudan, whose Scots burr seemed to deepen, smiled. "Come, come. We all know whose ships have brought such changes to the balance of power in the New World, and whose presence has emboldened men such as Admiral Tromp to engage the Spanish head-on. And so, have made them the permanent irritant that Admiral Banckert just mentioned."

Eddie nodded. "Yes, that would be me. But my ships are not what caused the changes in the New World. In point of fact, they are simply the result of changes that were already occurring."

Coapland cocked his head. "Your words are clear but their meaning is not, I fear."

Eddie kept himself from looking at Tromp and van Walbeeck; technically, this was about the Dutch, not the USE, and so, not his debate. On the other hand, the conversation was moving into the realm of global implications, so . . . "Councilor Coapland, the changes occurring in the New World are not a product of Grantville's technology, but its knowledge. Specifically, that which is contained in its library."

Banckert made to interrupt but Eddie pressed on. "No one in this time foresaw that the New World would be the root cause of the power shifts that would occur during the coming centuries. That's because they failed to realize that the real wealth was not in gold and silver, but in resources and land.

"But this time, there's a big difference. In my world, explorers and prospectors first had to *find* that wealth. That took centuries. But in this world, we have maps that give us a pretty good idea of where all the major mineral deposits are. We know where the fishing is best. Which soils and regions are best for which crops. Which areas are joined by what rivers."

He swept an arm from the north, through the west, and ending on the south. "Kings and queens didn't—couldn't—know how much they should invest in all those unknown places because they didn't know what they'd ultimately be worth. Well, now they have the answers to *both* those mysteries. And we're lucky that the Spanish have been so stuck in their notions of short-term conquest and wealth extraction at gunpoint that they haven't acted upon that new information yet. But they will. Every nation's scholars spend days and weeks in our library. If we hadn't arrived in the middle of what our historians called the Thirty Years' War, I'm pretty sure there would be a lot more national flags flying from topgallants in this part of the world, by now.

"So our choice was between standing around while

the knowledge from Grantville's library drives a radically new history, or to have a hand in shaping it. And these islands are among the places where those changes will come the fastest and the hardest."

Joost Banckert's frown was no longer impatient but somber. "There is much to think about in what you have said, Eddie. But none of it shines a light on how mariners such as us, bred to pursue profit individually and aggressively, can make money when we are all part of one navy with many restrictive rules."

Eddie smiled. "You really think there's a short answer to that question?"

Joost's frown lessened. "I know you cannot show me the whole tapestry of that new reality, Commodore Cantrell, but a quick sketch of the general design would suffice. For now."

Eddie shrugged, drew in a deep breath. "Okay. So, there will still be profits in taking ships, and there will still be crew shares, just like now. The difference is that the total value will be set by a prize court which will operate under the auspices of..."

Eddie Cantrell was, somehow, still standing as the last sliver of the sun sank down toward the almost-purple sea. He distinctly remembered hitting the head (such as it was) once, maybe twice. He was pretty sure he'd eaten an extremely crumbly cassava roll with bacon specks baked into it. He remembered watching all the goods get trundled past, either on their way to being sold or out to the wharf and a waiting lighter and thence to a buyer's ship.

The biggest draw of the day were the down-time manufactured steam engines. To his eye, they were heavy, inefficient, and overengineered, but on the other hand they were rugged and designed for ease of adaptation to a variety of purposes: for wheels or propellers, for electricity generation, for grinding. The stall right next to that one seemed to specialize in saws of all types, including several which had cranks. And—surprise, surprise!—it just happened that their rotary mechanism was the right size and shape to facilitate easy connection to the steam engines, once the crank was removed. Where the fuel for the engines would come from was another issue. St. Eustatia was not densely wooded, and shipping it from other islands simply to burn it would have been an expense that would increase as a function of distance from the source. But upon studying the firebox, Eddie discovered that it too was modular insofar as it was clearly designed to be swapped out. He'd thought a moment, wandered over, and asked the self-styled "engineer" peddling the engines if they could be modified to burn bitumen. He had to back away in less than thirty seconds, so eager and emphatic was the sales pitch with which the purveyor of engines assaulted him.

Sometime in the late afternoon, various important passengers debarked from the Dutch frigates: the general and former governor of Recife, Diederik van Waerdenburgh, was received with as much ceremony and pomp as van Walbeeck and Tromp could muster. Following soon after, they toasted the arrival of two military commanders who'd distinguished themselves under him: Major Berstedt and the legendary Hermann Gottfried van Stein-Callenfels. It added a bit of official solemnity to complement the last ferocious commercial surges of the day.

Svantner, delivering a list of engineering issues that had been detected on the two new destroyers during their Atlantic crossing, watched as the martial luminaries passed into the fort for a combination inspection/reception that Eddie would soon have to attend. "Why?" he'd asked when the stout doors had closed behind them.

"Why what?"

"Well, you have pointed out that officers in a combat... er, zone, should never cluster together, even if they believe themselves to be in a friendly place. They make too easy and tempting a target. So why have them disembark and arrive as a group?"

Eddie had smiled. "To give the Spanish spies something to look at and get excited about."

Svantner's frown deepened. "Is that wise?"

"It is if we want them to believe that, having seen the arrival of those commanders, they've seen everything that's worth seeing."

Svantner's mouth made a soundless "Ah!" He showed enough perspicacity not to inquire after those items or matters from which they were meant to distract Spanish attention.

Shortly after, he'd trudged into the fort, so tired that his Dutch was beginning to fail him as he met and attempted to converse with the new warships' post captains, several of whom spoke almost no English. Those two hours felt more like two weeks, and when he finally emerged into the street, it was everything he could do not to limp on his prosthesis. It was far more comfortable than the old one, and much more rugged, but the fact remained that when he was on his feet—well, foot—for an entire day, the amputation site and proximal muscles began aching and spasming. He steadied himself on the wall for a few moments, and then made his way home, resolved not to appear weak in front of his energetic bride, who had every reason to expect that he would have been home at least two hours earlier.

Eddie crept up to the bedroom door, leaned his ear against it. No sound. He sighed. On the one hand, even when he was dog-tired, returning to Anne Cathrine was one of the best parts of his day. Even if it was just to collapse into sleep beside her. Seeing her smile, touching her face, smelling her scent were—well, it made his senses and his heart silently affirm, *home.* Not merely that he had "come home"; she herself was home, to him.

He released another sigh, longer but no less controlled and quiet, and with it he exhaled the tension and nonstop activity of the day. He turned the latch and slipped in.

Anne Cathrine was on the bed. Not in it: *on* it. Bolt upright. She was on her knees, but Eddie had never seen a less coy or submissive posture in his life. Her eyes were bright. "So. You've come home." Her voice was not reproachful, but it was—tense?

Eddie nodded, rushed to the end of the bed, tried not to limp but failed. He took her two hands in his. "I'm sorry, Cat"—only he used that name for her, and only when they were alone—"but it was exactly the kind of day we expected. I thought you might be asleep, already." Like the rest of the denizens of the seventeenth century, Eddie had gradually come to live in accord with the sun, rising and setting when it did. Well, mostly: the predawn rising crap was still a pain in the—

Anne Cathrine squeezed his hands gently. She was wearing a nightgown—or robe, or something—that left very, very little to his always-active imagination. "I knew you would be late. I waited."

Eddie nodded, kept from frowning at her unusual demeanor and almost distracted tone of voice, almost as if she was speaking in her sleep. Which she never did. "Are you okay, love?"

"I am very well. And I am very glad you are home."

For a moment, Eddie wondered if he should send for Dr. Brandão. Anne Cathrine speaking in short, simple sentences that declared the obvious? With barely a hint of animation? Was this the onset of some unusual tropical disease?

She slipped her hands out of his, reached up toward him. "I love you, Eddie."

He smiled, moved in to give her a hug, knowing, beyond a shadow of a doubt, that he was absolutely the luckiest man in the—

Anne Cathrine grabbed him: hard. Her mouth was on his faster and even harder. She was already breathing like she'd just finished a marathon. All of which he noticed as, with her hands firmly on his shoulders, she twisted sharply at the hip.

Eddie, exhausted and leaning over into what he had expected would be a gentle embrace, fell, her arms guiding and turning him as he did. He landed on his back, too surprised to react, at first.

But Anne Cathrine was not waiting for his response. She turned with his fall, wound up straddling him. He had a fleeting thought that he sure was glad she loved him, because given the expression on her face, her only other possible intent would have been to *kill* him.

In fact, her hands and arms moved with the speed, force, and focus of an assassin's. She pushed him down with one hand, grabbed the front of his shirt with the other. She pulled: not merely hard, but savagely. Buttons sprang loose with dramatic snaps and pops, the force of which sent them flying.

They sprayed in all directions, rolling under doors, down between planks, never to be seen again.

Chapter 21

Oranjestad, St. Eustatia

Anne Cathrine, daughter of King Christian IV by morganatic marriage (and so, not a princess) yawned, stretched, fended off the sunlight that eked in through the slight gap in the hurricane shutters. They were just slightly ajar, held there by an adjustable hook and eye that had been set just so.

She smiled into the morning light. That had been done by her wonderful, kind, thoughtful Eddie. Her war hero, ducal, up-time machine-wizard Eddie. Her adoring, innocent, and—because of that—so very, very alluring Eddie.

She sighed, let herself fall back on the same bed that had been theirs on *Intrepid.* She stretched her full length upon it, happy in her body, in the softness of the layers beneath her, and buried her face in the pillows which smelt faintly of sandalwood. She exhaled, inhaled, considered her great good fortune to be with Eddie, to be in this warm and beautiful place, and began sobbing uncontrollably.

✧　　✧　　✧

An hour later, Anne Cathrine was striding purposefully from the door of their house. She was moving so quickly that Cuthbert Pudsey, the guard that Eddie had firmly insisted accompany her everywhere, had to grab the separate bits of his breakfast, weapon, helmet in order to scramble after her. "Where to, Lady Anne?"

Just as Eddie called her Cat—*no; mustn't think of that pet name, of him, of our bed*—the much-displaced Pudsey was the only one to call her "Anne." Not because of a special bond between them, although that was certainly present, now, but because the Englishman seemed incapable of remembering her full title. It wasn't his regard or respect that was wanting. If anything, that could easily be adjusted a notch or two lower, given his unwonted proclivity for bows and hat-doffings. It was simply that Cuthbert Pudsey was what Eddie called a "total yeoman." Loyal, respectful, practical, bighearted, fundamentally guileless, and as incapable of recalling protocol and honorifics as he was of running to the sun and back before dinner. Occasionally, Eddie referred to him as Sam or Samwise, but she had yet to discover why.

"I say, Lady Anne, is it to the Gov'ment House we'd be going?"

"Not immediately, Cuthbert. I am meeting my sister at Dr. Brandão's."

"Ah," he said as he drew alongside. He glanced at her attire. "If you'll pardon me sayin', m'um, you're not in your volunteering clothes, an' this isn't your volunteering day. 'Asides, you've the party to prepare for, eh?"

She smiled up at him; he smiled back, missing a few teeth but as cheery a face as imagination might paint. "There is no fooling you, is there? You are right; I am going to observe a medical case."

Cuthbert grew a bit pale. He was a redoubtable fighter—he'd proven that beyond any doubt during last year's attack by the Kalinago and the French—but was not enamored of doctors, or "chirurgeons," as he still called them. As he once explained it, it wasn't the blood or gore that bothered him; it was the "fiddly messing about in one's flesh" that made him feel like he might lose the lunch he had not yet eaten.

Pale as he might have grown, he straightened up a bit and put back his great, if rather curved, shoulders. "Right, then: to the cutter's!"

Anne Cathrine managed not to reveal her dismay by putting one fine tooth on one equally fine lip. She had counted on Cuthbert's aversion to Dr. Brandão's infirmary as the means whereby she would shed his constant oversight. So what could she—? *Ah!* "Mr. Pudsey . . . I . . ."

"Why . . . yes, Lady Anne?" He knew that when she called him Mr. Pudsey, she was about to say something Very Serious Indeed.

"I . . . I must ask a favor of you."

"Why, fer you, anything. Anything at all!"

"I must ask your discretion."

He frowned. "My . . . my discretion? In what way, m'um?"

She affected being unable to meet his eyes. "I will require privacy. When we reach the doctor's."

"You'll . . . ?" Then he leaned far back from his concerned forward hunch. "Ah! Now I see it." He nodded, leaned in, floated a sotto voce question. "A lady's matter, izzit?"

"It is," Anne Cathrine answered in a hushed voice, not lying but using her reticence to inveigle him into making some very erroneous assumptions.

He was frowning, however. "Given that the little doctor is the finest I've ever seen—though I see as few as I may—I'm surprised that he's, ah, tending to, er, the fairer sex."

Anne Cathrine managed not to roll her eyes or punch his beefy shoulder. While she still viewed many of the up-timers', well, more relaxed relations between the sexes with some reserve, there were two areas in which she was a complete and vociferous convert: the rights of women and the elimination of segregated medical treatment. She found the latter particularly infuriating, and particularly here and now in the New World. Granted, it was rather uncomfortable to be disrobed in front of and examined by a male, but if their expertise was superior, then that was who she wanted administering her care.

Fortunately, she only had to playact with Cuthbert, not argue for sweeping changes in social attitudes toward the practice of medicine. "I did not say that Dr. Brandão would be there, just that the matter will be addressed at his infirmary."

"Ah, well, I should have realized!" Pudsey smote his flat forehead with his equally flat palm. "Apologies for assumin', m'um."

"No apology required. However, I will require privacy."

"Well, of course you will. Where shall I wait for ye?"

"At the western pavilion that has been erected alongside Government House. I should not be very long, but do remain there, even if I am detained."

Pudsey smiled and frowned at the same time. He was obviously glad to be of service but didn't want to agree to staying put if her absence was so extended that he became unsure of her safety. "Well, as you say, m'um. And here we are."

"Keep walking, Pudsey; I do not wish to enter through the front door."

"Ah. Right, then. No need to feed the gossipmongers, eh?"

"My thoughts exactly. Now, I shall slip in through the smaller door in the rear, just there. Remember, wait for me at the western pavilion."

Pudsey frowned, but waved and kept walking toward the canvas wing protruding from one side of Government House where preparations for tonight's fete were in full swing.

She watched him go, then slipped in the door.

"About time!"

Anne Cathrine started, whirled, fist coming back— and saw Leonora staring wide-eyed at her. She dropped her arm, and managed not to utter several of Eddie's extremely tepid curses. "Sister, do not startle me so."

"Who were you expecting? A pirate?"

"I was expecting to be able to see you plainly if you were here before me, not hidden in the shadows."

"Anne Cathrine," Leonora said in a voice that would have been quite appropriate in a governess twice her age, "if the objective is for us to remain unobserved, it would be rather foolish of me to arrive here and then stand in the middle of this sunlit room, would it not?"

Anne Cathrine silently admitted she had a point but was also silently resolved not to admit it to her fourteen-year-old sister. "Is Sophie here yet?"

"Yes."

"And is he?"

"No, but it is still early."

"Then lead on."

"Me?"

"You got here first, and you know the best hidden vantage point, do you not?"

"Dr. Brandão keeps the bolt thrown on the doors to both the supply room and the surgery. The latter has an ill-fitting door, made of driftwood. We should be able to see and hear even while leaving it locked."

"Perfect." Anne Cathrine waited. "Well?"

"Well, what?"

"Lead on!"

Leonora did, and Anne Cathrine was fairly sure she was supposed to overhear her annoyed mutter, "Why do I have to do *everything*?"

They saw the increase in sunlight in the infirmary's front room, heard faint, polite voices: Sophie's as she arrived and Dr. Brandão's as he left.

Crouched beneath her taller sister so they could both see through the crack between the door and the jamb that had started out as a hatch coaming, Leonora released a long, muffled sigh.

"What now?" Anne Cathrine whispered.

"This is ridiculous," hissed Leonora.

"It is not," Anne Cathrine hissed back.

"Either we should enter and be known, or we should leave. I do not understand why you would—"

"Let us just stop at that statement: that you do not understand. We shall remedy that later. But for now, let us watch and listen."

"But why? If, as you suspect, Sophie's feelings are greater than she admits, then is it not—?"

"Leonora," Anne Cathrine muttered sternly, "Sophie Caisdatter Rantzau may be the most intelligent woman I know beside yourself. And she seems equally limited in her understanding of things—things of a personal nature. We are here to observe so that we might help."

"Seems to me we are here to spy on matters that are manifestly none of our business. And how is it that Sophie's understanding of personal matters might be lacking? She is a widow, she knows—"

"Her marriage was arranged for her. Just as Poppa had planned for you and me, until we were saved by the changes wrought by the up-timers. Now be silent or begone!"

"This is wrong," Leonora grumbled. But she craned her neck to get a better look through the crack of the door.

The knock at the infirmary's front entrance was so gentle that they barely heard it. The door itself was not in their line of sight, but the soft-voiced greetings confirmed that the newly arrived patient was just who they expected: Hugh O'Donnell.

Anne Cathrine listened as pleasantries transitioned into medical practicalities. He explained how he no longer felt any pain in it, and attributed that to both her skill and her solicitude. Anne Cathrine smiled. *Good!*

Sophie breezed past that compliment—and opportunity to shift the conversation to a more personal level—by pointing out that it was difficult to know when a healing process could be considered complete, and commenced to bombard the earl with a battery of inquiries: Did the amputation site, or remaining digit, ever feel hot? Did it ever feel numb? Did it ever swell? Did it ever, and did it ever, and did it ever? Anne Cathrine hung her head: bad, very bad. A string of questions that had all the veiled romantic potential of a bouquet of rotting parsnips.

Hugh answered patiently, a bemused smile growing on his face as Sophie's barrage continued. His eyes rested upon her more and more; hers were upon him less and less. Unless you counted the mauled finger: her gaze was fixed upon it. More out of desperation than clinical focus, Anne Cathrine suspected.

When Sophie finally ran out of queries, Hugh smiled broadly and declared himself the most fortunate of all patients. So fortunate, that he was half-glad to have been wounded in the first place.

Sophie was baffled. "I do not understand, Lord O'Donnell."

He shrugged. "Well, if I hadn't been wounded, then I might never have met you."

The unthinkable happened: Sophie blushed. "Nonsense. A soldier should never wish for a wound, even in jest! And certainly not one that costs him a part of his body!"

Hugh tilted his head, and his smile grew very wide and so, became very bright. "Well, now, that's a question of exchange, isn't it?"

Sophie's color returned to normal as she frowned, asked, "A question of exchange, Lord O'Donnell? I do not understand; what is this question and what exchange?"

His eyes became a little less jovial, a little more serious. "It is a question of whether losing half a finger is a fair price for meeting you." He paused, waited until he had her eyes on his. "I'm thinking it to be a most excellent bargain, Lady Rantzau."

Anne Cathrine felt like she might jump out of her skin for want of rushing in and shaking even minimal instincts for courtship into Sophie. Even Leonora murmured wordless approval of Hugh's soulful wooing. They leaned forward, straining at the aperture between the door and the jamb, listening for Sophie's crucial response—

"As I said at the outset, Lord O'Donnell: purest nonsense." But as unpromising as the words were, her tone was playful. And the smile that followed them was wide and radiant. "Now let us see how it is healing."

"Truly," Hugh protested, "it is quite healed already."

"I will be the judge of that," Sophie countered as her smile changed.

Anne blinked: was that how Sophie looked when she was being...being...*coy*? Was "coy" even possible for Sophie the Norn, who reminded the sisters of those spirit-women of Nordic legend, those pronouncers and makers of Fate?

Sophie rose and gestured to the bench that also served as the infirmary's couch for examinations. "Kindly be at your ease on this chair, with this hassock beneath your feet. Good. Are you comfortable? Now, just relax."

Sophie undertook the unwrapping of the finger with deliberate—almost languorous?—care. By the time the savaged digit was revealed, the procedure had begun to border on the sensuous. She looked, saw him watching her. She returned the stare, smiled slowly. "I work best when I am not under observation, Lord O'Donnell."

He smiled, nodded, closed his eyes.

Sophie made a genuinely thorough and attentive inspection of the still-discolored lower half of his small finger, the top half of which had been shredded by the fragments of a French grenade during his relief of Oranjestad. The remains had been promptly amputated, but Brandão had recommended against searing it, for fear of locking infection in, and his skills had been desperately required by others with far more grievous injuries. In consequence, the tip of what remained was uneven and still somewhat raw.

"I do not like the look of that," she pronounced. "Sepsis could still occur. I have half a mind to forbid further travel until that danger is clearly past."

Hugh smiled. "Lady Rantzau, my finger is as fit for duty as the rest of me. It was untroubled by my travels, whether at sea or in pestiferous jungles."

Her eyelids flew wide open. "Unacceptable! I will not hear of—!"

He reached a hand toward her, not touching, but imploring. Gently. With a gesture that hinted at a caress. "I am perfectly fine, now," Hugh reiterated. "I would not lie to you. Lies, even those little ones we tell to calm the concern of those who we hold in high regard, become barriers. And I would not have any barriers between us."

She rose very quickly. "I am glad you believe yourself to be well, but as I already told you, *I* will be the judge of that, Lord O'Donnell!" Anne Cathrine smiled. Sophie was marvelous when she drew herself to her full height and became lofty and almost imperious. Anne was almost a little jealous of her.

O'Donnell was shaking his head. "I'm never one

to contradict a lady, and certainly not one so skilled and determined as yourself. Besides, it's exhausting."

"Exhausting?"

"Well, that stands to reason, doesn't it? Here I stand—well, recline—not only laboring to change your mind, but to remember your name."

Now Sophie was confused. "You have difficulties remembering my name?"

"Well, it's more a matter of remembering to call you Lady Rantzau, because in my mind, you're Lady Sophie. For which I apologize: I've a most unruly and unreliable mind when it comes to remaining formal with those who've become special to me. But so long as you address me as Lord O'Donnell I'm fated to address you as Lady Rantzau. Whereas it would be far less exhausting to simply call you Lady Sophie." He paused, once again made sure she was looking directly at him. "I would so much rather call you that."

Sophie didn't respond immediately. She had rapidly transitioned from looking quite composed and happy to appearing confused, and not exactly sure why she was. Anne Cathrine wanted to shout out what she might do next, to keep this ridiculous charade of a medical examination moving in the right direction.

But Sophie found her own answer. "Well," she said with purposefully overplayed seriousness, "in the interest of making your final recovery less taxing, I do suppose that a more relaxed environment would be congenial to that purpose. So let us dispense with titles altogether. If that would suit you... Hugh?"

He smiled. "It would suit me very well, Sophie." He said her name as if he were about to sing it.

"Well, then, I... I will get the linens for one last

dressing. To cover it while the scar tissue becomes stronger. I shall return momentarily." She went to the supply room.

He smiled as he watched her go, kept watching the door as if some faint hint of her image might have been imparted to it.

Anne Cathrine wanted to stamp her feet in wild happiness, relief, and a bit of exultation. The only man she had ever seen more smitten than Hugh O'Donnell was her own darling Eddie.

Leonora, however, was looking up at her, frowning. "Yet *another* dressing?" she complained, forgetting to whisper. "That is totally unnecessary. His finger is perfectly fine. I can see it from here. Her so-called precautions are actually quite baffling and obtuse."

Anne Cathrine patted her hand. "As are you, some-times, dear Leonora. As are you. Now be quiet! You were entirely too loud. So let us leave before we are detected." As she said it she stole one more glance through the crack of the door.

Hugh O'Donnell was looking straight at her. He couldn't actually see her, she told herself, but, well, he was certainly staring at the door. And yes, he was focused on the crevice between it and the doorjamb. He turned away, chuckled noiselessly, and put his hands behind his head and laid back.

Anne Cathrine grabbed Leonora's arm and they left the infirmary as quickly as stealth would allow.

Chapter 22

Oranjestad, St. Eustatia

Moments after retrieving the already-anxious Cuthbert Pudsey, a familiar voice with a Dutch accent inquired, "Do you approve of the preparations, Lady Anne Cathrine?"

She turned after an instant's delay: the time it took for her to be sure that she had successfully pasted a smile over her expression of surprise and fear that, somehow, someone had seen her eavesdropping in the infirmary.

Maarten Tromp was standing just to one side, hands folded before him. As he often did, he radiated fatherly approval and regard—which at this moment, made her feel incongruously like a naughty, sneaky child, even though she had now almost reached the unthinkably advanced age of eighteen. "Why yes, Admiral," she answered, glancing at the sail-derived pavilion and the crude tables beneath it, "I could not approve more. Not that my approval is of any particular importance!"

Whereas Leonora nodded and announced, "They seem quite wonderful!"

He smiled, beginning to stroll as he gestured at his intended path, inviting them to walk with him. "I must differ with you regarding the importance of your approval, Lady Anne Cathrine. You and your sister have seen more of such events than anyone else here. With the exception of the others that came with you from your father's court, none of us are well acquainted with the staging of such large celebrations." He chuckled. "I fear that you will have to be willing to tolerate a large measure of what burghers and the gentry consider 'an entertainment.'"

Anne Cathrine did not have to summon or amplify her responding laugh. "Admiral, if you could only imagine how dull and downright plodding the majority of state affairs prove to be. Most of the men are too old, busy, and 'dignified' to dance, whereas their wives are equally old, busy, and self-conscious of the infirmities that impede their grace. And for every such infirmity that is actual, there are a dozen that are imagined, though they may be painfully real in the minds of those who believe themselves afflicted. The food is plentiful, and so, wasted in quantities that would feed whole villages. The wine and drink is equally plentiful, but the opposite problem obtains; so much is consumed that felicity becomes besotted carousing."

"And conjugal incapacity later on," Leonora added casually. When she noted Tromp's startled stare and Cuthbert's delighted surprise, she blinked. "What? Are we not simply speaking truths that society is typically too polite to utter?"

Anne Cathrine smiled winningly, while thinking, *Dear sister, would that your social sensibilities were so well tuned as your intellectual gifts.* Aloud: "My sister's convictions, and the courage with which she shares them, are among the rarest of gifts. Alas that she hasn't the time to share more."

"I don't?"

Anne Cathrine tried to make sure that her smile did not evolve into a grimace. "You have forgotten? That you and Sophie agreed to prepare for the party together?"

Leonora's eyelids opened wider. "Oh, yes! I quite forgot! You must excuse me!"

The others waved her on her way. Anne Cathrine was simply glad that the excuse was genuine; Sophie and Leonora had indeed felt that it would be pleasant for them to help each other primp for the great event. Whereas, had Anne Cathrine fabricated a groundless excuse on the spot, Leonora would almost certainly have argued that there was no such appointment, rather than taking the hint. Instead, she ran off with the blind abandon spawned by that sudden fixity of purpose observable in fourteen-year-olds the world over, nobility or not.

Pudsey looked around for her escort. "Er, Lady Sophie, about your sister..."

Anne Cathrine was doubly relieved. "Go with her until she is safe in our house, Cuthbert. I am sure that the admiral or one of his staff will see me safely home."

Tromp smiled at the mercenary-become-protector-of-noble-ladies. "My word on it."

"Obliged, sir!" Pudsey answered and trundled after Leonora.

Before Anne Cathrine could speak, Tromp began

walking, murmuring, "I am glad for this opportunity to speak with you."

"What about, Admiral?"

Tromp made a huffing sound that took her a few seconds to recognize as a heavily suppressed chortle. "Merrymaking."

She smiled. "I doubt I am your best resource for that! I have attended many balls and dances and dinners, but have not spent a moment ever planning one or observing the process."

Tromp nodded as they strolled out from under the west pavilion and crossed in front of the entrance to Government House. "And yet you have more experience of them, from which we may hope to interpolate what must go into their making."

She tried not to frown. "Admiral, I am flattered that you reside such trust in my opinions, but at this late hour..."

He held up a hand as they stopped in front of Government House. "I fully realize that this is an extraordinary imposition, made more so by coming to you at, almost literally, the last possible minute. But before you object, please, let me explain.

"Lady Anne Cathrine, as you could not have failed to notice, I am not a man who has spent much time observing society, let alone the ways of the nobility. All I know about entertainments, regardless of their type, is whether I am enjoying them or not. My colleagues and officers are cut from the same cloth; our involvement has always been in matters that are intensely practical, if not barbaric. We are military men, after all.

"In consequence, we planned carefully for these days

when so many people would come to Oranjestad, for this opportunity to fix it in so many minds as a hub not only of commerce and power, but society, opportunity, and entertainment. So naturally, we always envisioned a party, but particularly a dance, an event where new romantic friendships may be kindled and so, start to bind all our islands together with even stronger ties. But in all of those considerations, no one ever stopped to ask: 'but who shall oversee this party?'"

He looked up at Government House, the façade of which was three stories high. Its wings and the rear extension were only two floors. "We considered the space we needed; we allowed for food and drink, where they would be prepared and in what quantities. We asked for volunteers to help with that service and promised tariff relief as an incentive, and so accrued more willing hands than we know what to do with. We even contacted the musicians among us, who used the last two days of strolling the streets as a time to rehearse and prepare."

He sighed. "We were military men approaching this objective as we would any other: identify and gather resources at the time and place where they are needed." He huff-laughed again. "But somehow, we missed the final analogy that should have been the first thing we determined: to recruit a knowledgeable commander for this enterprise." He glanced at Anne Cathrine.

"Admiral, even if I was capable and willing to take on this great enterprise"—*God forbid! I'm better at a council table or commanding defenders, and I'd prefer the dangers of either before the drudgery of this!*—"I am expected to be *at* the party. I was honored to have so many notes sent to my house expressing the fond hope that I might reserve a minute of the evening to spend with its sender." She smiled. "I also know what those requests really mean. They are oblique attempts to gain access to my ear. The majority of those correspondents hope to enlist my support, or acquaint me with an issue germane to their own interests, or speak to any one of a number of important people who are routinely in my circle of acquaintance: Hannibal Sehested, Governor van Walbeeck, you, my husband, even my father."

She put a hand to her head; it was really rather dizzying as, speaking it out all at once, she realized just how big a fish she had become in this little pond. "I agreed to dozens of such brief meetings that will, I am sure, all go on too long. Governor van Walbeeck prevailed upon me to do so, if for no other reason than these are all persons who are wealthy, influential, or ambitious. And the more of them who know that they will be able to speak with me, the more of them will attend. And the more of them who attend, the more prestigious the event becomes, and so the desire to be seen at it spreads like wildfire. And so it has. And so I may not be absent from the event, given the role to which I am already committed."

At about the halfway point of her explanation, Tromp had again folded his hands patiently in front of him. "That is why I am asking you to give us only an hour now. To answer the questions of the volunteers and servers, not officer them through the event. We lack the knowledge to tell them what will please the guests the most, what music and dances were last in fashion, how and when to best serve food and drink."

"But I do not know these things."

"Perhaps not, but they will listen and obey what you tell them, Lady Anne Cathrine." He smiled. "You may constantly point out that you are 'only' a king's daughter, but they still refer to you as 'the princess.' Without that voice of authority, they will continue to bicker with each other. You need not be knowledgeable, but even so, you will have far more knowledge than any of them, simply by dint of having been present at such expansive entertainments."

An hour. She really didn't have the time. But on the other hand—

Her future was here, she realized in a sudden rush. This New World, this place far away from the viper pits of Danish—no, of European—nobility: this was where she felt more vibrant, more alive, more *useful*, than she ever had in her entire life. And maybe, just maybe, she could have a hand in guiding it to evolve toward . . . toward what?

Toward something better, affirmed a blunt, practical voice in her head. Toward a community where one's daughters and principles and "friendships" were not employed as chess pieces in a sweeping, unending, and insufferable game of accruing and preserving power. She did not envision a Utopia; she already knew too much of human nature to consider that anything more than a quixotic dream. But she could help make this New World better, perhaps much the same way that Grantville had wrought wondrous changes in the old one.

She turned to Tromp. "Yes. I will help. Would you be so kind as to escort me there?"

Three hours later, Anne Cathrine emerged from the same door, where Tromp—who had been called to other matters—had agreed to meet her when she sent for him. She was exhausted but energized. She did not care much for the topics upon which she had been called to make decisions, but, well—she most certainly did like making decisions. And here in the New World, she was not being pushed behind those who held power; she was being drawn forward to wield it. Her thoughts flashed to Eddie, and she felt blood rushing to the places where thoughts of him usually hastened to.

But upon seeing Tromp, she stilled that as best she could and nodded at him. "I believe you shall find that this evening's entertainment will still be chaotic, but at least its delivery shall not be divisive."

He bowed deeply. "Lady Anne Cathrine, you have done all that I could have hoped and more."

"Then Admiral, I wonder if you will do something for me in return."

Tromp was too experienced to be giddy at the prospect of furnishing recompense for her efforts; it was the way of kings and their families, and it was one of their least welcome habits. He stood, almost stiffly. "Certainly."

She gestured at Government House behind him. "This place is a mystery. I would have you explain it to me."

He frowned. "I am not sure what you are referring to, Lady Anne Cathrine."

"It was originally built as the Governor's House. I remember the first time I saw the inside of it."

Tromp nodded. "The New Year's party. Just six months ago."

"Yes. A quaint and intimate event compared to what will be held here in but four hours. But between that first event and this one, and without any announcements, it became Government House. Two immense wings to either side, an even greater expansion to the rear to create a great hall." She began walking in the direction of the house she and Eddie had been given as the senior representatives of a foreign power. "Why these changes?"

Tromp put his hands behind his back, head down, and considered a moment before answering. He resembled a school master, again.

"There are ticklish subjects involved in this explanation. I will trust that you will not share them with anyone except your husband."

"He is not already aware?"

Tromp shrugged. "Very possibly. It was not purposefully kept from him. But he was busy with the planning and preparations for the interception of La Flota, and there was no reason to distract him with such details.

"So: when the time came for Jan—Governor van Walbeeck—to take up residence in the Governor's House, he decided it would be unwise. After seeing the almost desperate merriment of the New Year's Party, he came to realize that the building was sorely needed by the community as a place to gather, whether to celebrate, debate, or mourn.

"He also perceived that, although it is a colonial tradition that the governor should have a separate, and large, residence, there were political frictions here on St. Eustatia which made that inadvisable. Too many of our people were still living in tents. And if resentment for that privilege struck even the smallest sparks of resentment, our political opponents—this island's stubborn and increasingly obstreperous slaveholders—were likely to attempt to fan those sparks into a conflagration."

Anne Cathrine frowned. "Could they have succeeded, do you think?"

Tromp shrugged again. "Even if they had not, van

Walbeeck foresaw that if the slaveholders made so overt an attempt to undermine our authority, that act would draw permanent battle lines. Even if the colonists were indifferent or unfriendly to their cause, the resulting pall of discord and animus would not readily dissipate. Morale would have suffered when we needed it to be strong. So van Walbeeck elected to retain his apartment in the fort until a more modest domicile could be built for the governor's use.

"Within weeks, however, we began discovering yet another reason why we needed to convert the Governor's House into Government House; we needed more space for our administrators and officials. More specifically, with the USE's fleet permanently in the New World, and trade ties rapidly increasing between the cast-off communities that had once been England's possessions, we found ourselves appointing a harbormaster, a customs and tariff office, a sheriff, a court of justice, a deeds and titles registry and archive."

Anne Cathrine raised an eyebrow. "I have been told that Spanish colonies often do without such formalities for years, even decades."

Tromp nodded. "And that is quite true, but that is because their leadership in the New World follows the true nature of governance in Spain itself: highly centralized autocratic power. They only introduce additional layers of control when they must, which creates a rigid, tiered hierarchy in which even the lowest positions are as often filled by nepotism as proven qualifications."

Anne Cathrine smiled. "Whereas you innovative, independent, and contentious Dutch rely on public offices not merely for order, but to prevent excessive centralization of power." She smiled wider when Tromp glanced at her sharply, surprised, but also pleased. "My father has made quite a study of your government. He admires it. He also fears that if that model becomes popular in Denmark, it might undermine his throne."

Tromp chuckled. "Yes, because our system is *so* much better: a marginally competent civil service shot through with a double skein of bribery and cronyism."

They shared a laugh. They then walked in silence for almost a minute.

Anne Cathrine looked up at him. "So, you do not feel the Dutch system is much better than a monarchy?"

Tromp frowned, head down as he walked and reflected. "I simply meant to underscore that it is by no means perfect, or even particularly fair." He paused as they arrived at her door. "But I will not serve an absolute king, and would die fighting to keep my country from having one. If I felt otherwise, our half century of struggle against the Spanish means we were not fighting for our freedom, but over whose collar we would wear."

She smiled slowly. "I shall see you again tonight, Admiral."

"That shall be my honor and my pleasure, Lady Anne Cathrine. Here comes Pudsey; my happy duty escorting you is at an end." He bowed and left at a brisk walk.

Pudsey approached. "That seemed a most serious talk you were having with the admiral, Lady Anne." He tried to inject a lighter tone. "From the looks on your faces, it seemed as if you might be solving the problems of this old world."

"No," she mused, looking after the admiral's retreating and entirely average figure, "we were talking about how best to build this new one."

Chapter 23

Oranjestad, St. Eustatia

Leonora was grumpy. Yes, she had reason for disappointment, but it went beyond that. First, the seamstress who was to make necessary changes to the one gown she had brought from Denmark was overdue and her services were absolutely required. Leonora was still only fourteen and just six months' worth of bodily change—much of which was quite welcome!—absolutely required alterations or profound embarrassment might ensue.

Secondly, after spending half an hour fretting over the tardiness of the seamstress and ineffectually primping, Sophie returned—announcing her arrival with a set of sharp knocks to the door of their shared toilet. Leonora had been deeply involved in her third attempt to adjust her hair and the surprise turned her untrained touch into a brief eruption of startled fingers that ruined her already dubious handiwork.

And of course, once Sophie had settled in to her own pre-dance preparations, Leonora had to stay calm and casual in her choice of topics while her curiosity—her desire to know how the earl of Tyrconnell had departed, and how Sophie felt, and what she meant to do—was threatening to burst out of her mouth, as if it were a rabid mink spinning and clawing inside of her.

She settled down for another attempt at her hair, this time with the benefit of Sophie's calm advice. Indeed, Leonora was so set upon her efforts that the end of her tongue protruded from her lips, as if it were an external rite meant to placate the demi-deities of Focus and Determination. But no sooner had she made some appreciable progress, than the door banged open and Anne Cathrine came racing in, the overdue seamstress following just behind. Even more startled by this second interruption, the consequent ruin to Leonora's hairstyling efforts were still worse and, to add insult to injury, she had nipped the tip of her tongue.

Anne Cathrine excitedly discoursed about Government House and Tromp and a New Start in the New World and having to make an immense number of decisions about the party that sounded unbearably dull to Leonora. In other words, it was more evidence that the universe did in fact revolve around Anne Cathrine, who punctuated her departure with a hug that ruined yet another of Leonora's attempts to tame her hair. Despite entreaties that Anne Cathrine very likely did not hear, she did not return to help fix the damage she had wrought.

Leonora was missing—for the fifth time in as many minutes—her older sister's skill in the arts of efficacious primping and improvised makeup when there was yet another knock on the door. *My word, are we to prepare for a party or answer summonses?*

Sophie Rantzau glanced at Leonora. "A reply to

a knock is at the discretion of the king's daughter," she murmured.

Well, bother; I suppose that's true. "Yes?" Leonora called toward the door.

"It is I, Edel Mund. May I enter briefly?"

The two young women exchanged glances. Leonora knew what she wanted to do: ignore the Medusa-in-mourning who had inexplicably come to their doorstep at this most unprovidential moment. But instead she said, "Yes, of course, Lady Mund."

The door opened, and Edel Mund, more spare and pale than ever, entered and nodded severely at Leonora and Sophie, her eyes questing into the further corners of the room.

"My sister is not here," Leonora explained. "She is preparing for attending this evening's entertainment, I'm afraid."

Edel Mund nodded again. "I see. Then I will ask you to be so kind to convey to her the message I share with you here. I extend my apologies, ladies, but I must refrain from attending that affair, despite your sister's kind solicitation for my presence. It would still be—unseemly for me to do so."

"*—even if I were disposed to go,*" Leonora finished silently for the middle-aged woman. "I hear this news with regret, but fully understand." *What I do* not *understand is how long you intend to mourn your husband.*

"Also, I would be most grateful if, when next you see Dr. Brandão, you would tell him that I wish to volunteer my services to him, as well. I expect I would be a passably capable nurse."

Leonora nodded, quite sure that what Edel lacked

in bedside manner and compassion she would make up for in efficiency and reliability. "I am sure Dr. Brandão will be delighted to welcome you into our little hospital."

Edel made no response, other than to bow slightly, her black shoulder wrap hanging. "Ladies, I am sorry to have intruded at so inopportune a moment." Without any sign of haste, she was nonetheless out the door with remarkable speed.

Leonora blinked, shrugged, returned to the task of securing yet another errant wisp of hair in its proper place. "Lady Mund is a most peculiar person," she observed. "And I can only imagine that her continued mourning intensifies her peculiarities."

Sophie Rantzau, whose long, gleaming hair remained infuriatingly perfect without any apparent effort on her part, looked at the closed door with solemn gray eyes. "I suspect we are seeing more than the oddities of her character or the distraction of extended mourning."

"What do you mean, Sophie?"

"I mean that, in the terms of life as she has chosen to live it, volunteering to help with the sick and wounded is a form of penance."

"Penance? But for what? Edel Mund is hardly a model of Christian charity or joy, but neither does she seem a great sinner. What could she have done to make her feel compelled to do penance?"

Sophie Rantzau's tone suggested she was sharing a secret rather than a comment. "For many of us, penance is owed not for what one has done, but for what one did not do."

Leonora looked overcautiously at Sophie. The tall young woman was still staring at the back of the door.

"You said that with great conviction. Personal conviction." Leonora was tempted to say more, but knew that she could not, not unless she wished to chase her silent friend's own emerging truth—or confession?—back into whatever deep hiding place it had inhabited before Edel Mund's odd visit had summoned it forth.

"My name," Sophie said softly. "Has it never struck you as strange?"

Leonora, who had been holding her breath in anticipation of a great revelation, was taken off guard by this strange redirection. If it was, in fact, a redirection. Perhaps it was merely an oblique means of approaching the painful core of whatever truth Sophie kept buried. Because certainly, no one would be as laconic as she unless they were, in fact suppressing *something*. "I have never thought there is anything strange about your name. Also, I am unsure which name you mean: your Christian name or surname?"

Sophie smiled. "My surname, of course."

Cautiously now, Leonora! "What is strange about it?"

"That it is still affixed to my person. You know, of course, that I was married."

"Y-yes." It would not do to let Sophie know how very much Leonora knew of this. Her personal curiosity could easily be misunderstood as mere nosiness. "Your husband died in the Baltic War, did he not?"

"Yes, he did. So I am familiar with the many ways in which mourning can become a burden more trying than the grief that may underlie it. Or not."

Suddenly, Leonora was unsure that she wanted to hear Sophie's unuttered truth. But she was also aware that there was no way to stop it now. To flinch away from it, to smother it before it could leave Sophie's lips, would be to show herself a coward, to be unworthy of trust, and so, to be unworthy of further shared revelations. And so Leonora took what she knew to be a fateful step: "I am unsure how best to understand that statement, dear Sophie."

Who smiled. "That was well and delicately put, Leonora. I thank you for being so patient with me. This is difficult to speak of. Not the least because I fear it will make you—your sister, too, but particularly you—think ill of me."

Leonora did not know what to say: she simply shook her head.

Sophie drew in a deep breath. "I was married to Laurids Ulfeldt in October of 1631, had our child in June of the following year, and lost that child soon after. But by that time he had been sent to serve under Anders Bille on the island of Osel. Which is where he died, early in 1633, trying to intercept a boat of Swedish couriers. Which only occurred because Gustav did *not* die at Lützen, which in turn led to your father's eventual war against him. So, in point of fact, Laurids died when he did because the up-timers arrived and changed history."

Sophie turned to face Leonora directly. "You are not the only one to spend much of your life transported to other places and other times in the pages of a book. As is true for so many of us, I became curious about what had happened to me in the up-timers' world. Last year, I finally had the chance to peruse their collected histories." She smiled. "It was a humbling thing, to see what little mention there was of me at all, other than that I was a 'rich heiress' who had married Laurids Ulfeldt. Who, I discovered, was to have lived much longer. And with whom I was to have had four children."

Leonora felt tears rise into her eyes, but did not blink, did not let them escape. At the age of seven, harshly treated by the parental surrogates who had raised her while she was away from her father's court, she had resolved never to shed tears again.

Sophie's eyes widened. She reached out and touched Leonora's cheek. "No. Do not weep. Not for me. And most of all, not for what you think is my grief."

"What?" Leonora croaked.

"My dear friend, you know what the Ulfeldt family is like. Laurids was the best of them, true, but they are not...not warm men. Nor sensitive, nor compassionate. He was more physically vital than most of them, but not what one would call vigorous. He spent most of the few days we had together immersed in his books, pursuing his 'historical projects,' as he called them."

Sophie laughed, shook her head. "That was to have been the great bond between us, you see: books. Except that he used them as a means of making things smaller, as a way to fit all life—what had come before and what was transpiring around him—into neat compartments and categories, whereas I used them to rove far and wide, to the ends of this earth and beyond." Her rueful smile faded. "I suppose one could say nothing defined the differences between us so sharply and so sadly as the reasons for which we embraced books. Which was the majority of the embracing that occurred in our marriage."

For the first time since Leonora had met Sophie, the young woman averted her eyes. "So you see, Leonora, I know what it is like to mourn and yet not feel grief.

I am not saying that this is what is occurring behind the hard façade that Edel Mund shows to the world. Frankly, I think something different afflicts her. But I know what it is like to wear black, and step slowly and heavily because it is what is expected of a mourning wife, but to feel nothing but relief within. And in that relief, feel oneself base and monstrous."

"But how? And for what?" Leonora blurted out. "For being rid of a man you did not love, never wished to marry? Because, Sophie, it was no secret that your mother engineered that marriage, in no small part to secure allies who would protect her from my father's wrath. What would you feel but relief in escaping from such a union? And why, therefore, should you feel such guilt?"

"Because my guilt does not arise from escaping my marriage to Laurids," Sophie explained hollowly, "but from dancing away to my freedom upon the ghost bodies of three more little children to whom I never gave birth. And for living past my time."

Leonora did not breathe. "What do you mean?"

Sophie's eyes rose back to Leonora's. "One of the other things the histories revealed about me was my date of death: May 1635. Just as we were preparing to leave for the New World, I had, in that other history, left the world entirely."

Leonora went from horrified to confused in the space of a single second. "But then, how did you have four children—?"

Sophie shook her head. "In that other history, Laurids was only briefly on Osel. With Gustav dead, the Baltic War never occurred; the tensions were brief, and he returned. But here, he never returned from

Osel and so, did not father three more children. For which I am unspeakably grateful. And for which I must certainly be damned."

"Damned?"

"How can I not be, Leonora? I wake every morning and breathe a sigh of relief that I am no longer married to Laurids Ulfeldt. And then I remember, in the next breath, that my freedom comes at the expense of his life and that of three unborn children. How does that not damn one?"

Leonora forced herself to become calm. "Sophie, you did not act to deprive Laurids of his life. And whatever you may have felt about your marriage, I do not believe you wished him dead, did you?"

Sophie shook her head mutely.

"And you only learned of the three other children afterward, so they could not even have been a part of your initial reaction to his death."

Sophie looked up. "What point are you driving toward, Leonora?"

The young woman considered. "You have read much of the up-timer literature?"

"As much as I can, but it was mostly histories, since that is what fascinated Laurids. Ironically, the copies he commissioned arrived two years after he died."

"How much of the up-time 'psychology' have you read?"

"I know the word, and the basic principles, but nothing specific."

"I see. Well then, when you have the opportunity, you must come to peruse the complete copies that my father has in his library. And once there, you must look up the term 'survivor guilt.'"

And Sophie asked, as Leonora had hoped: "What is survivor guilt?"

"It means that when, in a group of people, only a few survive, those survivors may feel guilty not to have lost their lives, too. It was often observed when the up-timers' ships sank or their flying machines crashed. It happens with them much, much more than with us, because so many people of our time are convinced that God chooses, with great purpose, who shall live and who shall die." *And there is a statement that damns me, Sophie: "many people of our time are convinced that God chooses . . ."—but not me. Not anymore.* "There is much more to it than that, of course. And, since I am a wallflower at these dances and parties, I shall have ample time to explain more of it this evening, if you so wish."

Sophie smiled. "I do so wish. And thank you for not insisting on returning to the matter of my surname."

Leonora blinked. "To be truthful, I had quite forgotten about it. I take it you were referring, then, to why you are not using the name Ulfeldt?"

"Yes, that is part of it. Although it wasn't even my own doing."

"I do not understand."

"That is because you are not the daughter of my mother. It was she who compelled me to keep my name Rantzau, so that the estates in my father's name would not be so easily subsumed into the growing treasury of the Ulfeldt family. And also to ensure that my name did not strike the ear of your father with an immediate spark of pain and annoyance."

Hearing those words, Leonora felt her very own spark of pain. "Well, that is truly said."

Sophie's hands flew to her mouth. "Oh, Leonora, I am so sorry. I was too deeply involved in my own regrets. I forgot that you, too—"

"There is nothing to be sorry for. The dissolution of my betrothal to Corfitz Ulfeldt is past and done. Do not trouble yourself with any thoughts of it. I don't," Leonora lied.

Sophie's eyes remained upon her, gentle but steady. "You are a strong young woman, Leonora, and driven by a quiet but firm will that many might miss. I can even imagine it extends to embrace the idea that one finds in so many of the up-time attitudes, and in their later writings: that a woman need not be defined by any man, not even her spouse or father. A fearsome thing for many of this world. Conversely, it is a refreshing, even life-saving, freedom to a few of us. But I wonder—"

Leonora heard that last fragment of a sentence for what it was: a baited hook, which, if inquired after, would catch her on a question she might regret. But as ever, her curiosity was greater than her fear: "What is it that you wonder?"

"Whether any girl, at the age of eleven, has ever been completely indifferent to having a betrothal struck aside by her royal father? And to a powerful man who, I am told, showed as much affection toward you as he ever has toward anyone else."

Yes, as much as that was. And would have been more properly avuncular, since he is more than twice my age. "It was a disappointment, yes, but even then, I realized that although father's first thought was to protect himself and the throne, his nullification of our betrothal was a blessing to my future happiness." She leaned back, vaguely remembered that if she did not triumph over her annoying, mousy brown hair, she could not countenance going to tonight's party at all. "I remember quite clearly when my father's first agents returned from Grantville, just before summer, 1633. Corfitz, who had been his favorite courtier, had not only been a traitor to him in the other world, but the documents revealed that he had already commenced pursuing the earliest of those same treacheries in this one. There was no explaining the future events as a sad set of unfortunate circumstances in which some combination of flawed perception and momentary lapses of integrity had led him down a path that history contrived to paint in unflattering hues. No, his flaws of character were revealed to be many and monstrous. Indeed, in retrospect, much of the wit and charm with which he had captivated my father upon his arrival in court had barely masked a scheming mind overwhelmingly shaped by two principles: ruthlessness and ambition."

"I have heard," Sophie ventured, "that although he has committed no overt crime against the throne, your father's rejection of him has made him so vituperative and disruptive in the *Rigsrad* that it might be best if he were to be banned from it. Given that the new trade and cooperative industries with the up-timers are bringing Denmark far more silver than Corfitz's own fiscal proposals, there are very likely enough sympathetic nobles to make such a dismissal possible."

"Yes. I have heard the same things whispered," Leonora said with a nod. "But I suspect that my father has reservations about doing so."

"Your father is, of course, quite politically prudent."

Yes, Sophie, he is. But prudence is not why he has foresworn what would amount to a public crucifixion of Corfitz Ulfeldt. The question is, should I share the actual reasons with you? Are they too hurtful? And will the subjectivity of memory—my memory—do them justice?

As if magically summoned by that final concern, her memory seemed to wipe away her sight, expanding and unfolding until, quite suddenly, she was in that past moment, almost a year ago this very day...

Chapter 24

Oranjestad, St. Eustatia

Leonora remembered the quiet servant who came to her room, delivering a summons that interrupted her preparations for another party, the one her father had held to honor her and Anne Cathrine before they departed for the New World. Ironically, it was her father who was now demanding that she immediately make her way down to his private audience chamber.

When she had arrived, flushed and slightly winded, he had smiled and guided her by the hand—for he always treated her like a shy little girl—to her customary seat, the one right next to Anne Cathrine's. But this time, the room was empty except for herself and her father.

At first she wasn't sure why he had summoned her. That his conversation did not plough immediately and directly to the topic at hand was nothing new. Christian IV was in his element when discoursing passionately upon three topics at the same time, leaping back and forth between them and integrating his arguments with insights that were as often illogical as they were inspired, leaving his audience with the impression that he was part savant and part madman. But today, Leonora's royal father was rambling among, not hunting after, his subjects. Had she not known better, she might have suspected she was witnessing the first signs of a decline into dotage.

But his lack of vigorous direction was a reflection of the multifaceted misgivings and uncertainties that occupied his ruminations that day. He began by muttering vaguely about history—that what is recorded about the past is not the full story of that past, and may often show some persons in a better light than they deserve, and others far worse. Without segue, he veered into revealing that he had begun to give serious thought to setting aside his mistress, Vibeka Kruse. Although he did not explain the topical connection, Leonora knew it well enough from her own readings of the up-time histories. Vibeka Kruse was a viperous enemy to all of the children Christian IV had with other women, but most particularly those of Leonora's own mother, Kristen Munk. And, just as the up-time histories had opened his eyes to the true character of Corfitz Ulfeldt, so too had it swept aside any self-delusions that he could actually effect some rapprochement, or at least modus vivendi, between Kruse and his children.

Her father had fallen silent after once again affirming that he felt great ambivalence about using these future histories to judge those around him. After staring moodily into his empty goblet for the better part of a minute, he startled her by bursting out with: "I did him a favor by dismissing him, you know. A favor."

"Who, father?" Leonora asked with a blink, knowing precisely whom he was referring to. "You did who a favor?"

Christian IV looked away, and she knew the expression on his face all too well: furtive and guilty, like a toddler caught perpetrating some naughtiness. Whether that guilt was in reaction to ruining Ulfeldt's career or for breaking Leonora's betrothal to him was unclear until he spoke again. "By dismissing Corfitz Ulfeldt, I saved him. In the other world, I gave that wolf a taste of royal blood and he came to crave it for himself. I was so pleased by his wit, so pleased that he seemed to like you, that I did not stop to see what I should have suspected: that it was all calculation and connivery."

And she had thought: *Yes, you were so pleased to learn that even your half-ugly duckling might now be wed someday. Pleased even though the man who was supposedly attracted to her was twenty-four, that the glow of royal approval was heating his ambitions to a tumultuous boil, and that the object of his supposed affection was only nine years old. Could you possibly have thought that his interest in me was anything but* political?

But Leonora had long before learned to school her features to impassive attentiveness, and when her father stole a glance to judge her reaction, he learned nothing. He looked away again before continuing. "My overeager embrace of him was irresponsible. Conferring royal favor upon an overambitious man is like handing a drink to a drunkard: you are encouraging his worst behavior. For the sake of his own soul, to say nothing of the health of Us and Our State, it is better that he becomes a bitter anti-royalist. Even though he continues to pour almost treasonous accusations into the public ear from his seat in the *Rigsrad*. The other course of history, in which We kept him close to Our chest and Our favor, led to his becoming a traitor entertaining plots of regicide."

Having shared his thoughts, he sat staring at the wall. He did not ask her opinion of what he had said, nor how she felt about having her betrothal and future plans evaporate at one snap of His Royal Fingers. Several very long minutes of silence passed before he rose, muttering about servants who couldn't even keep their king's goblet full, and stalked off in search of refreshment. He never returned to the chamber and, in consequence, she arrived late for her own party.

But that had not been the end of her education in regard to Corfitz Ulfeldt, although in some ways it marked the beginning of her education about her up-time self. A subject in which she was uniquely self-taught. But that memory—of receiving the book that was to guide her through all those unhappy studies—was so unpleasant that it catapulted her out of recollections and back into present perception.

Sophie was watching her calmly, but there was a hint of concern in her gray eyes.

"I am sorry," Leonora said. "I was ... remembering what my father said about Corfitz."

"I see."

Do you? Leonora wanted to say more, to explain so many things to her much older friend, but she couldn't—not until the air was clear between them. Which she undertook with a lack of preamble that startled even her. "I must begin by apologizing, Sophie. For the opinion I held of you back then, when your mother was our governess, and you came to visit."

Sophie waited while Leonora struggled to find a way forward and the courage to follow it. "Yes?" she said.

"Sophie—my sister Sophie, that is—assured me that you were now betrothed to . . . to Corfitz Ulfeldt. That I had been . . . replaced by you."

Sophie's look of surprise was utterly genuine. "What? No! There had been some earlier talk of that, if I recall, but I refused outright. He was . . ." She seemed to be grasping after a word that would not come to hand. "He was . . ."

"—too plain?"

"Heavens, no! I mean yes, he was not, erm, a man memorable for his looks. But that was not what decided me against any suit from him. He was too . . . too clever."

Leonora frowned. "And you would reject a man seeking your hand because he was too *clever*?"

Sophie sighed. "His cleverness was often in bending words so that, although what he said was not untrue, nor was it clear, complete, or forthright. 'Too clever' was not the right way to describe him; he was too *shrewd*. But to return to your question, no, Leonora; Corfitz did not visit me to press a suit of his own. He was sent to plead the case of his brother, Laurids."

"Your late husband?"

"Yes. Did you not know that was why Corfitz visited me? To act as the liaison between us?"

Leonora frowned and looked down. "I did not. And my sister Sophie told me differently."

The Norn-Sophie's small answering frown gradually became a small smile. "Ah. So it was she who told you that Corfitz was seeking my hand. To make you jealous."

"Yes. And . . . and that is the only one of her many ploys against my happiness that ever succeeded."

"Dear Leonora, why did you not simply ask me about this, then or since? I would have made the truth of the matter quite clear."

Leonora squirmed. "Because—because at that time, you were the Two Sophies." When her friend's eyebrows raised high and quizzical, she hastily added, "That is what *she* called the two of you, at any rate. And she claimed to have your confidence and love besides. You were the sister she wished she had, she said."

Sophie Rantzau shook her head slowly; her long dark hair swayed. "I do not know what I ever said or did to excite such enthusiasm for my person. I was not frequently at court, you may recall. I was an—an impediment to my mother's designs."

"Yet I always saw you with my sister Sophie! You seemed inseparable!"

Sophie may have blushed. "There may be truth to that, but . . . Please understand: I do not wish to insult your sister, Leonora, but that devotion was entirely one-sided."

"You mean she was just following you about?"

Sophie shrugged. "I was twelve or thirteen during the time you relate. She was, I believe, ten? Her interests were in court gossip. Mine were not. Yet my mother encouraged me to spend time with her. And she seemed eager to do just that." Sophie lifted an upward palm. "I did not wish to be cruel, so we were often together."

Leonora leaned forward. "I recall. And I recall you looking serenely on while she taunted me about Corfitz!"

"Is that how you saw it?"

"I did, then. Just as I believed it when she recounted, in great detail, your resounding agreement with her most bitter characterizations of my person."

Sophie's smile was back, but tentative. "And now you know differently?"

Leonora squirmed some more. "Mostly."

"What persists in troubling you about those days, my friend?"

Leonora didn't want to whine, and she succeeded in that—but only because what emerged from her was closer to a wail. "Then why did you not take my side when she tormented me in your presence? I was only eight or nine!"

Sophie nodded. "Yes. I understand. But if, in your presence, she had ever claimed that I was betrothed to Corfitz Ulfeldt, I would have contradicted her immediately and clearly. I do remember her being a most unpleasant older sister to you, but do you recall me ever being present when she made such a claim?"

Leonora thought hard. "Well, . . . no."

"And tell me one other thing, Leonora: if I had in fact defended you, against your own sister, what do you think she would have done in response?"

Leonora stopped. She had never considered that. "I—I am unsure. But I am *quite* sure she would have concocted an even nastier and vindictive attempt to undermine my happiness."

Sophie nodded. "Which was what I foresaw. Had I rebuked her for treating you so, she might have *wished* to make trouble for me, and so, for my mother, but she would not have dared do so. Even at that age, she would have realized how badly that would rebound if its origins in her pettiness had been discovered. However, I was quite sure that she could and find ways to make *your* life far more miserable. Which she eventually did anyhow, by poisoning the next governess' opinion against you, if I recall correctly."

"You do." Leonora's spine slumped against the backrest. "So you—you were protecting me?"

Sophie patted her hand. "I wish I could say that helping you was uppermost in my mind. But I had been warned by my mother not to become close to you or any of your sisters. I realize now that she was simply attempting to prevent any complications that might arise from either affinities or animosities between her child and those of the king. But at the time, I thought it was simply because the relationships among all your siblings were so decidedly—peculiar."

"What a charming new synonym for the word 'unpleasant.' Although Anne Cathrine and I were always true sisters."

Sophie shrugged. "Of which I was unaware until we all traveled here together. She was being thrust into older circles by the time I arrived at the royal castle. Even though I am a year older than she."

The corner of Leonora's mouth quirked. "She was my father's first—and eminently—marriageable daughter. He was prompt in capitalizing upon whatever alliance could be secured by making her the property of some doddering old *adelsmand*. He might also have settled for some younger suitor of lesser means but singular capability and ambition."

Sophie smiled. "That was obviously why he initially welcomed Corfitz's interest in you. Until, that is, the up-timers' histories revealed how your father would be undone by his shrewdness."

"Yes," Leonora mumbled. "About that. There were many things written about these matters in up-time histories. One of which came to light just before we departed and was forwarded to me by my most horrid governess, the one who came after your mother."

"You mean, Hannibal Sehested's sister?"

"The same. She brought me a gift from none other than Vibeka Kruse. An item of historical significance that an agent of hers had located in a private collection in Grantville." She could still see the book as she took it in her wondering hands. *A gift? From Vibeka Kruse? Who barely reads at all? What might this tome be?*

"And what is in this history that makes it worth specific mention?"

"Well, it is not so much a history as an account. And it is not the contents themselves that made it particularly significant for me. It is the author."

Sophie waited a moment, then asked, "And who is the author?"

Leonora drew in a great breath and exhaled it all behind one word: "Me." Leonora had never seen Sophie look surprised. It was quite reassuring, in a petty way.

"You?" her friend murmured. And then smiled. "Ah. Of course. The you who married Corfitz. The you who probably continued to believe that I originally had designs on him for myself."

Leonora squirmed and told herself that she was not a three-year-old. However much she might feel like one at this particular moment. "Evidently, I was never disabused of that belief. Even by my own husband, apparently. And my autobiography was so painstaking in such details that I would certainly have mentioned such a revelation. Which proved to me that history's—and my father's—judgment of Corfitz's character was correct down to the last, despicable particular."

"And so, that Leonora's opinion of Sophie Rantzau never changed."

Leonora closed her eyes. "I confess: it did not. I also freely admit that I think I became a gifted liar.

At least to myself. And I became petty. Well, *more* petty. And that person who I became savored the arch bathos with which I depicted my enemies—either real or perceived." Leonora could barely speak her final judgment, for it was the one that had the most overlap with who she knew herself to be in this world, as well: "I was quite insufferably pleased with myself."

Sophie took the young woman's hands in her own. "And now that you are done excoriating the other you, you should take a moment to thank her."

"For what?"

"For an unintended gift: to see who you *could* become. Because, to the extent that you reject the up-time version of Leonora Christina Christiansdatter, you now have the clearest possible path—a veritable instruction manual—to avoid becoming her." She stood. "Now, unless you feel a need to do so, let us speak no further of this. That is part of a universe that shall never be. Whereas in this world, we shall soon be wanted at a party."

A sudden knock on the door seemed to underscore that reminder.

Sophie's lip curled ruefully. "Again, it is the prerogative of the king's daughter—"

"Yes, yes, Sophie." Louder: "Who knocks?"

"Mr. Michael McCarthy, ma'—er, Lady Leonora."

Sophie and she exchanged quizzical looks: was anyone on St. Eustatia *not* going to come knocking on their door as they were preparing for the party? "Please do come in, Mr. McCarthy."

The up-timer entered, sun hat in hands. Although a singularly grounded and competent man in most situations, and possessed of that peculiar species of confidence that accorded no special place to the title or birth of anyone around him, he seemed ill at ease.

"Ladies, I hope you'll forgive the intrusion. I know you must be trying to get ready for your ball—erm, party. But I've been looking for my friend, Hugh—er, the Earl of Tyrconnell. Someone remarked that one of you might know his whereabouts?"

"Yes," Leonora replied, turned toward Sophie, and saw the surprise, and then suspicion, in response to her young friend's confident assertion.

Leonora turned back to the up-timer. "I am mistaken. But Lord O'Donnell cannot be far. I saw him walking near the infir—the Government House this morning. I remember because his hand was still bandaged."

"From the finger he lost? That's still bothering him? I thought he'd have recovered by now. Is it infected, or—?"

Leonora waved a stilling hand, smiled. "Lord O'Donnell is quite well. Before he was allowed to return to his men on Trinidad, Dr. Brandão himself assessed the injury and pronounced it safe from reinfection. And the doctor is quite expert at assessing and treating injuries in the tropics. Shall we summon someone to help you find the earl?"

McCarthy stepped back. "And wait here in the meantime, keeping two lovely girls from getting to a dance on time? Hell, no—I mean, gosh no, Lady Leonora."

"Then would you be so kind as to allow us to complete preparing for that party?"

He bowed, and backed out. The door shut firmly.

Sophie stared at it. "We should lock it," she observed.

Leonora nodded. "And then pretend we are not here."

Chapter 25

Oranjestad, St. Eustatia

Eddie ended the preliminary dance with his arm around Anne Cathrine's waist and would have happily stayed there for another few seconds. Or maybe an hour.

But the musicians were already launching into another tune: a galliard, he thought it was called, and there was no way he could manage one of those with his prosthesis. Besides, with all that hopping and leaping it looked a little, well, a little too showy. Like kids trying out for the cheerleading squad or to be dancers for the spring musical. Not his speed, even when he had two of his own feet.

Anne Cathrine was already tugging him off the floor. "What's the rush?" he asked.

"Oh, it is this gown!" she complained. "I just had one hem mended and now the other is—ah! There she is!" Anne Cathrine waved at a small group of bystanders among whom he recognized exactly no one.

"Who?"

"The seamstress."

"Seamstress? Here?"

Anne Cathrine finished towing him off the uneven floor of Government House's half-filled great hall. "Yes, here! Eddie, understand: we brought our oldest gowns to the New World because we did not expect to need them, and also thought it quite likely that they would get ruined by—well, by something. So they are falling apart."

"And so you've got a—a seamstress on call?"

"Yes! It is a wonderful idea, isn't it?"

He smiled. "Let me guess: you thought of it."

She swatted him. "Well...not exactly. One of the helpers here suggested it, and I agreed. There were always servants back home to take care of such things, even in the middle of a ball. And this puts some additional money into the community!" She slipped from his arm, turned, kissed his ear, whispered two words which immediately made him conscious that these formal pants were waaayyy too formfitting, and with a grin that had the slightest hint of a leer, dashed off to get her gown fixed. From where Eddie stood, admiring her go, there was absolutely nothing wrong with her attire. At that same instant, he realized that appreciating Anne Cathrine's appearance wasn't helping his "pants situation" in the least.

He turned a sharp right face and marched himself over to the least stunningly dressed among all the most prominent guests. "Gentlemen," he said by way of greeting as the music started once again. One dance and the musicians were already improving how they worked with one another.

"Eddie!" exclaimed van Walbeeck. "Freed at last from the delicious clutches of your wife?"

Tromp put a cup—well, a lopsided clay mug—of

punch in the up-timer's hand. "No rum," he murmured in assurance.

"Commodore!" barked Mike McCarthy as he snapped a fairly crisp salute.

"Aw, c'mon, Mike; you're twice my age."

"Yeah, but I'm not twice your rank," rebutted the mission's master mechanic. Although, more broadly, Eddie and everyone else knew that his real title ought to be Go-To Guy for Technical Problems. Particularly for problems that didn't have readily discernible answers.

Hannibal Sehested frowned, glanced at Tromp. "I was under the impression that Mr. McCarthy did not have a rank at all."

Hugh O'Donnell chuckled. "Don Michael is just— what's that expression of yours?—pulling Eddie's leg."

"Ah," murmured Sehested, who was watching as various volunteers began converging on the main entrance. They were all men, and none of them were small.

Bouncers, Eddie thought with a grin. And actually, in the sense of ensuring some measure of crowd control, that was the job they'd soon be performing.

Van Walbeeck was watching them also, nodding approvingly. "All Lady Anne Cathrine's doing, you know."

Eddie choked on his punch. "What? The bouncers?"

"The what?" they all asked.

Except Mike; he laughed, explained, "The men getting ready to open the doors and make sure we don't have a stampede."

"Ah!" answered van Walbeeck. "Yes, them: her idea. It was inevitable, though, given her other orders."

"Her other orders?"

"Why, yes; didn't she tell you? She was the one who

realized if everyone was allowed in at once, it would be madness. But she also realized that the normal order of entrance at the entertainments hosted by aristocrats would not be suitable here."

"Huh?" said Eddie.

"Quite right," agreed Sehested, who probably had more experience with such events than the rest of the group put together. "Normally, the less prominent guests are admitted first."

Mike McCarthy frowned. "Yeah, so that the big shots have an audience to 'ooh' and 'ahh' over their entrance."

Sehested frowned but continued. "However, here, all may attend, so there is no practicable way to follow that convention. Besides, she rightly foresaw that once all the attendees are within—or under the pavilions—the persons of prominence will have no respite."

"You mean from us smelly, unwashed masses?" Mike almost growled.

Sehested turned toward him. "No, Mr. McCarthy, from the unremitting torrent of introductions and requests that will surely consume the rest of their evening."

Van Walbeeck jumped in before Mike could reply. "Lady Anne Cathrine foresaw that and other potential problems, and saw that the answer lay in how the entry of attendees could be structured to answer all of them."

"I'm all ears," grumbled Mike.

Van Walbeeck smiled congenially. "If the most prominent attendees were to have any time to themselves—such as we are having this very moment—it had to take place before the actual festivities began. And while we were here, having small samples of the refreshment, and, in the case of those so inclined, dancing, the volunteers had practice performing all the functions that they must soon perform for twenty times more people."

Mike nodded irritably. "And the musicians got a chance to get their act together. Mostly."

"Precisely! Now, here is the further genius of her plan. The sound of the music drifts out into the area surrounding Government House, not only working like a siren song but priming those who have gathered outside for the festivities." The second dance concluded; that time, there had been no musical train wrecks. "And now, we shall see her concluding masterstroke."

Van Walbeeck gestured toward the doors, just as the bouncers—because that was what they really were, damn it—threw them wide and stood in the openings, hands raised until the crowd quieted and the simple instructions were given: women first.

Given the speed and numbers with which females of all ages started flooding through those entrances, Eddie surmised that his amazing wife had probably instructed the volunteers circulating among the pavilions to make preparatory announcements to the crowd.

As the torrent of ladies increased, the dancers came off the floor quickly, as much to cede it to newcomers as to avoid being trapped in a rapidly growing throng. Two of the last to escape were Leonora and Rik Bjelke. Eddie didn't recognize his sister-in-law for a moment because the galliard seemed to have transformed her. He had never seen her so flushed, loose-limbed, and frankly radiant as, arm slipped through Rik's, they rushed over to join the group.

Van Walbeeck led an impromptu round of applause for their performance, which of course no one had seen. "You are grace personified, Lady Leonora!"

"And you are an inveterate, if completely dear and charming, liar," she giggled in response.

Eddie wondered if instead of being nonalcoholic, Tromp had slipped him a cup with a double shot in it. Because clearly, his senses were beginning to deceive him. Leonora *giggling*? What was next? The Second Coming?

There was a different miracle occurring, though: the musicians had completed the last dance without any perceptible wobbles, let alone disasters. They started the next piece almost immediately: the rhythm was slow and stately but you could tell that it was going to pick up. Ladies collected in groups, those who were familiar with the steps helping those who were not as they began to dance together. Which seemed like a really good idea to Eddie, since most men were such awful dancers.

A few of the other notable personages in the great room decided to join in. Governor Warren's and Lieutenant Governor Jeafferson's entire families recognized the tune and took to the floor with glad cries, recalling times past. Councilor Coapland was drawn in by the St. Christophers' contingent. And, entering along with the rest of the women was Sophie Rantzau, who was a striking figure in flowing white. But she took one look at the dancing and swerved away, to the side of the hall opposite Eddie.

Hugh saw her, too: she was impossible to miss. But Eddie had the distinct feeling that the Irishman would have spotted her even if she had been shrunk to half her size and rendered invisible by ancient Norse magic. O'Donnell put aside the punch he had been nursing and clapped a hand on Eddie's shoulder. "You'll excuse me, gentlemen. I believe I hear my name being called."

Tromp looked around, baffled. "I hear no such summons."

Eddie smiled at his big friend and drawled, "I didn't know you could hear with your eyes, Hugh."

Hugh's smile widened. "I'm a man of many strange and unexpected talents, Eddie. Be well; I'm off." And he was, striding across the great hall toward the tall figure in white.

Mike was grinning after him, took a glass of punch. "Well, we always seem to talk politics at these shindigs, so let's get to it. I'm not staying long."

Sehested frowned. "I'm sorry if our sharp words have disinclined you from enjoying the festivities."

He glanced at the Danish nobleman in surprise. "Has nothin' to do with it—although those are kind words and I appreciate them, Lord Sehested. In point of fact though, if I stayed, I might dance. And I don't dare do that."

"Come, come," protested van Walbeeck. "I have the musical sensibilities of a rockslide, Mr. McCarthy, and even I shall assay a gavotte, when one is finally played."

Mike shook his head. "Not afraid to cut a rug." He saw the confused stares. "I'm fine with dancing. But I'm a married man."

"Surely," Sehested said, "that does not preclude the purely social dances done in groups, though?"

Mike shrugged. "I try to keep my life simple. To do that, I live by simple rules. The rule tonight is, if you can't scratch an itch, then don't go where you're going to be tickled by feathers. Like the ones that some of the ladies are wearing in their hair tonight." He glanced at Eddie. "So what are the topics du jour?"

Eddie shook his head. "Sorry, Mike: no confidential confabs tonight. Too risky, now."

"Killjoy," Mike groused.

"OPSEC," Eddie corrected.

"I beg your pardon?" asked Sehested.

Eddie grinned. "Sorry, 'OPSEC' is shorthand for operational security. Spies are going to be thick here, now."

"You have intercepted some already?"

"Not yet."

"Then how do you know any will hear us this night?"

"I don't. But we've got to assume that, with all the people passing through here in the past three days, at least one would be willing to trade information for coin. After all, spies are to Spain what corn is to Kansas...Uh, well, would have been." That didn't help. "Spies are to Spain what wine is to Italy."

Expressions of sudden understanding quickly transformed into wide grins.

Van Walbeeck struck one heel upon the floor. "Secrets can wait, but celebration cannot. We are alive, gentlemen. Starvation is a distant memory and all is well with us and our little corner of the world. Besides, there is a segment of our population that would have revolted had we not had a party!"

Sehested glanced at the lively dance floor. "The ladies were so insistent?"

"Ladies? My dear Sehested, I fear that your mind is so filled with the calculus of logistics, statecraft, and keeping your mercurial monarch pleased, that the simple math of our local reality has eluded you." In response to the Danish aristocrat's puzzled gaze, van Walbeeck threw wide the hurricane shutters and gestured outside. They all looked.

They saw a sea of faces. Flushed faces. Eager faces. Male faces.

At least three for every woman now inside the hall.

The song ended, the dancers clapped their appreciation, and the doormen began to lift the bars that had shut the doors against the male horde waiting just beyond the threshold.

"And now, gentlemen," Tromp murmured, "behold bedlam."

Chapter 26

Oranjestad, St. Eustatia

Anne Cathrine was not a particularly pious person. She felt that, when it came right down to it, God—if there really was one—had a great deal of unpleasantness and injustice to answer for. But this night, she was tempted to believe in deity, because it certainly seemed that her prayers had been answered.

Hugh and Sophie had been dancing for almost an hour. Between their exertions—they were both thrillingly sure-footed—and the music, they only spoke intermittently and in short bursts. But the discourse of their eyes would have been plain to a blind man. And when they did speak, Sophie was either smiling or laughing.

Sophie was laughing: her head back, her fine throat stretched up as if she was finally breaking above water that had been drowning her. And even as the breath was rushing out of her in peals of mirth, her friend knew that she was also gasping greedily at the first breaths of life-giving air her Norn heart had known in years.

Anne Cathrine dabbed away a tear of joy from the corner of one eye, marched over to Eddie, grabbed his arm, and tugged him toward the dance floor, never giving him a chance to resist or refuse.

Sophie watched Hugh go to get them refreshment, fanned herself with a long hand. *This* was dancing. Without eyes watching, measuring, judging. Without having to worry who she must partner with and who she must not, which dances were appropriate and which were ill advised. It was a perfect moment—

"Lady Sophie?"

She started, knew the voice before she turned to welcome the unwelcome intruder upon her reveries. "Lord Sehested. Are you enjoying the evening?"

"I am, although not so much as I enjoy seeing others enjoy it." He edged closer. "There is no courtly way to broach this topic, but I have admired your composure and resolve to remain aloof from the uncharitable comments and...and speculations that I have heard, even here, in relation to your mother. Particularly in light of how many of those same calumnies touch upon your good self, as well. With no basis, I know, but it must be quite difficult to—"

"There you are!" cried Leonora, who ran up with Rik Bjelke in tow. It was unclear whether she was on his arm, or he on hers. "Come with us! The musicians have finished resting, the lazy louts! The floor is filling, even now."

Sophie struggled to keep her composure, emotionally whipsawed between the ominous knowledge that Sehested clearly possessed about her past, and the adolescent enthusiasm of her oblivious friend.

Leonora did not wait for a reply but tugged on her arm. "There is dancing again! Come!"

Sophie allowed herself to be pulled away from Sehested. Away from the prospect of being forced to relive the wounds and disgrace that, until this moment, she thought she had left behind in Denmark. But clearly, she had not.

She did not look back at Lord Sehested as she joined Leonora and Rik and told herself that she must not vomit.

Across the dance floor, Eddie saw Hannibal Sehested approach Hugh, who was carrying two drinks and looking around, expectant. As the Danish noble launched earnestly into whatever topic he meant to press upon the Irish earl, the much taller man began to scan the great room, evidently looking for the vanished Sophie. Granted, there were a lot of ladies wearing some shade of white (including age-yellowed) that evening, but none so strikingly as Sophie Rantzau. Or so it seemed to Eddie.

Which was why he was able to quickly pick her out of the crowd on his own side of the room, the musicians blocking Hugh's line of sight to her.

But she had clearly positioned herself where she could see him and Hannibal Sehested. Actually, from the way she was peering between the musicians, it looked like she was furtively watching the two of them with something like apprehension or even terror. When Sehested eventually nodded farewell and departed, she recoiled, almost bumping into a volunteer bringing in a fresh bowl of punch. Flustered, she moved further away with long, accelerating strides—

"Eddie! Will you not save me from Governor van Walbeeck?"

He looked around, saw his laughing wife abandoning the very red governor who seemed loath to leave the dance floor. Anne Cathrine's escape ended with her grabbing his arm, glistening and beaming. "Jan is relentless!"

Van Walbeeck's smile was huge. "I am inspired by my company and overjoyed at this evening's success! Who would ever *want* to stop dancing?"

"I would," Anne Cathrine almost giggled, "unless my husband is ready again."

"Well, I—"

"Oh, come, come, young Cantrell! If your limbs are weary, put some spirit back into them!" He apparently meant that literally; he handed Eddie a mug of punch.

"Governor? I don't drink. Remember?"

Van Walbeeck smacked his forehead so sharply that half of the surrounding merrymakers stopped to see what that loud, meaty slap had been. "Apologies, my dear Eddie! It seems unnatural to me, that any man should foreswear those natural spirits that raise our own!" He glanced thoughtfully back at the impromptu down-time equivalent of an open bar. "And such a marvelous diversity of spirits has certainly heightened mine an extra measure!"

"It seems you are not alone," Tromp observed, watching couples stumbling and laughing as they re-paired for the next *allemande courante*. "I suspect such high spirits shall lead to spirited courtship."

Inspecting a newly arrived bottle of calvados, van Walbeeck chuckled at his friend's comment. "Ironic, how all these different expressions of 'spirit' were made possible by our Spanish antagonists. Although certainly not willingly."

Eddie laughed. As he prepared to follow his wife out to the dance floor, he quipped, "Yeah; I wonder how *their* spirits are, right about now?"

Chapter 27

Santo Domingo, Hispaniola

Admiral Fadrique Álvarez de Toledo poured his first glass of rioja almost to the rim. It recalled the manners of a peasant, not a *hidalgo*, but right now, he didn't care.

To his right, Don Eugenio de Covilla, a captain who had proven invaluable during the previous year, raised an eyebrow but said nothing. Well bred and even better educated, he was judicious enough to genuinely respect his superiors, his elders, and those who held his fate in the palm of their hands. Which meant that he showed Álvarez three times the deference he might have shown another man.

To the left, another captain, Manrique Gallardo, had not even waited for the others to fill their own glasses, and so make a toast. He was already slurping noisily at his own liberal portion. *Another hidalgo in name only*, Álvarez concluded silently. Of course, there were far more of those in the New World than the real article.

At the other end of the oval table, their host,

Governor and Captain-General Juan Bitrian de Viamonte y Navarra, glanced briefly at Gallardo and then at Álvarez with a look of amused resignation. Gallardo was a capable soldier and there was a silver lining to his ignorance or impatience regarding the manners of polite society; he was utterly frank and unstinting in his reports and assessments. For which he'd been included in this gathering.

De Covilla glanced at his host. "Shall we begin, Your Excellency?"

Don Juan Bitrian de Viamonte nodded, suppressing a shiver despite the still, sultry night. There was no breeze off the bay, and in the streets beyond the compound of the Governor's Villa, the voices were loud and irritable. Tempers were short and emotions ran close to the surface when the humidity reached such levels.

De Covilla waited for de Viamonte's almost spasmodic trembling to subside. Fadrique stared at his wineglass but through it, was able to assess his friend's health.

After an absence of three months, it was little changed, at least so far as he could tell. The left arm looked slightly more shriveled, but on the other hand, his color had improved and he seemed to have more energy. He had inquired after the nature of Juan's ailment during his time in Havana, and learned that it had not been congenital as he had speculated but the strange result of a small wound received in combat over a decade ago. It usually did not make itself felt as anything other than a nuisance, but would occasionally send fevers and chills through him which, at their worst, might confine him to bed for a week. De

Viamonte always recovered, but always a little weaker than before.

His shivers either fading or mastered, the invalid governor's eyes snapped over to catch Fadrique, as if to say, *caught you looking*! Álvarez simply let a small, sad smile crumple his lips.

De Viamonte's gaze did not waver. "Normally I would ask Captain de Covilla to provide us with any updates. However, Admiral Álvarez de Toledo has not only received and reviewed the latest intelligence, but is newly returned from Havana, where he was often closeted with Governor Gamboa. So I suspect he best knows the order in which we might most profitably consider the new challenges before us."

Fadrique nodded, thinking: *That may prove to be the most dubious honor that has ever been conferred upon me.* Because there was no jest nor irony in his voice when, eyes still upon de Viamonte's, he asked frankly, "Your Excellency, I know that you have been occupied with many matters here on Hispaniola, so I shall address those matters with which you are least likely to be fully familiar." He sighed. "Which is to say, which disaster would you prefer me to detail first?"

Even Gallardo stopped slurping his rioja. "It is as bad as all that, sir?"

De Viamonte, maintaining formality since there were subordinates present, simply waved two pale fingers in Fadrique's direction. "Admiral, you may proceed as you think best."

Fadrique folded his hands and leaned forward over the reports. "La Flota has been lost. Entirely."

Gallardo's mouth hung open for a moment before he snapped it shut. De Covilla's response was hawkeyed attention; he'd heard the basic news, no doubt, but not the specifics. Which Fadrique did not need to follow on the papers before him; he knew them by heart. Would probably never forget them as long as he lived.

"We do not have all the details of how it happened, or the final fate of several of the ships which escaped, but here is what we do know..."

He set it all before them: the galleons sunk, the hulls suspected as having been taken, the number of estimated survivors who presumably were still marooned on a pair of small islands off the southeast tip of Guadeloupe.

De Covilla leaned forward. "Admiral, a question if I may."

Fadrique waved casual permission. "A pleasant formality, asking allowance to speak or inquire. These matters are too serious to cling to such frippery. You may both"—he caught Gallardo's eye as well—"speak when and as you wish."

De Covilla nodded polite gratitude. "How do we have this intelligence, sir? Spies? Our...auxiliaries?" He stiffened as that sanitized euphemism for *pirate* slipped through his rigid lips.

Álvarez shook his head. "No. There were three pataches with the Plate Fleet. They escaped."

"They did not fight?" Gallardo asked indignantly.

Maybe you're not as smart as Juan claims. "Had they fought, they would have died, and we would only now be wondering if possibly the fleet had been late leaving Seville. As it is, not all of them survived the experience. One was especially bold in keeping the enemy fleet in sight, and once La Flota's survivors had been marooned, tried to slip in under cover of night to reclaim the most senior among them to convey back here."

Álvarez waved a fly away from his wine. "All they achieved was their own deaths. A Dutch jacht had apparently been detailed to keep surreptitious watch for just such an attempt. It had the advantage of the wind gauge, guns, and surprise. The outcome was never in question.

"Fortunately, the other two patache captains were more prudent than daring and returned with what they saw. Their information is incomplete. But we do know this: the enemy took great pains to capture rather than sink our ships. We must presume they are being repaired and will be used by the Dutch."

De Viamonte frowned. "I would have thought the United States of Europe would have claimed and crewed the majority of those prizes. It was their steamships which, according to the account, were the true source of our defeat, and their ports are not blockaded."

"Neither are the Dutch ports. Not anymore," Fadrique explained.

"There has been a change in the status of the Netherlands?"

"There has indeed. In addition to persisting in styling himself as King in the Lowlands, Philip IV's brother has taken further steps which suggest he is consolidating those lands as his own. Including some kind of detente with the Dutch and their Stadtholder General, Prince Hendrik Fredrik."

"So they have begun sending supplies and new forces to the Caribbean?"

The admiral shrugged. "If so, we have yet to get wind of it. But they might be on their way or already arrived."

Gallardo frowned. "But are we not watching St. Eustatia, and for that very reason: to determine when and if they begin to receive reinforcements and supplies?"

De Covilla leaned forward, waited for Fadrique's nod. "Watching St. Eustatia has proven problematic. We strongly suspect that Tromp's home fleet is there, but he, with limited assistance from the English on St. Christopher, maintains a patrol that screens those islands. In the past six months, we have lost two packets probing them. Between the high ground from which to observe all approaches, highly refined optics, and radio communications which guide their patrols to intercept our ships, the heathens have thwarted our efforts at reconnaissance. We have, instead, contacted and recruited confidential agents through intermediaries."

Gallardo growled. "You mean, through the pirates we've retained."

De Covilla shrugged. "If they flew our colors, what good would they do us in this matter? Besides, after the admiral"—he nodded toward Álvarez—"all but expunged the English presence on St. Christopher's eight years ago, the population had no choice but accustom themselves to such visitors. The only regular trade that colony could count upon was with independent ships that flew no colors and held no allegiance."

"In other words, as I said: pirates," Gallardo summarized.

De Covilla nodded, turned to Álvarez. "There is one factor I find puzzling about the interception of the Plate Fleet. How did these so-called 'allies' know when and where to find it? La Flota's point of landfall varies, and the date of its arrival is subject to the many vicissitudes of both politics and weather."

Fadrique tidied the papers that he did not need to consult. "Although the lowest in La Flota's chain of command, the captains of the escaped pataches offered some insight into those matters. Last November, His Excellency Governor Riaño y Gamboa sent three advice boats from Havana to Seville to convey word of the USE steamships and the havoc they wrought at the Battle of Grenada. That report startled and worried both the persons responsible for organizing this year's Plate Fleet as well as Philip, who, it is said, was angered by Olivares' initial dismissal of it as 'alarmist.'"

Gallardo frowned again. "Did the duke doubt its veracity?"

Álvarez shrugged. "Patache captains are not privy to such details, Captain. However, I suspect that Olivares' reaction was not motivated by any profound dispute with the contents of our report."

"Then why would he dismiss it as overwrought?"

Fadrique was not about to answer so pointed a question, not after having run afoul of Olivares earlier in his career. He glanced at de Viamonte, whose difficulties with the duke had been less pointed, and whose infirmities emboldened him much in the way a clearly mortal wound inspires otherwise prudent men to acts of suicidal bravery.

De Viamonte saw the look and smiled. "Captain Gallardo, when the up-timers developed their steamships for use in the Baltic, King Philip was assured that their ambitions did not extend to the waves of the wider ocean. And the person who spoke these assurances, often with less information than conjecture, was none other than Don Gaspar de Guzmán y Pimentel Ribera y Velasco de Tovar, comte d'Olivares et duc de Sanlucar la Mayor." He nodded as Gallardo's eyes narrowed. "So, you see now."

The gruff captain nodded. "I see that Olivares can't admit to the full danger upon us now, without making his earlier advice look idiotic—and himself an ass for spoon-feeding it to our king."

Fadrique took a moment to admire Juan's ability to show Olivares' self-interest and incompetence merely by acquainting Gallardo with the facts. That was why Juan was a statesman and he wasn't. It would have taken him the better part of a day to figure out a way to do what Juan did by reflex, and without uttering a single politically risky word.

"So," Álvarez resumed, "while the report sent to Spain raised concerns, they did not center upon La Flota's arrival in the New World, but what it might encounter afterward. Accordingly, the doctrine for landfall was unaltered: the ships of both the New Spain and Tierra Firme fleets were to remain together while the pataches went ahead to scout the first stretch of each fleet's respective course. The objective was to enter the Caribbean swiftly and undetected. No one was thinking about the possibility of interception.

"As to why Dominica was chosen as the point to make landfall? Firstly, it is one of the most common islands used for that purpose. Its height makes it an excellent landmark for correcting any minor navigational errors; it is detectable from almost seventy miles into the Atlantic. Secondly, news of the Battle of Grenada and the allied fleet's presence in that area was given serious consideration by the planners. It disinclined them to pursue alternatives such as breaking off the Tierra Firme fleet earlier to make landfall near

Trinidad, or to risk sending it through the constricting clutter of the Grenadines.

"It is not clear why they chose not to make landfall further north. However, the patache captains relate overhearing conversations which supported our projection that Tromp had established himself in the Leeward Islands, particularly because our probes there prompted his move against Santo Domingo. It is presumed that La Flota's planners were of the same opinion.

"Taken in sum, these many concerns resulted in La Flota being directed to enter the Caribbean between Guadeloupe and Martinique. Which is just where our enemies were waiting."

"So they committed so much time, energy, and concentration of assets on the hope that they had guessed our own projections so accurately?"

Fadrique shrugged. "Doubtful. It is likely they had confidential agents watching preparations being made in Spain, even shadowing the fleet as it left. From that information alone, they could have had confirmed their hypotheses on our actions this year, committed them to the plan they had been preparing."

De Viamonte nodded, added, "We can expect greater details at our next meeting. Just yesterday, one of our patrols watching the Anegada Passage and surrounding waters notified me that they had discovered some of La Flota's survivors who had escaped and survived a perilous journey by small boat. One of the patrol's boats brought word to us. The other conveyed the survivors to Puerto Rico."

Gallardo frowned. "Why not here? A boat that carries news of survivors could have carried them to us just as well."

De Viamonte held up a hand that stilled Gallardo like a dog told to heel. "It is quite likely they needed to recuperate before yet another voyage. I expect we shall have them and their depositions soon enough. But frankly, those details, while informative, do not materially affect our planning. Because the real issue that stands before us is not how our enemies captured La Flota, nor even how they knew when and where to find it."

Álvarez heard his cue. "Indeed. Our question must be this: how did we fail to foresee this?"

"Well," Gallardo temporized, "it *is* unprecedented."

"Yes, but therein lies the lesson: taking unprecedented action is proving to be our enemy's *pattern*. They are changing their strategic thought and plans at least as quickly as we adapt. And that is by design, not chance."

De Covilla nodded. "We devise a counter to their strategy, just in time to discover they have shifted their emphasis to a different strategy. In short, we are allowing them to control this war. We are always reacting, not acting."

Gallardo's eyes were carefully focused on his own hands, so that it was unclear to whom he meant to address his muttered interjection. "You tried 'acting' at Vieques. What great victory did that get you?"

De Covilla's retort was swift. "We lost more ships than the enemy, but most of them were pirates."

"And more importantly," de Viamonte added, "it saved this city. They meant to come here and destroy us. The Battle of Vieques compelled them to turn back. But while we are on the topic of our 'auxiliaries,' Don Álvarez de Toledo, I presume this touches upon the other disaster you mean to address?"

"How well you know me, Your Excellency; it does

indeed. Frankly, I am inclined to agree with Captain Gallardo: Vieques was a defeat."

The captain stared at the admiral in stunned disbelief as Juan impatiently waved away Fadrique's assertion. "Historians will bear me out on this matter, Admiral. I will concede that it was not the outcome we had hoped for: pulling the allied protection away from their supply ships so that our privateers might sink them. Which would have crippled their ability to move troops or keep their steamships supplied with ammunition and fuel."

"Now *that* would have been a victory!" Gallardo exclaimed.

De Viamonte smiled indulgently. "I cannot disagree. But we won our survival, and because of that, our foundries and ways have been building weapons and ships for half a year, unmolested. Whatever the future holds, Santo Domingo and Havana have, between them, replaced many of the losses suffered last year and have begun making important changes. Our diving bells have allowed us to recover many of the cannon and other ironworks that we lost in that battle and elsewhere. But I suspect that the admiral does not mean to tell us how Vieques was a disaster, but rather, how that describes the outcome of our attempts to make privateers out of pirates."

Álvarez sipped his wine before beginning. He disliked this topic almost as much as the loss of La Flota. "It was to our advantage that so many of the costs of Vieques were among our privateers. But there is also a heavy cost to us, strategically. They have become far fewer in number and now perceive the arrangement with us to entail far greater risks than they conceived. They also suspect that we always meant to spend their lives far more readily than ours."

Eugenio shrugged. "Well, they are not entirely wrong in that."

"No, but they will not hear the logic that we would never have paid so much silver for their loyalty simply to have so many of them sunk. Which is also true. But they are unconcerned with caveats; they only know what they have lost. And because they fear raiding our enemies and have sworn not to raid us, the price of their cooperation has grown. Alarmingly."

Gallardo frowned. "Is it still worth it?"

De Covilla sighed. "For now, we have little choice."

"Why? What purpose do they serve? Whom have they attacked?"

De Covilla seemed to spend a moment taming impatience. "The privateers are responsible for more than half of the patrols and reconnaissance we conduct beyond our own waters. And without their ships—numerous, lighter, self-sustaining—we would have little to no contact with those who tell us what our foes are doing in their own ports and colonies."

"But they are not sacking such places?"

"Rarely, if ever."

Gallardo looked around the table. "But then how are they surviving? Raiding the few remaining native tribes that persist in the Antilles? And even if they are, I'm quite certain that does not slake their three great thirsts: women, rum, and coin. And did I mention coin? I did? Well, let me say it one more time: *coin*.

"And I'll say this as well: even if they were being supplied with all they desired through the largesse of our treasuries, that would still not make answer to their truest, deepest lusts."

"Which are?" asked de Viamonte.

"As if you need me to tell you, Juan?" Gallardo replied, his use of the governor's given name revealing that the connection between them was more personal than Álvarez had guessed. "Men become pirates not just for material gain, but because they are restless. And because they thrill to the sight of an enemy's blood. It is in their nature." He leaned far back in his seat. "So I will be happy to learn how it is that the impulses of their nature are being sated."

De Viamonte looked around the table. "I too find this puzzling and gladly anticipate a solution to the mystery Captain Gallardo has identified."

De Covilla sat very straight. "As you must surely perceive, Your Excellency, it is not a mystery at all." De Viamonte just stared at him, waiting for a statement that was substantive rather than evasive. "The captain is of course correct," Eugenio resumed. "Pirates are incapable of inaction. It is one of the reasons their crews are likely to depose a prudent and patient captain, no matter how successful his raids might be, and no matter how much of that coin they still have in their pockets."

De Viamonte frowned. "All known to me and in no way a useful response to the question I posed. However, I am certain I shall soon have the answer to how our pirates are being both provisioned and satiated. What I am not at all certain about is why a subordinate is attempting to distract me with declarations of the obvious while his superior allows him to squirm under my gaze rather than furnishing that answer."

And he looked straight at Admiral Fadrique Álvarez de Toledo.

Chapter 28

Santo Domingo, Hispaniola

Álvarez suppressed the reflex to blink in surprise at the governor's sudden stare, then suppressed the reflex to smile at the clever trap his friend had laid for him. *Oh, you sly fox, Juan. So that's why you have Gallardo here. So you do not have to joust with me directly. Very well, I tried to keep the dung from sticking to you, but if you must have it, then have it you shall.*

Fadrique put two scarred fists on the table. "You are very frank. I hope you will not think ill of me if I am frank in asking a question in return."

"And what question would that be?"

"Merely this," Fadrique said slowly. "If I understand the wording and nature of your oath to the king, whatever enters your ear, you are required, in turn, to whisper in his. Is that not so?"

"You know it to be."

"Then I pray you understand my dilemma. Together, we have taken steps that we abhor. None more so than retaining the services of degenerate and godless thieves, murderers, and rapists. But if those who

manage those 'privateers' directly must make further...
accommodations to secure their continued cooperation,
and those details were reported to you, then you
would have to report them to Madrid. And knowing
you as the honorable man that you are, you will take
responsibility for having given us the latitude to act
as we must. And so, if any of those actions should
displease Philip—or Olivares—your position here would
be jeopardized. In fact, it might be in grave doubt."

De Viamonte nodded. "I am aware of this as well.
What I am not aware of is your apparent belief that
it is part of your job to protect me from the consequences of my own oaths of fealty."

"Not just you," muttered de Covilla. "All of us."

Juan frowned. "Now this I do not understand."

"Don da Viamonte," growled Fadrique, "in all my
long years of serving the crown here in the Caribbees,
you are the first person who has occupied this villa
who was a man of principle, intelligence, prudence,
and action. I swear on Our Savior's Own Wounds that
before you, we counted ourselves fortunate to have a
governor with just *one* of those qualities." He raised
his chin. "If we were to lose you to Madrid's wrath
or Olivares' scapegoating, we would not see your like
again. And neither Spain, nor those of us who serve
her in this distant place, can afford a lesser man
than yourself in that chair. For that is surely what
we would get."

De Viamonte's posture had become slightly straighter.
His voice was no longer pointed, but it had not diminished in firmness. "And yet, despite the kindness you
mean to do me and the service you mean to render
to our empire, I ask you: how are the pirates being

sustained in a relationship that is intrinsically antithetical to their very nature? It is my *duty* to know."

De Covilla leaned forward as if to speak, Álvarez waved him back: *no reason to let the young and the valiant sacrifice themselves for the old and the devious.* "The details of our privateers' letters of marque are worded thus: that they 'shall not molest our convoys.'" Fadrique paused. "'Our *convoys*.'"

De Viamonte frowned at the repetition. "So they remain free to attack any of our ships that happen to be traveling alone?"

"The language of the letters of marque does not prohibit it. But bear this in mind also, Don de Viamonte: with the exception of advice packets, we have forbidden the movement of individual ships."

"A provision that has existed for years, and has been ignored for just as long."

"Yet we took pains to repost it in all our ports."

"And in the other viceroyalties and audiencias?"

De Covilla raised his well-manicured hands in a gesture of both uncertainty and powerlessness. "It was communicated to them, along with the rest of our advice and requests that Governor Gamboa echoed last year. But if either Armendáriz in New Spain or de Murga in Cartagena saw fit to publish or promulgate the reminder that ships are forbidden to travel alone, we would never hear of it."

De Viamonte rubbed his eyes for several seconds. "This legal sophistry toes the very brink of validity."

"But it has not fallen over the edge, your Excellency," Álvarez pointed out, "and soon, we hope to be able to extricate ourselves from our disastrous arrangement with these privateers."

De Viamonte nodded. "Because of the larger pataches and even some shallow-draft galleoncetes that are coming off the ways in ports such as Campeche and Portobello."

Fadrique nodded. "Soon, we will no longer require our 'privateers,' and our fleet will grow beyond mere replacements for last year's losses. Spain has accelerated shipbuilding to support us, despite a considerably increased indebtedness. And within the same week that your advice boats arrived there, the crown sent word to the East Indies that a goodly number of Manila galleons are to brave the passage around Cape Horn and add their guns to ours."

He lowered a broad palm to the table. "But this—all these details—do not show the way ahead. Critique is the handmaiden of analysis, but that means doing more than just acknowledging and compiling a list of our failures. They must form the basis of our new strategy, our new action."

He looked into each of the other faces in turn. "Governor Gamboa not only agrees with that principle but has already acted upon it. Because if we are to win this war, we must think far beyond where we shall move our pieces on the game board. We must change the rules by which we have been playing.

"The first way we must do this is to no longer think as though we are the master of the region and every battlefield within it. We most obviously are not, and the longer we refuse to acknowledge that, the deeper the strategic deficit we shall accrue."

Gallardo was nodding. "Impressive words. They make a man want to jump up and take action. But where, and for what reason?"

"Excellent questions, Captain, because they exemplify one of our habits of thought that must be changed." Fadrique steepled his hands. "As long as we deluded ourselves into thinking that the so-called 'allies' were but a nuisance, that we were still the undisputed masters of the New World, we continued to choose targets the way a rich man chooses his meals; what do I feel like today?"

He leaned forward. "Now that we acknowledge that we are no longer so wealthy, we must instead ask: where can I get a meal, even if it is a smaller and meaner one? Because it is only by seizing every opportunity to nourish ourselves with a victory that we are likely to survive.

"Up until now, we have thought in terms of defeating the allies in one or two great battles, believing that our prowess and numbers could not help but carry the day. We have now been proven wrong no less than three times: at Grenada, then off Vieques, and now in the shadow of Dominica. So let us put aside the visions of trying to draw our adversaries into great battles. Such engagements no longer favor us. Quite the contrary."

De Covilla was nodding, eyes narrowed. "So we choose smaller targets and attack them with smaller forces."

De Viamonte shook his head, but was looking at Fadrique. "No, my young captain. I suspect the admiral means that we should choose smaller targets but attack them with massive forces."

Yes, you still think like a military man, my friend, Álvarez thought as he nodded at Juan's emendation. *Why did you never tell me you have worn a morion, too?* "His Excellency sees my meaning with complete clarity."

Gallardo was sitting forward in his chair; his face showed the same vicious species of excitement as a man wagering on a cockfight. "So at what may we strike?"

De Covilla shook his head. "I believe our first step must be to define where we may *not* attack, and why."

The governor nodded. "Precisely. We cannot engage the allies as we did at Grenada, where we were unwitting. Nor can we presume that any of our formations are traveling in complete safety, which was ultimately what led to the defeat at Dominica."

"And surely, we may not hope to engage their steamships in a conventional engagement on the open seas. Even at Vieques, where numbers and darkness were on our side, they proved invincible."

Gallardo looked from one man to the other. "So Gamboa and the admiral say 'attack!' and you are speaking of how we cannot? Do you propose that our new strategy is ultimately to defend rather than sail against our foes?"

Fadrique was beginning to see how Gallardo might grow on a commander. "We speak of where we must defend first so that we may be sure to reserve sufficient forces to keep them safe. And we need no complicated equations to tell us which places we must defend: those cities and strongholds where we build ships and receive supplies from Spain. In short, the places that are most directly and powerfully necessary to our war effort."

"So we are to abandon our smaller cities and colonies?"

"No, but we cannot afford to reduce the forces

we have left—those with which we may attack—by sending any to defend them."

Now de Covilla was steepling his hands. "Frankly, if our adversaries elect to diminish their concentration of force to cripple such secondary targets, they will then lack sufficient mass to attack our true strongholds. And so, in sacrificing one or two such places, we have achieved our essential objective and kept them from mounting major offensives elsewhere."

De Viamonte was frowning. "I have one reservation. Let us take our most fortified city as an example: Cartagena. Even if we turn more of our essential cities into such citadels, is that enough to ensure that they are adequately defended?"

Álvarez laid his hands flat upon the table. "Let us leave aside the matter of procuring more large guns for such defenses, if for no other reason than this: our guns are more likely to deter rather than defeat an allied attack from the sea. Rather, let us concentrate on the decisive factors in determining their ability to protect themselves: do they have ample available materials to create comparable fortifications, and the masses of labor required to build them?"

Juan raised an eyebrow. "You have read what the USE ironclad's guns did to the fortifications at Hamburg less than two years ago?"

Fadrique nodded. "I have."

"And you believe that, for some reason, our fortifications will not succumb to the up-time guns?"

"No. What I believe is that the up-time guns will not have either the same concentration or freedom of action that they did there. Because this is a large sea and they cannot be in all the places they are needed at once. Nor can they expend their special fuel and their special ammunition with the same surety of ready resupply."

De Covilla's smile was satisfied and a little predatory. "Could the up-timers presently destroy any target, even the greatest of our fortified cities, if they dedicated themselves and their resources to that project? Yes. But can they do it in multiple places, and an infinite number of times? The incremental damage we would inflict upon them and the drain upon their special ammunition and fuel tells us the answer is 'no.' And if we are striking at other targets and forcing their steamships to sail hither and thither to repel our forces, they will have less and less freedom to even conceive of such major strikes against us."

"So," said Gallardo, who sounded glad to be returning to the part of the discussion he found most energizing, "where should we be striking to achieve that?"

"Trinidad," de Covilla said flatly, as if it was already decided. "They have been there less than a year, it is quite valuable to them, and we have allies in the local Arawak tribes. Its distance from their center of power in the northern Antilles also makes it vulnerable. If we strike undetected and quickly, their steamships cannot respond before the engagement is decided."

"But if it is so valuable to them, then will they not strive to retake it, even if they can't spare their steamships for the task?" Gallardo was genuinely puzzled.

"All the better," Álvarez said. "We have no particular need to own Trinidad—other than to keep them pinned to it, like a fly mired in the pitch which they so covet. So let them come retake it. And then we shall take it back. And so forth and so on, a constant drain on their time and resources. Besides, it will not be our worry; it will be Cartagena's."

"You mean, the fleet that was sabotaged at Puerto Cabello last year?"

De Covilla nodded. "The same. Happily, their losses were not in ships, but supplies. They hadn't the stores to sail soon enough to meet our fleet at Grenada. They are recovered, now. And at last word, they received orders from the Escorial that they are to carry home their attack this time."

De Viamonte rested his chin into his good hand. "Is it known how the allies determined that the Cartagena fleet was staging out of Puerto Cabello for an attack? Because if that mystery has not been solved, then how may de Murga of Cartagena be certain his efforts will not run afoul of the same impediment this year?"

Fadrique raised a palm. "Like most things that occur along Tierra Firme, it is likely we shall never know the cause. But one of the patache captains from La Flota reported overhearing the admiral of the fleet tell how Olivares had, often and in the hearing of many others, railed against the lack of action against the Dutch captain Thijssen, who was confirmed to have been in Curaçao. Which may well have been the venue by which Trinidad got word of the fleet preparing in Puerto Cabello. So he is being urged to consider Thijssen seriously."

"Very well," de Viamonte affirmed with a nod. "With any luck, the forces from Cartagena should not have to contend with any of the difficulties that they, or we, encountered during our attempt to retake Trinidad last year. Not unless the up-timers have left one of their steamships there, that is."

De Covilla shrugged. "It is difficult to foresee how or why they would do that, Your Excellency. I have done what reading I can of the few technical articles that we have available from the Grantville library, most of which are in the hands of our shipbuilders in Havana. From what I can deduce, their steam engines may burn wood, but cannot operate for very long with that fuel. I suspect they may use coal or oil."

"Oil," mused de Viamonte. "Could they have seized Trinidad to secure Pitch Lake? That bitumen burns, I am told."

De Covilla shrugged. "We do not have complete intelligence on what has been transpiring upon Trinidad, Your Excellency. But what we do have does indeed suggest they have taken it to gain access to the oil that they knew to seek there because of information from their library."

"That damned library will make an end of us yet," growled de Viamonte. Álvarez did not interrupt to point out that although the phrase Juan had chosen was usually used in a figurative context, it might well prove literal in this particular case. "So they *do* plan to use the oil to fuel their ships."

De Covilla's carefully controlled expression suggested he was trying to find a polite way to correct his superior. "That is certainly a possibility, but the more we learn of their mechanisms, the more *unlikely* it is that their steamships were built to burn oil, Your Excellency. You see, oil engines do not readily accept any other form of fuel, whereas a coal engine may burn wood as well.

"In addition to this greater operational flexibility, consider also that Grantville has, from its first arrival, been at great pains to secure sufficient supplies of oil for numerous crucial machines and projects. While it may hope for a different situation in the New World, it is difficult to foresee how or why the USE would build an entire class of ship which requires a fuel source that is, and will for some time remain, unavailable in its home port in Europe. Coal is in more ready supply everywhere, and, although not currently available here, there is certainly no shortage of wood."

Fadrique could not determine whether de Viamonte looked more relieved or vexed at de Covilla's answer. "But then why would they have gone to the trouble and expense of securing Trinidad's oil?"

"Because oil is so precious to them, so essential for the function of so many of their most crucial mechanisms, that they may mean to ship it back to Europe."

"Can they do so in sufficient quantities?"

De Covilla shifted in his seat. "Before the hearing of La Flota's sad fate, I would have said no. At least I would have said, 'not yet.' The USE does not possess a ready excess of hulls that could be tasked to transport oil, certainly not of the right kind."

De Viamonte frowned. "But now you have a different answer? Why? And what does the loss of La Flota have to do with it?"

Fadrique put his forehead in his hands as he realized what de Covilla was driving at, and damned himself for not seeing it until now. "*Madre de dios.* This was part of their plan. That is why they went to such lengths, took such risks, to capture so many of our ships."

He looked up, saw that only he understood what de Covilla was intimating. "Our ships . . . or rather, our naos. Don't you see? They could easily be converted to freight liquids in bulk. And oil is lighter than water, so they will perform more admirably with that filling their holds."

De Viamonte's face was white with suppressed rage. "So *we* provided them with the convoy ships they needed?"

De Covilla's voice was careful. "That would both validate and explain the extraordinary ambition and risks of their plan. Conversely, it would be difficult to believe that our enemy could have spent so much time and care considering all the ramifications of that operation without perceiving that naos could be tasked to provide the means of getting Trinidad's oil to Europe.

"No doubt they would have—and still will—build special hulls to serve in that capacity. But with the Ottomans attacking and the USE's resources stretched thin to answer that southern threat, there could have been a very long delay in realizing that ambition. This, however, is an immediate and elegant solution. Having our naos to transport the oil now is an operational bridge between this moment and the time when their shipbuilding resources may be retasked to create specially crafted oil convoyers."

"Very well," de Viamonte agreed angrily, "let us presume that they seized parts of Trinidad for its oil. But if so, then why do you think they will not protect it with one of their steamships?"

Fadrique grunted. "Frankly, I'd be delighted if they *did* leave one behind. That's one less somewhere else. And individually, they actually have some vulnerabilities. But I do not think they will leave one at Trinidad simply because I doubt they would station it so far from their one safe port.

"The strategic importance of that port, on whichever island it is, far outstrips any other consideration. It is where they must house their troops, cache their supplies, perform their maintenance, coordinate their command staffs. If they were to lose that, they would lose everything else in short order. Conversely, if they keep that port, they have reason to hope that they may eventually regain whatever else they may lose. No, the Cartagena fleet will not need to face the up-time guns, fortunately."

"The question is," mused de Viamonte turning toward de Covilla, "how many Dutch ships will they face if they try to seize Curaçao?"

The young liaison smoothed his silk vest. "The day of our last council, I sent word to Governor de Murga in Cartagena of our resolves, and of the expedients we planned to employ here in the Antilles. We had a packet back from His Excellency just two days ago, bearing word that he had received our messages, was moving with all haste to coordinate his actions with ours, and that he was giving our plan for 'recruiting auxiliaries' serious consideration. As it turns out, he had already established contacts among Tierra Firme's so-called Brethren of the Coast. He considers them a 'distasteful' solution to the problem of Curaçao, but conceded that it was prudent and probably the only reasonable alternative to attacking it himself. Which would probably alert the defenders of Trinidad to his ultimate designs on them and so give them enough time to summon and receive reinforcements. But as to whether he has acted as he intended, or fortune has seen to interfere in some fashion, that is beyond my power to determine, Your Excellency. I can only add that, in the matter of de Murga settling affairs at Curaçao, Olivares' desires and exhortations were in alignment with our own."

De Viamonte nodded. "This is most reassuring, Eugenio. I just wish we could coordinate these far-flung actions as swiftly as our foes do."

Fadrique nodded, thinking, *But we never will. Not so long as we are relying upon packets and advice boats tacking across headwinds while they have radios that send messages in—literally—the blink of an eye.* He saw from de Viamonte's frown that he still had misgivings about Curaçao. "Your Excellency, as to the conditions along Tierra Firme, I would not task myself with worry. De Murga is a good man and resolute. He will do what needs doing, when it is needed." *Even if he hates having to do it.*

"So, where else?" asked Gallardo impatiently. "The English colonies, perhaps? They are small and vulnerable, without any succor from a king that has utterly abandoned them."

De Viamonte held up a hand. "Be not too hasty, old friend. St. Christopher and Nevis are almost certainly within the protective ring projected by the Dutch base. It is not inconceivable that it might be on one of them, in fact. And the others are simply too far, at this point. Barbados is well east of the Windward Isles: a far reach for us. The Somers Isles are an even farther reach, and we haven't the ships to consider such far-flung attacks. Better we use what assets we have to pin down the location of the allies' center of power."

"And once it's located," Gallardo said eagerly, "maybe the pirates could be induced to sack it!"

De Covilla glanced at Fadrique. "The admiral has expressed doubt that they could do so successfully."

"Until we know what is there, we cannot even hazard a guess." He shrugged. "I would presume they would invest in its protection. They might even tie down a steamship to protect it, although they are just as likely to be unwilling to purchase that safety at the expense of foreswearing so many opportunities for mounting swift attacks and counterattacks. But if it proves to be poorly defended, our privateers would enthusiastically overcome and sack it, and so do great damage to our foes' strategic locus."

De Viamonte turned an unconcerned wrist in the air. "And if it is strongly held, then it is they who suffer the costs of that discovery, and we who shall benefit from the report of those who survive to reveal its actual location."

De Covilla leaned forward to speak, but paused, abashed. Fadrique nodded encouragement, sat back as the young *hidalgo* began speaking softly. "In the interests of Spain and our king, I am honor bound to point out that we also enjoy an advantage that is, in itself, an instrument of no honor at all." The others looked blankly at his puzzling words. He sighed, said more loudly, "Our spy network is vastly better than any our adversaries employ. If they even do. And our mission from Holy Mother Church would seem to allow us the use of such creatures insofar as we are her chosen servitors and her survival and success is therefore tied inextricably to ours."

Fadrique could almost read De Covilla's self-loathing subtext in glowing words above his head: *Or, to speak more frankly: the side that can exploit espionage and treachery most effectively is the one with the fewest scruples. All hail us, the pure-hearted champions of Holy Mother Church! No irony, there.*

But what Fadrique said was: "I quite agree. But we have thus far employed them in a general sense—to merely bring us information of interest. Are you proposing something more...focused?"

He nodded. "I am. In managing our affairs with the privateers, I have learned that they use many of the same agents we do."

"No surprise, there," Gallardo snarled. "Faithless to one is faithless to all, no?"

De Covilla sighed. "I cannot deny that, even if I wanted to. But there is an advantage in this. We can use the privateers as conduits to an increased number of agents. And based on their reports, begin to discern those who are suitable for more than reporting on strategic gossip for the price of a goblet of wine."

De Viamonte perked up. "For what would you use such confidential agents?"

De Covilla shrugged. "Nothing too complex or dangerous. They would simply be required to gather and remit information specifically pertaining to the movements by our enemies' military forces, ships, or anything unusual or novel in their region."

De Viamonte frowned. "Even with regular contact, such reports almost always come too late for us to act upon them. And I fear that, until we have radios, this shortcoming will persist."

"And indeed it would, if we were attempting to gather intelligence for immediate action. What I am proposing, instead, is to seek patterns in their movement, in their refurbishment, in their use of facilities, of where they billet troops, warehouse spares. Simply knowing where they are positioning what kind of supplies tells us much about what they may be planning to do, what operations they may have given priority. For now, that may be the only way we can anticipate their actions because, to date, they never follow up any of their successes in accord with the time-honored habit of most combatants: to do the same thing, only on a larger scale and with more at stake. As was said at the outset, their pattern is that they refuse to follow a pattern—and so become unpredictable."

De Viamonte was nodding. "There is merit in this. Write your proposal in greater detail for me. Now, what else may we use against our foes?"

"Their overconfidence," Gallardo muttered sullenly.

"In what way?"

"Don't know yet. Still thinking. The way they don't use the same kind of plan over and over again means that whatever habits they do have are harder to see. But no one has that many successes without coming to rely on tools or outlooks that helped make those successes happen. Just don't know what they are yet."

The best thing about Gallardo, Álvarez reflected with a smile, was that he was as much of a son of a bitch to himself as everyone else. As if to prove the point, the hard-bitten captain shot a hard look at the admiral. "What about you? You've been awfully quiet."

"I am reflecting upon how we may inspect our own assumptions and situation with such fresh eyes that we shall see every alternative, every advantage, that exists for us."

"It seems like we just did that."

"We have not." Fadrique felt oddly young as he heard the words pour out of his mouth. "We must not merely think of new places to attack, new stratagems to employ, what new kinds of ships we must build, the new guns and carriages we need for them, or even the best way to build them. We must ask more fundamental questions and see where they lead."

De Viamonte rubbed his well-groomed goatee. "Questions such as?"

Álvarez knew what a losing war looked like and knew there was only one way to turn this or any other around: by reassessing everything. On the other hand, he had existed at the upper tiers of the Spanish political and military elite for years, and knew that impolitic words or unconventional opinions could get one sent into retirement. Or worse. It had already happened to him once and he refused to let it happen again. But between the family that had been taken away by disease and the years that had accumulated upon his brow, he suddenly discovered that he'd rather die than give up, just as he'd rather die than go back into obscure disgrace.

So this is what is meant by "do or die"; not to charge into battle recklessly, but to speak one's mind, without any restraints or misgivings. He took a breath and began.

"We must consider each order that comes from Spain and ask, 'will this lead to victory or defeat?' And if we discern it is the latter, then we must ask ourselves, 'then what is a better option and why?' In short, we must look to ourselves for *different* answers, for our own path toward victory.

"I can foresee that meaning we must change our industries, and with that, our economies. And if that is required to prevail, then we must not shirk considering it."

Gallardo was staring at him. Fadrique couldn't tell if he was about to kill him or propose undying fealty to his cause. De Covilla's eyes were wide and he was flushed; with excitement or panic, there was no way to tell.

But de Viamonte was simply gazing at him, index finger propping up his high-domed head. "My friend, I would take care where I say such things."

Álvarez shrugged. "I will take what care I may, but it is urgent that we begin to wage this war, and to love our king, without blinders on. We can only be so politic when asserting that Armendáriz must be brought in line by any means necessary, because we need the power of New Spain behind us in this. Or when we assert that we must employ any means at our disposal to compel the viceroy of Chile to send de Murga more resources and to push the rest of Tierra Firme to take action. As I said last year, we will live or die by how well we achieve these. Or not."

De Viamonte smiled sadly. "I agree. And yet it is also true that you, Fadrique Álvarez de Toledo, may live or die by where you choose to speak such words—or not."

The admiral heard the response coming out of his mouth unbidden, like a long unuttered truth that finally had a chance to leap out into daylight and be irreversibly seen and heard. "I pledged my life to king and country decades ago," Álvarez said, "and have been called upon to risk it for far less compelling reasons and for far lower stakes than these. This battle is the one I have been preparing to fight my whole life. Accordingly, in order to win it, I am ready to lose my life in battle, or to lose my head to the king's executioner."

Chapter 29

Oranjestad, St. Eustatia

With the dance behind and several weeks of frantic trading concluded, the carnival pace—and hours—in Oranjestad had finally begun returning to normal. The market was once again quiet at six a.m., the only sounds coming from regular day-start activities: fishermen and laborers leaving their houses, breakfasts being cooked, chamber pots being emptied, some in unauthorized areas. All of it had a faint sense of sleepwalking about it, as if all the recent bartering and dancing and drinking had been a pinnacle of merriment and energy and that now, even the buildings themselves wanted nothing more than weary repose.

In the midst of the morning's leaden yet dogged activity, there were few to obstruct or even notice a few crude wains being drawn from the head of the dock by the garrison's three oxen. They made their way into Fort Oranje under the none-too-watchful eyes of still-drowsy guards. The loads in the wagon beds were bulky and in nondescript crates, some covered by old sail canvas. Hardly a commercial parade to quicken mercantile, or any other kind of interest.

Yet, had the procession attracted any dedicated observers, and had they been looking toward the tops of the fort's walls, and if they had been able to see far enough into the crisp, black morning shadows, they would have seen marksmen of the Wild Geese, each with a rifle patterned on an up-time .40-72 Winchester lever-action. Half were tracking along with the slow, dull progress of the wagons. The other half were in slow, subtle motion, sweeping all the buildings that overlooked or had immediate access to the wains' route. Inside three of those buildings, four-man teams of Wild Geese waited for the signal that would bring them charging out into the street to ensure the safety of the wagons. Or more precisely, their contents.

But there was no such noise or excitement this morning. The gates to the fort swung wide and the wagons entered, one creaking piteously, before the gates closed behind them once again.

Maarten Tromp glanced at the team of stevedores who were unloading the boxes for what Eddie called "eyes-on confirmation." A clinical-sounding up-time term meaning that one could not simply trust a manifest and a handwritten—or in this case, printed—bill of lading. Peering inside was the only way to be sure that what had gone into the crate was what came out at its final destination.

What was unusual about these cargo handlers was they were in matching, if unexciting, uniforms. Which seemed to be a motif about everything that came from the two new steam destroyers, *Harrier* and *Relentless*:

standardized objects, routines, orders. In this case, it was evident not only in the dress but the actions and demeanor of the men, who began opening the crates without a word, without even meeting the eyes of the persons who were watching them work.

The two political witnesses to the unloading and confirmation of what were nominally secret cargos looked at each other. Then the taller, thinner one asked, "Granted, these crewmen are most efficient— most efficient!—but why were they tasked to this work rather than troops stationed here at the fort?"

Mike McCarthy, Jr. pointed up at the second-story windows that looked down into the compact marshaling yard; it was too small to be called a parade ground. "What do you see up there, Lieutenant Governor Corselles?"

Pieter glanced up. "I see closed storm shutters," he observed in a wry tone that suggested he thought it witty in its profound obviousness.

"That's right," Mike answered, "and they're all closed. And current patrols and checkpoints are being manned by the Wild Geese. All for the same reason that these newly arrived destroyer crewmen are doing the unloading and the unpacking: they already know about the cargo. They were responsible for it during the crossing of the Atlantic, so they already know the codes on the lading. Similarly, if any of the boxes had to be repaired or checked during the voyage, that, again, would be their job."

The other civilian nodded, eyes narrowed. "So, by having these men do the work, no new eyes see the cargo. And thus, no new tongues may wag about it."

Tromp suppressed a sigh. It was no surprise that

Phipps Serooskereken saw and understood the significance before Pieter, his immediate superior.

Eddie Cantrell had moved forward to stand alongside the senior councilor of St. Eustatia's *Politieke Raad*. "And since their ships are both heading away again in a few days, and since those crews already had their liberty ashore, we can be sure that even these men can't spread word of what they did or saw today."

The only woman present—Ann Koudsi, who had come up with Jol and Hugh from her work at the Trinidad oil rig—smiled. "So, are you going to tell us what's behind door number three, Eddie?"

Tromp and the other down-timers smiled politely. As so often occurred with up-timers, he and his countrymen hadn't the faintest understanding of her comment, except that it was yet another allusion to some ubiquitous aspect of the world they would never see again. But this at least sounded as though it was relevant, probably some reference to revealing an unknown or secret object.

Eddie smiled sideways and started walking around the boxes and pointing into one after the other. "Either in their entirety, or in parts, we have: rifles, pistols, ammo for all, second-generation Aldis lamps, tools for darn near everything, telegraph wire, portable smelters, powder grinders, shell molds, steam engines with driveshaft adapters, signal pistols, heavy flare launchers—"

Joost Banckert interrupted. "Those flare launchers. They look like the deck guns on your steamships, the, eh, 'Big Shots.'"

Eddie nodded. "They're modified models, designed to fire flares at a higher arc and to a much higher altitude than the signal pistols. A lot of new colors in the mix, too. And some go off like fireworks; you can see them really easily. We call those Tomshots."

Mike McCarthy, Jr. rolled his eyes. "Let me guess: because Tom Stone came up with them."

"The chemical magnate who now dwells in Padua?" Corselles asked. "That Tom Stone?" Tromp heard awe and a hint of ready sycophancy in the lieutenant governor's voice.

Ann Koudsi chortled. "Is there any other Tom Stone?"

"You know him?"

The up-timers looked at one another. Ann was still smiling, but there was a hint of a frown creasing her brow. "Yes, Lieutenant Governor. Kind of hard not to. There weren't many of us in Grantville when the Ring of Fire hit, and with a few exceptions, we all knew one another. Whether we wanted to or not." She exchanged knowing glances with the other two up-timers; they all nodded and rolled their eyes. Ann pointed her dainty chin at the most distant row of boxes. "So what's in those other crates?"

Eddie grinned. "Patience, patience. There's actually a lot more that you're not seeing because there's just too much of it, and there's no reason to unload it."

"Like?"

"Well, a *lot* of ammunition and powder charges for the eight-inchers, even more for the down-time cannons, three more mitrailleuses—uh, machine guns, sort of—and another eight-inch naval rifle. And coal. Lots of coal. Lots and *lots* of coal."

Tromp smiled. "So, we have another of your wonderful naval rifles. A spare?"

Eddie sighed. "No, a hand-me-down."

Tromp felt his smile invert as he puzzled out the colloquialism. "It is—it is used? Then why was it sent to us?"

Again, the three up-timers exchanged looks. Mike McCarthy, Jr., the oldest person present, crossed his arms like a patriarch about to deliver news sure to disappoint his entire family. "It was sent to us because it was, well, free."

Corselles frowned. "That cannot be possible. It *must* be costly! Your naval rifles are so large and carefully crafted that surely—"

Again, it was Serooskereken who provided insight for his superior. "I believe Mr. McCarthy simply means that it was no longer of value to the USE. So they were willing to send it to us."

Mike sighed. "Actually, unless I'm wrong, that's the case with a lot of this cargo. Those rifles and pistols? Older models or newer ones that they didn't want to spend the time and money refurbishing. The mitrailleuses? Either salvaged from a wreck or decommissioned." He shrugged. "We're like the little kids in a family, getting what's left of the big kids' clothes."

"Well," Eddie added, "it's not quite *that* bad. Admiral Simpson has been pushing hard for newer systems, naval and otherwise. Constant upgrades."

"And how does that help us?" Banckert asked with his family's trademark irritability.

Eddie shrugged. "Because the moment a piece of machinery gets replaced, one of three things happens to it. It's junked, it's put in reserve, or it gets sent here. So by constantly pressuring Grantville's government to spend on new systems, Simpson is not just pushing the leading edge of our technology forward, he's creating a stream of decommissioned equipment for us."

"Yes," Banckert grumbled, rather like a dog that wasn't quite ready to give up a bone, "equipment that we have to spend our time fixing. If we can."

Eddie's tone was clearly intended to coax the bone out of Banckert's argumentative jaws. "See those seven crates of tools? We can fix anything you see here in front of you. And a lot more, besides."

"And that sounds like more jobs and apprenticeships to me!" said Corselles happily.

Tromp nodded. "Assuming they can be trained to the necessary standards, I see no reason why not." He glanced at Eddie. "Do you have objections?"

Eddie shook his head. "Not at all."

Phipps Serooskereken frowned. "I confess I was expecting a different answer, Commodore."

Tromp kept his face motionless as he silently berated himself. His remark about allowing civilians to repair military items had been an innocent slip, but Phipps had seen the implications. *Oh well, my mistake to fix.*

Tromp waved the stevedores into the hulking mass of the fort proper, waited until the heavy-timbered door closed behind the last of them. "Now, Phipps: why did the commodore's answer surprise you?"

"Because since you have observed strict secrecy unloading and revealing these cargos, it is not consistent to then turn some of them over to civilian artisans for repair."

Tromp sighed. "You are completely correct, Senior Councilor."

"Then which is it, Admiral? Are they to remain secret or are they to be given to civilians for repair?"

"Both."

"Huh?" said McCarthy.

Eddie smiled sheepishly. "Welcome to 'secrecy theater,' Mike."

But Serooskereken had jumped ahead with a thin smile. "Of course. The Spanish will learn of the new ships and convoy, and they will presume that it has brought us many necessary goods and tools, some of which would logically be new, advanced war matériel.

"However, if their agents do not hear of any cargos being unloaded separately and secretly, they would become suspicious; equipment designed or made by up-timers is almost always of strategic importance. So your 'slip' in allowing some of it to be repaired by civilians will be seen as a 'security error' that reveals exactly what the Spanish expect: improved weapons and machines." He frowned, glanced quickly from Eddie's face to Tromp's. "But this charade is only necessary if you have truly secret cargos that you want them to overlook."

Tromp shrugged and turned his palms outward in resigned affirmation.

Banckert's irritability returned. "So you have evidence of spies among us *already*? And I was not informed? Maarten, you and I had better—"

"Admiral Banckert," Eddie broke in, "we don't have *any* information on Spanish spies. But, look: the Spanish have us totally beat in humint." The young commodore saw the uncomprehending stares, even from his fellow up-timers. "Uh, 'human intelligence': the kind gathered by living, breathing agents. So let's just assume that whether or not spies are here yet, they will be and that they are sure to find the weak spot in any routine activity that we're trying to keep secure. Consider the items that need fixing and all the handoffs they *have* to go through. From shipment to off-loading to refurbishment to reassembly and testing to quartermaster and, eventually, back to maintenance. That's a long chain. There are going to be links that can be bribed or blackmailed . . . and the Spanish will find them."

Van Walbeeck folded his hands. "And they will not restrict themselves to the obvious channels."

Corselles looked frightened. "What do you mean?"

Van Walbeeck shrugged. "I shall answer you with questions, Pieter. Do you clean your own house? Clean your own clothes? Who takes care of your daughters? Who cooks your meals?" Van Walbeeck nodded at his subordinate's increasing pallor. "All potential conduits to the Spanish. Families, particularly important ones, often forget their servants have ears and eyes as well as hands and feet. Just as they forget that those hands and feet serve them out of need, not love. Because, in the end, their possible love for you will not buy the food or clothes or medicine that their own children certainly need. And if some unknown traveler is willing to trade coin for tales, why would they refuse to share seemingly harmless details from overheard conversations?"

Phipps nodded. "So you are acting on the presumption that the Spanish already know that St. Eustatia is our fleet's haven."

Eddie shrugged. "If they don't already, they soon will. But that was inevitable."

"Why so?"

Tromp turned out a palm in appeal. "When our

ships were fewer and we had no supply from home, there was wisdom in hiding. But now that we are growing both in size and our contact with allied colonies, hiding has become impossible. They will find us soon enough, and from that moment, they will not rest until they are rid of us."

Ann Koudsi was craning her neck to get a look at the farthest row of boxes. "So are you going to tell us what's in those, or is there more stuff that you're not showing off here?"

"Oh, there's a lot more of that."

"Because it's the really secret stuff?"

"Some, yeah, but more of it is just too big for show-and-tell."

"Like what?"

"Well, in addition to the first production run of steam engines for ocean tugs and Hale rockets—"

"Wait: so now we're not just kids getting hand-me-downs, we're guinea pigs?"

Eddie smiled. "That's why this whole mission was supposed to be a shakedown cruise."

"Yeah, supposed to be. Okay; so rockets. What else?"

"Three standard observation balloons and two of the first hot-air dirigibles that were built back in Grantville: all decommissioned or refurbished. And there's something else we couldn't have unloaded if we wanted to, and is arguably the biggest secret of all: the new rotary drilling rig for Louisiana."

"Still no word from Larry Quinn?" McCarthy asked.

Tromp inclined his head. "I promised I would tell you immediately, Michael, and I will. So, no: nothing."

Ann was smiling shrewdly. "So that's why *Patentia* is scheduled to depart with the other ships: she's the only lumber ship we've got—or any stern loader, for that matter—so you've got to transfer the drill string and the well casing over to her." She considered. "Which means that she's going on to Louisiana without stopping back here. And since you'd never allow her to go without protection—"

Banckert laughed. "Miss Koudsi, you think like an admiral. Perhaps you should consider changing careers, hey?"

"I think I'll stick with drilling for oil." She smiled at him.

He smiled back and bowed deeply. "I understand that without your expertise, we would not have received the first shipment, of both oil and bitumen, so quickly."

She started for the furthest row of boxes. "Well, my boyfriend and about a dozen rig hands from the USE had a little bit to do with that as well, but since I'm the only one here, I'll say it for the rest: 'you are very welcome, Admiral.'" She punctuated that with a nod, and then looked at the boxes lined up before her feet.

"You look like one of my daughters at Christmas." The very end of Mike's comment was tinged with bittersweet recollection.

"Better not be shoes or gloves, then. I want to see *toys*!" Anne muttered. "Well, are you going to open them?"

Eddie obliged and when the lids had all been removed but one, he stood back.

Ann stared for a full five seconds, then put her hands on her hips. "What the hell is all that, Eddie? Looks like boxes of science projects I used to have in my basement."

"Well, Ann," Eddie answered, running his hand

through his hair, "you're not far off. You're looking at components for three inclinometers and three electric firing systems. Two are for the guns on *Intrepid* and one is for that new naval rifle, which is eventually going to be mounted up on The Quill."

"Then what's in that box? The one you left covered."

"Ah," said Eddie as he exchanged smiles with Tromp. He lifted the lid carefully, removed packing materials that took up almost ninety percent of the crate's volume, then waved a hand at what lay revealed: radios.

"There are seventeen," he explained with a hush in his voice that Tromp found vaguely disturbing; it was simultaneously reverent and lustful.

"Seventeen radios?" Mike repeated in what sounded very much like disbelief and puzzlement. "What are you planning to do with all of them? Start a Top Forties station?"

"A what?" Eddie asked.

Mike recoiled. "Wow," he exhaled with a shake of his head, "I really *am* getting too old for this. A Top Forties radio station was—oh, never mind. Why so many?"

"Michael," Tromp answered before Eddie could, "if I had a hundred, I would still want more. Nothing has been half as valuable, as decisive, as your radios. I wish we had one for every allied settlement and colony that will allow us to have a permanent presence. Which is ironic, actually."

"Why?" asked Corselles.

"Because," van Walbeeck volunteered with a grin, "every time we have explained what the radio enables, they invite us to send one to their island, along with its operators!"

Joost van Banckert nodded. "It certainly made it easier to bring Bermuda closer into our orbit," he muttered. "Their governor, Waters, understood the advantage right away. He also understood that it made him very valuable to us, as well."

"Why so?" Serooskereken asked.

"The commodore understands this much better than I, but it has to do with their location being closer to Europe and to the mainland. Just as ships have an easier time journeying between closer ports, so it is with the signals sent by these radios."

"Which of our other neighbors have radios, now?" Corselles said with a frown, clearly wondering why he hadn't been informed of that development.

Van Walbeeck thought. "Nevis and St. Christopher's, of course. Montserrat last month. Trinidad since it was taken, Tobago just recently. And there's one on the way to Barbados right now."

Ann's face was a cluster of perplexed creases. "So if you already had enough radios for all those places, what are your plans for these?" She waved at the contents of the crate.

Tromp spoke the answer as if he were thanking God for impending deliverance. "One for every major warship. One for every balloon and dirigible. And it will take a few more to establish our weather-watching network."

Corselles now looked thoroughly perplexed. "What is a weather-watching network?"

You'll learn soon enough, thought Tromp. But what he said was: "We have seen all that there is to see. Let us continue our business over breakfast."

Chapter 30

Oranjestad, St. Eustatia

As Eddie had suspected, breakfast was simply a glorified term for juice, carob "coffee," cassava rolls, and goat cheese. He'd hardly finished what he intended to be his first helping, when Pieter Corselles proclaimed cheerily, "So, you have rid us of the French, Commodore! Well done! They shall not be missed. And in doing so, did you also tame the faithless savages allied to them?"

After Eddie had managed to control the sharp pulse of anger elicited by the Dutchman's slur about "savages" that needed "taming," he'd confirmed that, yes, a lasting peace had indeed been made with them. However, when he announced that said peace had been secured by guaranteeing the Kalinago perpetual and unbothered possession of the islands they still inhabited—Dominica, Grenada, St. Vincent and the Grenadines, St. Lucia, Martinique, and Guadeloupe—the result was shock, then disbelief, then outrage.

As he had anticipated, the objections came from Banckert, Serooskereken, and particularly Corselles, and were purely practical. With the exception of St. Christopher, the Kalinago were now the sole owners of all the islands that were well watered and most favorable for agriculture. What was left for colonial expansion? That the Kalinago might actually have an intrinsic right of ownership over what were in fact their own homes didn't seem to enter into their considerations at all.

Eddie had held on to a slim hope that by listing all the islands that were still open to them, and by pointing to why so many of them were uninhabited, he would rouse their slumbering—not to say comatose—consciences. Specifically, in addition to the islands they already possessed—St. Eustatia, St. Christopher, Nevis, Montserrat—the Dutch could yet add St. Croix, St. Maarten, Anguilla, and the entire Bahamas. Why? Because the Spanish had depopulated them, mostly by raiding for slaves, but also because they perceived and treated the native peoples the same way they did rats: vermin to be exterminated. The other islands of the Lesser Antilles—Antigua, Barbuda, Saba, St. Barthélemy—had been long uninhabited, even before the Spanish came. Either they didn't have enough water, were too rocky and uneven for husbandry, or both.

And now, looking into those three stony faces, Eddie saw the reactions he had, sadly, expected. They were neither mollified by the promise of that additional real estate nor softened by the fates of the islands' past inhabitants. While not devoid of all sympathy, they were hard-nosed pragmatists who saw the legacy of spilt blood as akin to spilt milk: no good crying over it now.

That dismissive attitude was clear in Corselles' eyes and tone as he led the charge. "Commodore, I cannot be overly concerned with the past when the needs of the present are so pressing. Yes, you have identified islands without populations and yes, the natives have no objection to our possessing them, but that is only because they are all inferior sites for settlement. Small wonder that the Kalinago were willing to agree to such a treaty, since it effectively ends our ability to establish new, profitable colonies in the Antilles."

Tromp held up an index finger. "I beg to differ."

"How? The commodore made it quite clear that the Kalinago have sole, permanent rights to their islands."

"True. It was your other statement which wants correction."

"What? You mean to imply that Kalinago *do not* hold all the choicest islands in the Antilles?"

"Ah. But he was only speaking of the *Lesser* Antilles."

Serooskereken looked confused. Judging from the annoyance knitted on his brow and at the corners of his mouth, he was not accustomed to the sensation and disliked it intensely. "But, Admiral, that is exactly what he said. He listed all the Antilles and . . ."

Tromp's index finger rose again. "Ah. There is the error, yet again. Commodore Cantrell did *not* list all the islands you say he did. He omitted those of the *Greater* Antilles."

Banckert appeared both perplexed and aggravated. "There are no major fertile islands what we might colonize in the Greater Antilles, Maarten. I—"

"Again, I beg to differ. Indeed, we are free to colonize *all* the islands of the Greater Antilles." He waited for his implication to set in. It did not. So he gave them the list, slowly: "Jamaica, Puerto Rico, Hispaniola, and Cuba."

Only van Walbeeck had seen it coming; he smiled. But the other three Dutchmen were wide-eyed.

"Cuba? And . . . and the rest?" muttered Serooskere-ken. "Admiral, do you not anticipate that the Spanish might make at least a trifling objection if we attempted to settle their most crucial colonies?"

Tromp shrugged. "Not when they no longer possess them. Not when the tide has turned that far."

"Do you think it ever could?" Pieter Corselles sounded hopeful and disbelieving in equal measure.

"I think it must, for they will not brook our presence here. It is us or them."

Banckert opened his mouth but closed it again. Whether out of respect, fear of ruining a friendship, or startled admiration for so bold a vision was unclear. Eddie suspected it might be all three.

It was Ann Koudsi who spoke. "That is . . . a most ambitious projection, Admiral Tromp."

"That was tactfully put, Miss Koudsi. But whereas you may feel I am obsessed by improbable visions of conquest, I consider this the minimal resolution for survival. If there was a middle course, I would pursue it. Gladly. Avidly. Thankfully. But the Spanish will not have it so."

His tone became less declarative, more reflective. "The price of their resolve will be a tidal wave of blood. The only consolation is that when that red tide recedes, slavery will be carried away with it."

Banckert seemed to shake himself back into animation. "Let us return to the less fantastic and very immediate topic of our own defense. You were talking at length about radios. I certainly understand the value of those magical boxes, but then you seemed to link them to a network of weather stations?" He shook his head. "How does that add to our defense of St. Eustatius?"

Eddie nodded. "Admiral Banckert, what I'm about to say may sound like a pointless semantic difference, but I assure you it is not. I'd like to talk about the radios and the weather-watching network in terms of *security*, not defense."

Banckert shrugged indifference, but Serooskereken leaned forward. "I would like to understand that difference as you mean it, Commodore."

Eddie had hoped the question would arise; it would make everything else a lot easier. "Defense is pretty much the opposite of offense, the way the phrase 'to defend' is pretty much the opposite of 'to attack.' Would you agree?"

Now it was Phipps' turn to shrug indifference.

"Okay," resumed Eddie, "but security is about *everything* that concerns our safety. It's the whole picture. Defense is part of it, absolutely; walls, guns, ships, men, and all the other assets which, to borrow Admiral Banckert's words, can be used to defend St. Eustatius.

"But what about our ability to attack, the threat we pose to the enemy, all throughout this region? What about our ability to know his whereabouts, or to conceal ours? And what about our ability to protect our assets against weather and other natural forces? That—*all* of that—is what I mean when I talk about security."

It looked like Serooskereken grasped that shift in concept even faster than Banckert did, whereas Corselles was frowning in desperate uncertainty. "Very well," said Phipps. "Lead on, Commodore."

"So: radios. One at every community. That would be good under any circumstances, but it's particularly helpful here in the Lesser Antilles. Look at this map." He unveiled the big hand-drafted but freakishly faithful map of the Caribbean. There were green lines drawn between each island-to-island gap, from the northernmost of the Lesser Antilles, Anguilla, all the way down to their southern terminus at Grenada.

Phipps Serooskereken assessed it through squinted eyes. "It looks like a guide for jumping from one stepping-stone to the next. Which is why you are showing it to us, I presume."

Eddie smiled. "Exactly. But those green lines aren't just a route; they are measures of the distance between each island's closest northern neighbor and its closest southern neighbor. The biggest gap is the twenty-nine and a half nautical miles separating Guadeloupe and Montserrat."

"We know this," Banckert grumbled.

"I was sure you did. I am equally sure that you know this island chain is three hundred and eighty miles long as the crow flies. Or, if you want to hop from stepping-stone to stepping-stone, it's four hundred and seventy-five miles. And if you want to include Trinidad, it's five hundred and fifty."

Banckert folded his arms. "And you are going to point out that even if your steamships can only make ten knots, they can still cover the whole distance, from Anguilla to Trinidad, in less than two and a half days." He shrugged. "That means we can certainly send powerful assistance to any threatened area quickly. But until the majority of our ships can move just as fast, our offensive range will not change much."

Eddie nodded. "I agree. But that's not the primary impact that this geography has upon our security strategy." Banckert tried not to look deflated as Eddie pushed on. "Right now, I don't want to talk about moving. I want to talk about watching. Because if you take that maximum separation of twenty-nine miles, and then you consider the highest points on each island, it means that every single one of these"—he tapped the green links—"also represents a clear line of sight."

Koudsi saw it first. She ran her finger along the long, lazy, east-leaning curve of the Lesser Antilles. "You can keep this whole arc under observation. Any ship that is moving from the Atlantic into the Caribbean has to pass between at least two of these islands, and would be visible to both." She frowned, thinking, and so did not notice that Tromp and van Walbeeck were exchanging delighted glances over her head. "But it's got limitations. It's porous."

Corselles nodded vigorously. "A ship could easily be missed it if passes at night. Or in high weather. Or when the haze is thick, as is usually the case."

Eddie nodded. "As Ms. Koudsi says, it is porous. But to the Spanish, who just had a fleet grabbed away from them, this string of observation posts would be, at the very least, a huge inconvenience. At worst, it tells them that their disaster at Dominica could happen again. At any time. And it's even more likely for any ships they might send along the chain's long axis."

Banckert frowned. "Might their ships be seen? Yes. But does that portend disaster?" He wagged a finger. "Only if we have ships nearby. But Commodore: is this even practicable? How do you mean to keep this vast expanse of water under observation? From isolated

watch posts on all these islands? Many of which you
have just agreed never to set foot upon again?"

Eddie smiled. "Yes: we put observation posts on
all the islands. Each one furnished with your fine
Dutch optics. As for having outposts on islands over
which we have no jurisdiction, well, if we're good
neighbors, there's growing evidence that our hosts
would be happy to have a small number of us working as lookouts, way up on peaks they don't frequent.
Because our watchers will be under orders to share
everything they see with any persons so authorized
by the local cacique."

Koudsi was nodding, Banckert was rubbing his jaw,
Mike was staring hard at the map. It was Serooskereken who asked, "And assuming that you had a force
close enough to intercept ships crossing this line of
observation, how would that force be ordered to do
so? Do you mean to furnish each of these observation
posts with radios?"

Eddie shook his head sharply. "We don't have
enough. Besides, that would be like handing sets
over to the Spanish. Once they become aware of our
watch posts, they'll surely learn—or deduce—that
if they can't see signals going back and forth, then
we must be using radios. And I suspect the Spanish
would go to extraordinary lengths to get their hands
on that technology."

Banckert nodded. "I agree. They know these radios
are what is defeating them almost every time."

Phipps looked and sounded a little less predatory.
"So without radios, how do they communicate?"

"Mostly by heliograph. With good reflectors at
preplotted locations, sunlight or even firelight will

work. Any detection starts a chain of relays that sends the news on to the closest radio-equipped outpost.

"There would be a finite number of those, each placed so that every heliograph is within three relays of a radio. They'd also be defensible and have provisions for, and personnel trained in, destruction and disposal of the radio on extremely short notice."

Banckert was no longer frowning. "Very well. But the gap between Trinidad and Grenada is much greater than thirty miles."

Eddie nodded. "Trinidad is a special case. For now, I suggest we leave it aside to keep things simple."

"Simple?" Corselles echoed, shaking his head. "It sounds anything but! All sorts of delays and failures could befall such a system."

Tromp folded his hands. "As the commodore has emphasized, this plan has flaws and is unavoidably porous. The worst problem will be haze over the greater distances. But the true strategic value of this system is not that we may sortie out after any ship which crosses our line of observation, but that, so far as our enemies know, we *might*."

Van Walbeeck nodded, but looked grim, possibly the first time Eddie had ever seen that expression on his face. "Some here today will not know that, before coming here, my work was in the East Indies. Lands of infinite and, to our eyes, trackless jungles." Van Walbeeck looked like he was seeing—or remembering— ghosts. "The possibility, and fear, of native ambush was constant." He gestured to the map. "This shall instill the same species of unremitting trepidation and anxiety in the Spanish. Will they be intercepted every time? No. When they are, will we always respond with a whole flotilla? Of course not. But since the Spanish cannot know when we will detect them or if we do have a flotilla to send, they must build that perpetual possibility into all their calculations. And that will cost them time, money, and tactical flexibility.

"And the cost to us? Negligible, for being able to observe almost everything they bring into this region. We shall have a measure of their numbers, whereas they will find it hard to estimate ours."

Serooskereken grimaced. "Until they start building more of their own ships here."

Eddie nodded. "Which will be the single greatest game changer. Which is why we must press these advantages now, because they are not permanent."

Mike leaned back from studying the map. "And unless I miss my guess, you haven't told us the other half of the reason for those watch posts."

Of course it was the mariner among the skeptics who saw it first; Banckert was nodding before Mike had finished. "These are also your network of weather stations. All on high ground, all able to detect heavy weather from great distances and send that information promptly. Fast enough for it to actually be of use to a captain." He leaned back, crossing his arms. "And not a moment too soon. We are in hurricane season. If we can preserve ourselves against that misfortune, we will be glad of it." He cocked an eye at Eddie. "So, you have made good your initial point and promise: this discussion of our security has gone far beyond our combat capabilities. I am satisfied."

Serooskereken smiled. "I am, too, Commodore . . . but judging from your stance, I suspect there is at least one more security issue you wish us to consider."

Eddie took a deep breath: *all in, now.* "There is. And I believe it to be so urgent that, if we do nothing else, we must address this: our fleet needs a home port."

Corselles seemed ready to spit in frustration. Banckert's frown was back. Ann Koudsi just shook her head.

But Phipps Serooskereken was smiling. "I suspected, since you saved this for last, it would also be the most confounding. Please: explain this quickly, or I will need to fortify myself with a measure of rum."

Eddie smiled back. "Okay. So earlier, Admiral Banckert pointed out that the proximity of all the islands in the chain wasn't as helpful as it looked because it still means that almost all of our forces have to stay pretty close to St. Eustatia."

Nods, except from Tromp, van Walbeeck, and Mike: they knew what was coming.

Eddie didn't let up. "No one disputes that we are strong here. This is where we've stationed all our ships, except for those protecting Trinidad. Same for land forces. It's where we have our government, our intercontinental radio, the great majority of our population and food production, and now, with a real town and trading hub developing, where we are seeing some local industry starting."

Serooskereken was frowning, Banckert almost as much. Corselles looked lost. Koudsi looked suspiciously from Eddie to Mike and then back at Eddie before observing, "We've got all our eggs in one basket."

Phipps was nodding. "If we site all our power on St. Eustatia, we are inviting its destruction."

Banckert nodded. "Which encourages the Spanish to concentrate all their forces here, because if we lose this place, we are done. They have many options when they must retreat, regroup, repair. We have but this one."

Corselles was looking from face to face, as if everyone in the room had become suddenly unrecognizable. "So we build quickly! We line our shores with batteries of the cannons that were taken from La Flota! We have many new workers and artisans among the newly arrived! We have new wealth and new weapons."

Koudsi shook her head. "That's just putting more eggs in the same, single basket."

Eddie nodded. "The more you keep building up, the more you make St. Eustatia, and particularly Oranjestad, an irresistible target for the Spanish. To use an expression from my time, attacking it becomes the strategic equivalent of one-stop shopping for them."

Banckert frowned. "'One-stop shopping'?"

"Yes," said Koudsi with a small grim smile. "It means going to a store where you can buy everything you need, all under one roof. So, if you put all your economic and military and industrial and agricultural power here, you're inviting—you are *forcing*—the Spanish to come at us with everything they have, casualties be damned. Because if they win that battle, they win the whole war. We'd be done."

Eddie nodded. "And that is why the industries and facilities that are essential to our defense must *not* be located here. Because—"

"—because," Phipps picked up with a shrewd smile, "St. Eustatia's *security* cannot be assured by *defenses* we build here. The only way to make it less vulnerable is to make it a less decisive target." He nodded. "So, what do you propose?"

"Okay, this is going to sound *really* weird—"

Banckert snorted. "We have come to expect no less, *jonger!*"

Eddie smiled. "So, what if our primary military power was near enough to engage any enemy that threatens Oranjestad, but is so difficult to reach that it's hard to attack?"

Serooskereken was rubbing his chin. "And where would that be?"

Eddie wasn't religious, but he had a fleeting desire to cross himself, just for luck. Or grace. Or whatever the hell you got by crossing yourself.

Banckert's growl brought him back to the moment. "Where is this place?"

He nodded eastward. "Antigua."

Corselles threw up his hands. "You up-timers baffle me. You make such progress in this world by learning from history, and then, at just those moments when its lessons are the most clear, you ignore it. Commodore, if I recall the up-time accounts correctly, Antigua did not develop until much later. As you related, it has almost no fresh water, has limited arable land, and, crucially, is a full thirty nautical miles east of the leeward seaway which is so salutary to our economic development."

Eddie nodded. "Which is exactly why I am proposing it as the home of our military power and essential industries."

"I see," Corselles drawled sarcastically. "So even though St. Eustatia is well situated and well favored for commerce and agriculture, we should instead build another port with new defenses on an island that shows no promise for either enterprise?"

Ah, there it is. You're thinking about the dollars and cents—well, guilders and groots—that might get taken out of your rice bowl. Eddie put on his best easy smile. "Actually, Lieutenant Governor Corselles, my plan will help St. Eustatia's economy, not diminish it.

"Take a good look at the bay the next time you're taking a seaside stroll. It doesn't have much of an anchorage. That's why it got so crowded so quickly while the market was at its peak.

"Now, imagine how much more room there would be if most of the fleet's hulls weren't out there. How many of the billets currently holding soldiers could be freed up for new colonists, merchants, warehouses. And how all the men in the fleet and in industries over on Antigua would be coming back here regularly, with lots of coin and a powerful urge to spend it."

Corselles looked sideways, frowning. "Go on."

"First, last, and foremost: Antigua is a better home for the fleet. For starters, it's the only hurricane hole in this part of the Caribbean."

While Banckert nodded emphatically, Koudsi frowned. "'Hurricane hole'? That sounds like a bar for beach bums out on the Keys."

"Yeah, well, the Keys *wishes* it had a hurricane hole. Here's why: a hurricane hole is a harbor, usually a long narrow one with a leeward mouth, where ships are most likely to be able to ride out even the worst storms. And that's just where the up-time town of St. John's was built: at the end of a long, leeward-facing harbor of unusual depth. And, because it is the easternmost of all the Leeward Islands, it is a great "first landfall" point for any flotilla or merchant convoy coming across from Europe. And put a star next to that if you want those arrivals and the cargo they off-load to remain less likely to get seen by the eyes of casual informers.

"Also, because it is so far to the east, Antigua is sheltered from direct Spanish incursions . . . because they'd have to travel *over* our line of observation posts in order to get to it. Also, they'd be sailing straight *into* the wind as they're trying to 'quickly slip past' the two most populated islands in the area: St. Eustatia and St. Christopher."

Eddie looked at them and knew he had them. Time to stop, despite all the other advantages he could cite. But still . . . he couldn't resist putting the truly sweet icing on the cake: "And when you get a chance, take a look at the distance from St. John's Harbor to the leeward sides of those same two, highly populated, islands that the Spanish might think of attacking. Fifty-five miles. Let me put that in terms of *defense*.

"Just for a moment, forget that when you're sailing here from Antigua, you can count on following seas and winds over your quarter. Forget everything but this: a cruiser steaming along at twelve knots solely under its own power can reach the intervention point for either of those islands in just *four hours*.

"Now, add this into the equation: if the Spanish are coming at the islands from up or down the Lesser Antilles, they'll be spotted dozens of miles away. Let's say only twenty. Now let's say that the Spanish are doing four knots, because God really *is* on their side—"

Banckert grinned. "Twenty miles would take them five hours. So the steamships from Antigua would be there to greet them when they arrive. And it would be even worse for them if they were sailing straight out of the west: they would be tacking across a headwind." He leaned back. "I support this idea of a base at Antigua."

Phipps' glance went from Tromp to van Walbeeck, and briefly over to Mike. His slow smile was sly. "The commodore would not have been allowed to make his case today if those three gentlemen were not already of a similar mind." He leaned back. "As am I. Pieter?"

Corselles threw his hands up one last time. "It sounds prudent." Which clearly meant, *I don't know, but I trust your judgment. I guess.*

Banckert rubbed his hands. "So, we are done! Now, where's that rum?"

Chapter 31

Oranjestad, St. Eustatia

Sophie Rantzau opened the door to the infirmary, simultaneously reflecting that it really should be fitted with a lock, while also being delighted to live in a place where locks were simply not necessary. "Dr. Brandão?" she called.

A very unexpected voice answered. "Dr. Brandão is elsewhere, for the nonce. I informed him there was an urgent case."

Sophie was glad she didn't gasp in surprise—or at the sharp twist of conflicting emotions: the voice was Hugh O'Donnell's. She turned, saw him in the shadows, leaning against the wall. It was dim, but it looked like he was smiling. Insufferable! But also very...appealing. "You lied to Dr. Brandão?"

"I did not."

"Then what case is this, that so needs his immediate presence?"

"I didn't say I told him it required his *presence*. Indeed, at this particular moment, it needs his absence.

As far as whose case I was telling him about . . . well, it's yours."

She didn't know which surge of indignation to release first: that Hugh—that *anyone*—would presume to know what she needed, or that he had revealed her private affairs to another person without any right or allowance to do so. She unleashed the latter without even attempting to limit the archness of her tone. "So you took it upon yourself to involve Dr. Brandão in our, er, my—?"

Hugh smiled. "I involved him in nothing, dear Sophie. He is a wise man. All I had to say was that you were suffering from, well, a long-standing heart ailment. He understood that right enough."

"He did?"

Hugh stepped closer. "Sophie, I must apologize for taking the liberty of making this personal observation—"

"Then don't!"

"—but your reserve is at odds with your nature. For those who get to know you, well, that's as plain as black on a witch's cat."

"And you presume to know me so well, Lord—?"

"I am Hugh. We agreed. I am not Lord O'Donnell, or any other title, to you. Not now or ever again. And I do not have to know you so very long to also know that something has wounded you deep in your heart. The heart that rose up and danced as you did, just a few weeks ago."

Sophie remembered to breathe. And to hold on to some vestige of her entirely justified indignation: "Well . . . well, you might have come to see me personally, rather than resorting to this subterfuge."

Hugh's answering grin was crooked. "Oh, you must

mean I should have called upon you at home? Which I tried twice a day after the dance, and then every day since I came back from another trip to Montserrat. At first, I actually thought you might be ill, since your servant reported you to be 'indisposed.'" He sighed. "It had me thinking that perhaps the experience of dancing with me was so very revolting that you were nauseous for days on end."

She shook her head in sharp denial before she could check that honest reflex. Or before she saw his smile straighten and one eyebrow lift in response to her reaction. Despite herself, despite her resolve, she smiled back, then laughed softly. "You are incorrigible."

"If you'd be seeking an insult to cut me to the quick, you'll need to find another, Sophie. I've been scolded for that failing since before I was in long pants. Not sure I was even out of the crib." His eyes grew serious and very soft. "Now: tell me."

"Tell you what?"

"Tell me what had you running out the door instead of dancing the rest of the night with me?"

For the shortest instant, Sophie did not see Hugh, but a forked pathway. One branch was well known and dark; the other was unfamiliar but very bright. And in looking down the latter, she discovered herself seeing Hugh's face again, half-lit by a ray of the morning light slipping in through the unlatched storm shutters.

"I did not avoid you out of aversion, Lord . . . Hugh. I avoided you out of shame."

"Shame?" His face was truly puzzled.

Sophie's breath caught. Perhaps Sehested had been kind, or at least moderate, when recounting the sordid details and disgraces of her family. But it was impossible to think—to hope—that anyone could both tell the truth and make those events anything less than appalling or, frankly, revolting.

"Shame?" Hugh repeated with growing perplexity. "Over what?" His frown softened. "I *do* know your history."

"I do not think you know it all, Hugh. Or rather, I do not think you understand what it did to me, to my—soul. Do you know the specific circumstances surrounding my marriage? Well, more to the point, my betrothal?"

"No, but your past is of no account to me. We are creatures of this world, now."

"We may be," she said, consciously suppressing a pained sigh: *I will not invite pity!* "But we bring our nature with us wherever we may go. Perhaps my meaning will be clearer if I share some facts that are well known in my country, but probably not so well in the ones—and in the circles—in which you have traveled."

"That might indeed be clearest. And wisest."

"You know, of course, that I was married to Laurids Ulfeldt in 1631."

Hugh nodded.

"And you also know that Leonora was to marry his brother Corfitz... well, sometime this year."

Hugh nodded again. "Well, at least you get on, together. It seems like she would have been a fine sister-in-law."

"Under those conditions, I am not so sure. But I doubt she would have preferred the woman who would have been her other sister-in-law."

"And who is that?"

"My mother."

Sophie had never seen Hugh surprised, or even troubled. His men said he was unflappable. Not so now: his very blue eyes grew very wide. "Sophie, did you say—?"

"My mother," she repeated. "My mother married Knud Ulfeldt in 1629."

"So you and she—?"

"Became sisters-in-law when I married Laurids. It has been many years, but I have not yet decided whether I am more horrified by the cold-blooded political pragmatism of the unions she orchestrated, or the almost incestuous quality of them."

Hugh blinked. Whether that was in reaction to the facts she'd revealed, or her sarcastic scalpel cuts, she was not certain. Probably both. Either would be enough to send most men fleeing after a hasty and final bow.

But he was still standing before her. "So, all the Ulfeldt brothers—"

"Were equally determined and cold-blooded about the matter. As true creatures of their class, marriage was not about love. It was part of their greater game to accrue more power. The web of marriages which they meant to finish weaving—and did, in the up-timers' world—was a cat's cradle of leverage to be exerted upon the throne. Their collective influence in the *Rigsrad*, wielded according to Corfitz's singular political acumen and access and the power attained by more than doubling their wealth through marriage to both my mother and me, was to have so stalemated Christian's royal prerogatives that it would be they, not he, who would have effectively ruled Denmark."

She gathered her skirts and sat, keeping her back

very straight. "Even in an age when marriage is routinely informed by prudence and political alliance, the blatantly monstrous ambition that wove this crown-snaring web was so plain to see that it would even have startled a blind cow." She smoothed the folds of her dress where it went over her knees. "Is my shame more clear, now?"

Hugh sat next to her and frowned, but she perceived it was from trying to find the right words with which to reply. Granted, she understood that responding would challenge the tact of the most silver-tongued diplomat.

But he sidestepped that challenge altogether. "These were horrible dishonors and disservices done to you, and it would be strange indeed if you felt no anger or resentment at being so horribly used. But that's only the half of it, isn't it?"

She felt her eyes narrow. "What do you mean?"

"I mean it's a mean enough existence to suffer such insults, but to have them known publicly? There's as much salt as there is wound, that way. What's worse, you're nobility and so people talk. And what little they know gets shared and grows larger and more monstrous in each sharing. So I pay but little mind to the stories that accumulate around supposed 'scandals.' Beyond the barest facts, if you can even learn them, most of the rest is invented and the remainder is misreported or misunderstood."

She found his perception both surprising and refreshing. Then understanding replaced the surprise: "As nobility, your life, too, would excite conjecture and rumor." She frowned. "So why is there no such talk of you?"

Hugh smiled and rubbed his fine, straight nose.

"Well, among my own people, there's not much to say, is there? I'm an exile of no account. But beyond them, in the continent's great castles and courts that are home to those of your stature . . . Well, I'm not really nobility, not to them." His smile bent a bit. "I'm a savage from a land where the bards are all dead, the scholars do not go, and the bright students leave as quickly as they may. *If* they may."

He raised a palm along with the animation of his expostulatory lilt. "And of course, I'm not even really from my 'homeland' at all. I was still in swaddling clothes when I arrived in the Brabant." He smiled at her. "But *you*, from head to toe, are a true aristocrat, born and reared up in a land with commerce, and universities, and science, and power. Of course the mighty—and all who aspire to, or envy, their position—will talk of *you*, Sophie." He shrugged. "But I'm an earl in name only; the title is attainted, along with every square inch of my family's lands in an obscure country."

She nodded tightly. "You tell the cruel truth of your family with ease and aplomb."

He grinned. "I've had more than a bit of practice at it."

"Jest if you will, but it marks you as the true noble, between the two of us."

He frowned. "Now, how can I possibly believe there's a whit of truth behind those foolish words, Sophie?" He almost seemed to sing her name.

Just as he had in the infirmary during his final visit. And as he'd done during the dance, so many times . . .

She fought to keep focus. "You are wrong, Hugh. What I have said of my circumstances, and changed self, is too true for me to bear or for you to ignore. Today I am...reasonably collected. But I do not always have much equanimity of opinion or expression when I speak of my family, Hugh. Which is why I do not do so often. And also, I'm not sure they deserve any better. So when I do speak of them, I cannot in good conscience mediate the bitterness that rises up at the merest recollection of who they are."

"Even if the only one still being injured by that poison is your good self?"

She faced him squarely. "Hugh, the sad tale of your background is ultimately about what was done to your family. But my story is of what *my family did to me*." She closed her eyes, couldn't bear to see the world around her as she uttered the truth she had never yet spoken aloud. "And by my family, I mean my mother, whose love can be as comforting as the edge of a razor and as gentle as a scorpion's touch. And just as healthful." She spat out a mirthful laugh before she could stop it. "You see? Are you not impressed by my loving tone, my compassionate recollection of her sacrifices on my behalf?"

"Sophie—"

But once again, she couldn't stop. "And of course, I am no longer the beneficiary of her wealth, since she promised to disown me if I traveled with the daughters of her arch enemy the king, and up-timers whose histories exposed the Ulfeldt's perfidies and so undid all their plans.

"So you see, I am far more impoverished than you are, kind Hugh. You now have oil revenues, the love of your men, and a chance at restoring all your fortunes. I have nothing left, not even the one person I could truly call family in this whole world. Besides, the king wanted a companion to his daughters, a capable person who could be of assistance to those agents he sent to grow his domains in this New World." She managed a smile. "As the up-timers say, 'Hey, it's a job.'"

Hugh nodded. "Losing one's birthright can be a liberating experience. It certainly has been for me."

"In what way?"

"Many. But chief on my mind right now is how my definition of wealth has changed. It is no longer shackled to land and money and title and my duty to accrue them in order to regain a birthright stolen from me. The real wealth is the world around us and the people in it. Which I always knew, but now... well, freed of all those dutiful presumptions, I breathe what feels like freer air. And am free in ways I never before knew I was missing."

"Such as?"

"Such as the freedom to write poems."

"You are crafting poems? How wonderful! What topics?"

"Well," he smiled with a hint of color in his cheeks, "just one poem so far. And the topic... well, see if you are familiar with it." He held out a small, much folded piece of paper toward her.

She took it carefully, but as she touched one of its corners with a finger that was trying to tremble, he rose. "You mean to go?"

His smile almost seemed nervous. "Although I would be glad to watch you do anything, Sophie, it's rightly said that watching another read is hardly a spectator sport." His smile flattened to match a somber hint in his tone. "Besides, some things are best done in private. This might prove to be one of them." He reached out his hand slowly.

Unsure, she took it. He held it longer than would be expected as part of any meeting or parting of friends. Much, much longer.

He whispered something she could not hear, nodded into a half bow, and left the infirmary quickly.

Sophie teased open one corner of the paper, then another, and then, cross with herself, opened the rest briskly and started reading...

Chapter 32

Oranjestad, St. Eustatia

When Leonora arrived in the infirmary and said hello, Dr. Brandão's response was unusually muted. Sophie did not respond at all. In fact, she wasn't moving at all. She was sitting in a chair, pushed back against the wall on its own, reading something on a piece of paper. Or simply staring at it; Leonora could not tell which.

"Sophie," she asked, "are you well?"

After a long moment, Sophie answered without looking up. "I am well. I was given a poem. Written for me."

Leonora glanced at Brandão, who ducked his head into his work in order to hide a smile.

"I see," said Leonora. Unsure how to proceed, she sought a way to bridge the topic of receiving a poem with something she could comment upon meaningfully. "Oh!" she said aloud as inspiration provided an answer.

Sophie glanced up.

"Well," Leonora explained, affecting an offhanded tone because they never came naturally to her, "your comment put me in mind of the poems I have received from Rik—er, Lord Bjelke. Well, I suppose most of them are *treatises*. I know my answers are. Poems are too indefinite. Although, I do like them. Well, some."

This was not going well at all. "What I mean is that Rik and I exchange writings of ours," she added lamely, "but sometimes, he writes a poem." Leonora gritted her teeth, was quite sure that if Anne Cathrine was here, this was one of those moments when she should sigh and rest her suddenly heavy forehead in her suddenly weary palm.

But that was forgotten when, looking up, she noticed that Brandão was now holding himself very still, as if he might start quaking. His face was almost as rigid. His color was increasing. "Doctor, are you quite well?" she asked hastening in his direction.

He held up a hand quickly, arresting her approach. "Yes, quite well." It sounded like he had his jaws and throat clenched, as one does when trying to stifle a yawn or laughter.

"Are you quite sure?"

"I am in perfect heh-heh-health," he gasped out, covering his mouth as his eyes began to water. He looked away and cleared his throat several times. When he mastered himself, he turned toward Sophie. "Now that Lady Leonora is here, I see no reason that you should not use the day to find some serenity." He smiled and his eyes crinkled. "So long as you may."

Sophie answered with a wry smile and a nod. She rose, kissed Leonora on the forehead, and walked out of the infirmary into the bright Caribbean sunshine.

Leonora watched her go, turned back to Brandão, who seemed to have recovered from what she now surmised to have been a suppressed laughter, but at what, she could not imagine. "While we have a moment alone, Doctor, I would be grateful if you could answer a question for me."

He nodded, his face a study in careful self-control.

"I have been wondering: if I was contemplating the medical arts as my life's work, would you recommend commencing those studies here, or back in Europe?"

When Brandão turned to her, speechless, his face was as she usually beheld it, except more serious. Grave, even.

"I ask this," she carried on, filling the unexpected silence, "because I have been weighing the two options in terms of what I see as their respective merits.

"If I remain here, I shall accrue much practical experience in a frontier region where both common and novel medical challenges will present themselves. And of course, I would be working at the side of one of the foremost doctors of our era. I am inclined to think that is the superior option, because the opportunity is quite unique."

Brandão might have been preparing to respond, but Leonora did not notice his slight shift in posture until after she had resumed. "But in Europe, there are universities and libraries. Not the least of which is the one in Grantville, although I hear most books with any medical significance have been copied and recopied for inclusion in the collections of every major medical faculty. And of course, I might be able to apprentice myself to one of the up-time practitioners and learn their advanced techniques firsthand."

It looked like Brandão might be trying to interject something again, but Leonora reasoned that with her discursus so near its end, she might as well finish it. "However, all those universities and books and up-timers will still be there in the years to come. But this opportunity with you, here, at this pivotal time in the Caribbean, will not last. So my thought is to remain *here* to prepare for subsequent work *there*. What is your opinion, Doctor?"

And she sat to wait for his reply.

Brandão sat also, although he looked exhausted. Which was peculiar because he had barely moved an inch since she had started talking. "Lady Leonora," he said eventually, "in the first place, I am honored. Far beyond my ability to convey, given my limited mastery of English."

He moved his stool closer. "But secondly, I must be frank: you should not remain here." She frowned and started to open her mouth, but he shook his head and raised a quelling finger. "Attend, dear child...and I must be so bold as to address you that way, to give the necessary, added emphasis to my recommendation. Although my station is far, far beneath yours, I hope you will not be offended that I have fatherly feelings toward you, and that, more crucially, I offer my advice in that fond context."

Leonora was so surprised, and so touched, and so fearful that she might start crying, that she could only nod. She could also imagine Anne Cathrine across the room, sighing in relief at her continued silence.

"You are the most promising young assistant I have ever had, and a more extraordinary student than I believed our species could produce. And in working here with me, you have seen what is involved in this work and so, have had ample opportunity to consider and distinguish whether your affinity for it is a passing fascination or a true calling. Which is arguably especially important in *your* case, my child."

Leonora nodded, but Brandão continued too swiftly for her to slip in a comment. "You would continue to learn by staying here, certainly, but over the past ten months, you have already reached and exceeded that plateau of knowledge and experience which readies you for the next step: acquiring mastery in the deepest foundations of the medical arts. Indeed, because you have seen so much, and learned so quickly, there is another skill that you must acquire. And no one may teach it to you but you, yourself."

She blurted the question so he could not smother it with more of his own words: "And what skill is that, Doctor?"

He smiled like a grandfather might have, and she realized, suddenly and almost painfully, that here was the relative she had always wished for without even knowing it. That he was a small, withered, Sephardic *murrano* whose acquaintance she would never have been allowed to make back home only quickened her appreciation of, and devotion to, him.

She realized he was still smiling, but had not answered. "What skill must I teach myself, Doctor?"

Brandão reached out very slowly, as if hazarding to touch a wild creature that had wandered close. He held her chin gently in his sunbaked, wrinkled fingers. "You must teach yourself how to hold your tongue, you wonderful young woman. Not to be silent: that is a different lesson, and one I hope you *refuse* to learn!"

"But . . . but what is the difference between holding your tongue and being silent?"

"Holding one's tongue is akin to a hunter holding one's fire until the right moment. Being silent is to accept that it is not your place to be a hunter, and so never firing at all. Ever." He nodded grimly. "I have seen too many young women forced to accept the latter."

She nodded, but also could feel her face contorting into one titanic frown. "I understand that."

"Yes"—he smiled—". . . but?"

"But how do I know when it is time to fire and when not?" she almost wailed. "There is so much illogic in the utterances of so many persons. Thinking in the midst of that is like . . . is like trying to remember and hum a complex tune in a crowded market, with a bedlam of voices crying wares in every language. Discerning the right moment to speak, and what might be heard and received, is frustrating beyond couth description, Doctor."

He waggled her chin before releasing it with a sigh. "And that, child, is what you must learn to do, nonetheless. And it is more important for *you* to achieve than any other student or assistant I have ever had."

She pouted. "Because I utter such nonsense?"

He shook his head. "Because you utter such insights as will shock others. Or they may fail to fully understand them. Which is worse.

"The most influential among those 'others' whom you might shock or baffle are learned professors, experienced physicians, and men of power and title. With rare exception, they will not welcome being routinely shown to be no more perspicacious than a girl who is barely on the cusp of womanhood. Indeed, if you are not careful, you will unintentionally yet clearly show them to be your intellectual inferiors. This you must avoid at all costs. Your own noble birth and relations will shield you from some of the consequences that might result, but it will also inspire jealousy and resentment."

"And you would send me back to... to all that?"

He nodded. "I would. Because you must now go there to learn the foundations of this art, that you may grow to your full potential in it. And, unless I miss my guess, leave a profound mark upon its development." He smiled sadly. "But my dear, as a woman, there are many who will be determined to impede you, to make your path difficult, even humiliating. You must be prepared for that."

"And yet you suggest that it is worth my while to try."

He leaned forward. "Leonora Christiansdatter, I do indeed say it is important for you to try. But moreso, it is imperative for *us* that you try. For all of us. In most of the world, medicine has excluded half of humanity—*your* half—from its ranks. It has done so to the detriment of *all*. I grew up in that tradition, and only learned the human cost of it when I came to the New World, where women were giving birth without the aid of midwives. I could not stand by; I helped where I could and where I was allowed.

"But you could change all that. Your skill, your birth, and your access to up-timers through your already close relations with them could change the face of medicine. In every regard."

Leonora felt her earlier big frown threatening to return. "But I haven't the acquaintance of any up-time physicians."

Brandão waved away the objection. "That will be

yours for the asking. And if you can be accepted as an assistant to an up-timer, I would commend you seek out one above all others: Sharon Nichols."

Leonora felt her heart rise up. "Yes! She who performed surgeries before the most esteemed doctors in Venice. Do you think she *would* have me as an assistant?"

Brandão raised an upended palm of uncertainty. "I cannot say. Who but she may? But I suspect she would advise you as I would: attain the foundations of this art before you work alongside her."

Leonora could not see an oblique way to approach the topic, so she headed at it directly. "Do you know her? Could you write to her on my behalf?"

The wizened physician smiled. "That letter is half composed already." Seeing her surprise, he tapped his temple and added, "Right in here." He rose. "I see our friend with the early onset of gout is coming back. No doubt he overindulged at the dance and the sequelae have yet to relent. Let us be ready to receive him."

Chapter 33

Oranjestad, St. Eustatia

From the window overlooking the street, Anne Cathrine watched as Leonora rushed up the stairs of what was coming to be known as Danish House, and then, after charging around the corner from the foyer, burst into the chamber that had evolved into the ladies' sitting room. Clutching a handful of papers, she checked to see that Sophie and Anne Cathrine were both there. Evidently satisfied in her expectations, she nodded and sat herself down at the table in the middle of the room.

Sophie leaned toward her. "Are you well, Leonora? You look quite flushed."

Leonora nodded, still panting, and shook the papers under her friend's graceful nose. "I've got it all. Right here. Took me hours. Tracked down a dozen people. Some didn't want to answer. Had to try others. But I've got enough. It's complete."

"What's complete? What is it?" Anne Cathrine asked.

"A dossier. On him."

"Who?"

She stared at Anne Cathrine like she feared her older sister had gone irremediably insane.

"Who?" she shot back. "Why—him!" She spun toward Sophie. "HAO!"

Sophie frowned, repeated the letters carefully. "H. A. O. And that is—?"

"Hugh Albert O'Donnell! How can you be so wise and so...well, slow. It takes too long to say the name. Or write it."

Anne Cathrine noticed she had put that opinion to use: the dossier was labeled HAO.

"So here's what I learned about him."

Sophie held up a hand. "Leonora, I am grateful, but—"

"See here," said Leonora with a hint of frustration in her voice, "I was at the dance and saw you. With him. Everyone did. There is no secret what was happening, just as there is no secret about what is likely—very likely—to happen next. So, although you have learned a great deal about HA—um, 'Hugh,' I took it upon myself to put details to the...the broad facts we have of him." But her concluding tone added, *Which is to say, the details any sensible woman should have in hand before she considers a proposal of marriage.*

Sophie and Anne Cathrine looked over the top of Leonora's almost steaming chestnut hair and exchanged shrugs. Sophie sat back. "I am most grateful, Leonora. Please do share with us."

Anne Cathrine leaned in sharply. "Share the *short* version," she said, sending her *trust me on this* look to her tall friend. Who answered with a small smile.

Leonora shot a cross glance at her sister's qualification and, in a disappointed tone, began. "So I will omit all my arduous research into the time he spent at Archduchess Isabella's court in Brussels and his interactions while there. I shall also omit the details of the attainting of his lands. I shall also omit the unsolicited comments of the Wild Geese here in Oranjestad. They seem very fond of, but also very familiar, with him."

Anne Cathrine asked the question before she could stop herself. "But do they *respect* him?"

Leonora stared at her. "They consider him their prince-in-exile and king-to-be. And when any one of them made too broad a jest at his expense, dark looks from the rest stilled that. Immediately. Why do you ask?"

"Just a reflex," Anne Cathrine answered, but she was using her casual tone to conceal the instinct that caused her inquiry: *because capable leaders who lack respect are done before they begin, whereas capable leaders with complete respect can only be stopped by fate or a bullet.* "I'm sorry for interrupting."

"No matter," Leonora answered irritably. "It seems that once all the details are removed, this is indeed a very, very short version.

"Lord O'Donnell is the godson of the Archduchess Isabella and her late husband, the Archduke Albert. From whence comes Lord O'Donnell's middle name. His mother was in some vague combination of house arrest and lady-in-waiting at the English court. I cannot discover much that suggests she made any great effort to have him restored to her, or for her to be reunited with him in Brussels. I am equally unable to discern if this was pragmatism or from a want of maternal affection."

Anne saw Sophie's eyes become slightly more reflective, but she remained silent.

"However, his godmother remained childless and it seems that all those instincts, ambitions, and hopes were vested in the young Lord O'Donnell, whose progress to the New World seems to have been motivated by two of her clear objectives: to protect him from English assassins and to provide him with a solid financial basis.

"He was a page at Isabella's court until he began his education at the University of Louvain where he completed his degree, even as he trained in the martial skills he used in the service of the Spanish Lowlands. By the time he was twenty, he had led infantry, artillery, and cavalry units and had been made a Knight of the Order of Alcántara for his service. It was also intended, no doubt, to keep the Irish securely attached to their Spanish patrons.

"Who, in his case, was none other than King Philip himself, and through whose intercession, he had occasion to correspond directly with the pontiff of the Roman Church. He speaks English, Dutch, French, Latin, and Gaelic fluently. He is less accomplished in Greek. He is known to have some skill in Italian and German."

Leonora glanced up at the ceiling so she didn't meet anyone's eyes. "I suspect he may now be acquiring a facility in Danish, as well."

She returned to her reading. "In conclusion, the legal contortions and casuistries whereby the English king attainted his title—done only after Hugh's accused father died—was widely denounced. Quite vociferously, in several cases. The ranking nobility of the continent, regardless of their relationship to England, expressed profound questions as to its ultimate legality." Without stopping to breathe, she looked up and asked, "Is that helpful?"

Sophie's eyelids fluttered as she sought a suitable response. "It is overwhelming," she murmured.

"In what way?"

Sophie had recovered enough to smile. "My dear Leonora, you . . . you might have left me some mystery."

Leonora frowned. "Why would you want that?"

Anne Cathrine approached from the side. "Many people feel that mystery quickens feelings of . . . romance."

"Well, that's ridiculous," pronounced Leonora, who also did not note that "romance" had, in this case, been intended euphemistically. "A man and woman should know all they can about each other so that they may proceed forward in a productive and harmonious fashion."

Anne Cathrine suppressed a smile of her own. *Oh, sister, when you fall in love, you will not know the top of your head from the soles of your feet.* Aloud: "That is a wise and noble sentiment. And this was very useful information. Now, let us—"

"Hold," interrupted Leonora with surprising firmness. "Have I somehow been in error? Is what everyone is *saying* will happen not actually *going to* happen? By which I mean: Sophie, are you not soon to be betrothed to Hugh?"

Sophie's smile was sad and maybe a little weary. "In truth, I do not know."

"Well, what is he about, then, writing a poem for you and conspiring with Dr. Brandão to speak to you alone in the infirmary? No, do not interrupt me,

Anne Cathrine, and it does not matter how I found out. Suffice it to accept the obvious: that I did. Now, Sophie, what does Hugh mean with all these attentions, then?" Leonora pressed, almost crossly. "Has he spoken of marriage, or not?"

Sophie laughed, at which Leonora's frown deepened. Sophie stretched out a hand toward her friend. "I do not laugh at you. I laugh at the idea of knowing the mind of another. And I also laugh at the mere notions of proposals, of etiquette, of marriage."

Leonora flinched as if struck. "You . . . laugh at marriage?" Anne Cathrine had the impression that her younger sister was about to transition from Sophie's friend to physician, concerned with a sudden onset of hysteria, delirium, or both.

Sophie shrugged. "I only speak for myself, for my own life. I know quite well how blessed that union can be"—she glanced at Anne Cathrine—"and with what joy it may rightly be anticipated," she finished, taking Leonora's hand. She shook her head. "But for me—I do not think so. Not any longer."

Leonora snatched her hand away; Anne Cathrine could read in her face that it wasn't malice or disapproval which drove that reaction. It was fear. "Then what—how do you proceed?" she asked in a tone at once worried, baffled, and reluctant. "How do you— how does any woman, regarding of rank—deepen their, their, well, *friendship* with a man without such a union as the intended, honorable outcome?"

Sophie stretched, arms high above her head; the long limbs made her look like a lance aimed at a limitless sky. "I do not know, and I do not care."

"You don't *care*? How could—?"

"Leonora," Sophie said, lowering her arms and her tone, "do remember: I have been betrothed, wedded, bedded, and a mother. This is not some sudden philosophical discovery, my dear young friend. This is clarity. This is a view of the world unobstructed by the demands and the conventions of others, of society."

"And what does this view, this clarity, show you?"

Sophie settled her hands calmly on the table. "It has revealed the sobering fact that as I think upon my existence back home—well, back in Europe—I can no longer abide the notion of returning to that life. To the stultifying constraints of lineage, and inheritance, and propriety, and legality, and honor. I do not know how my relations with Hugh shall progress, but I know this: it will not be on those—on *their*—terms. It shall be on *ours*."

"And this is his suggestion?"

Anne Cathrine put a hand on her sister's shoulder. "Just listen."

Sophie nodded her thanks, took Leonora's hands in hers. "I do not know, nor could I anticipate, what Hugh might think of all this. Hugh would not even think to ask such questions of me. And he would not ask me to compromise myself. But I no longer feel that, by breaking with the rules of society, I would be doing so. I would simply be jettisoning all the encumbrances of a society besotted with status, prestige, and power.

"What that means for me, for him, for us, I do not know. How can I? In the old world, we could not even dream of joining, of existing, outside those limits, those shackles. But here?" She stretched her arms again. "This is in all regards a New World. And it would destroy the possibilities of true discovery for us to hastily impose the shapes and impediments of the old world upon it."

Leonora did not lean, so much as fall, against her chair's backrest. "Well," she said, and then was quiet.

Anne Cathrine patted her shoulder, met her friend's eyes. "And Hugh . . . Hugh has not heard your thoughts on these matters? At all?"

Sophie shook her head. "Not yet. I would hardly know where to begin, for I am yet new in finding my way through these revelations. I feel like a toddler walking into a mostly unlit room. I am not afraid of what might be there, or falling or bumping into unexpected objects, but I do not yet know its shape, cannot responsibly call to another to come see what I have discovered." She smiled sadly. "But we have both been so ill used by the old world—so utterly neglected or abused by those whose responsibilities to us should have been inviolably rooted in blood, in law, or both—that our bonds to the lands of our birth are frayed unto breaking."

Anne Cathrine nodded understanding, but said, "He is the last heir to the throne of Ireland. People look to him. They may call upon him to restore their country."

She nodded. "Yes, I know this. But as he has said, he can help them best from here by securing the oil from Trinidad and through it, amassing funds that may be used to advance their interests, and one day, perhaps, their cause. And if he must eventually go to his land, then that will be addressed when the time comes. I cannot know what I shall do so far in the future when I do not even know what tomorrow will hold."

Anne Cathrine nodded. "Such an array of possibilities must be exciting. And terrifying."

Sophie nodded. "It is both. And more."

"Do you mean to stay here, then? Permanently?"

One half of Sophie's mouth hinted at rueful irony. "Do you not?"

Anne Cathrine felt a flush as she realized she had no answer, no certainty that her growing sense of purpose here in the New World was not also diminishing the ties that bound her to the old.

Suddenly, both her home in Copenhagen and Eddie's in Grantville seemed impossibly far away.

Chapter 34

Nezpique Bayou, Louisiana

The sound of a distant rifle shot, and then another, echoed unsteadily through the bayou's trees and Spanish moss. The sound seemed to shimmer through the air the way light passes through a waterfall. Very different from the sound that the same Winchester .40-72 made in the grassy, rock-sided valleys of Germany, Larry reflected.

Katkoshyok looked up at the twin reports, cocked his head to clarify the direction, and nodded. "Our men find the bison near the lick. I will send others to help with the kill."

Larry nodded his thanks. "As ever, we are grateful to the Ishak."

Katkoshyok smiled. "You are a most polite visitor to Ishak lands. Maybe too polite." Although his smile did not diminish, he looked up and met Larry's eyes directly. "When tribes live together for a month, it is tiring to always be thanking. Be at ease, Larry. Be with us and of us."

Larry nodded, barely stopped himself from saying

"thank you" yet again. And discovered why he kept saying it: because the alternative was to offer a tangible reciprocal favor or courtesy of some kind. And that was dangerous and uncertain ground.

Yes, there'd been exchanges of gifts. The Ishak highly prized the simplest of iron implements, and steel was almost literally the stuff of magic, to them. And yes, they'd traded visits to each other's homes. The two-day trip to *Courser*, now anchored just beyond the mouth of the Mermentau, filled the Ishak with wonder and cemented their friendship in some quiet but profound fashion that it took several more days to figure out. Namely, that no white visitors to their lands had yet brought them to see their ships, much less board them, and certainly had not patiently answered their questions about how the various systems operated. The secrecy that their prior visitors had always maintained about their far more rudimentary technology had purchased an aura of wizardry but at the price of aloofness and distrust, and therefore, anything like true friendship. So far, Mike Stearns' history-altering strategy for how to initiate contact with Native Americans, at least in this part of the country, was working extremely well.

So well that, when Larry almost embarrassedly confessed why they had come searching for the Ishak, Katkoshyok and Tulak simply shrugged and offered to help seek the source of the strange oil that he sought. Larry explained that in his time, it had been found by gases that burned, rising up from uneven ground, or possibly by a strange smell that could be detected near open ground or greasy sands almost from the limit of bowshot. The Ishak leaders shrugged again. They knew of no such things or places, but would happily help their new friends find them. But what did they want them for?

Larry thought that would be the beginning of a long discussion about oil, and power, and machines, and technology. But the Ishak heard the quick version— that the oil powers the most important machines on their ship and the motorboat—and nodded their understanding and welcomed them to take as much as they liked.

At which Larry had fallen silent. To take "as much as they liked" meant something very different to the Ishak than to Europeans. Although Larry tried to impress on Katkoshyok and Tulak the scope and size of an oil well and its immediate infrastructure, he kept coming away with the impression that he was failing to impart the almost factorylike aspect of industrial resource extraction. He mentioned all the wagons, and the steam pinnaces and barges on the Nezpique and Mermentau, and the processing plant they would probably have to build where the Mermentau first flowed into Big Mud Lake, but to the Ishak, these all seemed like interesting places where they could always visit their new friends, partake of the wonders being built there, and trade stories and goods. And, if Larry read his Native Americans correctly, they might also be imagining them as places to find wives or husbands, since mixing gene pools was a known benefit to almost all tribes, and furthermore, built bonds of alliance and mutual support.

Or such was the case in their world. Treachery within families or bonded groups was not unknown among the Ishak, but was so unusual and reviled that such incidents lived long in memory. Unlike Europe, where backstabbing family members had long ago been raised to an art form that was still in its full flower. Mike Stearns had laid out some pretty principled and firm rules about dealing with the native peoples of the Americas, but even so, Larry wondered if they could really understand what they were agreeing to. On the other hand, to deprive them of the choice to agree—to become their "legal guardians" in a kind of parental caretaking role—would be a disrespectful and demeaning reassertion of the "Great White Father" concept garbed in robes of futile political correctness. At times like these, Larry almost hoped that his expedition's one enduring and crucial failure—failing to find oil—might persist, even become permanent.

As if to punctuate that thought, Karl Klemm came trudging down the game path from the marsh swards that predominated just inland, which they tentatively identified as being close to the up-time town of Evangeline. "Any luck?" Larry asked.

Karl stared at him, flopped down and accepted a cup of fresh water with a grateful nod.

"I guess that means 'no'? And where's Vogel?"

"Herr Vogel is a minute or two behind. Two of our Ishak guards are teaching him about local game tracks." Karl shook his head. "I am sorry to be so cross, Major, but it is most frustrating. We have excellent information, reasonably good maps, know the specific signs to look for in this oil field, and have only three or four square miles to cover. At most. And yet, we have found nothing. Nothing." He knocked back the water, stared moodily at the bayou, nodded at one of the Ishak dogs wading out after two small children who were playing "touch the strange red boat": the most popular game among the tribe's four- and five-year-olds. It required them to go out to the limit that their parents permitted and indulged their endless fascination with touching and running their hands along the smooth, red sides of the boat. However, the dogs, while not averse to the water, usually did not join in the game, since it did not involve chasing or tugging anything.

Tulak nodded sympathetically. "A small place can seem very big when a man searches for a very, *very* small thing within it. Do not despair. We shall continue to assist you."

"Tulak, friend, you are very kind," Karl replied, swatting at flies. "Perhaps too kind. Your people have better—necessary—things to do other than help us look for these burning gases or slippery sands."

Katkoshyok smiled. "We do have other things to do. But we are doing them more easily because of how you help us." He jerked his head in the direction that Larry had heard the shot come from. "It might have taken a day and half a dozen arrows to wound and wear down a bison to the point where it may be killed. My ears tell me that one of your rifles has just killed it at the first ambush." He stared up through the hanging mosses. "It is not yet midday. The whole of the kill will be here by nightfall. So you save us more time than you cost us. But either way, that is nothing among friends, Karl."

"Thank you, Katkoshyok."

Katkoshyok looked at Larry as if to say, "you are *all* too polite," just before the dog following the children in the bayou began barking. That surprised one of the children who had been reaching for the side of the boat. The small figure toppled over in the water and disappeared beneath its surface with a gurgling shriek of surprise and panic.

Larry was running toward the weed-choked banks before he was conscious of having risen to his feet. And in between strides, the full mosaic of unfolding disaster became clear.

The barking dog had only been part of the reason the child had stumbled and was now in over its head. The more urgent fact was that the last coil of the mooring line had obviously been lazily laid and, with the persistent, gentle motion of the water, had slipped free. That extra play in the mooring line had allowed the boat to drift three or four feet farther from the shore, where the shelflike apron of mud and sand gave way to a steeper drop-off into five feet of water.

But the dog's bark had not been a warning of deeper water ahead, but rather, predators inbound. As his long strides carried Larry closer to the edge of the bayou, they also put more of the tunnellike tree canopy behind him. The increased periphery of sightlines showed him what the dog was barking at: a pair of mostly sunken narrow logs drifting downstream in the direction of the children. Except those were not logs.

They were alligators.

"*Ciwā't!*" cried Larry in Ishak. "Two of them. Karl, get my gun!"

"What?"

"Get my gun and shoot those gators."

"What are you doing?"

Jeez, whaddaya think? "I'm getting the kid." *Thereby proving myself to be the stupidest person on this planet.* "Just start shooting." Larry shrugged off his pack, kicked off his shoes.

"But Larry, I'm not very good at—"

"*Just fucking shoot, will you?*"

And then Larry was into the water. After two steps in the foot-sucking muck, he realized that swimming would be faster. He gulped in air, aimed at the place where the child had gone down, and, as he dove, was almost hysterically glad to hear the roar of the .40-72, along with the ferocious, I'll-take-on-Godzilla barking of the dog. *Gotta love dogs.*

Larry was a passable swimmer, but had never planned to go free diving in a zero-visibility mud-hole choked with weeds and what looked like coffee grounds. He pushed ahead, heard two dull reports, then muffled screaming. Wondering what the hell he would do if the alligator had already reached the child, he clawed his way back up to the surface.

And found the child screaming straight into his face. She had fortunately resurfaced on her own, but was coughing up brown bayou water in between wild sobs of panic. *And she hasn't even noticed the gators, yet. Best keep it that way.* Larry made himself smile at her, hoped she didn't notice his eyes look over her shoulder to gauge the distance to the gators: about fifteen yards. *C'mon Karl*, he thought angrily, as he slipped an arm around the child and started to tow her back to shore, *start shooting the way I know you can, you god-damned—*

The Winchester barked, probably the fourth time, and the lead gator flipped and thrashed in the water. Probably only six feet from toe to tail tip, the predator disappeared under the water, the heavy .40-72 game round having either killed it or, more likely, convinced it to go off somewhere to nurse its very probably mortal wound.

But the second gator was the larger of the two, and was not deterred by the apparent fate of its fellow. It came on with slowly increasing speed. The little girl, who was already flailing against being towed on her back, saw the approaching serpentine back-ridge of the beast and screamed long, loud, and impossibly shrill.

Larry tried to remember that good swimming form made you fast in the water, while sheer brute force made you flounder, but it was difficult to maintain that discipline, knowing that an alligator was quite literally coming to bite your butt off. He stroked and kicked past the dog, which was barking and snarling and standing its ground with the wild abandon of a canine berserker. *Well, given that the adversary is an alligator, more like a kamikaze . . .*

And then came the sweetest sound Larry thought he'd ever heard: the sustained and much closer roars of a Winchester .40-72. Between each report was a smooth *shk-klak!* of the lever being cycled, and the third shot must have hit the gator, which splashed fitfully for a moment, but then bore on, only a few yards behind Larry.

The fourth shot splashed in the water well behind the gator.

Dammit, Karl, I know you don't want to hit me, but tighten up that aim and lead *the son of a—*

The fifth shot seemed to hit a grenade. Or at least that's what it sounded and looked like. The gator, an eight-footer, exploded into a swirling rage of what must have been death throes. Glancing over the girl's quaking body, he caught only a brief glance of the beast's head and a front limb slashing back down into the water in something like a desperate fury—right before a second Winchester started firing, sending round after round into the creature.

Larry, not trusting that the two gators he'd seen were the only ones lurking and cruising for prey, stood while he was still in three feet of water and heaved the girl toward the shore in the direction of Katkoshyok, who was already halfway to him. On the riverbank, Karl was hastily reloading his Winchester with smooth, professional efficiency while Vogel, the only one of the Hibernians who had not gone out with the morning's bison-hunting party, scanned the water for further targets, his rifle up and ready.

Once the girl was on shore and being tended to, Larry called the dog out of the water, just as the two guardian hunters who had been traveling with Vogel and Karl waded in to fetch the carcass of the alligator. Katkoshyok looked into Quinn's face as he panted toward the shore. "Well," Larry commented, "that was exciting."

Katkoshyok's hand came down on his shoulder. "You have our thanks, Larry Quinn."

Larry shrugged, then grinned. "What is it with you, Katkoshyok, always saying 'thank you'?"

Katkoshyok blinked and then laughed. "That is well said. And you, Karl: you are a warrior this day. Not many men slay the *ciwā't*, the great monster of these bayous."

"With respect, Chief Katkoshyok, I was not so much a warrior as I was simply a man with a gun who kept shooting at the alligator until I hit it enough."

Larry nudged Karl in the ribs. "That's how we all start, kiddo. Pretty much how we all finish up, too. There's only one bit of bad news about being a soldier."

"And what is that?"

"Over time, it's easier to succeed at the job, but it never gets easier to do it."

"Which is why I am a scientist, Herr Major."

"Yeah. So you say. In the New World, I think we've all gotta be ready to kill our own gators." He walked over to where the little girl had begun vomiting spasmodically. Thick black ooze came out along with the water. "Is she going to be all right?"

"Yes," Tulak answered. "She has just swallowed some river mud."

Larry looked at the viscous black pool that had collected next to her. "Huh. Closest thing we've seen to oil," he sighed.

Tulak raised an eyebrow, looked at the small black puddle, looked back up at Larry. "That is what oil looks like?"

"Why—yes," he replied. "Didn't you know?"

Tulak shook his head. "No. You spoke of strange smells, greasy sands, and fiery gas. You never spoke of black liquid."

Well, son of a—"Karl?"

Klemm was suddenly very red. "Major, you and I followed the same protocols. We described the findings, and the prior signs, that the Grantville sources indicated were seen by the discoverers of the Jennings oil field."

"And you didn't think to give them a physical description of oil itself?"

"No, sir. Er—did you?"

Well, damn it. I guess we were both so busy staying close to the data we had that we shot straight past the obvious. And past the realization that the Ishak have never seen this oil we're talking about. "Tulak, tell me, have you ever seen a liquid like this, rising up from the ground, perhaps?"

Tulak was frowning at the slick of bottom mud the girl had coughed up. "Not exactly. Although when the bayou here rises and floods into nearby fields, there is a place that sometimes—not often, maybe once or twice in a generation—bleeds like this."

"'Bleeds'?" Karl echoed.

"Yes, as though the floodwaters wash away an old scab covering some deep wound in the ground. The blood of that wound is black like this, thick and strong-smelling, as earth blood would be. Might that be the oil you are looking for?"

"It just might be, Tulak," Larry said before he smiled and punched Karl in the shoulder. "It just might be."

Chapter 35

Governor's Palace, Cartagena

Francisco de Murga y Ortiz de Orué, governor of Cartagena, stared glumly out his window at the cerulean perfection of his city's bay. And it *was* his city, damnation. Made safe from *cimarrones* and the excesses of the Inquisition alike since he'd arrived in 1629. Cartagena now had walls that were the envy of even Old-World cities famous for their fortifications.

Soldier and engineer de Murga had not been idle since taking the post at age fifty-nine. "Too old for the job," they'd scoffed behind his back when he arrived. Well, half of those scoffers were dead from pirates, pestilence, or the pride of thinking themselves indestructible in a wild land that specialized in destroying the overconfident. Whereas he was still here, building walls and defeating Spain's foes. Which was the topic of today's business with Captain Gregorio de Castellar y Mantilla and his lieutenant and field engineer, Juan de Somovilla Tejada.

De Murga sat before them sternly, his scowl an intentional reminder of how poorly they'd handled their attempt, last year, to chase the English Puritans off their privateer-harboring colony on New Providence Island, just off the coast of Nicaragua. They were not incompetent men, but nor were they much more than competent, and the English had been innovative and dogged in repulsing the Spanish. So this was a chance for these two *hidalgos* to redeem themselves. Frankly, de Murga wished he could have sent some of his better, younger men to command the land forces that would soon begin embarking for the mission to Trinidad, but de Castellar was too senior to be passed over. "Well," de Murga said and then discovered he really didn't have anything to add. "Well," he repeated. "Are you quite prepared?"

"Quite ready, sir. All nineteen warships and four transports are in complete readiness and the men in fine spirits."

"They'd better be. It's a long trip to windward," de Murga muttered.

"That is so, sir. But just yesterday, the winds began coming around in our favor. So we are eager to be off."

"And I shall not hold you. But there will be no last meeting with Captain Contreras. He has sailed ahead of you."

"To Puerto Cabello?"

"No. I shall not send more ships to Puerto Cabello, not after last year's disaster." And it truly had been a disaster. Only one ship lost, but the supplies that had been collected there to support his final push on Trinidad had been sabotaged by, of all possible adversaries, Irish mercenaries who had once served Spain herself. That they had evidently now sided with the Dutch was every bit as strange as their seizure of

Trinidad. Unless the reports regarding the oil there were true. In that case—well, the world seemed to be turning to stand on its ear, so why not that too?

Castellar glanced sideways at his silent companion before asking, "If we should face heavy weather or other dangers, may we still make for Puerto Cabello?"

De Murga kept himself from uttering a wordless snarl. Just what he did not want to deal with: a completely reasonable and prudent question. "In the event of an emergency, of course. But you are not to lay over there any longer than necessary." He rubbed his eyes. "It is beyond countenancing that last year's raid was chance. The saboteurs either had specific report of our fleet being provisioned in that port, or conjectured that we were preparing to respond to the seizure of Trinidad and knew that our protocols name Puerto Cabello as the final staging area. That's why we built all the warehouses there: to resupply any fleet that must travel all the way to the eastern end of Tierra Firme against its headwinds and contrary currents."

The two officers were nodding like automatons. Castellar broke out of the repetitious motion first. "Your Excellency, you mentioned that Captain Contreras has already departed, but you did not reveal his destination."

"Contreras is overseeing the action that will be taken against Curaçao."

Castellar and Somovilla exchanged long looks. "Governor, did I hear you correctly? Captain Contreras is departed for Curaçao? Already?"

"Yes. Better than a week ago." *Closer to two, actually, but who's counting?* "We have secured the allies and support necessary to deal with the Dutch raiders there. Consequently, you will not need to detach any of your ships to address that problem, thereby preserving your full offensive strength to apply against the usurpers on Trinidad."

Castellar's eyes opened a bit wider. "Governor, does this mean that Captain Contreras has succeeded in, er, negotiating successfully with the Brethren of the Coast?"

De Murga suddenly felt queasy. That Contreras, the finest officer he had, was necessarily sent to secure the cooperation of brutes that should have been drawn and quartered in the public square was a deep blemish of shame upon Spanish arms and policies. Too many bribes, too many sinecures for noblemen's sons, too much opulence, too much self-indulgence, too much embezzlement of funds earmarked for military expenses and maintenance: Spain was getting soft, and so, like Rome in her dotage, she took that fateful step of relying upon mercenaries. Or what was worse, murderers. "Yes, Captain Contreras has made the necessary arrangements. Consequently, even if you should happen to encounter a known pirate upon your journey to Trinidad, do not engage him unless he makes to engage you or other ships flying our flag."

"Captain Contreras has secured the cooperation of *all* the Brethren of the Coast?"

"Of course not. But many. And it will be some time before I receive a comprehensive list. In the meantime, we must err on the side of caution and desist from meting out whatever punishment these dogs might have warranted a week ago. Because they might be *our* dogs now, you see." De Murga fairly spat his conclusion.

Castellar stood. Somovilla followed suit. "I shall refrain from troubling you further, Governor, but I must ask: originally, you had indicated that I would at least be rendezvousing with Contreras near Curaçao. To relay orders, possibly provide him with additional munitions, supplies, troops. Am I still to attempt to—?"

De Murga shook his head sharply. "You are to bypass Curaçao. It is no longer necessary that you bring news or matériel there." *And it is absolutely essential that you do not go there and carry away tales of what you might see, of the lengths and depths to which we must now go to protect our rightful places in the New World.*

Which was the doing of that bootlick Olivares, who kept insisting—against all reason—that Tromp had abandoned Recife for Curaçao. Total idiocy. On more levels than he could bear to list. But above all, it was simply a matter of scale. You might—*might*—be able to fit all the ships Tromp had reportedly had in Recife in St. Ann's Bay, but they would have been bulkwark to bulkwark in that small anchorage with an extremely narrow mouth. Tromp was too clever an admiral to put his fleet in such an easily blocked bay.

But with the Inquisition still seeking ways to get back at him, and the unspoken blame when his fleet was not there to stand along with the one Cuba sent to meet his at Trinidad made him all the more vulnerable. Even worse, after the fleet was cut to ribbons in the Grenada Passage, he had still not been able to assure Gamboa and Álvarez of the Antilles that he could fully participate in their greater plans. His own position was potentially at risk, so he had no choice but to act upon Olivares' idiot notions, despite the overwhelming tactical and strategic evidence that Tromp was somewhere in the Leeward Islands. And now with the loss of La Flota off Dominica, de Murga did not doubt that if he failed to follow Olivares' instructions, he would not merely be relieved of his governorship but very possibly his head.

He tried not to let his thoughts influence his expression, but he feared he was glowering at the two soldiers still standing across from him. "By the time you are returning with news of your victory at Trinidad, the Dutch will be gone from Curaçao."

"Gone?" asked Somovilla. "You mean relocated to become slave laborers, such as have built our walls?"

De Murga did not meet the engineer's eyes. "I mean they will be gone. Fare well, and bring glory to Spain."

Chapter 36

Oranjestad, St. Eustatia

Eddie exited his office in Fort Oranje, a box under each arm, and noticed light coming in from the end of the hall: the door to Maarten's office was ajar. Eddie glanced at his watch, wondered how much longer he'd be able to enjoy that convenience. Everything broke, sooner or later.

It was 0530. Not early for Maarten to be up, but early for him to be in his office. Eddie padded quietly in that direction, although with the prosthesis, stealth wasn't really his forte. Not that it ever had been. But in case it wasn't Maarten, it would be prudent to get closer before he—

"Come in, Eddie. I didn't want to disturb you when I arrived, but I am glad you came by."

Eddie slipped into the room, had flashbacks of having been grilled there by three Dutchmen, less than a week earlier. "Okay, Maarten, how did you know?"

"That you were approaching? I heard you."

"No; I figured that. I mean, how did you know I was in my office? The door was closed."

"Ah. Yes, it was closed, but your storm shutters must have been open. The morning wind from the sea: it can make the doors rattle on that side."

Eddie narrowed his eyes. "C'mon, what else? For all you know, the storm shutters could have blown open during the night."

"Well, yes, but there was a faint play of shadows under the door."

"Pretty impressive," Eddie allowed with an approving nod.

"Also," Maarten added as an afterthought, "I asked the sentry."

Eddie gaped; Maarten Tromp had been gaslighting him? No way! He laughed. "There I was thinking you were like some admiral-ninja."

"Admiral what?"

"Ninja? You know, Japanese assassin types who—? Yeah, okay: never mind about ninjas. But instead you were—"

"Hauling your leg, yes?" Maarten was grinning widely.

"Uh... *Pulling* my leg, but yeah, you sure were!" He looked around the large office; it was set up for another meeting. "Ooohh," he said. "Last time all those chairs were around that table—"

"You were being roasted on a spit." Maarten filled in with a much smaller grin. "Have the burns healed yet? Hair still singed?"

Eddie nodded. "Who's on the menu today?"

"I am," Maarten sighed as he tidied papers, sorted them, slipped them into different leather portfolios. "Many of the same cooks, as well. Serooskereken, Corselles, and now Servatius Carpentiere, too."

"Servatius is a good man. What's the occasion?"

"Slavery. The end of it."

Eddie whistled. "All at once? I thought—"

"Not all at once, but faster."

"But none of them are slaveholders."

"You are right, but they are all on the *Politieke Raad*. And they will be the ones who bear the brunt of the slaveholders' anger."

"Are you changing the terms you set out last year?"

Tromp stopped moving his papers around. "Eddie! You do not seriously think that I would—"

"Maarten, I'm not thinking anything in particular. But I know how you feel about slavery, and you know I'm right there with you. So no judgments on my part if you found a loophole. Or three."

Maarten resumed putting his papers into the down-time equivalent of a filing system. "I am changing nothing. I am adding incentives."

"Ah! The carrot instead of the stick."

The admiral tilted his head. "I do not think most of the slaveholders will see it that way. Now, I do not wish to delay you, but has there been any news from Admiral Simpson about the Marines that he planned to send?"

"They left, but just two days ago."

"Such a long delay. Weather?"

"Money. It's pretty tight right now. Well, always, actually. It was supplies and payroll questions and— stuff. Lots and lots of stuff."

"I know how that 'stuff' can be. When are they to arrive?"

"Too early to say. I'll send a new ETA as soon as it shows up in the next secure pouch. Or the next. Or whenever."

"So, their arrival is . . . er, 'need to know'?"

"Absolutely."

"And once you have the ETA, there will be no further communications with them?"

"None. We only hear if there is another schedule change, but within a week, they'll be out of sending range anyhow, so from there on, it's all guesswork. Unless the Bermuda station comes online. Any idea when that agreement will be inked?"

Tromp shook his head. "*Nee.* The smaller the remaining points of negotiation to be settled, the slower the process. It is not uncommon."

"Yeah, I'm starting to see that. Any info you have for me?"

"Just that we have finished cataloging all the cargos from La Flota. You would not believe how much contraband and secreted wealth was on those ships. But there was one strategically significant find: a balloon."

Eddie put his boxes down. "You mean . . . one of ours?"

"Not exactly, but it is a very close copy of the same one that the Wild Geese have."

"So it's French? Made by Turenne?"

"I doubt his shops manufactured it, but it was certainly made by someone who had that pattern to follow, and understood it intimately. According to letters found on the same ship, there was a Frenchman traveling with it. Apparently to instruct the Spanish in its use."

"Could he have been killed in the battle?"

"Unlikely. That ship did not sustain a great deal of damage. But we certainly did not have time to survey the dead. And if he had accomplices to help hide him, or if he was one of the wounded who was not responsive, he could have slipped through. Quite easily."

"So we should assume he did."

"Exactly."

"Maarten, you don't seem very concerned."

"I am not. If he survived and reaches Havana or Santo Domingo, he will certainly make a frank report to their governors there. Unlike a Spaniard, he has no reason to curry favor with the grandees and their proxies. Rather, he'll be appreciated and rewarded for the frank speech they know they will not get from their own people."

Eddie picked up his boxes again. "Well, I guess I'll see you tomorrow." He started to turn away, turned back. "Maarten, I didn't want to say anything at the time, but . . . but why did you have Corselles and Serooskereken with us when we looked at the secure cargos and then the meeting after? I mean, I get the part about telling them about the settlement with the Kalinago, but the rest?"

Maarten sat on the edge of his desk, studied Eddie, smiled. "You already have a suspicion, don't you?"

Eddie smiled, was afraid he might have blushed. "Yes," he admitted.

Tromp nodded. "I can tell from your voice what you already suspect."

Eddie shrugged. "Security test?"

"Yes. They are the only two civilians who will hear certain parts of that information for quite some time. And several facts are actually incorrect."

"I noticed. That's why I guessed. Because if we ever hear about someone suspicious asking questions about those particular matters, then we know one of them is a leak. Either intentionally or just out of carelessness." He looked around the room again. "And that's what you're doing with today's meeting, too? Testing for leaks, but in a slightly different pipe?"

Maarten smiled. "Eddie, you've only just started moving your things, but already I am starting to miss you." He became thoughtful. "Eddie, I have been giving this a great deal of thought. I would very much appreciate it if you would take Kees with you, when you leave for Antigua."

"Evertsen? Why? Won't you need him here?"

"I need him on one of your ships. Learning."

Eddie nodded. It made sense; Kees had a knack for up-time technology. Not just the individual pieces, but how they worked together. But: "Well, if you mean to have him as an XO on one of the Quality class, wouldn't he learn fastest on an active ship?"

"*Resolve* will be active in word only, unless the Spanish force our hand and we must put to sea. But more importantly, you and Mike will be building the future on Antigua. And much of that echoes the very foundations of what built *Resolve*. Not many of us will understand that so rapidly and so completely as Kees will. He should be with the two of you to see, to help, as it comes into existence."

Eddie studied Tromp, realized why the admiral had balked at asking until now. He was uncomfortable making the request because—"You need to make me redundant, Maarten. Replaceable."

"Eddie. Please understand, I do not wish—"

"No, no, I get it. And I agree. I mean, what if something happened to me? Right now, Rik is the only one who could really take over. You need someone who can fill the role I've been in." Eddie shook his head. "Damn. I should have thought of that myself. Not like I get to choose whether or not some Spanish ball sends me to meet my maker."

Tromp's gaze was calculating. "No more than it is your choice when you might receive orders to sail back home. Which is a far more likely occurrence than death in battle."

Eddie smiled. "Your lips to God's ears, Maarten. I'm not in a rush to be fish food, but hey, I'm not invulnerable."

"None of us are. But it is also true that none of us are without superiors who may require our services elsewhere. And until the Spanish can match us ship to ship, I consider it far more likely that you will be called away by John Simpson than by Our Creator. Now, I must ready myself to be broiled by politicians."

Phipps Serooskereken inspected the crack that had snaked halfway down the mug which held his carob coffee. "Well, Maarten, I am glad to hear you do not mean to undo the promises you made this time last year regarding slaveholding."

Jan van Walbeeck held up his left hand, all fingers extended upright. "Five years and then immediate conversion to bondsman status."

Servatius Carpentiere stared solemnly over the rim of his own cup. "Then why are Lieutenant Governor Corselles and Phipps and I—the councilors most vocal in support of the elimination of slavery—all here, and all so early that it is unlikely that anyone else will ever know of this meeting?"

Tromp smiled. Servatius was the most quiet of the group, the most imperturbably calm, and the one who missed nothing. "So that you may know what is coming."

Phipps smiled sourly. "Yes, and to convey it to the council. Whose leading slaveholders are not present, I notice. For a man who routinely stands in the way of cannonballs, Maarten, you haven't much stomach for political argument."

He'd meant it as a good-natured joke, but Tromp elected to answer it seriously. "I haven't much *patience* for it, frankly. In part because it is interminable, and in part because it is rarely conducted with frankness and clarity of actual intent. Whereas the intent of an approaching cannonball is very, very frank indeed." Even Corselles chuckled at that.

Phipps was still smiling. "Point made and taken, Maarten. Now, what do you have in mind regarding the five-year transition away from slavery?"

Tromp nodded toward Jan van Walbeeck. "We mean to accelerate it without changing it."

Corselles put down his cup, worry etching creases across his forehead. "How? And I remind you: the landowners' profits are still dependent upon unpaid labor."

"Speak plainly," Carpentiere muttered darkly. "They are dependent upon slaves."

Pieter shrugged. "As you say. But the point remains. The landowners know that in five years, their costs will increase. Dramatically. So in that time, they must accrue even more profit, just to survive the costs of the transition to . . . to paid labor. And now you mean to shorten that time, even though they are still prohibited from growing tobacco or cotton?"

"Which they can't plant and freight to Europe before some time next year," Phipps retorted. "And it would mean burning off and losing their coming cane crop now to replant. At least they can sell cane for local refinement into products with regional value: rum, pure alcohol, syrups. They will get by."

Corselles grew more animated. "Yes, they get by, but that is not why they came to the New World. They came to get rich. To do that, they must have markets and free labor. Now, after the past ten months of victories over the Spanish, even the slaveholders agree that the sacrifices made to achieve that were not only worthwhile, but wise—and this from men who have little enough love for you, Maarten."

"I am surprised to hear they have any," Tromp replied calmly.

"Well, depending upon what you have in mind, that may come to pass. Our plantation owners sold a great deal of sugar to the convoy and are relieved to trade with European markets once again. But to survive the coming transition from slaves to bondsmen, they must sell a great deal more cane at a similar profit. To do that, they must keep their slaves as long as they may. What possible incentive can you offer to compete with that?"

Van Walbeeck answered. "Five years' freedom from all tariffs on all trade between us and all the countries that are our partners here in the New World. This would apply to both export and import excises."

Servatius Carpentiere frowned. "That will simply result in the slaves being worked to death over that time, so that their owners may maximize their profits. Why should they care if any are left alive at the end of five years? So I say what I have said since we left Recife: why not simply forbid slavery right now? Why tiptoe about the edges of it like a cautious house cat?"

And there, Servatius, thought Tromp, *is why your sovereign could not trust you with more responsibility, why he could not empower you with the broad latitude to carry out mandates in his name. Because although you wish to do the right thing, and are so very calm, you are also rash.*

"As tempting, and satisfying, as the direct and immediate prohibition of slaveholding would be, we would be endangering all the inhabitants of this colony were we to take that step. The slaves most of all."

"I suspect their masters would be at far greater risk if they attempted to defy that law," Carpentiere murmured. "Particularly from the slaves themselves."

Van Walbeeck spread his hands in appeal. "Yes, and that is exactly the outcome we must avoid. Because if the slave owners defy the law, will the slaves calmly sit by and wait for our soldiers to secure their release? I do not think I would!

"But then where does that leave us? With slaves killing their owners to break free. And many of the slaves being killed by the better-armed and -trained owners in the process. And for every slave so killed, two more who loved that martyr will spring up to carry on the fight. Which will then become as much about vengeance as justice."

Van Walbeeck closed his eyes. "I have seen how quickly these conflagrations rage out of all control, during my time in the Pacific. Once the fighting becomes personal, the resentment and hatred of the slaves combust wildly with the bigotry and fear of their owners. And after the fires have finally guttered out, it is impossible to sort out who injured who first and with what measure of justice.

"This is because although the commercial class might have no affinity for slavery, the slaveholders are often tied to them by marriage, by faith, by language. So do the merchants and artisans stand by to see all the slaveholders consumed by a two-day fire storm of retribution? No. And so, because of those personal ties, townspeople invariably enter the fight on the wrong side. But once the first of them is killed, it becomes their fight, too."

Van Walbeeck shook his head. "No, there is a better path. And we have already taken the first and crucial step in that direction. About which: you are aware of the dozens of slaves whose labor this government has 'leased' from their owners? The ones who we are secretly shipping to Antigua to help build our new facilities there?"

All three of the politicians nodded. Corselles murmured, "Of course."

"Well, during their absence, two things will occur. Firstly, the owners of those slaves will make a considerable amount of money. Not immense mind you, but money without risk. Also, their investment in the slaves themselves is not at risk. The labor leases stipulate that this government must repay the owners the purchase price for any slaves who might die in accidents or escape."

Carpentiere's face was unchanged, but his eyes seemed to ignite. "So, you mean to free them, then? To pay the insurance as the price of their freedom? That is as bold as it is just."

"And is also financially insupportable," Serooskereken grunted with a hint of regret.

"It would also be unwise," Tromp added. "As Jan said, we must avoid abrupt action, lest that become the catalyst for an equally abrupt reaction. And if a large number of the leased slaves were to strangely 'escape' while on Antigua, their owners would know that was not the result of error, but intent."

Servatius folded his hands. "So if you do not mean to pay for their 'escape' to freedom, then how do you propose to achieve that less 'abruptly'?"

Van Walbeeck grinned. "The up-timers have an interesting axiom about that. It involves cooking frogs."

Serooskereken's face contracted into an asterisk of wrinkles centered on his nose. "You mean, as the French do?"

Jan laughed. "I am not speaking of a recipe, my dear Phipps, but an axiom. And here is the gist of it:

"You put a frog in a pot of water, so high-sided that he may not escape easily. Now, if you put that pot over a roaring fire, the frog will feel that rapid increase in heat and hop out, struggling as may be needed. But if you raise the temperature slowly, ever so slowly, the frog never feels it. Rather, he keeps adapting to it . . . until he is cooked."

Corselles shrugged. "Yes, yes, and so how do you propose to—er, slowly increase the heat on the land-owners?"

"Well, it's already started, of course. By making money from the leases, they do not have to watch over their slaves nor worry about whether the weather will produce a good crop. So we're already introducing the landowners to a new way of life; less money than they'd envisioned, but also not as risky, expensive, or exhausting to make.

"The second phase will start when, in a few days, we shall announce the incentive I mentioned earlier: a five-year exemption upon both export and import. Their profit margins shall thus be drastically increased."

Phipps nodded. "I believe I see where you are going with this."

Tromp smiled. "I suspect you do. Not long after that, we take a third step. We announce that our partner nations have imposed one requirement upon those who wish to take advantage of the exemptions: the recipient may not be a slaveholder. Or, in the case of speculators, the goods exempted may not have been produced by slaves."

Carpentiere was solemn. "At which point, the actual intent of the exemptions will be writ clear: to get the owners to free their slaves. Why not simply announce the exemptions and the stipulations all at once?"

"Because," Jan twinkled, "that's the time over which we are boiling the frog, their initial resistance to the idea. By putting some time between those two announcements, the landowners will have had time to consider which future seems more prudent and more pleasant. They can either keep their slaves without the enjoyment of the exemptions and yet with the surety that they will have to free them within five years, or—"

"Or," Phipps finished with a slow smile, "they can convert their slaves to bondsmen immediately. Yes, the rate of production will go down and expenses of labor will go up, but the exemptions will make up for most of that."

"Still, some will not like it," Servatius cautioned darkly. "There are men among them who like holding slaves, and whose visions were not of merely a comfortable life, but of ever-increasing wealth. And dominion. And frankly, satiation of their lusts."

"Exactly," Tromp agreed. "And they will likely leave."

"You think they will simply leave?"

Jan nodded. "Actually, I do, *mijn Heer* Carpentiere. Most men simply wish to keep their families safe, their bellies full, their prospects bright, and their lives pleasant. Very few will set aside all those benefits in pursuit of unlimited wealth and unbridled power. Some will, and many of those did indeed come to the New World.

"But they are not the majority, particularly now. In addition to the soldiers and sailors, most of our new arrivals have no such ambitions.

"However, when we first arrived from Recife, who had the time to think of such things? Contending with the ever-imminent threats to survival was the daily reality and that uncertainty made the community fragile. And for those who had no overpowering greed to serve as a counterweight to the terrible risk, their humbler hopes could hardly be seen as worth the cost: living in constant fear of pirates, the Spanish, the Kalinago, and even the French.

"And those are only the external threats. This time last year, nine out of every ten people beyond those storm shutters were living in tents. Sanitation was a daily struggle. Food was short, water almost as much. The great majority of them would gladly have climbed aboard ships and returned to the Lowlands from whence they came, preferring the grim and limited lot of that life to the constant terror and unsurety of this one."

Van Walbeeck cocked his head in the direction of the window. "Go out and ask them what they want now. Now that they have full bellies, peace with the Kalinago after repelling them last year, and three historical victories over the Spanish in the same space of time. Now, every day when they rise they walk out into real streets lined by real if humble houses. They see the mighty fleet now in our bay, the various wondrous machines of up-time manufacture or inspiration, the wares and wealth from all the islands with which we have now made common cause—not the least of which is the oil, which Don Michael McCarthy has rightly dubbed 'black gold.'

"So go into that street and ask almost anyone you meet if they *still* wish to return home. Because with the convoy still at anchor, they can leave if they wish. They are no longer marooned in this world, and even the land they came from is now at peace and with largely autonomous rule."

"Yes, yes, Jan," Corselles muttered, waving his hand as if to push all those factors behind him. "The people are now as content and hopeful as they were desperate and fearful this time last year. But how does that concern slavery in these colonies? The people of whom you speak are not slaveholders."

Van Walbeeck's cheeks flushed. "But my dear Pieter, do you not see what that means about the great majority of our colony, about those families that came here merely seeking a better life, not boundless wealth and dominion? It means they have decided that here, in this world, they are achieving all those things that do matter to them: the comfort and safety and homely pieties that make for happy families and a good life."

Phipps nodded, frowning. "And I suspect—as you and Maarten clearly do—that many of the present slaveholders will feel similarly, and will free their slaves. That will relieve them of much worry, and for many, nagging guilt."

Servatius nodded solemnly. "Many of the smaller landowners cannot reconcile owning other humans with the precepts of their faith. But the others?" He shrugged. "Their voracious appetites are not merely the evidence of sin. It suggests a deeper depravity." He glanced at Tromp. "So what is to be done about them?"

Maarten took a moment to respond. "I have given much thought to that. In general, I like to think myself a tolerant man, in that I judge not lest I be judged. Even if I find my neighbor's actions or beliefs highly . . . idiosyncratic, we can only live in peace because their right to exist as they please in their house is the only guarantee of my enjoying the same freedom under my own roof.

"But depravity is a different matter. I do not want such neighbors who derive gratification from treating others worse than they would an animal of the field. Because—and mark this—any who accepts that *one* human can be property will come to accept that *any* human can be property."

"So you are saying we are better without the ones who would leave?"

"I am. And the sovereigns and presidents to whom we answer are unanimous in that feeling as well." Tromp stood. "This is what shall be announced in the coming weeks. I wanted you to hear it from us well in advance."

Phipps rose with a sigh. "And so give us nightmares in advance? You are most considerate, Maarten."

"Well," van Walbeeck mused, "you could always do what I do."

Servatius stared balefully at him. "Tell me that it does not involve rum."

Jan just smiled beatifically.

Carpentiere sighed. "I knew it."

When all three had walked out, silent and somber, van Walbeeck closed the door behind them. He stared at it for a moment, and muttered, "'Dead men walking.'"

"What? You think they shall be killed for bringing the news to the slave owners, when the time comes?"

"No, no: it's an up-time expression I've heard Eddie and Mike use. It means seeing men who are acting as if they're walking to their own execution. Which is just how those three may feel, since we may be quite sure that de Bruyne, Haet, and Musen shall skin them alive when they hear the news."

Tromp found it very easy to envision the island's three most prominent slaveholders relishing such an activity. "As long as that remains a figurative description of their exchange, I shall be pleased."

Van Walbeeck paused. "Still no word of Curaçao or Thijssen?"

Tromp shook his head. "Nothing." Van Walbeeck's question had acquired the routine of a ritual, and the admiral understood why. He was to have sailed to Curaçao with Thijssen, but the disaster at Dunkirk undid those plans. Jan seemed to feel as if he should be there, sharing the greater danger of that far more vulnerable colony.

"Not even word from our privateer with too long a name, Moses Cohen Henriques Eanes?"

Tromp sighed. "Moses can no longer make port at Curaçao. As it is, too many of the 'Brethren of the Coast' have already become suspicious of him, of where his true allegiances lie."

"I thought they were always suspicious of him."

Tromp nodded. "They are more so, now. It was inevitable that they would learn that he and Calabar have not just been taking Spanish and Portuguese prizes, but pirate hulls, as well. And while it is true that there is no honor among thieves, and that they often strive against each other when there is great profit in it, they may have had whispers of his occasional rendezvous with Jol."

"So Curaçao remains quiet."

Tromp frowned. "Let us hope it *is* quiet . . . in every way."

Chapter 37

Willemstad, Curaçao

Captain Alonso de Contreras watched another pair of pirate sloops approach the two smaller raiders that had already lashed themselves to opposite sides of the Dutch jacht trying to clear the mouth of Curaçao's harbor. If the Dutch spotted the two closing ships, they gave no sign. While they were still narrowly getting the better of the fight against the less numerous raiders who had come over their gunwales, they had their hands full just keeping their ship. However, when the two sloops finally lashed themselves to the smaller hulls already grappling their target, the contest would effectively be over. Fresh and eager for combat, and with muskets and pistols loaded and ready, the freebooters' combined numbers would sweep the deck of the jacht.

Contreras watched one of the tallest of the boarders from the first ship, a *cimarrone* who had probably been born a Spanish slave, slash at a wall of Dutch cutlasses with a falchion in either hand. After a few moments, however, a Dutch officer behind the skirmish line finished loading his musketoon, raised it calmly, and discharged the weapon into the pirate's body from a range of three paces. The fellow kept swinging for a moment, then slowed, looked down at his much-ravaged abdomen and staggered sideways. He disappeared behind a flashing whirl of Dutch cutlasses. Contreras, watching the first of the sloops now making itself fast to the portside raider, reflected that within minutes it would be the Dutch suffering the same fate they had meted out to the *cimarrone*. Such were the fortunes of war.

Beside him, Captain Ramon Berrio gestured repeatedly back toward the channel-like anchorage that led into Curaçao's St. Ann's Bay. "At last they've decided to crawl out of their den. They must have finished their gin. Which we'll find out as soon as our devils open up their bellies!"

Contreras glanced toward the harbor, where the only true warship of the four Dutch hulls was fatefully venturing out. Square-rigged, she had the advantage of a wind out of the northeast, but that did her little good against the nimble fleet of almost thirty craft arrayed against her. Several angled in from windward, leaning over as the breeze came into their sails on a broad reach, musketeers waiting on their decks, gunners holding their *petereroes* level. By the time they had cleared half the distance to what was almost certainly Thijssen's own flagship, another three of the smaller pirate ships had heeled over to follow the first wave. And so it would go, the fore-and-aft-rigged picadors coming in to throw their darts and dashing out again, hopefully before the square-rigged Dutch bull could turn its heavy half-cannon horns in their direction.

"Ah, this will be good sport," Berrio muttered to the two masters of the galleoncete that was not so much directing the pirate attack as it was watching its execution. Contreras reflected that feral smiles and breathless anticipation such as Berrio's had probably been common sights at Nero's coliseum, as well. And, although his armor and body were adorned with crosses and other signs of his so-called devotion to Christianity, the criollo would probably have been rooting for the lions. Because, after all, whatever he professed and whatever prayers he said, it was clear enough that his holy trinity was War, Blood, and Rape. Usually, but not necessarily, in that order.

The masters of the twenty-six-gun galleoncete with the horribly ironic name *Santa Maria de Gracia* were little better. Juan Garcia and Pedro de la Plesa were a pair of opportunistic cutthroats who'd made their living as Dunkirkers until they began to snatch the occasional Spanish fishing smack in lean times. Quitting the Old World for the New before any warrant could be made out against them, they now plied a similar, legitimated trade as "captains" of Tierra Firme's Garda Costa. Operating mostly from pataches and barca-longas, they ostensibly eliminated various pirate threats and kept a finger on the pulse of such activity.

It seemed to Contreras that, as de Murga had expected, this pair excelled at their job largely because they had surreptitiously become part of the scourge they had been set to eliminate. But their years in Dunkirk had taught them the dangers of incautious opportunism, so they applied a different strategy in their new roles.

During the season when the Flota and the smaller ships that converged upon its ports of call made their westward progress along Tierra Firme, Garcia and de la Plesa were veritable lions of the coast. Their success at finding and exterminating pirates during those months was prodigious. However, once La Flota had passed—which was to say, once Mother Spain's interests had been secured—their anti-piracy efficacy plummeted precipitously. And, among those who knew to look for it, a curious pattern evolved. Wherever the galleoncete of the white-locked Garcia "Blanca" patrolled, searching vigorously for "pirate scum," there would be calm and tranquility until a week or so after he moved on to his next port of call. That calm was frequently shattered by the appearance of a small, well-armed pirate band with extraordinary luck at finding and looting the richest prizes in the town that Garcia Blanca had just visited. That the small and quiet Pedro "Pistola" Plesa (so called because he was almost comically useless with a sword) was not with the older Garcia on his patrols excited little comment. And if anyone had thought to look for him hidden aboard that extraordinarily lucky pirate ship which shadowed Garcia's rounds, they would have found their investigatory visit lethally rebuffed.

Garcia Blanca puffed out his white mustaches, nodded in the direction of the inrushing pirate sloops. "They'll break to windward."

"What?" exclaimed Berrio. "Head into the wind and closer to the land to escape?"

"Why not?" Contreras offered with a shrug. "They have shallow draft and can sail quite close-hauled. If Thijssen turns his ship to bring his guns to bear on them, he loses the following wind and is heading the wrong way: directly toward us and away from his only reasonable course of escape."

The newly lettered Brethren of the Coast had approached from the east of Curaçao, ensuring that they would have the weather gauge for this engagement. It also encouraged any Dutch who might escape their narrow anchorage to flee before the westward wind, and so right into the clutches of the six barquentines and large sloops that lay in wait behind the headland of Cape St. Marie.

Garcia Blanca was nodding approvingly, no doubt trying to curry favor with Contreras, who would be carrying a report back to de Murga. "Captain Contreras has an excellent grasp of pirate tactics." His dazzling, avuncular smile was beatific. "One might almost think he'd been fighting pirates as long as I have." Contreras would have enjoyed voicing his speculations that Garcia's skill came not from fighting pirates, but competing with them. And sometimes, apparently, cooperating: it was striking, how quickly he had managed to get the word of a Spanish-sponsored attack upon Curaçao to the Brethren of the Coast, and how facile he had been in negotiating the pecking order among those contentious and ego-driven captains. It was almost as if he already had personal knowledge of them all . . .

The first wave of sloops had come to within a hundred yards of Thijssen's ship. The *petereroes* sent out smoke and a dim, thin rumble. No response from the Dutch warship of almost forty guns. The pirate musketeers lined up on the leeward gunwale, aimed up toward the sail handlers in the Dutchman's rigging, loosed a ragged volley. Several small black forms tumbled down from the yards and ratlines, small white eruptions marking the points where their descents met the lightly ruffled blue of the sea. And still no response from the Dutchman.

"Hah!" cried Berrio. "Too much gin in his belly, and not enough fight!"

"Watch," counseled Contreras, narrowing his eyes against wind and sun.

The second pirate sloop followed in the wake of the first, but, emboldened by Thijssen's lack of response, closed to fifty yards before discharging her *petereroes* and the four demi-culverins she carried on her port side. Still no response.

At forty yards, her musketeers stood, readied their pieces—

The boom of the Dutchman's fore-and-aft-rigged mizzen swung sharply. The big ship angled toward the smaller one.

Seeing almost twenty culverins swinging about with purpose, the sloop's master called her hard over. Her jib fluttered wildly as she bore into the wind, leaning, righting, and then beginning to heel again as her canvas came into a close-reach.

But that rapid set of motions played havoc with the musketeers, whose volley was ragged and wild. If any of the crew on the Dutchman had been hit, there was no sign of it. And as the sloop's bow came through the wind and her speed dropped, the Dutchman straightened her mizzen's yard, held course, and stabilized.

"Now," said Contreras.

As if the Dutch gunners had heard that as an order, the portside battery thundered. At seventy yards range, the shooting was quite respectable, considering that the target was a much smaller ship: three balls hit. One simply tore away rigging and a stay. Another crashed into a cluster of musketeers gathered near the gun closest to the bow. Kindling and bodies spilled out into the water, scattered backward onto the weather deck.

But the third ball went straight through the quarter-deck, gouging a huge, saw-toothed hole in the planking from which a thin stream of white smoke began to emerge. The sloop veered unsteadily toward a broad reach, trying to make maximum speed away from the Dutchman while her badly depleted crew labored to stabilize the mast that had lost its stay. Seeing this, the second wave of sloops swung from a broad reach to run before the wind. Being fore-and-aft rather than square-rigged, this reduced their speed of approach, but left them with considerable freedom of movement.

Contreras could tell from his peripheral assessment of the posture of the men around him that they had all shifted to face him more directly. Garcia was the first to speak. "You have spent more time on ships than you have revealed, Don Contreras."

"Strange. To my recollection, I have not revealed anything about how I had spent any of my time prior to our first meeting last month."

Garcia blew out his mustaches again, offered a large but discomfited smile, and gestured back toward Thijssen's ship. "As we see, the gin drinker's brief victory was to no avail. See how they box him in."

The inevitable was occurring: the moment the Dutchman had turned to port, the sloops waiting leeward off his starboard bow began tacking in aggressively. And as they did, two larger craft—up-gunned pataches from the look of them—began approaching him bow-on, just as the second wave of port-side sloops began edging in again from windward. Whichever direction he turned, he would be offering one of the attackers an undefended facing, and no matter how good his gunnery was, he could not defeat them all.

"As I said," Berrio shouted, "excellent sport! And more to come!" He gestured toward the two fluyts, waiting behind the warship in the channel. Small skiffs of pirates were angling in toward them with almost suicidal eagerness. Contreras frowned, wondering what their pilots had seen that so emboldened them, raised his spyglass to inspect the fluyts more closely.

And saw women hurrying belowdecks. He saw smaller boats following the fluyts from further back in the narrow harbor channel, a trail of them leading all the way back to the rude wharf of Willemstad.

Contreras lowered the spyglass, felt his stomach hardening. So. The Dutch had read the writing on the figurative wall against which they were to be executed. They had discerned that since there was not a single Spanish flag on the ships attacking them, that this was a purely piratical attack regardless of its instigation or backing. It might mean that some men would survive, those who were willing to throw their lot in with the pirates and seemed earnest enough in doing so. But what it meant for the women, and even the girls—

Contreras turned his back on the scene. But it was no use. Looking astern, all he could see was a ragged parade of ships brimming with rageful, lustful, unshaven faces, over which swords and axes and pistols were brandished.

Cannon spoke behind him. First the heavy Dutch guns, then the lighter pirate ordnance.

"You are missing great sport, here," Berrio almost shrieked. "Dutchmen killing pirates and pirates killing Dutchmen. All the devils of the world killing the other devils! I could watch this all day."

Contreras conceded that Berrio probably could. He also realized that, when the criollo captain ostensibly supervised the landing that the pirates would conduct however they chose, he would need to be watched. War was the business of killing and Berrio was authorized by his crown and his faith—God forbid!—to do so. But beyond that, the man's nature was too close to that of the pirates whom he claimed to despise. So much so that he might join in on the other atrocities, just to show the uncivilized and brutish sea dogs the proper manner in which to commit mortal sins.

Footsteps and creaking planks ascending the companionway from the officers' cabins told Contreras that the landings were indeed at hand. The Spanish commander that Thijssen had driven off Curaçao last year, Lope López de Morla, heaved his considerable bulk up to the quarterdeck. His belly hanging over his belt in multiple folds, he showed many of the signs of broken-spirited dissipation. Addiction to food, to wine, and to women had each left him with different ailments, all of which were converging and conspiring to ensure that he did not live to see another decade of the seventeenth century, or possibly the end of the next year. Hollow eyes staring out of sallow sockets, breathing heavily through his mouth, he glowered at the coastline of Curaçao with an expression that seemed partly one of longing and partly one of intense hatred.

"Don López," Contreras prompted, "we have want of your expertise now. That is why Señor de la Plesa had you summoned, I believe."

"Yes," López replied slowly. "You have already landed men to either side of the harbor?"

"Three miles to the west and three miles to the east of the channel, respectively, yes."

"How many in each party?"

"Two hundred." Which was as close a count as anyone had been able to get from the pirates. With this many hulls of the Brethren this close together, there was no shortage of infighting, defection, even desertion of malcontents who meant to form their own band. One group of a dozen had commandeered a native piragua and demanded recognition as a new ship. Which Garcia had granted with suitable officialese and modest pomp, observing immediately afterward that they'd probably be slain by lead or liquor within the first fortnight, so it was hardly a worry to have given them a piece of paper which would soon cease to have meaning.

"Two hundred," López repeated dully. "Well, that ought to do. Have each group spread out, extending inland until they come to the wide, shallow inner harbor, which the Dutch call the Schottegat. Keeping the sea on one shoulder and the Schottegat on the other, they should advance until they are a mile away from the Dutch town. Willemstad, I think they call it now." He spat.

"And once they are there?"

López blinked. "They wait. As I told him"—he jerked his head at Berrio—"all the Dutch live in the town, and if you approach it as I've just instructed, you have cut off the two means of land escape to the rest of the island."

"But we have seen roofs further inland—"

"Native huts. They keep a few to work the salt marshes. And as strikers, to bring in turtle meat. They won't fight for the Dutch. I'm surprised they work for them at all. We had to keep hostages to get an honest day's labor out of them. The brown bastards."

"And is there anything else we should know about the island?"

López hooked a thumb at "Pistola" Plesa. "I told him. Weeks ago."

"I see. Well, it never hurts to hear the most important facts twice." Or at all, since de la Plesa had never informed Contreras that he had debriefed López.

López shrugged. "There's not much to tell, except that this is where I died, Don Contreras. On September 19 of last year. Thijssen still has his four ships, I see. If everything else is consistent, he will have about two hundred sailors for them, and about two hundred and fifty soldiers. They have a foreign captain, a Huguenot heathen named Pierre le Grand who previously served the Dutch in Brazil. Their governor is some old Dutchman named Willekens. A true whoreson."

"He was a hard man, then, when you were his captive?"

López looked away. "Worse. He was damnably agreeable, and convinced Thijssen not to work us as slaves. Met our request for being deported to Coro. And smiling, all the while. Didn't say much, and made a great show of seeming patient, sympathetic. Damn him and his somber, gloating daughters. They all deserve what's coming to them. Punishment for their false virtue is long overdue." López's hands were upon the rim of the gunwale now. They were white with grasping.

"This gets better and better!" whooped Berrio. He pointed to a large pirate barquentine, at least twenty guns, maneuvering straight toward the Dutch ship, which was now closely beset from three sides. She had damaged another pirate sloop and one of the pataches, but had taken a variety of hits, one of which had taken down the top half of her foremast. Wisps of smoke trailed behind her as she struggled to protect herself and fight to open a gap in the swarming pirate ships through which she and the two fluyts might sail. Several hundred yards off her starboard bow, the Dutch jacht was now thoroughly overrun with pirates. The defenders had disappeared beneath the attackers like badgers under a swarm of army ants, and the torturing of the wounded had begun. Faint shrieks reached Contreras over the rushing of the one-foot seas and intermittent gunfire.

Berrio stared at the barquentine's swift progress directly toward Thijssen's ship. "What is that madman doing? Ramming?"

"That is no madman," Pistola Plesa snarled. "That's a traitor."

López glanced at the weasel-like man. "What?"

Contreras cleared his throat. "The barquentine is captained by a renegade Dutchman, Mahieu Romboutsen. We asked him to wait for a moment such as this to press home his attack."

"Why?" asked Berrio suspiciously.

Garcia provided the answer. "Because he can read Dutch captains and crews better than anyone else. He knows the pace of their actions, the significance of any resetting of their sails and rigging." He nodded at the barquentine. "And I believe he has found the opening he was looking for."

At only forty yards range, the boom of the barquentine's mizzenmast swung quickly as her daggerboards dipped down into the water. She heeled sharply leeward, her starboard battery coming around swiftly. Whereas she had been heading bow to bow, her amidships were now at right angles to Thijssen's bowsprit.

"He'll finish her, now that he's crossing her bow," Contreras explained.

Romboutsen demonstrated the effectiveness of his maneuver in the following moment. The guns of his starboard battery sent forth a loud blast, a wall of smoke, and, faintly, a humming of murderous bees.

"Grapeshot," Garcia explained. "And probably some sangrenel."

The Dutchman's foremast splintered and came down. Deck gunners sprawled, dim maroon sprays marking those who'd had arteries severed by one of the infinitude of small balls, bullets, or nails which raked the length of the weather deck. The lower mainsail shredded. Several figures on the quarterdeck were struck down and flopped like hooked fish. The ship lost way, swung back toward a running position, her wheel unmanned or her whipstaff damaged. Or possibly both.

The pirate sloops and pataches swung close, sails out into the breeze like so many stooping, white-winged vultures approaching a dying beast.

Berrio fixed his morion on his tight black curls with a slap and a laugh. "And now Dutch killing Dutch? I don't know if this day can get any better, but I'm going to find out!" He cried down to the weather deck. "Ho, boy there! Ready my skiff and send word to my sergeants. We shall lead our 'allies' ashore. But don't raise the signal pennants until we're in the water. I don't want those piratical bastards getting ashore before us!"

Alonso de Contreras had only seen an actual crucifixion once before. It was in New Spain, used to punish a recidivistic mestizo whose return to pagan beliefs had led to a small and ultimately inconsequential uprising. Two Dominican friars had been killed, along with two soldiers, the criollo overseer of a minor hacienda, and a number of *griffos*. Some dozens of mestizos who had joined the uprising had been summarily put to the sword in their villages, along with their families. Since the uprising had been caused by, and subsequently targeted, members of the Inquisition, the suppression had been put in their hands as well. And the Inquisitors of New Spain were often of the opinion that it was a benefit to the ever-backsliding natives of the region to kill them before they could sin again. Or at all.

Illustrating that same ready ardor to save the souls of the races over which Spain had been granted paternal care by the Holy Father in Rome, the Inquisitors had made a special effort to capture the mestizo ringleader alive. Apparently missing the irony of which part in the reprise of Christ's story they were playing, the Inquisitors decided to crucify the poor fellow in the middle of a large native village, with a round-the-clock guard of well-armed troops.

Contreras had not seen the barbarity himself. He had passed through the town in the aftermath, on the way to deliver a particularly sensitive parcel of messages to Vera Cruz. The mestizo who had renounced the savior whose name and origins had probably been meaningless to him was still hanging in the town's center, however, much to the unremitting delight of the vultures.

Now, as Contreras stepped out of a skiff and started up the smooth, gentle slope to Willemstad—or rather, what was left of it—two crosses stood starkly against the red glow and black smoke of the fire behind them. It might well have been a scene from hell. And Alonso de Contreras, who had seen barbarity aplenty in the service of Spain, had to wonder if, having had a hand in the events of the day, he was seeing a foreshadowing of his own eternal torment.

In the rude streets that converged on the crosses, the Brethren of the Coast were celebrating the freedoms that were their ubiquitous social bonds: prodigious appetites for murder and violation. The only individuals being spared were, apparently, the smallest children. But then Contreras realized that they were being kept alive to witness what was being done to their fathers, mothers, brothers, sisters, and even grandparents. Clear streaks marked the passage of tears down their smoke-smeared faces, many now beyond crying or even making a sound. Contreras saw one child—he could not have been older than three—abandoned against the side of a burning house, quaking. He had become too unresponsive to be of any amusement to his tormentors.

As Contreras walked up a lane flanked by two long tableaux of saturnalia more savage and sadistic than anything ever envisioned by Brueghel, he was confronted by one of the pirate captains, Diego de Los Reyes, striding with long, stiff legs back down toward the shore. Berrio was at his heels, berating him. "Get back into the fight, you mulatto dog!" the criollo captain shouted at the tall pirate's back.

De Los Reyes gritted his teeth and kept walking, saw Contreras, put a question in his eyes: *And will I get the same order and insult from you?*

"Captain de Los Reyes," Contreras said with a nod, not three yards away from where several reivers from the Mosquito Coast were testing the sharpness of their knives on the limbs of a wounded man. "Please respond to Captain Berrio's charge against you. Are you deserting in the face of the enemy?"

At first, de Los Reyes' face became rigid with anger, but then Contreras' calm tone and expression evidently registered and he realized he was being asked a serious question by a reasonable man. "There is no enemy anymore," de Los Reyes asserted. "They are all defeated. I have taken my spoils and have sent my men back to my ship."

Berrio's objection was shrill behind the tall pirate's shoulder. "The Dutch may be defeated, but they are not all dead! And it is our mission, our holy mission, to slaughter the heathens wherever we find them. Those orders have come from Olivares himself!"

For a moment, Contreras could not speak because he was unsure whether he would scream or laugh at Berrio, who could make speeches about holy missions while other human beings were, quite literally, being raped, tortured, strangled, vivisected, and crucified all within twenty yards of him. So Contreras turned back to de Los Reyes. "Captain, I commend the discipline you maintain over your men, that they have not joined in this barbarism. You are free to return to your ship."

De Los Reyes nodded, started past Contreras—

"He may not go!" Berrio screamed. "He earned his letter of marque by agreeing to this campaign. He must repay Spain—"

De Los Reyes turned on Berrio. "I must repay Spain? By doing to others what was done to me?"

Berrio blinked. "What nonsense are you speaking? What does this have to do with—?"

"Idiot. How do you think I was born, was *made*? Why, do you think, I am Diego the Mulatto? Do you think for a second that it was my *mother* who was white? No, one of you great and noble hidalgos did to her what is being done to the women here—right here!" he shouted, pointing to a scrum of distracted men clustered in the narrow alley between two smoking ruins, all staring at something taking place on the ground. He spat in their direction, resumed his rapid progress toward the shore.

"Godless dog!" Berrio shouted after him. And then, falling in beside Contreras, who resumed his approach to the crosses atop the slight rise in the center of Willemstad: "The mulatto is not reliable, you know. It's said that he helped that gin-drinking cripple Peg Leg Jol raid Campeche. Well, him or some other *griffo* like him."

Contreras stopped and looked back. He saw that Diego de Los Reyes had himself stopped and was looking down at the three-year-old boy propped against the wall of the burning house. The flames were approaching the child.

Abruptly, the tall mulatto pirate captain leaned over, plucked up the boy, and resumed his rapid pace toward the ship waiting for him.

Berrio had resumed his rant. "But I suppose we can't expect loyalty, or even obedience from reivers. Particularly of *his* type. They are half animal, after all. You can see that clearly enough in their—"

"No," Contreras interrupted. "Men such as him—and they *are* men—have been tormented by a life of being refused the dignity of being called, or even thought of, as human. So if they are now animals, it is not because they were born that way. You made them thus."

"*Me*? How is the mulatto's bestiality *my* doing? I didn't whelp him on his mother!"

Contreras sighed. Of course Berrio would be insensate to figurative language. Contreras continued past the flames, the shrieks, the moans, the cowering children and came to the foot of the crosses.

Upon the larger one, fashioned out of a splintered yardarm lashed to a high post, a tall, thin elderly man was affixed. His eyes were closed and there was no sign of motion in his face or his body. The pirates had managed to nail his feet to the pole, but had apparently failed, despite repeated attempts, to affix his palms similarly to the yard. The curve of the wood and its many cracks rendered it unsuitable for spikes. So they had simply strapped his arms over it.

The other cross was not really a cross at all. It looked more like some kind of drying rack—for fish? for skins?—that had been propped up by a pair of stays and had been fitted with a thin plank for a crossbeam. Hanging from that beam was a young woman—she could not have been older than fifteen—with a wound in the center of her chest. If she was still alive, there was no sign of it.

Contreras felt his jaw muscles bunch in rage, forced his voice to be calm. "Berrio, what do you know about this?"

"What? You mean the woman?"

Inhuman idiot, why were you not taken by a random bullet? "Let us start with the woman, then. Why has this been done to her?"

"We're to kill the Dutch. So we have." His voice was defensive. His eyes skipped sideways.

"The truth, Berrio. Now."

"She—resisted."

"Being captured?"

"In a manner of speaking."

"Berrio. I will not warn you again. Speak clearly or answer to de Murga. Personally."

"She resisted the attentions of my men."

And you too, you worthless filth? "And so, you shot her?"

"No! She did that to herself. When Raul climbed on her, she saw the pistol in his belt and—"

Contreras could not tell if his body was trying to laugh, to sob, or to vomit. "So she is up here as an example?"

"Yes."

Contreras checked the girl more closely. "I doubt she was still alive by the time you finished doing this."

"She was," murmured a hoarse, accented voice.

Contreras turned, saw that the old man on the other cross had raised his head slightly. He stepped quickly over. "Berrio, cut this man down. At once!"

"Captain, this is the chief enemy of Philip our king! This is Jacob Willekens, the governor of this den of heathen raiders."

"Do as I say, Berrio, or I shall—"

"Señor," pleaded Willekens, "no. I do not wish more pain. I only wish to be rejoined with my last daughter."

"Very well. I shall bring her here."

The old man looked over at the dead girl on the adjoining cross. "She is already here." He glanced at the pistol on Contreras' belt. "Please," he said, "for the love of the one we both call Christ, send me to Him, to her."

Contreras pulled the pistol, placed it gently against the old man's heart. Who nodded, smiled, and closed his eyes.

And as Contreras pushed the muzzle more tightly against the narrow chest and pulled the trigger, he thought: *I wish it was Berrio.*

Part Three

August–October 1636

Liquidly glide on his ghastly flank
—Herman Melville,
"The Maldive Shark"

Chapter 38

Oranjestad, St. Eustatia

Eddie woke to the sound of gulls. He lay a moment, listening. *Calling me out to sea again, huh, guys? All right, all right: I'm coming.* He opened his eyes.

Anne Cathrine was sprawled, leonine, beside him. Well, not exactly beside him; one of her legs was still on top of his, trapped there from when she'd finally half-dismounted, half-fallen off him.

Images of the prior night came back, along with the recollection of, *Three times? Damn!* Not that Eddie Cantrell had any problem with that whatsoever. His attitude about hot sex was simply "the more, the merrier." Except in Anne Cathrine's case these days, it was "the more, the hornier."

And that was a change. If anything, he'd been the one who'd always been up for round two, occasionally three. Not because she wasn't into it but because when she finished, she really finished. As in "wake the neighbors, scare the dog, rattle the windows" finished. That was just who she was: extremely vigorous, amazingly passionate, and very physically fit—to say nothing of damn-near double-jointed.

But, particularly since the dance, her lovemaking had been, well, different. Whereas she used to be Miz One-and-Done to the point that she slept like someone had slipped her a Demerol cocktail, now she seemed to get more determined to go again, and even again, until she was more spent than he was. Given his prosthesis and how that impacted their respective levels of exertion, some imbalance was nothing new, but that was part of why she hadn't been frequently ready for round two: she was ready to become comatose, often for nine hours. Of course, when she woke up, fully recovered...

Eddie shook the memories out of his head and the smile off his face. *Focus, man, focus.* The sex had been different in another way. Not only had she been initiating encores, but when she did, the lovemaking was more...what? He sought for the right word. It was almost, well, desperate. As if she'd been told that she was never going to make love again.

He looked at her, resisted the urge to move a bang of red-gold hair off her cheek. *Is she afraid I might not come back, that something might happen to me?* If he'd been weighing anchor to cruise into battle, well, yeah, maybe then. But today he was just sailing to Antigua from St. Eustatia: the down-time equivalent of driving to the back-roads convenience store where you never saw another car. So, no; fear for his safety wasn't the cause. Besides, this trend had been growing for a while now. But last night had felt like some kind of final surge, that whatever forces were at work in her had sparked each other into overdrive.

The mystery was easy enough to solve, of course; just wake her and ask. Well, ask *after* she had a cup of faux coffee and cuddled and dozed a bit and then stretched and then...well, maybe asking her wouldn't be so easy after all. Because it would sure take a bit of time—

Time!

Oh, for the love of—! Eddie swung out of bed, using his prosthesis as a very efficient pivot to slip over to the window, lean the storm shutter further out, and squint into the sunshine.

The very crude, yet very precise, wooden sundial in the square told him exactly what he feared it would: if he didn't get a move on, he was going to be late for his own predeparture meetings!

He pivoted back away from the window, lifted his waiting uniform off the gentleman's valet, and headed for the door. He stopped, looked at Anne Cathrine sleeping, her lips slightly parted. His heart just about turned into mush. He tiptoed back over to her side of the bed; the resulting sound—*sfft...tak! sfft... tak!*—reminded him that with a prosthesis, "tiptoeing" was not only a half misnomer, it was only half-quiet.

He kissed her cheek and backed away. She made a sound like a lioness purring through a sigh as he headed to their dressing room.

Eddie left the dressing room by the door that communicated directly with the hall—and almost ran straight into Anne Cathrine. "You—you're awake!"

She nodded and glanced away. Her eyes were sort of puffy—and—red? Had she been *crying*? "Cat, honey, what's—?"

She intercepted his hand, held it so it did not reach her, but clasped it so firmly Eddie thought that she would never let go, break it, or both.

"Anne Cathrine, what's wrong? Please, tell—"

"I have given it serious thought, Eddie. And...and I have decided not to come down to the dock to see your ship depart."

He put his other hand on hers, moved the one she held so that now he had her one hand in both of his. "Okay...but why? Did I do someth—?"

She shook her head hard, smiled like her face might break. "No. No." She squeezed his hand again, *really hard*. "No. But I do not wish to embarrass you."

He had to stop himself from laughing at the notion that she could ever do something that would embarrass him, because her face clearly told him that now was *not* the time for levity. "Sweetheart, that's not going to happen. It's simply not possible."

"It could."

"How?" He couldn't help but smiling slightly, just enough to be reassuring. "Just how are you going to embarrass me?"

"I might cry."

Eddie once again had to stop himself from laughing. "Cat, that wouldn't embarrass me. I'd be—"

"Then I do not want to embarrass myself." She reached up and took his shoulders, looked him in the eye. "Eddie. Please. This will be better for me. For us. Now go. You will be late. As you so often are these days." Her brief smile was so pained he thought that *he* might start crying. "You are the most wonderful husband in the world." She pulled him in and hugged him so hard it made him think of what water-safety instructors had told him about how drowning people often react to rescuers; they clutch you so hard, there's a risk that you could go down with them.

Then she was walking, stiff-legged and fast, back to their bedroom. She closed the door behind her quickly, leaving Eddie speechless and wondering.

Sophie looked up at the rap on the infirmary door. Had somebody burned, cut, or crushed a finger or toe already? Her hands full with hanging her good dress so that it would not wrinkle, she called over her shoulder, "Please come in. It is unfastened." Because Brandão *still* had not acquired a lock for the door.

Which opened to admit a beam of sunlight that then reflected off the red highlights of a head of auburn hair.

"Hugh!" Sophie hung up the dress quickly—wrinkles be double-damned!—and stepped quickly over to him as he slipped in. She didn't stop until there was only a hand's width separating them. He was looking down at her and said, "Sophie," and for a moment she thought of stepping just a little bit closer—but no: the old shibboleths of decorum rose up, along with the internal voice that reminded her, *You don't know how* he *would feel about that. Yet.*

"I didn't expect you," she said and wondered if any human could possibly sound more lame uttering the perfectly obvious. "Why are you here? Are you not leaving, after all?" She controlled her voice lest she sound too hopeful. "Has there been a change in plans? In your orders?"

He smiled ruefully. "No, seems that I'm still wanted

back down south to sort out some possible silliness involving my old Spanish employers."

Sophie stepped back so she could take his hand without fumbling her own along his body. "Please. Do not make light of such things, Hugh. In my experience, flippant words tempt fate."

"Heh. Funny thing for a Norn to say."

"A Norn?"

His smile became one of perplexity. "What? You've not had word of the girls' nickname for you?"

"I am the Norn?"

"Yes. Well, *a* Norn. Not sure as if they've identified other Norns or not. But that hardly matters now, does it?"

She wasn't sure how to feel about such a fate-filled nickname. "The Norn are severe creatures, Hugh."

He closed the distance between them so that it was back to a palm's breadth. The ends of her fingers hovered near his abdomen, and his near hers. "Well, now, you *are* a bit severe, when you've a mind to be. And—don't deny it!—you're often of just such a turn of mind. But I see beyond that, and so do those two sisters. And they love you not in spite of your being a Norn, but because of it."

"And you?" she asked. She heard her voice buzz, deep in her throat, as she said it. "Do you have—regard for me in spite of, or because of, my being a 'Norn'?"

Hugh's smile slipped away, but not because he was pulling back from her, but because he was suddenly serious, his head closer. A full second passed. Maybe two. He was looking at her, but his eyes were also someplace else.

Then his head elevated back to its prior, more

upright position. He slipped his hand out of hers to reach into his pocket. "There are some lines I've been working on over these weeks. They've been contrary, they have. Not wanting to flow straight.

"But then, I saw the sun come up this morning and I thought, 'well as a wise man once said, carpe diem.' But I still wasn't sure if the words had ripened enough. Plenty of time to share them when I get back, I reasoned. Never show much of an important work too soon."

He had more to say, but she didn't care. "Hugh, I know where you are going and why, so please: do not tempt fate by presuming that you can be certain of sharing them when you get back. Because, since none of us may know which moments will be our last, no moment is 'too soon.'"

He nodded. "Those were my very own thoughts when I saw the sun in your eyes, just now. Besides, you asked a question about whether my regard for you is in spite of your Nornish qualities or because of them. As chance would have it, those troublesome lines I've been mulling over speak to that—and you're entitled to an answer." He slipped a wax-sealed sheet out of his pocket.

She stared at it. "Is it another poem?"

He was smiling again. "Well, now, I don't quite know what label would most suit it. It started as a letter, but halfway through it turned into a poem. It ended as what I believe the up-timers call 'free verse.'" He held it toward her. "Why don't you take a look, and tell me what *you'd* call it?"

She had to take a step back to make sure she took the paper without any unwonted contact, felt the new part of her damn the old part as either a creature of trained reflexes, a hypocrite, or both. *If you would be quit of the hoary old bonds and shackles that almost strangled your soul past resuscitation, then be quit of them all. If some prove wise, add them in later: learning as you go will not kill you. Think for yourself. Live for yourself.*

She studied the wax seal: it had been impressed with a signet ring. No doubt that of his family, of the earl of Tyrconnell. She suddenly wished to see his homeland, then just as suddenly realized that would not magically bring them any closer into each other's orbit: he had never seen those green fields himself. Besides, that land was part of the Old World, and all they had spoken about in their times together were how they felt about this New World, both its perils and possibilities. And above all, its uncertainties, which were, after all, the wellspring of the other two qualities. Anything might be possible here.

And that might be his topic, she realized as she broke the seal and unfolded the paper: a heartfelt embrace of what they might become individually, even together, in such an untamed and unshackled place as this. Her eyes ran greedily over the first lines, drinking them in.

Then she felt her eyes slowing, encountering words she had not expected. He had written them beautifully, lyrically, soulfully, but—

She took another step back, held up the paper. His eyes went from puzzlement to worry.

She struggled to find words of her own, truly her own, in every way. But her surprise, and her dread, were amplified by waves of emotion crashing headlong into each other at the very core of her being. Speechless, she waved the paper once.

And then ran as fast as she could. Out of the infirmary. Down the street. Then down the next. She did not know where she was going.

And she could not stop or think long enough to care.

Tromp was waiting at the far end of the dock, where the last skiffs from the three remaining steamships would arrive. *Harrier* had left eight days earlier, ostensibly as part of the escort for the first ships heading down to Trinidad. Those larger ships, mostly carrying supplies and new gear to expand its oil field, would not all arrive there, however. *Patentia*, carrying the more complex rotary rig needed for the Jennings field, had split off for that destination only one day out, escorted by *Harrier* and a pair of speedy jachts.

Turning to look back at the head of the dock, he caught sight of the primary architect of the misinformation and misleading movements that would hopefully leave the Spanish baffled as to the actual numbers, types, and deployment of their vastly expanded fleet. Eddie Cantrell, his stride almost normal, was weaving through the stevedores, deckhands, and pursers that were making their last-minute preparations and adjustments.

Maarten took the moment to watch the young up-timer's approach. It would be peculiar not to see him in his office and around the halls of Fort Oranje for so many weeks. It would be stranger still not to hear the cheery banter that was his hallmark, even though he was not aware how often it lifted others' spirits, particularly during the dark days when he had first arrived.

And now he was going off, with Michael McCarthy and Kees in tow, to build a naval facility on Antigua.

Which would also require initiating a host of ancillary projects to ensure an adequate training program, site defensibility, fresh water, smelting and repair facilities, and local husbandry. All of which he accepted with a rueful reference to how much time and labor each would take—but without ever doubting that he could, in fact, achieve what was required of him. Not because he was arrogant, but because he simply did not waste time doubting his abilities.

Maarten frowned as Eddie threaded a tight and winding course through two different groups of lightermen who were busy loading, unloading, or cursing the incompetence or inconsideration of their fellows. There was so much riding on the young man's modest shoulders. After ten months, Tromp still could not decide if it was a curse or a blessing that Edward Cantrell did not fully understand just how exceptional he was. Probably because, having come from unremarkable (at best) origins, and having an agreeable nature, no simmering dissatisfaction had boiled to his surface. What had happened instead was that he rose to the needs of a completely unprecedented occasion and, in the course of so doing, revealed a completely unanticipated depth and breadth of skills and aptitudes.

He approached with his customary grin and complete lack of reserve. "I'm on time!" he shouted.

Maarten managed not to smile. "So you are. You might even consider making a habit of it."

Eddie chuckled. "Yeah, it'll be a lot easier on Antigua." Realizing how that statement might have sounded in the context of the inevitable difference between his early morning activities there and on St. Eustatia, he blushed. "Well, you know what I mean."

Tromp couldn't suppress the smile anymore. "Yes, I believe I do." He turned to look out at all the ships. "I shall be sad to see so many go," he mused. "They are a comforting sight. But that is the nature of expansion. Now, I mean to talk to you about your determination to offer the leased 'laborers' military training. You have enough on your hands. And it could be politically...sensitive."

Eddie put his hands on his hips, squinted out over the bright water. "Well, Maarten, if you're right about what could happen here in the worst-case scenario, I'd like to give the slaves returning to St. Eustatia a fighting chance if the garrison won't enforce the protections that are now a matter of law. Besides, I'm not doing the training. I'm going to have a lot of bored Wild Geese on my hands, as well as German ship's troops. Better than giving them make-work. And with Captain Arciszewski coming along to supervise the fortifications, I might even have the nucleus of a school. Might want to set up a naval academy, while I'm at it."

For a moment, Maarten was preparing to plead against such youthful optimism, to be more realistic about how many projects he could oversee—until he saw the hint of a grin twitching the corner of the up-timer's mouth. The admiral laughed. "I almost believed you."

"No, I was just hauling your leg."

"*Pulling* my leg. I have finally learned that idiom, thank you very much. And those schools may actually be a fine idea. Eventually. But for now, Ove Gjedde is producing fine sailors at a respectable pace, right here. And he sends his regards, but is out on the water, making lives miserable for more would-be navigators."

Eddie was looking at the timepiece he called a

"wristwatch," and then glanced back along the dock. "Maarten, I know Houtebeen keeps his own hours, but do you know if he is actually going to show up? My skiff is going to be here in—"

Tromp smiled and nodded over Eddie's shoulder. "And here he is."

Jol's own skiff was completing its approach from the nearby *Achilles*. The admiral had evidently spent his last night in Oranjestad sleeping aboard: a good choice, in that it precluded any hedonistic excesses that would leave him suffering from indigestion, exhaustion, or a hangover when he was supposed to be weighing anchor. At least, that was the theory.

And on this occasion, it just might have worked: Jol waved off the hand Eddie offered, and swung up to the dock unassisted. "I'll not be troubling a fellow member of the One-Legged Fraternity to help me do what I must be able to do on my own. *Intrepid* looks as ready to leave as my *Achilles*, Eddie, aye?"

Eddie smiled. "*Intrepid* is shipshape and ready to get underway, Admiral Jol."

Who laughed. "And next you'll be calling me 'Cornelis'! Maarten, this young fellow is entirely too well mannered. You must give me charge of him some week, that I might teach him the rarified pleasures of—oh: wait. My pardons. A married man. Well, you'll be a fine example to children, then. Very respectable. Too respectable. Never mind; here, this fellow trying to climb around me to get on the dock is the one I told you about."

He stepped aside, and a tall dark man, probably about Eddie's age, more or less leaped up to stand upon the dock. It was an impressive feat of not only strength and agility, but a well-honed instinct for the rocking of the waves and swells.

Tromp's first thought as the muscular man stepped into the group was that he was the same physical type as Hugh O'Donnell: a lithe, tigerish build combined with natural grace. But this fellow was younger, was as dark as Hugh was fair—he was clearly of mixed race—and carried an aura of brooding menace whereas the Irish earl radiated a glow of fellow-feeling and easy confidence.

The new arrival surveyed the group, his eyes flickering uncertainly as they grazed over Eddie.

Who, to his credit, responded by sticking out his hand: "I'm Commodore Cantrell. And you are?"

The tall man—taller than Hugh, even—looked down at Eddie and frowned. "Your English, it is strange. I apologize; I am distracted by that. The name of my family is no longer important. My baptized name is Diego. Where do men speak English as you do?"

Jol glanced at his taciturn friend. "You have heard, perhaps, of a town in Europe that appeared in a ring of fire from the future?"

"Yes," answered Diego. "I hear it in the mouths of the same jug-lovers who tell of cities on the back of sea tortoises, dragons a league in length, and other wonders magical and impossible."

Tromp nodded. "But in this case, the story is true; Commodore Cantrell is from that future town."

Diego nodded somberly, cast an eye over his shoulder: it was fixed on the three remaining steamships. "They are yours?"

"They have been placed under my command," Eddie amended. "And yes, their differences are due to devices shaped by the knowledge we brought from the future."

Diego scanned the group again. "You sail against the Spanish. You are allies with the Dutch." He was clearly seeking confirmation, although it was uttered as a statement.

"I do. I am. And my name is Eddie."

The newcomer screwed up his face. "Ed d-ee?"

"Short for Edward."

Another nod. "My friend"—he glanced at Houtebeen—"has asked me to remain here while he sails to Trinidad. He says you might wish to speak with me at length about what I know of both the Brethren of the Coast and the Free Companies."

"Unfortunately," Eddie said, "I will be departing shortly. But I wonder if I could send questions to Admiral Tromp and if he might convey them to you?"

Diego nodded. "That is well. Besides, I must speak to Admiral Tromp. And I suspect he will have many questions when he hears my news."

"Which is?" Tromp asked, surprised.

"Curaçao," Diego said. "It is no more."

Tromp had half-expected that news but had not anticipated a messenger such as this one. He considered Diego for several seconds. "Were you there?"

Diego nodded. "It was my shame to be there."

"With the Spanish?"

Diego stared. "Yes. But I did not know that when I was approached by the Brothers of the Coast. After that, all I could do was leave as soon as possible."

Jol interceded, glancing nervously at Tromp. "Diego has very important information. He arrived just last night, delivered to *Achilles* by some . . . er, professional acquaintances."

"I see," said Tromp, trying to keep his tone level.

"Diego, allow me to be clear. Oranjestad is an open town, but not to those who might be our enemies. And unless I miss my guess, you have been—or are—a member of one or both of the pirate groups you mentioned. Be warned—"

"I am of them no longer. I joined them only to sail against the Spanish. Now, both groups have become the whores of the Spanish. I am done with them. I am here to aid you against your enemies, because they are mine. May I stay in your city?"

Tromp, overcoming the surprise at hearing anyone refer to Oranjestad as a "city," nodded. "Yes. And we shall discuss the news you bring. Soon."

Diego nodded, turned to Eddie. "I shall hope to hear from you, Eddie, if I may be of assistance." He slipped to the outer edge of the dock and set off toward the roofs of the "city."

Tromp frowned after him. "A man of few words."

Jol waggled his unruly eyebrows sadly. "Because he's a man of many hardships and sorrows. Mother was African or part. Father never acknowledged him. He wasn't many years into manhood before he was affronted on that account."

"Killed a hidalgo?" Tromp speculated, his eyes unreadable.

"Worse. The Spanish aristocracy is not honor bound to answer a challenge from one who is as lowborn as Diego. He became a laughingstock. He repaid Spain and Havana by raiding them whenever possible. Now he's disgusted with the raiders."

Tromp nodded. "Because they now take Spanish coin to attack us."

Jol nodded back. "Something happened at Curaçao that so disgusted Diego that he refused to sail with them any longer. That meant abandoning his own ship and crew as they passed leeward of Montserrat, on their way back to Tortuga."

Eddie leaned forward. "He knows Tortuga?" He waved to his approaching skiff.

Jol nodded, frowned. "Your inquiry does not sound casual, Eddie."

"It's not. I really am going to send you questions for him, Maarten." Eddie started toward the boat from *Intrepid*. "What Diego knows...well, it could prove to be quite important."

Tromp nodded. "I will make sure that Diego receives all your questions." Jol was staring at Eddie as if trying to figure out what lay behind his sudden urgency over news of Tortuga.

Tromp stepped to the very edge of the dock as Eddie clambered down into the skiff. "Fair winds and be well, Commodore Cantrell."

Eddie saluted. "I will, Maarten. And you be careful, too!"

Tromp returned the salute, let it fall, and Eddie did as well. Then, already seated on the skiff's center thwart, he started talking to his sailors as they began leaning into the oars.

Jol nodded, looked questioningly at Tromp. "Why's he so eager to speak to Diego?"

Maarten looked after the skiff. "Houtebeen, honestly: do you think I know what goes on in the mind of an up-timer?"

But in this case, Tromp suspected he did.

Anne Cathrine stood at the second-story bedroom window that was furthest from the still-unmade bed.

When the servant had attempted to make it up, she had wordlessly indicated in the negative. And again, when she failed to appear downstairs, the same servant asked if she would like some nourishment. Again, she silently shook her head.

Intrepid was moving. Anne Cathrine could not see the whole of the cruiser over the top of the fort, but her immense sails distinguished her as she gathered speed toward the small northern headland that framed that side of the bay. The fluyts from Amsterdam had left along that course an hour before, getting a head start before the up-time vessels and the fast, nimble jachts came out after them.

She watched until they were gone.

But even then, her tears did not stop.

Chapter 39

Oranjestad, St. Eustatia

Seated at her writing desk from *Intrepid*, Anne Cathrine had just set aside her current book and was reaching for her clay mug of "coffee" when the door banged open and Leonora barged into the bedroom—and stared, shocked. "You're up. And you're *reading*!" She had begun the exclamation in a tone of surprise; it had transmogrified to baffled horror by the end.

"Yes, do come in," Anne Cathrine replied, careful not to let her tone transmogrify as well, but from wry facetiousness to arch annoyance.

Their exchange was, she allowed with a small sigh, just another sign of their changed existence. In the wake of so much activity and so many new visitors and so many ships coming and going, Oranjestad's retraction to its normal size and pace brought a matching emotional undertow. So even if its commerce and industry were still basking in a modest afterglow, the social mood was one of deflation.

But life went on in the town and the fields and in Danish House. They had even extended yet another invitation for Edel Mund to come live with them. After all, she was still a noble; her husband's Icelandic tract had been conferred upon her by a sympathetic Christian IV. In a rare show of unalloyed unanimity, the *Rigsrad* had declared him a national hero. Which had only made her more bitter at herself and her prior focus upon status and comfort. When she did talk, it was of how by driving her husband to the risks he took, she had vouchsafed deathless fame for him. After all, it had only cost him an untimely death and her any chance of happiness or even peace.

Perhaps, Anne Cathrine mused as Leonora inspected her from a safe distance, it was fortuitous that Edel Mund refused their invitation. Danish House was quite dour enough, now. Whatever had happened between Sophie and Hugh on the day he departed was unclear, but it had driven her back into herself, and she had deflected any question or conversation that might have become an entrée to gentle inquiries. And as for Anne Cathrine herself, well—

"You are worrying me," Leonora declared from the other side of the small table. "This is most unlike you. First, you have spent weeks moping—yes, moping! You can glare all you like; I said it and I mean it. Now, it was natural enough, I suppose with Eddie gone. But this—this!" she concluded, waving distressed fingers at the open book. "How long has *this* been going on?"

Anne Cathrine allowed a small grin to emerge. "I do read, you know."

"Well, yes, I suppose you do...sometimes...well, not often...but I mean, really! The first thing in the morning? Is *this* why your first appearance downstairs has become later and later over the past month? I thought you were just sleeping even more than usual, but—"

Anne Cathrine reached over, closed the book, picked up her lukewarm carob concoction, and shook her head. "No, I have been reading. Quite a lot."

The way Leonora sat next to her—close, eyes alert, leaning slightly forward—was identical to the way Anne Cathrine had seen her receive new patients at the infirmary. And her query was the same one with which she typically began those conversations: "Do you feel quite well?"

"So, if I am reading, that is a sign that I am not well? Thank you very much, darling sister!"

"Well, no, that is not what I meant, exactly . . . but it is a dramatic change in behavior and habit. And that is a significant diagnostic result." She leaned back. "But of what, I am unsure."

Anne Cathrine smiled. "You cannot imagine how relieving"—*and gratifying*—"it is to hear that you are actually unsure of something. Of anything!" Anne Cathrine leaned in so that their shoulders touched briefly. "Clearly, this day is off to an excellent start."

Leonora frowned and smiled in return. "Thank you . . . I think." She craned her neck to get a look at the book's cover. *"Appendix G: Race in the New World,"* she read aloud. "It looks very well printed indeed. And I would know. But an appendix? To what?"

Anne Cathrine sipped at her mug. "Before beginning this 'reconnaissance mission,' Eddie was tasked to assemble a comprehensive review of all up-time documents pertaining to what we might encounter here in the New World." She smiled, partly at the surreal notion of learning about one's own world from the books of a future that would now never be, and partly because talking about the book made her think of Eddie. "It was an immense undertaking and he had numerous assistants responsible for locating and recommending pertinent selections. Not just from the high school library, mind you, but from the entirety of Grantville. The resulting document was so long that it would have been unusable unless special topics were broken out separately." She touched the cover of the appendix gently. "This is one such."

Leonora stared at it, fascinated. "And you are allowed to read documents which were prepared for military purposes?"

"Some were not prepared strictly for commanders, but for selected political and even religious leaders. Such as this one. It is . . . most illuminating."

"I want to read it, too," Leonora declared. "When you are done, of course. And when do you think that will be? I have been meaning to—well, never mind that. You must get dressed—oh, you are! Come downstairs to help me."

"With what?"

"With Sophie. Her mood has become—well, intolerable." She stopped, considered. "And I love her."

Ah. "I see. And her mood has become intolerable because you have not been able to snap her out of it." *And because coaxing her—or anyone—is simply not within your compass, is it, my most wonderful sister?*

Leonora looked cross, probably at herself. "She is intractable," she muttered, "or at least, unreachable. By me, at any rate. So, I admit I have failed. But you have been absent so much that you've really not tried in almost three weeks, now. It is time that you did." Leonora got up. "Well? Aren't you coming?"

❖   ❖   ❖

After ten minutes of expertly parried attempts at starting small talk on personal matters, and other potential gateways to affairs of the heart, Sophie put down her own book—more up-time poetry—and stared squarely at Anne Cathrine. Who tried very hard not to suddenly feel like a little sister pestering an older one.

"Yes?" asked Anne Cathrine when Sophie's stare was not accompanied by any statement.

"Please, if you must ask, just ask."

"Ask what?"

Sophie seemed about to roll her eyes, but shut them instead. "I am distracted, not dense, Anne Cathrine. You have not been down before noon in at least two weeks, and your heart is not truly invested in the mission upon which it has embarked." She opened her eyes; they were gentle. "I suspect it, too, is distracted."

Anne Cathrine suppressed a gasp. *Does she know? How could she? Is there something that I—?*

But Sophie was continuing. "It must be very difficult."

Ah, so perhaps she is only thinking of Eddie's long absence. Which, just yesterday, had been extended another unbearable two weeks. "Not as difficult as the emotional weight you seem to be bearing, Sophie."

"Which I have kept to myself. And which I shall not be allowed to continue, as is revealed by your presence now, and"—she closed the book—"the very subtle scrutiny of your sister."

If staring, unblinking Leonora were sitting and leaning any closer to Sophie, Anne Cathrine would have presumed her sister intended to sit in the taller woman's lap.

"So please," Sophie concluded, "ask your questions, so that we may all go forward in peace."

Anne Cathrine nodded gratefully, found what she suspected were the right words to ask about Hugh—

"Well, what happened?" Leonora blurted out. "Did he ask for your hand or not? Why are you so glum? No, that's not it . . . Why are you so *detached*?"

Anne Cathrine wished she had worn a sun hat, just so she could sweep it off and whap Leonora over the head with it.

But Sophie merely sighed. "It is not so simple, so black or white, as that. Hugh wrote me a wonderful, thoughtful, searching missive that at times lapsed into poetry." She smiled so sadly that Anne Cathrine discovered she had a lump in her throat.

"Searching for what?" Leonora persisted.

Sophie's smile became small, personal. "For answers. For what place we may occupy in this New World. In each other's lives. But I am not sure that we have, or can, draw the same conclusions from all that. Or make the same decisions."

Leonora blinked. "Well, that all sounds far too much like philosophical theorizing. It is far too intellectual, so far as I'm concerned." It took her a moment to realize that the other two women were staring at her, both with mouths slightly open. "What?" she demanded. "Do you disagree?"

Anne Cathrine tried to struggle past the idea that her sister had insisted that something—anything!—was "too intellectual."

Never one to tolerate a silence when she was always so ready to fill it, Leonora plunged onward with a sharply assessing gaze at Sophie. "Entirely too intellectual. Which makes me wonder if there are . . . other underlying insufficiencies that might be causing your reluctance." She squinted, if that might help her see some answer hidden behind Sophie's eyes. "Are you not attracted to him?" Leonora asked.

Sophie's casual gaze hardened into a long, unamused stare, if she was waiting for the younger woman to figure out that, in fact, two plus two did indeed equal four.

Frowning, Anne Cathrine shot a sideways whisper at her sister. "Leonora, really: you have in fact *seen* Hugh, have you not?"

Leonora frowned at her sister, genuinely perplexed. "Of course I have. Such a strange question!"

Anne Cathrine managed not to roll her eyes at her sibling's guileless literalism.

Sophie shook her head slightly, which seemed less like disapproval than it did an attempt to shake off the shock of an unexpected blow. "Leonora, I assure you—in the name of all that I or you or anyone holds sacred—that Hugh's, er, attractiveness, is not something I find wanting." A small bitter laugh escaped her taut lips. "Not in the least."

Leonora's frown deepened, as if a sound hypothesis had been stunningly disproven. "Then if you are so suited to each other in all regards, what is it that might be holding you back? It is almost as if you fear happiness."

Because the young woman had thrown it out as a notion hardly worthy of consideration, she did not immediately see what Anne Cathrine did: the color rushed out of their friend's face. She leaned forward. "Sophie? Is there something to that?"

"I . . . I do not think so," she answered through pale lips. "I have not been so happy, so ready to sing and dance, in . . . in more years than I can remember. Certainly, I did not fear that."

Anne Cathrine heard a lingering tone, an unspoken "but . . .", and risked another question. "Or is it that, in embracing happiness, you are also risking its loss?"

Sophie became very still. When she spoke again, it seemed she was speaking as much to herself as the two sisters. "My father and mother loved each other. That is not just the idealization of a child. Then he died, and I saw her change.

"All her laughter was premeditated, either to appear appropriate or to influence those who heard it. The same with every smile, every touch, every meaningful glance. It was all theater. Because when we were not out in society, she was . . . she had become an automaton. Hardened by loss and driven by the fear that she, as a woman, would neither be allowed nor able to keep her own wealth and that which she had inherited from my father."

She blinked and started, as if stuck by a pin from her memories. "Flirtation, betrothal, marriage, offspring, even trysts arising from irresistible passion: no, she now travels in circles where all those things are merely means to other ends. But if such mean and meretricious ends had no grasping, amoral manure in which to take root, then maybe the beauty would be restored to all of those celebrations of life, love, and family."

"And that is what you felt here, in the New World. As you said after the dance."

"Yes, but as I also said then, I did not yet know what that sudden sense of freedom, of boundlessness, meant."

"And now you do?"

Sophie's face seemed to sag. "I think one cannot know what it may hold without walking forward into it. And even then, what one discovers there will continue to evolve for as long as one lives. But at least one immutable truth has become increasingly clear: one cannot become free while still wearing the shackles of custom, or what one perceives as such."

Leonora's frown cleared. "So he did ask for your hand!"

Sophie shook her head. "I would not lie to you, dear girl. Not to save my soul. No, he did not propose marriage. But his letter was so full of..." She closed her eyes, struggled either to find words or to say them aloud. "It was so full of considerations, of accommodations, of bows made toward matters that only exist back across the ocean in the lands we left behind...I knew where such a discussion would lead. And how any acknowledgement of the expectations and conventions of those lands would compromise the freedom we—or at least I—might find in this one."

Anne Cathrine nodded. "But if you do not ask, how do you know he wouldn't join you in rejecting all that? As you pointed out, you have both been used dismally by so many people and institutions, there."

Sophie closed her eyes. "It is wrong to ask that of another. It is also unwise." She opened her eyes; they were very bright, now. "It must be his choice, not my plea, that would put him on a similar journey. Otherwise...time and regret wear hard when we assume a shape that is not truly ours, but one we took to make another happy. Better early grief over what might have been, than a later tragedy of two who find their ways ineluctably growing apart after many years and much devotion."

Anne Cathrine murmured, "And yet you do not sound reconciled to this."

"I do not know if I ever shall be." Sophie's eyes sent out fast, thin rivulets, yet neither her voice nor her color changed. "But that is not the greatest misery in this."

Leonora leaned forward. "Then what is?"

She looked from one to the other. "Do you not see? Whether or not I deserve it, Hugh loves me. It shines from every line he has ever written, and from every moment we have spent together, and nothing I said or did seemed to dissuade him from that feeling. And then, he comes to me on the day he leaves, lays his heart out in both prose and verse . . . and I run from him. Unable to even say why. Like a wild animal scampering off upon hearing a crack of thunder. A fear that arises out of instinct, out of reflex, not reason.

"And that is how I bid him farewell, how I let him go off to war against the Spanish who deem him a traitor. I sent him away with a heart as heavy as mine, just when he needs every iota of focus and awareness and energy to prevail, and so, survive. That was my parting gift: to undermine his best chance at survival."

"You cannot take this upon yourself," Anne Cathrine soothed.

"Can I not? Should I not?" Sophie retorted sharply. "I may bear him love, but that merely adds irony to tragedy if he dies because of it. As I warned him at the outset, I am not to be trusted." She laughed bitterly. "And here I have been, dreaming—as that Englishman's play says—of being one of the goodly creatures in this brave New World. That all would be transformed, and all could be made anew." She uttered a single, hollow laugh. "What was I thinking?"

Ann Cathrine reached out and took her hand. "You were thinking that in a new place, love might be greater than the crushing weight of duty, convention, and religious prejudice. And you may yet be right, that this is indeed that brave New World."

Sophie looked up, her eyes as gray as rain upon a winter ocean. "Perhaps no world can ever be *that* new." She shook her head and repeated, "What was I thinking?"

Neither sister could find a new or better answer.

in his steely, intense, far-off way. Had that been in behind his foppish—? No matter. Scarcely breathing, Tromp picked up his cutlass. A few last feet—

He burst around the corner and into a circle of men, all silhouettes in the early morning light—but he knew their shapes. With a shout that was all wrath and no words, Tromp charged the closest one, cutlass raised high—

Chapter 40

Oranjestad, St. Eustatia

Jan van Walbeeck was gratified to have his walking stick with him. A nice, tapering length of teak from his East Indies days, capped with a ball of brass, palm-brightened on its upper surface, brown-patinaed on its lower. Yes, a wonderful day for a walking stick.

Particularly in case he needed it.

Maarten Tromp was staring at his desk somberly.

"Well, are you or aren't you?" Jan asked him.

"I am still considering."

"Well, if you consider much longer, you are going to miss your stroll with that ravishing king's daughter."

Something in what Jan said seemed to decide Tromp. He reached into the desk and pulled out a smallish snaphaunce pistol that he'd carried from his earliest days as an officer. "Do you wish to walk with us?" he asked as he closed the drawer.

"More than ever, seeing you pocket that antique. Now, be sensible: if you think it best have that with you, shouldn't you reconsider today's walk? After all, the three wise men only informed the *Politieke Raad* about the stipulations for the tariff exemption five hours ago. Tomorrow the slaveholders will be much calmer."

Tromp raised an eyebrow as he opened the door. "Will they? But that is beside the point. I am not Oranjestad's governor." He smiled, poked Jan in his broad chest before starting down the corridor. "You are."

"And why do you think I am carrying this fine-looking skull crusher?" van Walbeeck replied, hurrying after him. "This is an unnecessary risk for you. You know how the slaveholders are. They will see you behind this. They are benighted, but not stupid. They know your fervor for ending slavery, and they know that only you had the political contacts back home to bring the matter before all the allied nations and get their approval."

Tromp shrugged. "Well, if they think that, then it is all the more important that I am seen out there"—he thrust his chin toward the town beyond the fort's inner walls—"than be suspected of cowering in here. Even if this is not necessary—and you are right; it is not—there can be no room for anyone to perceive and characterize my absence as fear or weakness."

Van Walbeeck did not want to agree, but had to. "You are right in that regard. But... well..."

"You are still convinced that we should have introduced the stipulations in stages, rather than in one announcement?"

"Well, to be frank, yes. Is it truly wise to push them so hard and all at once?"

"Maybe it is not wise... but it is necessary."

"Necessary? If it causes a revolt? Maarten, we have lived with slavery for years. Surely we can—"

"I am not saying that it is a moral necessity, although

that I aver that as well. I act with such dispatch because freeing the slaves is essential to the survival, let alone the security, of this colony.

"Historical parallels teach one unexceptioned lesson: if the slaves on this island had not been assured that they would be converted into bondsmen, and then have clear opportunities to pay those bonds off in a reasonable amount of time, we would not even be here to discuss the matter. They would have either joined the Kalinago during last year's attack or stood aside. And no one debates what either outcome would have been."

Jan shrugged. "If they had sat in their hovels, the invaders would have pushed past The Quill that much more swiftly, certainly before that handful of colonists and troops could have gathered to hold them at the outskirts of Oranjestad. And had the slaves joined the Kalinago? Flames and ruin. The colony would probably have survived, but the cost—particularly given the rising hostilities with the Spanish—would have been disastrous."

Tromp nodded. "A slow death rather than a quick one." They had arrived at the gate leading out to the streets of Oranjestad. "So: do you wish to join us, Jan?"

Van Walbeeck considered. Partly because he wanted to ensure the safety of his friend, and partly because he found Anne Cathrine's presence delightful in every conceivable way, he answered, "I'm sure I will regret it, but lead on."

Van Walbeeck stopped in the middle of the street. "Repeat that, if you please, Lady Anne Cathrine."

She had rarely seen the governor stunned. She

also struggled to remember her exact words, couldn't, gave up, and settled for a rephrasing light on details. "According to the up-time history books, before the Dutch West India Company began its coastal conquests in Brazil in 1630, they had never considered entering the slave trade themselves."

Van Walbeeck simply nodded and gestured for her to continue.

"They—well, *you*—did have slaves but almost all had been taken from ships seized from the Portuguese and the Spanish. It was only when sugar production in Recife began to grow that a number of captains proposed acquiring their own slaves from Western Africa. But they were opposed by several men who said that this would be the end of the colony, saying that greed is the cancer that kills conscience. They went on to assert that they would have no shortage of affordable workers, thanks to the escaped slaves already fleeing to them from the Portuguese territories."

Van Walbeeck put a hand on his forehead while his other maintained a firm grip on the cane for support. "Well, your history has turned me into 'several men,' apparently."

Tromp actually smiled. "They probably mistranslated a phrase such as 'a man as large as several smaller ones.'"

Jan sniffed. "If there was any reference to a superfluity in my person, it would have been of my wisdom and discerning taste in wine, I am sure."

Anne Cathrine wondered if she was staring like one of the young up-time girls that Eddie laughingly remembered as "groupies." "That warning—those words—they are yours, Governor?"

He shrugged. "I suppose it is possible that more than one person has uttered the phrase, 'greed is the cancer that kills conscience.' I only know that I did. And at that exact time. Of course, after Dunkirk, Recife had no way to ship its sugar, so the need for more labor, let alone slaves, ended almost before it began."

Tromp nodded sharply. "And we shall make sure it stays that way. This is not merely a matter of prudence. The Ring of Fire was our redemption, it seems. Or a second chance."

Anne Cathrine almost gulped at the words, "a second chance." *Exactly how I have thought about the Ring of Fire, ever since Eddie and I were married. I could hardly believe my good fortune, right up until the end of the ceremony, fearful that someone would coming running into the cathedral, would appeal to my father, would say or do something that would make me what I was before Eddie entered our lives: marriage chattel. A "gift" to be bestowed by a grateful king in exchange for sufficient aid to his throne: a young, reasonably attractive, almost grown daughter who would join the recipient's family to the king's by joining her body with—*

Anne Cathrine slammed down a mental portcullis on that train of thought, decapitating it like a loathsome dragon that threatened to slay her right here, at the northern end of Oranjestad's as yet unnamed main street. *No. Don't follow those thoughts further. Mustn't follow them further.*

Besides, there was so much else that deserved the attention of her bitterness and resentment. Not the least of which was the blithe manner in which such marriages were arranged, and later, tolerated. After all, kings and councilors in every land of Europe—indeed, in every "civilized" nation of the word—accepted the wisdom that, in order to maintain peace and prosperity, it was necessary to marry daughters not only to advantage, but to forge bonds that disinclined all the parties thereto from warring against one another. Yes, that was the wisdom of kings and councilors, who— regardless of their differences in language, culture, religion, even goodness—had one glaring thing in common: they were men.

To be fair, those disparate rulers shared another almost universal presupposition. They accepted the burdens of leadership as a solemn duty that was either explicit or implicit in their culture's holy writ: that their rule was clearly the intent of deity. Because, of course, only the mind of a man would be able to hold converse with the mind of God, would know His will—despite the fact that sermons in all faiths routinely asserted that God's mind was unknowable. Had the consequences upon her sex been less grim, it would have been quite funny how that implicit contradiction never occurred to, or at least never perturbed, them. Probably because they never saw it. Probably because they were its beneficiaries.

And at that moment, as she realized her two walking companions had begun to frown at her distraction, Anne Cathrine understood—yet again, but as if anew—one of the reasons she had fallen ardently, absolutely, passionately in love with Eddie: he was a man who didn't require external validations of what he intrinsically knew himself to be. His status as a man was not dependent upon competing with other men, nor blindly protecting the privileges and presumed superiority accorded to his sex by the religious, political, and social shibboleths of this time. Eddie was simply—

"Lady Ann Ca—?"

"I apologize, Admiral," she interrupted. "I find that, with the reading I have been doing, I see so many things in a new light. I often get lost in those thoughts." They turned the corner into Oranjestad's northernmost square. "I can never tell when even a subtle act or remark puts me in mind of—" She stopped, the word *slavery* frozen behind her lips as she stared at the scene in the square, first confused, then disbelieving.

Tromp and van Walbeeck had stopped in mid-stride as well, the admiral's frown hardening into a deep scowl. The governor sighed, glanced at Anne Cathrine. "Would this be one of those 'subtle acts' you were remarking upon, my lady?"

It took that long for her to sort out the elements in the bizarre tableau that dominated the northern end of the square. And still the meaning—or rather, the purpose—was not entirely clear.

Approximately thirty slaves, almost all African, were lying facedown in the northward road, their numbers extending into the wide intersection it formed with smaller streets. They were arrayed in rows and columns, like some perverse game board made up of dark-skinned humanity. All ages and sexes were represented.

Walking in the narrow longitudinal and latitudinal lanes of the arrangement were four slaveholders and their senior foremen, all carrying whips. Machetes and pistols were stuck through their belts. If any of the slaves moved, even if it was merely to scratch themselves or brush away a fly, one or more of the vigilant men would hasten in that direction, shouting and raising their whips.

Anne Cathrine looked at Tromp, wondering what he would do, would say . . . but started at the look on his face.

Fury such as she had never seen before. Oh, her father was capable of rageful storms, but they were more in the nature of tantrums. But this? Admiral Tromp—kind, wry, gentlemanly Maarten Tromp—did indeed look like a male incarnation of a Fury from Greek myth, poised like fate itself: not simply determined, but devoid of any other human feeling or purpose. Now, there was only an avatar of dispassionate and unstoppable annihilation looking out of his once-mild eyes.

Several of the men paused. One, Hans Musen of the *Politieke Raad*, gestured toward the admiral and van Walbeeck. "Ah, perhaps these good men can help us," he cried with histrionic flourishes. "Their voices—the authority of the governor's office and the Fleet, combined—must surely be able to compel obedience where we have failed."

The most restless slaveholder—Councilor Jan Haet, if Anne Cathrine remembered correctly—guffawed, throwing his head back and his belly out as if he was a giant rather than five and a half feet tall. "Well, thank God! The authorities are here!"

Cuthbert Pudsey, who had remained a discreet distance behind Anne Cathrine and her two walking companions, came up close behind her.

Tromp's face had become somewhat human again. His voice was loud, but calm. "Move these people. At once."

"We've tried, Admiral," Musen explained. "We've

pleaded and begged and cajoled, but they refuse to move." The men snickered. "But maybe, just maybe, if a powerful man like you were to ask them . . ."

The small crowd that had been watching the spectacle was growing. The men's raucous laughter seemed to bring townspeople from all directions.

"End this foolishness," Tromp said sharply. "Tell your charges to move."

Musen did so. When none of the slaves complied, he shook his head sadly. "And so we see the disorder that occurs when lesser beings refuse their Heaven-ordained role: to submit themselves to the authority and orders of better men. Even though those men are—by *law*—their owners. What are we to do?"

Van Walbeeck's face was carefully devoid of emotion, feigned or otherwise. "You will not provoke us. You have made your point. Leave. Take your *people* with you. These matters are to be settled in the council's chamber, not the street."

Musen affected sudden understanding. "Ah, you must be referring to the chamber where you hold your weekly puppet shows?" His smile became savage. "Because that's what it is, no? A parody of participatory government? You summon us, we attend, then you tell us what must be, and we are expected to continue capering and nodding like agreeable puppets."

"Makes you wonder who are the slaves, after all," one of the foremen sneered.

The sharpness of Tromp's voice reminded Anne Cathrine of the report of Eddie's up-time pistol. "Move them, Musen! Now!"

Musen looked at Haet, who looked back. They shrugged, and then started walking along the rows and columns of slaves, some quaking with fear. "Move! Move, you dogs!" They brandished their whips, ordered the other men to do the same. The slaves quivered but remained rooted to the ground.

Musen turned back to Tromp. "You see? They will not move." He turned to Haet. "What shall we do?"

"I suppose we will have to whip them, won't we, Hans?"

"Why I suppose we will, Jan." Musen swung his wrist so that the tightly coiled whip widened into loose loops. "But what if they still won't move?"

"Then I suppose we'll have to keep whipping them," Haet answered, flicking his wrist. His whip lashed out, snapping testily.

Tromp held up a hand. "Halt this nonsense. Let us talk, instead." Without missing a beat or turning his head, he muttered sideways at Anne Cathrine: "Lady Anne, please return to the fort at once. Send two squads to us, on my direct orders."

Musen was rubbing his chin. "I don't know if we really have time to talk, Admiral. If we wait much longer, the cane growers in town on business will be unable to return to their plantations, just as the paid farmhands coming the other way will be blocked from their homes."

"*Ja*," Haet grinned mirthlessly, "the time for talking is past. It's far too late for that." His smile made the double meaning of his comment venomously clear. He snapped his right arm and wrist; his whip cracked less than half a foot above the back of a boy no more than eight years old.

Now Tromp did glance at Anne Cathrine. "Why are you still here?"

"Because—because I am not leaving," she discovered as the words came out of her mouth.

"Lady Anne Cathrine, I do not have time to argue—"

"You're right," she interrupted. "You do not have time to argue. You must fetch your troops, who will follow *you* immediately and without any debate. So hurry back here to stop this. Before it grows worse."

"I cannot leave you in the middle of—"

"With respect, sir," Cuthbert Pudsey muttered, "the first one of that lot what tries to touch the lady will be meeting his Maker—or more'n like Old Scratch—before he can draw another breath."

"I shall stay also, Maarten," van Walbeeck said. "These are creatures of my government."

"Which makes them more likely to harm you than me!"

Haet grinned as more whips cracked just above the backs of the slaves.

Now it was van Walbeeck whose face wore an expression Anne Cathrine had never seen there before: a complete lack of animation. Pure composure and calculation. "Admiral, if they harm you, not only is our defense compromised, but their violation will be a hanging offense. So you must go, and quickly, if you mean to keep this from becoming a massacre."

"We will have words on this matter," Tromp said, glaring at the two of them. Then he turned about, jaw rigid, the crowd parting and closing behind him as he stalked rapidly south toward the fort.

Haet laughed at the admiral's vanished back, glanced at van Walbeeck. "Heh. I thought you'd be the one who'd be too delicate to stand the sight of blood."

"I have seen more blood than you can imagine, Jan

Haet. That is why I'm staying: to convince you not to do this. Do not take this fateful step."

"What step? You mean, whipping my slaves? Did you start early on the rum today, Governor? Because what I know of the law is that you do not have the right to tell me what I may or may not do with my own property!"

"In fact," said Musen, putting a hand on his excitable friend's shoulder, "it seems like we're going to have to whip them, in order to *obey* the law. We've been ordered to get them to move. If they will, that is."

Without warning, and with startling speed, Hans Musen spun and brought his whip down across the back of the eight-year-old boy. A deep red seam opened up, from his shoulder to his buttocks. He screamed. "Are you asking for another, with that noise?"

The boy shook his head, whimpering.

"Well, get up!"

The boy was suddenly still, but Anne Cathrine could hear, even at a distance of almost twenty feet, that his teeth were grinding.

"Well," Musen sighed with a philosophical shrug and monstrous smile at van Walbeeck, "that didn't work. Want to try using your gubernatorial authority?"

"Child, rise," van Walbeeck shouted. "Get up immediately. Do not fear these men. Get up and run behind me."

But the boy didn't move, except to bury his face in the dirt, as if it was not merely his body that was in danger of being torn apart, but his mind.

"No?" said Musen. "Well, I guess we'll have to keep trying it my way. The way a master actually keeps control over slaves." He reared up, the whip swinging high behind him.

"You are an animal! An *animal*!" a woman's voice screamed. A haggard figure in a worn shift broke free of the crowd and ran toward Musen. Who turned, hand on his machete so quickly that the crowd shrank back and the woman stopped.

It was Edel Mund.

Chapter 41

Oranjestad, St. Eustatia

When Musen discovered who it was upbraiding him, he threw back his head and laughed. "'Animal'? I think you have me confused with my property, *Lady* Mund. Now, since your delicate feelings are offended by my attempts at getting these dull beasts moving, you should go back home." His smile became a threat. "It's safer there."

Mund circled Musen. Haet tracked her with his eyes. "I am not going anywhere!" she shouted, without the earlier edge of hysteria. "I am going to keep shouting until the whole of Oranjestad is here to witness that you *are* an animal. No: I correct myself. No animal is so driven by spite and malice to conceive of a charade such as this. This is the work of a monster."

Musen laughed—and then leaped at her. The crowd gasped and Mund scuttled back, almost into Anne Cathrine...but it had only been a feint. Musen laughed again, turned his back on her. "Like I said, go home to your hovel. I'm sure the ridiculous leaded windows in its ugly walls will trick you into believing that you

476

really *are* in your manor house again, curled up around that grim manikin you used to call a husband. Heh: not much different, now that he's dead, eh?"

Anne Cathrine almost leaped past Edel Mund's suddenly sagging shoulders. "How can you be so brutish?" she yelled. "Those windows are her one indulgence!"

The slaveholders and their foremen laughed; Mund's home was a shack made incongruous by having the only glass windows in Oranjestad. "Yes," Haet taunted, "those windows are certainly an indulgence—of her pride, of her desire to remind us of her 'fabulous wealth'!"

"No!" Anne Cathrine shot back angrily. Edel Mund turned curious eyes upon her. "We invited her to come live in Danish House. She refused; she does not want to burden anyone else with her grief."

"*Ja*, that and Danish House doesn't have glass windows!" one of the foremen cackled.

Anne Cathrine suppressed a string of insults that would certainly have shocked her father and might have sparked an attack. "Lady Mund is a private person, but shutters make a house dark. So why should she not have glass if that gives her sunlight, even though her grief keeps her inside?" Edel Mund's face was not merely surprised, but wondering as Anne Cathrine revealed the unspoken truth behind the widow's daily life.

"Yes, yes, such poetic excuses," Haet drawled. "If she is so unhappy, she should get back across the ocean. Or drown herself in it, for all I care. But she has no business remaining here, no business interfering in our community." He turned toward Edel. "I give you one last warning: go home, you withered crone."

"How dare you!" shouted Anne Cathrine. "You are speaking to a noblewoman of Denmark—and my friend!"

The entire group of slaveholders and their men became motionless for a minute, staring at Anne Cathrine. Pudsey came up close behind her.

Musen nodded at her slowly. "And you mind your own business, too, 'king's daughter.' You're no princess, so don't start thinking you can order us about as if you are."

Haet took a step toward her. "You should leave with your friend. You're not welcome here, either." A surge of disagreeing murmurs among the crowd was the unanticipated response to Haet's assertion.

"Shut up!" he screamed, rounding on them. "You're no different from townsfolk back home: always ready to lick the first aristocratic boot that comes in range of your tongue."

Van Walbeeck folded his hands. "I wonder how much longer you will be able to remain a councilor, Jan Haet, insulting your own neighbors in a public—"

"I wonder how much longer you'll be aboveground, van Walbeeck," Haet spat back, moving in the direction of the governor.

Anne Cathrine stepped forward to interpose herself, but three hands stopped her: van Walbeeck's, Pudsey's, and Edel Mund's. The older woman's eyes smiled even though her mouth did not. Then she moved her hand to Anne Cathrine's shoulder, squeezed it once, turned and began walking back toward the landowners and their thirty terrified slaves.

But instead of approaching Haet or Musen, she crouched down beside an African woman, not quite as old as she. "Will you move, if I ask you to do so?"

The woman shook her head, trembling.

"Lady Mund..." van Walbeeck called anxiously.

But Mund wasn't listening. She smiled at the slave. "Because your master told you *not* to move, yes?"

Before Haet could react, the woman had nodded.

"Bitch!" Haet screamed, charging forward.

"Are you speaking to me?" Mund asked coolly as she straightened.

Haet came to an abrupt halt, managed to smile. "Lady Mund, how could you even think such a thing?"

"I only require you to answer 'yes' or 'no.'"

Musen yawned. "Or you will do what?"

"Oh, I will not need to do anything more. I have already revealed, in the presence of these good people and their governor, that Jan Haet is a liar. Either for denying that he plainly called me a bitch, or for shamelessly maintaining the deceit of this grotesque spectacle: that these slaves remain where they are because you have told them they must, on pain of death. By your hands."

Anne Cathrine heard van Walbeeck's breath suck in through his teeth.

Haet started forward. Reluctantly, so did van Walbeeck.

Mund was simply smiling at Haet, who stopped five feet away from her. Whether that was because of her utter lack of concern at his approach, or van Walbeeck's advance, was unclear. Mund's smile was now serene. "And you still have not answered; am I the 'bitch' you were addressing?"

Haet's voice was more like a snarl. "And what if you are? What can you do to me, old woman?"

"Firstly, I suspect I am not much older than you.

But as to what I might do to you, well, if you fear I will notify my king, whose subsequent complaint to the Stadtholder would make special mention of your name—No, *mijn Heer* Haet, I will not do that. I am not a coward like you. I fight my own battles. Indeed, I have fought yours, as well."

"What raving is this?"

Mund shrugged. "It is not raving; it is common knowledge. Ask those gathered here. Those who saw me in the shallow trenches alongside them. Many of them wanted to know why almost none of the slave owners came to defend the town when the Kalinago attacked last year. Most presumed you were simply cowards. Others speculated that you were traitors. I have wondered since that day: which is it?"

Van Walbeeck emitted a sigh that was almost a groan, and Anne Cathrine suddenly understood his efforts at calling Mund back. He was not just worried for her safety, but that her words were leading toward this point of unresolved contention. Ultimately, the calls for an investigation of the slaveholders' inaction had foundered on two points: the community's unspoken need to remain undivided, and the lack of any testimony supporting the assertion that their failure to defend Oranjestad had been intentional. The landowners' improbable excuses ranged from having believed their own homes were in imminent danger to complete ignorance of the attack until it was over. And of course, no slaves would assert anything to the contrary, particularly since their testimony was neither admissible nor likely to be deemed impartial.

But now, the issue had been resurrected in the most tense and ugly impromptu town gathering that

Anne Cathrine had ever witnessed. And Edel Mund was not letting go of it. "You still have not answered, Jan Haet. And you may tell me that, as a Dane, I have no right to ask, but *they* seem to want an answer"— she swept her hand in a semicircle that indicated the tense crowd—"and you are oddly silent."

"I gave my answer."

Mund shrugged. "Give it again. Either they've forgotten it or don't believe it."

Haet's face surged red and he leaped toward her, his whip moving. Pudsey and van Walbeeck started forward.

But Edel Mund, in circling away from Haet, had also moved further away from her would-be protectors. "Ah, *mijn Heer*, and now you mean to beat *me*, eh?" She stopped, her face thrust toward his. "Well, try it, coward. Go ahead! *You* are the animal, not these poor beings you torment. And now that your little rodent brain is emptied of lame rebuttals, you resort to force. So please, show the world your superiority. Beat the widow; show how your whip makes you the better being."

Haet started forward again, but Musen came up behind him, and put a firm hand on his shoulder. He steered him away from Mund and kept him in tow as he walked over to the same African woman that Edel Mund had approached and questioned. Musen studied the slave's shaking back. "She is not as old as you," he mused, "but seems close in size and health, *ja*?"

Mund shook her head; her frown did not signify an answer in the negative but perplexity at why the slaveholder was asking such a question.

Musen made his intents clear so swiftly that many

blinked: he spun and slashed the whip across the woman's back with surprising force. He was clearly an expert; an extremely wide, bloody seam had been opened but no bone exposed. The woman screamed and then wept through the moans that followed. He nodded to Haet, who grinned and readied his own whip.

Musen considered the ashen-faced Mund. "Councilor Haet may not have the permission to beat you, Lady Mund, but I suspect he will be able to make you *wish* it was you under the lash." As he smiled at Mund, he nodded.

Haet swung the whip in a wide serpentine and slashed down. The woman's scream was not just one of agony but terror. Haet slashed again; the slave shrieked. A man beside her wept. Somewhere else in the group, a younger female voice cried out, probably the woman's name: a rush of panicked syllables that sounded African in origin.

Musen held up a hand; Haet stopped, panting . . . but not from exhaustion.

Musen assessed Edel Mund, who seemed about to fall over. He gestured to the steps of a home that fronted on the square. "This may go on for quite some time, Lady Mund. You will find it less taxing to sit until it is over."

"How many lashes do you mean to give her?" van Walbeeck asked through clenched teeth.

"I do not know." Mund looked back at Haet, who shrugged. Mund cast an assessing glance at the slave's bloody, shining back. "She is not strong, but she is relatively tough. It could take as many as sixty lashes."

"Sixty lashes?" Anne Cathrine cried, looking from Pudsey to van Walbeeck to the sobbing woman. "What can you hope to accomplish with sixty lashes that ten would not achieve?"

"Her death," Musen answered.

"But she—she did nothing!"

"True . . . except for refusing to move," Mund amended with a gloating grin. "Because, as God is my witness, none of *us* ever told her that she must continue to lie there. Yet because of her, here we are, obstructing the road and so, breaking the law."

Anne Cathrine could not decide which urge was stronger; to vomit or kill Musen where he stood.

"But," he continued, "since the law also prohibits my friend from whipping Edel Mund, I have lawfully chosen to give him the full use of my property. That way, he is legally beginning to clear the road . . . and showing Lady Mund what he would otherwise have done to *her.*" Musen's eyes narrowed—right before he nodded.

Haet threw his body into moving the whip up high and hard. Screams erupted from the crowd. Edel Mund rushed at Haet's back, hands curved into talons. Without having thought to do so, Anne Cathrine discovered she had sprinted after Mund, was grabbing her shift, pulling her back.

Slave owners reacted to the sudden eruption of motion, brandishing weapons. Townspeople shrank away. Haet turned, whip forgotten, drew his knife when he saw Cathrine dragging Mund to safety. He leaped after them . . . but Cuthbert Pudsey rammed into his blind side, sprawling him in the dust.

Soldiers appeared among the slaveholders and the crowd. Haet reached for a pistol as he rolled to face Pudsey—whose own flintlock was up, cocked, and aimed at the small Dutchman's chest before he'd laid a hand on his weapon.

"Enough!" Tromp's impressively loud and sharp voice froze the tableau, which struck Anne Cathrine as how Brueghel might have depicted a battle among the inmates of an asylum.

Tromp stepped into the center of that imagined painting, pointing his index finger at the slaveholders as if lightning was ready to leap from its tip. "You will leave immediately. Sergeant, the first squad will watch to ensure that the remaining slaveholders allow their... *charges* to rise and return home."

The landowners looked uncertainly at one another, weapons still in their hands.

"Sergeant, the second squad is to intervene if anyone obstructs the first squad from carrying out its orders. They shall take all such persons into custody."

"And if they resist, sir?"

"Then your men are authorized to use force. To the final degree, if needed."

Some of the landowners and all of the foremen made their whips and weapons as inconspicuous as they could.

Tromp was not finished. "Lady Mund makes an excellent point when she brings up the question of those whom we may depend upon to defend Oranjestad. And considering how that spontaneous militia was so very nearly swept away, and how capricious slaveholders have been in providing for the health of those voluntary defenders who were also their charges—"

"Our *slaves*!" Haet shrieked.

"—both the governor and I, given our respective duties to protect this colony, now have both the grounds and obligation to ensure the continuing well-being of those same voluntary defenders."

There was a sudden hush among both the slaveholders and the townspeople.

"Maarten—" began van Walbeeck.

Tromp did not seem to have heard him. Or if he had, he did not care to listen. "Beginning tomorrow, designated individuals—although we shall consider volunteers with skill in medicine—shall commence regular but unannounced visits to the plantations of all the slave owners present here today. They shall be escorted by troops, as the visit is military in nature."

"And what is the purpose of these intrusions? Harassment?" Musen asked loudly.

"Not at all. The designated individuals must be given private access to your slaves so that they may assess whether they remain fit to once again assist in the defense of this island. Any report of mistreatment or neglect shall result in those *individuals* being made temporary wards of the state—"

"What?" screamed Haet.

"—who shall be released back into the custody of the owner at such time as they are deemed recovered. Assuming that no investigation has been brought against their owner."

"What kind of investigation and why?" asked Musen suspiciously.

"Any second confirmed report of mistreatment or neglect will necessitate an investigation to determine if this colony may continue to reside its confidence in the loyalty and support of the slave owner in question. If not, the community's only recourse, both to secure its own safety and that of the mistreated slaves, is to immediately convert them into bondsmen. Without recompense to the owner."

Musen's objection was faster, strident. "This is nonsense, Tromp! How does any of this secure the safety of the colony? Slaves aren't soldiers; they can't—"

"Your slaves," Tromp interrupted, "were far more enthusiastic in joining the defense of St. Eustatia than you were. Several took the risk of slipping away from your tracts in order to do so. Now, this is a particularly confounding fact, since many of those same slaves belong to and reside with owners who claim they had no knowledge of the impending attack. Perplexing indeed."

There was no reply or even grumble from the slave owners and their men.

"More to your point, though, *mijn Heer* Musen, it also demonstrates that, left to make the choice for themselves, your own slaves would, and many did, come to defend Oranjestad. Should we need that loyalty and courage again, military prudence dictates that we cannot allow those defenders to remain under the control of men who do not share their zeal. Or who show, as today, that they will not comply with the rules of the colony, and who have no discernible regard for most of their fellow citizens. I trust that answers your questions?"

Haet spat. "Well, it certainly answers the question of who is the real government around here. Tell us, Jan van Walbeeck, do you need the admiral's permission before pissing, too?"

The laughter was not entirely limited to the ranks of the slaveholders.

But van Walbeeck was one of those laughing as

well. "Why, yes...if I had to relieve myself during a *battle*. Because that is Admiral Tromp's domain of authority. But as far as the civilian administration of this colony is concerned, that very witty gibe could not be more wrong."

"Then why did Maarten speak, instead of you? Scared we might taunt you, big cheeks?"

"Why no. I was simply concerned that my patience had grown so short that I might tell some truths that none of you gentlemen slaveholders wish to hear."

"And what truths are those?" Musen asked.

"They remain unspoken truths but, after today, are obvious to all. Specifically, that while your collective ignorance, stupidity, and greed are very notable traits, they pale in comparison to your cruelty and depravity. So you see, it was very fortunate that *Maarten* spoke to you. Because I surely would have lost my temper and said such things." Van Walbeeck held up his hands, still smiling. "How lucky that I did not do so."

Laughter rose up from the townspeople, but hushed when the eyes of the remaining slave owners roved among them, seeking the identities of those who had laughed.

"And now," Tromp announced, "you shall comply with our orders. Move these *people* from the square."

Haet, more defiant than smart, retorted angrily "And if we don't?" Musen put his palm to his face and shook his head.

Van Walbeeck folded his hands. "I understand why you did this. You wished to show that there are no clear boundaries defining what a slave owner may or may not do with their 'property.'"

"And we broke no laws doing so."

"Actually, you did. *Mijn Heer* Musen has already alluded to it: you used your property to obstruct a public thoroughfare. If you do not act now to correct that situation, we shall take appropriate action." When there was no immediate reaction, van Walbeeck produced a sheaf and one of the crude but useful pencils which had sold by the hundreds the first day the convoy's market had opened. "Shall I start making a list of those who are not complying?"

A muttering began, but so did movement among the plantation owners. They approached their slaves and ordered them to return home, often with words and a boot that the meanest man would not use on his dog.

Cries of "Fire! Fire!" were what woke Anne Cathrine, rather than the dull banging of Oranjestad's makeshift gong. She flinched upright, grabbing for Eddie, found empty space instead, and felt her heart plummet even as she leaped out of bed.

She pulled on the shift she sometimes used as a nightgown and got to the front door just ahead of Sophie. She thought she heard Leonora yelling after them as they burst out of Danish House and almost ran headlong into the stumbling, sleep-dazed Cuthbert Pudsey, who swerved after them, stumbling.

Townspeople stared mute after the two young Danish women racing toward the bright glow over the near rooftops. More than a few followed them. Two corners and a twisting alley later, they burst onto the street where a small house was afire.

Edel Mund's house.

Anne Cathrine looked wildly for water to douse the flames, but it appeared that the neighbors had already done so and used what little was ready to hand. But where was Sophie?

As if summoned by the thought, Sophie Rantzau appeared out of the nearby building: the tannery. She had an immense and heavy bucket in either hand. She was bowed under their weight, but Anne Cathrine wondered if she was also staggered by the sour, acrid stink coming from them. She passed one to Anne Cathrine and nodded toward the flame-covered door.

Anne Cathrine understood, and even as she ordered the surprised neighbors to get more of the tanner's urine to fight the blaze, Sophie pitched the contents of her bucket at the entrance.

The liquid hit the flames like a palm swatting them away, released a choking reek in the process. But the wood was still burning, threatened to reignite.

Anne Cathrine heaved the contents of her own bucket, was pulled forward by the heavy pendulum momentum, and went with it.

The urine splashed and smothered the flames the instant that Anne Cathrine hit the door with her shoulder. It gave and she plunged through the fumes into the hovel.

In response to the new source of oxygen, the fire leaped at her like a demon from Saharan myths, reaching for her face—

And then she was flying backward, airborne as Sophie slung the smaller woman past her hip, hauling her bodily out of the doorway with such force that Anne Cathrine was briefly airborne before landing in the dirt. Sophie, hands warding off the outgushing flames, backed away along with the others who had been fighting the fire.

But she quickly brought her hands down to lay hold of Anne Cathrine, who, without thinking, was trying to plunge into the small inferno, determined to find and save—

"Anne Cathrine!" Sophie shouted into her face.

Anne Cathrine started, looked from her friend into the flames.

"No," Sophie said, townspeople gathering around, witnessing the spectacle of two night-clothed, urine-stained, smoke-smudged ladies of Denmark huddled and firelit in the dirt of the street.

"But . . ." Anne Cathrine pointed at the hovel. "But we have to . . ."

"Lady Anne Cathrine," said the closest of the faces ringing her, "Edel Mund is dead."

Chapter 42

St. John's Harbor, Antigua

St. John's Harbor was beautiful, as it was every single day. And today, because there wasn't a cloud in the sky, it was pretty, too.

Which weren't the same thing for Eddie Cantrell, because when he looked at St. John's Harbor, he rarely saw its natural loveliness. The bright blue waters, the lush growth clinging to the volcanic rocks and cliffs, and the white gulls wheeling in the sky were almost invisible, to him. What he saw was its *real* beauty.

Which was to say, its naval beauty: a long deep-draft waterway; an entry only nine hundred and seventy yards across between two promontories that formed a natural choke point; a deep inner anchorage that was one of the Caribbean's most famous hurricane holes. And even if a threat managed to avoid detection as it passed St. Eustatius or St. Christopher, or avoided them altogether and came out of the northwest, the local highgrounds—ranging from four hundred to thirteen hundred feet—enabled constant observation out to a distance of thirty nautical miles. More, in most directions. Which in tactical terms translated to ample time to get any warships out of St. John's Harbor and deployed into its approaches while still under the defensive umbrella of the batteries on the highground that lined that part of the coastline.

No, mused Eddie with quiet satisfaction, an island didn't get any more exquisite than that. And he and the work crews were making it better all the time.

He looked away from the window to the exacting copy—enlarged—of an excellent map of Antigua. It covered the far wall, and beside it was a smaller, less-detailed version. That one was now festooned by pins of various colors: all the current projects and the ships in the bay.

Which looked pretty impressive, Eddie admitted. It wasn't just *Intrepid* which had been bound for Antigua under the cover of escorting the convoy on the first leg of her return to Europe. While *Resolve* had returned to St. Eustatia after only a week, and it had been leaked that *Intrepid* was still in the Caribbean somewhere, *Relentless* and three of the four USE frigates had also doubled back to St. John's Harbor. And there was also a steady stream of Spanish prize hulls that were undergoing repair, or in the case of any undamaged trade galleons, conversions that optimized them for war.

All those ships' crews had not only swollen Eddie's available workforce, but boasted a much higher than average percentage of artisans. In consequence, St. John's Naval Base already had half as many buildings as Oranjestad (most of them larger, too) and almost twice the number of (again, larger) warehouses.

St. Eustatia was an additional source of workmen— Eddie grimaced every time he remembered they were actually leased slaves—but yesterday's planned allotment had not arrived. The almost terse reply to his telegraphed inquiry indicated that all was well, but the situation there was "fluid." Which made Eddie smile: that telegraph message had definitely come from Tromp, whose acquisition of select up-time terms and idioms had become some kind of weird guilty pleasure.

Well, whatever floats your boat, Maarten, thought Eddie, who almost groaned at his own pun before snagging the report on the progress the work crews had made on *Intrepid*. Mike's writing was on the cover. Moment of truth.

Eddie pulled at the corner with a fingertip; he always hesitated before opening Mike's updates on *Intrepid* because, in some ways, it was the most crucial single project being undertaken. But again, as always, he got annoyed at himself—*don't be gutless, Cantrell; waiting won't change the news!*—and opened it abruptly.

He sighed in relief: the inclinometer was finally, *finally*, working. The device was tricky, and it had taken Mike McCarthy half a week just to get it to function at all. It was really quite ambitious, too. Two sights, one fixed, the other a "floating element" that was responsive to the roll, pitch, and yaw of the ship. When the system was activated and the two sights were in perfect alignment, a circuit closed. That sent an electric pulse which fired the gun. Instantaneously. Having to read the waves and the chop would be unnecessary. And now, finally, it worked.

However, there was a further challenge: the module that allowed the gunner to quickly adjust the entire sight for different ranges had yet to be added. It was still in its shipping crate and had come with warnings that it was notoriously finicky. But that was another challenge for another day. *Right now, Eddie, take the win.*

Eddie closed the report, saw Mike's writing on the cover again. Where would he be now? Eddie checked the down-time pendulum clock that would have long since become the world's biggest, strangest, most expensive paperweight if his orderly didn't remember to keep winding and adjusting it.

It showed 1000 hours. Which meant that Mike and Kees should have just about reached the first stop on their weekly tour of the project sites.

Mike McCarthy's butt told him that it was going to be a very long day. He knew that because he'd only been on horseback an hour and already he could feel the ache coming on. And if he wasn't careful, the hemorrhoids would come back. *No, please, God; anything but that.*

Next to him, Kees Evertsen, who was usually the picture of youthful vigor, wasn't faring much better. Yes, he was a down-timer and so, had a much greater acquaintance with horses as essential forms of transportation. But he had been a mariner his whole life. Horses hadn't figured very prominently in his youth and since then, travel meant being on a deck, not in a saddle.

The younger man pointed higher up the rocky bluff as they neared its edge and the sea breeze buffeted their shirts and hair. "We are expected, Michael!"

Mike returned the wave of a lively, agile figure at the crest of the rising road that hadn't even existed six weeks ago. "Let's see what he's done with the guns." They urged their mounts up the slope.

Usually, Mike didn't require anyone to hold his horse while he dismounted, but today he felt achy and creaky enough that he didn't object when the site supervisor put a steadying hand on the mare's bridle. "Welcome, Don Michael."

I will never forgive O'Rourke for telling everyone that's how I prefer to be addressed. "And a good morning to you, Krys. What's news up here at Loblolly Point?"

"Excellent progress!" answered Krys, who was actually Captain Krzysztof Arciszewski, a Polish soldier and engineer with a legendarily unpronounceable name. He'd been with the Dutch at Recife, and had been a noble back home. However, it seemed as though he had commenced his career as a mercenary just ahead of a murder charge that may or may not have involved a duel or dispute over another nobleman's wife. The details were not plentiful and it was a certainty that Krys wasn't going to furnish any himself.

All that aside, Mike had found the captain to be as determined as he was indefatigably optimistic, and if he almost always reported "excellent progress" that was because . . . well, he'd made really excellent progress.

This day was no exception. He led them to the walls that had been built overlooking the mouth of St. John's Harbor. Kees whistled. "Captain, these are almost finished, no?"

"No," Krys corrected with a laugh. "We have a good deal of work still ahead. But they'd serve in a pinch. And come see!" He led them to a rectangular pit. "Measured for one of the Spanish forty-two-pounders, but it could rapidly be made optimal for one of the thirty-two-pounders as well." Workers appeared from over the rim of the new earthworks of the next, more northern battery. They were a mix of crews from one of the Dutch frigates and laborers leased from St. Eustatia's slaveholders. There were all soaked in sweat. The Dutch seamen looked downtrodden; the bond laborers were animated, energetic.

Kees Evertsen frowned. "Are the African laborers just starting their day?"

Krys raised an eyebrow. "Why?"

"Well, they seem . . . much less exhausted."

"Ah," the captain answered. "It is always such. I suspect they find the comparative freedom here—equal food, equal work, equal conditions, equal treatment—extremely invigorating. Frankly, I do not know how you will get them to return to their masters."

Mike meant to say it soberly, but it came out as a growl. "That's the idea, actually."

For a moment, Arciszewski's wonderful mustaches and wind-and-sun-burnished features were less remarkable than his almost comical look of confusion. Then he smiled. "Ah. I see. Well, Michael, would you like a look at the other battery?"

Mike waved it off. "A little later. How are you set for supplies, tools?"

"All is adequate," Krys replied. "Although any increase to the water ration would be appreciated. This is strenuous work."

Mike nodded. "We're working on that. For everyone, of course, but your fellas are first on my list. This is backbreaking work, up here."

"It is not the simplest I have overseen, but it is hardly the most taxing, either. There is one other thing I would like to know, however."

"What's that?"

"When may we expect receipt of the guns themselves?

It would be good to have one or two as models, to make sure we are leaving sufficient margins for safe operation around them." It was not unusual for excellent engineers to also be excellent artillerists. Krzysztof Arciszewski was one such.

Mike shook his head. "I wish I knew the answer to that myself, Krys. But we've got a problem: insufficient draft animals. Almost all the horses here in the New World are for riding, and oxen aren't plentiful in the Lesser Antilles. We're waiting on two more. Both were just bought from a plantation owner on St. Christopher. Cost us an arm and a leg, too. They'll probably be here within the week."

Krys nodded. "I hope that you may locate more. For if those two and the three we currently have are the only ones available for the work of bringing the guns up these slopes, then I fear they will quickly die from the work. Perhaps before all the cannon can be moved to the various batteries."

Mike nodded back. He feared the same thing. They had fifty-eight guns, all gigantic Spanish forty-two- and thirty-two-pounders taken at the Battle of Dominikirk. They had to be moved into three batteries guarding the approaches and entry to St. John's Harbor: twenty-four for James Point across the bay, twenty for Barrington Point a few hundred yards further west, and fourteen for here at Loblolly. Given the size of the guns, that was either going to require a lot of rest days for just five oxen, or it was going to kill them. On the other hand, even if it was never going to have Cartagena's walls, St. John's would have some of the most numerous and heavy-hitting shore batteries in the New World. Which reminded him: "Krys, did you get Eddi—the commodore's note about reserving that little rise behind the Barrington battery?"

"Yes. What use does he intend for it? Observation?"

Mike smiled. "Well, that too, but eventually, we want to mount some naval rifles up there. That would increase our effective threat range by a factor of ten." Mike began walking back to his horse. Krys fell in beside him, Kees remaining slightly behind the two older men.

When Mike was in the saddle, Krys looked up, imploring, "If I may reemphasize, Michael: any increase in the water ration would be most helpful."

Mike nodded. "That's where I'm heading now." He twitched the reins and headed down the pseudo-road.

Eddie stared at the folders on his desk. Which one next? Did it matter? Naval work was like the game of whack-a-mole. The moment you whack one job down, another springs up. He frowned. No, creating a naval base from scratch was the advanced version: whack-a-*hydra*. Where every time you finish off one job, *two* more spring up in its place. And from the crowding on his desk, he was not winning this game: not even close. Too many papers, too many reports, too many letters, too much of everything—

Except pictures. No pictures. In every office he'd ever seen as a kid—either the real ones he had occasion to enter, or the innumerable ones he'd seen on TV shows—desks had pictures on them. Pictures of things beloved or special to the desk's user.

Eddie looked at his desk. No picture of Anne Cathrine. The only thing he would have gladly put on his desk was one of the objects you just couldn't get down-time. Oh, he could probably commission some micro-painting of her, with the obliging artist wondering the whole time: *why so small an image?* But that just wouldn't be the same as an actual photograph of her.

If he closed his eyes though, he could see her. Her smile, her hair, her neck when she laughed, her shoulders when she—

Whoa, and hold on there, Commodore! Those are dangerous waters! He blew out an anxious breath, surprised at how readily *that* had come to mind. Or maybe not, given how big a change arriving on Antigua had been from a conjugal perspective. It was like going from a feast—hell, a nonstop banquet with mandatory seconds and thirds of every course—to an absolute famine. Why, over the course of that one last night...

He stopped himself yet again. Tried to think about something else, noticed his mouth had grown very, very dry. He'd never realized that thinking about your spouse and sex could be thirsty work. He reached out for the clay pitcher on his desk.

It was light. He shook it. No sloshing sound.

He closed his eyes. Once again, he'd already blown past his water ration.

The ride out across the grassy plain just south of the harbor was a whole lot easier on Mike's butt. But it kept threatening to start aching again because of the uphill jouncing with which the day had started.

Kees, on the other hand, was demonstrating the enviable and infuriating resilience of youth, sitting his more energetic mount with verve. Three miles south of the harbor, they'd angled up a slope following what looked like a game trail that had been widened by the occasional passage of draft animals. After passing through a mile and a half of mixed rainforest, bushes, and elephant grass, they had to dismount to continue.

They tied the horses in the shade of a wide, spreading tree, under which a lean-to had been thrown together. From there, it was a quarter mile of steep, jungled switchbacks to Antigua's one constant supply of fresh water: Christian Valley falls. Another label that would carry over from up-time sources since there was no known down-time name for it.

After fifteen minutes, they reached the work site: six men building a sluice from halved and hollowed tree trunks. Given the bugs, the humidity, the growing heat of the day, and the rudimentary tools, Mike and Kees exchanged looks that readily translated as, *I sure am glad I don't have to do this*. The looks they got from the men were the logical corollary: *I sure do wish I didn't have to do this*.

Mike didn't see anyone he recognized. "Where's, uh, Carver? Wasn't he in charge?"

"Was," one of them sighed. "Got sick. Fever. Two days ago. Bound back to St. Christopher."

Mike wondered how Lieutenant Governor Jeafferson would take the news that the work he'd agreed to support on Antigua would cost him more of the time, or maybe the life, of one of his most accomplished builders of wells, dams, *ghut*-flumes, and millruns. "Are you in charge now?"

The fellow who answered shrugged. "Not really. But I think I'm the only one here who speaks English."

What the hell? Mike wondered. *Did I just time-shift onto the set of* Apocalypse Now? But Mike just nodded and tried his passable Dutch instead. "Do more of you speak this?"

All of them said yes, but also confirmed that no one was really in charge. They had been told what to do, so they kept on doing it. And no, they hadn't thought to inform anyone about Carver, because he'd been taken away by the soldiers—or maybe sailors?—when they came to cart down the water barrels two days ago. Hadn't those men told anyone when they got back to the harbor?

Mike shook his head. "If so, I never heard about it. Okay, so which one of you is best with numbers?"

Two men put their hands up hesitantly, one of whom was the English-speaker. Three of the four others looked very embarrassed.

Kees was looking sidelong at the empty barrels by the side of the flume. Mike noticed the direction of his gaze, nodded. "Okay, men," he said in Dutch, "here's what you're going to do. First, you fill those barrels."

"But Mr. Carver said we had to—"

"Mr. Carver's not here anymore and I suspect he thought you'd get more done. This is less than half the progress you made last week. So for now, you have to stop extending the sluice. Your primary job is to get a water ration ready every day. Everyone in the harbor depends on it, and a shipment every other day is just not enough.

"As soon as we get more workers up here, you'll go back to running the sluice down the hill to the lean-to and building a catch tank there. After that, you'll get to the scheduled improvements: covering the sluice, sealing its joints, and improving the path to the shack so that we can get a wagon up here: a specially made water wagon."

"What?" said Kees.

"Two emptied wine tuns mounted and framed

sideways into the bed of a regular wagon. One trip with that will give us half again as much water as all these damned barrels." He raised his voice. "Do you need anything?"

"Two of our axes broke," said the other man who could count.

"We're running out of food," said one of the embarrassed ones.

"When do we get paid?"

Mike got out a small pad, scratched down hasty notes. "I'll get you answers. And I'll get a new boss up here for you within two days. My word on it."

They headed back down the path, never having seen the falls. Oddly enough, they had yet to do so. They heard them, but there was always something that needed fixing or decisions that needed making, so they never even saw the source of the water. Another item on the to-do list: to get a team to follow the falls up to their source. It hadn't been clear in the one up-time reference that mentioned them whether the water came from an actual spring or, like most Caribbean water, was runoff from condensation on high rock faces. In this case, Boggy Peak.

When they were mounted again, Kees observed. "Well, that was disturbing."

"Yeah," Mike grumbled. "For a minute there I thought two of them were going to pull out banjos and do the scene from *Deliverance*."

"What?"

"Never mind. Let's keep going."

Eddie put down the report on Curaçao. So much for the unbroken string of Dutch successes. Add one

Dutch disaster. And a horrifying illustration of just what the Spanish meant when they said, *no peace beyond the Line*. They meant no discussion, no mercy, no prisoners, nothing but extermination. Unless you wanted to count the preceding rape and torture as separate activities.

Worse yet, it showed how dangerous an adversary pirates could be, presuming they were given time to gather together and could cooperate long enough to be aimed at a relatively easy target. Problem was, almost all of the allied colonies and ports were just that: easy targets. Of all of them, only three might not have to worry about the same kind of attack: St. Christopher's because it was too large, St. Eustatia because it was too strong, and Bermuda because it was too far.

Eddie leaned his chin on his palm. On the other hand, the pirates of Tierra Firme hadn't been trimmed back by Cartagena's fleet last year because it had been focused on Trinidad and then got its resupply sabotaged at Puerto Cabello. And now this year, the mightier half of La Flota, the Tierra Firme fleet, never showed up at all. So the pirates of the Spanish Main hadn't really had their numbers thinned out in well over a calendar year. So they were probably stronger and more numerous than they had ever been.

But that wasn't the case regarding the pirates that were an immediate threat to St. Eustatia and its allies. Tromp and Eddie had bloodied the pirates of the Greater Antilles and Leeward Islands pretty badly at the Battle of Vieques. And they'd been pretty quiescent since then. According to Diego's answers to the questions he'd sent, a lot of them weren't happy with the deal they had made with the Spanish and frankly, didn't like the odds of sailing against the Dutch and their near-magical allies. Which meant they were weak. Both in terms of numbers and cohesion.

Eddie's gaze shifted to the wall map across from him, drifted to Guadeloupe and Martinique. *When an enemy is weak*, he had said to the Dutch admirals and captains when proposing to go there, *you take him off the board. You simplify your strategic equation.* And that had worked. But it had been comparatively easy.

His eyes drifted northwest on the map, stopped on Tortuga. Now *that* would be difficult. Much more strongly held. A well-established base. *And besides, we don't have the forces to spend on that. But if we did, oh, if we did...*

Mike's last stop was as reassuring as the one at the water project had been depressing. They could see it from a mile away. Rather, they could see its glare. And best of all, there was a friend working there.

When he and Kees rode down into the small valley closer to Antigua's windward coast, Mike shouted, "Don't be sleeping on the job, you lazy bum!"

"Don't tell me how to do my job, you taskmaster!" Bert Kortenaer howled back as he moved away from the solar boiler. Mike and Kees had to put up their hands against the glare. "Damn, Bert," Mike grumbled, squinting and wincing, "how the hell do you stand working around these contraptions?" Two others, offset one hundred yards to the north and the south respectively, were similarly painful actinic flares.

"There's a secret, Mike, which I'll share only with you and Kees," Kortenaer explained, ending on a conspiratorial whisper. But when they leaned close he roared, *"Don't look at them, you idiots!"* He laughed loudly, as did the other four men working with him, all leased laborers.

Mike jerked a head at them. "How goes the off-site revolution?"

"Just fine," Bert grinned as he adjusted the reflectors of the central solar boiler. "All of them are taking the basic military skills instruction that the Wild Geese started teaching a few weeks ago. And we've been talking strategies for reducing the time to buy their way out of being bondsmen. They had some ideas about collective work that were very impressive."

"Such as?" asked Kees.

"Well, if they are all working for themselves, each winds up going slowly, as slowly as their respective masters can finagle. But if they designate one as having a skill that will pay significantly more money, it may speed things up if they pool their resources and buy out his bond all at once. Then most of his money goes to buying the next one out, and so forth and so on."

"And they trust each other that much?" Kees wondered.

"*Ja*, right? We Dutch could learn a thing or two from them just about now."

Mike smiled, nodded at the solar boiler. "And how are these coming along?"

"Mike, they are wonderful. Yes, the reflectors are very expensive. And yes they need constant tending to keep the reflectors focused enough to boil water, but come look." He walked them around the back of the unit and pointed: a hillbilly-style still.

"Really?" laughed Mike. "It works?"

By way of answer, Bert handed him a small jug. "Try."

Mike did, sputtered. "Damn, that is some strong moonshine, Bert my boy!"

"I don't know what moonshine is, but yes, that is strong. Ninety percent pure. And we can do better. And at these temperatures, we can use this for working with light metals, such as tin and pewter. And if we can find a way to build it so that we can combine its heat with that of a small wood furnace, we should be able to work copper and still save immense amounts of wood."

Which was, of course, the whole point of the solar boilers. If they were going to bring even light industries to these islands in the next year or two, they had to make sure that they didn't wind up consuming all their trees for fuel. He clapped a hand on Kortenaer's shoulder. "Bert, I could almost be convinced to stay awhile. But I have to get back in time to send a telegraph for relay from The Quill Array."

"Report on the progress here?"

"No, another attempt to reach my wife. Been too silent back there. I need to make sure everything's all right. And Bert?"

"Yes, Mike?"

"You leave some of that hooch for me!"

Three hours later, Eddie was startled by a knock on his door—the first all afternoon. But evidently someone he knew, since the guard was allowing the intrusion. "Come in, Mike!"

The older up-timer entered, shaking his head. "Staying in these islands is giving you a voodoo vibe, Eddie."

"Yeah, sure. How'd it go?"

"Good, but we gotta prop up the Christian Valley water project."

Eddie nodded. "Saw the report on Carver an hour ago; got buried in other stuff. We'll work that out tomorrow morning first thing. Why don't you call it a day, Mike. You look beat."

"I am. By the way, the radio to Vlissingen is up again."

"Didn't know it was down."

"Yeah, a few days."

"Was the problem on their end?"

Mike shook his head. "Nope. Weather or atmospherics. Or both. At any rate, I sent another message to Susan."

"Did you get an answer to the first, yet?"

"No, but I sent that one so close to when the signals started dropping that the wifely unit may never have received it. So I resent it just half an hour ago. Added a few homey details. Should be hearing back any day, now."

"How long since you sent home, Mike? I mean, the first one weeks ago?"

He considered. "Jeez. Probably seven weeks?"

If Eddie didn't trade telegrams with Anne Cathrine every seven days, he felt like part of him had died. "Well, hopefully, you'll get an answer soon. And now, if you'll excuse me, I think I'm going over to the comms shack and send a few words to someone on St. Eustatia."

Mike smiled. "Color me shocked. Say hi to the missus."

Eddied nodded, picked up a message pad as the

door closed behind Mike, thought about what to write, but stopped. *Seven weeks? Damn, I know the personal sends to Europe are pricey, but...seven weeks? Damn.*

Eddie started writing but it was difficult, because the only thing in his head were memories of how Anne Cathrine looked, and sounded, and felt, and smelled. But every so often, the thought came back:

Seven weeks?

Damn.

Chapter 43

Oranjestad, St. Eustatia

"So," finished Maarten Tromp, "as I understand it, you refuse to allow your charges to fulfill the leased-labor contracts you signed with the government of this colony."

Of the three men standing before him, only Jehan de Bruyne had spoken so far. "Until the government rescinds the stipulation that the five-year tariff exemption only applies to persons who do *not* own slaves, yes. We must. It is the only way we may resist this change, which is clearly designed to make it more costly for us to honor those leased-labor contracts."

Van Walbeeck, who occupied one of the only two chairs in the room, shook his head. "That is incorrect. You signed those contracts well over a month before the tariff exemption was announced. So it was neither explicitly in existence at the time you signed the contracts, nor implicit in any other transactions or announcements."

"But you knew about it!" Haet shouted, finally losing his obvious struggle to control himself. "You baited

509

us into taking those contracts! And now, even if we wanted to take advantage of the exemption, we can't! We *have* to keep our slaves so long as they are working for you!" De Bruyne's jaw worked in impatience and frustration at his fellow councilor's outburst. "By God, we're members of the *Politieke Raad*! If anyone was told ahead of time, it should have been us!"

Van Walbeeck sighed. "In the first place, all the current labor contracts will be over long before the exemption is put into effect. Secondly, the exemption is not just at the order of the Stadtholder, but is a joint decree by leaders of those nations that are not only our allies, but our business partners on Trinidad. Our little colony hasn't the power to promulgate or alter such policy, only to enforce it."

"'Allies'? Who are these 'allies'?" demanded Musen.

Van Walbeeck made an exasperated gesture, as if he were swatting away an annoying insect. "It's an informal term. Although the Netherlands and the United States of Europe have no official alliance, our relations are cordial and sometimes quite closely aligned—nowhere more so than here in the New World. And one of the issues on which the two nations are firmly agreed is the need to eliminate slavery and the slave trade. The slave trade, immediately, and slavery as soon as possible."

"Hah!" barked Haet. "I wonder what the new king in the Lowlands' brother—Philip IV of Spain, you might recall—thinks of that arrangement! To say nothing of Olivares!"

Tromp shook his head. "It doesn't matter what either of them thinks. At this moment, they have no more desire to go to war with the Netherlands than we have to go to war with them. They will continue to look the other way so long as the pact remains informal and commercial." He indulged in a sly smile. "'No peace beyond the line,' is *their* watchword, you may recall. They will ignore any violence so long as it stays on this side of the Line of Tordesillas."

He looked to van Walbeeck. "Continue, if you would."

The governor nodded. "Lastly, while we were aware of the possibility that the leaders of the allies were considering such a measure, we did not have advance knowledge of the exact shape it would take, nor that they would later add the stipulation that it could not be enjoyed by slaveholders or those trading their goods."

Tromp made sure his face remained immobile, but he appreciated van Walbeeck's ability to tread so close to the limit of what might be called "the truth." No, they hadn't known the *exact* shape the policy would take, but there was every reason to suspect that the allies would agree to the detailed program that he and van Walbeeck had proposed. The same went for the tariff exemption and the exception pertaining to slaveholders. In fact, the leaders of the various nations *had* actually introduced two changes that made the exemption even more attractive to the slaveholders than the initial model he and the governor had set forth.

But the admiral and the governor were not the only crafty gamesmen in the room. De Bruyne smiled slowly. "You didn't *know* in advance? Of course you didn't *know*; kings are fickle. Sometimes they even make a few changes to documents, even those pushed under their noses by trusted advisors. But did you have *reasonable expectations*, I wonder?"

Van Walbeeck shrugged. "You may wonder all you like. We have told no lies."

"I suppose misrepresenting the truth can't be called a lie, then, can it?" Musen snapped.

Tromp glared at the man. "*You* would speak to us of misrepresenting the truth? The architect of that threadbare charade in the square? Asserting that you could not clear it because your...your *charges* refused your orders to move?"

Musen's chin came up. "I do not have mastery over any 'charges,' and so your statement is meaningless." De Bruyne seemed ready to intervene, but stopped himself with an annoyed wince. "If you are speaking of my *property*," Musen finished with a smile, "say so plainly. If these are to be legally admissible proceedings, you may not use euphemisms."

Tromp thought he might be ill if the word "property" came out of his mouth. No, his years of slavery among the Berber pirates of Salé had not in the least resembled the soul- and body-shredding labor of plantation work. He had been more of a hostage, mostly held for ransom but also put to work imparting knowledge of the sea to his captors. But this—what he saw every day on this very island, and what he had seen two days ago—this was...

Maarten stopped the thought. If he continued down that path, he was not entirely sure he could refrain from throwing the men before him into the windowless cells of the fort to which they had been summoned. Or he might shoot them all where they stood; his new Hockenjoss & Klott percussion cap revolver had not yet been removed from its small but sturdy shipping crate. It was therefore untried, yes, but this seemed a particularly fitting test of its potentials...

The men in front of him had leaned away slightly,

their eyes wide and fixed on his face. Haet had gone pale. Even van Walbeeck was looking at him, alarmed.

De Bruyne, however, leaned forward. But cautiously, as if approaching a wild animal that might suddenly attack. "Maarten, are you quite well—?"

"I am Admiral van Tromp to you, *mijn Heer* de Bruyne!" he barked "Christian names are for those on cordial terms. We no longer are. Your companions wish legal precision? Then here it is.

"By your own admission, you are in breach of contract. You are legally bound to ensure that your... your *property* completes the labor contracts for which you have already been paid. You have refused to comply. As that labor involves projects directly related to the military security of this colony, I am empowered, by the Stadtholder Prince Hendrik Fredrik, to unilaterally determine and enforce any penalties and punishments I deem suitable.

"Firstly, no slave owners, nor any of their family, workers, or... or property, are now allowed to enter Oranjestad."

Haet gaped. "But how will we—?"

"Furthermore, if our inspectors remove any slaves from your oversight to protect them from suspected abuse, they shall remain in our care until you have convinced us that they are no longer at risk. This you were told. However, the standard of proof for their return is now even higher than it was after your shameful display at the square. Additionally, as long as those slaves are in our care, we are crediting them with wages.

"Furthermore, I am convening a legal tribunal comprised of military, political, religious, and freeborn representatives to determine what damages you will be expected to pay in recompense for your breach of contract."

"How dare y—!"

"Compensation must be paid in currency if you lack sufficient credits with which to offset what you owe in damages."

"Credits?" Haet seemed lost.

"Credits," repeated van Walbeeck. "The admiral just mentioned that any of your property which is working for us while in our protective custody accrues wage credits. Those can become the earner's money at such time as they may have possessions of their own. Or they may confer it to you as a credit for the payment of the damages, but also the redemption of their bond price."

"For what?" Even Musen wasn't picking up on it just yet. But De Bruyne's mirthless smile was the facial equivalent of him saying, *Yes, of course you would do that.*

Van Walbeeck spread his hands out. "Let us review what has been set forth. The tribunal will assess damages for your breach of contract. However, we do not wish to take money from you—well, more accurately, from your ability to care for your dependents.

"So we will consider the value of other items: namely, and preferably, your slaves. We shall value them at their purchase price. Happily, we have those records, both from here and from Recife. For any slave you fully release, we will credit their original purchase price as payment toward the damages you owe. Similarly, for any contract labor done while a slave is in our protective custody, the credits that slave accrues in the place of actual wages are extra credits you may add to his or her value when paying the damages.

"Now, do you have any other questions, *mijn Heeren*?"

The two behind de Bruyne both had their mouths open to speak, but he stilled them with a raised palm.

Tromp suppressed a bitter smile. *Until now, the pack leader has stayed well back from the rabid beasts in his pack. Now, he stalks forward as the ostensible voice of reason. Yes, you always were the smartest—and most dangerous—of your breed, Jehan de Bruyne.*

Van Walbeeck nodded at the senior of the three councilors. "Yes?"

De Bruyne didn't even look at him. Instead, he faced Tromp. "Maarten, it is not like you to overlook the terrible pain you will be causing women and children."

"You will address me as Admiral Tromp. And you must be more specific; what terrible pain will I be causing, exactly?"

"You decree that our families and our slaves may not go to the cisterns in Oranjestad. All the other fresh water flows down from The Quill along narrow *ghuts* that are now on tracts reserved for military use. So, how shall our families, slave and owner alike, not die of thirst?"

Tromp shrugged. "If they do, that will be your doing, *mijn Heer*. Because you can prevent it merely by honoring the contracts you signed, all of you. Once your slaves return to the work for which we hired them, and for which you have been *paid*, you may have full access to the town and its cisterns once again."

De Bruyne heard the grumbles rising behind him, waved a palm at the floor. Silence. "It seems we have little choice but to submit to this extortion. Which we shall protest at the highest levels and in the town, as well."

"You are welcome to try your luck with any of the allies' leaders. As far as protesting in the town, you may do so peacefully. But I cannot answer for your safety."

De Bruyne's frown told Tromp the ringleader had not been expecting that. "*Our* safety?"

Van Walbeeck's drawl forced De Bruyne to look at him. "The nature of Edel Mund's death has spawned a great deal of speculation, particularly since it is quite clear that she did not even have any kindling in her home. In fact, neighbors attempted to press some firewood upon her just a week earlier. She refused."

De Bruyne raised his chin indignantly. "And so you leap to the conclusion—without any evidence—that one of our workers was moved to commit arson."

"One of your workers . . . or one of you. As for who is leaping to conclusions, you will have to look beyond these walls."

Haet sneered. "Leave it to townfolk. Always have to have something to gossip about, no matter how outlandish it is!"

Van Walbeeck regarded him with a quizzical stare. "Outlandish? Really? Would you care to guess how many people heard you and Musen say, loudly, that you intended to beat that poor slave to death only because it was illegal for you to visit that fate upon Lady Edel Mund?"

De Bruyne turned to look at his two fellow councilors. His glower was a mix of disbelief and withering contempt.

"Ah," van Walbeeck said to the back of his head, "I see the other councilors' report of the incident may have been less than complete."

Squirming under de Bruyne's glare, Haet shouted at van Walbeeck. "You cannot prove—uh, *know* that it was one of us! That fire could have been started by one of those bastard townsmen, trying to make us look bad! Or one of them might have come to their senses and thrown that brick through Mund's pretty glass window to remind her she'd best mind her own business and let Dutchmen take care of Dutch affairs!"

But van Walbeeck was smiling. "*Mijn Heer* Haet, what causes you to believe that a brick was thrown through Lady Mund's glass window?"

Haet went whiter than usual. "I...I heard it. From someone. I can't remember who."

"Well, you must think hard: who told you?"

De Bruyne did not look back at Haet, but his upper lip twitched.

"A townsman. I overheard it," Haet said in a rush.

"Really?" van Walbeeck pressed. "Are you sure?"

"I—I don't know. All I can think of these days is how you're trying to ruin us!"

"Right now, *mijn Heer* Haet, we are talking about Lady Mund, and how her life was not merely ruined, but ended. Now, I ask again, do you remember who told you that a brick went through her window?"

For the first time, Haet did the smart thing; he shook his head instead of opening his mouth.

Van Walbeeck interlaced his fingers where they rested on his belly. "Allow me to tell you exactly how many people know of the brick that went through Lady Mund's lovely stained-glass window, her lovely *indulgence*...as some called it." Van Walbeeck's smile was arctic. "There are five people who know. Three are military men: the soldier who discovered the brick, the sergeant to whom he showed it, and the officer who received the brick from the sergeant. None of them have left the fort since those events. The soldier has been kept confined so that none may question whether he, well, spoke inadvisably of what he found. And all of you are personally acquainted with the officer in question: our garrison commander, Lieutenant-Colonel von Schutte, whose discretion and loyalty are known to you from our days in Recife."

"You said there are five men who know of the brick; who are the other two?" Musen asked with a frown.

De Bruyne closed his eyes. "Look in front of you, Hans. You can *count*, yes?"

Musen seemed to see Tromp and van Walbeeck anew. "Oh."

Van Walbeeck smiled, turned his gaze back upon Haet. "So you see, *mijn Heer*, I am baffled as to who could possibly have told you about the brick that went through Lady Mund's window and hit the oil lamp that started the fire."

"So . . . so you have determined that it was an accident! That it was not intentiona—!"

"Shut up, Haet!" de Bruyne spat over his shoulder. He sighed, stared at Tromp. "The slaves whose labor we contracted to you shall be at the work sites by lunchtime."

When the three sets of dejected footsteps had receded so far down the fort's echoing hall that they could no longer be heard, Jan van Walbeeck leaned back in his seat. "Well, that tears it."

"And about time," Maarten growled.

"How so?"

"Jan, tell me: just how long could you watch this go on? How long could you stand for this dainty dance of legal manners, tapped out upon the bloody backs of fellow men who are slaves for no other reason than the God-given color of their skin?"

Van Walbeeck shrugged. "I do not disagree. Yet, you said it yourself, Maarten. Rebellion will kill this colony. And you may have just started one."

"Well," muttered Tromp, "if I did, at least I take comfort that I am on the right side."

"Again, I agree. But I wonder how much that would matter if the outcome of such a rebellion is that the Spanish hear of it and arrive to strike us at our weakest. They could make all of us *their* slaves." He sighed. "Or worse."

"Well, Jan, I think that is far less likely now, given the forces that have joined ours and the opening of Amsterdam and our other ports. By the way, did you notice? Not one of those three had any advance warning of the exemption or the exclusion."

Van Walbeeck let out a long sigh. "And de Bruyne was too surprised by the ineptitude of his lackeys not to have tipped his hand. So it seems that I was right; even though Pieter Corselles is less, er, resolute than Phipps and Servatius, he is not giving away information to the slaveholders. And if he cannot be corrupted by them, I find it inconceivable that he would knowingly be an agent for the Spanish. He has no reason to do so, and every reason not to."

Tromp nodded. "Yes, but 'knowingly' is a very important qualifier, Jan. I am convinced of Corselles' loyalty, but not of his discretion."

Jan shrugged. "I would disagree if I could. So we

will have to continue to be very selective regarding what we discuss in his presence. And share as much as we might so that he will not feel excluded. While we are on the topic of confidential information, I assume you have seen the telegraph from the Stadtholder."

"You mean his warning that Fernando is sending a direct representative to New Amsterdam? A royal governor, no less." Tromp nodded. "I glanced at it. Just before the meeting. It was waiting in the overnight pouch."

"Maarten, do you really see it as a warning? He specifically assures us that our much-beset King in the Lowlands has no intent of giving us orders. Or sending anyone to the New World with the power to do so. He is scrupulously obeying both the letter and spirit of the agreement he made with Fredrik Hendrik in order to reunite the Netherlands. Yes, Fernando officially controls the foreign policy of the Lowlands—but 'officially' leaves a lot of maneuvering room for Dutch forces in the New World. I find it very reassuring."

"That is because you are an optimist, Jan. I find it very logical."

"It is, in many ways. And you seem to have a particular one in mind."

Tromp nodded. "If there was any hint, any shred of evidence, that King Fernando was giving orders to forces directly opposing those of Spain, his brother Philip IV could not abide that. Even if he was willing and wanted to."

"A king cannot appear to be weak or irresolute," van Walbeeck agreed. "I am sure that is part of Fernando's calculus, too. But I suspect that means he will send a most discriminating and circumspect fellow to be the extension of his authority in the New World. And I found it significant that the message specifically stated that he would be the royal governor of the New Netherlands—*not* all territories of the Low Countries in the New World. That would exclude the Caribbean and all its islands."

"Time will tell," allowed Maarten. "And assuming you are right, it might be wise to put some forces at his disposal."

"I'm sure he's already coming with some, Maarten."

"So am I. But in the event that the Dutch on the mainland resist this fellow's authority—and it is easy to see how they might—they would find it more difficult, or at least confounding to do so if we send along a ship or two to give him not merely some extra strength, but the informal imprimatur of the Stadtholder and his senior representatives in the New World."

"Meaning us!" murmured Jan, affecting the palm-rubbing glee of an adolescent.

"Yes," Tromp agreed with a laugh while wondering if van Walbeeck's reaction was entirely an act.

"Seamstress?"

She did not stop so much as dragged to a halt. Just going to *Heer* Musen's home to pick up his wife's garments was unsettling enough; working there made her nervous, almost fearful. Of what, she was not sure. She was a free woman and he had need of both her overt and covert services. But she had seen the pinch-faced man exorcise his demons, and exercise his lusts, upon his slaves and was always eager to leave. However, he was evidently not ready for her to do so just yet. She was ready to grit her teeth before replying when he walked into the room. She started. "Yes, *Heer* Musen?"

He smiled at her pulse of fear. "You have my wife's party dress?"

"The one that you needed done by tomorrow? Yes, sir." *And you are a fool, demanding "immediate repairs" for a party dress when there is no talk of any party in the foreseeable future. Everyone is too busy talking about what you and your cronies did in the square, you beast.*

But Musen was determined to make his intent singularly clear. "You are sure you know the dress I mean? The special one?"

"Yes, sir."

"And you are familiar—you have actually met—the gentleman who shall be picking it up?"

"He patronizes my business regularly, sir. Many of my customers trust him to pick up their . . . garments." *And the confidential messages hidden in the seams.*

He smiled. "Of course they do." He produced a *stuiver* from his pocket.

The seamstress shook her head. "I am sure the gentleman will convey the—er, *your* payment to me when he picks up the lady's dress."

"I am sure he will. This is from me. Just from me."

"For . . . for what, sir?"

"I simply wish to express how much I appreciate your lovely lips . . . and how much I appreciate your ability to keep them closed." When she hesitated, he added, "It would . . . irritate me if you refused it."

She edged toward him—but not too close—curtsied, and snatched the coin before almost running out of the house. His laughter followed her as she shut the door and then dashed down the footpath, back to the ribbon of wheel ruts that was the road, this far out from Oranjestad.

It was strange to think that a gratuity might be paid for her ability to keep secrets; after all, that was the most basic requirement of any confidential agent. But she would never have believed that having a coin, a gift, pressed upon her could also imply the mortal cost of failing to remain silent.

Until now.

Chapter 44

Santo Domingo, Hispaniola

The Frenchman mopped his brow. He glanced toward the door through which servants came and went. "Governor de Viamonte, I would welcome another glass of water."

Fadrique Álvarez de Toledo smiled as his friend Juan nodded and casually raised a finger. A mixed-race slave came through the door almost instantly, bearing the glass of water before any request for it had been (apparently) conveyed. *You may be infirm, de Viamonte, but you play the wizened wizard passably well.*

The Frenchman, who, like many of his kind, seemed to pride himself on alternating between blasé indifference and haughty sangfroid, sat a bit straighter.

Ah, Juan got you at last, Fadrique exulted inwardly. *Now that the oyster has opened a crack, we'll pry and see what's inside.*

He was not alone in that anticipation. De Covilla stroked his mustache to hide the shade of a smile that passed over his lips. But Gallardo, the oaf, leaned forward expectantly. If the Frenchman saw and interpreted the gruff soldier's reaction as betokening a new, keener level of interest in what he might say, he gave no indication of it.

Indeed, the Frenchman seemed busy gulping down the water. Almost desperately. While he was not burdened with any outwardly noticeable ailments, he was neither young nor had he aged well. He was pale, clearly shortsighted, and frail. He was probably about sixty, but looked closer to seventy. Or death. Whichever came first.

De Viamonte let him finish his water. "We very much appreciate your account of the savage ambush of La Flota, Monsieur Hargault. It is very illuminating." It wasn't really; it had mostly been a confirmation of what they had already learned. "However, there is one final matter on which we hope you may enlighten us."

Hargault nodded, suppressed a leathery little belch. "The balloon I was accompanying."

"Yes. I confess it is a puzzlement to us."

"Why?"

De Viamonte glanced at de Covilla and leaned back.

The hidalgo captain, who seemed a great deal less young than he had a year ago, leaned forward. "I believe the governor means to suggest that, up to this point, our nations have been, well, let us say, competitors in the Caribbean."

"True," Hargault replied before the pause became pregnant. "But times have changed."

"Yes. The Dutch and their allies have apparently seized all the possessions of His Eminence Richelieu's *Compagnie des Îles de l'Amérique.*"

"I am not a diplomat," Hargault sniffed. "But I feel it safe to say that the ruination of one of Richelieu's pet projects shall be a cause of intense delight for His Majesty Gaston."

Gallardo was, as ever, shockingly blunt. "So your king has no interest in the Caribbees?"

"I cannot be sure, but given the current circumstances, I very much doubt it. And now that our presence in this region is at an end, it allows him to focus on a much greater prize."

Only de Covilla evinced no momentary confusion. "Of course. His great prize would be the North American continent itself." Álvarez and the other two Spaniards stared at him. He shrugged. "I have had the opportunity to read widely in the up-time histories. France found its greatest successes there. And historically, their greatest—indeed, their only—important competitors were the English."

"Who are now, truly, insular," Álvarez mused. "So," he asked Hargault, barely believing he was being as direct as Gallardo, "there is no continuing interest in our regions?"

"As I said, I am not a diplomat. But I know several, and they talk in their cups. Nothing too specific, of course, but they love intimating more influence and access than they have. This is why it is significant that none of their talk even touches on your territories." He saw the uniformly uncomprehending stares and expanded. "I discount ninety percent of what junior diplomats say as self-flattering lies. However, it is also true that they lack the imagination to lie about a region that is not on the lips of the court. So I feel it safe to conclude that little or nothing is being said about Spanish possessions, even where I may not hear it. Otherwise, they would be lying about those, too."

De Viamonte quirked a half grin. "There is logic in that."

De Covilla frowned. "Your Excellency, is your meaning that in this regard, a trend that is historically consistent with what happened in the up-time world may indicate deeper parallels that will impart a similar strategic impetus here, too?"

"That is possible, but that was not my meaning, Eugenio. I refer simply to the political pragmatism that is implied in the king of France's willingness to sell his competitors a balloon. Spain's fortunes have been waning since the Americans arrived. So have France's." He turned toward Hargault. "Our master Philip, and your master Gaston, have ample reason to at least refrain from antagonizing each other, even if they have not made common cause."

Not yet, Álvarez mused silently, with a pull at his beard. "Tell me, Monsieur Hargault; are you the—what would you call it?—architect of the balloon? Its builder?" He certainly didn't look like the latter.

Hargault flipped his wrist in dismissal. "I am a scientist and a professor, formerly associated with the *Université d'Orléans*. As such, I was consulted on both the design and the fabrication of the balloon, but did not carry out either, myself."

"Then why were you sent with the balloon?"

"As I said, I am a scientist. And I have a passing familiarity with engineering. We knew, however, that for those unfamiliar with the operation of the device, there could be two difficult—not to say fatal—challenges: learning how to operate it and addressing any unforeseen complications."

Fadrique nodded. "I understand the first challenge. We have no balloonists, so someone must teach them. But I am unsure what you mean by 'unforeseen complications.'"

That was the question that opened the Gallic oyster. As the cagey Frenchman warmed to his favorite topic, he also grew less guarded. So, by the time he had explained the many local variables that might require adjustments to both the balloon and its operation— different levels of heat by the combustion of animal oils novel to the New World; unforeseeable high-altitude wind patterns; new molds and fungi that might show an appetite for the envelope; a dozen others—he was also talking about the transaction whereby it was sold to Spain. Who had been involved, the dickering over price, the obstruction, the months of waiting for decisions to emerge from the Escorial, and some religious objections which even the most devout Frenchmen found absurd.

This was the opening for which Fadrique had been waiting. "So, I gather that you and the others who created the balloon had been hoping to sell more than just one."

"*Vraiment*! It was most frustrating when we did not. That is why I was sent along with the device: to ensure that it would perform properly. Successful operation was the condition for additional purchases. Frankly, though, I remain skeptical of that promise. I mean no disrespect to your nation or its sovereign, gentlemen, but it was most...trying to arrive at terms with its representatives." He grunted. "You gentlemen are refreshingly frank."

"So much so," Fadrique followed, "that I wonder if you would consider a business arrangement in addition to the one you have with Spain."

Hargault's face was a study in perplexity; the others' were studies in surprise, tinged with fear. The Frenchman's frown deepened. "I do not know what meaning I should derive from that statement, Admiral."

"I simply mean that there are gentlemen here in the wealthiest colonies who find the idea of, er, 'ballooning' most intriguing. And we expect, most invigorating. And insofar as those of us here have ready access to all manner of products and coin that you might find interesting, would you and your associates be amenable to furnishing, oh, say, half a dozen of us with our own balloons? For private use?"

At the words "half a dozen," Hargault's thin, wrinkled lips parted. They were shiny and becoming wet, as if he had smelled his favorite food. "I am relatively certain we could. But how—?"

"We will speak of specifics soon enough, my friend. And we will make a ship available to convey you safely back to your home. No need to expend the extra travel, time, and paperwork that would be necessitated by returning through Spain itself. Now, I am certain that Governor de Viamonte would be happy to keep you as his guest until such time as we have worked out the details and readied that ship, yes?"

Hargault nodded eagerly; de Viamonte's similar affirmation was more studied.

When the Frenchman had left, there was complete silence. *Well*, thought Fadrique, *at least I haven't been run through. Yet.*

De Viamonte nodded, eyes narrow. "That was

extremely well played, my friend. It may also get us killed."

Álvarez reached out and poured a half glass of wine, although he felt quite ready to down the bottle. "No, it may get *me* killed. Hear me out. That means you, too, Gallardo." He took a long swig. "In my next conversation with Hargault, I will explain that I am hoping to make a commission for myself in this 'sale' and that the rest of you have no interest in the balloons and were outraged that I dared to use an official meeting to conduct personal business."

De Covilla cocked an eyebrow. "Admiral, Hargault has been to our homeland. Asking him to believe that personal business is not conducted at official meetings would be much like telling him that in Spain, we do not speak Spanish. He will not believe you."

But de Viamonte was nodding. "Hargault does not need to believe the admiral, Eugenio. He only needs to be able to claim, truthfully, that this is in fact what he was told. That way, if the transaction is discovered, the responsibility begins and ends with Don Fadrique Álvarez de Toledo, God save his soul." He raised his glass toward his friend.

"So," Gallardo asked, looking at the others, "we mean to get balloons from the French, rather than from the crown?"

"Yes," Álvarez answered, "not that it should make much difference, because that is obviously where the Crown vouchsafed the one lost with La Flota. We are simply using our own funds and our own initiative to get far more of them, and far more swiftly."

"I know, sir, but—"

"Gallardo." The governor's voice was stern. "I share

your reservations. And I suspect no one at this table has greater reservations than the admiral himself. But he did what a military leader must sometimes do: seize a sudden and unexpected opportunity. Is there risk? Always. But if this works—well, it is as he said: then he, and all of us, will be lauded as heroes. But I will ensure that it is he who is recognized as the architect, that it was he who was willing to take a bold gamble to change the fortunes of our empire. He did no less than the conquistadors."

"Well," Fadrique muttered, "if the histories are accurate, this involved a lot less dysentery and a lot fewer insects."

The laughter was more than polite, but was still subdued. "This is still serious business," de Covilla said to no one in particular.

"Yes," de Viamonte agreed. "So serious that I believe we must speak to Admiral Antonio de Curco y San Joan de Olacabal once again."

"As well as the other La Flota survivors who were rescued with him?"

"No, Eugenio. This time, we shall speak to him alone."

So now you're trying to make me nervous, Juan? Álvarez thought. But he doubted it, in actuality: the governor seemed deadly serious as he had de Covilla brief the low-level grandee-made-sailor. Whatever he meant to do by bringing back the one surviving admiral of La Flota for a second interview was unclear, but Fadrique was the first to admit that if his own style was to take risks and seize on sudden opportunities, Juan's approach was invariably serious, well considered, and without logical flaws. So he had something in mind. But what?

De Covilla was finishing the summary that had not been shared with the survivors, lest it impact their reports of the battle off Dominica and what they observed and did on their often-perilous voyages back to Spanish territory. "So, considered in conjunction with what His Excellency de Murga has relayed to us about the battle and assessment of Curaçao, we have been confirmed in our speculations. Tromp was not based out of Curaçao. In fact, he was never there.

"Rather, informers on St. Eustatia confirm that it is a, and quite probably *the*, center of Dutch power. They also confirm that the attack on Trinidad was apparently motivated by the island's oil resources, which have not only been accessed for local use, but are being shipped back to Europe. De Murga's fleet is moving to retake Trinidad and, if feasible, begin to operate the oil extraction ourselves."

De Curco y San Joan, his skin still peeling from the horrible sunburn he suffered before being rescued off Puerto Rico, frowned. "Is de Murga's fleet strong enough for that task? Several galleons detailed to protect the Tierra Firme fleet along half its voyage were to have permanently remained with the Cartagena fleet. I suspect that His Excellency may have considered them integral to success at Trinidad. Is he still confident he can take it without those ships?"

"He expressed no doubt over the outcome. And the knowledge that it is not the primary power center of the Dutch and their USE allies makes him just that much more confident of victory."

De Curco y San Joan nodded, but was still frowning.

"What I do not understand, though, is how you or anyone plans to prevail against their steamships. They are too fast to catch. And they are too deadly to close with, anyhow. How do we defeat such enemies?"

Álvarez shrugged. "Until we have machinery like theirs, we cannot do so. Not with our current ships and conventional tactics, at any rate. Every time we have tried cases with them we have lost."

De Curco y San Joan shook his head; his voice was almost a groan. "So we cede the seas to them? Everything is lost?"

"No. But everything must change."

"What do you mean?"

Fadrique gestured out the window. "Do you see those three galleons currently in the ways, almost completed?" de Curco y San Joan nodded. "Those are the last galleons that will be built in Santo Domingo in the foreseeable future. But I suspect they are among the very last of their kind that will know the touch of the waves. Ever."

Flakes of shedding skin flew off de Curco y San Joan, he started so violently. "What?"

Álvarez shrugged. "It is merely one of the inevitable consequences of fully acknowledging, and then acting upon, my earlier assertion: if we only change our tactics and objectives, we cannot win. We can only delay the inevitable. In order to win, we must reinvent the way we make war here in the New World."

The younger admiral looked as if he wanted to move to the other side of the room. "This is all very good to say in a council chamber, but it is easier said than done. How we may wage war here is largely determined by the ways our colonies must operate to serve Spain."

"Yes. So that must change, too."

"Such words could easily be mistaken for treason." From the tone of his voice, it sounded more than likely that de Curco y San Joan was making that very mistake.

Álvarez folded his hands and squared his arms and shoulders to the mirrorlike tabletop. "Tell me, does *this* sound like treason? I will do anything—*anything*—to protect Spain and see her victorious in the New World."

"Those are the words of a true and devoted son of Spain."

"Well, then let me explain why ending the construction of galleons, and all the 'traitorous' choices and changes that it entails, is the only way we can hope to achieve that glorious outcome for our king and our country.

"You have seen how slow our galleons are compared to our enemies'. And not just the steamships, but almost all of them. Until now, this was not a great concern. Our galleons were stout enough to withstand most Dutch guns. They were floating forts, equipped with cannon that meant death to any who tarried beneath them too long.

"But now, they are simply very big, very slow, and so, very easy targets for the up-time guns. So we are now laying down smaller, faster ships. Here and in Cuba. I suspect de Murga is doing the same in Cartagena, but given his run-ins with the Inquisition, he has more eyes eagerly scrutinizing his activities, eager to get him recalled to Spain. Either into retirement or a grave, depending upon the severity of his violations. The point is, we must build ships that are faster, smaller, harder to hit."

De Curco y San Joan shook his head. "Pataches will not win battles."

Fool! Of course not! "I am not speaking of pataches, but galleoncetes and more crucially, fragatas."

The other man shook his head again. "Even the largest of those hulls have fewer guns, and you cannot mount our heaviest pieces in them. The recoil would shake them to pieces, and their gundecks haven't the beam to accommodate their full range of motion. Our forty-two-pounders would be crashing, cascabel to cascabel, at the centerline. It would be ruinous in every way."

Álvarez nodded. "Which is why we must follow the Dutch model: more guns with less throw weight and so less recoil. And that fire far more rapidly. However, enough of this. There is ample reason for urgency, for risk-taking, but not for despair." *Not yet.* "We have other means of defeating our foes."

"Such as?"

De Viamonte gestured on the map that was painted on the wall that faced the bay. "We have long familiarity with these seas, these lands, their weather. The Dutch are comparative newcomers. The up-timers only know what's in their history books. We have begun systematically examining our knowledge to identify useful items that we know but they do not. Most will prove useless, but others could be decisive.

"In the meantime, it is crucial that we acquire two of the technologies upon which they rely but are simple enough to be produced by Spain currently. The first are the balloons, which enable them to see us so far in advance that they may avoid us at will or engage any target of opportunity they happen upon."

"I presume the other technology is the radio," de Curco y San Joan added quietly.

"Yes. We sent our request for them directly to Olivares

and the others who are our direct superiors. Did you happen to hear if any were included in La Flota, or if any news of our request escaped the labyrinth of the Escorial to reach outside ears?"

De Curco y San Joan pursed his lips. "I cannot be sure if radios were secreted in any of the holds of La Flota, but I doubt it."

"Why?"

"Because those responsible for the fiscal success of the fleet were particularly attentive to the possibility of acquiring radios, both for use and trade. Given their role in the reversals you experienced last year, it was assumed that some of these devices would certainly be shipped and a fine profit made. But all inquiries met with silence. Stony silence."

Gallardo frowned. "Any idea why? Sir?"

"None, although there are those I could ask." De Curco y San Joan smiled wanly. "That is, if I dared to return."

"So," de Viamonte probed, "you fear your reception, back in Spain?"

"Not in Spain, not even with Philip."

"Ah," Álvarez muttered, "Olivares, then."

De Curco y San Joan actually shivered. "Sir, I am an admiral of merchant ships. I haven't your expertise, as is surely obvious. I was, to be frank, fourth down in the actual chain of command responsible for responding to attacks. However, I doubt anyone could survive an engagement against the up-time steamships, particularly without advance knowledge of their capabilities. To say nothing of their proximity.

"Yet, for this blame not to descend upon Olivares's head, it must be shifted to another. I am the ranking officer remaining. And Olivares can easily assure that his story of what occurred, and of my 'culpability,' will be the only one ever heard. And certainly, the only one recorded."

Álvarez sighed. "So the blame will descend upon you. Or more narrowly, upon your neck."

"I am a dead man," de Curco y San Joan concluded with a nod.

"No," murmured de Viamonte, "you are not."

The other man's answering smile was sickly and rueful, but also the slightest bit hopeful. "I mean no disrespect, Your Excellency, but Olivares does not hold you in such high regard that you might successfully intercede on my behalf."

"Let us speak plainly. Olivares loathes me. So I plan no attempt at intercession."

"Then how in the name of our Holy Mother do you imagine you may forestall, let alone prevent, my appointment with the headsman?"

"By making sure that for now, you are already dead."

De Curco y San Joan blinked. "Your Excellency, I do not understand."

Álvarez regretted his occasionally earthy outbursts, but this one caught him by surprise. "Oh, I like this!" he guffawed. "I like this a great deal."

De Viamonte glanced at de Covilla. "Eugenio, we will need to emend the report you are crafting in my name regarding what we know of the loss of La Flota. You are to add this to the beginning of the roster of losses we have estimated."

"Yes, sir?"

"That since the great majority of the crews and passengers of La Flota remain unaccounted for, we cannot know if the information we relay will be definitive.

Logically, others may yet be discovered alive who will add, or give additional context to, it."

"Very good, sir. Anything else?"

"Yes. You will include the names of all the civilian survivors that we know from the accounts of those who have reached us by small and makeshift boats. However, you will *not* include any names that came to light solely through our conversations with Admiral de Curco y San Joan and his companions."

De Covilla smiled. "Because they will now be listed as missing without a trace, after setting off to reach Puerto Rico?"

De Curco y San Joan's jaw dropped.

De Viamonte was still crafting the revised letter. "Yes, and add that storms, pirates, and enemy forces were all reported in those seaways at that time, and so, may have either delayed or made an end of them."

"It appears I shall not hang alone," Álvarez said with a broad smile.

"But...but, why?" de Curco y San Joan stammered.

"Firstly," de Viamonte replied calmly, "because if I can save a true servant of Spain from Olivares, I shall. Also, because you clearly have contacts in the Escorial who can tell us what is actually transpiring there, yes?"

He swallowed. "My brother. And my cousin."

"Excellent. You also have knowledge and expertise we need right here. And lastly, I can be sure that you will not speak of our activities, because as you pointed out, your mere existence marks you for death." He smiled. "Until you may resurface as a hero of the Empire. Is this agreeable?"

✧   ✧   ✧

No sooner had de Covilla escorted the weak-kneed de Curco y San Joan out of the council chamber than he popped his head back in.

"We have an unexpected visitor with an unexpected report."

"Who?" Álvarez felt it justified that his query came out as a growl, since his belly had started growling at him.

"Captain Equiluz, who brings information of profound interest, I think."

"Equiluz?" de Viamonte wondered aloud. "The fellow who was the primary liaison with our 'privateers'?"

"The same, Your Excellency."

Equiluz marched in looking somewhat worse for wear. He eyed the wine longingly, but got straight to business. "Captain Cibrian de Lizarazu, commander of our garrison on St. Maarten, reports Dutch claim jumpers have landed on the southeastern extremity of the island and are making intermittent use of the salt flats for curing fish."

Gallardo let himself fall against his chair's backrest. "Are they mad?"

"It is more likely that they are desperate, Captain. It is unclear, but the use of slaves in the Dutch colonies may be waning, possibly prohibited."

"They *are* mad," Gallardo concluded. "Has de Lizarazu not driven them into the sea?"

Being the same rank as Gallardo, Equiluz simply shook his head. "His men were struck with a fever in July. He claims he has not enough left to evict the heretics."

"Where are they from? St. Eustatia?"

"That is the presumption, but that detail was not

included. This was one of several dozen reports that were almost overlooked in an intelligence packet being gathered in Puerto Rico."

De Viamonte nodded. "From whence you came. And you are still in the clothes from that journey. Correct?"

Equiluz nodded.

"And in the course of consulting the files concerning St. Maarten, you came across something else, something that made you feel it necessary to travel here without stopping?"

"I did, sir. And I suspect it may incline you to send one, or maybe many more, fast ships to that island."

"Show us."

Equiluz spread out a recent Spanish map of St. Maarten. "Thanks to the generosity and foresight of both Your Excellencies," he said, nodding to Fadrique and Juan, "I also had ready access to this: a common up-time map of the island. Not suitable for navigation, of course, but as you see, that is what makes it so interesting."

They stood and inspected it and, almost in unison, leaned forward sharply. "We are certain—certain—that the current up-time maps are identical to this one?"

"Thanks to the information that has been coming to us from one of my agents with a contact on St. Eustatia, yes, sir. That contact has seen the maps being used by the leadership there. It is identical. In every particular."

Álvarez nodded to himself, looked over at Juan. Who was already looking at him. "This could be the decisive piece of superior knowledge that we've been looking for."

De Viamonte nodded. "My thought exactly. Equiluz, we will require a detailed report on the current conditions of this feature." He thumped his good index finger down on the map.

Gallardo was frowning. "Maybe I'm superstitious, but I'm worried about the lack of true hurricanes this season. If the sea decides to make up for that lack..."

Álvarez clapped him on the shoulder. "Gallardo, you morose old ape, if we get a blow, that is always to our advantage. We can keep building ships here, training crews here. We have a population that will restore our losses so that we may sally forth again. And again.

"So if a hurricane comes when both our fleet and the enemy's are at sea, then we must hope that if God cannot spare us, His biggest waves will hit us both. For we can recover those losses. But they cannot."

Gallardo shrugged. "Yes. I suppose. But still, this difference between the maps: it makes no sense."

De Viamonte compared the maps carefully. "It might make sense...if the feature on the up-time map was man-made."

De Covilla rubbed his well-manicured chin hairs. "Yes, they could do such a thing. In the up-timers' world, their nations moved earth and water in most extraordinary projects. They dug a canal from the Gulf to the Pacific. That was a hundred years before their town was whisked away. And in the intervening time, they flew up to the Moon. To think of it! They meant to colonize the Moon!"

Álvarez shook his head. "Nonsense; it is too hostile. They could not make any use of it nor survive there. That, surely, is why they stopped such flights into space."

Juan noticed de Covilla's awkward glance away. "You know differently, Eugenio?"

"I only know what I read about the cessation of their flights to the Moon. It was a collection of commentary, not rigorously provable data or an official statement."

"And what did the up-timers themselves say about why they ceased going to the Moon? Its inhospitability?"

"No."

"The expense?"

"Not exactly."

"Then why, *exactly*, did they not go back?"

"Most contend that there simply wasn't the desire to do so."

"No desire? Be plain; they had the desire to go in the first place!"

"They did, but once they had done so . . . well, they lost interest." When de Covilla confronted the resulting ring of baffled faces, he explicated: "Having done it, and then proven they could do it at will, they—well, they became bored. It no longer captured their imagination."

"Surely, they *are* mad," de Viamonte agreed.

"Sounds it," Gallardo grumbled. "At any rate, I'll want sappers. Dredgers, too, I suspect."

Now he was the one ringed by baffled faces. De Viamonte was the first to find his voice. "Manrique, you mean to go to St. Maarten, to oversee the work yourself?"

"Well, the parts on the land, yes." He returned their stares. "You think I'm going to stay here and miss all the fun?" He snorted. "What? Do you think I'm mad?"

Chapter 45

Oranjestad, St. Eustatia

The sun was beginning its slow fall toward the rim of the sea before Anne Cathrine was finally able to extricate herself from the day's duties and callers and set forth with Cuthbert Pudsey. As they arrived at their sad destination, she looked over her shoulder and ordered, "Wait here." She was through the door into the charred ruin of Edel Mund's hovel even before the big Englishman had muttered, "Yes'm."

She had come straight from the infirmary, having volunteered not only to help the stricken as to be a companion for the mostly silent Sophie Rantzau. Consequently, she was already wearing clothes that would want washing. So, she reasoned, what's the harm in adding a little soot to the mix?

Unfortunately, "a little soot" proved to be a profoundly inadequate projection of the reality with which she was now confronted; the completely gutted interior yawned at her like a roofless, carbonized maw. *Well, if I look like a chimney sweep when I'm done, so be it.*

Except—how would she know when she was done?

What should she look for? How could one get any clues as to how the fire was set, or who might have set it, just by wandering around the shell of a building in which every combustible object had been reduced to ash?

It took almost fifteen minutes of largely aimless puttering before she realized that her question had actually contained its own answer. Which was to say: if everything combustible was gone, then, assuming that any clues still existed, they would necessarily be found among the nonflammable remains.

But that, too, was frustrating. The hearth was blackened rock. Its andirons and tools were scorched, but otherwise uninteresting. There were intact shards of clay pots and a few better plates, but not enough to piece together, and besides, what would that reveal? Covered in much, much more than "a little" soot, she rose from where she had crouched to inspect a lump of lead and headed for the door. Perhaps this was as foolish an errand as Leonora had believed; if any clues existed, certainly Tromp's men would have found them. They had been over the gutted hovel at least half a dozen times, and still, there was no word of how the fire had been set.

She slowed as she approached the door. In some indefinable way, she felt that once she recrossed the threshold, she would have said her true farewell to Edel Mund. That in accepting her inability to learn any more about the woman's killer, Anne Cathrine was also accepting that this chapter was closed and that the dead widow's memory had to be just that: a memory.

She touched the crumbling, fire-ribbed remains of the door-jamb—and stopped. The window just to the side of the jamb was different. Not like the other.

But why? She stepped backward into the house, not examining either of the windows closely, but taking them in as generalized images.

These had been Edel's prized stained-glass windows. They were both ruined by the blaze. The lead had obviously melted early and the panes held by those mullions had collapsed into a heap.

Or rather that's what had happened to those in the window to the right-hand side of the door. The lead had pooled and rehardened in the lower sill of the window, some on the floor, and although many of the colorful panes were shattered or missing altogether, about half had fallen into the lead that had once held them in place, now stuck in the resolidified metal like multihued dragon's teeth.

But on the left, only a fraction of that amount of lead was melted into the sill. Similarly, there were fewer panes left, and far more were shattered. So where had the lead and the panes gone?

Anne Cathrine turned, went back to the piece of lead she had found on the floor, kneeled, broadened her focus again...and discovered she was crouched at the far end of a fan-shaped litter of broken panes and beaded lead drops that widened as it got further from the window.

This window hadn't melted like the other. Something had gone through it, sent pieces flying into the house in an arc, which were then punished by the heat at the center of the de facto crematorium and subsequently crushed and punted around under the feet of the investigators. But now that she knew to look for it, that progressive wedge of shattered glass plain to see. Which meant...

She turned, paced along the trajectory implied by the center of the debris fan...and found herself staring down at the modest remains of the dead woman's Roman-style oil lamp. It had been on a table which was now ash, and the small clay shards were few and scattered. But on the stonework of the hearth that had been right behind it, there was a sharp-edged chip at just about hip level.

She stood next to it, leaned over, closed one eye... and discovered that it was indeed at the end of an invisible line that went from the window to the lamp to the fireplace.

Anne Cathrine lifted the hem of her dress, spat on it, and rubbed frantically at the flaw in the stonework. When the soot came away, the sharp, fresh edges of a recent impact not only stood out more, but the wound in the rock itself was creamy white. It was impossible to say if the flaw was only a few days old, but it certainly had not begun to dull with age.

She stood, realized she had to report what she had found to Tromp. But first, she needed to find the conclusive piece of evidence: the object that had been thrown into the house to shatter the lamp and so, start the fire. And which had very possibly dented the hearth at the end of its flight.

She bent at the waist, started examining the ground all over again...and stopped. She straightened slowly. She had spent her first fifteen minutes scouring the hovel's small interior for a sign of...well, anything. If there had been an object that could have broken through the window and still retain enough force to shatter the lamp, let alone take a chip out of the fireplace, she would have found it. But since she hadn't—

The realization snapped her spine straight as she looked around the hovel: *Tromp knows. Because his men must have found what was thrown. Which means he has decided not to tell the town about what actually happened here.*

She nodded. Of course he'd do that. Tromp might still be investigating. Or he might have decided—probably accurately—that if the town learned he'd discovered a "murder weapon" (although it had more likely been manslaughter, she realized), some people might very well take matters into their own hands. Given present sentiments, she could imagine them storming out to Haet's tract or Musen's or some other, armed and angry. And if they had actually drawn blood, they would probably have lost some of their own in the process. And God only knew how wildly that might spin out of control.

So, yes, as the guardians of the colony's greater safety from external threats, Tromp and van Walbeeck would almost certainly have elected to keep this bit of information quiet. It was, she admitted angrily, their duty.

But, she thought, *it is not mine.*

The sun was setting over Fort Oranje, which meant that there was almost no light left in the narrow lane that ran past her shop and humble rooms. She opened the storm shutters on her only window, reached out, and turned the sign hanging from the weathered hook in the top sill; now, the word CLOSED faced the world.

What faced inward was SEAMSTRESS. She looked at that word for a moment, almost wistfully. If only life could be as simple as that, once again.

She closed her mind to that thought at the same moment that she closed the storm shutters and turned to make sure that her day's last labor, a recently re-hemmed dress, was hanging evenly. Even though it would ultimately be conveyed to rough men who would tear it apart simply to get messages out of its seams, she still insisted that it be hung just like the garments she repaired or altered for her actual clients. She did so in part because it was wise not to call attention to the items of clothing used to send secret information to her anonymous "patrons." But she was also proud of her business, of her work as a seamstress. And if anyone happened to call, even at this late hour, they would still see a tidy workplace in which all the garments were hung in an orderly, wrinkle-defeating fashion.

A knock on her door startled her; the sun still had not set. Why would tonight's contact come so early? Was there something amiss? Had she been discovered? Whatever it was, she told herself not to panic. It was probably nothing. And if it was, then panic was not her friend but her enemy. A disordered mind made it less likely that she would be able to think, flee, or fight her way out of a bad situation.

As if she were putting on a hat, she put on a tentative and mildly confused smile, gave herself a moment to minutely arrange and settle into it, and then opened the door.

She stared. The tall dark man standing on her doorstep wasn't either of her two contacts, one of whom worked for the Spanish, the other for the "adventurers" who roved among the islands. "Yes?" she said. "What do you want?"

"I want to speak to you."

"It is late, and I do not recognize you."

His lips crinkled; it wasn't really what one could call a smile. "My name is Diego," he murmured. "I am not surprised that you do not recognize me. But I recognize *you*. From another port. Well south of here."

She had always thought that the saying "my blood froze" was odd; even when fearful, she'd never experienced that kind of sensation. But now, she understood that it was not merely a fanciful expression. Her limbs and extremities were suddenly chilled, although the growing dusk was still, even sultry. "What—what do you want?"

"It is as I said; I want to speak to you. And that is *all* I want."

There was something about the way he said it which also seemed to be a grim guarantee that he was speaking truthfully, that if he wanted more, he would take it without dissembling to get it. She opened the door and stood aside.

He entered and turned toward her as soon as the door was closed; she was trapped with her back to it. "You do not know me," he said.

She shook her head. "No, but I know what you are."

"Good. Then this will be quite simple." He waved behind at the dresses without looking at them. "I know how this is done. I know what to look for. And I know faces from Curaçao. From Willemstad. Before the recent"—he grimaced—"misfortunes there."

"I do not know what you mean." Her upper lip was sweating and she could not meet his eyes.

"I refer to events late last year. When the Brethren of the Coast were starting to gather information on

Curaçao. You were there. You did their work. When you were finished, one of their Dutch captains, Mahieu Romboutsen, removed you. He took you to a boat that was waiting off Tobago. It was a pink of no particular nationality, if I recall. Just one of the dozens of small, independent hulls which trade in those waters. It carried you to the Dutch colony there, New Walcheren.

"And now you are here. But you are no longer working just for pirate coin. I have seen who comes here. The other man may be paying you in Dutch guilders, but behind them are Spanish reales." When she blinked in surprised terror at his unfailingly accurate narrative, he nodded. "I did not lie to you. I know how this is done and what to look for."

She shivered. "Have you told them? The Dutch?"

"If I had, where do you think you'd be now?"

"At the bottom of the sea with a millstone around my ankles."

The man frowned. "Some of them might do that. Tromp would not. But no, I have not told anyone. Obviously."

"So I . . . I may still escape?"

Diego shrugged. "If that is your wish. But you must also decide if you will redeem yourself, first."

"How? To whom?"

"To yourself. You know what is going on here. Edel Mund's death may have been an accident. But the door to violence has been opened. It will not close now. Your actions made that possible by making the slaveholders bold. And you are making it possible for them to hope to bring slavery here in full force. As only the Spanish can."

She felt her eyes grow wide. So he knew that she

had also been the channel through which the Frenchman from St. Christopher had communicated with the slaveholders, prior to the Kalinago attack.

He was nodding at her, as if reading in her eyes the realizations that were darting through her mind. "Yes, I know that, too." He paused, pointed to his face, then hers. "Look at us. Look at our stations in life. Who might we have been, had we been born in places where the color of our skin was of no consequence? That is the world the up-timers and Tromp and the Danish princess are trying to bring about."

"She's a king's daughter, not a princess."

He swatted away the distinction with the same gesture he would have used to shoo an annoying fly. "Only one thing matters, right now. Will you flee for your life without stopping to help, without helping to set things right for people like us? Or will you redeem yourself by helping to change what is happening on this island? It may change nothing. Or it could change everything, could set these lands on better course so that we, or at least those who come after us, will not have to live in terror and suffering—or die trying to rise out of it."

He started toward her; she dodged to the side.

But he continued past her to open the door. He looked back at her, his large brown-black eyes steady and unblinking upon hers. Then he closed the door behind him.

When she remembered to breathe again, she ran to the door, opened it to see where he went.

The street was empty.

Pointe Blanche, St. Maarten

Captain Cibrian de Lizarazu cursed his slow progress up out of the surf toward the narrow strand between the sheer rocks on the bayside flank of Pointe Blanche and the surly waves crowding around that promontory into St. Maarten's Great Bay. Would the weakness inflicted upon him by that damned fever never relent? Was he to become a cripple like that busybody de Viamonte?

He shrugged off a helping hand offered by one of the newly arrived soldiers: eighty in total, half of whom were sappers. Well, at least the governor of Santo Domingo was a helpful busybody, although the sappers weren't subject to his orders. And they had brought word that a far more senior captain than himself, some old warhorse by the name of Gallardo, would soon arrive with more troops of various types and would take overall command of St. Maarten's land forces.

But in the meantime, the new troops were just what Lizarazu had needed to get the God-damned Dutch claim jumpers off of his island while it was *still* his island.

Panting as he finally dragged his feet up beyond where the waves stretched themselves out and disappeared, he saw the Dutch—well, the ones who were still alive—staked out in the sand. One, a heavy man, was screaming in agony. Sounds like a little girl, or a rabbit, he thought with a grin.

Off to one side, the trespassers' Moorish slaves were huddled, shivering as if the setting sun was a dire omen for what would soon befall them, too. It wasn't, not in any immediate sense: the Empire always needed more slaves. He'd have them interrogated, find out what they knew how to do. But for now . . . "Morca!"

His corporal came running over. "Yes, Captain?"

"Those boats we saw, did our skiff catch them?"

"No, sir. They both turned out to be sloops. Bermudan, from the look of their lines. But they went in different directions. One south, the other north. And that last one wasn't set to run like the ships of the Somers Isles. She was rigged more like—well, like a pirate."

Lizarazu frowned at the unexpected development. Why can't anything ever be simple? "You mean 'privateer,' Morca. Remember that. One of ours, do you think?"

"No way to know, sir. Not running any colors."

The captain looked after the boats. "Did both boats come from the same direction?"

"No, sir. Different directions. When they got enough breeze to run, they chased back along the headings that brought them here. They seemed to be as surprised to see each other as we were surprised to see them."

Wonderful. A mystery. Well, maybe there were some clues. "What have you learned from the, er, prisoners?"

"They are from St. Eustatius, as you conjectured. They were salting fish, but I think they were here for another reason, too."

"Yes, and what would that be?"

"I—I'm not sure. The leader, whom we are currently questioning"—more cries, then a meaty *krakk-kk!* and a long shriek—"keeps asking . . . well, sir, it seems like nonsense or delirium, to me."

Lizarazu rolled his eyes, drew his pistol, and stalked to where the Dutchman was staked out. He waved at the surrounding soldiers to undo his bonds. "Sit him up," the captain sighed. *If you want a job done right, you have to do it yourself.*

He looked into the Dutchman's pain-clouded and ashen face. "You! What is your name? No, stop: I don't care. Why are you here? And I don't mean the fish." He cocked the pistol's hammer meaningfully.

The man, dazed, did not respond to the sound. It took a few moments for his eyes to focus on the captain's face, then he winced and looked down at his leg. The left tibia was splintered and protruding through a bloody ruin of pulped flesh. He started screaming, staring at the wound, which portended an amputation in his immediate future.

Lizarazu sighed, held the gun away, reached across his body with his other arm, and backhanded the Dutchman, full force across his face. A cry of surprise, a sudden rise of color, and the heathen's eyes were back on Lizarazu's. "Now, again: why are you here?"

The Dutchman looked around, saw the last white fleck of the south-running sail dip beneath the horizon. "Him. Maybe. I think."

"What? What do you mean, him? The man in the boat?"

"I . . . I don't know. Please!" he screamed when Lizarazu pulled his hand back for another blow. "Please! I— we are here to salt fish, yes, but also to meet someone."

"To meet someone? Who?"

"I don't know—really! Really! Why would I lie? The man we were to meet knew to come here, to look for us. He was supposed to give us a message—a time, date, and place for a meeting."

"Who with?"

"Planters. From Eustatia. Haet. Maybe Musen, too. Please, that's all I know. Please, please!"

Lizarazu stood, dusted sand off his hands.

"What does it mean, sir?" Morca asked.

Lizarazu shrugged. "Damned if I know. Probably some buggery having to do with contraband or some other nonsense that is of import only among the squalid tent slums these heathens call home. Well, no mind. Any left to question?"

"No, sir. He was the last. We tortured all of them, as per your orders. He's the only one who knows anything of interest."

Lizarazu nodded. "Well, then, let's not be late for dinner."

"What?" cried the man, who evidently understood Spanish. "You mean to leave me like this? Why? I told you what you wanted! I told you everything I knew! And you're just going to leave me . . . leave *us* here? Even after you did this?" His hands floated above his leg, not daring to touch it. "I'll never walk again!"

The captain frowned, tilted his head, considering. "You have a point. You should not be burdened by the endless worries of such an infirmity." He raised his pistol and fired.

A bloody crater appeared in the center of the man's forehead. He fell back.

The dim whimpering of the other Dutch ended abruptly.

"What about the others?"

"Gather the slaves; they'll either bring coin or be useful."

"And the others?"

Cibrian tossed his chin toward the dead Dutchman. "Like him. But hurry up. I'm getting hungry."

Chapter 46

Pitch Lake, Trinidad

As the dinghy from *Orthros* ground to a stop on one of the few scree beaches of Trinidad's southwestern shore, Hugh O'Donnell barely recognized Fort St. Patrick, or for that matter, Pitch Lake. The signs of industry were all about it: shacks, wagons, and pots that looked similar to oversized tryworks from whaling ships but were not. And there were barrels, and barrels, and more barrels.

As Hugh threw a leg over the dinghy's bow, Kevin O'Bannon was there to offer him a hand. Hugh took it and smiled. "You're a sight for sore eyes, *Major*!"

Unflappable O'Bannon lived up to his reputation; he raised an eyebrow. "One foot out of the boat and already he's handing out promotions. Good to have you back, Lord O'Donnell."

"That 'Lord' nonsense must stop. Colonel is enough."

O'Rourke muttered darkly as he swung his leg over the other side. "Colonel is enough for *military* use."

"So says my keeper," Hugh laughed. "Show me what fine heights of industry you've reached in my absence."

O'Bannon did so. The originally simple fort had been improved by the extension of a sea-facing ravelin from its eastern side and a lunette that curled down and around to protect against any flank attack that followed along that same shore. The last of the tents and sheds had been converted into barracks and the first of the barracks had undergone their final trans-mogrifications into two-story blockhouses. However, the big new sea-facing outer walls that would screen the fort from slightly beyond its western palisade all the way to the start of the ravelin on the east weren't really walls yet. They were just—well, mounds of dirt.

Hugh stood before those mounds and rubbed his chin. "Well. Major, it was my understanding that you expected this to be ready by now."

"An' sure it would have been. But you left other orders that unexpectedly prevented that."

Hugh frowned. "Did I, now?"

"Aye, sir, though I have had much reason to doubt you ever imagined such a conflict of intents might arise."

Hugh waited, then: "You'll not be keeping me in suspense much longer, I'm hoping?"

"No, sir. It was, er, well, your most important directive, actually. Not so much an order as the most basic requirement of our mission here."

Hugh felt his eyebrows rise. "Relations with the natives? Don't tell me that McGillicuddy couldn't help exercising his strange charms upon the local ladies?"

"No, sir. Not this time, at any rate. No friction between us at all. Except over building these outer walls. Which we stopped right quick."

Hugh felt his eyebrows descend into a frown. "The Nepoia were averse to our having walls?"

"Well, no, sir. It wasn't the *having* of them that rubbed 'em wrong, sir. Like I said, it was the building of them."

"O'Bannon, you're a great man for decisive action and clear orders, but you're not bringing those fine traits to this conversation. What, specifically, are they objecting to? Are we digging on sacred ground?"

"They've no problem with us shoveling the dirt about, sir. It's the trees. The cutting of them. They didn't expect that."

Hugh sighed and nodded. "So since you've made no great progress on these, I'll project that it wasn't something they were willing to chat about with your fine self."

"No, sir. Their cacique, Hyarima, said it was a matter to be settled between chiefs. Between friends."

Hugh glanced at the executive officer of his tercio. "He said that, did he?"

"Conveyed in person, and in fluent Spanish, sir."

Hugh nodded. "How are you communicating with them, these days?"

"Well, they only send scouts out here, now. As much to say hello as keep an eye on us, I think. I'll say this, though; Hyarima has turned the game right around on the Arawak, he has. Now it's the Nepoia who own most of the island, and the Arawak who are huddled in the southwest."

"So faster if we send an advice packet over to Port-of-Spain, then?"

"Almost certainly so, my Lo—Colonel."

"Then send a runner down to the *Orthros*. They're to carry this message to the Nepoia, to the immediate attention of my friend Hyarima. Be sure they say that, mind you: my *friend* Hyarima."

"I've the sense of its significance, sir. What else?"

"Just that I look forward to discussing the trees and other matters that friends may wish to raise at a time and place of his choosing. I would be honored and pleased to invite him to Port-of-Spain, but I am sensitive that he may wish our words to be spoken beneath an open sky rather than a Spanish-built roof."

"It's on its way as soon as we're finished, sir. And judging from Ms. Koudsi's eager waving back over by the access road to Rig One, I'd say you're wanted elsewhere."

Hugh raised an eyebrow. "It's Rig *One*, now?"

O'Bannon smiled. "There's been no slouching in your absence, sir. Not by anyone."

Ann Koudsi and her boyfriend-foreman, Ulrich Rohrbach, were all smiles at Hugh's approach.

He affected, with some difficulty, a storm-cloud frown. "And exactly when were you going to tell me that there's a second well, Ms. Koudsi?"

She laughed. "As soon as I knew. The signs were right, but it sent out a lot of high-pressure gas early in the digging. And with cable rigs like the ones we're using here"—she waggled her hand in a gesture of uncertainty—"I'm not confident that reading the spoor will tell us what might be coming next."

"You mean, not like the rotary rig that's en route to Louisiana, currently?"

Ann's smile dropped away. "Who told you?"

Hugh laughed. "Well, as it happens, you did. Just now."

"What? Why you—" But she was smiling. "When did you know?"

"As I said, just now. But for anyone who's at meetings where ship movements are discussed, 'twas quite clear that Eddie and Tromp were occasionally shuffling information about and changing topics. F'rinstance, last year *Courser* departs the fleet, before we're in sight of St. Eustatia. And then nary a peep out of her. But also, no report. A strange silence, if a ship of that importance was thought lost. But if not, then where is she and what is she up to? And then this year, her sister ship *Harrier* escorts us part of the way down and then disappears into the west. And a day later, *Patentia* and another jacht go off on their own merry way. In the same direction.

"Now if that wasn't enough, my dearest godmother, who near as raised me as any one living person did, sent me the occasional telegram last fall of a project in Germany that she hears tell of. Something regarding a different kind of drill. A bit hushed, as it were. And then, just before Christmas passed, all the whispering stops. So do the occasional updates from, well, shall we say, 'interested parties.'"

Ulrich almost smiled. "That is a very interesting synonym for 'spies,' Lord O'Donnell."

"It does have a much a prettier sound to it, doesn't it? And Ulrich, if you don't start calling me Hugh, I'll be telling Ann about your scandalous reputation among the ladies back home. Heartbroken, every one."

For the slimmest sliver of a moment, Ann fell for it. "Okay, okay, Hugh," she said through a chuckle. "So you know about the other half of the oil project."

"I just know that it exists. And the secret is safe with me. Because I can well understand why you don't wish it bruited about. Sounds to be in the backyard of my old Spanish employers, I'd wager, given what I read of oil discoveries along North America's Gulf Coast."

Ann nodded. "So: are you going to tell Tromp and Eddie, or should I?"

Hugh thought. "You, I think. If there are any 'interested parties' of the other side getting a peek at our communications, they'd be watching me more closely for messages of military significance than you. No insult intended."

"None taken, and better you in their sights than me! Now, come take a look at the new rig."

When they reached it, Hugh noticed that while the drill was mechanically identical to Rig One, the layout was slightly different. As Anne had explained shortly after arriving on Trinidad, it was a certainty that they'd make their biggest mistakes with the first rig. That's where they'd come to know its mechanical idiosyncrasies, but also get their first practical acquaintance with the soil, the rock, the plants, the water table: all the things that make drilling different from place to place. Rig Two's layout suggested that all that knowledge had been implemented.

In addition to the crew currently working the rig, a young man of better than middle height and solid build was watching the activity, back to them.

Ann called to him. "Phil?"

The fellow turned, smiled—an easy expression—and sauntered over, sticking out his hand. "Hello, I'm Phil Jenkins. I'm guessing that you're Colonel O'Donnell."

Before Hugh could reply, Ann added. "But he prefers 'Lord O'Donnell.'"

Hugh turned on her. "Now, Ann Koudsi, that's no laughing matter! I'll have you know—"

But Ulrich intervened. "I think everyone has evened the score, *ja*? Phil, Ann is correct. He is the Earl of Tyrconnell."

"Which," Hugh added, "having now been said, may now be as quickly forgotten. I'm pleased to meet you, Phil. You're another scientist?"

Phil chuckled. "Not hardly, Your Lor—uh, Colonel Tyrconnell. Wait; no—"

"See?" Hugh remonstrated, shaking a histrionic finger in Ann's direction, "you've confused the lad beyond all sensible cogitation. See here, now, Mr. Jenkins: let's make this simpler, yes? I'm Hugh. You're Phil. Easy enough?"

"Yeah. Uh, yes . . . Hugh."

"Splendid. See?" Hugh grinned at Ann. "So much better." He turned back to Phil. "So if you are not one of Grantville's scientists, what's your intentions here, then?"

Phil shrugged. "Trained to help run a rig, is all." As if an afterthought, he added, "And I've been here before, so I thought this would be kinda fun."

Hugh smiled. "I knew your name sounded familiar! You're the fellow who came here—what? Two years ago, now?"

"Wow," said Phil, "Lookit: I'm famous!" He laughed at the notion.

Hugh grinned. "Well, famous enough that Don Michael McCarthy—Junior, that is—had full knowledge of everything you reported about Pitch Lake. And about your travels in general, by the way." He frowned. "But it seems like a young explorer like yourself might have ambitions in addition to working oil machinery, no?"

Phil shrugged. "I don't know that I'm what you'd call a really ambitious guy, Lor—Hugh. But everything was, well, kinda boring after I traveled here. It was weird, going back to high school, hanging out and kicking around Grantville again. Which had really gone through some changes while I was gone. So when it was getting close to graduation, people started asking me what I wanted to do, what I was interested in, what jazzed me."

Hugh nodded, realizing for the first time, the profound differences in the vernacular and idiom of young up-timers.

"And you know what I realized?" Phil continued. "I always wound up talking about what I did or saw back here. So," he finished with a shrug, "I learned how to operate a rig. And here I am."

Hugh smiled. "Yes, but when you did all that talking, what were you talking *about*? Did you always see yourself coming back here to drill for oil?"

"Naw, that was just a way to get back. What I talked about . . . ? Well, you know the Dutch ship I sailed with was looking for rubber, right? And so I got interested in that." His eyes opened a little wider and he started speaking more quickly. "So, did you know that all the way back in 1445, this guy named Prince Henry the Navigator set up a trading post on Arguin Island, which is just off the coast of Africa? He was able to get gum arabic there and send it to Portugal. But they didn't really know what to do with the stuff, I guess. Neither did the Spanish, because it only took off when the Dutch came in and took over the trade. So I started wondering, 'Hey, if the Dutch are already looking for gum arabic, you can be darn sure there's going to be money in it. I mean, do you know how many up-time machines really need rubber?" He pointed at Rig Two. "Do you know how much easier it would be to make that cable drill? Heck, if we had enough rubber, I'll bet Grantville would have tried to develop a rotary rig by now. It would be so much easier to do with rubber, and it would be so much easier to get to the oil really quickly."

At the end, Hugh and Ann were exchanging raised eyebrows behind Phil's head, which was clearly awash with images of personal memories, more distant history, and what might come to pass.

Ann was the first to lean forward, grinning. "Well, *someone's* been doing their homework. Sounds like the idea of rubber really got you thinking hard. Maybe thinking about whether farming gum arabic would work here, now?"

Phil nodded. "Yeah, I thought about it some. I mean, it really made the Spanish and Portuguese and the Dutch rich, but that's because all the work was done by slaves. So without that, it might not be very profitable. But then again, rubber's one of those things that you may never miss if you've never had any, but boy, once you do have rubber, you start realizing how many things you just can't make unless you have it. And with Grantville jump-starting those kinds of industries all over the place, I just kinda thought, you know, before long, the price might go up a lot higher than it was back in the up-time seventeenth century." He looked around Rig Two's jungle clearing, as if he expected to spot people just within the tree line. "Do you think the local Indians—I mean, native peoples, would want to farm it?"

Ann shrugged. "Maybe. Maybe not. I kind of think not. But if it's valuable enough, and they don't have to lease a lot of their lands for European growers, then maybe it might work."

Phil nodded. "You know, that would be kind of cool. I guess I always kind of figured, or at least hoped, that I'd come back here. And I gotta say, it just *feels* right."

"Why?" asked Ulrich.

Phil scratched his head. "Not sure, exactly. But back home, well, if you're an up-timer, everybody expects that you're going to be a whiz with gadgets. Or science. Or something else that people can make money from. Because almost everyone from here expects that you'll have some kind of up-time skill or ideas that will be really valuable." He shrugged. "That's not me. But I liked traveling here. And I was thinking about going into forestry anyway."

Hugh smiled sadly. "I'm sorry to say that your first task in our forests might be to help us cut down trees."

Jenkins shrugged again. "Suits me. But why?"

"We'll need them to expand our fortifications."

"Wood won't hold out cannonballs, er, Colonel."

"You are very right. But I don't want the wood to stop cannon balls. I want the wood to shore up berms of hard-packed dirt that *will* stop cannon balls."

Jenkins grinned. It was a ready and guileless expression. "When do we start?"

Hugh sighed. "Just as soon as I get the owners' permission."

"The Arawaks? They're not likely to give you permission to breathe."

"No, they're not. But they are also not the owners, anymore. I mean to talk to the Nepoia."

Chapter 47

Port-of-Spain, Trinidad

Hugh awakened from dreams of being in the belly of a ship... and realized that reality had been seeping into his dreams. He was once again in the "dignitary" cabin of Pieter Floriszoon's *Eendracht*.

When the advice packet he'd sent to Port-of-Spain returned with Hyarima's prompt reply, he'd meant to sail there with the *Orthros*. But inasmuch as that ship carried few and lighter guns and would be traveling alone, O'Rourke persisted in loudly opining that the unusually swift and heavily gunned *Eendracht* would be a far better choice. And damn it if O'Bannon and even Floriszoon didn't agree with his aide-de-camp-become-nursemaid.

However, by the time that debate had been resolved, and other matters requiring his orders had been settled, it was late afternoon and *Eendracht* was still replenishing her supply of fresh water for the journey. The winds were acceptable, but it was a twenty-five-mile sail from the southern to northern reaches of Trinidad's coastline on the Bay of Paria. Consequently, it was dark when the jacht arrived, which meant dinner and sleeping aboard.

After a breakfast of half a cassava roll and a few slices of guava, Hugh was in armor, on deck, and wondering where Pieter was. O'Rourke was already waiting, as was the oversized dinghy that would take them to Port-of-Spain, where a few more of the once predominant *ajoupas* had been replaced with walled buildings. Hugh asked his aide, "Where's that Floriszoon?"

The other jutted his square jaw back in the direction of the jacht's modest quarterdeck. "Cuddled up wi' invisible lightnings." Which was one of O'Rourke's many colorful euphemisms for the radio.

When Pieter did come on deck, though, his face was not that of a man who had been cuddled up with anything. Except, perhaps, a porcupine.

The two Irishmen stood. "I'm thinkin'," O'Rourke muttered, "that it's not a happy Dutchman we're looking at."

Hugh shushed his friend and nodded at Floriszoon. "Bad news is a bad start to any day, Pieter. What have you heard?"

Floriszoon gestured to several barrels that would be unloaded after the two Wild Geese had been ferried to shore. "Well," he sighed, "we knew it was coming. For a year now."

"Ah," Hugh nodded, "the Cartagena fleet. Where's it been spotted?"

"Just east of Puerto Cabello. Three hundred fifty miles over the shortest water route, but they won't sail between Isla Margarita and the coast. They'll go around to stay in open water. So, say, three hundred and seventy."

"How old is the news?"

"Six days. It was either Moses' ship which saw them or one of the captains he helped get started."

O'Rourke shook his square, shaggy head. "That Hebrew fellow's patache is a wonder, 'tis. Largest I've ever seen and the fastest, as well. He's given us a good start on making ready."

"How long until the Spanish arrive?"

Pieter shrugged. "Well, they're fighting the westward current and headwinds. Tacking in those square-rigged monsters will increase the actual distance by half again, I'd say. So, three hundred seventy miles becomes five hundred and fifty. They might make a knot and a half, at best, so sixteen days from where they were spotted. But the news is six days old."

"So they could make the mouth of the Bay of Paria in ten days."

Floriszoon nodded. "Probably more, of course. But I agree: plan on ten. Any extra time is just that much more for preparation."

Hugh frowned. "We've other worries, though."

Pieter nodded. "The oilers."

"The what?" O'Rourke asked.

"Oilers. Most of the naos taken at Dominikirk have been, or are still undergoing, conversion into hulls for carrying liquids. The first half of them are on their way down here now, in convoy with some of the galleons taken at the same time."

Hugh frowned. "Do any of them have a radio aboard?"

Floriszoon nodded tightly. "Only one, and it's not the best."

Hugh shrugged. "It will have to do. They have to

be turned around. It sounds like we've got a job for Ed—eh, Commodore Cantrell's observation network."

Pieter shook his head. "It's several links short of finished, Hugh. The Kalinago of the Windward Islands are not trusting people. If that chief from Guadeloupe, Touman, wasn't trying to convince them, they wouldn't be talking to us at all."

Hugh sighed. "Very well. Then you have to sail to meet the convoy, to send word."

Pieter's eyebrows raised. "Well, we'll have to see what Houtebeen has to say about that. And besides, Hugh, it's a wide sea. There's no guarantee that we'll approach close enough to be in range during the limited intervals we can send. Those batteries don't give us many minutes, you know."

"I do. That's why it can't be just a single ship reaching out to find them. It has to be two or more. On divergent courses. As you say, the seas are wide, so we'll need a wide net to be sure of catching that fish."

O'Rourke looked sideways at his friend. "I should like to hear what Admiral Peg Leg will have to say about sending his fastest picket boats out chasing that fish while the Spanish are bearing down on 'im."

Pieter put up warding hands. "You're welcome to take my place and be the one to bring the request before him."

Hugh leaned forward. "Pieter, I'm not suggesting this merely as the commander of the Wild Geese. I'm making an urgent request as one of the owners of the Trinidadian oil enterprise."

Floriszoon looked uncomfortable. "Hugh, you are only a five-percent holder. As a Dutchman, Jol represents almost ten times as large a share of the ownership."

"Yes, but I am an actual shareholder. The Dutch portion is in the hands of the Stadtholder, Prince Fredrik Hendrik, and this is a matter of state authority, not military command."

Pieter turned the palms of his still-warding hands upward. "And if the admiral agrees to your request, is there a course of action you wish conveyed to the convoy?"

Hugh shrugged. "The obvious. They are to return to St. Eustatia, scatter if intercepted. But above all, they cannot come here until Admiral Tromp receives confirmation that Trinidad is secure."

"Which is why Jol may resist your plan. If he reduces the flotilla to send out these fast ships, then he could lose Trinidad and the wells."

Hugh stood. "Then we will take them again. But if we lose those converted naos, then what's the good of producing oil we can't move? Because we'll wait quite a while before we find ourselves with a fleet of oilers again. Now, I don't want to keep the ruler of Trinidad waiting."

O'Rourke slapped his palms down on his knees before rising. "I wouldn't be eager to tell the cacique that his old foes are on their way. And in greater numbers than he's ever known."

"I assure you, old friend, it's not the way I had hoped to start our friendly chat." They headed toward the waiting boat.

Hyarima waved a dismissive hand at Hugh's announcement of impending invasion. "Do not be troubled by bringing us this news, Hugh. It is already known to us."

Well, beat me like a blind donkey. "You already know?"

"Of course," Hyarima said with a casual sweep of his hand toward the west. "We are friends with the Arawak of the mainland. They brought this news. That is why we are finishing our war with the Arawak here."

"You are making peace with them?"

He gazed at Hugh as if he doubted he had understood the Irishman's words. "No, I am killing the last of their men. If I do not, they will join with the Spanish again. They have done so many times. We shall make an end of them and those worries. Now, we have shared food and drink and soon we shall smoke. But first, I hear upsetting words of your people. They are cutting down trees in forests that are not theirs. At the far end, near what you call Pitch Lake. Did they do this with your permission, Hugh?"

Hugh sought for words. "I did not think to either permit or forbid them. The fault is mine, for not asking if the lands around Pitch Lake were free for our use, since you had agreed that we could use the lake itself."

Hyarima frowned, but nodded. "It is a reasonable confusion. The limits of the farms and buildings we gave to you were clear; how and where you may use the lake is not. We will correct this. But for now, tell me: how much wood do you need there?"

"Perhaps a hundred trees, to improve our defenses. But there are others we may wish to cut down."

Hyarima reflected. "All men may use what the forest gives, but not so much that it dies away. And this is what the Spanish and Dutch have done. We have seen this. How can I know how many trees you mean when you say there are others you may wish to cut down?"

Saints above, thought Hugh, *how will I be able to*

explain oil prospecting? But he took a deep breath and gave it a try.

Hyarima's first reaction was dubiety, then a sideways glance as if he'd just discovered that his newest friend was also quite mad. But finally, as Hugh described the uses of the thick black liquid that lay deep beneath the lands close to Pitch Lake, relief and understanding prevailed. "I understand, now, all the strange activity and machines that have arisen there. Very well, then how many of these 'well sites' will you require?"

"Not more than ten or twenty at any one time, I believe. And only for so long as there is oil to extract. Once the well is dry, the land shall be returned to the forest, shall be made as it was." Hugh hoped Ann's descriptions of drilling what she called "clean, policed wells" were accurate rather than optimistic.

"Then you are welcome to the sites you require. If you discover you need more, we shall speak again. Now, we shall smoke."

Hugh, who had never acquired a taste for tobacco, prepared to honor his host. But before he did, there was one last matter: "Hyarima, it is not right that my people should have all the oil that comes from the ground. I cannot speak for the others, but I wish to give a measure of each barrel to you."

Hyarima stared, almost smiled. "And what would I do with this black blood of the earth? I have no machines that require it, so I have no need to share in it."

Hugh was glad that none of the more business-minded Dutch were present, as they would certainly have wanted to strangle him for what he was about to say. "Hyarima, your generosity is that of a brother. So, to be as a brother in return, I strongly, *very strongly*, advise you: take this share of the oil, or the value it brings, for the good of your people."

Hyarima looked at Hugh a long time. "The more we speak, Hugh, the more I hope to meet other pale men, that I may improve my opinion of people from over the sea. But my fear is that you are not like them." He held up a hand against Hugh's objection. "The wisest elders tell us that for everything we know to be true, there is at least one exception. I hope that you are not such an exception among your people."

"Hyarima, I am not. Indeed, I am nothing like the best. I simply keep my word."

"Which is rare enough, in my experience. But if there are more who are like you"—his eyes flicked to O'Rourke—"and like him, then why have they not come to our lands also?"

Hugh sighed; there was danger talking in generalities, but the upper limits of vocabulary and available time allowed nothing else. "My friend, most of us who first came to your shores came for wealth. It was that which made them leave their homes and sail at peril to unknown shores."

Hyarima frowned. "Liars and cowards rarely do such brave things. Were they starving?"

"Some, but not all. And few were so poor that they lacked either food for their bellies or shelter for their heads."

"Then brave though their doing may be, it was also foolish." Hyarima looked out over his lands. "And evil, if they came to enrich themselves by taking what already belonged to others." He looked back at Hugh. "And you came here to do their bidding?"

Hugh frowned, sighed. "In a manner of speaking."

Hyarima frowned. "Those words say nothing. We are friends. Speak plainly."

"Hyarima, when I arrived last year, it was to earn coin. To feed my men. We were soon to be as the Nepoia were: struggling to survive and without much hope that we would.

"But then"—Hugh turned a palm toward the sky—"then I saw what was happening here." He forced himself to keep his eyes upon Hyarima's. "You know the Spanish were my employers until I left to come here. They gave me titles and privileges. They told me that their deeds in the New World were one with the will of God Himself."

He shook his head. "As a child, I believed that. But the older I grew, the more I doubted. Then I learned that they meant to break the promises they made to my people, to betray us. So, when I left their service and came here, and saw what they have done—well, I am that child no longer." He looked Hyarima in the eyes, wondering what would happen next. "Do you understand?"

Hyarima nodded solemnly, and put forth his hand, resting it on Hugh's shoulder. "I do understand, my friend. You were never evil, merely ignorant. A man whose leaders had lied to him, from childhood onward. There is no tribe, no nation, no town which is unfamiliar with such persons." He sighed. "It is sad that most children follow the path set before them without ever questioning its rightness. You did not. You are a man of honor, of . . . 'principle' is the word, yes?"

Hugh felt his eyes getting wet. "It is the word you seek. Whether it describes me is another matter. But I aspire to it. With every fiber of my being."

Hyarima removed his hand, nodding. "This I know. This I saw behind your eyes when first we met." His tone became reflective, almost sad. "People who have always known the straight path, who have had good and thoughtful parents and leaders, are the ones who may claim to have always possessed these high principles. And yet, there is at least as much nobility in those who must search and fight to attain them. As you have."

Hyarima stood. "You shall have your wood. We shall share in the wealth of the oil, and that shall be your lease to us for all you require and more besides. And you shall have our friendship. And our spears and guns against the Spanish."

Hugh shook his head. "No! I am not here to ask you to fight the Spanish! Too many of your people have died already. As I said at our first meeting, the Spanish are our problem. We shall deal with them."

Hyarima smiled. "I wonder how much it would please the wives and children of your men, to hear you increase the hazard to their husbands and fathers by refusing our help. Besides, we have both the need and the right to fight for these lands. If we do not, can we feel they are truly ours?"

Hugh drew in a breath, prepared a rebuttal he had not yet composed.

Hyarima raised a hand. "And lastly, Hugh, you will *need* our help. You will. The Spanish are many. Perhaps you will prevail without our aid in the battle that is coming. But the greater the cost to you this time, the more likely you will not be able to resist their next attack. And they will keep attacking until they vanquish you, or you vanquish them. That is who they are.

"Now, we smoke."

Chapter 48

Oranjestad, St. Eustatia

"Lady Anne Cathrine? Is that you?"

Anne Cathrine stood up quickly, almost falling in her rush to do so before she recognized the voice behind her. She turned, smiling, "Yes, Dr. Brandão, it is I. You are up early, are you not?"

He leaned on his walking stick. "I agreed to see a fisherman who must be out upon the waves shortly after the sun's rays sparkle upon his outward course. But you, what are you doing in this sad place?" He stared around the blackened, sagging shell that had been Edel Mund's home.

"I . . . I find it a helpful place to look for answers. To understand why she died." Which was technically true.

Brandão evidently heard her comment as a metaphysical euphemism, rather than as the ruthlessly clinical intent that had brought Anne Cathrine back to it. "Ah, yes," said Brandão, putting both hands atop his stick, "it is difficult to see the world through the eyes of the person who perpetrated this tragedy. Particularly for one so caring as yourself. Well, I shall leave you to your meditations, dear lady—"

"Doctor, a moment. If you please." *Should I really do this here? Now? Well, when else will you be sure of finding him alone?* "Doctor, Leonora has told me that your practice of medicine in the New World, and Recife in particular, has been . . . well, atypical."

Brandão's smile was accompanied by a frown. "That is true in so many ways, I cannot know which atypicalities you might have in mind."

"Well, as she seems to be seriously considering following in your esteemed footsteps, she often mentions how, since Recife often had but one or two midwives, you witnessed women die in childbirth who would likely have survived had that not been the case. Or had they been willing to have you as their physician."

He nodded. "Sadly, that is quite true."

"Whereas, those few who were willing to consign their fates and privacy to your hands, to the hands of a man and a physician—almost all of them survived. And their infants, as well."

Brandão was frowning again. "And that, too, is true."

By God, how do I do this? "Doctor, it seems to me, therefore, that with your unusual combination of general medical knowledge, and familiarity with the most delicate matters of a woman's health, that you might also have expertise in . . . or some insights . . . That is to say, you might have, in the course of your practice—"

Brandão's eyes were now closed. "Lady Anne Cathrine, beholding you tongue-tied by your own self is a wonder I never thought to witness in this lifetime." He opened his eyes; they were as kindly and welcoming as his smile. She thought she might sob. "Now, what is it you wish to ask me? You may trust to my discretion. Implicitly. Completely."

"Doctor, I am so happily married to my husband, to Eddie."

His eyes twinkled. "That is quite evident."

"And our happiness is complete, you understand. In every aspect of our, our...union."

His eyes twinkled even more. "That is, if you will pardon my qualifier, outrageously evident."

"Well, then...you see, I cannot understand why—"

"Why, Lady Anne!" Cuthbert Pudsey's voice shouted. "There you are!"

Anne Cathrine closed her eyes. "Yes. Pudsey. Here I am."

The Englishman panted as he ran up and leaned on what was left of the doorjamb. He stared and nodded at Brandão, who stared and nodded back.

If Pudsey had any sense that it might have been a propitious moment to take a few steps back to allow a private conversation to come to a natural conclusion, there was no evidence of it in his face or demeanor. "Bless me, Lady Anne, you are sly as a cat when you want to be, and three times as fleet of foot! You were down the street from Danish House before I had my pants on to be able to run after you. Why'd you go running out into the dawn on yer own, like that?"

"To find this." She opened her palm.

"Wot? Bits of a brick?" He looked at her with a sad, assessing gaze.

"It looks like the pieces of a corner," Brandão murmured, peering into her hand. Then with a bow, he withdrew. "I shall be happy to continue our conversation whenever it might suit you, Lady Anne Cathrine."

She nodded her farewell, and closed her eyes again. *So close. So damnably close.* Then she stood. "Well, come along then, Pudsey. Let's go searching."

"Fer wot, Lady Anne?"

"Bricks," she grumbled.

Two hours of wandering the rapidly changing, and expanding, streets of Oranjestad was as unpromising as it was fruitless. Owners of buildings built before the arrival of the Recifean refugees were made from all different shades of bricks. Only a few might once have matched the almost hay-colored shade of the fragments she'd found scattered within a few feet of the impact point on Edel Mund's hearth. And the owners of those buildings whom she discovered at home were usually not the original owners. It seemed that many of the colony's founders had moved on, either by giving up their stake or giving up the ghost: fever and want had intermittently stalked its first few streets.

Ironically, more recent constructions had bricks of similar provenance. Until last year, the call for brick had been infrequent and small enough that those needed could often be harvested from the ruins of the island's few abandoned buildings. And the spate of new constructions that incorporated bricks were being put up by resettled Recifeans who'd purchased the bricks through the town's two general merchants and did not know whether they were locally manufactured or not, since ships occasionally carried them as ballast and then sold them when no longer wanted or needed.

Anne Cathrine was tired, hungry, thirsty and just about to decide that the house she was examining didn't really have the right color brick after all, when a vaguely familiar voice asked solicitously, "Lady Anne Cathrine?"

She sighed, tried to compose herself. *So, here it is: the first veiled inquiry after my mental health. Because after today, there are sure to be more. How soon before I go from being Lady Anne Cathrine of Denmark, to Crazy Anne Cathrine, Her Lady of the Inscrutable Brick?* She straightened, made sure her smile was serene, and turned.

Her seamstress—well, the far better one of the only two in Oranjestad—curtsied. "I . . . I saw you and your man examining houses earlier. And now, again. Are you—are you looking for something?"

My wits, Anne Cathrine was tempted to reply. *It's what you're thinking, after all. And you might just be right. So the lamp was hit by a brick. Maybe. What would it prove, even if I could find it, much less where it was made?* But Leonora wasn't the only stubborn daughter her father had sired: "Actually, I am looking for a brick. Well, bricks. Of a particular type." *Yes, she* did *sound mad. No doubt about it.*

But the seamstress frowned. "Why? What kind of brick?"

Anne Cathrine elected to ignore the first question and answer only the second. "It is a yellowish brick, rather like this color, I think." She held out the fragments from Edel Mund's hovel.

The seamstress squinted at them. "Lady, would you be so kind as to follow me?"

Anne Cathrine did, albeit suspiciously.

But in the shadow of a recently built granary, and well away from the town's habitations, there was an old livestock trough, fed by a sluice from a cistern. Except the cistern's capacity was being expanded by extending its sides upward by adding four courses of brick.

Hay-colored brick.

Anne Cathrine stared at the cistern, then at the seamstress. "You have done me a great service, and I shall not forget it."

The seamstress—pretty, lithe-limbed, mostly Tupi she guessed—shook her head. "Think nothing of it, Lady Anne Cathrine. I was pleased to help. But why are you so interested in this kind of brick? Do you require them? Are you expanding Danish House?"

Eureka! "We are considering it," she lied. Well, fibbed. For the female denizens of Danish House, the matter of how it might be expanded was a source of inexhaustible conversations that were safely disconnected from any likelihood of actualization. As such, the topic was modestly interesting while remaining completely uncontentious. "Do you know where such bricks might be procured?"

"Indeed I do, lady. You should be able to purchase them directly from the man who makes them." She suddenly seemed uncomfortable. "Although, as I think upon it, you might wish to seek another source."

"I am not particular about the source. Who makes them?"

"*Heer* Hans Musen."

"And *Heer* Musen just started making bricks again recently?"

"Since the New Year, milady," said the West African slave in surprisingly good English. "Before, he made them occasionally. Usually when another landowner had want of them. But now, the kiln is going all the time."

"There much call for them, now," another slave explained in a strange polyglot pidgin. She seemed to be a mix of many peoples. "Now that coin is in townfolk hands, and no Spanish boats come, more building. Because sure they stay."

Logical, thought Anne Cathrine. She turned to the youngest of the four she had found working in Musen's farther fields. "And you saw two men come from *Heer* Musen's house the night after Whipping Square, and each take a brick before heading back to town?"

"Yes'm," he said in a singsong accent. "They make me scared."

"Why?" *What I* should *ask is, "why more scared than usual?"*

"They drunk," he said, eyes checking over his shoulder. "Lotta rum when they come back, that evening. All come here. Haet and his men, too. It was bad. We scared. All of us."

Anne Cathrine nodded eagerly, even as she asked herself, *Are you really doing this? All over a few crumbled bits of brick? What would that prove? Lots of bricks come from here. And even if the brick that hit Edel's lamp did come from here, there is no way to show who threw it or why. What* are *you doing?*

"*Ai!* Lady, they come!" yelped the smallest slave, a young woman who hadn't yet said anything. As if jabbed with pitchforks, Musen's four slaves bolted, running back to their tasks as if pursued by rabid hyenas.

Which, Anne Cathrine reflected, was quite close to the truth of the situation: Hans Musen was running down the slope toward her, his prim wife not far behind.

She stood straight, turned to face them directly. For

the first time since she'd cleared Oranjestad's buildings and began sprinting, she regretted having left Pudsey panting far behind. But that had been her intent, it was her doing, and she would fend for herself. Pudsey might not even see her, given the trees that obscured this part of Musen's tract from the one wagon track that led to the island's various plantations.

"What—what do you think you're doing?" Musen shouted as he came bounding and panting through the pasturage.

She waited until he was close enough that she did not have to shout. "I was conversing with your slaves, *mijn Heer* Musen. They are quite well spoken."

He stopped abruptly. Whether that was to avoid running into her or out of shock at her calm, casual reply, was unclear. "Well . . . you have no right to do so!"

"I am sorry, sir. I was not aware you insisted that freeborn people avoid discourse with your slaves. Indeed, I am not aware that you have the power to constrain the actions of freeborn people at all."

"This is my property. This is trespassing. You will leave! At once!" He produced a muzzle-loading pistol. Just a single barrel, but that would quite suffice.

"I will leave quite soon," Anne Cathrine said, "but I think it only fair to indicate what I have learned. So that you will not conceive of unfortunate plans regarding the slaves with whom I was conversing."

"What? What are you talking about?" Musen shouted. But over his shoulder, his wife's eyes were keen and assessing.

"I am talking about the investigation that is sure to commence as a result of what they have told me," Anne Cathrine lied. Well, bluffed. "I'm sure you already know if it was one of your bricks that broke Edel Mund's window and oil lamp. Your own son, perhaps? Either way, I am sure you know which one of your or Haet's men did it—because you are all braggarts."

"That isn't proof!" Musen shouted.

"No, but testimony is."

"Testimony?" Mistress Musen asked quietly.

"Yes. You see how it is, of course. When there was nothing more than vague suspicion, no townsperson would have been willing to reveal what they might have seen. They fear you landowners. As well they should. But now the investigation begins with a simple request to confirm what we know happened. Those interviewed need not make an accusation, or identify who did it...because that is almost as good as known, now. And once one witness confirms it, more will surely follow.

"A shattering window is not silent. Nor are drunken men. And I suspect they were in no fit condition to move swiftly and quietly away from Edel Mund's house by narrow alleys or past unoccupied buildings."

While Musen's mouth was working to find words to utter, his wife turned and strode at a surprisingly rapid pace toward the smallest and quietest of the slaves with whom Anne Cathrine had been speaking. The slave turned from her work on the near side of the trees, saw Musen's wife approaching, started to bolt away, but stopped when the Dutch woman barked at her, commanding her to halt or be beaten until she was unrecognizable. The young woman stopped, weeping, turning from side to side, as if she was trapped in an invisible cage.

Anne Cathrine felt a pulse of panic; Musen's wife

had the movement and face of an automaton. She just might be capable of—

And without thinking, Anne Cathrine was running after her. She heard Musen behind her. She was more fit and nimble, but he had longer legs.

As Musen's wife reached the girl, she grabbed her hair, dug in her apron and pulled out a small pistol. She cocked and put it against the slave's temple in one smooth, well-practiced motion.

Anne Cathrine stopped instantly. Musen ran past her, toward his wife.

Mistress Musen pulled the young woman's hair so her skull was tight against the muzzle of the gun. "So, now you will leave. And you will stop making these accusations. Or this . . . *person* dies. And if you report that we have abused her, and an 'investigator' comes to find out, we will see him coming. And she"—Mistress Musen yanked the young woman's hair, got a piteous cry in response—"she will never be found. So sad. They take their own lives sometimes, you know."

Anne Cathrine felt as though she had jumped into the ocean, her body had become so suddenly and completely drenched in sweat. Why had she done this? Or was this, this very moment, *exactly* why she had done this? "You must know that cannot be, *mejvrouw* Musen. I have told others of my suspicions." *Another lie, but why stop now?* "My silence will not stop the inquiries. And they will come out here, as I have, asking questions. Do you mean to kill all your slaves, then?"

Musen looked nervously at his wife. Who didn't even blink. "If necessary," she said, "but it will not be. I have seen you. I have heard you. You are not ready to know that your actions caused this creature's death. You will do as I say."

"It doesn't matter if I do as you ask. Investigators *will* come. What you are doing is now illegal."

Musen's wife's answer was a spray of spit. "I am the wife of a *vrijburgher*. This is my property. I may do with it as I please. No law says I may not. And if you penalize me for doing so, the others like us will resist. Your choice, 'king's daughter': are you ready to start a civil war, as well?"

The brush rustled behind her. "Lady Ann, I—wot's this?!"

She turned, hoping to wave Pudsey back, but the big Englishman had his own pistol out already—and then stopped, eyes wide and staring over her shoulder, face losing color. Anne Cathrine turned to see what had frozen him like Medusa's stare—and found herself staring down the barrel of Mistress Musen's gun.

She cocked her head, staring into Pudsey's eyes. "And you will kill me? A woman? I think not. Lower your gun."

"No. I reck it may be the only thing keeping Lady Anne alive."

More rustling and Sophie Rantzau burst out the bushes behind Pudsey. Hans Musen brought his own gun up again. "This is madness. Get out of here!"

Sophie took a knee in the tall grass, folded her hands upon the other. "I will leave with my friend. And not before."

Musen's wife snapped irritably at him. "The English oaf means to shoot me. You have a gun! Will you not defend me?"

Musen went closer to her, gesturing toward the

motionless Pudsey with one hand. "This is not wise. And his weapon is not full upon you. Be calm. This cannot go further." His voice became pleading as she finally glanced at him. "We . . . he . . ."

Anne Cathrine finally breathed again. Even Musen was trying to step back from the brink upon which his wife's actions had put them. Pudsey seemed to be relaxing a bit, as well. Now, if only—

Musen's wife sighed contemptuously—"Flaccid fool"—in the same instant that she snapped her gun sideways slightly and fired.

Anne Cathrine's senses told her the blast, the smoke, the bullet were all coming straight at her . . . but instead, she heard the bullet whisper past, a foot away—*zerp!*—answered instantly by a grunt from Cuthbert Pudsey. She turned in time to see him tipping backward, the gun falling out of one hand, the other grabbing up toward a bloody patch above the bicep. As he fell and rolled, Sophie stooped over him.

"Geertje!" gasped Hans Musen. "You have—!"

"I have missed, is what I've done. I knew he hadn't the mettle to shoot a woman. What are you standing there for, Hans?" Her face rigid with rage, she threw aside her spent weapon, grabbed the pistol out of her husband's numb grasp, turned it over quickly, and rammed it into the trembling slave's temple. "It is clear to me that you need proof that I will do what I say to my property. So, if you wish the other three wretches—and more—to die, just remember I did this." She darted a scornful glare toward her husband as she cocked the much larger pistol's hammer. "Now you will know I play no games."

From behind Anne Cathrine came an unexpected

answer: "I haven't played at anything since I was thirteen." She turned: the voice, the tombstone face, the erect sideways posture, and the muzzle aimed unwaveringly at Geertje Musen, all belonged to Sophie Rantzau.

"You will not shoot me!" Geertje hissed.

"Be assured, *mej Vrouw* Musen, that if you discharge that pistol, or move to train it on anyone else, you will never see the results of your handiwork. A bullet between the eyes has a tendency to ruin one's vision."

"And that would be the end of you, too! You are disgraced in your homeland—it is well known. You would be an embarrassment, cast out, maybe offered up for Dutch justice. Because you will have killed the wife of a *vrijburgher*. Who committed no crime in destroying valueless property."

Sophie's gray eyes did not blink, did not move. "You counted upon chivalry to protect you in the moment Mr. Pudsey could have used this very pistol upon you. But there is no appeal that can protect you from me, Geertje Musen, because I no longer care about the consequences. So unlike him, I am not on the horns of a dilemma."

"Are you not, *Lady* Sophie? I know you and your kind. You are born to wealth and made soft by it. Weakness and irresolution is in your very blood. You stand there, making brave noises, but tell me: are sure you are ready to kill another human being?"

Sophie sighed as if she was bored. "I was at the barricades when the Kalinago came within thirty feet of overrunning us last November. You were not. Perhaps you should ask those who were there with me if I can kill with a gun, before you make the rash—and

perilous—assumption that I will not." She sighted down
the barrel and dipped it slightly. "Should you press
me to prove my resolve, I must apologize in advance
for shooting low. I am a hunter's daughter and would
normally make a quick job of it, would shoot for the
head. But I am out of practice, and so, might miss
such a small, small target."

The color drained completely out of Geertje Musen's
face. She took her index finger out of her weapon's
trigger guard, eased the hammer back down, then
pulled the slave to face her directly. She spat into
the young woman's tear-streaked face and stalked
away, her pace and speed as machinelike as they had
been earlier. With one baffled backward glance, Hans
Musen chased after her.

Anne Cathrine raced past Sophie to kneel beside
Pudsey. "The blood—"

"He will be well," Sophie said in a distracted tone.
"The bullet passed through, and no bones were broken.
It was a small gun, the kind provided for ladies and
assassins, who must keep them inconspicuously upon
their person."

Those words released a torrent of tears that Anne
Cathrine hadn't even known were inside her. "Curse
you, Cuthbert Pudsey!" she cried. "You told her I was
coming here?" She punched him in his unwounded
arm, even as she felt a smile stretching her face so
wide that it was almost painful. "Can I trust no one?"

"Ow!" complained Pudsey, whose wooly brows gathered into a great frown. "Lady Anne, now see here:
I took an oath to protect you. Keeping your secrets
was not part of that bargain. Especially when keeping
those secrets might get you killed! So yes, I told Lady

Sophie, and bloody glad I did, too!" He was flustered when she hugged him very tightly, then mumbled. "Er, pardon the blasphemy, milady."

"Oh, shut up," she wept happily.

On the walk back to Oranjestad, Sophie explained that it was Brandão who had started her searching: "When I arrived at the infirmary, he mentioned you had been behaving strangely. Then I heard about the bricks."

Anne Cathrine looked over, expecting to see Sophie's wry almost-smile. But she was expressionless.

"People knew what direction you had gone," she continued. "Then I saw Pudsey. Following him meant finding you, so..." She shrugged.

"I owe you my life," Anne Cathrine injected into the silence that followed.

Sophie shrugged again. "Being sent on this voyage with you, I counted myself dead. Then I met Hugh and I wanted to live again. And then today, I didn't care if I lived or died. But now I know again: I want to live."

Anne Cathrine nodded. "I understand. Sometimes, I have felt that way about my Eddie. I go from feeling that I cannot live without him, but then feeling that if he died, I must—*must*—continue on, that—"

But Sophie was shaking her head. "No," she said, "that is not what I mean at all. I no longer care what it costs to fully return Hugh O'Donnell's love, nor the obstacles we might face. The freedom to try—to walk that path, or any other—is what makes life worth living. But that is also why, if Hugh O'Donnell died tomorrow—and in this New World, he may well—I would still want to live. More than ever, perhaps. Here, I am not just free from all the meanness and hypocrisy of the Old World, but I am free to work against its infection of this one. I was a child of privilege, but I was also its prisoner. Here, I am neither. And in that is the first real freedom I have ever known. Maybe it is the only real freedom to be had in the world."

Anne Cathrine did not know what to say to her friend, who simply kept moving forward, as if nothing in the world could stop her from where she was going, and yet was in no hurry to get there.

Chapter 49

Oranjestad, St. Eustatia

Van Walbeeck stared at the white-scorched brick on Tromp's desk. It was missing a good chunk of one corner. "So, how long do we just stare at that?"

"Probably forever." Tromp was opening the secure pouch that had just come from the telegraphy station that handled The Quill Array's coded traffic. "That brick is enough to enrage the people, but not enough upon which to mount a conclusive investigation." He scanned the comm reports, which, for some strange reason, Eddie sometimes referred to as "flimsies," even though they were written on the same, stiff paper that was used for all other purposes on St. Eustatia. "It seems that the commodore has been keeping the wind—er, *air*waves busy communicating with both Admiral Simpson and Governor Waters of Bermuda."

Van Walbeeck waited for two seconds, then loudly complained, "Well, do not keep me in suspense. Read it!"

Tromp considered doing so, scanned down the sheet, shook his head. "I am not about to read all these bits and pieces of sentences, punctuated by 'stop' and 'stop' and 'stop' yet again. I accept that they are optimal during battle, but that is where I draw the line. They give me a headache. I shall synopsize."

"Well, then, do that, already!"

Tromp scanned further down the sheet. "Bermuda has allowed us to put up the antenna." Which, for now, was just a glorified term for a very long piece of cable held up by a very tall pole. A more worthy successor would be in place shortly. "It has been successfully tested and will enable communications with New Amsterdam, although that will, for now, require an offshore relay."

Jan shrugged. "Seven hundred nautical miles is at least a workable distance. At fifteen hundred miles, there was no way we were ever going to be able to establish direct radio contact with the mainland. And we are . . . what? Nine hundred nautical miles from the Somers Isles?"

Tromp nodded, barely hearing his friend. "As part of the agreement, the Bermudans require that the Allies—spelled with a capital 'A,' mind you—provide a security flotilla. Reasonable," the admiral commented, "because when the Spanish learn of it, they will certainly wish to eliminate that communication hub."

Van Walbeeck sighed. "It was only a matter of time before our war spread to Bermuda. Have they agreed to our requests to build port and layover facilities there?"

"Yes, if we can broker an agreement with Warner of St. Christopher's for a regular exchange of convoys, mostly for trade in comestibles. And in other news . . . Eddie indicates that we should stand up the crew for the first of the ocean-going tugs. He says that the sturdy old blunt-bowed pinks we acquired from Nevis and New Walcheren were, and I quote, 'capable of being retrofitted' for the down-time steam engines. Two of which, he notes for our interest, were manufactured in Holland."

"Well, hooray; and I shall toast the industriousness of our homeland with an extra gill of rum this night. Anything else?"

"An offhand remark that his desk is almost clear of project folders." Tromp looked at his own clutter. "Enviable." He smiled. "But as you and I know, old friend, the last few items on a desk are generally not there because they are the easiest to resolve."

"Do not remind me," van Walbeeck groaned, "or I shall have to take that gill of rum much earlier than I intended."

St. John's Harbor, Antigua

The sun was going down over St. John's Harbor, but there were still two reports staring up at Eddie Cantrell from the top of his desk. One was good news, the other was . . . well, not bad news so much as it was paralyzing news.

Since he feared he might never get beyond the paralyzing folder, he snagged the good-news report first, opened it, and sighed in relief.

Finally—*finally!*—the inclinometers installed on *Intrepid*'s guns were fully functional, including the range adjustment module. The basic link between the two sights—so that the gun would fire automatically when they were aligned—had been reliable enough that his gun crews had been practicing with them for several weeks. However, calibrating the floating sight so that it could include adjustments for other targeting variables, range foremost among then, had proven a thorny challenge. And without it, the entire sighting system was damned-near pointless.

With a typical gun, the means of compensating for any projectile's increasing rate of drop over the course of its flight was pretty straightforward, if tricky: you aimed "above" the target. That way, the projectile's drop put it right where you actually wanted it. A lot of math was involved, and if there was any significant wind, or the powder was weak, or even if there was high humidity, your calculations could be perfect and you'd still miss. To Eddie's mind, gunnery involved as much zen as it did math.

With the inclinometer though, there was only one really good way to compensate for distance (and eventually, other variables): by adjusting, or "re-zeroing," the position of the "floating" sight. Because you still had to line up the two sights to complete the circuit and fire the gun.

Unfortunately, the offsetting mechanism on the floating sight had proven to be finicky and sensitive. And because Simpson had only been authorized to send over the two hand-me-down systems originally used as second-generation test beds, these particular mechanisms came with some unique quirks all of their own.

But there, on the top of the report he'd opened, was Mike's terse summary:

Inclinometer targeting offset module functioning to within 0.1 tolerances of projected baseline. Performance refinement continues.

Eddie leaned back with a sigh, rubbed his hands over weary eyes. That was huge: *huge*. It meant that they could now use *Intrepid*'s—and eventually all the other steamships'—eight-inch naval rifles at longer ranges and in rougher conditions. Additionally, they'd spend only half the number of rounds finding the range and getting on target. Or, to put another way, Mike's two-sentence update meant that they had increased *Intrepid*'s effective firepower by—well, by a lot.

There was an inquiry attached to the cover of the report, but it was from the chief quartermaster, not Mike: "Retire percussion-lock firing mechanism upon upgrade?" Eddie scrawled his reply in capital letters: "NO!!!" Yes, the inclinometer would revolutionize naval combat—until the damn thing broke. Once this shiny new toy had repeatedly proven itself to be rugged enough and resistant to the vagaries of combat conditions, *then* Eddie would allow the old firing mechanism to be mothballed. Maybe.

He put that folder aside with a fond, farewell glance and picked up the one that was sure to induce paralysis, both to his brain and productivity. Which was why he'd left it to the end of the day. He sighed and opened it.

It was the planning file on Tortuga, a mostly rocky island off the north coast of Hispaniola that was, even in Eddie's time, associated with pirates. In addition to all the available up-time information, there were maps from different periods and detailed descriptions from Jol, Diego, Moses, and anyone else who'd ever been there or whose speculations upon it were deemed reliable.

Its first settlers had been French hunters, whose

name—*boucaniers*—indicated their primary product: smoked meat. Originally, that meant sea turtles. However, markets for that meat and the shells proved to have limits, along with the local sea turtle population. So they also began hunting the island's plentiful boar, but trade still remained marginal. Plantations were tried, but like so many early French efforts in the Caribbean, they foundered for lack of cohesion and support. So the forerunners of the region's buccaneers made trading their primary activity—specifically, trading in goods that had either been stolen from, restricted to, or prohibited by the Spanish. And after becoming successful black marketers, it had been only a few short steps to sailing under the black flag.

The increasing flow of forbidden goods from the island, the buccaneers' raids upon the northern settlements of Hispaniola, and the increasing number of true pirates who made it their home port, prompted the Spanish to mount a sustained attack upon Tortuga, using troops from Santo Domingo. Occurring less than a year before Grantville popped into this world, the Spanish succeeded in driving the raiders out of their makeshift home port, but the inhabitants simply fled into the densely wooded highlands until the galleons left.

Months later, an English "privateer," Anthony Hilton, initiated what was to be the last attempt to establish a legitimate colony on the island. With the support of the same backers who founded the Puritan colony on Providence Island, Tortuga's plantations were renewed, but ultimately failed again. However, as a base for English-authorized raiding of Spanish shipping, it was a great success.

That was the point at which local and up-time history diverged considerably. According to Diego and Moses, the moment that King Charles relinquished England's Caribbean claims to the French, the ownership of the island became a matter of fierce dispute between the mixed French-English population. The Puritan influence was the first casualty of that friction and shortly after, Tortuga's only port, Cayonne, became a true pirate enclave, supported by an inland mountain fortress.

The only firsthand information subsequent to that came from Diego, who had been there as recently as a year ago. Apparently, Hilton had either left or been killed and, perhaps because of the changed fortunes of both England and France, no further support had come from either nation. Tortuga was known among its piratical inhabitants as Association Island, the home of freebooters. They sorted themselves into what they called Free Companies: a noble-sounding euphemism for loose collections of like-minded raiders.

They had been growing steadily stronger until large numbers of them were destroyed at last year's Battle of Vieques. Whereas the up-time Spanish had returned to, and sacked, Cayonne and its fort, in this timeline, the emergence of consolidated Dutch opposition caused the Spanish to reconceive the pirates as potential privateers.

Now, however, the ranks of those mercenary pirates were sorely depleted, and the ones still operating were doubly wary of continuing to take Spanish silver. Many were convinced that they would lose more of their own blood earning Spanish coin in pitched battles than what they would shed if they simply returned to their own free-booting activities.

Eddie sighed. Which meant that the pirates were close—*really* close—to leaving Spanish service. On the gameboard of the Caribbean, they were a piece which, with the right push, would no longer be controlled by his opponent, but would return to random activity. Or, if sent the right kind of message, would actually consider it safer to go after Spanish ships than his own.

Eddie leaned back in his chair and rubbed his hair in frustration. But how could he give them that push? Tortuga wasn't big, but history had shown that conventional attacks upon it had always been costly, and taken longer than expected. And any force large enough to mount that kind of assault was one they would surely see coming.

Eddie scoffed; as if he had any forces left to devote to such an operation. All his own game pieces were already tied down and overextended, both geographically and operationally...

He jerked upright in his chair. All his pieces except *one*. He smiled, imagined a cartoon lightbulb suddenly flashing into existence over his head. But would it work? *Could* it work?

He leaned back and ruffled his hair again, even more rapidly. He was contemplating the kind of plan that Simpson characterized (in rare moments of crudity) as being "more balls than brains."

But if Eddie could bring that one available piece on to the gameboard, in the right place, at the right time, then maybe, just *maybe*, it would be the sucker punch the pirates of Tortuga would never be looking for.

Eddie started rearranging all his sheets, laid out a planning calendar to his left, and opened the telegraph pad and code book to his right. Although the sun had only recently begun accelerating its descent for the horizon, he glanced at the small table across the room, wedged into the narrow space where the floor-to-ceiling map of the Caribbean ended and the windows of the bayside wall began. On that table were two full pitchers of water, a soursop, a pineapple, goat cheese, and four loaves. There were also three stoppered clay jars of lamp oil. He smiled at the latter.

Who knew that one day I actually would *be burning the midnight oil?*

Eddie was started awake by a knock on the door. He raised his head from his desk, looked at the clock. Just after midnight. "What is it?" he called, belatedly realizing he had sounded more like a grumpy college kid than a commanding officer.

"Highest priority signal sir."

He was suddenly very awake. "Bring it," he ordered. The first line told him most of what he needed to know:

SPANISH FORMATION SIGHTED OFF SOUTH COAST OF ST. MAARTEN.

"How old is this intelligence?"

"Hours, sir. It was confirmed before relay to us."

"How did we get it?"

The orderly seemed puzzled. "Er, radio from St. Eustatia, sir."

Eddie managed not to roll his eyes. "Yes. I mean, who collected it and when?"

"Earlier today, sir. From a Bermudan sloop coming

down to freight smoke. They saw the ships a few days ago, sir. The Spanish were apparently reinforcing the island, landing troops. They ran a skiff out after the sloop. The Bermudan captain showed his heels, escaped, but it took him quite a while to get clear."

"Why, if he escaped them?"

"Because he ran south and ran straight into a much greater number of Spanish, sir. Mostly fast ships."

"Pataches?"

"Larger than that, sir. Galleoncetes or upscaled fragatas, according to the report."

Eddie thought for a moment. "Do you have your pad and codebook?"

"No, sir."

"Well, get them! Smartly!"

"Yes sir!" The runner banged the door behind him as he ran back to the comms shack.

Eddie leaned his head back into his hands. He had known it was going to be a late night. Now, he'd be lucky to finish while it was still early morning.

Oranjestad, St. Eustatia

Making sure not to drip any blood on the infirmary floor, Anne Cathrine bundled up the rags that had served as the first compress for Cuthbert Pudsey's arm. Sophie had been correct; the wound had been mercifully minor, to the extent that a gunshot ever is. But the ball had been small, and very likely not made of lead; it had gone through cleanly, without the terrible, wider wound left by a bullet that was deforming and expanding.

She had sent Sophie to see that Pudsey went to his

room and stayed there while she remained behind to clean up and close the infirmary for the night. And while doing so, she had kept on imagining how she might approach Tromp, what she might say to convince him to take action, yet not so overtly that it would endanger the lives of the Musens' slaves.

But as she played the many permutations of that scene in her mind, it always ended the same way: Tromp with a pained look on his face as he explained the many reasons he could not take action. And he always ended on, "And if I do as you ask, knowing in advance that all I can do is make an accusation without any clear evidence or witnesses to the act, do you know what the people of Oranjestad will say? That I have become Danish, instead of Dutch."

Which was an entirely likely outcome and an entirely reasonable reluctance on the part of the admiral. As a foreign dignitary who had the luxury of having her needs provided for, Anne Cathrine had possessed the freedom and time to act and speak as the workaday Dutch colonists could not. But it also meant that she was an outsider whose investigation would appear to be motivated by the fact that the victim had been a woman of her own country.

And so, at least in the greater scope of things, the Musens had won. It would never be known who had thrown the brick that led to Edel Mund's incineration, nor would the near-murder of one of their slaves ever be called to account.

She heard the front door open softly. "Yes?" Anne Cathrine called, walking back toward the infirmary's main room. "Is your condition urgent, or can it wait until morning? Dr. Brandão is not—"

She stopped; the seamstress was in the room, closing the door quietly behind her. Anne Cathrine was sure of the answer even as she asked, "Are you unwell or injured?"

"No, Lady Anne Cathrine, I am not." She stood, uncertain. Glanced at the door behind her.

Anne Cathrine took a step forward. "You were a great help today. It . . . it saved a life. Maybe more than one."

The seamstress nodded nervously. "I know. I saw."

"You—?"

"I followed your friend. When she started running. Just outside of town. In the same direction you did."

Anne Cathrine sat, gestured for the seamstress to do the same. "You see a great many things," she commented.

The seamstress remained standing, shook her head. "Too many."

"What do you mean?"

The young woman's eyes shone, although the only illumination was the moonlight that came through the open storm shutters. "I am going away."

Anne Cathrine, struck by the sudden change of topic, paused . . . long enough to sound composed and sage when she finally said, "I am sorry to learn that. Will you be back?"

Again, the expected answer: "No." Then: "Before I leave, it is important that I tell you something. About the men, the families, you are dealing with."

Anne Cathrine waited again, then said. "Go on."

"You must beware of them. You must be more careful. They are desperate. They will do anything."

"The Musens, or—?"

"All of them." The seamstress took a deep breath.

"I am quite sure they were bribed, or promised something, to remain in their homes when the Kalinago attacked last year."

Anne Cathrine did not remember getting to her feet when she spoke again. "That is a very serious accusation. Why do you believe this?"

"I do not believe it; I know it. Because I was the... the intermediary."

"You? You were—are—the liaison between them and—?"

"No, no. I simply pass messages between them and those who contact them."

"They have more than one, er, 'contact'?"

The seamstress nodded. "Two, now. But last year, just the Frenchman."

"There was a Frenchman here, conspiring with the slaveholders openly? Through you?"

She shook her head vigorously. "I only passed messages. Through clothes. In the hems. I cannot even be sure there were bribes. I only know the messages came from St. Christopher."

"And the man who brought them was French?"

"Different men brought them from St. Christopher, different men took them back there. I had never seen them before, and I never saw any of them a second time. They were Dutch, English, of mixed race."

"So how do you know that the person who bribed the slaveholders was French?"

"Because I was told that, under no circumstances, should I take commissions for passing secret messages from the English of St. Christopher's. Specifically, to avoid any dealing with representatives of Governor Warner or his associates."

"After the attack, do you have any knowledge of what became of this presumed Frenchman?"

"I do not, but just recently, messages are once again being exchanged that employ the same set of precautions as he used last year. That is all the information I have that may, *may*, pertain to the Frenchman. And I know better than to ask questions to try to learn more."

Well, that is sensible enough. "You say that you have a new—a second source of commissions, now?"

The seamstress nodded, seemed to be growing even more nervous.

"So, how did this new, ah, employer come to know of you? Through the Frenchman, do you think?"

"Again, I cannot say." The seamstress shivered, although the night was warm. "And it is perilous to ask. But this contact knew of the services I had provided before the Kalinago attacked. They asked me to do the same for them." She reflected a moment, moved her feet restlessly. "Well, not exactly the same. They do not ask me to pass messages. They have only asked me to send them confidential messages. Of my own."

Anne Cathrine frowned. "What do you mean, messages of your own?"

"They asked me to . . . to observe. Things. Here on St. Eustatia. To report what I see in the bay. Unusual visitors and travelers. When ships or soldiers come or go."

Now it was Anne Cathrine who experienced a chill that ran the length of her body. "Anything else?"

The seamstress shrugged. "They asked me to describe any maps or documents left out, any that I could see easily. I read, you know." Her chin came up proudly.

"Three languages, and a bit of a fourth. The priests taught me. Back near Olinda."

"With that skill, I suspect you may yet have other opportunities of employment."

"If I was a man, yes, but men do not like going to women for information, for understanding, they do not possess. Not even for something as simple as translation."

Anne Cathrine risked closing the distance between them by another step. "Why are you revealing this now?"

The seamstress looked down, shuffled her feet. "Several reasons. I fear being caught; I have always feared that, but more now. And weeks ago, they asked me to start copying things. Mostly maps. Then they asked me to steal some. And once they are missed, the owners will start wondering who might have taken them."

"Surely you knew that when they asked."

The seamstress nodded. "Yes, but once you start down this path, you may not stop. They offered more money for me to steal things, but it . . . well, it is really an order. If you say no, they worry that you may be changing your mind. And that if you change your mind, you might reveal what you have been doing." She shivered again. "They pay well for silence. The punishment for not staying silent . . ." Her concluding shrug was grimly eloquent. Before Anne Cathrine could ask another careful question, the seamstress looked up. "But there is another reason I am revealing what I have done. It is because of what *you* have done."

Anne Cathrine blinked. "Me? And what have I done?"

"Everything that I wished I had." The seamstress leaned forward, eyes rising to meet Anne Cathrine's and then falling away again. "Last year, I saw you at the barricades, defending the town when it seemed there was no hope left. Then I saw you at The Whipping Square. And then I saw you today. I never saw a noble lady who fought so hard for those who have no titles, no hope of ever being much more than they were born. And I...I have been paid by those who put and keep my own people in chains." She looked up again, eyes bright. "I cannot keep taking their coin. But the only person I could bring myself to tell is you. You *deserve* to know."

Anne Cathrine reached toward her carefully. "Where do you live? Where may I find you, before you depart?"

"My lady, you may not. I have sold what belongings I may, and will take ship before the sun is up."

Anne Cathrine frowned; it was exceedingly rare for a ship to begin a journey at night. Unless—"Are you leaving with one of the contacts of those who paid you?"

"No, lady. I can only survive so long as I remain unfound by my employers and their agents."

"Then where—?"

"Good lady, these are large seas with many islands. I have had three names before the one I used here. Taking another is of no consequence to me. I just pray it is the last. Please do not look for me, nor cause the admiral to send ships in pursuit of any that set sail tonight or tomorrow. It would be my death, and I have told you all I know."

Anne Cathrine did not want her to go, realized that there was an opportunity—for both the seamstress and the allied nations in what she had revealed: "We could protect you, here. Indeed, if these employers still believed that you were working for them—"

"No, lady. There may be some who thrive telling lies, and are happy to grow wealthy through them. I am not such a person. And to tell lies in two different directions? No. I cannot." She looked down, shaking her head as if that negation might erase all that she had done. "I did not seek this employment. But after leaving Recife, my sister and mother succumbed to a fever. To survive on my own, I had to choose between two mortal sins: lying or harlotry." She shrugged. "I chose this. I thought it was safer. It is not. Nor did I see how it would become a tool whereby others—so many others—were killed."

"And now?"

She shrugged again. "And now I have money and have learned a respectable skill. It is one with which I may find employment anywhere. Garments, sails, even sacks: wherever two pieces of cloth require joining, there I may earn enough to survive. There are many such places within a week's sail of here. And more than that I may not tell you."

"Thank you, Mistress . . ." Anne Cathrine trailed to a halt, smiled. "I still do not know your name."

"As is best. And thank you, kind lady, for allowing me to depart."

Anne Cathrine tried to think of some appeal that might get her to change her mind, to remain to bear witness against the men she'd named and the enemies who had employed her. But those nascent schemes faltered before Anne Cathrine's deep reluctance to jeopardize another woman because of deeds that she might never have committed, had she not run afoul of the machinations of men.

And by the time that inner struggle had been resolved, the seamstress had fled out the door and into the night.

Chapter 50

Near Nezpique Bayou, Louisiana

Larry Quinn stared at the tall rotary drill rig. He listened, one ear cocked in its direction.

"You hear that?" asked Mason Chaffin, the project manager, his eyes wide.

Larry heard what sounded like a subterranean granite whale suppressing a belch.

"There! That! You hear it?" This time, the question came from Jennifer Garrett, who'd led the final survey. Morgan Hart, who oversaw most of the hands-on construction and running of the rig, was leaning over her, grinning wildly.

Larry stared at his fellow up-timers, who, until now, had mostly complained about insects when they weren't complaining about having too few hands to move all the gear for the rig and to construct the derrick. Now, they were suddenly like kids at Christmas, standing fifty yards away from the drill site.

The granite whale released a second, more modest burp.

"You mean *that*?" Larry asked. "That's *it*?"

"That's it." Mason seemed disappointed in Larry's response.

"Well...damn, guys: where's the excitement in *that*?"

Mason, who'd been a surveyor and civil engineer up-time, sighed. "Larry, when it comes to oil wells, you don't want excitement. Kind of like your time in the military. Excitement is the sign that something is going *wrong*."

"Oh," said Larry. "Oh," he repeated because he'd never thought about it, and because he was still kind of disappointed. "So...no gusher?" A thrilling, Hollywood montage of fountains of oil, blasting upward toward wide-open Texas skies streamed unbidden past his mind's eye.

"No gusher," Mason grumbled, wiping the back of his neck with a sopping handkerchief, the funk of bayou foliage stronger than the faint petroleum smell. "We don't want a gusher. Anything but that. Before coming over here, did you ever read about the disasters connected with gushers?"

Larry shook his head. "You mean, like, fires?"

Jennifer nodded; she seemed the most ready to forgive Larry for his lack of excitement. "Fires. Major environmental damage. And so, so wasteful. You've heard of Spindletop, the Texas oil field a couple hundred miles in that direction?" Her index finger jabbed westward. "Totally uncontrolled gusher. That was what they—well, now 'we'—call a blowout. Didn't have a way to cap it until the pressure let up by spewing out oil—to the tune of one hundred thousand barrels a day. For nine days. That's probably more oil, right there, than we've pulled out of Weitze field since we got here."

Morgan nodded. "Yep. That's why we've been going so slowly. Particularly since Tuesday."

Larry had a vague recollection that they'd told him something about *garblegarblegarble* and the well on that day. "So, what happened on Tuesday, again?"

Mason's brow was a straight, disapproving line. "We started getting some sand and then a little oil in the drilling mud. And then the drill string got lighter."

"What?"

Morgan took over. "It's the early sign of what's called the 'kick.'" He used his hands to demonstrate: one fist stacked on the other, the top pushing down while the bottom pushed up. "The upward pressure being exerted by the oil and gas and anything else down there resists the weight of the string—the drill shaft—that's pushing down from the top. So up here, that makes the string seem lighter."

Mason couldn't seem to keep his grump going; his voice sounded excited again, even if his face didn't show it. "When that started happening, we were pretty sure we were getting close. So Morgan did a machinery check, made sure the blowout preventers were all in place and ready. And now, finally, the oil is starting to come in. We've got the pressure balanced pretty well, which is the real trick at this stage. The first few hundred barrels are likely to have a lot of junk in them; sand, grit, water. Probably no salt, though. The few records we have say they never hit salt here in the Jennings field." He turned and put his hands on Larry's shoulders. "But let me put this in terms that are meaningful to you, son. Your whole secret mission to the Gulf Coast and all the obstacles you overcame? Well: *mission accomplished*."

Well, hell, when you put it like that . . . Larry smiled. "Well, yeah: I'd drink to that!"

If only they had something to drink . . .

Karl Klemm's excited, if distant, voice was the buzzkill that ended his coalescing vision of a cold beer. "Herr Major!"

Larry turned. Karl was as soaked as if he'd just climbed out of the bayou. Sweaty place, Louisiana. You couldn't even tell it was fall.

The young German ran up, breathless. "You must come to the communications shack, Herr Major."

"Jeez, Karl, when are you going to learn to call me Larry?"

"I am sorry. It is difficult. The way I was raised . . . well, I will try. Larry." When he uttered the name, it looked like he was swallowing one of the monstrous palmetto bugs that made Larry feel like he was living on the set of some creepy sci-fi flick. "You must come! Now."

Larry shrugged and started moving, felt the others fall in behind him. "Lead on, Karl."

When they were all done staring at the radio in disbelief, Larry asked. "How the hell are we even getting these signals? We were out of range from halfway across the Gulf. Where the hell is that coming from?"

The wireless operator turned, nodded a salute, shrugged, went back to trying to find the precise frequency.

Karl crossed his arms, thinking, then leaned over the operator's shoulder. "How many repeats?" he asked.

"Twenty. Sometimes we don't get half. It usually takes us about ten of their sends to build the complete message."

Larry frowned. "So, what's the best guess? That The Quill is boosting the signal, but it's still just barely enough to reach us?"

Karl shook his head. His arms were still crossed, a frown still fixed on his face. "No. I think not."

Larry waited for him to think some more, then rolled his eyes. "Karl, what's going on between your ears? What's happening here?"

"What's—? Oh, I beg your pardon. I was considering."

"Considering what?"

"Apologies. I shall explain. The signal is not coming from the St. Eustatius array."

"What?" Larry and the drilling team chorused.

"There are several indicators of this. Firstly, while I have not seen the array myself, I am aware of its basic properties. While its range could be boosted, I am skeptical if it could be done to a degree that would allow it to reach us here."

"Because it's aimed at Europe, not us?"

"Precisely, Herr Major. This is a crude analogy, but the power that would need to be added to produce a geometric increase in the signal as it would be received in Vlissingen would, at best, barely cause an arithmetic increase in the signal strength we receive here."

"So maybe they built a new extension, on the west-facing slope of The Quill?" Jennifer guessed.

"Possible, but unlikely. It would be an immense undertaking, very expensive. More importantly, it is not needed at this time. Rather, I think something much simpler and—for now—advantageous has been done."

Larry leaned forward. "Stop the mystery theater, Karl: what's been done?"

"I suspect that Admiral Tromp and Commodore Cantrell have adopted the expedient of a dedicated relay ship."

Quinn smacked his forehead. "Holy shit, of course." Then he frowned. "Wait: so why didn't they do this before?"

Karl gestured to the begrimed experts from the drilling team. "It is implicit in the news they brought, Herr Major. This idea had been raised before, but there were insufficient ships to spare. There were not even enough for basic shipping or defense."

He nodded at the group again. "However, the news that arrived with the rig, of La Flota and cooperation with distant islands like Bermuda and Barbados, suggests that the shortage of hulls is at an end. And wires strung along the tall masts of one large galleon could accomplish what we are witnessing today." He shrugged. "With a little time and a map, I could narrow down the area in which they are probably operating."

"That won't be necessary. But, hey: we can signal back now, right?"

Karl straightened. "Firstly, Herr Major, I very much doubt the ship is in range to send signals back to The Quill Array; it only receives them and sends them on to us. But more important, I strongly—*strongly*—advise against sending any signals. If I may confirm my suspicion?"

Larry blinked. "Uh, sure."

Karl turned sharply to the radio operator. "Have you been instructed or invited to reply?"

The operator shook his head.

Karl turned just as sharply back toward Larry. "Headquarters means for us to maintain radio silence."

"What? Why?"

"Herr Major, it was no different in your time; it is by sending a response that you may be located. The same principles apply."

"Yeah, but we had electronic warfare units working on both sides of the border, and directional finders and . . ." Larry slowed to a halt. Then: "Of course. Directional finders."

Morgan scowled. "C'mon, Larry. That's bonkers. The Spanish probably don't even have any radios in the New World yet. And they sure as hell don't have directional finders."

Larry shook his head. "Mason, if they have radios here, then they *do* have directional finders. Of a sort. Picture this: every once in a while a Spanish ship passes within a hundred miles of here, maybe two hundred. And their radio just happens to be on and scanning frequencies when the folks on the relay ship are sending to us. First time it happens? The Spanish write it off as a . . . a freak of nature."

"Anomalous meteorological conditions," Karl supplied quietly.

"Right," affirmed Larry, nodding. "That. But then it happens a second and a third time. So they start plotting where it's been happening. And—"

"And then they start drawing the same circle on a map that Karl was just talking about," Mason said, nodding.

"Yup," Larry agreed. "Karl, you have made your point. In spades. Inform all the radio operators: do *not* reply until asked to do so."

"Herr Major, if I may suggest an emendation: they are not to reply until asked *in code*."

Larry smiled at his new up-timer oil experts and

hooked a thumb over his shoulder at Karl. "That right there is my number one weapon. Do it like you said it, Karl!"

"I shall pass the word immediately." Klemm proffered a strip of paper. "Also, here is the completed content of the first coded message, Herr Major."

"Karl? I'm Larry. *Larry*. Repeat after me: *Laaa-rreeee*."

Karl smiled as though he was being pinched. Hard. "Yes, sir. We are receiving another coded transmission now. It is in a blind code, I believe."

"A what?" asked Jennifer.

"You probably have another name for it, Ms. Garrett. The message's prefix indicates that it is not a cipher. These are words, or a phrase, which are sent in the clear, but have special meanings, known only to those with a codebook defining what each of those words or phrases means. We call it a 'blind code' because deciphering it still does not provide any useful knowledge. Indeed, in some cases, dummy, or meaningless, code words are sent just to give the enemy the impression that there may be an ongoing operation, when in fact—"

Quinn closed his eyes since he could not close his ears. "Karl?"

"Yes, Herr Ma—Larry?"

"Get me the incoming transmission as soon as all of it has been received."

"*Jawowl* . . . eh, at once, Herr Ma—" He looked like he was passing a kidney stone. "Larry."

Morgan looked over Larry's shoulder at the first message and frowned. "What the hell is all that?"

"Coordinates. Codes for rules of engagement. Target date for mission completion."

"What mission?" asked Mason suspiciously.

Larry shook his head, pushed back at the rising annoyance. "Grantville says we're to send a contingent to search for the Lake Salvador oil and gas deposits, just a day's walk from the banks of the Mississippi. Not too far from New Orleans, apparently. And they're asking us to cajole the Ishak into helping us." He laughed.

"And that's funny . . . ?" Jennifer asked with a frown.

"In the worst possible way. Best I've been able to figure out, the Ishak are not exactly on friendly terms with those particular neighbors." He crumpled up the message, was tempted to throw it into the soggy weeds. "Damn it, we have enough to do here. Hell, they don't even know you guys have finally hit oil and the big shots in Grantville are already shoving us at the next site?"

Mason took Larry aside; Morgan and Jennifer had become interested in the ongoing attempts to sort out the incoming signals from background noise. The older man lowered his voice. "Larry, I don't think this is just about the oil. It's about the Mississippi."

Larry nodded. "Yeah, I get that. The North American arterial system in the form of a single river. But what is Ed Piazza thinking? That if—well, *when*—the Spanish tweak to us here, and then get an inkling of what we're doing, they're going to make a grab for these oil fields up near New Orleans?"

"Sure. That, and put a roadblock between us and the rest of the continental U.S."

"Well, not the 'continental U.S.': that's never gonna exist in the here and now. But yeah, I see what you mean. But since this continent sure as hell isn't ours, what's the motivation? To keep the Spanish from grabbing their own oil field? Denying them access to the interior's resources? Or just us protecting the indigenous peoples?"

Mason's smile was rueful. "How about answer D: all of the above?"

Larry glanced at him. "You know something I don't. They talked to you. About what comes next."

Mason shrugged. "You know how this works, Larry. You're not the only one who gets orders they can't discuss."

Quinn looked off into the mists. "Yeah, I was afraid you'd say that. But let's say the real answer is D, all of the above. How the hell do we achieve all that with this small group?"

Mason looked away, evasive. "Well . . . we probably don't do it at all. At least not yet."

Quinn frowned. "That has the stink of shitty orders given for shitty reasons. Come clean, Mason, at least on this much: what's the concept of operations? How are we supposed to achieve 'all of the above'?"

Mason shrugged; the gesture was not entirely relaxed or comfortable. "Recruit the locals."

"Why? So they can be bullet sponges for the Spanish?" This didn't sound like Piazza, or even Stearns. "Who's pushing this agenda?"

"All the leadership, so far as I know. And the idea is not to have the locals fight the Spanish. They're to come inform us when the Spanish begin nosing around. We're going to do the fighting."

Quinn looked over his shoulder at the meager camp. "Oh, yeah, that's not anything like suicide."

Mason sighed. "Look, we don't have perfect answers right now. Particularly not with the crap that's starting back home."

Larry frowned. "And what crap would that be?"

Mason leaned closer, lowered his voice. "The Ottomans."

Larry leaned away. "No shit? Well, that explains why everyone's still acting like we're as confident as church mice and as overextended as a rubber band in a tug of war. Because that's pretty much our situation if the Turks are on the march."

"And they have been," Mason added quietly. "For months."

Jennifer came trotting back. "Larry, Karl's got complete copy on the second message."

"Well, that was quick." They started back to the comm shack. "Better reception, this time?"

"No. Still a lot of atmospherics ruining the signal. But it was really short. So the fifteen passes went pretty quickly."

Larry nodded just before they met Karl as he exited the shack, Morgan right behind him. "Major, this is most peculiar."

"What's the code?"

He frowned. "I don't know. It is only four characters. C, colon, C, R." He looked at Larry. "C:CR: what does this mean?"

Larry suddenly felt quite cool despite the heat and humidity. In fact, he felt a chill run out from his spine along his shoulders. "This is one of about a dozen Emergency Contingency Codes."

Karl nodded solemnly. "May I ask what it stands for?"

"Well, the message prefix didn't lie; it is what you call a 'blind code.' The Emergency Contingencies are only initials, though. This one," Quinn sighed, "is 'Contingency: Class Reunion.'"

"'Class Reunion'?" Morgan repeated with a laugh. "What the hell does that mean?"

"It means exactly what it says, Mr. Hart. It's telling us that there's a special event and we've all got to go back home for it."

"Yeah, but what—?"

Larry Quinn was on the move. He stuck his head in the radio shack. "Signalman, immediate send to Captain Haraldsen. *Courser* and *Harrier* are weighing anchor in twenty-four hours. Coordinates for course will be relayed soonest. All ops and provisioning teams are to be recalled immediately. Except wood-gathering parties. They are to remain active until the last possible hour.

"*Patentia*, the jacht *Vogelstruis*, and USE frigate *Svarta Hunden* are to maneuver into the Lower Mud Pond, staying in the deepest anchorage, close to the Gulf."

He turned to openmouthed Jennifer Garrett. "You're the expert on crude oil separation, right?"

"Well, I'm not really an exp—okay; yes, that's me," she gulped.

"Have you separated the first flow from the well?"

"Just today. It's hard to say if—"

"I need you to separate out as much as can be used for combustibles in the next twenty-two hours. Your operations have priority over all others."

"Are you looking for bunker oil, Larry?"

"I'm looking for anything in which we can soak wood so that it will burn hotter and faster." His eyes went to Morgan. "How much lumber do you have left over from building the derrick?"

"Uh, about a whole second derrick's worth."

"I need half of that on the steam launch in two hours. I need it out of the Nezpique and into the

Mermentau by day's end. I need it alongside *Courser* and *Harrier*, ready for transfer, by morning."

"Yeah, but—!"

"And Karl?"

"Sir?"

Larry smiled. "You need to brief your assistants on how to take over for you. You have twelve hours. After that, you are on the next boat back to *Courser*."

"Sir? But . . . but my job is here!"

"Karl, you don't have just one job. Hell, you're our Renaissance man."

Karl frowned. "According to most of your up-time academics, the Renaissance would now be considered over. This is the Age of Enlightenment."

Larry laughed. "Better still. Even more than I knew, you are a man of your time. And just the man I need. Your work here is done. Ready for a new adventure?"

"I am not sure."

"Well, it should be a welcome change. You'll be using both new and old skills."

Karl frowned. "Given my past, I remain unsure that I find the sound of that appealing."

"Unsurety and change are the only human constants, Karl. As a man of science, I'm sure you can't argue with that. So you might say this is just changing your current collection of unsureties for a whole new set of them. And here's the bonus: on this new adventure? No mosquitos. Hell, no bugs at all."

Karl straightened. "I am ready, Herr Major!"

Larry patted Karl on the shoulder with a cheery nod. "I knew you would be!"

And, silently: *Oh, if you only* knew *how ready you are . . .*

Chapter 51

Staubles Bay and Fort St. Patrick, Trinidad

Bram Ditmerszoon stared westward over the Bay of Paria and pushed aside his plate of cassava loaves, smoked goat, and papaya. It was sound food, to be certain, but it was also horribly predictable, since that is what the Nepoia brought to the main garrison at Port-of-Spain every week. Without fail. And without variance.

The culinary boredom that Bram and his five fellow coast watchers experienced was, however, the lesser part of his food-related concerns. His deepest worry was the dozens, maybe hundreds, of Spanish prisoners clustered on nearby Nelson Island, survivors from last year's Battle of Grenada. It was possible that they might ultimately be driven to desperation and attempted escape, since they enjoyed even less variety in their diet. Granted, it was unlikely they would get very far. Although the Nepoia delivered the food to Port-of-Spain, from whence the newly planted Dutch garrison could effect its delivery to the Spanish on the now denuded island, those natives never returned home immediately. Instead, in shifts, they squatted by the shore and stared out at Nelson Island. They had agreed that the Spanish would be allowed to stay there, unmolested, until a means of repatriating them was worked out. But the Nepoia had endured many decades of slavery and abuse at the hands of landowning hidalgos, and so, were not content to rely upon six Dutchmen stationed over a mile away on a headland to monitor their foes via a spyglass. Accordingly, the natives had taken to crouching in the underbrush just off the shore, spears and bows in hand, waiting—perhaps hoping—for one of the Spanish to attempt an escape. So far, none had tried.

Fortunately, overseeing Spanish prisoners was only a secondary job for Bram and his small detachment from the garrison in Port-of-Spain. Their primary duty was to maintain a day and night watch on the narrow northernmost expanses of the Bay of Paria, those which communicated with the Dragon's Mouth and the Caribbean beyond. It was through that stretch of water, visible from their four-hundred-foot perch, that a Spanish fleet must come.

And so, once again fulfilling that dull, uneventful duty with a bored sigh, Bram snatched up the spyglass with which they watched for the Cartagena armada and aimed it westward, seeking the thin green rim that marked the Paria Peninsula on the other side of the deep blue bay.

But on that wave-stippled expanse, a scattering of black waterbugs topped by white pennants was entering the northern extent of his field of vision. And those bugs were precisely what, at this range, ships looked like. Big ones. At least twenty-five of them and all headed south.

"Gerlach!" Bram shouted. "Gerlach! Are you at the radio?"

A sleepy voice answered. "Yes. I'm manning the radio. In my hammock."

"Damn your lazy ass! Get on your feet and crank up the wireless. The Cartagena fleet is coming through the Dragon's Mouth!"

Fort St. Patrick, Trinidad

O'Bannon joined them on the second floor of the blockhouse. "The Spanish will be here by tomorrow noon. The *Tropic Surveyor* and jachts hiding up in Scotland Bay have received the message as well and are setting out now."

"And will they beat the Spanish here?" asked Ann Koudsi, who found war much more frightening than oil wells.

The Dutch admiral named Cornelis Jol, but whom everyone called Peg Leg (or its Dutch equivalent, Houtebeen), smiled. "Those ships are not supposed to beat the Spanish here. Not quite." He looked away without offering any further clarification. "When will you launch the balloon?"

At a nod from Hugh O'Donnell, sprightly Tearlach Mulryan answered with a smile. "Not until we can see them clearly."

"Doesn't that rather defeat the purpose of observing them?" asked the big, Danish-born Dutch captain Hjalmar van Holst.

Hugh shook his head. "No. Because in this case, we're not using it for spotting at a distance but for tactical information. If they knew we have the balloon, they might take steps to minimize its effectiveness, to adopt a formation that gives as few clues to their intents as possible. This way, if they do not see it until they are within a few miles, it will be too late to change or disguise their plans. But we will still be in a position to see when and where they are sending landing parties, and the like. If they are trying to outflank us, we shall know. If they are landing a second wave of troops, again, we shall know. And if they have spotted your ships where they are hidden and are separating some of their own to engage you, we can use the wireless to alert you. You will have complete information on how many ships, how many guns each, how fast, and on what heading."

Peg Leg nodded. "Yes. That will be the important information in this battle. Given that the greater part of our little fleet is hiding to the southwest, behind the little nub of land the maps label as Point Fortin, we'll need that coordination to know exactly when to weigh anchor and join the battle. And hopefully, we'll catch them by surprise once they've all navigated closer to land to duel with your cannon."

Doyle, the engineer, smiled, big teeth dominating his thin face. "Yes, I'm eager to have them make that mistake, given all the work we've done pre-ranging the guns and plotting their precise impact points."

"Their what?" asked Ulrich, who seemed tense as he stood beside Ann in his wildcatting coveralls.

"The guns of our fortifications will start this battle waiting to engage targets at preset ranges," explained O'Bannon. He gestured at Doyle and the other officers of the Wild Geese. "You see, when these fellows took possession of the artillery you salvaged from the defeated galleons at the Battle of Grenada Passage, they started calculating where they themselves would position ships to bombard the fort. Then they pre-targeted those areas. That's why you've heard them firing all the captured Spanish pieces for which they've dug a battery into the braced earthworks before the fort and the ravelin that extends beyond it to the east."

Ulrich shrugged. "I am certainly no soldier. I simply believed that they were firing the guns to make sure they still functioned."

"Well, that too," commented Doyle, who was making minute corrections to the many maps and charts spread out on the table before them, "but it was equally important to see just where they'd hit, given a fixed battery position, a precise measure of powder, and a precise weight of ball."

Ann frowned. "'Fixed position'? You mean, the guns can't be moved?"

"Oh no," Doyle said with a smile, "we'll be able to work them about again after the first discharge. The damn iron beasts will jump off their chocks, fer sure. Nothing less than the hand of God could hold them still when they go off. But the first time they speak in defense of our walls—well, let's just say they've been waiting for weeks to be called upon to do just that. And if they don't hit right away, we'll have a good measure from which to adjust when we roll them back into their marked positions."

Ann looked around the council of war and asked the question that had been gnawing at her since she and Ulrich had been summoned from the oil separation facilities. "There's one part of all this that I don't understand. Why are we"—she included Ulrich in her gesture—"here at all? For safety?"

Hugh glanced at Peg Leg. They shared a sly smile. "No, Ann," answered O'Donnell. "We called you here to share your expertise and your resources."

A sharp, surprised laugh flew out of Ann's mouth before she could stop it. "Our expertise? So, you want us to pump some oil for you? In the middle of a battle?"

Hugh's smile only grew more sly. "In a manner of speaking, Ms. Koudsi, in a manner of speaking..."

Ann Koudsi wiped the back of one oil-reeking hand across her brow as she picked up her empty bucket. She turned her back on the timber-and-plank-littered expanse just east of Fort St. Patrick and started walking back toward its walls.

Ulrich, waiting patiently in front of the berm-fronted trench line that ran from and extended the south-leaning curve of the earthwork lunette, smiled at her. "You are done, then? Finally?"

For the first time in half an hour, Ann looked around. She was, in fact, the last of her crew to leave the dumping ground that had started as the graveyard of ship timbers that had washed ashore after the first Battle of Fort St. Patrick. She also discovered that the half hour which had passed since her last check of the area had, in fact, been closer to two hours. She smiled back at Ulrich. "I'm a determined woman. When I set my mind to something, I get it done."

Ulrich's smile suddenly became private, reminded her of similar smiles in their shared bedroom. "Yes," he commented. "How well I know that."

"Yeah," she smirked. "And you love it."

"I most certainly do. As I love you. Which is why you are leaving this place. Now."

"Okay," she agreed. "But why the urgency?"

"Because," he said, pointing out into the Bay of Paria, "the Spanish are not as late as we hoped they might be."

Ann turned north and drew in so sharp a breath that she once again became painfully aware of the acrid petroleum stink in the air all around them.

She had been updated on the precise numbers and types of the Spanish hulls—eighteen galleons and galleoncetes, five apparent transport or supply ships, and a single patache—but had not imagined that they would look so daunting when they appeared, all at once. "That's a lot of ships," she gulped. Not compared to all the ones she had seen in Oranje Bay, perhaps... but those had been *friendly*.

Ulrich nodded, motioned toward the earthen glacis that now shielded the lower two thirds of St. Patrick's palisade. "We should get inside with the rest of the workers." She heard a resigned finality in his voice.

"What? And stay in there? That's where the Spanish are going to be aiming their guns!"

"True. But they are also sure to land hundreds of troops, who may rove anywhere once they come ashore." He tugged her arm. "Come, Ann. We shall be safer in there than out here."

For the first time in her life, Ann had a sensation that she imagined might be a close cousin to claustrophobia. She held back. "No, I've got to check—"

"The fuses are fine. And the bamboo tubes protecting them have been buried, so you cannot check them without disrupting them." He cupped her chin in his broad hand. "I know you do not wish to be locked inside the walls of the fort." He smiled. "That, too,

is part of who you are. I think it is why every time I
bring up the subject of marriage, you quickly change
the subject: you feel the walls of eternity closing in
around you. But now, this one time, you must put
aside that fear of walls if you are to survive. Please,
Ann: come with me now."

She looked at the field of broken strakes and planks
behind her, then out at the Spanish fleet, then at the
Dutch gunners, hunching behind the immense Spanish
cannon that pointed toward the oncoming sails. She
nodded. "Okay," she said.

Ulrich smiled, started to lead her toward the fort,
found her arm still resisting his pressure to move. He
frowned. "You said okay, did you not?"

She nodded and gulped. "Yes, I said okay. I'm just
trying to get used to the idea. It's hard for me."

"Being in the fort will not be—"

"I'm not talking about the fort," she interrupted.
"I'm talking about marriage. But I think I'm okay
with it, now." Refusing to react to Ulrich's sudden,
flabbergasted smile, she snarled, "Now let's not stand
out here talking. I'll be damned if I become a widow
before I get to be a wife."

For young Tearlach Mulryan, who was the senior
aviator among the Wild Geese, being aloft in the balloon had become second nature. Indeed, on peaceful
days, when the air was clear and the winds mild, he
caught himself nodding off in the harness, lulled to
sleep by the distant murmur of the waves and the
serene blue that was both below and above him.

But he had no problems with drowsiness at the
moment. He signaled for McGillicuddy, chief of the

ground crew, to stop playing out the line when, for the fourth time today, he reached five hundred feet. Experience had shown that even the best shots found it all but impossible to hit a man at that height with down-time weapons. Projectiles lost their power quickly when fired at so steep an angle, and correcting fire was problematical. Even the smallest variation in weight of the ball, or the amount or fineness of powder in the charge were variables that confounded precise adjustments over multiple attempts at such a target.

If the Spanish were interested in experimenting with such long-range, high-angle marksmanship, they had not given any sign of it. As if thoroughly unconcerned with the presence of the balloon, they had set about their business with a supremely confident disregard for any such minor surprises. When they had reached the two-mile mark, they had shortened their canvas, slowing and assessing the earthworks that had been thrown up before and to the east of the fort. Then they had fully unfurled their sails once again and resumed their approach.

Three of their transport/supply noas lumbered off even further to the east, making for the promontory bearing the name Pitch Point. Separated from the fort by slightly more than half a mile, there was a strand just west of it that offered optimally shallow landing conditions for longboats filled with armored troops. In the weeks of planning prior to this day, it had been presumed that the inevitable Spanish attackers would choose that very spot for that very purpose, and after much deliberation, it had been decided not to contest a landing there. Struggling in the open field against the presumably superior numbers of the Spanish was, as Colonel O'Donnell had put it, fighting the enemy's battle. The two hundred and thirty Wild Geese and one hundred and eighty Dutch soldiers and artillerists would shelter in their defenses, a (hopefully) tempting target for the gunnery officers aboard the approaching galleons.

But that plan had presupposed at least a reasonable wind from the northeast or the east. That would have allowed Peg Leg's flotilla of seven ships—his own *Achilles*, van Holst's *Vereenigte Provintien*, *Amsterdam*, *Sampson*, *Overijssel*, *Thetis*, and Jochim Gijszoon's jacht *Kater*—to catch the wind in a close reach and head northward. They would then have pushed a mile past the headland that was the fort's western flank, Point Galba, and come around through the wind, close-hauled as they backtracked southeast to engage the Spanish ships that would presumably be crowded close against the land to conduct a bombardment.

But today the wind was uncharacteristically blowing from the northwest, which forced Peg Leg's small fleet to tack aggressively just to get around Point Galba. Consequently, although it had been three hours since the Spanish topgallants had peeked over the horizon, Peg Leg still had an hour of tricky sailing left before he could round Point Galba, and, turning it, head directly into battle. A northwest wind meant he'd at least have the consolation of winds on a broad reach when he turned toward his foe, and so, unexpectedly gave him the weather gauge, albeit narrowly so.

However, for any of that to matter, Peg Leg would still have to arrive in time. Originally, it had been hoped that his fleet would worry the Spanish enough to compel them to abandon any plans to land troops.

But with his flotilla so badly delayed, the burning question had become whether or not the Spanish shelling would sufficiently reduce Fort St. Patrick to allow their landing forces to carry it, despite the surprises O'Bannon and Doyle were waiting to spring on them.

The Spanish were apparently impatient to put their own rather predictable plans into action. Arrayed in two echelons of ten and eight warships respectively, the five lead galleons were now cruising within three hundred yards of the steep twelve-foot drop that separated Fort St. Patrick from the Bay of Paria. They reefed sails as they approached the positions from which they meant to conduct their bombardment. Which were, in two cases, precisely the positions that the Irish and Dutch officers had anticipated.

While the Spanish had no doubt predicted that the guns of the fort would respond to their attack, and had perhaps even predicted that their enemy had guessed the positions from which they might do so, they had apparently not foreseen or detected that the guns arrayed along the earthworks, the ravelin, and even the facing corner of the lunette were nothing less than forty-two-pounders. The roar of these twelve pieces and the sudden storm cloud of smoke they sent tumbling outward toward the galleons seemed to hush the tableau beneath Mulryan's feet into a moment of stunned stillness. Then, frenetic activity seemed to start everywhere at once.

Three of the twelve balls found their marks on the two galleons that had been targeted, from which planks and strakes flew upward. The sail handlers on those galleons, and their three unattacked fellows went back to work with a will, unfurling their sails yet

again to catch the wind and carry them further out
and, at least for now, out of the action. Meanwhile,
the Dutch gunners were busy swabbing their pieces
and readying the next charges. The two nao that had
almost arrived at Pitch Point hastily began lowering
their long boats. The two others were loitering at
the six-hundred-yard mark, evidently waiting for the
outcome of the first landing force to determine where
they should put their own ashore. But at the sound
of the fort's guns, they came about slowly, putting
more distance between themselves and the shore.
The telegraph clattered at Mulryan's side, requesting
updated observations of what Commodore Cantrell
called "the battlespace."

Mulryan tapped his reply almost as easily and famil-
iarly as if he had been speaking it aloud, watching as
the second echelon of Spanish ships seemed to react to
the allied cannon fire as well. That made little sense,
since those eight warships were still almost a half mile
offshore. But then Mulryan saw that their reaction was
in response to an entirely different stimulus: *Tropic
Surveyor* and her two escorts, the jachts *Leeuwinne*
and *Noordsterre*, had now appeared on the horizon,
directly behind the Spanish, running fresh and fast
with the wind.

The ships in the Spaniards' second echelon broke
into two parts. The smaller element, three galleons,
actually bore closer to the shore, but stopped short
of joining the first echelon. They were apparently
now a closely positioned rearguard. Meanwhile, the
larger part of the second echelon, three galleons and
two galleoncetes, came about and struggled to find at
least a beam-reaching breeze with which they could

make northerly progress. No mean feat for square-rigged vessels, although the galleoncetes clearly had the easier time of it. However, if their mission was to intercept and defeat the three enemy ships which had appeared to their rear and which possessed more suitable rigging and the weather gauge, they had little choice but to struggle northward however they might. And as Tearlach watched, the three galleons of that group fell into irons, losing way entirely.

Mulryan frowned. If the northbound Spanish ships were now in irons—

He scanned the galleons more nearly below him. They were now turning their prows more confidently to the northwest and began shelling the fort from almost four hundred yards range. The Spanish patache, which was patrolling near Point Galba, now filled her sails directly from the north.

God's balls! Mulryan blasphemed silently as he sent the observation swiftly down the wire to the ground station. The timing could not be worse for the wind to shift and come straight out of the north. Although that would help Peg Leg pass Point Galba a little sooner, he would no longer have the weather gauge when he rounded it. Both he and the Spanish would have the wind abeam. Which meant that after their long delay, the Dutch ships would not even enjoy much maneuver advantage when they confronted the Spanish. And if *Tropic Surveyor*'s light squadron did not engage the five northbound Spaniards soon enough, they could come about and add themselves back to the force that would be confronting Peg Leg.

Mulryan put the spyglass to his eye, twisted westward in his harness. Less than half a mile from Point

Galba now, the six warships and one jacht of Cornelis Jol's command were nearing that point at which there would be a clear line of sight between them and the patrolling patache. Which would surely signal the eight remaining warships addressing the fort.

The Spanish would likely break off from their bombardment, and if joined by the small three-galleon rearguard from the second echelon, that would give them nine galleons and two galleoncetes. And if the two galleons that had been wounded by the fort's guns swung back in, Peg Leg would be outnumbered almost two to one and facing a weight of shot that was three times his own. Mulryan lowered his spyglass and suddenly felt sick low in his stomach.

That was the same moment at which the Spanish musketeers in the highest rigging of their ships began filling the air beneath him with small, zipping balls of lead.

Well, he thought, *I guess everything is going to hell all at once.*

Lieutenant Juan de Somovilla Tejada did not like close-up soldiering, which was why he had become an engineer. But not a mere sapper, no. Hidalgo status and a modicum of silver had ensured him of education sufficient to perform those rudimentary mathematics needed to oversee, rather than merely physically effect, sieges and both the construction and destruction of fortifications.

But today, off the coast of Trinidad, his so-called friend Gregorio de Castellar y Mantilla had insisted that he land and personally survey and assess the fortifications at Pitch Lake. So, after having managed to spend years as a soldier who fought wars solely from tents containing map tables and ample supplies of sherry, he had at last come to the scenario he had always dreaded: being within musket shot of his enemies.

Beneath him, the longboat bucked as it crossed the low bar that sheltered the shallows of the beach beside Point Pitch. "Pardon, Lieutenant," offered the boat's pilot, "I am not familiar with these waters."

Somovilla grunted, then started as several Dutch guns around the fort spoke again, in near-unison. *Coño! Those are* our *guns, forty-two-pounders! Where did the heathen ass-lickers get them?*

And they had once again found the range. One of the two already damaged galleons, having lagged behind as her crew struggled to repair two snapped mainstays, took two more balls in her portside gun decks. One barely penetrated, but the other broke through her timbers, causing God only knew what carnage and chaos within.

As the white sand beach rushed at him and his seasoned troops held their pieces high in the anticipation of entering a few feet of water, he looked back at the nao that had landed them and saw her coming about. She was sending signals urgently, apparently in response to flags from one of the ships preparing to resume shelling the fort. But the glare from the sun-shimmering water was too severe for him to make out the message, and then the longboat tugged to a soft, grinding halt.

"Out!" yelled his adjutant and company leader, Sergeant Casañas, to the armored troops. "Run the ten paces into the trees and then take cover! Look for natives and kill anything that moves. We've no friends left on this part of Trinidad." He turned to Somovilla, stared quizzically as the men around them leaped into the low surf, a few brandishing outdated matchlocks over their heads, blowing on glowing, wrist-wrapped match cords to keep them from being doused by the spray. "Sir, the men and I require your orders."

"Of course," Somovilla replied. Annoyed—at the unexpected unfolding of the battle, his supposed friend Gregorio de Castellar y Mantilla, and life in general—he threw one leg over the side and into the surf. "Have the men find the game trail that is said to run along this coast. We shall wait for the boats to complete their second trips before moving toward our objective."

Casañas shielded his eyes with his gauntleted hand, scanned the nearby waters, frowned. "That will delay us an hour, at least, Lieutenant."

"Then it will be an hour," snapped Somovilla as he entered the surf. "None of us know this land. All our enemies do, and have had the opportunity to set traps and ambushes. We shall not run into them piecemeal and not until we have our full strength."

The sergeant saluted and looked relieved, probably not so much at the plan, Somovilla conjectured, as at the decisive tone he had used. Spanish sergeants liked being given orders by someone who sounded certain that they were the right orders to give. That the orders themselves might be disastrous was quite beside the point.

But not to Somovilla, who stared into the jungle and saw in it the certainty of more of the surprises that the Dutch and their allies had obviously prepared for them this day.

Chapter 52

Fort St. Patrick, Trinidad

Tearlach Mulryan watched *Tropic Surveyor* brush past one of the galleoncetes which had been sent to intercept her, discharge a broadside, and then swiftly heel over as soon as her stern passed the Spaniard. The responding fire missed, falling behind the speeding frigate-built bark or splashing into the water to either side of her. Meanwhile, her two escorting jachts darted in between the other Spanish ships, tempting them into perilously close-hauled positions in order to return broadsides at the swift craft. Although the speedy northern contingent of the fleet under the Swede Tryggve Stiernsköld had been tasked primarily to pull Spanish hulls away from the main fight before the fort, it seemed quite possible that they might inflict some damage of their own. The galleoncete which had come under *Tropic Surveyor*'s guns had been hit by multiple balls and no small amount of chain shot. Several of her shrouds were down, and her portside ratlines were shredded.

Mulryan sighed, made himself swing his glass westward to what he knew would be a far less cheering sight.

He was not surprised. Peg Leg Jol's small contingent of ships had finally come to grips with the Spaniards who had been near the fort and who had since pulled away from it. In one sense, that was good news, because the Spanish bombardment had been short and largely ineffectual. One ball had blown a forty-two-pounder in the ravelin off her carriage, apparently killing most of her Dutch crew. But otherwise, the allies' ground defenses were virtually undiminished.

However, so short a bombardment had not been part of the plan, nor had the early discharge at the Spanish ships. O'Donnell and Jol had wanted the Spanish settled in to shell the fort when Peg Leg came sweeping around Galba Point, and so, take them by surprise with the wind abeam and ultimately in a broad reach as they turned into their foes. But with the wind having blown against Jol, surprise had been impossible, to say nothing of swift and decisive maneuver. And so O'Bannon had probably fired his battery early with the hope of disabling ships, since he knew the Dutch were no longer moving quickly enough to pin the Spanish in against the shore, surprise notwithstanding. And the two ships that O'Bannon's artillerists had savaged were indeed nursing their wounded rigging by continuing to move away from, not toward, engagement with the Dutch, so that at least was helpful.

But it seemed like it could not possibly be helpful enough. The picket patache had run before the Dutch lead ship, Gijszoon's *Kater*, which reluctantly gave chase. That pulled him far enough out of position to expose the flank of the Dutch van to the two Spanish galleoncetes, but still did not allow him to catch and trade shots with the Spanish packet. The *Amsterdam* had moved forward in an attempt to plug that hole. She was now fending off two galleons with her forty-four guns: more than the number carried by either of the Spaniards, but of smaller bore and lighter shot.

Whether it was a trick of the wind around Galba Point or a momentary lapse of seamanship, the Dutch van had also split into two parts. Peg Leg, leading the way to the point, had continued on past it with the *Thetis* in his wake, apparently attempting to court the wind so that, by heading a little further upwind, he would be able to swing around and still have a slight advantage of the weather gauge when he cut southeast to engage the Spanish.

However, Hjalmar van Holst's *Vereenigte Provintien* lost the wind as she came around the point more closely and struggled to make headway. That ultimately brought her bow around to point due east before her sails bit into the wind, still quite close-hauled. Evidently taking this as a sign that the flotilla was to split into a small anvil and an even smaller hammer, the other ships followed van Holst, which slowed them even as they steered into a head-on course toward their Spanish enemies. And now those four Dutch warships found themselves trading blows with six galleons and three more closing in rapidly.

Until, that is, the breeze began to die. In three minutes' time, the imminent naval battle became a feckless combination of sailing and drifting as all the ships—Dutch and Spanish alike—struggled to grab any useful piece of wind. However, the Spanish old-style galleoncetes that had been in the main echelon took advantage of these baffling winds to lower their rarely used oars into the water. They began boxing in Hjalmar's fragmentary van, becoming a screening force between him and Peg Leg's two ships.

The Spanish, possessing longer and heavier guns, and probably thinking themselves to have greater reserves of powder, began firing at two hundred yards range. The several balls that did hit inflicted considerable damage, particularly to the bow of *Overijssel*, but were not in any way crippling. As the Dutch stoically, and practically, held their fire, muskets began sputtering between the closer ships. A few men fell, but again, at such ranges, the effects were minimal.

However, as the ships drew slowly closer together, Mulryan forced himself to send the update that he had anticipated with both fear and loathing:

```
—MESSAGE  BEGINS—
    BOTH  FLEETS  ALMOST  BECALMED  STOP
    SPANISH  HAVE  MORE  SHIPS,  GUNS,
  TROOPS,  POSITIONAL  ADVANTAGES  STOP
    DUTCH  DEFEAT  LIKELY  STOP
    UNCONTESTED  SHELLING  OF  FORT
  COULD  COMMENCE  AT  DAWN  STOP
    GOD'S  LOVE  BE  WITH  US  ALL  STOP
  —MESSAGE  ENDS—
```

Juan de Somovilla Tejada stared across the three hundred yards of mostly open ground from the western edge of the forest and studied the fort the usurpers had constructed. It was not large, but the stockade had been improved by berms that were set five meters out from it, and were given shape and reinforcement by a stout wooden backing. Perched beyond that, and extending past the stockade's eastern extremity was a lower ravelin, built almost to the edge of the drop to the Gulf of Paria. All but two of the captured Spanish guns were mounted in these two positions.

Slightly beyond the eastern end of the ravelin was a lunette, a crescent-moon-shaped free-standing redoubt, that protected the balance of the battery and was, obligingly, without any rear protection other than a low berm that trailed directly inland before tapering away, too low to offer cover. Which meant that eliminating the lunette, or at least chasing its gunners from their pieces, could be achieved by maneuvering to its rear flank, which could be achieved by approaching to approximately eighty yards.

That position would also put Somovilla's attackers approximately one hundred yards from the walls of the eastern wall of the stockade. The enemy's defensive arrangement was thus far from perfect, but on the other hand, they may not have had the time or manpower to do much more than maximize their protection from naval bombardment. Either way, a direct attack on the lunette's eastern flank seemed to be in order.

Happily, the enemy had also used the open land between the fort and the forest as a dumping ground for driftwood beams, strakes, and other wooden debris. Just beyond the midpoint of the three-hundred-yard expanse, partial frames of derelict ships littered the ground like the ribs of so many vulture-picked carcasses. Somovilla nodded approvingly at the rubbish: it was a convenient point at which to take cover and regroup for the final assault. It also offered an excellent position from which to more closely assess any enemy preparations that might lie lower to the ground, unseen behind the heaped piles of distaff wood.

He looked behind, saw the forward edge of his six hundred morion-wearing troops milling ten yards in from the tree line. Casañas, hovering over Somovilla's right shoulder, glanced expectantly at him. "Sergeant," Juan asked, "are our men ready?"

"Yes, sir. There was a bit of confusion after running into the ambushes, but I've sorted that out."

Somovilla nodded curt approval. The usurpers had, predictably, seeded marksmen into the woods, sniping through clear spots in the foliage as the Spanish followed the game trail. Their balls had killed or incapacitated almost twenty of his men. In return, his troops had given chase and dispatched four of the attackers. The Spaniards who had cornered the first of the slain ambushers were taken aback when their quarry turned and unleashed a short but deadly barrage of pistol fire upon his pursuers. The source of that brief shower of lead had been Somovilla's first surprise of the day. It was a pistol such as the engineer had never seen before, having five separate primer-fired barrels bored into a rotating cylinder, each of which held a shot in readiness. Not up-time manufacture from the look of it, but unmistakably up-time influenced.

The second surprise was the appearance of the ambusher himself, whose freckled skin was as pale as his hair was red. A cross around his neck marked him a Christian, and a pocket with crude pictures of the saints annotated in an indecipherable language marked the fellow as either an Irishman, or one of the rarer Scots Catholics. A strange fellow to be fighting against the Spanish, and stranger still to be found doing so on this mostly forsaken island.

But Somovilla had little patience for mysteries and had less time to waste. The original landing plan had simply involved a first wave of troops to overwhelm the presumably rude defenses. Having discerned the prepared fortifications, Captain Gregorio de Castellar had revised that plan, deciding instead that the first landing group should assess the enemy's preparations from greater proximity and also sweep the area around the fort to locate and eliminate any relief or counterattack forces in reserve. That plan did not survive the hour in which it had been formulated, but changed again when the enemy's battery spoke in the rolling, thunderous voices of captured Spanish forty-two-pounders. Now Somovilla was charged with disabling or disrupting the batteries, starting with those in the somewhat vulnerable lunette and then pressing on along behind the ravelin, rolling up the artillerists there. And all of that meant closing with the enemy.

"Sergeant."

"Sir?"

"I want our fastest men as a skirmish line of fifty, leading the rest. They are to be carrying swords and pistols so that they are only lightly encumbered and may clear any enemy who may be behind that debris in a short, close fight."

"Yes, sir. And the rest of us?"

"We follow those skirmishers at a range of fifty yards, pieces loaded. Our first objective is to reach the driftwood barrier and take cover. Once there, we will more closely observe the enemy positions and decide upon a plan of attack. Ready the men."

Casañas gestured sharply to the less senior sergeants, who passed the gesture quickly along the tree line. At various points, more lightly armed and armored men, most of them quite fit, moved a step beyond the main lines. They looked toward their sergeants for the order to charge.

Casañas nodded at Somovilla. "We are ready, sir."

Somovilla rose to a crouch and shouted, "Then Santiago and at them!"

Overhead, Tearlach Mulryan heard a sound as faint as a butterfly spitting. He looked up, saw that another near miss from a group of musketeers below had popped a small hole in the envelope of the balloon. Too tiny a leak to be of any concern, not when he was equipped with Don Michael McCarthy's wondrous and altitude-boosting Coleman hand burner, but worrisome, even so.

Not as worrisome, however, as the naval battle unfolding beneath and before him. Several miles to the north, *Tropic Surveyor* and her two jacht escorts were keeping the Spanish occupied, but only by engaging them directly. At the faintest hint that the lighter allied ships might be showing their heels, the galleons demonstrated that they were more than happy to come around and head for the main fray just east of Point Galba. In consequence, the three allied ships were now continuously trading blows with vessels much larger than they, and had it not been for their superior maneuverability, would have been battered beneath the waves long before now. As it was, the *Noordsterre* had taken a good portion of a galleoncete's full broadside and was trailing smoke and shattered spars.

However, their fight was not in vain, for had those Spaniards been free to join the main combat unmolested, they might well have turned that desperate fight into a complete slaughter. Although the wind had freshened somewhat, it did so from due north, conferring the weather gauge upon neither fleet. Peg Leg Jol's *Achilles* and the *Thetis* were finally bearing down upon the tangled melee of ships closer to the shore and would have both the wind gauge and an advantageous position when they arrived. But that would be at least twenty more minutes, and Mulryan saw quite clearly that in that time, all could be lost.

The Dutch ships were beset from all sides now, and only their masters' superior seamanship and gunnery kept them from falling afoul of a lethal sequence of overlapping Spanish broadsides. But as the fight went on, the superior Spanish numbers were able to further constrain the Dutch maneuver and the ranges between ships were growing ever smaller: a harbinger of the kind of close action and boarding battles that Peg Leg had desperately wanted to avoid.

Only one of the Dutch ships, Hjalmar van Holst's *Vereenigte Provintien*, was a match for the largest Spanish galleon that was still roughly at the center of her fleet. And yet, when a path in the seas between the two stood suddenly clear, and the almost black-sided Spanish forty-eight-gun beast put her prow toward the big Dutch ship, van Holst responded in kind. It was unclear whether he was heading directly toward the Spanish flagship, her somewhat smaller starboard escort, or the one-hundred-and-fifty-yard-wide span of water between the two. The latter would be the worst, naturally, since then Hjalmar would be subjected to broadsides from both port and starboard. Unfortunately, that looked to be just where he was heading.

In a brief lull between the mounting cannonades, Tearlach heard another sound: a distant cheer that was vaguely familiar. He scanned the ground and discovered both its source and familiarity in the same moment. Three companies of Spanish troops, close kin to those he'd served alongside in the Lowlands, had come bursting out of the eastern tree line. Their battle cry was a distant echo of his first battlefields, and he felt a twinge of regret at being opposed to his old allies. But then again, Tearlach Mulryan regretted the need to lift his hand against any man.

However, it did not make him hesitate doing so. He sent his observation of the Spanish infantry's numbers, armaments, and direction to the ground station and breathed a sigh of relief. *Well, at least one thing is going according to plan.*

Somovilla was among the first in the main ranks to reach what looked like the shattered prow of a Dunkirk cromster. The fifty skirmishers who had preceded them were already behind cover, wondering that the defenders had not used the considerable piles and scattering of wood as cover, or at least concealment, for their own troops.

It was Casañas who first remarked on the pungent smell that seemed to permeate the air around them. "I had heard that the Pitch Lake has a stink, but this!"

Somovilla did not comment. He was too busy assessing an unpleasant but not disastrous surprise laid by the defenders. Evidently they had employed the ship-parts graveyard as a blind, to prevent the attackers from observing the positions they had prepared on the partly open rear-flank of the lunette: a short, shallow double trench line, each one covered by a low, outfacing berm, such as the one he had seen extending inland from its outer corner. But the personnel and equipment in those trench lines remained hidden, except for what looked like stands or tripods arrayed along the further berm. Approximately eighty yards away, the trenches were a screen against any close attack directly into the rear of the lunette. But the broader tactical wisdom was still a puzzlement to Somovilla: Why would the defenders leave such cover as the wreckage and driftwood within far musket shot? Why not groom the three hundred yards of open ground between forest and fort to ensure that any attempt to charge across it would result in it becoming a monstrous killing field?

"Captain," the sergeant said. "That smell, sir. It's not just Pitch Lake."

Annoyed, Somovilla supported himself on a blackened fragment of gunwale and turned. "What? What do you mean?" And then he had the answer to his own question. Beneath his supporting hand, the wood was slimy, even viscous, as though it was coated in—

Two of the skirmishers shouted something about smoke. A burst of sparks—a fuse end that evidently snaked up out of the ground from beneath a concealing plank—ignited a small puddle of something flammable.

What happened next was not a sequence of events so much as a collage of near-simultaneous disasters. The fire from that small puddle of burning liquid raced along the driftwood, spreading faster than the eye could follow. At two other points in the debris, similar fuse ends revealed themselves in bright, momentary flares. One failed to ignite anything but the second made up for it. With a breathy *phwuuumphh* the largest piece of wreckage, a sizeable section of hull, burst into sudden, fierce flames. Dozens of men who had sheltered behind or rested against the fuel-oil soaked timbers were suddenly alight, screaming, clawing to shed clothes, armor, gear.

The invaders' ploy was abruptly, perfectly, horribly clear. They had left the wood precisely so that the Spanish *would* take cover behind it—and so, anoint themselves with the flammable coating that was, as Casañas' nose had detected, much more powerful and pungent than mere pitch.

Somovilla flinched away from the ruined bow of the cromster before the racing flames reached it. He was checking to see if there was a clear path of retreat when the sergeant raised his sword. "Out of these flames and at the heathens!" he cried with a confirming nod toward his lieutenant as he charged beyond the quickly building inferno around them.

"Yes, charge! Charge!" shrieked Somovilla. Who did not join them, but rather, continued to look for a safe path rearward through the mounting flames.

Ann Koudsi had known that this moment would come, steeled herself for it, but still lacked the impassivity she had hoped to achieve. One moment the Spanish, hundreds of them, had been huddled behind the driftwood that she and her workers had soaked with bunker oil: the most plentiful product they were distilling from Well Number One's crude. The very next moment, the debris field was burning in two places.

Two of the Wild Geese who had a crude proficiency with a bow looked toward Hugh O'Donnell, who eyed the burning rags secured to their nocked arrows. He shook his head. "No need. The flames from the two successful fuses are spreading quickly enough."

"Good thing we buried five fuses in those bamboo tubes," murmured Ulrich. "Two of them didn't even go off."

O'Donnell nodded. "And that's precisely why we laid five, and why we had these lads waiting with their fiery arrows." He squinted into the rapidly mounting flames. "Any moment now, the Spanish will—"

Out of the smoke and flame, a roaring—and in some cases, smoking—horde of blackened Spaniards emerged at the charge. Ann had grabbed Ulrich's sizable bicep before she was aware she was doing so. Even though they were safe behind a murder slit that had been cut between the upright logs of the fort's palisade, it was a fearsome sight, seeing all those armored men approaching with no thought other than to kill them.

In the lead trench, Fitzwilliam the marksman turned toward the section of the wall where he obviously knew Hugh was observing.

"At the second range marker, Fitzwilliam!" O'Donnell shouted. "As we planned!"

Fitzwilliam nodded, turned, head just barely above the berm fronting his waist-deep trench.

"'Range marker'?" Ann echoed.

Hugh pointed. "Can you see the white-washed stakes facing us, but concealed from the Spanish behind smaller bits of debris?"

"Yes, now I see them."

"Well, when the Spanish reach the second one—"

Which was the very moment when the bow wave of the charging soldiers reached it. In response, the forty Wild Geese lying in wait behind the first low berm rose high enough to lay upon the berm in a slanted prone position. Each one laid the muzzle of his long rifle into a V-shaped notch in the mound's rim, formed by two embedded, down-angled shingles.

The Spanish came on another six paces before the muskets discharged in a long, rolling sputter. A surprising number of the first rank of Spaniards staggered or fell in their tracks, most groaning, a few ominously still. But the wave, although broken, continued onward, albeit hesitantly.

That was when the occupants of the second trench, mostly Dutch gunners, heaved no fewer than ten different kinds of swivel guns up into the waiting mounts, tripods, and pintel posts. The lead rank of Spanish slowed. Having reached fifty yards, they now had a clear view of just what it was they were facing.

At the same moment that a few of their veteran sergeants screamed to resume the charge, the swivel guns fired their loads of shot into the ragged ranks. At some places, the carnage was horrific; at others, only a few men went down with annoyed curses. But what the marksmen had left of the front rank, the swivel guns almost completely swept away. And with that rank, went the courage of those behind it.

Because in the next moment, the Spanish saw the first trench of musketeers bring a fresh set of preloaded weapons to bear upon them, and gunners on the wall of the fort uncover two sakers that were already aiming downward.

The Spanish formation started to break away, first

in small bits, then in chunks, then en masse. Most headed left: north to the beach. They had seen no enemies there, the footing was sure, and for those who needed it, there was water to put out their still-smoldering clothes and boots.

The Spanish who had been on the southern side of the assault broke inland, racing around the edge of the burning driftwood and making for the jungle. And a few very desperate men who had been at the central point of the charge ran straight back toward the ragged flames, vanishing into the thick black smoke. Of the three or four hundred Spanish who had emerged, charging, from that smoke, perhaps a quarter lay still or were attempting to crawl or hobble after their routed comrades.

"It was a good choice, bringing some of the swivel guns taken from La Flota down here," Ulrich remarked.

"I wish we'd taken more," Hugh muttered. "Because we had to take some from the fluyts hiding behind Point Fortin, to the south. If the Spanish prevail at sea and find that anchorage, it will have been a very bad choice indeed."

Ann was still staring at the bodies littering the field before them. "I know it's stupid to feel this way, I know they would have shown us little or no mercy if our situations were reversed, but it just seems wrong. Wrong to slaughter all those men who never had a chance."

O'Rourke appeared from behind Hugh's shoulder, had possibly been there all along. "No soldier likes the killing, Miss Ann. At least not any of the sane ones. But it's just as you say. Once battle is joined, it's them or us."

Hugh turned and began walking back to the block-house that was the stockade's headquarters. O'Rourke looked after him, closed the shutter on the murder slit. "There's no good that's ever come of the dirty business of war, except ending it with your friends still alive and your flag still flying. Which might not be what's happening off Point Galba. You can see for yourself, if you wish." He gestured to the roof of the blockhouse.

Instead of going up there, Ann wanted to find a very deep hole, close it after her, and shake for a very long time. But she said, "Yes, I'll come up with you."

Tearlach Mulryan watched, unable to think or even blink, as Hjalmar van Holst's forty-eight-gun *Vereenigte Provintien* continued heading directly for the lane of open water separating the even larger Spanish flagship from its smaller starboard escort. *Does he know what he's doing? That it's tantamount to suicide?* the young Irishman wondered.

But just as *Vereenigte Provintien* was starting to come between the two galleons, she veered sharply southward. It was an easy maneuver, since the wind was from the north, and gave her stronger way and better speed. But now she was on a collision course with the Spanish flagship.

Which, Mulryan realized with a gasp, had been van Holst's intent from the moment he had started running head-to-head with that massive galleon. Both she and her escort had been expecting a duel of broadside to broadside at pistol shot, had probably expected to pinch in toward the overconfident Dutch warship, trap her in a vise and hammer her from less than thirty yards. But now, with the *Vereenigte Provintien* heading obliquely toward the flagship, the tactical situation had radically altered. The two largest ships on each side would now come into boarding range, and the Spaniard's escort would be hard put to change course in time to arrive within the first ten minutes of the fight across those decks. Furthermore, she could only do so by turning hard to port, thereby putting her bow athwart the big Dutchman's port batteries. That would allow van Holst to send a raking broadside down the length of her weather deck.

The escort's only other alternative was to maneuver as best the wind allowed to swing about to approach the other side of Hjalmar's ship, more improbably, turn directly into the wind to get sternway and slowly back herself into a position alongside the *Vereenigte Provintien*. If the breeze, her sail master, the gunfire, and her captain's skill all permitted it, that is.

Van Holst had made an inspired and bold choice, Mulryan conceded, but still suicidal. The big Dane would never be able to break away from the big galleon once he'd grappled to it. And the other Spanish ships would surely converge upon *Vereenigte Provintien*, both to sink her and save their own flagship.

Which was already occurring. The galleons that had nearly boxed in *Sampson* and *Amsterdam* were signaling continuously, and showed signs of breaking off. They were probably trying to work out which one was going to double back to help their flagship. Given that brief respite, the two Dutch warships maneuvered in the fresher wind, regained running room, headed toward the enemy vessels which had worked in between them and Peg Leg. Clearly, they were now intent on tearing apart one side of the box in which they, and the van of the fleet, had almost been caught.

The flagship's smaller escort galleon was similarly undecided in her course for a few moments. First she angled closer, her gun crews huddling over their pieces. But she swung away when it became obvious that, by the time she delivered a broadside to the Dutchman, it was likely that some of her fire would hit their admiral's hull. As the escort came closer to the wind, she strove westward, evidently resolving to come all the way about and lay to on the other side of the Dutchman: an easier and more reliable maneuver, but longer in the execution.

Van Holst's ship had now reached the flagship and, breaking to port at the last second, came close alongside, the yardarms cracking into each other as she did. The ships exchanged thunderous broadsides at point-blank range, smoke and debris gushing outward in all directions. By the time Mulryan could see the decks again, the Dutch boarders had taken the more numerous Spanish by surprise, leaping aboard and throwing sputtering grenades in a wide circle.

But no: they were not grenades. They were what Eddie Cantrell had called "Molotov cocktails." Loaded with the heavy petroleum products of the oil well, their burning fluids kept smoldering and flickering even where they shattered in pools of water or upon wet objects. Another suicidal move by van Holst, since fire on the Spanish flagship could now easily spread to the *Vereenigte Provintien*. But it sowed confusion among the Spanish, who seemed uncertain which of their number should fight the Dutch and which should fight the fires. In that time, van Holst had leaped upon the Spaniard's deck.

As he did, his starboard battery discharged once again, before the heavier and more cumbersome guns of his adversary could. When the Spanish gun decks made reply, it was noticeably diminished.

But as the escort finally started to come about, and two other galleons maneuvered toward the duel between the great ships, Peg Leg's *Achilles* and the *Thetis* were gaining speed, closing with the wind behind them and gun decks fresh and ready. Perhaps van Holst's maneuver might yet allow the Dutch to fight the Spanish to a standstill, or even achieve victory.

But as the black-morioned masses of enemy soldiers kept pouring up to join the fight on the flagship's deck, they were winnowing out the ranks of the buff-coated Dutchmen surrounding Hjalmar, whose blond hair streamed to show where he had lost his helmet. And it was a certainty that before help could arrive, the escort would come along the *Vereenigte Provintien*'s port side and board her, pitting the crews of two Spanish galleons against that of one already-tired Dutchman.

Mulryan watched, the telegraph box forgotten at his side. Had Hjalmar van Holst been brave or reckless? Cunning or foolish? Given his eagle's-eye view, few had a better perspective from which to judge such matters than Tearlach Mulryan, and yet the only thing he knew with certainty was this: *Can one call a stratagem successful if it is also, intrinsically, suicide?*

Because, from the flickering of Spanish swords now hemming Hjalmar closely, that certainly seemed to be the price the Dane-born Dutchman was about to pay.

Part Four

November–December 1636

The port of serrated teeth
—Herman Melville,
"The Maldive Shark"

Chapter 53

Oranjestad, St. Eustatia

No one sitting around the large table in *Amelia*'s great cabin was even thinking of food as the last of Tromp's orderlies exited, rolls and fruit left on the side and already forgotten.

"Eddie," said Tromp, "thank you for traveling here overnight from Antigua."

"There's too much news, and planning, that can't wait, Admiral. The rest of the ships at St. John's Naval Base will be arriving later today."

Dirck Simonszoon raised an eyebrow. "Even before we've decided on a course of action?"

Eddie shrugged, which sent new rivulets of seawater down his back. He'd come straight off *Intrepid* to the meeting and his neck and hair were still damp from the spray of crossing Oranjestad Bay's predawn chop in a skiff. "Whatever plans we make, it's a sure bet all those hulls are going to be wanted."

Joost Banckert nodded. "It is a shame a few of them were not down in Trinidad."

Tromp sighed. "Which is the first order of business.

We have a full report now. The Cartagena fleet did not just disengage, but is confirmed to be withdrawing. Our own forces are too reduced and battered to give chase. Particularly since that would leave Trinidad undefended until the reinforcements arrive in approximately two days."

Banckert frowned. "What did we lose?"

Tromp sighed. "Too much, Joost. *Kater*, *Noordsterre*, *Overijssel*, and sadly, *Vereenigte Provintien*: all lost. Half of the remaining ships were badly damaged, so much so that few would have survived a second engagement. As you know from the first message, Hjalmar van Holst turned the tide but paid with his life. And now we have news that old Gijszoon died from his wounds. Good ships, good captains, and good friends all of them, the like of which we shall not see again."

"Crew casualties?"

"As usual, the losses were highest among the ships that sank. Excepting the *Vereenigte Provintien*, fifty-seven were killed, seventy-six were wounded."

"And on van Holst's ship?"

Eddie had never seen Tromp take so deep a breath. "Of her three hundred and thirty-one sailors and soldiers, two hundred and twenty-four were killed, remain missing, or were mortally injured. Thirty-eight wounded were able to swim to shore. Only sixty-nine made it off the ship unscathed, most by going through gunports or taking desperate dives over the bow and the stern. She never had the chance to put any boats in the water."

"Good God," said Eddie.

Tromp nodded. "When a ship is bracketed by adversaries, this is often the result. It did not help that the fires started during the boarding of the Spanish flagship spread back to *Vereenigte Provintien*. Both she and the galleon burned down to the water. But the Spanish won the fight well beforehand and so, were able to abandon their own vessel before it rolled."

Simonszoon's voice was carefully unemotional. "Are the guns, theirs and ours, in shallow water? Reclaimable?" The others at the table could only stare at the ruthless pragmatism of the question. Hannibal Sehested's eyes widened slightly.

Tromp nodded tightly. "I believe so."

Banckert's frown had deepened. "Trinidad is already becoming an expensive proposition."

Simonszoon's lips were taught, thinner than usual. "Just as we anticipated. How many of the Spanish did we sink or scuttle?"

Tromp exhaled. "Four galleons were sunk or scuttled, as was one of the two naos that had already landed troops. Three other galleons were abandoned as hulks."

Eddie did the mental math, based on the thumbnail data he'd heard about the engagement. "If Jol's ships were in such bad shape, I'm surprised that the Spanish considered themselves beaten."

Tromp shrugged. "They probably didn't, any more than we felt 'beaten' when we turned back at Vieques last year. But with half their troops dead, wounded, or routed, and their fleet split into two parts that could not support each other, it would have been dangerous for them to press on. The odds at sea were no longer strongly in their favor, the remaining transports were being threatened by *Tropic Surveyor* and *Leeuwinne*, and the fort and its considerable battery had not suffered any appreciable losses. In short, the Spaniards' primary objective, to land and expel us, had gone from being reasonable to very unlikely. And with their commander forced to transfer his flag, and the certainty that further ship losses would not be offset by replacements from La Flota, they made the same decision I would: to preserve what force they had left. Particularly after the near-massacre of their landing force."

Sehested's eyes remained wide. "That sounded particularly gruesome."

Tromp nodded. "It was. But as is often the case, flame weapons drive off far more men than they kill. Even including the volleys from our troops entrenched on that flank, only one hundred fifty of their infantry were casualties. And of those, less than half were killed outright or mortally wounded."

Eddie shook his head. "So there are four hundred fifty Spanish regulars loose on Trinidad? Well *that's* sure going to put a crimp in our oil prospecting and extraction operations."

"Yes," agreed Tromp, "although this new report indicates that the Nepoia have already accounted for more than one hundred of the survivors, as well as the great majority of the wounded. And I suspect those who remain are presently concerned with hiding, not attacking. However, until Hyarima can assure us otherwise, we must now presume our operations on Trinidad may be at risk from raiding and sabotage."

"And how many men did we lose on land?"

"Very few. Eighteen Dutch soldiers and artillerists were killed. A similar number were wounded."

Sehested, who was more familiar with land combat, frowned. "Why is the proportion of dead so high, Admiral?"

"A galleon hit one of the guns in the battery. Its entire crew was slain, as well as several men tending adjacent guns. Additionally, nine of the Irish mercenaries were killed and fourteen wounded, half during their ambush against the landing, the other half when those in the fort sortied to ensure that the Spanish retreat became a rout."

"Still," Eddie mused quietly, "it doesn't sound like the Spanish got a bloody-enough nose to stay away for very long."

Tromp nodded. "I am afraid you are right. Had La Flota arrived earlier this year, I doubt the Cartagena fleet would have withdrawn farther than Puerto Cabello."

"Or maybe Curaçao?" Eddie almost whispered the last word. The island had already become synonymous with rapine, lawlessness, atrocity, savagery. And not merely because of what the Brethren of the Coast had done there, but because they had stayed. It was now their own open port where anything, truly anything, could be had for the right price.

Tromp looked grim. "No. Not even the Spanish will use Curaçao. They are not welcome there, even though many of its 'inhabitants' remain on their payroll."

Simonszoon doggedly stuck to practical matters. "Was Jol able to save any of those three Spanish hulks?"

Tromp shrugged. "Just one, but it was so badly damaged that he can't repair it down there. Along with two of his own ships, they will sail to Antigua for refit as soon as the reinforcing flotilla reaches Fort St. Patrick. But he was able to strip the others of their cannons, canvas, shot, even cordage."

Eddie sighed. "I think we need to send one of

the new steam tugs down there. And yes, I know: I've been the one urging to keep them together as a strategic mobility reserve to help some of our other ships keep up with the steam cruisers and destroyers. But if Peg Leg had just one tug down there, it could have totally changed the outcome."

"How?" wondered Sehested.

"When they were all becalmed," Simonszoon muttered, "Jol could have used a tug to pull one of his bigger ships across the stern of an enemy galleon. Maybe two. Raked the decks, hammered them until they were junk. When the wind returned, the entire engagement would have been different."

Banckert nodded. "I agree. And while we are on the topic of better outcomes, we must also consider this: if Floriszoon's *Eendracht* and the patache *Orthros* had not been off on a wild-goose chase with their radios—as suggested by Colonel O'Donnell—they too, might have turned the tide."

Eddie saw Tromp fold his hands, knew that he was preparing to counter Banckert's criticism—which was fine by him. Let the Dutch argue with the Dutch, was the young up-timer's motto.

"I think that is a very debatable conjecture, Joost. They would have been part of *Tropic Surveyor*'s squadron, and as such, might have accomplished the same outcome with fewer casualties. But *Noordsterre* was doomed either way; she was the smallest of our jachts and was hit dead amidships by a forty-two-pounder at close range. It might as well have been the hand of God that smote her to the bottom. However, I have plotted the projected progress of the oilers had the earl of Tyrconnell's plan not turned them back.

They would have just arrived at Fort St. Patrick only a few days before the Spanish. They and their escorts would either have had to run and hide in a distant anchorage of the Bay of Paria and possibly be hunted or discovered, or had they remained nearby, could have been lost to us, along with the strategic and economic advantages conferred by the oil operations. As it is, only because *Eendracht* remained at Pitons Bay, St. Lucia, to serve as a wireless relay, do we even have these reports from Trinidad. Otherwise, we'd be meeting half a week from now, or more. Which, I think you'd agree, would put us in much greater jeopardy, given what we have learned since."

"I must echo Admiral Tromp's sentiments on this matter," Hannibal Sehested added, ignoring Joost van Banckert's annoyed glance. "Every day matters in mounting a swift and decisive response to the increasing Spanish presence on St. Maarten. As the representative of His Royal Highness, King Christian IV of Denmark, I am compelled to remind all of you that, at this time last year, we all agreed to the solution that Commodore Lord Cantrell proposed for settling our rival claims to that island. It was also agreed to postpone the retaking of that island until sometime in 1636."

He looked around the table. "Gentlemen, 1636 is rapidly drawing to a close. Furthermore, as the latest reports from our Bermudan allies now show, the Spanish have taken advantage of our lethargy. They are not only improving and reinforcing St. Maarten's defenses, but evidently creating an expanded and protected anchorage in one of its southern-facing bays."

He put the point of his finger to the surface of the

table as if he was pinning his Dutch listeners to a dissection tray. "The Spanish activity does not obviate our agreement. Rather, it makes it incumbent that we move with all possible speed to satisfy its terms. Any delay increases the risk to lives and matériel that would never have been at risk at all, had concluding this business been of sufficient import and urgency to all concerned." His stare at each of the Dutch naval officers left no doubt about whom "all concerned" actually were.

"I will make one final point. All your wonderful successes against the Spanish have been at sea, where you enjoyed the extraordinary advantage of the USE's ships and their up-time technology. But you have no such advantages on land, and if you wait too long, that is exactly where you will be forced to do much of your fighting for St. Maarten. Which, given the modest size of your regiments, could prove terribly expensive." He leaned back, crossed his arms, and waited.

Joost Banckert rubbed his chin. "I do not debate the truth of anything you have said, Lord Sehested. But we must be cautious. They know all this as well. They could be investing St. Maarten not so much because of any intrinsic value it has to us, but to bring us out. Either to ambush our fleet, which seems profitless. Or, more reasonable for them, to have a second force waiting to take advantage when we leave St. Eustatia, greatly reducing its defenses."

Well, thought Eddie, *this looks like the right moment to shock the bejeezus out of everybody*. He leaned forward and nodded. "I agree with Admiral Banckert. I think it is very likely to be a trap of one kind or another. But knowing that, and acting upon it, could actually be an advantage for us. Besides"—he turned to Hannibal—"as Lord Sehested points out, I was the one who proposed the solution regarding St. Maarten. So I feel it is incumbent upon me to support his request that we act to fulfill the final stipulation of the agreement before it becomes any more costly or difficult to do so."

Banckert's eyebrows rose. Dirck Simonszoon looked narrowly at Eddie, then glanced at Tromp and, noting the admiral's *lack* of surprise, was unable to hide the flicker of a brief smile.

If anybody in the room was flabbergasted, it was Sehested himself. "This . . . this is a welcome resolution, gentlemen. I shall communicate your ready cooperation to His Majesty, Christian IV. However"—he looked sidelong at Eddie—"I am not sure I understand what you mean by opining that walking knowingly into a trap could be to our *advantage*."

Eddie shrugged. "Well, if we move quickly, that is likely to make them think we're *not* suspecting a trap. That gives us a chance to turn the tables on the Spanish, who are likely to be lulled into false confidence by thinking that events are playing out according to their own expectations. Right down to what they will believe is our lack of suspicion and caution."

"Well, if we're not taking the time to act on our suspicion and caution, then how is that any different from, well, *not* being suspicious or cautious?" Dirck was grinning as he asked the question.

Eddie smiled back. "You tell me."

Dirck "the Smirk" Simonszoon lived up to his name. "Let me guess. Of all the reactions the Spanish expect from us, sailing against them immediately is the least likely. They're either expecting us to stare at the situation, looking for traps. Or that we jump past that gambit with one of our own. Maybe by using our long-range gunnery to stand off and bash at their fleet. Maybe by doing to them what they were hoping to do to us at Vieques: find and hit their supply ships.

"Either way, we dodge the land battle by wearing away their naval assets until they have to abandon their land forces. Which we then starve into submission. There are other scenarios, but the point is: by choosing the seemingly rash response, we're also taking the one they really haven't considered as much. We're still taking them by surprise."

Eddie nodded. "And regardless of any of those countermoves, we are there as early as possible to disrupt their attempts to secure St. Maarten."

Dirck leaned back. "Good as any other approach," he sighed. "I'm in."

Joost Banckert shrugged and nodded.

Still staring like a stunned owl, Sehested rose. "Gentlemen, my sovereign will want this news as rapidly as possible. Given the time difference, if I depart now to get it coded for transmission, he will likely receive it before the end of the day. Now, since I presume the rest of your discussion will be operational in nature, I would take my leave of you."

Tromp stood, joined by the others. "We would not delay you, and we thank you for your candid speech, Lord Sehested. It is an excellent way to begin our shared utilization of the island."

Hands were shaken all around and Sehested exited the cabin. His personal aide could soon be heard shouting along the weather deck for his lordship's skiff back to Oranjestad.

Dirck smiled, collapsed into his chair at a rakish angle, and drawled. "And now, Commodore, what's the part you *didn't* talk about?" He glanced at Tromp. "Or is Maarten going to do the honors, since it's clear both of you are in on it?"

Tromp's answering smile was small as he nodded at Eddie.

Who sighed. "Maarten and I were already on the same page about this before we even talked about how to respond. There is, however, *one* angle that is all mine. But that can wait. Here's why we have to tackle the Spanish now, regardless of the agreement with my father-in-law.

"First and foremost, everything I said to Hannibal is totally legit, strategically and tactically. The Spanish do have us between a rock and a hard place. If we wait, they get stronger and the job gets harder. But if we go right away, we don't have a lot of time to find out what they might be up to.

"But that leads to the second point, which is: we're as ready as we're going to be . . . right this very second. We've got no way to get better reconnaissance, we've got no intel pipeline to exploit, and we sure as heck aren't going to whistle up a few more ships from Trinidad when what we're doing is sending more down to them. We've finished all the ship repairs and conversions that started about five months ago, so we've got enough to guard St. Eustatia, have a decent regional reaction force in Antigua, and we've been running twenty-four-hour readiness drills. So our ships are topped up on consumables and crews are on short liberty or standby. Which is weeks faster than our opponents' reaction time, so we just might catch them with their pantaloons down."

He frowned. "But the third reason is that Spain is in trouble. Real trouble. No treasure fleet this year means only a trickle of silver getting home. Italy is a pig in a poke. The antipope in Rome is one of their own, who likes Madrid but who Madrid doesn't like. Meanwhile, Philip's breakaway brother is hosting the real pope who Madrid does like, but he doesn't like them. Here in their overseas empire, they just put a whole fleet in their enemy's hands, and because of that their chosen sons in the New World are, whether by choice or necessity, starting to play by their own rules. And although I have to read between the lines that Admiral Simpson sends, it sounds like Madrid has been under huge pressure to help against the Ottomans and is catching some nasty backlash for not doing so."

Joost Banckert shrugged. "So it's not a wonderful time for Spain. Other than finding some rum to toast their continuing miseries, how does that influence us?"

"It means," Eddie summarized, "that Philip, and Olivares even more, need a win. A big win. And the biggest win they could score, and also the one over which they probably have the most control, is to get the silver back home, shore up the economy, mute the grumbling, and in general look like they're back on top.

"Now, there are two ways to do that. Either destroy us so we can't stop them. Or avoid us."

"Good luck with destroying us," Dirck sneered.

"Exactly. So what does that leave?"

"Avoiding us." Simonszoon frowned as he saw the connection. "Yes. They might."

"Might what?" Banckert snapped.

"Might reroute La Flota."

"And what does that have to do with St. Maarten?"

Banckert persisted. "They already use different routes. They used to come through these very waters, sometimes. Sometimes the two fleets split much earlier, starting along the Spanish Main from Trinidad, the other—oh," Banckert stopped. "You think they'd send the fleet into the Caribbean near St. Maarten? Through the Anegada Passage? That's . . . that's madness."

"Is it?" Eddie asked. "Compared to trying to fight us, ship to ship? So let's say they actually follow the usual route for crossing, like this year. But as soon as they see Dominica pop over the horizon, they hang a hard right and head north. All the way north, and angle back into the waters between Puerto Rico and the Leeward Islands, which—if they own St. Maarten— gives them friendly outposts on either side. A place to stop, get the latest intelligence and then split."

Banckert nodded. "Yes. That wouldn't be so hard for the New Spain Fleet. They've sometimes come in almost that far north, touching at Santo Domingo and maybe Jamaica before heading down to Cartagena. But it would be a long, slow journey for the Tierra Firme Fleet to dodge the entirety of the Lesser Antilles by cutting southwest across the full expanse of the Gulf."

Tromp repeated Banckert's words with emphasis. "'A long, slow journey'? Yes. But isn't that preferable to 'the destruction of another fleet'?"

Joost just nodded.

"Besides," Eddie finished, "it's not like they'd have to do that forever. Just a year or two, they'd figure. Until they get rid of us."

Dirck's smile was wicked. "I think it will take them a little longer than that, now."

"I agree, but they're desperate for a solution. And

they have such outsized confidence in themselves that I could see them drinking that Kool-Aid—er, convincing themselves of just about anything."

Tromp was nodding. "This entire scenario assumes that one of two possibilities are true. Specifically, that either the governors of the Greater Antilles have a radio to receive such orders from Madrid—which I very much doubt—or they have realized this and have taken such an initiative of their own accord." He shrugged. "Which is far more likely."

"Or," Banckert threw out, "that they have some other entirely unrelated scheme that we have not foreseen."

Eddie shrugged. "That is a very distinct possibility. But can we afford not to take action because we're scared of a ghost? Which might not even be there?"

Banckert frowned. "No. We must act. I just wish we knew more about why the Spanish are clustering around St. Maarten like fleas heading for a dog's back."

Tromp nodded. "So do I. But one thing is plain: time is of the essence and we are ready to go." He looked sympathetically at Eddie. "Which means that as of now, you already have less than twenty-four hours to spend with a wife who has not seen you for months. Go, now. What your staff aboard *Intrepid* cannot handle, we shall."

Twenty-five hours later, Eddie closed the door of his cabin aboard *Intrepid*. As it had turned out, he got a lot less than twenty-four hours to spend with Anne Cathrine. First, he had to go back to *Intrepid* to get his ready bag . . . and walked straight into a pile of legitimately "must-do-now" paperwork and crew instruction sheets to handle the various inquiries that were likely to arrive in his absence. By the time he had also provided his staff with orders, priorities, and protocols to ensure that his squadron would be ready to sail in the morning, three hours had elapsed. It took another hour for the skiff to get him to shore, and then get himself to Danish House.

But Anne Cathrine wasn't there. In fact, no one was. Except Cuthbert Pudsey, who avoided telling him why his arm was in a sling, but revealed that Anne was volunteering at the infirmary. So, after dropping his bag in their room, he spun right around and left.

And somehow managed to miss Anne Cathrine at the infirmary. She had left only minutes before, Dr. Brandão informed him, with a strangely contemplative look on his face. It had evidently been a light day at the infirmary; there was no sign that anyone else had been in. "Easy day?" Eddie had asked. Brandão's look became one of perplexity; general hours had not yet started. He had reserved this morning for . . . and there he faltered for a moment. For private inquiries, he finished. But hadn't Anne Cathrine volunteered that morning? Brandão shrugged, simply remarked that she had indeed stopped by. The entire conversation seemed a little vague and off-center to Eddie, but his only immediate concern was to catch up with his wife. He started back to Danish House.

And that was where he finally found her, with only eighteen hours left before he was due back aboard *Intrepid*. The way she leaped up into his arms, you'd have thought he had died and come back to life. Sophie and Leonora had been there when he entered, but by the time he remembered to turn around and say hello to them, they had vanished.

When Anne Cathrine learned how little time they were going to have together, she went from almost adolescent hyperactivity to downright solemnity. She assured him that no, of course she wasn't angry at him. And he believed it. But still. It was as if this news made it necessary for her to rethink plans. Although that was kind of strange because how could she have made plans when he'd only been home for an hour so far?

Eventually, she reanimated, but more out of duty than anything else. She explained how Oranjestad's best seamstress had probably been passing information to the Spanish, almost certainly the pirates, and definitely between the landowners and the French. When Eddie heard how it was the latter exchange which had caused the slaveholders to stand aside during the Kalinago attack, he was half out of his seat to pass the news on to Tromp and van Walbeeck. But Anne Cathrine's grasp on his arm and appeal in her eyes put him back in his chair, and she insightfully suggested that this was probably the worst possible time for the colony's leaders to be distracted by such news, let alone crafting a suitably stern response. Not only was the fleet about to sail against the Spanish, but the other military commanders, although in support of Tromp's antislavery policies, were neither aware of his longer strategy nor did they possess his authority.

By the time that was settled, Anne Cathrine had genuinely perked up again, enough to point out that he probably hadn't had real food in months. So they ate and chatted and she started laughing again. Then she insisted on feeding him, and then she let him try to feed her, but she refused to hold still. So he got food all over her and—

And then, somehow, it was after midnight. He had no idea how often they'd made love, but he woke to the feeling of her fingers tracing his arm, up and down, and then his side, up and down, and then...

Sex with Anne Cathrine had always been cataclysmic, spontaneous, sometimes almost kinky. Well, kinky in *his* book. Before Cat, Eddie had been pretty much Mr. Plain Vanilla when it came to sex. Not like he'd had many opportunities to try other flavors, let alone visit the ice cream truck of carnal pleasure.

But that night's sex with Cathrine didn't just move a little further away from the playfulness that had been waning ever since he'd returned from Dominica. Now, intimacy had become *serious* business.

And seriously athletic. Olympic, even. But not so much like gymnastics or even wrestling. More like the marathon. And Anne Cathrine, who'd always managed to effortlessly switch back and forth between tigress and coy flirt, wasn't merely serious about the lovemaking. She'd become, well...determined. With a capital D.

And then there was the way she had clung to him afterwards, just before the sun started coming up. It was almost desperate. Damn: if they'd had the day together, he'd have sat her down and asked her what was going on, how he could help. And it might indeed take the whole day, because when they *did* have conversations about their sex life, their roles kind of flipped. Though she was the far less inhibited partner in bed, she was *far more* inhibited when it came to talking about anything that happened there.

Eddie wasn't eager to dissect their love life, and up until now, there certainly hadn't been any reason to. He'd always been an advocate of the old saying,

"If it ain't broke don't fix it." In the case of sex with Anne Cathrine, his personal motto was even more emphatic: "If it's perfect, don't even *look* at it!" But something had changed her from a bedtime playmate to a determined contender in the sex-athalon. So when Eddie got back, he was going to hold her hands and ask her to tell him what was going on, or at least listen while he told her that he'd felt the change and that he was there for her, whatever it might portend.

Intrepid's engines surged, and the deck seemed to shift under him; they were underway. Eddie glanced around the cabin. Although everything was just as he'd left it, was just as it had been when he'd returned a few minutes before, it was different. Suddenly, it no longer felt like a sanctuary, or a place of pride, or even of work; suddenly, it felt like a prison. Because although it had often carried him away from where he wanted to be, this was the first time it was carrying him away from where he *needed* to be.

Chapter 54

Governor's Bay, St. Barthélemy

Six hours later, *Intrepid* rode at anchor in Governor's Bay, St. Barthélemy, and Eddie was back on deck, greeting Maarten Tromp, who'd just been piped aboard with abbreviated ruffles and flourishes. "So, I take it you've brought your flag, Admiral?" the young up-timer asked, offering a smile along with his hand.

Tromp sighed, accepting both. "I succumb to the inevitable, Commodore. Joost Banckert has wanted *Amelia* for almost half a decade now, and he has her well in hand." He sighed. "As for me?" He shook his head. "After directing the fleet from *Resolve* at Dominica, I cannot in good conscience fly my flag from a ship other than one of your cruisers. The command advantages are too many and too profound. Let us walk."

Eddie fell in beside Maarten, pretty sure he knew the purpose of their private stroll to the taffrail.

"You and your lady wife were wise to decide that you should not share the information about the seamstress until you saw me today."

"Did you tell Governor van Walbeeck?"

Tromp shrugged. "Just the basics. He is of the same mind, by the way. He agrees that we lacked the time to decide upon a course of action, and that this would not be the right moment for it. Not until the battle is settled, we are back home, and can take well-measured steps. Whatever those prove to be. As it is," he sighed, "we have more than enough demands upon our attention."

Eddie leaned on the taffrail. "Frankly, I'd feel better if there was a bit *more* demanding our attention." He waved in the direction of St. Maarten, through the slopes that hemmed in Governor's Bay. "I was hoping to have some observation reports to read through, get a head start on figuring out what the Spanish are doing over there. But it's just like the observers on The Quill predicted. Even at fifteen nautical miles, today's haze is too thick to see anything. Even from the balloon, the island's outline was barely visible."

Tromp nodded. "Then it is unlikely they have seen us, either." He looked up at the peaks and ridges that rose up around them like an amphitheater for giants. "And they will not see us here tonight. By which time the transports will have reached this anchorage as well and we may array the ships to weigh anchor while it is still dark."

Eddie nodded. It all made sense. It would also be one of the strategies their enemies were likely to anticipate, even if they hadn't already seen them sail up along St. Eustatia's west coast and then beat to the northeast. Now, twenty-four miles later, they were concealed in Governor's Bay, from which they had a much shorter sail into tomorrow's fight for St.

Maarten. Completely logical. And therefore, completely predictable.

They'd follow that script starting at 0300, weighing anchor so that they could traverse the last fifteen miles while it was still early in the day: enough time to finish whatever battle would ensue. The lead elements of the fleet—*Intrepid*, *Relentless*, *Crown of Waves*, and two Dutch jachts—were to precede the rest by two nautical miles, balloon up and watching for ambushes or other unexpected circumstances. All those hulls had sufficient speed and maneuverability that they could almost certainly avoid any nasty surprises, and yet detect the same in enough time to give the main body sufficient warning to steer clear.

The body of the fleet was led by *Resolve* and consisted of five more jachts, ten larger Dutch ships carrying anywhere from thirty-six to fifty-five guns, and three steam tugs to help the slowest of those keep up and thereby increase the speed of the whole formation. The argument to take along some of the newly repaired and refurbished prizes from Dominikirk, particularly the purpose-built war galleons, were not part of the fleet for much the same reason: the power of their guns and thickness of their sides could not offset the loss in speed and maneuverability that their inclusion would entail. In consequence, they remained at St. Eustatia, a daunting addition to the already significant flotilla that had been detailed to Oranjestad's defense.

Beyond that, there was the normal array of preplanned contingencies for engaging different numbers of different adversaries in different locations and different formations. All standard procedure. But that's exactly what bothered Eddie about the various plans; they, too, were entirely derived from conventional doctrine. So, once again, they were completely predictable.

Tromp had evidently seen those misgivings on Eddie's face. "What is troubling you, Eddie?"

"Doesn't all this feel, well, a little too tidy?"

Tromp's grin was small and rueful. "That would be a pleasant change, almost. But yes, I understand; I have a similar premonition. If the Spanish were proceeding in accord with their stated doctrine, they would have closed en masse and attempted to catch us near our own port. Or intercepted us when we came out, or shortly after if they hoped to cripple us by destroying our supply ships. Just as they tried at Vieques."

Eddie nodded. "But at Vieques, I got the same vibe as now. Because, like here, we couldn't see where the threat was going to come from. We had no way of knowing that they meant to bring in dozens of pirates-turned-privateers from over the horizon. And this . . . well, this kind of has the same feeling. What the Bermudans saw, and maybe what we'll first detect tomorrow, is likely to be a ruse. Just like the fleeing galleons that drew us after them at Vieques."

Tromp's grin widened slightly but remained rueful. "Tomorrow, I will not be surprised if, in fact, the Spanish surprise us. It is one of the few effective weapons they have left. So I am resolved to the presumption that they will have yet again labored to craft a plan that we cannot foresee. And we, in turn, have taken every possible precaution and have readied ourselves to seize every imaginable advantage. About which: I presume your plans for Tortuga are well in hand?"

Eddie nodded. "Everything is on track for that. Our

piece is not only on the gameboard but has made the first few moves."

"Well, then, let us accept that we have attended to all that is in our power to control." Tromp shrugged. "Which, in war, is never very much. Now we are subject to the dictates of Fates. Or perhaps, eh, the Laws of Murphy?"

Eddie smiled. "Murphy's Law. And there's actually just one, Maarten."

"Yes, yes, I misspoke. 'Anything that can go wrong, will go wrong, and at the worst possible time.' That is the only law, yes?"

Eddie nodded. "It is." *But darned if that one law isn't enough, every single time.*

Pelican Point, St. Maarten

Fadrique Álvarez de Toledo completed his descent to the bottom of Billy Folly Hill, where the slope disappeared down into the water. Known as Pelican Point, his longboat was bobbing in the nearby swells, waiting to take him the long way around St. Maarten to rendezvous with his flagship's anchorage in north-facing Marcel Cove. As the coxswain started the process of putting up the stepsail, a patache came sweeping around the eastern side of the small headland, steering near to the rocks. It put a dinghy over the side—a bobbing bridge between the rocks and its gunwale—and the ship's master called up to Fadrique: was he in fact Admiral Álvarez de Toledo? Fadrique signaled an affirmative and waited as a messenger hopped from the ship to the boat to the rocks and then panted his way up the slope.

"Sir," the fellow wheezed, "the signal you have been waiting for: it was seen three hours ago. A fishing boat—a smack, as the English call them—sailing up out of the south and flying a red jib."

So, they are on their way. Sometime this morning, from the sound of it. "Where was the boat encountered? And did it attempt to rendezvous?"

"About eight miles northeast of Saba, and no, sir; as soon as we confirmed seeing their signal, they turned about and sailed back south."

Álvarez nodded. "They fear suspicion if they are absent too long, particularly if they are seen returning from this direction. You saw no sign of the allied fleet?"

"None, Admiral."

Fadrique grimaced. The same haze that kept his men's work unobserved, and hence potentially decisive, also concealed the details of his enemy's movements. Yes, the signal told him that their fleet had left Oranjestad. It also suggested, based on how long it had taken their agent to wait for safe departure and then journey north of Saba, that the enemy had sailed relatively early this morning.

But if they had been heading here, they would have been seen several hours ago by his observers on what the up-time maps labeled Flagstaff Hill. Although visibility was limited to twelve miles, the allied fleet would have reached that limit long ago, even had they been traveling at a leisurely pace.

Which indicated that they had not traveled to St. Maarten at all. It was unlikely that they had traveled either west or south. If that had been the case, the agent in the fishing smack would have deemed it safe to leave earlier, and so reach the rendezvous earlier as well.

So, by process of elimination, all facts pointed to the enemy setting out on an initially northbound course that had not yet brought them to St. Maarten, although it was less than a day's sail from St. Eustatia. That suggested one of three possible destinations: Antigua, Barbuda, or St. Barthélemy.

The rotating and often unreliable informers on both St. Christopher and St. Eustatia had occasionally included vague references to "possible" activity on Antigua, but so far, that had been their way of padding out otherwise scanty reports. Barbuda had never been mentioned and was notable only for being proximal to nothing of importance. But St. Barthélemy? Yes: they were there.

Álvarez was giving orders to the messenger even as he made his way hastily down to the patache still bobbing in the rollers running past the bottom of Billy Folly Hill. "Get runners to spread the word: the heretics will be here tomorrow. Early in the morning, I expect. Harbor pilots need to guide the larger galleons into the lagoon immediately. Tell Gallardo that his men and boats have to be ready by midnight. Same for the positions on this hill. And send runners to the outposts on Flagstaff Hill and Paradise Peak; they need to make sure the firewood remains dry overnight."

As he jumped into the boat and crossed it to the patache with the surefootedness of a life lived at sea, the messenger stood on the shore. "Sir... my boat?" He looked at the rowers in the admiral's own longboat, who could only shrug.

Álvarez noticed none of it: he was already climbing over the gunwale of the patache, ordering its master to get him to Marcel Cove before nightfall.

Chapter 55

Off the southern coast, St. Maarten

"Are they trying to burn down the whole island?" Svantner asked the air around him. He sounded both perplexed and outraged.

"Not according to the signals from the observer in the balloon," Eddie said with a shake of his head. "Although there sure is a lot of smoke."

"Yes," mused Tromp, eye still affixed to his spyglass, "so much so that I think we are seeing the opening gambit of the Spanish attempt to surprise us."

Well, thought Eddie, *they sure got a rise out of Svantner, and I'm none too comfortable about this myself.* "Comms?"

"Yes, sir?"

"Did the observer confirm his first sighting of the enemy's ships?"

"Yes sir, although the smoke is starting to obscure them."

"Report positions for plotting." Eddie nodded to Svantner, who turned his attention to the tactical plot with some reluctance.

The runner who'd brought up the observer's report from the intraship comms cubby began reading out the report that had come down the wire from the balloon. No reason to use the speaking tubes until the pace picked up. "As per two minutes ago, observer confirmed three galleon-sized vessels maneuvering near Simpson's Lagoon and the base of Billy Folly Hill. There may be one or two smaller ships with them; smoke and haze prevents full confidence of sighting.

"Off the leeward shore of the island, just beyond Marigot Bay on the far side of Simpson's Lagoon, there are at least twelve and as many as twenty galleon-sized vessels. Fires have been set on the lagoon's western barrier bank. The smoke has made positive counts difficult and will soon complicate keeping those ships under observation at all."

"So, a smoke screen," Eddie summarized.

"It could be a signal, too," Tromp added, before turning to the junior signalman, whose apprenticeship included working as comms' dedicated runner. "Any sign of activity along the southern shore itself?"

"None reported. But the observer adds that fires have been set there, as well. He no longer has visibility of the near edge of the lagoon, nor anything beyond the shore lining its southern barrier bank."

"And the mountain range that runs from north to south?"

"Still two very large fires burning near the top of the mountains tentatively identified as Flagstaff Hill and Paradise Peak."

"Those fires: has the observer been able to determine if they are widespread or concentrated?"

"Yes, sir. A single source in each case. Observer

reports a steady output of smoke, no evidence that it is spreading."

"And we can't see beyond that smoke?"

"No, sir."

Tromp raised an eyebrow. "Those hills are both quite high, Eddie. What would you expect to see over them, even if you sent the balloon up to seven hundred feet?"

Eddie shook his head. "I don't know. But I get the feeling those fires wouldn't be there if the Spanish didn't want to hide something. But since they are probably uncertain about just how high our balloon can actually go, they're not taking any chances."

Tromp accepted that explanation with an agreeable pout and a nod. "That is true. And they have gone to a great deal of trouble to cut all that wood, so high up, and have it ready to burn when they spot us. So if this is simply a...a stalking stallion—?"

"Stalking horse."

"Yes: that. If this is just a stalking horse, they spent a great deal of time and energy creating it."

Eddie nodded. "Yeah, I don't think this is a diversion." He clenched the hand holding the top of his pistol's holster, making sure the flap was secured. "I also don't like those ship numbers. And the way they're separated? It would take an hour for either formation to sail to the support of the other. It just doesn't make—"

The junior signalman came racing to the top of the stairs again. "New report, Commodore!"

"Good. Read it, Jetse."

"Activity detected on the shore-facing slopes and peak of Billy Folly Hill."

Tromp frowned. "That is at Pelican Point, just east of Simpson's Lagoon. Is there any sign that they have built a fort on its peak?"

"Unclear, sir."

"What about closer to the Great Bay, and near Fort Hill?"

"No activity there, sir. No ships, either."

Tromp frowned. "Now that is strange. They are ignoring what I have been told is the primary anchorage and the site of the original colony."

Eddie chewed at his lip. "I wish the Bermudans had gotten a better look at what was going on before they left."

"You can hardly blame them; they were being pursued."

"I know, but we're missing something. I just wish we knew what it was."

Tromp folded his hands, smiled calmly. "Well, Eddie, I think the Spanish mean for us to try and find out."

Eddie glanced sideways at him. "That sounds a lot like a 'go' order, Admiral."

"So it is. Case Theta Two, as we presumed. Mr. Svantner, have you heard if the fleet is still making three knots?"

"Confirmed within the last five minutes, Admiral."

"Then, Jetse," he said turning to the junior signalman, "tell the master signalman to send to all ships: commence evolution to second phase of Case Theta Two. All ships hold to three knots. Captains are to advise immediately if they are unable to maintain speed. Sound general quarters."

Marcel Cove, St. Maarten

In the narrow confines of Marcel Cove, Fadrique Álvarez de Toledo inspected the position of each ship in his squadron one more time. He could find no fault with their arrangement. So why was he still nervously checking them every five minutes, as if he was some freshly minted ensign, fearful of his captain's wrath?

The four galleons—his fastest—had already wended their slow, slow way out of the small, purse-shaped anchorage which was barely more than a notch at the northern end of St. Maarten's mountainous spine. Signals from a patache positioned from just beyond the mouth of the cove confirmed that they had reached and tucked in close to Eastern Point.

Fadrique calmed himself by recalling the calculations and what they indicated: the enemy balloons would have to be almost half a mile in the air to see the galleons behind that steep headland. They would also need to be able to see through smoke. And know exactly where to look. In other words, Fadrique concluded almost angrily, they could only be seen if God wanted them to be. In which case, God could go fuck Himself.

He breathed deeply. This was hardly a day for blasphemy. Despite all the planning, all the preparation, all the freshly launched fragatas and galleoncetes—the new models without oars—there were still many ways that the plan could fail. And, hearing an excited jabbering behind him, he was reminded of his greatest concern: the men responsible for carrying it out.

He turned. The captain of the largest of the Cuban

fragatas, the thirty-two-gun *Santa Ana la Real*, was walking briskly in an attempt to get ahead of Fadrique's own adjutant, the young and very eager Lieutenant Martin de Orbea. The tall captain glanced briefly at the admiral, who smiled understanding and barked, "De Orbea!"

The lieutenant stopped as if he'd been gut-shot by a *peterero*. "Sir!"

"Come up here and make yourself useful. Put this spyglass on your eye and keep a watch for the signal fires on Pigeon-Pea Hill."

"At once, sir!" The young officer—so young, *too* young—almost fell up the stairs to the low poop deck, bowed as he took the spyglass from Álvarez's hand, and rushed to the taffrail to stare up at the steep, facing slopes.

The captain, Juan de Irarraga, surprised Fadrique by also mounting the stairs to the poop, albeit reluctantly, and with a wary glance at de Orbea. He was a hard-bitten, no-nonsense sailor who had come up through the ranks and was more concerned with winning a fight rather than whether he won it according to the approved methods of the day. In other words, he was both exactly the kind of officer Fadrique liked and exactly the right man to have in command of this very new kind of ship.

He approached with a slight bow. "Admiral."

Álvarez waved off the gesture. "Let us dispense with the formalities, Captain. By the end of the day, we'll have seen blood and death together. No reason to postpone the bond that will bring us. Besides, I've just saved your life."

Irarraga blinked. "Sir?"

"I'm not sure how many more of de Orbea's expository salvos you could have withstood."

The captain's eyes opened wider, and he just barely managed to stifle a guffaw. "The admiral's keen eye is matched by his great compassion."

"He's a bit much, eh?"

Irarraga shook his head. "Sir, if you can weather that, you'd survive in an open boat for a month."

Fadrique elected not to mention that he had done almost exactly that when he was de Orbea's age. "We've many like him on our ships, today."

The captain's frown also had a hint of relief, probably because he was quickly learning that the admiral who was flying his flag from the stern was in fact a frank and like-minded fellow. "I cannot recall looking into so many eyes that have not yet stared into a cannon's muzzle."

Álvarez nodded. "The greatest losses we took last year were not in ships; these new ones are better. Nor in guns; we recovered enough of them. It was in the proven seamen that we cannot quickly replace. As it is, I had to pull every seasoned bosun and gunner and carpenter off the old galleons to give these new ships the crews they require . . . that they deserve."

Irarraga looked sideways at him. "So. That was you? Sir?"

Fadrique waved a hand. "It had to be done, and I have no love of crewing the galleons with such inexperienced sailors. They will have a hard-enough time of it, today. But if we would win, we must have experienced crews where they are needed most."

The captain nodded somberly, gestured toward the taffrail. "Your young pup's tail is wagging."

Álvarez suppressed a smile. "What is it, Lieutenant?"

"Sir, the signal tree! It is falling!"

Álvarez's eyes roved up the slope, locked on a tilting trunk with naked branches as bleached as a skeleton's grasping fingers. It shook, sank a little, then started into an accelerating fall.

So, they are at seven miles. Suddenly Fadrique was no longer anxious. The waiting was over; he was sailing to battle. "Lieutenant, watch for the smoke. Tell me how many fires, and which."

"Sir?"

God's Sacred Balls, do you not remember? "Watch the three points we discussed. Tell me, from left to right, which begin to put forth smoke."

"Oh, yes! A hundred pardons, Admiral!"

"Well, don't look at me! Look at the slopes, you igno—Just look!" As a young officer, Fadrique had hated those above him who insulted him, and thereby undermined his authority, in front of the regular crewmen. But sometimes, the temptation to tongue-lash de Orbea was so great, so exceedingly great—

"Admiral! Two plumes of smoke. The far left and the far right."

"Keep watching." He looked up the slope himself, could almost see them, he thought. But he dared not trust his unaided eyes any longer. "Still just those two plumes?"

"Yes, Admiral!"

"What does it mean?" asked Irarraga, who had not had any reason to be briefed on the complicated signaling protocols that the admiral had worked out with Gallardo.

"It means one-zero-one. The conditions are for plan of engagement number five."

Irarraga nodded. "So, we stay close to the coast for the first three miles."

Álvarez returned the nod as he waved de Orbea back to his side. "They are coming direct from St. Barthélemy on a northwest heading. They might be able to observe us for the first two hours of our run down the eastern coast. After that, the smoke and the highground of Pointe Blanche will screen us."

Irarraga waved understanding as he called over his executive officer, Lieutenant Francisco Rodríguez de Ledesma, to pass along the orders to get the fragata underway. As he did, de Orbea arrived with an expression of excitement and nonspecific terror.

"Lieutenant, signal to the squadron: weigh anchor and proceed to open water. Exit the cove in the order specified in plan five. Move!"

De Orbea leaped away, almost falling down the stairs to the main deck. Fadrique didn't know whether he wanted to laugh or cry or both. *But at last*, he thought gratefully, *we are underway.*

Underway to teach the heathens a final edifying lesson before we sink them deeper than the bowels of perdition itself.

Chapter 56

Off the southern coast, St. Maarten

"Sir, smoke rising up along the base of Billy Folly Hill."

Of course, Tromp thought, *why not*? Eddie had an up-time expression: that even the best officers might give disastrous orders due to "the fog of war." In his time, the phrase had become mostly figurative. Today, however, the Spanish were providing a singular demonstration of its literal origins.

Most of the western third of St. Maarten's southern coastline was obscured by smoke. And since much of that terrain was not heavily vegetated to begin with, it meant that the Spanish had invested an extraordinary amount of time and effort in cutting wood, gathering it, keeping it sun-bleached and dry, and then anointing it with oil and pitch to ensure that it burned quickly enough to put out a useful volume of smoke.

Tromp's own adjutant, a bright young fellow who had been Eddie's runner at Dominica, was waiting pensively at his elbow. He smiled over at the lad. "What is it, Caspar?"

"Another wireless from Captain Simonszoon, sir.

He asks that we remind you that his guns are loaded and he could close to firing range in four minutes."

"Send to the captain that he is to continue standing by." *Yes, Dirck, I know, I know. Resolve's guns could make quick work of those galleons close to the lagoon. But they don't seem to be going anywhere, and I need a moment to think.*

Tromp looked at the tactical plot and was quite sure that this was precisely the dilemma the Spanish commander had hoped to put before him. Directly in front of the allied fleet were the four—or now, maybe five?—galleons standing less than half a mile off the southern barrier bank of Simpson's Lagoon. The larger formation of other galleons standing off the western coast were no longer clearly visible due to the smoke, although final counts had increased their estimated numbers: eighteen to twenty. But they still had not appeared from around the western edge of the smoke concealing the lagoon, which meant that they had not been sailing to close with Tromp's ships.

It was very much like looking at a chessboard without any clear sense of your opponent's strategy. You could only imagine his unseen face grinning in a way that said, "your move." For a moment, he empathized with the senior admiral of La Flota, who'd no doubt had similar feelings as he'd watched the allied ships either waiting quietly or undertaking maneuvers that made no apparent sense.

Tromp shook off the comparison. It was not merely distracting and unhelpful, it was not accurate. His fleet had superior speed, firepower, and a consolidated position. So, if the Spanish were not willing to come out from behind the smoke, or wherever they were, it was time to take the pawns that were clearly unprotected. Without fully committing any of his own pieces in the process.

"Commodore, any signals yet from the two jachts we sent to our flanks?"

Eddie shook his head. "None, Admiral. *Vriessche Jager* just signaled that she is able to see around the smoke to the west. The galleons there are not moving. Their sails are reefed."

"Reefed, you say?"

"I repeat: reefed, sir." He smiled ruefully. "Looks like they're waiting for us, or someone else, to make a move."

"It most certainly does." *And since the Spanish typically expect us to lead with our steamships, that is exactly what we will* not *do.* He leaned toward the speaking tube. "Signalman, send to Admiral Banckert aboard *Amelia.* We are evolving to Contingency Epsilon. To confirm that contingency: he is to take our conventional men-of-war westward, but not proceed to engagement."

"Very good, Admiral!"

Tromp was already looking at the plot again. He pointed at the single blue symbol to the east. "And has *Zuidsterre* anything to report?"

Eddie didn't turn to respond. "No, sir. Last report is that she is now three and a half miles to our east. She's still running the 'all clear' pennant from her masthead." Eddie turned to meet Tromp's eyes. "Another half mile east-southeast and she'll be able to see all the way up the eastern coast as far as Babit Point." The up-timer paused. "She *is* a sloop, sir. Not much in a fight but as small and nimble as any ship we've got."

Tromp nodded. "You needn't jog my elbow. Caspar, signalman is to send to *Zuidsterre*: she is to tack as necessary to get that extra half mile."

"But sir," the towheaded boy started, and then shut his mouth with a snap.

Tromp managed to suppress a smile. "You have a question, Caspar?"

"No, sir."

Tromp added a note of sternness. "Caspar, I am your commanding officer. It is your sworn duty to tell me the truth. So I ask again: do you have a question?"

"Admiral, I—well, yes, sir. But I do not wish to seem impart—uh import, erm..."

"Impertinent?" supplied Tromp.

"Yes, sir. That. It's just that, well, we've already seen that side of St. Maarten. As we approached, sir. It was clear as a cup of spring water, sir."

"So it was...then. But the wind is fresh from the northeast today. An enemy who was waiting for us to pass the southeastern headland, Pointe Blanche, could have easily come from the north and sailed down the coast we believe to be clear behind us."

Caspar nodded thoughtfully, then looked at the comms tube. "But the Spanish don't have radio, sir... do they?"

"Not yet, but"—Tromp pointed at the tall pillars of smoke rising from the island—"they have other ways of sending messages. And almost as quickly, if they have arranged enough special codes beforehand."

"I understand, sir." He saluted—in the up-time fashion, no less!—and ran down the stairs to the pilot-house beneath them, calling out for the telegrapher to prepare to send to *Zuidsterre*.

"Are you happy, now?" Tromp said sideways toward Eddie.

The up-timer grinned. "Yes. And now you're going

to want me to bring the balloon down to one hundred feet, I'll bet."

"Eddie," Tromp murmured, "I appreciate a prudent measure of caution in a commander, but what do you expect to see from five hundred feet with the smoke in the way? Frankly, I would rather bring it down altogether. We have come to the point where swift reaction is almost certainly of greater value than distant observation."

Young Cantrell sighed. "I agree. I'll start retrieval. We should be secure for engines full in fifteen minutes, flank speed with full canvas in twenty-five."

A call came up the speaking tube from comms. "Admiral Tromp, message from Captain Simonszoon."

Tromp smiled. "Read it. Without all the insertions."

"Er, ahem . . . he asks, 'Do I have time for a quick nap?'"

Eddie managed to smother a guffaw into a rather ghastly sounding gargle. Tromp did not smile. Somehow. "Send this: 'Tromp to Simonszoon, CO, Resolve. No napping permitted. *Resolve* is free to engage. Jacht *Vliegende Hert* will be tasked to escort." Tromp frowned, thought, and added, "As well as frigate *Zwarte Tijger*."

"Having Kees keep an eye on Dirck?" Eddie asked with a grin.

Tromp shrugged, muttered, "Someone has to."

Off the eastern coast, St. Maarten

As the *Santa Ana la Real* drew abreast of Geneve Bay, Fadrique Álvarez glanced into it. There, along with their anchor watches, were two pataches. Captain Irarraga saw and followed his gaze. "Pickets?"

The admiral shook his head. "In the event we must evacuate."

Irarraga looked at the slope-walled eastern shore. "Where from?"

Álvarez pointed toward the notch between the hills that flanked the bay. "If Lizarazu must give up the fort, this is only two miles for his men. That bluff at the back of the bay will be a final, taxing uphill march from their side, but the rest is all downhill or flat."

"But that's just a fraction of the men who'd need to be taken off the island."

The admiral smiled. "That's why there are eleven more pataches waiting in Marigot Bay in the western." If all was going according to plan, and all indications were that it was, the majority of the sappers were there even now, awaiting the last of the soldiers who stayed behind to keep fueling the fires near the peaks and along the coasts. Some of the ones near the lagoon and Billy Folly Hill would find it difficult, if not impossible, to escape in the event of a general retreat. But there was no avoiding that. For the rest, at least, it was a swift run down the western slopes to reach the pataches and the safety of open water. "Still," he mused aloud without thinking, "I regret that I cannot ensure a safe escape for all of them."

Irarraga, not understanding the greater context, asked, "There are others to evacuate? Where?"

The admiral smiled. "Well, actually, right there, on Guana Cay." He turned to point in the opposite direction. To the southeast, a small, breaker-foamed elbow of rock rose above the swells.

Irarraga examined it dubiously. "That's barely five hundred feet long and fifty high."

"I believe both dimensions are even smaller. But if the Dutch decide to position a picket near Pointe Blanche, we have a half dozen coast watchers there who shall signal to us."

"Well, their job will soon be over," the captain commented, squinting at the headland that concealed them from the eyes of their enemy. "We're just under a mile and a half from turning round Pointe Blanche. With this breeze, that's thirty minutes. Just over twenty, if those galleons weren't slowing us down."

"'Those galleons,' sir?" a new voice echoed. It was Irarraga's executive officer, Lieutenant Rodríguez de Ledesma, who had come up the short flight of stairs to the low foc'sle. He smiled. "I thought you were one of the galleon's most ardent admirers." The tone was modest and jocular. Well, mostly jocular.

Irarraga stared at him. "You have a report, Lieutenant?"

Rodríguez bowed. "I do, sir. We just saw the last signal fires on Naked Boy Hill." He pointed aft; wisps rose skyward on the small green mountain a mile behind them. "The location of the two fires indicates that the allied fleet remains close by the center of the southern coast, but that some elements may be moving to the west."

"They could be moving on the lagoon," Irarraga said, watching for the admiral's response. "It certainly does not sound as if they are racing to engage the flotilla to the west."

Fadrique shrugged. "It is not essential to our plans that they should, although it would have been better. But frankly, I am unsurprised. Few Dutch captains would take that bait. They are bold, but they are always mindful not to split their forces unnecessarily."

"They did at Vieques, sir." Both men turned to stare at Rodríguez de Ledesma. His comment was not exactly impudent, but it had not been invited.

Fadrique faced him directly. "At Vieques, the allies did not divide their forces; the sailed ships made best speed to escape while the steamships remained behind as a rearguard. But I was not aware you were there, Lieutenant."

"It was my first battle, sir."

"What ship?"

"The *San Pedro*, sir."

Álvarez nodded. "That was Captain de Covilla's ship."

"It was, sir. He is a brave man."

"He is indeed." Fadrique pointed over the bowsprit to the furthest fragata, the one following just behind the last of the four galleons. "He is now captain of the *Espada Santa*. He will be the first to close with the enemy."

"As I said, he is a brave man, sir."

Álvarez nodded. *And he is stubborn, and a fool, leading from the front yet again! We need you, Eugenio. You have already proven your bravery and your ability and I will not allow you to risk your neck after this. Because upon that neck sits a very clever head that we cannot afford to lose.*

But Rodríguez was frowning. "Sir, I am uncertain what you mean. How would it be that *Espada Santa* will be the first to engage? Is she to come around the galleons and open the way for them?"

"No, Lieutenant." Well, there was no reason not to give Irarraga's executive officer a sense of the profoundly counter-doctrinal battle he would soon see unfold. "We do not expect the galleons to survive long enough to bring the enemy ships under their guns."

"Sir?"

"You were at Vieques, so you should understand. If we round Pointe Blanche and a steamship is anywhere in range, it will likely open fire at no less than six hundred yards. In good weather such as this, each gun will fire twice every minute. That is four shells a minute. Before long, they will be hitting at least fifty percent of the time."

"So, so . . ." stammered Rodríguez, "those fine ships, those brave crews, they are to be . . . to be Judas goats?"

"No," interjected Irarraga, "they are the strongest smoke ships we could fashion. With this wind behind them, they will make near four knots and the smoke will be rushing into the face of the enemy. And us—in these new swifter, smaller, and more maneuverable ships—shall close safely as far as we may, protected by their sacrifice. And Lieutenant?"

"Sir?" the younger man rasped.

"Mind your tone."

"Yes, but sir . . . galleons are Spain's mighty right arm!"

Álvarez assessed the distance to Pointe Blanche. They had time, and it was best that this young man understand why he was about to watch the greatest symbol of Spanish military might gored like a picador's horse. "Yes, Rodríguez," he agreed, "galleons have always been Spain's mighty right arm. But that arm no longer swings swiftly enough. Nor far enough. And I am not speaking of the steamships, now; we cannot get close enough to trade blows with those horrors. I am speaking of the Dutch ships, the new frigates that they have been building."

Rodríguez looked at the deck he was standing upon, then the fragatas and new-model galleoncetes that made up their squadron. "Yes, the Dutch ships fire more quickly, like these. But their guns are lighter and so do less damage. Again, like these."

Fadrique leaned away from the pale young man who, despite having been in combat only once before, was now—*God help us!*—an executive officer. "Lieutenant, do you know how long it takes to reload one of the forty-two-pounders that made our galleons the scourge of all seven seas? No? Well, as it so happens, I've spent my whole career waiting on those great beasts to be readied for a second broadside. So here is the only fact a young officer must remember about those guns if he wishes to survive: the Dutch load their pieces twice as quickly. So they always have more chances to hit you, even if you have the same number of guns. And in time, you will also realize that each Dutch ball that hits does not just damage your ship; it chips away at the morale of your crew."

Álvarez folded his hands, felt ridiculously like a schoolmaster rather than an admiral on the verge of a decisive battle. "So yes, a single hit from our greatest guns can cripple smaller Dutch ships. And yes, we've still been able to contend with the Dutch, although their ships are often faster, more maneuverable, and more quick to fire. But change is the only constant, Lieutenant. Our galleons are rapidly becoming great, ponderous Goliaths with fists too slow to hit what they swing at. Whereas our enemy's new frigates are like Davids: swifter still, even more maneuverable, shooting often, and readily dodging our greatest broadside blows."

De Orbea shouted from the midship gunwale.

"Admiral! Signal from Guana Cay, sir. One enemy ship has been sighted, tacking east. It is small and within a quarter of a mile of attaining a clear line of sight to us."

The admiral turned to Irarraga, seeking confirmation on what his senses were already telling him.

The captain implicitly understood the admiral's glance. His smile was narrow and pitiless. "The wind is perfect for these sails, sir. A bit wide over the quarter. We'll be around the point before the heathens can even signal we're coming."

"Excellent. I require signals, Irarraga."

He gestured to Rodríguez. "They are at your disposal, Admiral."

Álvarez indicated that they should walk with him as he descended the foc'sle and made briskly astern, speaking loudly so that the ship's masters and deckhands alike could hear him.

"We shall soon come around the headland to starboard, Pointe Blanche. The galleons will lead us out, the wind full in their sails and fires on their deck to raise smoke that shall conceal us as we follow behind them. When we are close enough, we shall come around and between them to set upon our foes."

"We'll smash those demon ships at last!" some sail handler shouted from the rigging.

"No, we shall not," Álvarez yelled over him. "Our job is to close with the *other* enemy ships, so fast and so near that those demon spawn cannot fire for fear of hitting them." Once amidships, he stopped and turned slowly to address all those in the range of his voice. "As we come at them from the east, our other ships shall round Gunner's Point to the west and stand as firm and unyielding as an anvil.

"And we...we shall be the hammer! And will do unto our enemies as they did unto our brothers-in-arms off Dominica! We shall see if the demon ships still venture boldly from their ports, as they have fewer and fewer minions to protect them from our wiles and ambushes." He paused and smiled around. "We may even have a holy lance with which to slay one of those great, smoke-maned lions today. But even if not, we can slaughter much of the pride. This time, and the next time, and the time after that."

He paused, felt their unblinking eyes upon him. "And then, when the demon ships are all that are left, *then* we shall see who truly rules these waves!" He resumed his journey to the stern, cheers growing and following behind him.

As did de Orbea, who asked, "Your Excellency, how do you mean to destroy their steamships? What is this holy lance?"

Fadrique glanced sideways. *De Orbea, my boy, you may not be much of an officer, but you are not blinded by stirring rhetoric. And that is a valuable trait unto itself.* "Lieutenant, there is only one kind of weapon which can kill such infernal adversaries: the ones they themselves create."

"So...so you have one of their guns? Or ships? Or—?"

Fadrique held up a hand. De Orbea might not be easily swayed by rhetoric but, alas, he was equally impervious to metaphors. "It is not a physical device at all, de Orbea. We shall undo our enemies through their prideful overconfidence in up-time wonders."

"You mean, confidence in their steamships?"

Fadrique smiled. "Those, too," he muttered and made for the poop deck.

Which left de Orbea to follow mute and wondering in his wake as the crew's cheers evolved into bellicose cries of eagerness for battle. That promising noise carried Admiral Fadrique Álvarez de Toledo all the way to the poop. It was still loud as he gestured Rodríguez toward the waiting signalmen. It persisted even as he nodded at the wide, fierce grins of the men around him and he thought:

Please God, I beg you: let everything I told them be true.

Chapter 57

Off the southern coast, St. Maarten

As *Resolve* came within a mile of the galleons waiting near Pelican Point, they finally began to move with dispatch...but toward Simpson's Lagoon's barrier bank.

Dirck Simonszoon could barely believe his eyes. Were they planning to run themselves aground? He looked through his spyglass. The smoke at ground level was thick, but he could still descry that they were proceeding directly toward the approximate edge of the land as quickly as a reaching breeze allowed. Simonszoon called for his foretopman to confirm if he was seeing the same thing, and got a cry of "Aye, sir!" almost instantly.

Simonszoon leaned toward his XO, smiled thinly. "Bjelke, I never thought I'd say this, but I cannot trust my own senses. I need your confirmation."

Rik Bjelke nodded vigorously. "I see what you do, sir, and I cannot imagine what the Spanish are doing. I do wish we could see the barrier bank better. Unfortunately, since it is almost level with the water and the smoke drifting over from Billy Folly Hill blocks observation from the crow's nest, there is no way to know if they are running as close to land as it seems. Perhaps they mean to bait us close to shore guns?"

Dirck frowned. "A reasonable guess, but how do they expect to see to shoot through their own smoke?"

Rik shook his head. "Sir, I have no answer. Indeed, I cannot think of any that make sense."

"Very well. We shall continue to remain under sail only. I want firing solutions from Mount One and Two for the closest ship. If they don't run like frightened hens beforehand, we shall open fire at six hundred yards."

As the leading galleon was slowly swallowed up by the smoke near the shore, Rik squinted at the distance. "I make their speed less than a knot, sir. We will reach range in six minutes."

"Which, if they hold their current course, is about the same time the last of them will run aground." Simonszoon shook his head. "Lieutenant, they say if you sail long enough, you will see everything. But in all my years at sea, I've never seen anything like this."

One after the other, the galleons vanished into the smoke, became dim outlines. Only the last one in line, their target, remained fully visible. But it too was approaching the smoke. "Rik, change in orders. Instruct Mount One to fire when we reach six hundred fifty yards."

Bjelke nodded, sent the instruction down the speaking tube, and a few moments later, the sound and rush of the forward eight-inch naval rifle buffeted them.

The azimuth setting had been correct, but the elevation was high; the shell punched a hole in the top mainsail.

"Adjust."

"Shall I steer another point to left to give Mount Two a firing angle?"

"Let's wait a moment, Rik. If the others come back out of the smoke, I want to be able to make them wish they hadn't." *But how could any of them hope to come hard about and toward us, now? They'd lose way before crossing the wind and be in irons for sure.*

"Mount One reports ready and target reacquired."

"Fire."

The gun sent out a long smoky plume that pointed to the shell's impact point, just abaft the galleon's waist. Planks, shrouds, stays flew outward, stippling the water. Dirck brought up his spyglass to inspect the degree of damage more closely.

. . . And watched as the shadowy outline of the galleon in front of the one they'd just hit sailed onto the land.

Impossible, of course. But at just under half a mile away, Simonszoon could measure distances between objects down to a few yards, and damn it, that ghostly galleon had just sailed right over or through where the lagoon's barrier bank began.

Or where we thought it began . . .

"I need steam!" Simonszoon cried. "Rik, get the handlers aloft! They need to catch more of this wind; I want five knots! Pilot, give me a point to port. Mount Two, acquire and fire. Mount One, give 'er another taste of our iron. Leadsman to the bow! Foretop, eyes ahead and keen on the coast! Christ's Own carbuncles, let's find out what the hell is going on here!"

"Admiral Tromp! Message from Captain Simonszoon!"

Eddie glanced at the paper as Tromp took it from Cas. "So does he tell us what he's been doing?"

"He does," the admiral answered slowly, "although I am no less puzzled now than I was before." He handed it off with a frown as he bent over the tactical plot. "It seems we must make an adjustment to the map."

"What?" Eddie said, right before he read:

```
FR: SIMONSZOON, CO RESOLVE
TO: TROMP, FLT ADM, ABOARD
INTREPID
—MESSAGE BEGINS—
    HAVE DISABLED 2 GALLEONS STOP
    2 OTHERS FLED INTO LAGOON VIA
  INLET AT BASE OF BILLY FOLLY HILL
  STOP
    INLET APPX 60 YARDS WIDE  STOP
    AT LEAST 6 MORE GALLEONS IN
  LAGOON STOP
    ALL BECALMED OR MOVING AT LESS
  THAN HALF A KNOT STOP
    INTEND TO ENGAGE SOONEST, PEND-
  ING YOUR APPROVAL STOP
  —MESSAGE ENDS—
```

Eddie held the flimsy away from him. "This makes no sense. *No* sense." He turned to Cas. "Get the operational atlas. You know where it is?"

"Yes, sir."

"Then run!" He turned back to the tactical map. "The Spanish couldn't have dug an inlet almost sixty yards wide and at least sixty long, not since we got word of them. They can't have. We'd have seen the dirt, the machinery."

Tromp nodded. "I agree. But here it is."

Eddie shook his head. "But it's not on our charts. Not on any of them!" Cas returned with a large up-time briefcase, and produced a venerable ring binder from its depths.

"Ah," Tromp mused, "The Holy of Holies."

"You seem awful calm about this, Maarten."

"Would it help to get upset?"

Maarten, I really do hate it when you get all . . . all adult *on me.* Eddie opened the ring binder to the section tabbed "St. Maarten." He flipped through the plastic-sleeved charts, each the product of hours of meticulous copying. He found those that showed Simpson's Lagoon and its approaches, then laid them out for Tromp. "The inlet is not there. Not even on these old maps, back to the mid-1800s. And this French one from 1775? Not there, either."

Tromp pointed to the center of the same stretch of barrier bank. "However, all of the newer maps *do* show an inlet here, about two hundred yards to the west. So perhaps there was some initial placement error made by one mapmaker that was picked up and repeated by those who came after?"

Eddie froze for a moment. *Omigod, how do I say this without sounding insulting?* "Maarten, here's the first problem with that theory: the older maps don't show any inlet *at all*. The second problem is that the inlet you're pointing at is man-made. Look: here are the four surveys conducted between 1943 and the Ring of Fire. And see? On the first one, there's no inlet anywhere along the barrier bank.

"But on the next three? There it is. And see how straight it is? That's because they dug it when they decided to turn Simpson's Lagoon into a marina. And it's three hundred and thirty yards to the west of Billy Folly Hill, not right up against it."

Tromp leaned back from the maps. "Eddie, we must make a decision, and quickly. And it seems to me that there could be a simple-enough explanation for this. Either the inlet we see before us now was filled intentionally at some later point in your world, or it naturally silted in over time." He shrugged. "So when they decided to make the lagoon a harbor, they chose the spot on your maps, instead."

"Yeah, but *why* move it from where we're seeing it now? Why not simply dredge along the natural channel?"

For the first time since meeting him, Maarten's voice took on a tone of carefully groomed patience. "If nature *did* fill in this inlet, that might have been what decided your up-time engineers against it. So they chose to dig a new channel with deeper approaches and less silting. Or what may have been more important"— Tromp pointed over the rail at Billy Folly Hill—"it may have been safer, away from all that loose rock."

Eddie frowned. "So you're saying that the inlet we're seeing is prone to rockslides?"

Tromp shrugged. "Entirely possible. Which might also explain why it is not on any of the earlier maps, at least not any of those you had in Grantville."

"What do you mean?"

"I mean, it may not be a permanent feature. Such things are common in shallow bays with shifting sand banks. Small islands can appear and then vanish in the course of a single decade, particularly in the wake of a great storm." The admiral glanced at the coast. "Here, a particularly strong hurricane might reopen this inlet by washing away silt and loose rock. Only for it to begin filling up again."

Eddie nodded. Yeah, and then it would make sense to create a better inlet, once you had the technology to do it. But something about this just wasn't right. "Look," he said, "I still have a bad feeling about this. Why not have *Resolve*'s escort, *Vliegende Hert*, go in first? It's got barely half the draft, so less risk grounding in the lagoon."

Tromp nodded somberly. "That is a reasonable suggestion. I will relay it, along with your reservations, to *Resolve*. But as Dirck is the commander on site, I shall leave the decision to accept or reject and escort to him." Tromp wrote a hasty message, passed it to Cas, who was off in a flurry of skinny adolescent arms and legs.

Eddie stared at the unchanged tactical plot for almost a minute before he asked. "Do you think Dirck will agree to taking the escort?"

Tromp frowned, shook his head. "I very much doubt it."

"So do I," Eddie sighed. *There's a reason he's called Dirck the Smirk; he's not shy about letting folks know that he's pretty sure he's right. About pretty much everything.* "But damn if this doesn't feel like a trap."

Tromp stared. "I don't believe I have ever heard you use profanity before, Eddie." He frowned. "Your misgivings must be grave indeed."

Eddie nodded. "Yeah, and it's not like I don't understand why this looks, and may *be*, a great opportunity to sink a lot of Spanish ships really quickly. Almost as many galleons as we sunk at Vieques. Or Grenada. And I totally get just how lame my counterargument is: I 'feel' like he's sailing into a trap."

Tromp nodded. "A good naval commander listens to his instincts. But Dirck's must take precedence, here. He is the one close enough to assess the situation, so his instincts are the ones we must trust."

Cas came running up the stairs, breathless. "Sir," he said, handing a new flimsy to Tromp, "I do not think I've ever seen so many signals come from Captain Simonszoon."

"No," muttered Eddie, "I'll bet not."

Tromp was still reading. "Shall I synopsize?"

Eddie just nodded.

"Captain Simonszoon is unconcerned about map inconsistencies, citing how certain features can change over time." Tromp raised an eyebrow. "Having approached the inlet, his leadsman and others have reported quantities of loose sand and debris consistent with a severe storm.

"He sees no reason to send the jacht ahead since the eight galleons are of comparable draft to *Resolve* and they continue to move toward the north. He suspects they are making for an inlet on the other side of the lagoon which will allow them to rejoin the squadron standing off the west coast."

Which, Eddie had to admit, was just where another inlet was likely to be, since that was where another postwar construction project had cut a second channel through the barrier bank.

Tromp was coming to the bottom of the flimsy. "Captain Simonszoon indicates that it is his intention to enter the lagoon, sink the enemy ships, withdraw, and rejoin the fleet with all speed." Tromp folded the flimsy, then his hands, then looked squarely at Eddie. "Commodore, do you have a concrete reason why Captain Simonszoon should not do as he proposes?"

Eddie sighed and shook his head.

Tromp nodded and leaned toward the speaking tube to the wireless room. "Send to Captain Simonszoon: you are ordered to engage the enemy in the lagoon until all are destroyed, or you deem it wisest to disengage and break off."

Chapter 58

Simpson's Lagoon, St. Maarten

Dirck Simonszoon slapped the flimsy with sharp, impatient vindication. "About time," he grumbled. "Engine room: I will be calling for steam within the minute." An affirmative cry came up the speaking tube.

Rik glanced at the galleons sailing slowly away. "Admiral Tromp has authorized the attack?"

"Yes, even over the obvious reservations of his up-time genius." He glanced sideways at Rik. "Don't tell Eddi—er, the commodore I said that. Frankly, he might well be a genius, and he's been right far more often than he's been wrong." He leaned toward another speaking tube. "Mount One and Two, track designated targets. We will be moving at one knot."

He faced Rik again. "But Bjelke, have you ever noticed how fearful up-timers are of . . . well, of making a mistake? How did *we* ever become *them*, as we obviously did in that world?"

Rik shrugged. "I have not given it much thought, sir. Other than that they are accustomed to having

715

so much more control over their environment, so many more options for . . . well, for almost everything. I suppose that when one has so many more answers from which to choose, one becomes accustomed to spending more time and research on each choice. Particularly the important ones."

Simonszoon kept his smile in check. "For a fellow who hasn't given it much thought, that's a pretty well-reasoned answer. Now, let's to business. As soon as we are into the lagoon, we will need to keep to the path the galleons took, and also, to angle ourselves so Mount Two may also bear. Understood?"

"Yes, sir. You wish me to tend to that, I presume?"

"Yes. Runner?"

"Sir!"

"What are you doing back there? Stand where I can see you, boy! Run this speaking trumpet to the leadsman. I need him to call out depth every fifteen seconds, and the moment we are at nineteen feet."

Rik spoke from over his shoulder. "You have steam for one quarter, sir."

"Tell them half of that and half again. Not more than a knot now, Rik. Mount One?"

"Target acquired."

"Fire."

At only four hundred yards, wood and dust erupted from both sides of the galleon's hull, the larger jet coming from the far side, where the shell had actually gone all the way through the ship. Dirck nodded in private satisfaction, ordered Mount One to fire again, and inquired about Mount Two's readiness, thinking: *now this;* this *never gets tiresome . . .*

"Sir," cried the leadsman through the speaking

trumpet, "depth is twenty feet. Thick weeds on either side of the channel."

Dirck managed not to roll his eyes. As if weeds on either side of a soil-sided inlet in the tropics were worthy of report. It would have been stranger if some growth *wasn't* there.

Mounts One and Two roared within a second of each other. One round was a near miss, vaporizing only the stern lantern before it shrieked out over the lagoon. The second projectile hit the hull where the maindeck rose to the quarterdeck; all manner of materials spewed out, and the ship seemed to stagger.

The leadsman cried out again. "Holding at twenty feet. Pushing through some weeds in the channel, now."

Dirck nodded toward the bow, but muttered, "Am I the only captain afloat cursed with a leadsman more attentive to weeds than depth?"

Rik had heard him. "Sir, it *is* odd that he remarks upon the weeds."

"Odd...or perverse. Look at all the growth." Simonszoon gestured to either side. "Some is bound to drift into the channel and the Spanish ahead of us just pushed most of it out of the way. Hardly worth reporting."

Rik frowned, his gaze moving from the overgrown barrier bank on the left to the still-smouldering foliage that climbed up toward Billy Folly Hill on the right. "But sir, if the Spanish have been using this inlet regularly, wouldn't it have already been clear of weeds?"

Simonszoon half turned toward his XO. "That is a very good, and somewhat worrisome point, Mr. Bjelke. Go to the side and take a look at those weeds."

Mount One spoke again. A fourth shell scored a third hit near the base of the mainmast. It tipped slightly, just before the mainstays started to snap, one after the other. Canvas shredding as it fell, the mast fell forward and smashed down hard on the already-savaged starboard weather deck. The ship listed, lost way, and it looked as if men were already leaping off the opposite side of her waist. So much for Spanish tenacity. Simonszoon leaned toward the speaking tube. "Firing solutions?"

"Both mounts have solutions on their next targets and are prepared to fire."

"Reload with standard round, fire, and then hold. Let's see if they strike their colors."

Two hundred yards further beyond her, the next target beckoned. He momentarily wondered why neither the last ship nor the two he'd hammered to pieces on the way into the lagoon had so much as fired once, at least in defiance. The crews seemed to be more interested in hiding beneath the gunwales and fleeing—however slowly—than fighting back. Of course, at the ranges which *Resolve* engaged them, their guns would have been lucky to hit a target the size of... Well, at four hundred yards, the only thing their balls had any chance of hitting was the sea. The odds of doing that, at least, were pretty promising. So long as gravity continued to function.

As the leadsman called out a depth of twenty-one feet, Rik Bjelke returned to the flying bridge. "Well," Simonszoon prompted, "are they weeds or not?"

"Sir, they are—but there are too many, I think."

"What do you mean?"

Rik indicated both sides of the channel through

which they had almost passed. "There is much loose or cut foliage all about us, sir. On the facing slope to our right and all along the bank to our left, from the seaside to the lagoon. Much of it is still burning—"

"Well, that's probably all you're seeing: the parts of the wood and the bracken they laid up to create all the smoke that haven't yet caught flame." He shrugged. "Some wound up in the inlet."

"Yes, sir, no doubt. But about the brush on the barrier bank; it looks as if a great deal of it was not *meant* to catch flame, and hasn't." He hastened on as Dirck's frown became impatient. "The parts that are burning, both near Pelican Point and on the bank, are all arrayed at the edge of or immediately overlooking the sea. Behind that, there is more of the same, but scattered. And it is not burning. Well, not much of it." Rik waved a frustrated hand toward the channel that was now behind them. "It is quite a jumble, sir. But I am struck by how much effort the Spanish expended bringing down not just wood, but cuttings, and then not doing a better job of setting it all afire."

Dirck found it vaguely disconcerting, but immediately chided himself. So was Dirck Simonszoon, terror of the Caribbean for almost twenty years, becoming as fretful as a twenty-three-year-old up-timer, imagining Spaniards hidden in every bush, terrors lurking behind every cloud of smoke?

He snorted aloud at the thought. "Keep on the pilot, Bjelke. I don't want the speed creeping up. And while you are at that..."

"Yes, Captain?"

"Send word down to de Ruyter. All ship's troops

are to load their pieces. I want half of the Germans summoned to the weather deck. Keep the rest, including those Wild Geese of his, below. But keep them ready."

Billy Folly Hill, St. Maarten

Captain Manrique Gallardo risked poking his head out of the makeshift command post and bunker on the rear slope of Billy Folly Hill. The enemy steam cruiser—half as long as the largest galleon ever built, but with only slightly greater freeboard—moved slowly past. The faint *chegg . . . chegg . . . chegg . . .* of its monstrous metal heart mimicked the pulse of a sleeping man. Even though its long, strange deck guns roared like thunder and hit like lightning bolts, there was still a palpable sense that the ship was moving cautiously.

No doubt part of that was explained by the busy leadsman. Gallardo doubted he would have been any more trusting of the "safe depth" along the path that enemy ships had navigated before him. But whatever other reservations the enemy commander may have felt, the lure of so many easy kills was, as Fadrique had predicted, irresistible. "Because," the admiral had confessed with a smile, "I am relatively sure it would be irresistible to *me*."

And he'd been right, as the grand old bastard usually was. He might be a hidalgo, might sip rather than swig his wine—well, usually!—but he was an old warhorse at heart and interested in only two things: Spain's dominion and winning battles. Which, to Manrique Gallardo, were damned close to synonyms and all he required in a leader.

He tapped one of his two runners on the shoulder. "Now, light the fuse."

The young fellow, eyes wide, almost left with his morion still on. Gallardo grabbed it, swatted the boy-soldier on the back of his head and resisted the urge to kick him down the hill. He refrained not out of kindness, but because a cloud of dust and tumbling youngster might draw the attention of someone on that demon ship.

However, the lad was fleet of foot, small of body, and stealthy when he ran. He made it down to the large, sun-bleached tooth of rock behind which they'd sheltered the heads of the covered fuses, and uncoiled the slow-burning match that was wrapped around his forearm. In the last five years, the arquebuses of Spanish soldiery had disappeared and the remaining matchlocks were mostly in the hands of native auxiliaries, but they still had plenty of the matches used to fire both.

The runner held the match to the fuse, which smoked, then flared, then burned its way downhill. Or so Gallardo imagined; except for the near end, the fuse was in a tube, concealed from sight and buried under a thin shield of small rocks along most of its course. Manrique realized he hadn't started timing it, so began at "three" instead of "one" and counted up toward ten.

At eight, he nodded at his other runner and they both ducked down beneath the lip of the bunker's window, covering their ears and shutting their eyes.

They waited. When Gallardo reach fifteen in his internal count, he stood. Downhill, the young runner who'd lit the fuse shrugged expressively.

"*Coño!*" snared Gallardo. He slapped the other runner on the side of the head. "Go tell the sergeants. The fuse didn't burn all the way to the charges."

"Anything else, Captain, sir?"

"Yes, idiot! Tell them to get out there and fix them! *Now!*"

Simpson's Lagoon, St. Maarten

Mount One fired, then Mount Two. The second of the galleons, its ribs already showing through its shattered starboard hull, was hit in almost exactly the same place as it had been by the last two rounds. Even before the bracings and pillars that supported it had finished flying outward to raise up dozens of geyser-like eruptions in the lagoon, Simonszoon heard another sound behind that rending of heavy timbers: a sharp crack, then another, then a long groan with a squeal of tortured wood rising up through its center. An immense section of the galleon's side simply gave way, the structural integrity too shredded to persist. Beams splintered and strakes came ripping off, down to and even beneath the waterline.

The groan of ruined wood succumbing to its own unsupported weight gave way to a long, greedy moan of inrushing water. As if the belly of the eviscerated galleon was sucking it inward, a vicious fuming rose up around the breach; the weight and pressure was such that a good deal of the ravenous flood was pulverized into vapor. The galleon started to list in the direction of that vast wound, and was settling rapidly as she did.

Simonszoon had seen many ships die in his many years at sea, but never one quite like this: so still and yet so grievously breached that she was sure to sink in less than a minute. But as she did just that, and her other side began turning toward the sky, the galleon's stern was also being dragged slightly to the right, pulled by the greater volume of water growling in up close to the bow. And as it did, and as *Resolve* steered to ensure that Mount Two would be able to bear easily upon the next target, Dirck saw that not only were most of the gunports on the port side closed, but those few with open lids were as dark and empty as a blind seer's eye sockets.

Simonszoon started into an erect posture. Unless all those cannons had broken free of both their breeching ropes and gun and train tackle at a mere twenty-degree list, those ports had been completely empty the whole time. Which now added to the speed of the galleon's death roll; since the starboard side that had faced him throughout showed all her muzzles, it meant that her port side hadn't that weight of cannon. And now, whatever lines had helped keep the counterbalancing ballast on that side tore asunder, cracking like a dozen titans' whips.

The suddenly released counterweight slid from left to right, bringing the ship over so quickly that, for a moment, her keel rose almost thirty degrees above the surface of the lagoon. Then she settled to the extent that she could in so shallow a body of water.

Dirck Simonszoon blinked in surprise at what he had seen—and as his eyes reopened, they showed him his surroundings anew. He was four hundred yards into a lagoon in which a galleon could not completely sink, even on its side. None of the ships were galleoncetes or pataches, although they had shallower drafts. As had been the first two galleons, all six remaining presented him with roughly the same perspective as he advanced: a view of their stern or starboard quarter. At no point would he see their portside hulls, as had the ship that had just gone down. A ship which, like half of those that remained, were among the darkest galleons he'd ever seen: so old that they warranted the adjective "venerable." Or maybe more significantly, "decrepit."

And the muzzles that had been facing him from their starboard and stern batteries: did they even have crews? Was that the reason, rather than the futility, that they had not even fired once? Was it why the deck crew had so readily leaped clear of the other galleons? Had there even been a full crew aboard, or just enough to move these ships along?

"These ships." Were they, in fact, really ships anymore? Or were they just—he struggled to find the right word—decoys? No; it went beyond that. These were just props. Which meant...

That young, duck-screwing up-timer was right!

Pointe Blanche, St. Maarten

With covered pots of burning oil arrayed on their poop decks, and combustibles stacked like hayricks near to hand, Fadrique Álvarez de Toledo's four galleons-become-smoke-ships picked up speed as they rounded Pointe Blanche, the strong Atlantic wind now directly over their starboard quarters.

Behind them, with *Espada Santa* in the lead, the newest hulls from the ways at Cuba and Santo Domingo had to keep their sails trimmed so as not to get ahead of the growing smoke screen. The Dutch sloop that had been spotted by the watchers on Guana Cay seemed to almost hop in fright as it heeled sharply southward, away from the enemy flotilla.

Álvarez was ready with spyglass to eye as the *Santa Ana la Real* cleared the headland and the crews of his smoke ships began removing the lids of what had been whalers' try-pots. He wouldn't be able to see beyond them for much longer, since their crews would soon start adding a mixture of sawdust, sugar, and niter to the flames, the resulting smoke making observations impossible until they passed the doomed galleons.

The glass revealed a scene not too different from the one Fadrique had envisioned. Approximately three and a half miles to the west, ten enemy ships were arrayed near Pelican Point. Another mile and a half still further to the west, about a dozen more were in a loose cluster. The purpose and nature of the farther group was obvious; it was the balance of the enemy's conventional men-of-war, set in a screen to intercept any attack by the galleons waiting off the west coast. But the closer squadron was the one that commanded Álvarez's primary interest . . . and concern.

Ten ships, four of which were small: jachts, almost certainly. Of the other six, four were decidedly modern hulls: a bark with French lines and three of the allies' newest frigates. Álvarez studied them as best he could from the distance and whenever there was a sufficient gap between his smoke-making galleons. Two of the frigates were similar to his own fragata, but the third showed even longer, leaner lines, retaining less of a quarterdeck and with almost all her guns in a covered gundeck: clear evidence of up-time design influence. And the last two ships were . . .

Fadrique almost crushed the spyglass against his eye: *two* steamships? Had the allies not taken the bait after all? But as he continued to look, his understanding grew. And so did the realization that while his ruse had succeeded, there was a new and wholly unanticipated danger with which to contend. Specifically, the second steamship was of a new, slightly smaller class. Which meant that the USE had not two, but *three* steam-driven warships in the Caribbean. The cold horror which came with that knowledge quickly gave way to grim gratitude; learning that was almost worth the losses he expected—he knew—his fleet would take this day.

And it also meant that the second of the larger steamships had likely taken his bait as the allied officers swung between alarm over the failure of their ever-so-perfect maps and the hunger to destroy all the galleons before and in the now navigable lagoon.

As the smoke in front of him grew and his enemies became hazy silhouettes, his final glimpse was of the anticipated inevitability of seeing them turn to face his own formation. They were steering smartly through the wind, ensuring that they did not lose way as they tacked to engage him, even without the advantage of the weather gauge. Of course, if that new steamship had guns like the other did, they still had reason for confidence.

But, thanks to the growing smoke screen, so did he. Time to share that, and a little bit more, with the men of his flagship. He put out a hand for the speaking trumpet, held at the ready by de Orbea. Irarraga appeared, seemingly out of nowhere, at his side.

"Sons of Spain and children of our Blessed Savior!

This is not merely a battle; it is a holy cause. We are not merely fighting men, we are facing heretics who have consorted with godless persons from what is now, by their own admission, a vanished future. They have already changed the world with their infernal machines, but here and now, we can fight to ensure that they change it no more! It is that for which we fight! It is for that reason that Philip IV's devoted servant, the Duke of Olivares, has sent orders that no Dutchman is to be spared! And by extension, the same applies to any who serve under their flag. You can expect no different from them. They are desperate and will not ask nor show quarter any more than we shall! Now, for God and Spain, let us send them quickly back to the Hell from whence they came!" The cheering after his speech was as deafening as had been the silence during it.

As de Orbea leaned over to retrieve the speaking trumpet, he murmured, "Sir, is that truly known? That they are so determined as we to show no quarter? I have heard that their actions after taking La Flota demonstrated quite the opposite."

Álvarez stared at his aide. "The truth of such matters may be reduced to this: if our men are now prepared to fight to the death, then what I have said is all the 'truth' they need to know."

With that, Álvarez turned and went to inspect the readiness of the fragata, trying to quiet his own demons of doubt: would her lighter, faster pieces really make the difference he was hoping for? He stared in the smoke-obscured direction of his enemies. *We'll know soon enough.*

Chapter 59

Simpson's Lagoon, St. Maarten

"Cease fire!" Dirck Simonszoon ordered. "Engineer, I need more steam. Now."

The pilot looked over, surprised. "Sir? Aren't we staying to shoot these fish in a barrel?"

"No, we are reversing course and leaving this lagoon with all possible speed."

The pilot met Simonszoon's intense stare. "Reverse course, sir? All the way back?" Glancing away, he stammered, "I . . . I'm not sure, sir. Not a thing I've ever trained for. Docking maneuvers and backing off a reef, yes, but . . ." He looked back along the four hundred yards to the inlet. "I can't make it at anything like good speed, sir. If at all."

Dirck nodded, started striding forward. At least the fellow was honest. Which was crucial, since he didn't have the time to try to sort out what his men thought he wanted to hear, rather than the unadorned truth. "Leadsman!" he shouted as he neared *Resolve*'s waist.

"Sir?"

"Any idea as to the widest part of the navigable path?"

The leadsman was hurrying back toward him. "Can't be sure, sir."

"I'm not asking for 'sure'; I need your best guess."

The old salt frowned. "About halfway in, we had readings of twenty and twenty-one feet for almost a hundred yards. It might still be just a narrow trench there, but from the play in the line, I'd say it was broader than that."

"Broad enough for us to turn around it?"

"Sir?"

"Backing engines is too risky. So I mean to turn the ship and make for the exit with better speed."

The leadsman's eyes were wide. "Sir, this ship is near on two hundred feet, prow to taffrail. Looking at the lagoon, sir, I can't assure you that she has the room to turn as you wish."

Simonszoon started as Rik Bjelke's voice came over his shoulder. "Sir, if I may?"

"Quickly, man!"

"We put down one of our longboats with another leadsman. That boat parallels us at a constant seventy yards' distance, taking soundings at the same interval. And if they discover a spot of sufficient depth—"

"—then they take soundings all the way back and prove a band of sufficient depth, perpendicular to the path back to the inlet. Yes, that will work."

The leadsman frowned. "That boat can't return to *Resolve* on a straight line, though, sir. They need cut back and forth, as if they were tacking wide. That's the only way to be sure there aren't spots that the keel might catch on while we're turning her."

"Not necessarily," mused Rik. "Even if there's just a fan of greater depth at a right angle along our path back out, we'd be able to turn. We back engines until our stern reaches the point where our boat found the useable depth. Then, once *Resolve*'s keel is perpendicular to the safe channel, we run ahead slowly, turning as our bow begins to come round toward the inlet and adjusting where we must." He smiled wistfully. "Commodore Cantrell calls the maneuver a 'K-turn.' Nonregulation terminology, I believe."

"Why not check the whole area first?" the leadsman asked with a frown. "Takes a bit more time, but there'll be no guessing and then the turning will be a single easy maneuver."

Dirck shook his head. "No. 'More time' is exactly what we don't have. And the longer you or someone else is out in a boat, the longer that some Spaniard with a rifle just might find the range."

The leadsman nodded. "I'll get a man for the boat," he said.

As *Resolve* finished reversing in the stretch of water that the leadsman had indicated as being deep enough for the maneuver, Dirck watched the ship's troops readying the heavy weapons on each quarter: two mitrailleuses and two of the so-called Big Shots. Others ran along *Resolve*'s sides, securing the crew's tightly wrapped sleeping rolls into the netting strung between the stanchions that held up the chain rails. Not as good as solid bulwarks against rifles and pistols, but they eliminated the spear-sized splinters that sprayed across a deck when wooden sides were hit by ball or shot.

As if summoned by his thoughts, a musket ball passed a few yards overhead with a dying whistle.

"From the barrier bank!" Michiel de Ruyter cried. "Stay low, men!"

Sage advice, Simonszoon thought, as *Resolve* started forward, holding true for the first twenty yards, but then slowly turning to port as she prepared to reenter to the safe passage back to the inlet, bow first. "Runner!"

The lad appeared in a moment. "Sir?"

"Tell the master signalman to send this to Admiral Tromp aboard *Intrepid*. Have sunk two more galleons. Am breaking off." Should he add that the galleons were decoys? No, that could wait. "Navigability of lagoon doubtful. Existence of inlet through western barrier bank cannot be ascertained." He nodded at the boy. "Get that sent and return at the run."

The boy shouted back an affirmative from halfway down the stairs to the main deck.

Now, he thought, raising his spyglass as *Resolve* continued turning, *was that musket ball meant for one of us, or was it ranging fire?* He swept it slowly along the debris-choked inner shore of the barrier bank. No way to tell where a single rifleman—or even ten of them—might be hidden among that dense mix of genuine foliage and unburnt cuttings, some of which appeared to be whole tree branches. No cover large enough to conceal a cannon, but still—

He brought his spyglass to bear on the inlet; it warranted close study, as they would have to slow and steer two points to starboard to put their bow in alignment with it. But as he did so, he found himself distracted by the hill and barrier bank flanking it on either side. More and more, that was looking suspiciously like a gauntlet. But whereas the barrier bank had no features or foliage large enough to hide guns, Billy Folly Hill had plenty of both. As *Resolve* finished its turn into the safe path back toward the inlet, Simonszoon began scanning its slopes...

...and saw a figure dash across his narrow line of sight. He snatched the spyglass away from his eye, and felt his stomach harden and sink.

Now that he knew to look for them, and where, he saw men scrambling among the rocky slopes overlooking the inlet. Their movement was puzzling, as if they were playing some desperate game of hide-and-seek as they ran back and forth, then up into the less vegetated higher ground and back down into the forested and cutting-choked base.

"Bjelke!" he shouted. "Eyes on Billy Folly Hill!"

At the same moment that the Norwegian evidently saw the figures—judging from his sharp intake of breath—Simonszoon noticed that, although their dress was plain, the enemy troops were nonetheless wearing some kind of uniform: brown and tan in color, with more straps and belts than seemed necessary. They weren't carrying any long arms or even pistols, at least none that Dirck could see. But still, they didn't look like artillerists either, who tended to wear colors or armbands that helped officers pick them out from the other specialists in the army. And while some artillerists had tools, all of these men were carrying picks, shovels, and axes. Just like sappers.

Sappers...

Simonszoon shouted down the closest speaking tube. "Engineer, ahead three quarters! *Now!*"

Bjelke grabbed hold of the flying bridge's railing

just as *Resolve* leaped forward. Others on the main deck, taken by complete surprise, sprawled with cries of alarm, anger, and in one case, pain. "Captain, I see no guns on the hill."

Simonszoon had turned to look west and what he saw there stretched his mouth into a bitter smile. "That's because they don't intend to fire on us. Look."

Bjelke did.

There was a tremulous hint of movement at several points along the arc of undergrowth and piled cuttings that lined the lagoon side of the barrier bank. As they watched, a wide skiff emerged. A moment later, it was surrounded by half a dozen Spanish soldiers, weapons held well above the surface of the lagoon, their morions glinting in the sun. As they dragged the boat clear of the rubbish so that they could board it, coronets pealed all along that stretch of the barrier bank.

Bjelke stared back at his commander. "B-but how do they mean to catch us, sir? We must be making five knots, already."

Simonszoon glanced back at Billy Folly Hill. "Oh, they won't have to catch us. Not if they can trap us in here with them by sealing the inlet behind us with charges. Then they can swarm us at their leisure." He saw confusion continuing to grow on Rik's face "They want *Resolve*, Bjelke. To capture and turn against us, if they can, but to copy, for certain. Now, stand by the pilot and give him any help he needs."

Dirck turned back to the speaking tube for the engine room. "Full steam, chief. Pilot, all ahead full for the channel! And don't worry about scraping her new paint; just get us out of here, dammit!"

Billy Folly Hill, St. Maarten

Manrique Gallardo waved his sergeants further down the hill. Yes, the bastards on the demon ship were sure to see them, but that didn't matter anymore. The immense ship was flying like a Bermudan cutter and whereas the engines had murmured low and cautious before, they now sounded like eager metal ogres, panting: *CHUGGA! CHUGGA! CHUGGA! CHUGGA!*

Two of Gallardo's runners started back up the hill; he waved them back down. Somewhere, in one of the tubes they'd buried—and had forgotten to mark, the idiots!—the fuse had burned out. Unfortunately, the failure point was not high up, but somewhere toward the bottom of the only slope that ran straight down into the water. To the right and the left of it, the slope flattened into a wooded shelf.

He smiled: and a most convenient wooden shelf it had proven to be. That hadn't made the job any easier, of course. It had been miserable work, first off-loading and readying all matériel, then moving all the rocks where they were needed, and then finally removing any sign that they had ever been there.

But still his men roved down the hill, looking for the section of protective tubing in which the fuse had burned out. It would hardly have been an urgent matter, if the heathen captain hadn't turned back, not even halfway to the shallows from which he would never have extricated himself. But now, in order to entrap the ship, they had to cut off her only route of escape quickly. And at the rate his men were going, they might not find the useable end of the fuse until they got within a few yards of the charges themselves.

Well, he sighed philosophically, *there are two bright sides if that's the case. First: Spain is made strong by the blood of just such martyr-heroes as they will be. And second:*

Better them than me.

Simpson's Lagoon, St. Maarten

At the last second, Simonszoon put his own hand on the wheel; the pilot was competent, but had been assigned more because of machine competence, rather than long years of sailing. And this would require a lifetime's worth of pure instinct and reflexes.

Rather than a smooth, slow turn to address the channel directly, Simonszoon called for only one-eighth less speed, counter-steered, and let the resistance of the side-slipping hull brake them. Two hundred feet of steam cruiser listed to port as her stern came around, screws churning the water. But even as the men on her flying bridge felt like they might be slung sideways into the water, that same slide brought her bow into alignment with the channel—without having to slow her engines. "Flank speed!" Dirck yelled into the speaking tube.

Which was the precise instant that chaos erupted everywhere, all at once.

Better than halfway up Billy Folly Hill's forward-leaning slope, a ragged roar of at least half a dozen cannons birthed a sound like a descending swarm of giant bees.

"Cover!" screamed de Ruyter just before the grape-shot began peppering the deck, the spars, the sails, and the water beyond the shadow of their starboard side. The crew manning the portside bow's Big Shot were riddled and slumped in the mount's "pulpit." Several deckhands went down either shrieking or without uttering a final sound. The spencer sail was clipped clean off the mainmast and the three balls that cut through the top of the funnel made a hollow metal sound: *thrunk-thrunk-thrunk*.

"Boats at two hundred yards!" yelled the spotter/loader of the rear mitrailleuse.

But Dirck was only partially aware of that or anything else as he grabbed the speaking trumpet and yelled, "Forward mitrailleuse! Target: two points port. On the slope. Sappers with charges!" The Spanish sappers weren't actually carrying charges, but the gunners got the basic idea. They brought their weapon to bear, checked elevation, hunched behind it, and set it to chattering. The slope erupted as if dozens of dust demons were breaking free of the ground, interspersed between writhing, tumbling bodies. Those who had not fallen dove for cover.

For the second time that day, Dirck Simonszoon both cursed and blessed Eddie Cantrell, whose obsession with drills—endless, repetitive drills that the crew hated—paid off. The weather deck was a sudden maze of men moving to ready guns, protectively reefing sails, scanning predetermined sectors for enemies, and checking damage. Others appeared on deck with the replacement splinter shields for the naval rifles, but in this case, propped them up as makeshift gabions.

"All stop!" Simonszoon shouted down to engineering,

then flipped over the five-minute glass. The sands started measuring out the minutes they had until the Spanish guns on the heights were reloaded. And if there were others, well, they'd surely speak soon enough. "Marksmen, shoot at anything that moves on those slopes!" Dirck yelled. "Section heads, report!" He got answers as various masters ran up or replied through the speaking tubes.

"Leadsman reporting less than nineteen feet! We need to exit slowly!"

"Sails reefed, in good shape."

"Main mounts cannot take enemy guns under fire, sir. Elevation is too acute."

"Marksmen reporting same, Captain. Their pieces are at approximately two-five-zero yards, but we see no targets."

"Enemy boats aft have slowed, sir. Seem to be waiting."

I'll just bet they are, Dirck thought. But when the surgeon said, "Casualties are—" Simonszoon stopped him with a raised hand. "You'll tell me when it is over. Orders!" he announced. "Master signalman?"

"Sir?"

"Update Admiral Tromp on our situation. Send until you get acknowledgment. Leadsman, how many knots can I have?"

"No more than two, Captain. Faster, and we may not keep to the path. It lays right atop a trench with sharply rising sides."

Of course, Dirck realized, *because the clever bastards dredged* only *that part. Like any good trap, it is easy to enter slowly, but disastrous if you try to get out quickly.*

But, still . . . two knots? That meant almost three minutes from where they were now to the moment they'd clear the other end of the inlet. *Which the Spanish must be anticipating, but we've got no choice.*

"Leadsman, I'll give you that two-knot limit, but keep us as far starboard as you can. Pilot, you heard that speed. Runner, get help to move this"—he waved at the tactical plot and everything near it—"down into the pilothouse. Make sure the armored shutters are in place. Pilot, once you're at the wheel below, take a mark on a fixed object to steer by, in the event we can no longer see our path." *Or they shoot our leadsman off his platform like a sparrow off a fencepost.*

After a brief upward sputtering of his troops' muskets, Dirck resumed. "I want all sail handlers, lookouts on deck, no one aloft. If you don't have a job, you help form those spare splinter shields into pillboxes, one around the base of each mast. Then pair up with the marksmen." More discharges aimed up Billy Folly Hill. "You are their reloaders. Marksmen, keep their heads down." *Because if those sappers fix whatever has gone wrong, I'm pretty sure we'll never see home again.*

A distant report from the barrier bank; a single musket ball buzzed over their heads.

"Mounts One and Two, affix rear shields and then bring your weapons to bear on the hill."

"But sir, we can't elevate enough to—"

"Bear on the hill—at zero elevation, Master Gunner. And load explosive rounds."

"To use against what? Sir?"

Simonszoon pointed to where the flanks of Billy Folly Hill met the channel. "There are sixty yards from the point where we enter the channel to where we leave it. Our enemies know we must pass through it slowly. That's not chance. That was in their minds when they built this trap." He straightened. "Be prepared for point-blank engagement on the port side as we go through. Any target capable of harming *Resolve*, you fire and keep firing. And I repeat: all explosive rounds. No reason to save anything. Same goes for all portside carronade batteries."

"And us?" It was the master gunner of the starboard battery.

"Keep a sharp eye out your gunports. If you see any movement on the barrier bank, blow it into the next world. Master gunner, report on the forward Big Shot."

"Weapon is inoperable, sir, but the position remains sound."

"I'll get something for overhead cover," de Ruyter called out. "I'll put one or two of the Wild Geese in there. With Winchesters: those are the guns for pinning down the sappers."

Simonszoon nodded. "Excellent. And men"—he checked the five-minute glass; it was just over half run—"those are thirty-two-pounders above us. They will be reloaded in another minute . . . and I mean that to be the last time we hear them. Three minutes to open water! Stations!"

Chapter 60

Inlet to Simpson's Lagoon, St. Maarten

Forty seconds later, Simonszoon nodded at the pilot and *Resolve* stirred forward again. Like hyenas following a wounded lion, the dozen broad skiffs that had emerged into the lagoon began paddling after her, but kept their distance.

"Sir," Rik said, "I have been wondering. If you suspect that the channel is a gauntlet that we must run, should we not first shell the banks on either side? It might inflict casualties or at least sow confusion."

Dirck smiled. "That is a fine thought and well worth trying, except for one thing."

Rik frowned, then nodded, understanding. "The time and the sappers."

"Yes: time and the sappers. We can't know exactly what they have planned, but every second we spend in the lagoon increases the chance they'll make sure we never leave it. Now, eyes front and alert. This will all happen very quic—"

The master gunner at Mount One stood high in his pulpit. He pointed portside, cried a warning Dirck could not understand over the bark of a Spanish musket that sent a ball ricocheting off the gun's splinter shield—

—and then it truly did sound as if hell was breaking loose.

Mount One fired at the same instant that three Spanish guns at the base of Billy Folly Hill roared back, their discharge and recoil sending concealing brush flying in all directions. Dirck's breath caught in his throat: Spanish forty-two-pounders. Probably from the lower decks of the decoys. At twenty yards.

Not even *Resolve* could withstand the punishment of those shells. Those that hit her portside hull sent strakes flying. The foreyard was blown free of the foremast, took three stays with it, shredding its topsail as the foresail ripped free of the flying spars. The whole hull shook in response to explosions that thundered low in her port side.

On the shore, half a dozen massive explosions tore at the Spanish battery at the base of the slope. Secondaries—ready powder—went off as well, but were almost lost in the overlapping blasts of the eight-inch shells. The concussive force sprang back from Billy Folly's stony sides and rocked *Resolve* to starboard. All along the hill-bottom shelf, fires were already raging. If there was any movement there, Dirck could not see it.

Resolve's damage bells were ringing. Men were shrieking in agony, more were shrieking orders. The engine room rang up. Before the chief could speak, Simonszoon yelled, "Are the engines damaged?"

"No, Captain, but—"

"Then hold two knots steady. For two more minutes." He turned to Bjelke, who was alarmingly pale but calmly giving orders to the starboard battery to help recrew the port battery's carronades while maintaining sufficient readiness among its own guns. "Damage report?"

"Still coming in, sir. Considerable structural damage to internal supports. Not taking any water. Two carronades gone, fires being fought. Three other breaches but all well above the waterline and afore the beam."

Well, there were two reasons for that. Firstly, *Resolve*'s bow was the first part of her that came abreast of the Spanish guns. But there was another reason the Spanish hadn't waited for a better broadside shot: if they hit the engines, they might lose their prize. And if a shell found the magazine, that became a near certainty.

Resolve's bowsprit was moving past the halfway point, the one stretch at the base of the hill where there was no shelf of rock and trees: just a sheer stone face that disappeared into the water. In thirty seconds, they'd begin drawing abreast of the next shelf, which probably had at least as many guns waiting for them. Another dose of that kind of damage might be crippling.

Simonszoon turned to Rik. "No reason not to use your idea now."

"Sir?"

"All remaining guns in the port battery, and Mounts One and Two are to fire blind at that second shelf. Aimpoint is at each gunner's discretion. Continue firing until we are clear. Make sure our guns' fire is spread across the length of the wooded area and—"

Up at the bow, the mitrailleuse was firing again, joined almost immediately by its twin on the port quarter. The enemy sappers had not been cowering, but moving; they rose up, much closer to the center of the slope, and began sprinting.

The two automatic weapons swept over them, tumbling most, sending a few scurrying to cover. The weapons ran dry at almost the same instant, which was just when the first of the portside carronades started firing blindly into the second half of the Spanish gauntlet. The thunder—of the guns, of the explosions—was deafening, rocks and debris flying back at *Resolve* from the impact points . . . along with another wave of grapeshot from the thirty-two-pounders high on the hill.

But Dirck Simonszoon did not allow himself to be distracted from the greatest threat to his ship: whatever the sappers were trying to reach. Which was why, in the midst of all the flying debris and deafening sound, and despite the peripheral sight of grapeshot blasting aside the mainmast's makeshift gabion and shredding its mainsail, he was the one who saw a new wave of sappers—at least two dozen—emerge from behind the cover of the sea-facing slope of Billy Folly Hill.

He snatched up the speaking trumpet, tried to shout a warning down *Resolve*'s weather deck to where most of his marksmen were clustered—and realized that he couldn't even hear himself. He grabbed Rik by the shoulder, tried shouting: again, nothing. He jabbed his finger in the direction of the approaching sappers.

Rik's eyes widened. He bolted out the side of the pilothouse, evidently meaning to run through the hellish flame and smoke and noise to direct their fire.

Some of the surviving marksmen had already seen the sappers, raised their pieces, fired, reached for the next readied rifle . . . only to discover that their reloaders had been killed or wounded by the latest wave of grapeshot. One or two still managed, despite the range and the uphill trajectory, to bring down one of the half-seen figures. The Wild Geese nestled alongside the ruined Big Shot brought down two more, feverishly cycling the levers of their Winchesters.

But that was not enough. The sappers had reached whatever site they had been striving to reach . . . just as the leadsman appeared in the starboard doorway of the pilothouse, bloodied and shouting words that Dirck could not hear until the man jammed his mouth against the captain's right ear.

As if struggling up from the depths of a cotton-filled mineshaft, Simonszoon heard the words, "Starboard. Channel. Twenty-one. Feet. Go faster." Dirck grabbed the fellow's shoulder, wondered how he'd managed to survive the swirling chaos at the bow—and was blinded by a splash.

He wiped his eyes, saw blood on his hand, wondered if he'd been hit at the same instant he noticed that the leadsman was no longer standing in front of him, but had fallen into the pilothouse. He was facedown, a bullet hole in the back of his skull, with a pool of blood widening around his head like a gory halo.

Simonszoon turned, grabbed the pilot, repeated what he'd been told. Amazingly, the pilot still had enough hearing to understand, nod, and eagerly comply.

Resolve began accelerating. More of her carronades fired into the second half of the gauntlet and secondary explosions rocked that shelf. Spanish gun crews, evidently fearing that they would die if they did not fire, or refusing to die without giving reply, threw aside the brush covering their guns. They hauled mightily at the forty-two-pounders, but the massive weapons did not budge easily. At least not before Mounts One and Two saw the activity, swung to bear, and put an explosive round into two of them. The carronades saw and followed the example.

By God, Dirck thought, *we just might make it.* Closing the pilothouse door before some other sniper on the barrier bank took another shot, he felt and saw *Resolve*'s bow sliding gently toward the deeper water to starboard, saw that it had just drawn abreast of the second half of the gauntlet, most of which was now aflame and in ruins.

God's Mighty Balls, we're going to make it!

Billy Folly Hill, St. Maarten

God's Hairy Balls, thought Captain Manrique Gallardo, *I'm not going to make it.*

But he accepted that sitting and staring at the surprisingly small hole that a bullet had punched in his rounded stomach really wasn't achieving anything. And since he'd been stupid enough to personally lead this last attempt the reach the charges, he might as well make something of it.

Swaying to his feet, he saw the ruin that had been inflicted on the demon ship. *You're not so mighty now, are you? Gaping holes in your side, two with flames and black smoke pouring out, that round iron chimney sheared away, two masts gone. Yes, you are quite a mess.* Of course, looking at what was left of his own forces—flames consuming the charred remains of men and guns—did temper his sense of achievement somewhat.

But not as much as the fact that the damn demon ship was *still* moving.

He'd originally considered running an extended fuse, to give himself time to get behind cover, but that was before the stupid little bullet had gone through his gut. Now, he was happy to use as short a fuse as he could.

He staggered the last few feet to where he'd directed his now extinct sappers to conceal the first of the string charges and sighed. At least he wouldn't feel anything. The only disappointment, he decided as he reflected upon his earlier philosophical musings, was that he didn't really *feel* like a hero or a martyr. He just felt like a fool for having run out here at all. Because as he'd rightly observed, "Better them than me."

But now, as it turned out, he was one of "them." As feelings went, that certainly wasn't a pleasant one. Still, he knew of a way to get rid of it.

He unwound the slow-burning fuse from his forearm, touched it to the fuse, sat back, and thought, *Yep; this is what comes of being a hero, you fool.*

Inlet to Simpson's Lagoon, St. Maarten

No sooner had Dirck Simonszoon surrendered to the opiate of optimism, than the universe slapped him in the face. Literally.

Despite his deafness, he heard an explosion loud enough to herald the end of the world. Its force blasted through the iron shutters, rattling the doors of the pilothouse and pushing him back toward the rear wall. Shaking off the sensation, he heard his men screaming in different languages, opened the shutters to see—

To see the channel-facing slope of Billy Folly Hill exploding upward as if it was, in fact, a bomb itself. Stones the size of wine casks and crates were flying in all directions, some toward *Resolve*. And through the bow wave of white dust rushing toward them, he could hear the stony growl of an upslope landslide building into an angry, descending roar.

Without waiting for instructions, the pilot had already pushed the throttle to half. *Resolve* leaped forward as he cheated the wheel another half point starboard. Dirck blinked, nodded. Maybe they could get out ahead of the tidal wave of angry stones—

The pilothouse's starboard side door opened and Rik stumbled through. He saw the dead leadsman, looked at Dirck, blinked—probably at the blood covering him—leaned close and screamed as loud and shrill as a little girl: "Starboard side. Floats rising. Out of the weeds." He looked back out the door and over the side. Simonszoon's hearing was coming back, enough to hear the Norwegian exclaim, "No, the weeds are planted *on* the floats! I think—"

Dirck didn't really hear the three explosions, but he felt them quite distinctly, because they went off in a rhythmically perfect sequence.

Each one hit *Resolve* like a hammer, staggered the pilot, who lost control of the wheel for a moment... the same moment that the rocks from Billy Folly Hill started crashing down upon—and in some cases, through—the deck.

Simonszoon closed his eyes, knowing what he would—and did—feel next. Even as his ship was still reeling from the pounding of the three mines on the right, the rockslide from the left pushed back. *Resolve* groaned, seemed to crack someplace deep within herself, and then, finally, the world was as still as it was soundless.

Dirck Simonszoon opened his eyes, ready to see the full measure of ruin, to help him witness and thereby believe the unbelievable:

Resolve was trapped, and it was all because of him.

Chapter 61

Off the southern coast, St. Maarten

Eddie Cantrell handed the flimsy back to Tromp, turned to Cas. "I need Mr. Svantner and the signalman's mate down here in my quarters. Smartly. Tell the master signalman he is to man the set until relieved, and his first job is to send this in the clear: 'Contingency: Last Dance.'" Eddie repeated the message slowly and precisely to make sure Cas understood every letter. As the boy raced past the door, he grabbed its handle and pulled it closed behind him without missing a step.

Maarten Tromp came away from the window of *Intrepid*'s not-very-great great cabin. He smiled faintly. "Technically, I believe it was my decision when to send that code."

Eddie smacked his forehead. "My apologies, sir. I'm—well, I'm a little distracted. A lot of problems to solve at once."

Tromp waved away his concern. "I suspect that is our enemy's intent. And I agree with your decision to send now. We can't allow our enemies to be the only ones who have impeccable timing, today." He sat at the table, leaving the head seat for Eddie. Who nodded his thanks, but shook his head and started pacing. "Whatever is behind those smoke ships three miles to the east is going to be on top of us in under an hour. Admiral, what do we do about *Resolve*?"

Tromp folded his hands. "We must determine whether she can be salvaged, first."

Eddie crossed his arms. "Frankly, sir, I don't hold out a lot of hope for that. But if salvage proves feasible, we got a good start on it when you ordered the two tugs out of reserve and to move toward the inlet at full steam. They'll probably get there about the same time as the two jachts you sent."

Tromp smiled. "Which is your politely oblique way of affirming that the plans for getting *Resolve*'s crew off and towing her are already well in hand. But also, that we must now decide what to do if she cannot be saved. I would hear your thoughts on the matter, Commodore."

A knock on the door. "Svantner?"

"Yes, sir. And Signalman's Mate Franz Croll is with me."

"Come in, and shut the door after you."

They did, and seeing Tromp, both gave up-time salutes. *Spreading like the flu, that*, Eddie reflected.

Tromp acknowledged them from his seat. "We are deciding upon the fate of *Resolve*. I believe the commodore is about to tell me that we must scuttle her."

Ignoring the goggle-eyed stares of the two new arrivals, Eddie frowned and muttered. "If we can. From what Dirck sent, I doubt it."

Svantner cleared his throat. "Sirs, *Resolve* is—is lost?"

Tromp glanced at the flimsy and read. "Cannot assess points of grounding or degree of damage. Slow flooding amidships may indicate breaches obstructed by sand or rock. Prepared to evacuate crew and destroy in place."

Svantner frowned. "Admiral, Commodore...doesn't Captain Simonszoon mean 'scuttle'?"

"That," replied Tromp, setting the flimsy down, "is precisely what we are going to determine now. And we have about two minutes to do it." He folded his hands and looked at Eddie.

Who realized he was chewing on the end of his thumb, which he hadn't done since he was thirteen. He yanked the offending finger away from his teeth. "Look. I'm gonna talk fast and without formalities. First, Dirck wouldn't say 'destroy' if he meant 'scuttle.' He's been a mariner and speaking that language since he could walk. Even if he *was* rattled, that's not a slip he'd make. Which means he's given us an assessment: that *Resolve* is lost."

Tromp nodded. "The damage is severe, clearly. But his hull is mostly intact, his engines are functioning, helm is responding, and has lost less than ten percent of his crew. He's lost two masts, but that doesn't mean a ship should be destroyed."

Eddie glanced at Tromp. "With all due respect, sir, do we really have time for you to play devil's advocate?"

The admiral's eyes opened a bit wider, his mouth grew stiff, but he nodded. "No, and you are right: it is not just the condition of the ship that is motivating him. After reading his first description of the channel, the nature of the ambush, and the restricted flooding despite multiple breaches, I believe he has concluded that *Resolve* is caught fast."

Eddie nodded. "And he reports a dozen boats with boarders approaching, and now infantry making their way eastward along the barrier bank. Put it all together, and it's only a matter of time until *Resolve* is in enemy hands." *And he and his crew are dead.*

Svantner looked from one to the other. "But—but, if we were to turn now, with our guns, and ship's troops, we would—"

"—we would make matters worse." Eddie didn't look at Svantner; he simply pointed east. "If *Intrepid* moves to conduct rescue operations, who and what is left to deal with what's coming toward us right now?"

"Well, sir, *Relentless* is—"

"Arne: *Relentless* is *one* untested steam destroyer. Its supporting ships? Three equally untested frigates that started their lives as prototypes, a thirty-two-gun bark, and two jachts. Because we sent our other two jachts to help the tugs with rescue and retrieval."

Now he did look at Svantner. "Lieutenant, look at the size of that smoke screen, and think like a Spanish commander. Is it worth going to all that trouble, and to surely lose the four galleons that are making it possible, to conceal ten ships? Fifteen? Twenty? Maybe twenty, but only if they are fast enough to hit us and live to tell the tale. But what we *do* know is that they intend to hide their biggest hammer until they swing it.

"So here's my question, Lieutenant: if either *Intrepid* or *Relentless* leave the fight that's going to occur right here, do you believe that any of our other ships will survive to tell us what happened?"

Svantner's eyes were as round as cannon muzzles and looked just as hollow inside. "No, sir. So then . . . what do we do?"

Eddie sighed. "We take a look, see if there's a chance we could pull her free. But I see two problems with that. First problem: she sounds as stuck as any ship has ever been. Maybe pinned in place by that landslide that came halfway across the channel. Second problem: the Spanish aren't just going to let us traipse in there and set up salvage and towing operations. They've still got thirty-two-pounders higher up Billy Folly Hill and boarders approaching *Resolve* from aft and starboard. I think we'll be lucky just to get the crew off in time."

"They are sailors and soldiers, sir," Croll said quietly. "They know that even the best commander cannot be sure of getting them all to safety."

Tromp sighed. "Unfortunately, Signalman Croll, the commodore's words are not simply motivated by loyalty and compassion. Many of those crewmen are like you in another way; they have been trained in the operation and repair of the technology that makes these ships so feared. If they fall into Spanish hands, it accelerates our enemy's acquisition of all this." He gestured to *Intrepid* around him.

Eddie nodded. "That's why Dirck was volunteering to stay behind to destroy her."

Tromp's face looked like it might crumble inward. "To lose *Resolve* is tragedy enough. To lose Captain Simonszoon is . . . well, I cannot even contemplate it."

Eddie shrugged. "You don't have to. I'll get him out." The room suddenly became very quiet and he realized that all three men were staring at him. "What?" he asked eloquently.

Tromp put a fist on the table. "Commodore Cantrell, if I must lose one fine commander and friend this day, that is more than enough. Two is unthinkable. Furthermore, your duty is to this ship."

Eddie shook his head. "Again, there's no time so I've gotta be blunt. Look: I know that ship. Maybe better than the people who built her. If anyone can assess her salvageability, it's me. And I can get Dirck off. So long as he's not being pigheaded." *Yeah, sure; that's totally likely.* "Besides, who else can do the job? Again, time's wasting."

It was Croll who spoke. "Commodore, your pardon, but . . . well, many of us crew on these fine ships may learn our jobs well, but we don't really understand how it all works, how it all fits together. So what I'm getting at is this: you up-time people have spent years teaching us how to use all these devices, but we still couldn't *build* them ourselves. So, do you really think the Spanish will be able to do so on their own?"

Eddie nodded. "Signalman Croll, I am completely certain that they would. And here's why: it was people just like them who *built* these ships. They were made by down-timers who, like you, were fascinated by machinery, but doubted they'd live to see half of what they imagined become reality. But then Grantville shows up, and poof!: you're the ones making and operating the very devices you dreamed of.

"Spain has plenty of people just like that. And every time we forget that, every time we start thinking we're smarter than the other guy, we get into trouble. Just like we did today. Because that's one of the major reasons that *Resolve* is aground on an enemy island with Spanish troops ready to capture and interrogate its highly trained crew. Because we forgot that sometimes the Spanish are *way* smarter than we are.

"So if we just hand them steam engines, and radios and all the rest, one day soon they'll be fielding their own versions. And we can't afford that day to come any sooner than it has to. So no, we can't leave *Resolve* behind."

Tromp opened his fist and lifted it from the table, held it hovering there. "Eddie, I am afraid I am much like Signalman Croll in that my understanding of your technology is woefully incomplete. So I doubt you have enough time to explain how you mean to destroy *Resolve* without sacrificing either yourself or Dirck."

Eddie smiled. "That's probably true, Admiral."

"Then I shall reside my trust in you. What do you require of me?"

"That you send an update to Captain Simonszoon and that you fight my ship." Eddie did not stop to acknowledge Tromp's wide-eyed surprise. "Mr. Svantner is a fine XO and will be able to acquaint you with any unfamiliar procedures or mechanisms. But you might want to turn the con over to Dirck, once he gets here."

"You think you will be able to send Dirck back here? So soon?"

"He's worth waiting for, sir, if you can. Captain Simonszoon will double the effectiveness of this ship against whatever is coming its way. Now, I've got to get a few things before I leave. Lieutenant Svantner, have Lieutenant Gallagher pick two of the Wild Geese. They are to report to me with full special tactics load-out. Make ready the captain's longboat, complete with the outboard motor. I want the same coxswain who put me ashore on Guadeloupe. Have him pick one assistant who's also qualified on the motor and handy with a rifle."

"Yes, sir!" Svantner almost shouted, and ran from the room, calling for Gallagher.

Croll bowed slightly. "Since you called for me, sir, I presume you wish something from me as well?"

Eddie nodded. "Indeed I do, Signalman Croll. I need you aboard *Resolve*."

Croll's eyes bulged. "Me, sir?" Eddie just smiled at him. "Yes, sir. Of course, sir. Is . . . is that all?"

"Just one more thing. I saw that you're qualified on all *Intrepid*'s electrical systems. I'm presuming you know where we've stowed the spares for the eight-inchers' electric ignition systems?"

"Yes, sir. I inventoried that crate myself."

"Good. I need you to pull a few parts from it . . ."

Chapter 62

Inlet to Simpson's Lagoon, St. Maarten

The bow of the motorboat rose slightly as they sped closer to Pelican Point. Eddie adjusted the buff coat that Gallagher had insisted he wear. It was a pretty good fit, as was the barbuta-style helmet, which had surprisingly good visibility. But sound didn't fare quite so well.

Ahead, one of the two jachts that were hovering in the area swept past the end of the barrier bank, which was burning fiercely, now. The Dutch ship twitched sharply to port. As if responding to that as a taunt, one of the thirty-two-pounders on Billy Folly Hill thundered, sending a ball on a long, descending arc toward it. Eddie half rose to watch, which was every bit as illogical as jumping up to cheer on the home team.

But the ball landed almost forty yards off the nimble ship's port quarter, kicking up a white flume of impressive height. Exhaling in relief, Eddie was about to sit when he saw more white, but in a place he didn't expect: the water reaching out from the inlet in which *Resolve* was stuck. Beyond the turbulence of where the sea crashed against Pelican Point and the swells abated, the water was more murky than he had ever seen in the Caribbean, especially on a sunny day. Closer to the channel itself, the water became a sickly white, like powdered milk mixed with quarry dust. That opaque stream pointed back toward its source where, visible despite the smoke, *Resolve* was pinned.

And she really was pinned. *Resolve*, which looked to be hogging slightly, was gripped like a bone in a bulldog's jaws. Barrier-bank mud and silt held her starboard-listing hull like brown glue; the rockfall from Billy Folly sloped down into the water from the other side, almost touching her sky-canted strakes near the waterline. They had all heard the cataclysmic explosion that ended two minutes of reverberating thunder from the western side of the hill, but no one had anticipated that half of the channel would be obstructed by boulders and stones from the now altered slopes behind Pelican Point.

Eddie wasn't a fan of defeatists. Although Captain Kirk could kinda be a jerk sometimes, he was all for the lesson of the *Kobayashi Maru*: no such thing as a no-win situation. But seeing *Resolve*, he shook his head. Ascertaining her seaworthiness was moot: she wasn't going anywhere. Not without about a dozen steam shovels and a couple of the big tugs that worked the heaviest loads in up-time harbors.

As they got closer, it also became obvious why Dirck and his crew hadn't been able to report just how hopeless the situation was. Eddie could now hear occasional musket fire from high up on the hill. And just as the coxswain gunned the outboard motor to close the remaining distance at best speed, one of the

Spanish thirty-two-pounders roared and grape whined down and stippled the water in a wide pattern that overlapped *Resolve*. No way he would have given—or obeyed—an order to venture out on deck into that, not just to get a better look at how hopelessly stuck the ship was. And the view out the gunports wouldn't have been much help either, given her list.

However, right as they began running in toward the mouth of the inlet, Eddie saw a hand waving out one of those same gunports. As it drew back inside, muskets coughed higher up the slopes: one round *blippt!* into the swells about five yards behind them. A few others spoke from a heap of smouldering thatch almost fifty yards down the barrier bank, quickly answered by one of the patrolling jachts as it swooped close and discharged three *petereroes* into the brush. Where the Spanish musket balls went, and whether the jacht's gunners hit anything, was a complete mystery.

Just when they were close enough that he expected the coxswain to race in, the gray-eyed German let the motor idle. "Why are we—?"

"Waiting for the sign," the boatman said tightly. "It has been arranged. One of the tugs sent word over the wireless."

"About a sign?"

"Yes, Commodore." He smiled. "You'll know it when you see it."

Eddie was readying another question when, from the same gunport where he'd seen the waving hand, the muzzle of a carronade appeared and discharged. He flinched away—

—right as the coxswain gunned the motor; the sudden acceleration made everyone sway backward.

Eddie looked back at the coxswain. "What are you—?"

"The smoke from the discharge," the German shouted forward. "Doesn't cover you for long. Go on! Stones are supposed to be only two feet down. There will be a Jacob's ladder out that port. Go *now!*"

The longboat swerved to run alongside the ragged apron of ruined stones near *Resolve.* Gallagher made sure Eddie didn't fall on the loose rocks underfoot as they scrambled over the side and waded into the smoke. As the longboard swung tightly about and powered off at high speed, Eddie and his team were guided forward by voices, then reaching hands which first helped them clamber quickly up the ladder and then pulled them through the gunport into *Resolve*'s portside gundeck.

Or at least, what was left of it.

When Eddie ascended the companionway into the armored pilothouse, only Rik Bjelke was there. "Commodore!" he exclaimed, a big smile suddenly shining out of his powder-grimed face. "I did not know you were coming! This is wonderful!" Then he frowned. "But...this is terrible! You must get away from here!"

Eddie sighed. "Let me guess; they hit the radio?"

Rik shook his head. "No, but it has failed. We are uncertain why. Our backup antenna was destroyed when a thirty-two-pound ball destroyed our mizzenmast. Or it could be a malfunction in the set. Either way, we did not receive any messages regarding your arrival." He frowned again. "Why *are* you here?"

"Yes," came another familiar voice, "why are *you* here?"

Eddie turned as Dirck emerged from the other companionway. Looking at him, he had a brief flashback to a Halloween costume he'd once seen: a postapocalyptic survivor turned crazed killer. Simonszoon's face was spattered with blood, his cheeks and brow sootcovered, his bright eyes staring out of a raccoon mask of pale skin that he had repeatedly wiped clear. His hair was wild and singed, his clothes rent and frayed, his breath horrible, and his mouth uncommonly red. Or maybe that was just the effect of the contrast.

Eddie made sure his voice was very level and calm. "Captain Simonszoon, I am here to get the crew off *Resolve*."

Simonszoon's blue eyes seemed to get gray and his thin lips seemed to be resisting something like a tic. "Commodore . . . Eddie, I—"

"Report your condition, Captain." Eddie let his tone become a little more conversational, if still firm. "And by the way, your day isn't over. Not by a long shot. Now, status report: smartly!"

"Taking water from four breaches. Sir. One is negligible. The other three, given placement, should be leaking more. I fear we are grounded so firmly that the holes are hard against the bottom."

Eddie nodded at each item of the report. The routine was bringing Dirck back around to a more normal voice and clearer eyes, so Eddie kept asking questions, even though he pretty much knew the answers. "Are you taking water faster than your pumps are handling?"

"Not so long as we keep up steam, sir."

"Hull condition?"

"You've seen her exterior, sir; I haven't. But I gather it's ugly."

"Captain Simonszoon, it's well beyond ugly; it's hopeless. There is no chance of getting *Resolve* to open water. And I am uncertain that her structural integrity would be up to the stresses."

He nodded. "As I expected. When those final explosions occurred, it . . . it felt like we were being crushed in a vise. First pinned when the rocks slid down to port and then cinched hard and tight-clamped when mines went off to starboard. Although I'm not sure that those mines were there to damage us, Commodore. I believe that was just another part of the Spanish plan to collapse the inlet and trap us in the lagoon."

He straightened. "Sir, I appreciate you coming to get the crew off *Resolve*. I shall see to her scutt . . . disposal. I have readied fuses and warheads from explosive rounds to—"

"You will belay those activities immediately. They are unnecessary. Besides, you'd be disobeying orders."

"Whose?"

"Mine. Specifically, the ones I'm about to give." He turned to Rik. "Lieutenant Bjelke, I brought an electrical specialist with me, as well as Lieutenant Gallagher. Please pair each of them with their equivalents aboard *Resolve* so that they may coordinate efforts. I also need your chief engineer, senior radio operator, and senior munitions specialists to become my shadows. Immediately. And you and I will need some assistants as we proceed with terminal operations. Deckhands and sail handlers will do." A blast high overhead, followed by the rain of grape on the deck. Eddie discovered he'd ducked; the other two officers were just looking at him.

As he straightened up, Rik nodded, snapped a salute,

uttered a clipped, "Yes, Commodore!" and scuttled down the companionway.

Eddie heard Dirck pull in a long breath, the way one does before launching into a long or difficult explanation. The up-timer spoke before the Dutchman could. "Here are your orders, Captain. Your work here is done, but this fleet needs you alive and ready for duty. Are you?"

"Yes, sir. But my duty is here, with my ship. Even if you do not require me to—"

"Dirck, shut up. There's a tug approaching. It's about ten minutes behind us. Bring every man that will fit. And stop with the allusions to a captain going down with his ship. In addition to that being an absolutely imbecilic tradition, you are the one other person in this fleet who really knows how to fight a cruiser."

He looked around at the ruin in which they stood. "Do I?"

"Yes, you do. And you don't have time to feel remorse, or responsible, or sorry for yourself. Did you get greedy for kills? Maybe. But you won't do that again today. Maybe never. Besides, Tromp won't let you. So get out to *Intrepid*, get to the bridge, and smash their fleet to pieces." Eddie stepped back and snapped a hard salute at the older, blinking man, who was apparently struggling to accept the sudden changes to the future he had decreed for himself. "Captain, here are your orders."

Startled, and not well versed in the formalities that Admiral Simpson had introduced to the USE Navy, Dirck returned the salute haltingly.

"Captain Dirck Simonszoon, you are to report immediately to *Intrepid* as CO. I shall take command of *Resolve* for the remainder of her service. Captain, you are relieved."

Simonszoon had to think for a moment. "I stand relieved, sir."

He knew to hold the salute until Eddie lowered his own, and then started moving. "Now get out of here, Dirck. And take all intelligence, all charts, all logs. And the radio, broken or not."

The Dutchman sighed. "I'm arrogant, not stupid." He grabbed a small crate holding the guts of the radio and three large leather folios. He stopped at the top of the companionway, looked around the battered interior one more time, muttered a string of mostly inaudible curses at himself, and was gone, effortlessly sliding down into the passageways just aft of the gun deck. Eddie heard him make his way into that cavernous expanse and start shouting: "Well what are you layabouts waiting for? Engineers and idlers will be taken off first. Gunners next. Then deckhands and ships troops."

"Jacob's ladders are ready to go out the gunports, sir."

"No, not from the ones abaft the foc'sle! It's too deep there. Only use Battery One's gunports. The rockslide is no more than two feet under the water, there."

If he said, or roared, anything else, Eddie couldn't hear it.

Rik called up from the same companionway. "All requested personnel have been gathered here, Commodore. Orders?"

Eddie nodded. As he started down the companionway toward the waiting ring of section heads and crewmen, he heard rifles firing out the starboard gunports, followed by the blast of a carronade. Either the Spanish were probing from the barrier bank, or the brush fire was dying down.

Once he was sure of his footing on the lower deck, he squinted into the dimness to look around the ring of faces. Those who'd come from *Intrepid* were markedly brighter: no powder smudges. "Gentlemen, we will be among the last to leave. Up until that moment comes"—he glanced at Gallagher—"we'll have to keep the heavy weapons manned. Sharpshooters will lend a hand, too. The rest of you will go either with me or Lieutenant Bjelke as we put together a couple of house-warming gifts for *Resolve*'s new owners."

"Sir?" said Croll.

"Bombs," offered Rik. "It's time to plant some bombs." He turned to Eddie. "Lead on, sir."

Southern barrier bank of Simpson's Lagoon, St. Maarten

"Captain Equiluz," reported one of the few sappers who had been assigned to the "Mechanical Appraisal Staff" that was sequestered well back on the barrier bank, "the enemy has closed two of the ship's gunports. Are they running out of ammunition?"

"No, they are running *away*." Equiluz sighed and scanned the top of Billy Folly Hill for Gallardo's pennant. Still no signal from him as to the next course of action, nor any sign that the veteran and much-commended ape was even alive. He had probably been buried under the apocalyptic torrent of boulders that had claimed almost all the other sappers that Governor de Viamonte had sent from Santo Domingo to carry out this most irregular mission.

The obvious fuse failure had been a costly business.

Gallardo should not have been called upon to fight or even step on to the field at all. The whole purpose had been to trap the steamship in the lagoon. That way, the allied fleet would have been torn between either saving that ship and its crew or fighting against Admiral Álvarez de Toledo's flotilla that would even now be flying in from the east. And from which the heretics would be unable to flee when the galleons came round Gunner's Point and blocked the west.

But because the steam warship had almost managed to exit the channel before it was stopped, the allies were now able to evacuate the wreck without any major effort from the other ships of their fleet. They had committed only two jachts and a pair of high-bowed, fire-belching pinks to the rescue operations.

Which meant that, against all odds, it was up to Antonio de la Plaza Equiluz to lead the Mechanical Appraisal Staff aboard the steamship. A ridiculous and optimistic label for the unit, and the only "staff" assignment in which Equiluz had ever been required to lie in hiding for hours, asphyxiated by smoke and devoured by insects as a comedy of errors played out on land, at sea, and in the lagoon.

But now, lacking any cue to the contrary, it was time for him to play his part. As soon as the steamship was secured, he would lead the six-man Appraisal Staff aboard, identify its key technological elements (many of which were described in absurdly general terms). They would also check for scuttling charges, although there could be no true scuttling in such shallow water, and certainly not after the channel they had laboriously dredged was now almost entirely filled in.

However, since the enemy could not dispose of the

ship in a sufficient depth of water, Captain Equiluz would have to be more watchful for bombs than usual. Which, by extension, meant that from the moment the ship was secured, he was probably in a race with one or more unseen fuses. If he won that race, he would be known as the man who had secured the greatest prize ever taken in the New World, and his greatest trouble would be in choosing between the many opportunities and assignations that would surely be offered to him.

And if he lost the race with the fuses . . . Well, he would certainly be saved the trouble of choosing among so many earthly alternatives.

Chapter 63

Off the southern coast, St. Maarten

Dirck Simonszoon clambered up the Jacob's ladder that had been let down over *Intrepid*'s starboard quarter and ignored the stares of the boat crew waiting there. Their attention was soon pulled away by the stentorian demands of Eddie's longboat coxswain, who was shouting for gasoline right now or the commodore might get overrun by the Spanish so do it now and I mean right now damn you all to hell!

Simonszoon could only hope that Eddie was not in such immediate danger, but could not take the time to worry about that. Or anything other than the task before him.

As he approached the rear of the flying bridge, he heard one of the mates call out, "Enemy smoke ships are at fifteen hundred yards, sir."

As he started up the stairs, he heard Svantner announce in a tone so deferential that it bordered on reverence. "Five minutes to range, Admiral."

As Dirck's shoulders cleared the top of the

pilothouse, he saw Maarten Tromp tilt his head very slightly. "Lieutenant Svantner, as I understand it, given the capabilities of the inclinometer and electric firing system, we have more than doubled our optimal engagement range. That would mean we are in range *now*."

Simonszoon reached the top of the stairs. The mates saw and heard him, but not the other two men.

Svantner's voice oozed patience. "Sir, those estimates are based on *tests*."

"Yes, but if I know Commodore Cantrell, any test of his includes exacting and realistic trials."

"Yes, sir, but—"

Dirck cut in, stepping forward. "Admiral, Captain Simonszoon reporting aboard. Request permission to assume command of *Intrepid*." He glanced at Svantner. "I'm sorry, Arne"—the Swede blinked, possibly as much because of Dirck's compassionate tone as his arresting appearance—"but I was there for one of those tests. I'm satisfied the system works, and I have a strategy to put that increased range to our immediate advantage."

When there was no immediate response from either of the surprised men, he faced Tromp directly. "Admiral, I implore you. Yes, *Resolve* is gone and it is entirely my fault. But right now, I know what needs to be done and exactly how to do it. Please, if only for the next thirty minutes, allow me to have the benefit of your trust once again."

"You never lost it, Dirck," Tromp smiled. "Now, what do you have in mind?"

Inlet to Simpson's Lagoon, St. Maarten

A runner poked his head through the magazine's open door. "Commodore Cantrell?"

"Yes?"

"Lieutenant Gallagher wants a word. If you've a minute, sir."

Well, I really don't... However, if anything, Gallagher was not *enough* of an alarmist. "Croll," Eddie muttered to the electrician from *Intrepid*, "keep at it. I'll be back in two minutes." *Probably a lie, but it* is *my intent.* He left with the runner. On the way, he passed *Resolve*'s engineer. "Has Rik put the charges in the engine room yet?"

"Not yet, sir."

"Good. Stave in the side of the smoke uptake, as far below the funnel as you can reach."

"But sir, the engine's smoke will begin spreading belowdecks. And it will get very thick indeed when the last of the gunports are closed."

"I'm counting on it," Eddie answered over his shoulder as he waved the runner on.

As soon as he reached the companionway up to the pilothouse, Eddie could hear that the tempo of the fight to hold off the Spanish had changed. The gunfire was no longer intermittent; it was steady. As his head came up to deck level, he heard two of the thirty-two-pounders go off in rapid sequence. Gallagher turned and said, "Head down, sir."

"Wha—?"

A sudden torrent of what sounded like crowbars battered the roof of the pilothouse. He heard a *thrupp-thrupp-thruppa* out on the weather deck. Again, he didn't realize he had ducked until he was raising his head.

Gallagher nodded. "Things are changin' a bit, Commodore. Started with that." He pointed at one of the jachts that had been providing cover for the tugs. She was trailing a steady wisp of smoke and listing, heading out to deeper water and beyond the throw of the thirty-two-pounders. "They finally tapped her near to five minutes ago. Started all the cards going down, it did. The last of the jachts is on her lonesome now, keeping the Spanish from laying into the tugs as they come close.

"But she's not enough on her own. The feckin' Spanish have sorted themselves enough that they've got marksmen out along the near sides of the barrier bank. Smart, they are. Hide, shoot, move, quick as a Cork pickpocket."

"At the tugs?"

"No, sir. At the swivel gunners aboard that last jacht. Can't be sure, but it seems the Spanish sharp-shooters are takin' a toll among those fellows. Sum of it is, the Dutchmen already 'ave their hands full, and now they're losing their fingers, as well."

Even as Gallagher explained the situation, Eddie watched the last jacht angle in. Her *petereroes* coughed at the shore. Muskets sputtered back. The small Dutch ship veered off, one of the gunners clutching his arm or side; it was too far to make out the details.

"That's when the boyos with the thirty-twos decided they've missed playing with us. Now the whole bloody battery is hitting us with grape."

"Losses?"

"Well, sir, not as such. But those splinter shields are damn near torn t' pieces and we've not many more. And every once in a bit, a Spaniard fires from the edge of that smoulderin' heap out there on the barrier bank. Wounded more than a few of our lads shooting out the gunports with their muskets. And now, with more of the gunners being taken off, the ranks are growin' a wee bit thin, below.

"Taken together, sir, the Spanish are givin' us a taste of what I've heard you call 'suppressive fire.'" Gallagher smiled, clearly proud he had both understood and pronounced the term correctly. "Right now, they're just fillying with us, to see how much we've got to fight back with. Every so often, one of the boats from the lagoon pokes its nose around the far corner of the channel, draws fire from the mitrailleuse or Big Shot—until I told 'em they're not to take that bait. Wait until they've a target they can't miss."

Eddie nodded. "Yeah, if they take every shot, they're going to shoot themselves dry in no time flat. But at some point, the grape is going to chew away the overhead cover on the heavy weapons, and then the boats will be able to swarm our stern. And their sharpshooters will keep our musketeers busy in the starboard gunports." He frowned. "Here's what we do. Seal up some more of the gunports. Start with those furthest abaft and afore. Task half of the remaining crews to load their carronades with cannister and hold at the ready. Have the other half start hitting the end of the barrier bank with explosive rounds. Shake them up there, keep them from organizing."

"A fine plan, sir, but a caution: all that smoke will

also be a friend to the fellows who want our blood. We may kill a few, but some could crawl in under the guns, crouch low in the water around us. A few grenades lobbed through the gunports from further down the tumblehome could mean no end of mischief to our fine selves."

Eddie nodded. "That's why you and the Wild Geese from *Resolve* have to be our rat catchers. You just told me you know what to look for and where to look for it. If that's the cost of keeping our carronades in action and whittling down both their numbers and morale, then it's your job to catch any rats that sneak up on us."

"Rat catchers, eh?" Gallagher mused as one of the Spanish cannons roared high overhead. "I like that, I do. Sorry to pull you away from your special work, Commodore. Oh, and one more t'ing." Grapeshot pounded down like iron hail. "I've told one of our fine Irish fraternity to watch over you. Opinion stands that we're not ready to have you go tattlin' on our sinful selves to the Holy Father, Commodore." He smiled. "Not just yet."

"That's a very kind thought, Lieutenant Gallagher, but there's no need to call someone from their post to play bodyguard."

"Ah, well now, yeh see, sir, it's already been arranged. He's down waiting for you outside the magazine." Gallagher winked. "Thomas Terrell. A true trial to Man, God, and 'is sainted Muther. But he'll keep you safe, Commodore. Now, I'll not bother you again unless the bastards are coming over the gunwales, which we don't seem to have on these ships."

Off the southern coast, St. Maarten

"Admiral Tromp, if I may?"

"Your ship, Captain Simonszoon. And I've no orders for the fleet, even *Relentless* and her guns, until the Spanish are much closer."

"Aye, sir. Mr. Svantner, please pass the following instructions to Mount One and Mount Two."

"Standing by."

"Master gunners. Targets: four galleons making smoke, dead ahead at thirteen hundred fifty yards. Northernmost galleon is designated Target One, the next as you count to the south is Target Two, and so forth until the southernmost galleon, which is Target Four. Send and confirm receipt."

The replies were almost instantaneous. "Target designations clear, sir."

"Helm, bring the bow over one point to starboard."

"Over one point starboard, sir."

"Mount One, confirm clear firing vector to Target Two, advise when acquired. Mount Two, same for Target Three."

Svantner sent the orders, turned to Simonszoon. "So, you mean to eliminate the two galleons in the center? To clear the smoke between us and the center of whatever formation they are concealing. And so, you will open a gap to target them as early as possible."

Dirck shook his head. "No, we follow by shifting fire to Targets One and Four." He heard voices from the speaking tubes declaring that both Mounts One and Two had their targets ranged and acquired.

Svantner, who as a Swede was not in awe of the

legendary Dirck "the Smirk" Simonszoon, hastily acknowledged the eight-inchers' status, and forgot proper protocol of address when he almost shouted, "I do not understand! Why waste time on the flanking galleons, once you have a clear lane of fire to the ships behind the smoke?"

Simonszoon glanced at Svantner. "XO, you will address me correctly. As for the tactics, you would be correct if the strategy was to destroy as many enemy hulls as we can. However, at this time, our objective is to compel them to flee. To stop this fight before it begins. Now pass on the word: first round, standard shell. Fire when ready."

In answer to the surprise on every face on the bridge, Dirck pointed back to the plume of smoke that marked *Resolve*. "We have an excellent crew and excellent officers back there, on an island that still has Spanish on it. If we want to get them back alive, we cannot also become entangled with whatever is behind that smoke.

"If we have to engage, we will. However, they are sacrificing four of their sturdiest galleons just to generate smoke and minimize the time under which we can take their true combat force under fire. So if we take that smoke away, the enemy admiral will have to choose between doubling the time he's willing to expose the best ships in his fleet to our best guns, or choose the better part of valor. It will be best for us if he chooses the latter."

Mounts One and Two roared.

Dirck, Tromp, and Svantner all raised their spyglasses.

Inlet to Simpson's Lagoon, St. Maarten

Rik came running around the corner, almost bumped into glum, silent Thomas Terrell just as Eddie was carefully closing the heavy door to the magazine. Rik was panting and sweat-stained, even more than before. "All charges in place. Also, runner from Gallagher. He says the jig is getting lively and we're down to two carronade crews. Forward mitrailleuse is out of ammunition."

"And I," replied Eddie, "am ready to go. Where are the others?"

"Ready to climb down the Jacob's ladder at portside Battery One, C gun."

"Okay. Send the runner back to Gallagher to tell him—"

"No need, sir; part of Gallagher's message was that he didn't need the runner to return. So I sent him forward to evacuate."

"And Gallagher?"

"He said he'll be down here in two minutes. Or less."

As if to emphasize the probability that it would be less than two minutes, they heard a rattle of muskets on the weather deck above.

"Not ours," Terrell grumbled.

The muskets were answered by a rapid fusillade of weapons with higher, sharper reports.

Terrell patted the Winchester .40-72 cradled in his arms. "*That* was ours. And way too close. Time to go, gentlemen. No need to be at home when the boyos with the pointy steel hats come knocking."

Off the southern coast, St. Maarten

Dirck watched the first shells from both mounts miss, but each by less than forty yards.

"Reacquire and adjust. Advise when ready."

The orders were passed on. Dirck raised his spyglass again, heard the mounts report ready, did not wait for Svantner to convey their status. "Fire," he said.

Again, the eight-inch rifles roared within moments of each other. Mount One missed Target Two, the shell's plume rising up only fifteen yards short of her bow. From one thousand two hundred yards.

More amazing still, Mount Two's shell hit Target Three's quarterdeck, the source of the smoke she was putting out. As expected, this evidently involved quite a volume of flammables, judging from the column of twisting flame that leaped high and caught up the mizzen's canvas in a bright, writhing death dance.

The flying bridge was silent as Dirck ordered, "Mount One and Mount Two, load explosive shell. Acquire and fire when ready."

The gun crews, perhaps because of all their training, or perhaps determined to make up for *Resolve*'s initially shaky gunnery off Dominica just a little over half a year ago, loaded and fired in just over thirty seconds.

Dirck waited calmly through the long moment of flight time...and was rewarded by a massive explosion on both ships. For the first time in his life, he did not meticulously catalog the effects. He had a generalized impression of masts falling, planks flying, fires catching, a secondary explosion on Target Two, and a set of them on Target Three as the battery just beneath her port quarter's weather deck ripple-blasted outwards like a string of firecrackers.

Tromp's smile was small, almost sad. Svantner's Adam's apple worked mightily before he asked, "Orders for Mounts One and Two, sir?"

"Yes, one more round on each target. Then move on to the other two galleons. Let's see if they have the stomach for it."

Chapter 64

Inlet to Simpson's Lagoon, St. Maarten

Gallagher came sliding down the companionway from the starboard forward hatch, landing into the first long-legged stride of a full-out sprint across to the gundeck toward where Eddie stood, waiting beside the open gunport on the opposite side. "Fire the feckin' piece!" the Irish lieutenant shouted.

Terrell made sure that Eddie and Rik were clear and fired the weapon which, being fired for smoke, had no shell in it. Eddie thought he might have lost his hearing for a moment, but then clearly heard Terrell say, "Move it, yeh great gobdaws!" He pushed Rik to the ladder, who couldn't object to being first without delaying the other three men who, along with him, were the last persons aboard *Resolve*. The Norwegian's grumbles threatened to become snarls as he went down.

Eddie jumped to the ladder, pivoted to swing his good foot over the gunport's sill ... and discovered he was poised over at least two dozen dead crewmen, sprawled in the grotesque poses of nerveless death, their blood staining the now gray water red. Immediately beneath him they were stacked so high upon the barely submerged rocks that the pile of death crested above the waterline. For a moment, it looked like a mound of infinite corpses, rising up from the deep. Rising up to claim them all.

"*Well, go, yeh eejit!*"

Terrell's walrus-roar reassured Eddie that he had not lost the smallest bit of hearing. He swung his prosthetic foot out, started down, began to slip, realized it was because he couldn't gauge how slippery the now blood-coated ladder was. Without a real foot inside the boot, he just didn't have the necessary sensory precision to compensate.

He tried descending another rung, almost slid off sideways, stopped himself by clutching the ladder's rope for dear life, and was suddenly swinging back and forth like a pendulum. He saw hands reaching for him, voices crying his name...and then had a thought as sharp and bitter as his sudden fury over putting other peoples' lives at risk: *Oh...fuck it!*

Eddie flung himself off the ladder. No way he was going to let the two Wild Geese be shot to pieces while they waited for him to get down a simple ladder.

Eddie landed on bodies, mostly. Which wasn't pleasant and sure as hell wasn't soft. His left leg had bumped down on rock at a bad angle, but since he didn't have a real foot there, he didn't get a real sprain or fracture, either. He tried to get up and immediately realized that the footing was treacherous even for someone with two intact feet. So, on his hands and knees he crawled beyond the bodies, toward the far margin of the rockfall where his longboat had originally deposited him. A handful of other crewmen, two wounded, was still there, waving to the oncoming tugs while huddling close against *Resolve*'s shattered bow.

What happened next was more a collage than anything like a clear sequence of events. Suddenly, there was a lot of musket fire coming off Billy Folly Hill. Eddie heard the lead balls zipping and occasionally thumping around them. Then two of the Spanish cannons fired. Terrell had already reached the ground, was shouting instructions at Rik while he brought his Winchester up and started levering rounds up the hill. Gallagher almost flew out the gunport and managed a midair grab of the ladder that allowed him to slide down in one unbroken movement. He landed awkwardly, but immediately started pushing rounds into his own empty Winchester.

That was when the grapeshot from the two cannons came down. One pattern hit mostly struck *Resolve*'s weather deck, raising a few curses in Spanish. But the other gun had evidently tried to aim for the pile of bodies and overshot . . . and so hit the closer of the two approaching tugs instead.

One of its three crewmen flailed as a ball almost removed his left leg. Another punched a hole up near the bow, and a third must have creased the boiler or a pipe because a sudden shrill steam-whistle whine cut the air, like an audio marker saying, "Here we are!" The tug lost way until one of the other two crewmen got it under control and, while it still had some steam, made back for open water, out of the range of the guns.

Eddie had just reached the water when a thin but strong hand got him under the right armpit and hauled him upright. It was Rik, smiling at him, his back toward the island. But over his shoulder, Eddie saw movement up on *Resolve's* deck.

Somehow, long familiarity and practice with how to keep upright if his good leg was slipping put the correct muscle memory in motion. Eddie kicked his prosthesis to the rear, planting it hard while he turned out of Rik's grasp to pull his HP-35. He got it up into a two-handed grip and put as many rounds as he could in the general area where he'd seen movement.

He doubted he hit anything, but the sharp, distinctive reports of the up-time pistol pulled Gallagher's and Terrell's heads around—not toward him, but to where his shots were going. Terrell cranked three fast rounds out of his Winchester, Gallagher two. Between all of them, they earned one pained howl and several curses in Spanish.

The last of the evacuees were getting on the second tug, which now had to take all the others that should have gone on the first. Terrell shoved forward, ordered the boat's master to make room for the commodore.

Eddie's shout was louder than that of the Irish bull walrus. "Belay that. Shove off. Best speed."

Thomas Terrell came around to stare at him. "You *are* an eejit! And *now* how do you get out of here?"

Eddie smiled. "Same way you do," he said, and pointed. His longboat, bow high and stern low where the outboard was churning the water, came sweeping in. As Terrell turned back to face him, surprised, Eddie shouted at him, nose to nose: "Now reload your guns and mind your tongue, mister!"

About the time they were finally settling in, more of the Spanish on *Resolve's* weather deck tried to get in a few shots over the bow and the sides. Eddie had a fresh magazine in the HP-35 and emptied half of it, while the two Wild Geese showed admirable precision marksmanship, which resulted in one cry of agony and one body that fell, lifeless, over the side of the crippled ship.

As the Spanish flinched back, and Eddie and the other three men were ready to motor out, the up-timer suddenly realized there was something he had to—*had to*—do. Making sure he still had one foot on the rocks just beneath the water, he shouted as quickly as one of those old-time radio ad announcers, "I-claim-this-island-for-King-Christian-IV-of Denmark! Now let's get out of here!"

Off the southern coast, St. Maarten

Tromp looked at the sagging, smoking wrecks of the four galleons. One of them, Target Four, had also been hit well back in the stern. While it resulted in a less spectacular fire—none of her sails caught—it must have run down into the lower decks and hit the magazine. Surprisingly, that did not blow the ship to pieces . . . probably, Tromp reasoned, because the enemy admiral had considered it unlikely any of the smoke ships would survive to reach cannon range. Still, there was a huge flaring hole in her side, and she was clearly taking water. If she did not roll within the next fifteen minutes, he would be quite surprised.

Behind the galleons, and now starting to break out of the smoke, were just what Tromp and the other officers had expected to see: galleoncetes without provisions for oars and fragatas whose lines showed the same trends of naval thought that were evident in the allied frigates now facing them.

Simonszoon saw the oncoming ships, sighed, then shrugged. "Mr. Svantner, build a target list. Until you have completed it, we will engage the galleoncetes by choice; they look slightly slower. Mount One, target: galleoncete, one point off starboard bow, range approximately eight hundred yards. When acquired, fire explosive round. Mount Two..."

Svantner leaned over toward Tromp, putting his finger on the western edge of the tactical plot. "Sir, may I point out that the enemy's other formation of galleons has now come around Gunner's Point in the west? They are facing Admiral Banckert's squadron."

"Yes, they are right where I want them."

"Sir? Granted our ships have the wind gauge, but they are outnumbered two to one."

Tromp smiled. "Are they?" He leaned toward the speaking tube for the wireless room. "Send this message in the clear at frequency reserved for Contingency: Class Reunion. To Major L. Quinn, aboard *Courser*. Confirm receipt of activation code for Contingency: Class Reunion. Code is: Start the Dance."

Fadrique Álvarez de Toledo had assumed, when his smoke-making galleons had been taking so many direct hits so early, that the up-time steamships had run in at full speed to close the range. It was a tactic he'd considered but deemed unlikely. Yes, it would allow them to eliminate the smoke screen as quickly as possible, but it meant either pulling their entire formation closer to his—yes, please do!—or sending the steamships forward unsupported to attain effective range and then steaming back to their main formation, which was almost as welcome.

But when the middle two smoke galleons lost way and he moved beyond their smoke, he witnessed the unthinkable: both the large and small steamships were still precisely where they had been first sighted. Which meant that one or both had begun engaging his smoke ships at a range of thirteen hundred fifty yards and had begun hitting them after one or two ranging shots.

Álvarez prided himself on being a practical-minded man who accepted both good and bad conditions. He'd never read, and had only encountered one brief précis of, the work of an up-time French-Algerian philosopher named Camus, but he readily understood the man's concept of "existential detachment." But this? For a moment, the admiral was not able to reshape his mind, and most specifically his tactical suppositions, around the inescapable facts of what had transpired.

The first coherent thought which came to him was eminently practical: *We cannot sustain this engagement. We must make a pass at their conventional frigates to the south, then sheer off. Or we will be ruined and unable to defend the ports where we build our ships.* He didn't need to summon or make any explanation to Irarraga, who was standing beside him. The captain's face was as pale and stunned as he imagined his own to be. He called for de Orbea, to whom he relayed the changed orders, including instructions for each ship that received them to confirm receipt and to immediately resend to others.

But he then wondered: would his captains see those

signals as they moved through the smoke? As they worked their sails to maintain every possible iota of speed? As they tried to formulate tactics to simply survive what should have been an effective attack with the full advantage of the wind gauge? Oh, for a radio *now* . . .

His misgivings were becoming reality before his eyes. Many of his ships had either not received any or all of the signals; too many raced forward through the thinning smoke as the last of the galleons, now shattered, fell behind. It was the logical course of action; if they lost the smoke early, they had to close as rapidly as possible.

But closing as rapidly as possible was just a more dramatic form of suicide. At what used to be its maximum range, the large up-time cruiser now hit with its second, or sometimes even its first, shot. One of the leading galleoncetes ran straight in and took a plunging hit straight down her centerline. It was like watching a knife gutting a fish. Starting in the foc'sle and running back along half its length, the deck planking and the supports beneath them flew up in a straight line, as if being cut by a plow. After also severing the foremast, the round still had enough force to so weaken the mainmast that the impact from the falling foretop brought it down, as well.

Another galleoncete approached the enemy, weaving slightly, and that did seem to ruin the aim of their first shot. But between the inevitable reduction in speed every time her bow crossed through the wind and the larger target she presented when turning across the axis of enemy fire, the second round hit her hard, staggering her. By the time she straightened and found her way again, an explosive shell hit her foc'sle, leaving a gaping, smoking hole that reached almost down to the waterline.

Álvarez swallowed, seemed to have a rock jammed in his throat. He had known he would lose ships this day, maybe many. And it was a worthwhile trade if they closed and did equal damage to the enemy's conventional men-of-war. The allies were unable to replace losses as swiftly as he could, and so, for them, an equal exchange of ships meant the surety of eventual defeat by attrition. But now, the speed and maneuverability which had been the admiral's tool to achieve that end was no longer sufficient. It seemed unlikely that the up-time guns had always possessed this accuracy, but it hardly mattered whether its sudden appearance signified long-standing suppression to effect this surprise or was the result of continuing up-time innovation. The brutal fact was that the tactics for which Fadrique had successfully orchestrated this scenario no longer held out the promise of success but, rather, the likelihood of complete disaster.

But at least half of his fleet had either received his orders or had come to the same realizations and were fashioning the same response independently. And leading them all was the fragata of Eugenio de Covilla.

The unusually swift *Espada Santa* had swung close around the southernmost of the galleons, whose destruction produced so much southwest leading smoke that it concealed his ship until it was only five hundred yards from one of the new enemy frigates. The smaller steamship attempted to take de Covilla's ship under fire, but after two misses, the allied frigate obstructed her aim and the two conventional warships closed to range.

Both captains were skilled, but the allied ship, not having the wind gauge, had to put her bows south to get the wind over her beam and so get speed. It was also a shrewd maneuver because, if *Espada Santa* decided to keep running in and rake her while crossing her stern, that put her closer to the smaller steamship, which would presumably fire as soon as the two conventional ships drew apart.

De Covilla evidently saw that, refused to sail to his own doom, and altered course to keep the frigate between him and the enemy's lethal guns. That also fulfilled another, more strategic purpose. As *Espada Santa* closed to trade broadsides with the enemy ship, he was also steering in a consistently more southerly direction. And just before he drew abreast of the enemy, he sent up a puzzling signal flag: FOLLOW ME.

Álvarez frowned, was momentarily distracted by the quick exchange between the ships. At fifty yards, they each scored hits. Planks flew and smoke rose from both. Then *Espada Santa* heeled over into a decided south-by-southwest heading.

"Where is he going? Toward St. Eustatia?" de Orbea wondered aloud.

"No," Álvarez realized, "he is keeping much of the wind and moving away from their guns."

"And giving them his stern!"

The voice that answered de Orbea was Irarraga's. "Yes, which means de Covilla is giving that smaller steamship the narrowest possible target. He's also sending more signals, it appears." He paused. "He indicates there is a threat further to the west. Beyond the Dutch men-of-war facing our galleons off Gunner's Point."

Puzzled, they all turned their spyglasses in that

direction. Two ships were just coming over the horizon, perhaps three miles southwest of the galleons.

And they were both sending up smoke.

No one spoke for several seconds as they strained to confirm what they had seen, and while doing so, discerned that these were not merely tugs. No, they were ships of the same size and shape as the smaller steamship that even now was firing after the fleeing *Espada Santa*.

"It cannot be," de Orbea croaked.

"My God, how many do they have?" Irarraga whispered.

"Too many for us," Fadrique declared sharply. "Eugenio is right. We must break off along that heading. Pass the signal to those who see us: crowd sail and follow. Or even run south-by-southeast. As soon as each ship is well clear of their guns, they are to make course due west. We regroup off Vieques and press on to Santo Domingo."

"And we just leave the others behind?" de Orbea almost blubbered. "The battle is over?"

"So the war can continue," Álvarez amended with a grim nod. "Now, keep sending those signals. We need to save every ship we can."

Inlet to Simpson's Lagoon, St. Maarten

Antonio de la Plaza Equiluz put out a restraining arm before the sapper who was about to swing into the companionway that led down from the savaged pilothouse. "Do not touch anything. Be careful where you step."

"Sir," he said, his face a fury of perplexity, "you just

told us we must move quickly. That there is a bomb on this ship and we will not have long to find it."

"That is true. We must move both very swiftly and very carefully. Now go."

Equiluz was one of the last down. "Report," he called into the gloom.

Calls echoed along in the thick air of the gun deck. No, the air was more than thick, it was . . . choking. "We must stop the engines. It is possible they might have been set to destroy the rest of the ship."

"Is that even possible?" asked the same sapper.

"I have no idea," Equiluz answered, "but we must presume it is until we know otherwise."

Another sapper coughed. "Besides, we have to stop the engines before they fill the air with their poison! Pope Borja is right! The up-timers must truly be demons, if they can breathe this infernal reek!"

"Do not be foolish," Equiluz snapped. "They could not work in this. But now we know why, in the fifteen minutes before we came aboard, there was less smoke rising up from where the chimney tube used to stand on the deck. Before they left, they found some way to redirect the fumes into the ship itself. Sergeant, you found the engine just abaft of us, yes? Excellent. Examine it and stop it as quickly as you can. If you have to damage it, that will be understood and excused. Report to me when you have stopped it. The rest of us will continue to search."

He turned to the others. "We have two tasks. Check the whole ship for bombs, but pay particular attention to the gun deck. The most important part to locate is the magazine. If you find it, do not open it. But come alert me at once. Now, get about it!"

It was not a long job. Although it was a very large ship, it had fewer decks, and with the exception of the orlop deck, they were very open spaces that followed exceedingly clean lines. Equiluz could not completely suppress a persistent sense of envy as he walked its length.

As it turned out, once he reflected on the design of the ship, the uniform bore of all the guns, and the incredible weight of the strange shells—eight inches in diameter and sixteen inches long!—he realized that what passed for ammunition portage in his time would simply not apply here. So he looked for, and found, signs of tracks for carts used to facilitate routine conveyance of heavy objects from one part of the ship to the other. It did not lead him straight to the magazine, but he was the first to find it nonetheless.

No sooner had he arrived than the sergeant he'd sent to deal with the engines found him. "Sir, the engine was fairly easy to stop. The controls are not complicated if you test them gently. Once the pressure in the boiling tank is reduced, it is relatively safe, I think. I also gave orders to open the gunports. Air it out."

"Excellent idea," Equiluz mentioned. He'd been so absorbed he'd never noticed the smell after entering. Instead his full focus was now on the object he had encountered directly in front of the door to the magazine: an explosive warhead, a slow fuse burning its way to what looked like some kind of ignition point at the rear.

The sergeant nodded. "We found one of those behind the boiler."

"Did you leave it, or—?"

"No time to waste, sir. I figured we had only five minutes left." He shrugged. "We cut the fuse."

"I told you not to touch anything."

"Sir, I wouldn't have, but I could hardly go to find you when the damn—eh, wretched thing might burn down and blow us up before I received your instructions and then returned to it. Besides," he added with another shrug, "if it's just a fuse as it seems to be, then the flame can't reach the bomb. But if it is some other kind of device, we'd none of us have any idea what to do except cutting it—and so, we were going to die one way or the other. No?"

Although Equiluz said nothing, he had to admit the sergeant's reasoning had an admirably primitive practicality about it. Other bombs were reported within the next few minutes, all of the same design. One by one, their fuses were cut, and no explosions, mundane or magical, occurred.

He cut the fuse on the one in front of the magazine. It seemed they were done. And it seemed too simple. He stared at the defused explosive. The sergeant leaned over. "Sir, what are you waiting for? Why are you staring at that?"

"This was too easy, Sergeant. They leave even this one out here, burning for us to see? It makes no sense." Equiluz paused. "Unless..."

"Unless...?"

"Unless they wish us to believe that, having disarmed this demon that guards the gate, it is now safe to open the door to the magazine." Equiluz stood back, glanced at the sergeant's aide. "You, try the door. Gently."

The soldier did so. "It's locked, sir."

Equiluz nodded. "Of course it is. Probably to keep us from getting to another bomb, locked inside as the fuse burns down." He sniffed around the jamb of the door. "I can even smell it, I think."

"How can you smell anything in this air, sir?"

"Do you still find it so foul? At any rate, fuses always leave a smell of niter."

And at that particular moment, given all the time they had already spent in this crippled hulk, that odor of niter was to his sense of smell what the ticking of a great, spring-driven clock was to his ear. A reminder of every second passing, burning away. Every second that could well be his last. *No time to wait.*

"Now," Equiluz said to the sappers who had brought the heavy tools, "you must break the lock so we may open it gently. But be mindful; there could be a grenade rigged to fall and begin burning if the door opens. Sergeant, have your man fetch a pail of water from the gun deck."

When everything was ready, the men with the tools started at the door's lock. It proved stubborn, and every moment the niter smell seemed to grow stronger, but Equiluz assumed that was probably his imagination. Probably.

Eventually, the lock succumbed to the tools. He took a deep breath, could tell that the men around him were tensed to sprint away. *As if you could outrun an explosion. Fools.* Equiluz kept hold on the door so that it could not swing in too quickly, then opened it a crack.

Just beyond the arc of the door's swing, he saw three fuses lying on the deck, bundled together and burning. He smiled. *A clever attempt at misdirection, to make me think there was another bomb, just like the one I disarmed out here, waiting for me inside. When in fact, the real danger is almost certainly...*

He reached around, probed carefully—and felt a taut cord. "A grenade," he said with a smile. "I can feel the mechanism. Now, hand me a knife."

"Sir?"

"A knife, fool! I have my hand on the grenade's fuse. It is quite short. If we had opened the door all the way and the grenade fell free of its cradle, that would have generated the spark that set the fuse burning. So now, with this knife"—Equiluz gently sawed, sawed more, then success—"I will just remove the grenade." Sweating heavily, he slipped the small bomb out of the narrow opening. He exhaled deeply, dropped the grenade in the waiting water bucket just to be sure, sighed, and, with a profound sense of relief and triumph, he pushed the door open.

As it swung past the halfway point, he heard a faint click at the same moment it revealed:

—a box filled with opaque, interconnected bottles;

—from which three wires ran in different directions;

—one of which led to a strange mechanical device;

—which was attached to yet another warhead.

Before the door had swung another fraction of an inch, the strange device sparked.

Off the southern coast, St. Maarten

Almost a mile south of Pelican Point, only Eddie and Rik were still watching *Resolve*, much as if they were sitting a vigil.

When its magazine exploded, the brightness of the flash made them blink. A mild wind pushed at them, having left behind the ripples that had been resisted and overcome by the currents of the sea. By the time the others in the longboat had turned, the actinic brightness was gone. Now it was just a neural memory pressed briefly on their retina as a diminishing fireball rose like a spinning fist up through the cloud that marked *Resolve*'s place of death.

Chapter 65

Santo Domingo, Hispaniola

Santo Domingo made Eddie Cantrell conscious of just how tiny and primitive Oranjestad still was. Many of the Spanish port's buildings were already called "The Old Town" and had been there for over one hundred and thirty years. Just to the east of its mighty stone pier was a winding inlet that led not only to a reasonable hurricane hole but an impressive complex of wharves and ways. And of course there were the forts, both the ones that had been here almost as long as the city itself, and the new constructions which weren't quite six months old but were leaping upward at an alarming rate. That was the part of Santo Domingo which had their attention today. Well, at least this afternoon. Nighttime would bring a major shift in focus.

Eddie turned to his companion on *Intrepid*'s flying bridge. Karl Klemm's face was motionless, intent, as if he was determined to discover something about the city he had not seen over the course of the week that he had spent examining it through the fleet's best telescopes and binoculars and then calculating, calculating, calculating. So much so that there were rings under his young eyes.

Eddie smiled. "Relax, Karl. This is simple compared to hitting the galleons at St. Maarten. After that gunnery display, you have nothing left to prove."

Except maybe that you aren't some kind of demon spawn. Eddie had heard about rare individuals who had that kind of skill with numbers, backed up by an eerie perception of the patterns that resided, invisibly, under the surface of them. Combine that with Karl's damn near photographic memory, and it added up to the traits associated with certain rare autistic persons. But the Bavarian's only social and behavioral challenges seemed to be the ones shared by other young people who had never quite "fit in." Which weren't half as severe as they might have been, considering that he had been orphaned at twelve and then made Wallenstein's human fire-control computer toward the end of what hadn't really become the Thirty Years' War.

Karl shook his head tightly. "With respect, Commodore, this is a very different set of problems. Hitting Santo Domingo's fortifications is not the challenge. But hitting them in the right place to cause structural failures, and with the right measure of powder, and to yet ensure that no rounds overshoot and land in the city as per Admiral Tromp's orders—well, there is very little margin for error."

Eddie nodded. "Still, if there's a man alive who can do this job, it's you. Ready to give the word?"

"Me, sir?"

Eddie shrugged. "You did all the work. Seems only fair."

Karl nodded, but not eagerly. "I see now why Admiral Tromp was adamant about not having any rounds fall into the city itself. It is one thing to aim and fire a cannon at an approaching enemy." He swallowed. "It is quite another to fire them at a peaceful city of tens of thousands of people."

Eddie sighed. "Yeah, except that the peaceful city sitting under our guns right now built some of the fastest ships that were trying to kill us just three weeks ago off St. Maarten."

Karl nodded, pointed at the speaking tube to gunnery. "I believe it is this one, yes, sir?"

"Yes. Just give the word, Karl."

The expat-Bavarian set his shoulder, leaned down and said, "Mount One and Two. Commence firing!"

The guns sent thundercracks toward the walls of the newest fortification, following just behind the two solid eight-inch projectiles that slammed into them, tearing immense stony divots out of the sleek-sided glacis. That was the moment that *Courser*, *Harrier*, and *Relentless*, riding at anchor near *Intrepid*, let their single guns speak also.

They watched as explosions blossomed along the walls like angry gray flowers, but did not even attempt to speak over the unrelenting roar of the guns.

Larry Quinn almost hit his head as he charged into *Amelia*'s great cabin. "Am I late? When do the fireworks start?" He glanced in the direction of the mural-sized window that reached almost all the way across the stern. Eddie found his eyes drawn to the tableau framed within it.

Santo Domingo was dark for the second night in a

row. That was rather pointless on a night with a full moon; as if the allied fleet was really going to continue their bombardment at night. And anyhow, what was left to shell? Two hundred and twenty-three rounds after Karl started the bombardment, there was little left worth shooting at.

The new fortifications went first and they were a bear. Engineering had come a long way since the first basic harbor forts had been thrown up to protect the city. They held up pretty well at first, but once Karl's selected target points had all been hit, sure enough, the wobble started showing. After about sixty rounds, all the new construction was coming down in chunks. By one hundred ten or so, it was pretty much leveled, and would take almost as long to clear away the rubble as it had taken to build it.

In all fairness, the real artistes among fortification designers and engineers made their best commissions from rich European kings who wanted to protect rich and valuable European cities. In the New World, it was a crapshoot what kind of designer you had working for you, and Santo Domingo apparently had a pretty uneven history in terms of the qualifications of their engineers, too. But there were still a lot of separate batteries and garrisons and armed towers to knock down before the bombardment finally came to an end.

At least the dust had settled. There hadn't been much worry about that, though; in order to make sure they'd have good visibility at night, it was agreed that the shelling would not go past 1600 hours. But at just after 1520, even Karl agreed that more rounds just meant bouncing the rubble.

And now, just eight hours later, here they were in

Joost Banckert's ship, sipping wine (or in Eddie's case, juice) and acting like they were waiting for a sporting event to begin. Which was kinda true if you had a really, really dark sense of humor.

Tromp was in an unusually fine mood. He liked to have meetings in his old ship, and Joost liked to host them. Probably because every time he did, *Amelia* felt a little bit more like *his* ship. So it was Banckert who suggested that Larry get some wine or schnapps and join them.

Larry and Banckert had hit it off right away. Neither liked it very much when diplomatic niceties got in the way of operational ease or clarity. Understandable, although Joost hadn't yet discovered Quinn's much lower toleration for "moral flexibility," a trait that had served Banckert and other Dutch captains so well for so many years. Right now, Larry Quinn was simply a rough-and-ready *and* competent up-timer who had appeared behind the flotilla of galleons facing Joost's own ships at St. Maarten and reduced them to kindling in just over an hour.

But it hadn't all gone their way. As Larry pulled out the chair next to Joost, cup of rum in hand, he asked "So, any more news about the wounded from *Neptunus?*"

Joost toasted the ceiling. "Thank God, it does not look as if any more will die. That Sephardic physician—Brandão—had to put three of them back under the knife to remove infections or arrest gangrene. And that Danish king's daughter—Eddie's sister-in-law, Leonora—has had her own successes, I was told. Spots a wound that isn't ready to heal almost as readily as the doctor himself."

While Eddie sincerely doubted that her skills had progressed to that extent, Banckert's appraisal was consistent with other reports. And it was fortunate for the men who had lived long enough to be returned to St. Eustatius that they were in such unusually qualified hands.

Eddie had seen the final casualty reports just before he'd met Karl on *Intrepid*'s flying bridge. Banckert's ships had stood off while *Courser* and *Harrier* arrived behind the Spanish formation; uncoordinated maneuver would only block their lines of sight and engagement. After losing a third of their number, including any that turned about in a bid to catch the wind and escape to the west, the remaining galleons had attempted to get in among Joost's formation. That meant sailing into the eye of the wind, and galleons were among the worst ships for making headway by sharply tacking across it.

They'd lost another six of their number by the time Joost was faced with the choice of either standing in the seaway and complicating the steam destroyers' gunnery or giving ground by turning southward into a reaching wind and getting out of the destroyers' field of fire. He had chosen the latter, signaled it to his ships, but before the Aldis lamps bumped it over to *Neptunus*, two galleons approached, striking their colors.

It was unclear exactly what happened next. The nearer Spaniard closed her gunports in response to instructions from the smaller *Neptunus*, which then moved alongside to board and take her in hand. However, at thirty yards, lookouts on the Dutch man-of-war saw several of the far more numerous Spanish crew moving aside canvas to better lay hands upon readied *petereroes.* A confused combat occurred between the two ships, with *Neptunus* getting the better of the fight on deck because more of her crew were already armed and ready. It was the same below because of the time it took for the Spaniard to open her gunports. By then, the Dutchman had put an extremely accurate broadside into her, inflicting particular damage to her lowest gun deck where the forty-two-pounders lurked.

Soon after, the jacht that Tromp had dispatched to keep watch on that formation of galleons, *Vriessche Jager*, ran in to assist *Neptunus*. But as she passed the second of the surrendering Spaniards, they proved themselves faithless, also, and discharged a full broadside at seventy yards. *Vriessche Jager* mostly flew into pieces and sank in minutes.

Vengeance came swiftly. *Neptunus* withdrew far enough for *Harrier* to destroy the already shaken galleon, and *Courser* saw to the other. That ended what proved to be the most costly engagement of the day: sixty-nine lost on *Vriessche Jager*, twenty-eight dead and forty-six wounded on *Neptunus*, twelve of the latter dying either because they did not get the prompt attention of a surgeon or due to postoperative infections.

Another ten had been in danger of succumbing to similar causes but were saved by Brandão after being carried to Oranjestad by two of the fluyts that had been sent to reprovision the fleet for its hastily approved push to Santo Domingo. All the senior officers were in agreement that in this region, the Spanish were now too weak to turn back another drive on the city the way they had at Vieques the year before.

Banckert was rolling a dram of his preferred gin

slowly between his palms, still glowering at the memories. "I should have let all those popish bastards drown."

Larry glanced at Joost's use of the word "popish." While not a Catholic himself, he had the same aversion to religious intolerance as most other up-timers. However, those prejudices remained predominant in down-timers, even those who fought against having (or at least showing) them. Quinn found a middle ground. "The men on those galleons were liars and backstabbers. So I'm not losing any sleep over taking care of our own first. Along with any other pressing matters." Joost nodded fiercely and downed his gin. "Besides," Larry reflected, "it was weird how many didn't even want to be rescued, at first. Scared shitless, most of them."

Eddie nodded. "I think we've found out why that might be. While we were patching up in Great Bay, near the salt pans, our troops were having a hard time finding any of the Spanish who we knew had been left on the island. Yeah, a lot of them got away on pataches from Marigot Bay on the west, but given all the men they had creating smoke screens, sending signals, and trying to trap and grab *Resolve*, it was a certainty they hadn't been able to evacuate all of them.

"But our troops couldn't find any. The Spanish had even abandoned Fort Amsterdam. Took a while to track them down, but they eventually came to freshwater sources and our guys were there waiting." Eddie shook his head. "It didn't make any sense at first: their half-starved guys with swords charging straight at our troops with muskets and pistols. Who were offering food. It was like Spanish banzai charges."

The Dutchmen looked at each other. "I'll explain later. But finally we got a chance to talk to some who were only wounded, and after some water and decent care, they came around and dropped the dime."

"Dropped the dime?" Larry asked. "On who?" This time the two admirals just shrugged and drank when they bounced off the up-time idiom.

"Olivares."

"What?" asked all three men.

"Yes," Eddie said, nodding. "The one and only epitome of self-interest, insecurity, and nepotism. According to the ones with more rank or seniority, they'd been told that all Dutchmen—and all their allies—should be executed. No prisoners taken. Because, of course, that's what all of us were ready to do to them."

Larry pushed back from the table with an expression that was equal parts dismay and revulsion. "Hey, I know it's war to the knife out here, but, really?"

It was Tromp who answered. "Olivares passed those orders a year ago. He issued the statement to the junta that oversees affairs here in the New World. It was presumed that this was simply one of his many vitriolic outbursts. But it seems he has made it an actual policy, this time."

"Well, that explains Curaçao," Banckert growled.

"And the massacre of the slaveholders' fish-salting camp back on St. Maarten," Eddie added.

Tromp nodded at him. "I understand you received our final casualty reports, this morning?"

Eddie nodded. "I did, along with other news that's worth sharing, I think." *Boy, is it ever!* "There were nineteen dead and thirty-five wounded on all other ships, combined. Except for *Resolve*, of course." He sighed. "Ninety-seven dead, mostly deck crew killed during the initial ambush, but also quite a few lost during the evacuation." He suppressed memories.

"Wounded?"

"Twenty-four convalescing, almost a hundred with minor injuries. All on the mend. They'll be ready for duty by the time we return."

"So many dead, and so few wounded?" Banckert wondered.

Eddie nodded. "I sympathize with what happened to the wounded aboard *Neptunus*, Admiral, because something similar happened on *Resolve*. Given how long they had to fight while surrounded, most men with serious wounds died because they couldn't move fast enough to avoid getting hit again. And of those few who were taken off, most died on the ride back out or because the fleet was engaged with the enemy and could not stop to take on wounded."

Banckert looked glum. "Well, I'm ready for some good news. Do we have a final count on how many of *them* we accounted for?"

Eddie paused. Banckert's concept of winning and losing was almost entirely in keeping with what one military historian had called "dueling kill counts," and that wasn't ever going to change. "There's no way to know how many Spanish seamen we killed. All told, twenty-one galleons, four galleoncetes and two fragatas were sunk or scuttled. Some of their crew survived and escaped in small boats, about eighty have been picked up. From what little information they're sharing, most of the galleons did not have full complements. Some only had skeleton crews, such as the ones *Resolve* encountered during its actions in and around the lagoon. I am not counting those ships as destroyed because they weren't actually combatant vessels."

"Lastly, one hundred and forty dead soldiers and sappers have been found, but given the fire, explosions, destruction of *Resolve*, and landslide, we are never going to have an accurate count. My answer to your request for an estimate of enemy casualties is 'a lot.'"

"Well," Banckert declared gruffly, "I'd say we did pretty well, then."

Tromp's reply was almost a whisper. "Did we? I tell you, Joost, I'd be happy to return all the ships they lost if we could have *Resolve* back."

Eddie nodded. "Yeah, because this wasn't just about capturing or even destroying one of our steamships. This was a lesson."

"And a blow aimed at our morale," Tromp added, "at our easy assumptions of invincibility whenever one of our steamships is present."

Larry Quinn put his cup down. "While we're on the topic of invincibility, I've been wondering: how long should we really stay here?"

Tromp frowned. "I am not sure I understand what you mean."

"I mean, we've got to start thinking about how long we want to remain anchored in front of Santo Domingo, almost five hundred miles from the closest friendly port. Particularly since we've given our enemies a lot of time to react."

"Come, come, Larry," cozened Banckert. "We have moved with excellent dispatch!"

"No argument on that," Larry replied, perhaps honestly, perhaps diplomatically. "But that doesn't mean we're not still racing a clock that could run out on us.

"Count it out: we spent five days refitting off St. Maarten. Then nine days sailing to the standoff point where we spent two days with the balloons and the jachts checking out the harbor and surrounding area to make sure we weren't walking into yet another trap. Then we wasted three days trying to talk sense into them. Their response to a flag of truce? They send out fire boats. We withdraw, sink them all. We go back in, they send out more, and we sink them, too. Lather, rinse, repeat. Then yesterday, because Admiral Tromp is really, really humane, he sends a second boat with a white flag. They meet it, get a very polite warning that we're giving them twenty-four hours to evacuate before we start shelling their forts, and what do they do?"

Eddie laughed. "What else? More fire boats."

"What is it with the Spanish around here?" Quinn stared in bewilderment at his audience and tapped his head in the universal *duh?* gesture. Then his face became serious. "That's twenty-one days. And so I'm asking you, the experts: what can they do to us in that time?"

"Very little," Tromp answered quietly. "Assuming the shortest course, average weather, and a generous estimate of the speed of their new ships, from St. Maarten it would take them thirty-six days to reach Cuba and then return here with a fleet—if it was already waiting for them. And there is almost no chance that they would encounter one that was already on its way here. Havana will not leave herself defenseless now that she has an adequate regard for the risk we pose."

But Larry was shaking his head. "Admiral, you've got me wrong. I'm not talking about Havana. I'm talking about Tortuga, about pirates. If the fleet at St. Maarten went straight to *them* for help, they could be here any day." He stopped when he noticed that all three men were staring at him. "What?"

Tromp smiled. "Eddie does indeed have some interesting news."

Larry looked at the young up-timer. "So? What is it, Commodore?"

Eddie picked up the flimsy on the table before him and read.

```
FROM: CPT. L. KLINGL, USEN
TO: CDRE E. CANTRELL, USEN
—MESSAGE BEGINS—
    MY PLEASURE TO SEND FINAL DATA
  RE: SUCCESS OF OPERATION "ISLAND
  HOPPERS" 48 HOURS AGO STOP
    PIRATE OPERATIONS TORTUGA TERMI-
  NATED STOP
    CAYONA PORT FACILITIES AND WARE-
  HOUSES DESTROYED STOP FORTRESS
  TAKEN STOP
    COMPLETE DEMOLITION UNACHIEVABLE
  WITH AVAILABLE CHARGES STOP
    3 SHIPS, 37 POW TAKEN STOP
    FINAL CASUALTY COUNTS FOLLOW STOP
    ENEMY CASUALTIES 89 KIA; UNK WIA,
  17 POW STOP
    NAVAL SQUADRON CASUALTIES: 14 KIA,
  37 WIA. MARINE CASUALTIES: 42 KIA,
  79 WIA, 12 MIA STOP
    AWAITING FURTHER INSTRUCTIONS
  STOP
—MESSAGE ENDS—
```

Larry blinked. "Holy sh—!" He broke off what an up-timer would have considered profanity and a down-timer might label blasphemy. "When—and how—did you do that?" He looked from Eddie to Tromp. Who merely sat in his chair, smiling. For him, that was the equivalent of a wide grin.

Eddie shrugged. "I'm guessing you chatted enough with the crew of the *Harrier* to know that there was supposed to be at least one more ship in the convoy that arrived in June."

Larry nodded, then his eyes opened. "They said there were supposed to be Marines sent along, maybe for Jennings. But something got tangled up ... ?"

"Oh, a lot got tangled up. Red tape. Budgets. Infighting. Horse-trading."

"So just like up-time."

Eddie nodded. "The more things change ... Anyhow, by the time the Marines were finally freed up and on their way over the Atlantic, I realized we needed to knock Tortuga out of this war. Too many reasons to go into here, but you can look at the OPORD, if you like."

Larry held up his hand. "Pass."

Eddie smiled. "Long story short, I diverted them so that they rendezvoused with some of our friends in Bermuda to resupply and recruit any interested auxiliaries. And also, guides around the Bahamas. Because this couldn't be a blind 'hey diddle diddle, straight up the middle' kind of attack. That would have been a disaster. But there are a bunch of Bermudans who make their living, and spend most of their life, in the Bahamas. And they knew all about how pirates go in and out of Tortuga. There are hidden signs, almost like hobo marks, where they get food, where they get powder, and so on. And not surprisingly, ever since the freebooters became pals with the Spanish, they got a lot more predictable. Some of them started evolving into bean-counting bureaucrats."

"Is there any other kind? And also: there's a few in every organization."

"Right. So the Marines, and their ship, and the 'indigenous auxiliaries' gathered intel for a few weeks, then nabbed an outgoing pirate smack, debriefed the crew, and got a ground plan. Using all the hobo signs and right approaches, they were to infiltrate in small boats and guide the Marines' ship in. At least that was the plan. And it looks like it worked."

Larry shrugged. "Except for trying to blow that mountain cave fortress apart, I guess. But I'll bet it was still quite a show. Hey, talking about a show, isn't tonight's about to start?"

Tromp rose. "It is. The dirigible should be over the target in a few minutes."

As they gathered at the mural-sized stern window, Larry steered aside to add a little more rum to his cup. "The air force is having a big day. Eh, night. Is this a first?"

"You mean a balloon observing and sending targeting adjustments to a dirigible?" Eddie frowned, shrugged. "It might be. Really haven't been getting those kinds of details regarding the battles with the Ottomans."

Banckert pointed to the east. "I believe I see it. That flash of light... there! Is that the, eh, device that generates the hot air?"

"The burner. Yes, Admiral," Eddie confirmed.

"It is higher than you said, I think."

Eddie nodded. "Right now, yes. It's easier to navigate from higher altitude, particularly at night. The pilot has instruments, but the best way to steer is according to terrain features. And the higher you go, the more the ground beneath you looks like the map you're using as a reference."

Although Banckert wasn't always a huge fan of technology, he was unabashedly fascinated and enthused about balloons and airships. "It is all quite ingenious. But I do not understand why you need the balloon up as well."

Larry leaned in. "Think of it this way, Joost. You're firing at a target you can't really see that well. But, you've got an observer who can see things really clearly from a different angle and who can tell you how to shift your aim to get on target. That's what the observer in the balloon will be doing. The dirigible has to descend to drop its payload accurately, but the observer will still be seeing everything from six hundred feet. He can see where the drop markers fall, then tell the dirigible pilot how to move to adjust his vehicle."

Banckert frowned. "And the pilot cannot see that even better, being lower and so close?"

Eddie smiled. "You know, I thought the same thing at first, but piloting a dirigible is kind of like being at the helm of a ship; the only part of the ocean you *can't* see is the patch you're right on top of. Also, the dirigible can drift with the wind a bit and you won't even notice it. The observer is a second, and often better, set of eyes to detect that. Which is useful because when you're flying an airship, that means trying to keep track of a dozen things at once. Besides, it is really noisy in the gondola."

Tromp crossed his arms. "It is beginning its descent, approaching the target," he announced.

Larry sipped at his rum while staring at the airborne oval. "Looks good. I heard there was some trouble with the launch?"

Eddie shook his head. "Just a security alert that turned out to be a false alarm. Escaped slaves. They got to Isla Catalina just two days before we did. They were trying to build a raft and not having much luck." He smiled. "So now we're giving them a lift aboard *Crown of Waves*."

The dirigible was now less than two hundred and fifty feet above the inlet that was also Santo Domingo's protected anchorage and moderately reliable hurricane hole. The Spanish must have seen her, but from twelve hundred yards, there was no way to tell if they were trying to fire at her. She crept forward slowly, reached the other side of the inlet and stopped. Something small tumbled down from her.

"What's that?" Tromp asked.

"White paint," Eddie answered. "One of the many reasons we were waiting for a full moon: so the observer can see and confirm that mark. It will take him a second to telegraph any corrections down to *Intrepid*'s radio room, which will then pass it on to the dirigible."

A moment later, the dirigible moved slightly closer to Santo Domingo's city walls and slightly closer to the coast. Another container of paint. This time, instead of moving again, larger objects began falling down from the airship.

"And there goes the first payload," Larry murmured.

The process was repeated, and then the airship reascended quickly and moved out over the bay.

"And now let us hope the jachts are able to do their part," Banckert mused.

"They are," Tromp said calmly. "And if they fail, we should be able to achieve the same end with explosive rounds from the *Harrier*; she is standing by to do just that."

Banckert frowned. "Is that even necessary? Can't the crew of the dirigible simply drop a burning oil lantern?"

Larry shook his head. "Nah, not reliable. That's why we didn't do that in the first place. Lanterns—most burning objects—are snuffed out during their fall, sometimes even when they hit. And tonight, you're going to want really fast ignition in a lot of places, all at once. So the Spanish just can't put out the fires."

As the airship flew beyond the left-hand frame of the window, two other objects moved in from the same side, but on the water: the jachts *Vliegende Hert* and *Dolphijn*. They sailed in swiftly, an unusually large group of silhouetted figures standing ready on their respective poop decks. Nine hundred yards from where the dirigible had dropped her payload, they heeled over, came fully about and laid two anchors.

"And we needed calm water," Eddie added.

"Now this," Larry added, "is where the observer in the balloon becomes even more important. The ships' ability to see the aimpoint is even worse than the view from the dirigible."

Once the jachts were still—well, as still as boats ever got, even in a calm bay—the figures on their poop decks began fussing with some kind of framework. At the same time, the sail handlers were reefing the canvas and drawing the yards as far away from the stern as they could. For no apparent reason, all the activity stopped.

After three seconds, Banckert asked impatiently, "Well?"

As if in answer, a rocket shot up from each of the jachts, not high like fireworks, but in a much lower and faster arc that carried them toward the general area where the dirigible had dropped its payload.

But it was truly only the "general" area; one went over a hundred yards farther into the moonlit waters of the anchorage, the other into the city itself. Tromp stirred at that, but made no sound.

They waited silently as correction advice made its way down the wire from the balloon to the radio room in *Intrepid* and then to the radio aboard *Dolphijn*. Two more rockets leaped toward the aimpoint; two more misses, but much closer. Another seemingly endless wait, and then two more rockets.

One exploded at the apex of its flight: a malfunction. But the other's arc terminated near the aimpoint. The explosion was bright but relatively small. Banckert seemed about to complain again . . .

The target area erupted into a sudden sheet of flame that raced along the wooden wharf with startling speed.

Two more rockets; two more misses. But the rocketry teams on both jachts kept at it, and by the time both had fired five rockets each, the city's protected wharves, docks, and ways were all ablaze, the fire climbing high into the night sky.

"And there goes Santo Domingo's contributions to the Spanish fleet, thanks to a little modern science and about seventy gallons of naphtha mixed with avocado and palm oil." There was a knock at the door, and Banckert called for the visitor to enter. "They will rebuild, of course," he added as he turned back to smile at the glow.

The runner who'd slipped in went straight to Eddie, a flimsy in hand.

"Of course they'll rebuild their facilities," Tromp nodded. "But during that time, they will not be launching or laying down new ships. We cannot ask for more than that. And now it is time to make ready to return home."

"Admiral," Eddie said, double-checking what he'd just read, "I don't think heading back to St. Eustatia is such a great idea."

"Why not?" Banckert snapped. "And why does *my* runner bring a message to *you*?"

"Because I am currently the first recipient of all communiqués from our weather stations." He remembered to breathe. "There's a hurricane coming."

Chapter 66

Santo Domingo, Hispaniola

Tromp folded his arms. "How close is this hurricane?"

Eddie swept a hand toward the map on the table. "Still hasn't reached Barbados, the observation station that spotted it." *And thank God they were happy to host a station and get a radio in the bargain.*

Banckert scowled. "Barbados? How can they even tell its direction?"

"Because they've been tracking it for thirty minutes. Not a lot of data yet, and they're still working to get a speed estimate. But the initial position change, as well as the local wind speed and direction, makes it reasonable to project that it's going to follow the standard hurricane path. But right now..."

"Right now," Tromp said with a nod, cutting off any further quarrelsome observations from Banckert, "we must prepare to get underway with all speed."

"All the ships are ready," Joost growled.

Tromp grimaced. "Yes, but not all are with us. *Crown of Waves* can remain where she is, since we'll be going that direction, anyway."

Larry frowned. "To the east? Against the wind? When we're trying to outrun a hurricane?"

Banckert shrugged. "Heading east means we will be slower at first but faster later. If I'm right about what Maarten has in mind, that is." He faced the admiral. "Unfortunately, the new Danish frigate, *Triumferende*, is a pig with its ass stuck in the fence. She's fifteen miles downwind."

Larry cocked his head. "I don't know, Joost. She seems like a pretty fast ship."

"She is, my up-time, land-loving friend, but she also has to wait for the airship to land. And then the ground crew has to break it down and load it, *ja*?" He finished by looking at Eddie.

Who nodded. "We can radio the dirigible's pilot to push the engines, but I'm not sure the minor increase in speed is worth the risk of pushing it harder. That could cause a malfunction. Which would really complicate matters."

"I agree," said Tromp, leaning over the map. "I know you chose the best landing site, Eddie, but I also remember you complaining that it was not a very good one."

"You remember correctly, sir. It's here." Eddie touched the map. "The airship's LZ is also where breakdown will occur, about a mile south of this spot labeled Playa Los Cuadritos."

"What's there?" Larry asked.

"Nothing. Not even in our time. No roads down to the shore. Some of the slaves that Calabar liberated from Hispaniola a few months back say it's not a good spot for boats unless you know where the rocks are. And there are *plenty* of rocks."

Banckert was frowning like an ogre. "Then why did we choose it?"

Eddie sighed. "First, we never thought we'd be racing the clock. Second, being a crappy spot for us means it's also a crappy spot for the locals. There's no beach and no good fishing, so it was never developed: not in our time and not in yours. That's what we wanted: a stretch of coast with no easy path and no good reason for locals to be wandering around where we mean to land, break down, and pack for removal."

"Which is accomplished how?" Larry was frowning, chin resting in his hand.

"Boat crews from *Triumferende* go in with skiffs and a purpose-built catamaran, all on towlines back to the frigate. Their draft is shallow enough to get in next to the shore. Envelope and engines are loaded and then they both row and are towed back out to the frigate."

Larry looked at him. "Towlines, huh? Sounds like you were expecting a hot extraction, after all."

Tromp shook his head. "That is to ensure that such heavily loaded boats can get beyond the breakers." He turned to Eddie. "Time until *Triumferende* is ready to sail?"

Eddie thought for a moment, adding the dirigible's remaining flight time, the average breakdown time, and the estimated time to get it out to the frigate. "Best case is one hour and forty minutes. Call it two hours."

"And we must presume *Triumferende* will take six hours to reach us, even if she hugs the coast and sails close-hauled. So we cannot leave any earlier than eight hours. And no, Eddie, I will not send the tugs after her. We need to conserve their fuel to help our slowest hulls keep as good a pace as long as possible as the fleet tacks its way eastward."

"About that . . ." Larry started to ask.

Tromp shook his head. "You will see why we are likely to sail east, since you are going to help us decide which is our best option. Now, I understand you have a particularly gifted mathematician aboard *Courser*?"

Larry smiled, winked at Eddie. "You could say that."

As Karl Klemm leaned back from the charts and laid the protractor aside, Eddie checked his watch: they were two hours into the hurricane countdown.

"Well?" asked Larry Quinn.

Karl sounded genuinely apologetic. "I am sorry, Herr Major, but of the two hurricane holes that we may reach before the hurricane is certainly upon us, Culebra is the far inferior choice. It would require tacking two hundred and ninety nautical miles due east. Even if we were to assume an optimistic average tacking speed of one and three quarters knots, the journey would require approximately one hundred and sixty-eight hours. And I am compelled to point out that we should not travel eastward any more than absolutely necessary, since that places us into an earlier part of the hurricane's probable track. Also, the closer we approach, the more likely that we would experience even stronger headwinds, which would make tacking both slower and more difficult."

Larry threw his hands up. "Well, it sure looked like the shorter trip. I guess this is one of those times when you just can't trust a map."

Tromp smiled. "You cannot trust a map *alone*," he amended gently. "So, Karl, what course are we committing to, then?"

"The plot to the hurricane hole at Bahia de Gracias is a much better alternative." He smiled faintly. "It is also the only one, Herr Admiral. Given a more realistic average tacking speed of one and a half knots to the eastern strip of Isla de Saona, and then a three-knot average given the various speeds we are likely to experience afterward, we would reach Bahia de Gracias in one hundred hours. If, that is, all our wind and current estimates are correct and there are no unforeseen variables. Which there always are."

Tromp nodded. "I agree. Opinions?"

Larry studied the map carefully. "So, once we turn due north just beyond this, uh, this Isla de Saona, the winds pick up?"

"Not exactly," Joost said, arms crossed. "And that's why you don't want to plot a course due north. You'd regret that."

"Joost is right," Tromp added. "The moment we round Saona, we are in a seaway where there are likely to be breezes from both northeast and due east. We will have to feel our way there. If the wind is strongest out of the northeast, following the coast would put us in the eye of the prevailing wind, but if the wind is strongest from the east, then that same course would allow us to sail close-hauled all the way, rather than tacking or beating."

Larry was trying to keep up. "So what do we do if the wind is strongest from the northeast?"

Joost's smile took on some of the piratical cast Eddie mostly associated with "Peg Leg" Jol. "Then we gird our loins and continue fifteen miles further east of Saona. A slow-going tack with a fickle close reach. And endless waiting to see if winds and fate are with you or not. Sure to tighten your nut sack."

"However," Tromp continued with a glance at Banckert, "once fifteen miles beyond Saona, we turn north. Now, any wind from the east is reaching, and we can even sail a northeast wind close-hauled, all the way to Cap del Engano. From there, the prevailing wind becomes our friend. It would rarely be worse than a broad reach until we round Cap de Samana. From there, it should be over our starboard quarter the rest of the way."

Quinn stared at the map. "So any extra time we spend tacking at first will be more than made up as we continue along the east and then north coast of Hispaniola."

"Larry," Banckert said in a cautioning tone, "a sailor never uses the word 'will' when speaking of the wind and its moods. That's tempting fate. 'Should' is better, but 'might' is the word I'd recommend." He glanced at Eddie. "Any further word on the storm? Has it hit land yet?"

Eddie shook his head. "That probably won't happen for another, umm, four hours, maybe more."

"What? How far off was it when they first detected it?"

"About one hundred and forty nautical miles, Admiral."

Joost stared. "That is not possible—unless, did you have a man in a balloon on Barbados?"

Eddie smiled. "No, we don't have that many. But we didn't need one: the weather outpost on Mount Hillaby is about three hundred thirty yards above sea level, and this storm system is at least a mile and a half high. So they started seeing a thin gray line poking over the horizon at a range of almost one hundred and forty miles. They couldn't be sure until it came closer. Now it's about eighty miles away and heading northeast."

Larry frowned. "So it's clocking in at about twenty miles an hour?"

"A little less, they think, but it fluctuates."

"Hey," Larry said with a resigned shrug, "it *is* a hurricane." The runner came in holding a message out toward Banckert.

"So the first projections remain reasonable," Tromp commented as the admiral sent the boy back out and scanned the flimsy. "Approximately eighty hours between first sighting and landfall at or near Culebra, one hundred hours to Luperón, the port in Bahia de Gracias."

"And it seems," Banckert sighed, "we shall have fewer hours to reach it, now." He passed the report to Eddie. "Add an hour until *Triumferende* reaches us. The boats capsized after they were loaded."

Eddie didn't curse much, not even inside his head. Now, he did. Like most operational plans that sounded easy, the retrieval of the airship had proven to be anything but. The landing had been okay, despite a shore breeze that kept trying to push the dirigible inland. The wind had continued being a nuisance as the ground crew deflated the envelope, folded, and secured it with straps. But when they finally had it and the gondola and the engines on the boats, they were still running on time.

But, according to the report, the chop along the surf line had become more lively than it was when the boats had run in, and the catamaran turned out not to be up to the task. The weight of the engine had her lower in the water than the tests reported, so her bottom was running closer to the rocks. One particularly lively swell lifted her up and when she rode down its back into an equally deep trough, her portside hull caught in the rocks. Before the crew could free her, another swell came along, tore the snagged hull partially away from the main beam. Crippled and with her bow in the water, the next swell flipped her.

Flipped a cat? How often did that happen? Then again, how often did you get your first genuine hurricane a week or two *after* the season for them? But at least the lashings held, and they were able to keep the catamaran afloat until more boats from *Triumferende* arrived to assist and bring the load aboard. However, the main components of the dirigible were so waterlogged that it wouldn't be safe to operate without a full refit.

Unfortunately, the captain of *Triumferende* had been a bit optimistic; the total delay was closer to two hours. So, eight hours after Eddie had started his mental countdown clock running, the Danish frigate rejoined the fleet, and Tromp gave the order to weigh anchor and begin tacking to the east. At which point, Eddie glanced at his wristwatch.

Ninety-two hours left.

Off Isla de Saona, Hispaniola

Two days later, almost to the minute, *Intrepid*'s taffrail pulled beyond Isla de Saona and her bow faced open water to the east. Eddie was on the flying bridge, Tromp alongside him.

"Well," the admiral said, "I am glad I am not on *Courser* right now."

Eddie smiled. "Yeah, Larry will be pacing like a caged tiger and twice as grouchy." Quinn had hoped that, at this point, they'd either be steering northeast for sure, or tacking fifteen miles west, for sure. But as the Dutch mariners had warned, the wind here was not merely irregular, but capricious. The moderate breeze that was coming out of the Mona Passage from the northeast continued to battle the usually stronger wind that ran westward along the southern extents of the Greater Antilles' largest islands: Cuba, Hispaniola, Puerto Rico. Finding the correct way to court the two winds would be an ongoing and uncertain process. Just the kind of situation likely to give Larry waking nightmares.

"Well," Maarten temporized, "he can console himself with the excellent job he did managing the firewood for the tugs. Without them, we'd not have kept to the one and a half knots we needed to stay on schedule. With *Neptunus'* repairs incomplete and *Prins Willem* being the slow sailer that she always is, they would have slowed us considerably."

Of course now, with the wood expended, it was the tugs that were being towed, one by *Harrier*, one by *Relentless*. But to be fair, Larry's anxiety wasn't just over the state of their wind and steam. He and Eddie shared another concern, one that now had to be voiced and resolved.

Eddie cleared his throat. "We're at a crossroads here, Maarten."

The admiral kept his eyes on the eastern horizon. Several long seconds passed. Then: "You mean, whether we should continue to send position updates to St. Eustatia?"

"Yes. Up until now, it hasn't really mattered whether or not we have informers leaking data from our weather stations. For the last two days, we've been on the only logical course for either of the two possible hurricane holes. Or home, for that matter. But to send our next position would be like drawing an arrow pointed at our intended destination."

"Do you really think the Spanish would come into the teeth of a hurricane to find us?"

"No. But if they've learned that it's coming, they'll sit in their home ports, wait until it blows over, and then come after us. And whereas they'll be in places where they can effect repairs pretty quickly, we'll be on our own, improvising. And hoping they don't find us until we can leave Luperón."

Tromp shifted his gaze to the southeastern sky, which had only a hint of atypical darkness. "I agree. I have been thinking about the same issue. Not sending another update is the safer course of action, certainly. But it means that after we send the cipher for, eh, 'going dark,' our own communities and forces will not know what has become of us. And soon after we turn north, our radio will not reach the relay at St. Croix anymore. So we will not even be able to, eh, squelch break to assure them that we still exist." He paused. "It will be very hard on the people of St. Eustatia. And for any who hope to have some word of the loved ones they may have in this fleet." He looked directly at Eddie. "It will be very difficult for Anne Cathrine."

And Leonora and Simpson and hundreds of others, but: "If we live through this, then at least we haven't told the Spanish where to go in order to finish us off. And if we don't survive this storm ... well, then it doesn't really change anything, does it?"

Tromp smiled. "No, I don't suppose it does. Very well. I am glad we are of a like mind, on this."

Me too, thought Eddie as he checked his watch.

Forty-four hours left.

Off Cap de Samana, Hispaniola

Eddie was ascending the stairs as *Intrepid* drew abreast of Cap de Samana. It was about an hour after dawn, so the eastern sky was still growing in brightness, but there was a persistent gray dimming the horizon in the southeast.

"You are early," Tromp said as the up-timer finished mounting the stairs to the flying bridge. It was stripped of its usual command and control elements, naked except for the frame of the bridge itself. The wheel and speaking tubes were covered, and those covers were tied off with multiple leather straps.

Eddie glanced at all the preparations, grinned, but could feel it was rigid, forced. "Expecting a storm, Admiral?"

Tromp's answering smile was smaller and no more an expression of mirth than Eddie's had been. "It is said that a person who can smile in the face of force majeure is, in and of themselves, a force to be reckoned with."

"Strange," Eddie confessed, glancing southeast, "I can't say I feel that way, just now."

"Nor I," Tromp agreed. They stood watching the

sky and the unusually low, slow swells for at least a minute.

"I have some news," Eddie offered into the suffocating silence.

"I hope it is good."

"It is. I think. You know that ship *Challenger* that came to Eustatia when I was on Antigua and you were assessing the repairs on the last of the La Flota galleons?"

"Yes, I do remember that ship. The master, he was an up-timer, too. Gordon Chehab, I think his name was."

"Yeah, him. Well, I got word from Klingl, the captain who just finished wrapping things up at Tortuga, that *Challenger* passed through the area again. Gordon told him that he was still hoping to airdrop those psyop leaflets you gave him to release over Havana, if he got the chance."

Tromp smiled. "I confess, I had quite forgotten about that. It would be a grand compliment to our activities in Santo Domingo." He grew somber. "I just hope Mr. Chehab has finished his aerial activities over Cuba and is already well beyond the path of the storm. He was most enterprising and I would have been glad if he had been able to stay and add his efforts to our own. He seemed like a nice fellow."

Eddie smiled sideways. "But not nice enough to give him a radio to replace the one he lost."

Tromp glanced sideways. "Now, Eddie. That is neither kind nor fair. You know very well that I had none left to give." He sighed. "We have more ships and more detachments? We need more radios. More allied communities and more weather and observation outposts? Again, more radios. And if I had given him our last set? Well, that was the one that went to Barbados. In which case—"

"In which case, *now* where would we be?" Eddie nodded. "Sailing casually back home and straight into a hurricane. I know. I was just making a joke. Trying to lighten the mood."

"Which I appreciate, Eddie, but I suppose that my mood is rather resistant to levity, just now."

"I understand." And like Tromp, he stared at the increasingly peculiar color of the sky in the far southeast. Another full minute passed. "Latest report puts it at eighteen miles an hour. We won't hear any more from the last relay, St. Croix. It's brushing alongside them right now."

Tromp nodded.

"That means the leading edge of it is due to hit Luperón right about when we're due to arrive there. Plus or minus thirty minutes."

"I know, Eddie," Tromp said quietly. He kept his eyes on the horizon behind them.

But Eddie's eyes were on his watch, as they had been for the last two days.

Twenty-two hours left.

Bahia de Gracias, Hispaniola

Sailing into Bahia de Gracias was the most hair-raising experience Eddie Cantrell had ever had while on a boat, even more than the speedboat run at the Danish ship which had cost him part of his left leg. That had been so sudden that there wasn't really time to be scared. And back then, he'd just been a kid in a speedboat, in way over his head. This time he knew what was happening, what was at stake, and that he was responsible for a fleet that could change the course of events in the Caribbean and Gulf for years to come. So, yep: he was still just a slightly older kid, still in a boat, and still in way over his head.

The final terror to be faced at Bahia de Gracias was the needle that the whole fleet had to thread into the bay: an S curve two miles long. And if you colored outside the lines with the hull of your ship, you were in shallows that had been the end of many ships. Although if you got stuck there in a hurricane, you really didn't need to worry: your fate was sealed and you couldn't do anything about it.

The growing westward winds that had been their blessing now became their curse. A strong, gusting breeze had pushed them along at four and then five knots ever since today's lightless dawn; the sun never broke through the looming cloud bank. But as the twenty-four ships of the fleet heeled southward, giving the headland's shallows a wide berth, they not only struggled to remain together, but to pass quickly through the narrowing passage at the middle of the S curve.

That curving passage was not much more than a hundred yards wide, so Eddie was glad that several of the Dutch mariners with more "mysterious" pasts had been here before. They had been able to give advice on how many ships could enter at once and in what order. In consequence, they had then been distributed to the most important or unwieldy ships in the fleet, tasked to function as the equivalent of bar pilots.

Nimble and sturdy *Salamander* led the fleet into

Bahia de Gracias, followed by *Relentless*, whose tow ropes were at the ready; her power and size made her the best choice for a rescue vessel. But as the other ships turned to slip through that narrow neck into the anchorage beyond, they were buffeted by rising winds to port that now drove at them directly abeam. Sail handlers, still aloft to trim the canvas, fought the unpredictable gusts, the growing rain, and the increasing roll of the ships beneath them. When they failed, so did the sails. And so did their luck, when the foot ropes gapped or snapped. Eddie watched three men not fall but fly from the slick, shuddering spars: small black figures that vanished, tumbling, into the gray of the sea and the rain.

Ships were pushed as unpredictably as the bearing of the wind itself. Fighting to keep her way, cumbersome *Prins Willem* swayed to and fro, endangering ships on every quarter. Trying to avoid a collision likely to shatter the big ship's rudder, *Omlandia* heeled sharply to port. *Neptunus*, not far off her port quarter and whose responsiveness was still compromised by her earlier damage, could not turn in time without risking other ships. The crash was louder than the growing thunder, which barely trailed the bright bolts that flashed between the darkening clouds. Signals being almost impossible, the other captains could only hope that neither vessel had sustained so much damage that they would sink.

What had seemed like forever turned out to have only consumed twenty minutes when finally, the last ship steered two points to starboard to exit those narrows and then slip through a slightly wider neck into the hurricane hole itself. They scattered to the sides of the protected bay, looking for the places that the bar pilots assured them were not only deep but broad enough for them to retain safe distance from other hulls.

Intrepid had just put down her third anchor when the hurricane actually hit.

The worst of the weather peaked about an hour later, and it had become no worse than a memorable squall three hours after that. There was no eye of the storm, no calm and resurgence, evidently because they had been south of its center. As many hurricanes do, it had "bounced off" the energy-diminishing land and its storm center had remained further out to sea.

But still, when Eddie and other captains could see enough to assess the damage, it was quite clear that had they not found shelter in the hurricane hole, many or possibly all of their ships would have foundered.

What had once been a forested coast was flat; whole trees, some uprooted, floated toward the small, and apparently shattered, port of Luperón. Five ships had come loose from their anchors or had chosen too shallow a mooring and were now grounded. *Neptunus'* bow looked like a pugilist's much-broken nose. And as reports of the missing came in, ship's boats were readied to search for survivors or the less lucky, as soon as the weather and visibility permitted. It also became clear that they were not the only ones who had headed to Bahia de Gracias for shelter. Captain Klingl's task force had tacked across the wind and the long miles eastward from Tortuga and had, fortunately, found suitable mooring in the further corners of the anchorage just a few hours before them.

When the senior officers were finally able to convene close to the end of the day, and the condition of the fleet had been determined, Eddie raised the one remaining challenge that the others had apparently been unwilling to bring up. "Luperón is not a large settlement," he explained, "but according to the sources from Grantville, it is a very old one. First Spanish town in the New World, although it was called La Isabela then, I think. How do we want to handle contact? From the look of it, we could be stuck here a long time, and we don't want the inhabitants to warn the Spanish. Or come after us."

Banckert and Tromp exchanged smiles. The latter leaned forward with folded hands. "I know this place is but a few dozen miles east of what you knew as Haiti, but I assure you that unlike what is shown in some of your most amusing up-time horror stories, you will not need to fight any zombies here."

Eddie blinked. "Huh? What?"

Banckert guffawed. "Because the only inhabitants here are dead! Everyone at La Isabela perished within ten years of its founding. There may be some wood shippers there, but from Jol's tales, they are seasonal and impermanent. If there are five loyal Spaniards in that wreck of a town, I would be surprised.

"Frankly, I'd be worried about having too many escaped slaves show up, and then spread the word that there are ships in this bay which, once afloat, would carry them all to freedom. We could be overrun with them."

Eddie felt his eyebrows rise. "You know," he said, "there just might be something to that..."

Part Five

January–February 1637

An asylum in jaws of the Fates
—Herman Melville,
"The Maldive Shark"

Chapter 67

Oranjestad, St. Eustatia

It's like a scene out of a movie, Eddie thought as the fleet sailed into Oranjestad Bay almost two months later. The fleet had learned just five days ago that the town's fears of its destruction had been growing since the New Year. But now, given the crowds lining the shores and even slopes around Oranjestad, it seemed that any gloom had inverted and become sheer, unadulterated joy. Probably along with considerable relief.

Normally, Eddie demurred when presented with the privileges usually given or offered to officers, particularly one of his rank. The same when it came to all the folderol over his position as "Danish nobility." *Yeah, right.* But this time, this *one* time, he literally pulled rank and was on the first boat heading to shore. And he made sure it was *his* longboat with the outboard motor mounted. Because, damn it, he just didn't want to wait. He took a moment to sweep his binoculars across the crowd along the shore and then lining the dock. *Not there.* He almost leaped down into the longboat and told the coxswain to burn all the gas he wanted.

The one thing Eddie hadn't taken the time to reflect on was that there were only three up-time motorboats in the New World. One was the real deal: a cherry-red 1988 180 Sportsman that Larry Quinn had been using in the bayous of Louisiana and which was still there. The other, just like *Intrepid*'s, had been lost along with *Resolve*; both cruisers had been equipped with one because it was deemed essential that the commanders of such pivotally important ships had quick means of getting around their fleet, to shore, or anywhere else they needed to go. His was the third and last, now running in toward the shore at such high speed that its bow was well out of the water.

Which meant that it was the most noticeable nautical unicorn in the whole of the Caribbean. Its fuming white rooster tail of spray and its distinctive noise drew almost every pair of eyes as it cut across the harbor, swerved around a few clueless fishing boats, and made for the shore.

He tried his binoculars again. Sweeping, sweeping, sweeping . . . "There!" he shouted at the coxswain. "Go there!"

"What? Run into the cliff beneath the fort?"

"No, no: run it up onto the beach."

"And then?"

But Eddie wasn't listening. He was focusing on the beach and his foot. Damn it, he was not going to stumble this time. Not here, and not now. So as the sand grated underneath the longboat's bow, he readied himself. Sit to the right of the prow. Left hand on the gunwale to support himself as—now that the boat was stopping— he could swing out the right foot. *Yeah: did it!* Then, moving fast, he used that momentum to keep going—

Straight into Anne Cathrine's arms, hugging her back as hard as she was hugging him, and—*yeah, what the hell: go for it!*—dipping her into a long kiss.

The reaction—other than delighted surprise from his laughing, crying, wonderful wife—was what you saw on TV ballgames when the announcer howled, "And the crowd goes wild!"

Because it really was just like that. When he broke out of the kiss and looked at his Cat, he didn't see the rest of it, but he sorta knew it was there, anyhow. People were mobbed around them, cheering, screaming, weeping. And it spread into the others packed behind the ones right around them. Some soldier up on the fort wall started banging his bayonet loudly on the ramparts. When others joined in, Anne turned and looked, her smile as bright as the tears on her face, her eyes lit with the wonder of a child at Christmas.

Feet were stamping, a ship's bell started ringing, then another, and it propagated, ship to ship, out into the harbor. And he and his bride were at the center of it all. Like in some impossible Hollywood musical.

Well, impossible until now.

Santo Domingo, Hispaniola

"It is impossible, simply impossible!" Generally, Fadrique Álvarez de Toledo despised people who shouted, except when it was absolutely necessary to discipline subordinates or be effective on a warship or battlefield. So he instantly regretted his outburst. He reiterated it in a calm tone, as if this version might somehow erase the first: "It is simply impossible."

"And yet it is true," Juan Bitrian de Viamonte said sadly. "The ships are not ours, and there is no mistaking their numbers. Or the significance of their course past Anegada and on into the Leeward Islands. And to think they were here, on Hispaniola, all along."

"And to think their fleet survived that hurricane!" added Don Antonio de Curco y San Joan de Olacabal. Fadrique considered him effective in his areas of expertise, but still prone to breathless, not to say histrionic, declamations. And until he had proven otherwise, not to be trusted half so far as he might be thrown.

De Curco y San Joan wasn't finished. "It is as if Our Heavenly Father means to punish us here on earth for all our sins."

Oh, I think he'll still reserve places for us at Satan's table...as appetizers. "It can seem that way when fighting up-timer technology and the heathens who make such careful study of its use. As must we, now. Unfortunately, despite our best attempts at St. Maarten, we have not yet secured the means to that end." *And it cost us dearly in ships and men and leaders that we shall not have again.* "About which, Governor de Viamonte, is there word on when de Covilla will return to us?"

De Viamonte smiled. "I am happy to say that Eugenio has almost fully convalesced from his wounds. He will be with us when we meet next week. In the meantime, I have other glad news. It seems that my old colleague and friend"—his tone was as sarcastic and spiteful as Fadrique had ever heard—"Viceroy Don Lope Díez de Aux de Armendáriz of New Spain has finally agreed to cooperate and coordinate with the initiatives that he would have gladly participated in from the first, 'had he been made aware that Olivares had approved them.'"

De Curco y San Joan made a baffled sputtering sound. "But, but...Olivares has not approved any of these initiatives! Many of them are in direct contravention of his policies."

"Of course," de Viamonte agreed.

"But then how can he say that Olivares has—?"

Fadrique's patience was not unlimited. "It is a misrepresentation that cannot be disproved when and if Olivares decides to hang all of us. De Armendáriz will point to a letter of his indicating that we implied or claimed that Olivares has given his approval to us. We would of course deny we had ever sent such a document.

"However, since he has dragged his feet for almost two years, now, it would indeed seem that he was the reluctant participant he claims to be. But us? There is no denying that we have been building new ships and deviating from approved doctrine in a host of different ways. So, since our own deeds prove us to be 'untrustworthy,' is anyone likely to believe that we never claimed to have Olivares' blessing? Why would a man who lies once scruple over lying again?"

"As least," said de Viamonte, "we have increased our capacity to build new and better ships at just the moment when we suffered such a terrible reduction in it." He kept his eyes from looking out at the piles of rubble lining the waterfront; the broken remains of walls that were to have rivaled Cartagena's would not be fully removed until March. "And with de Murga also committed, we shall be able to fight them on something like an even footing."

"Except that they have four steam warships, now!"

de Curco y San Joan cried. "Four! Meaning they had five until St. Maarten! I am amazed that they have not shelled our cities before now, have not hunted our fleets."

One half of a valuable observation, de Curco. "I am similarly puzzled, but I am less amazed than I am concerned. The allies are not as bold as we are, no, but they are not lethargic and they are not foolish. My question is this: what were they doing with those ships that we did not see? That is what worries me. Now, Don de Curco y San Joan, you sent word that you had heard from your brother in the Escorial."

"Not from him, Admiral. From acquaintances of his."

Oh, must we do the dance of perfect deniability? Yes, I suppose we must, you toadying whoreson. "And what have these 'acquaintances' discerned about the likelihood of receiving radios from Madrid?"

"I am sorry to say that it is most improbable. It seems to be a political matter of considerable embarrassment to the crown and to Olivares both. I shall endeavor to learn more about that in my next set of correspondences. However, these same acquaintances seem to have yet other acquaintances who would be able to procure wireless sets. For our personal use. If we so desired."

And so black-market goods can be made available if we are willing to swallow the markup for the procurement services of bureaucrats who specialize in graft and embezzlement. "Why, yes, Don de Curco y San Joan. We desire radios, don't we, Governor de Viamonte?"

Juan's smile was small, serene, and infinitely patient. "Why yes; yes, we do, Admiral." He turned to de Curco y San Joan, and his gaze had an edge. "We desire radios very much."

Chapter 68

Oranjestad, St. Eustatia

As Maarten Tromp stepped up from his longboat, he was met by Jan van Walbeeck and Mike McCarthy, Jr. and although it was not his wont, this was a special occasion and called for special allowances: in this case, drinking before noon.

Thirty minutes after extricating themselves from the celebratory crowds lining the bay, and well furnished with a selection of rum and gin in van Walbeeck's apartment in the fort, Tromp asked the inevitable, dreaded question: "And how are things with our irate and obstreperous landowners?"

Jan held up a hand. "Stunningly, they have been neither irate nor obstreperous since you left. Also, there has been some kind of division among them."

"How so?"

"Those who hold fewer slaves seem to have disassociated themselves from the cabal led by de Bruyne and Musen. The events at and after Whipping Square seem to have decided them to allow their slaves to be made bondsmen in order to realize the benefits of the tariff exclusion, to say nothing of the income from the bondsmen as they pay off their debt."

Tromp sighed. "It makes me sick to hear of any man having to pay off a 'debt' to have his freedom. But it will pass soon enough. Particularly when all the escaped slaves who came back with us from Hispaniola enter the community as free men and women. With any luck, the tide against slavery will turn even faster." He glanced at McCarthy. "You seem wholly unimpressed by the new possibilities of being rid of slavery, Michael."

"That's because I don't trust de Bruyne and his lackeys as far as I can spit...if I thought they were worth spitting on, that is. No, that bunch is up to something."

"And what do you think that is?"

"If I had any idea, I'd be digging and trying to root it out, but it's just a feeling. They've never been calm before, never able to just hold their peace and bide their time." He shook his head. "They're scheming at something we can't see. And I don't like it."

Tromp nodded. "And have you heard from your wife, Mike? Is she coming to join you soon?"

Mike grinned. "Damned if I can tell. Just got a reply a few weeks ago, finally." He shrugged. "You know, the basic married stuff. 'Glad you are well. All fine here.' Told me just enough about the kids so that I know they're alive. Then explained that the telegraph rates for private messages over the Atlantic are astronomical, so kiss-kiss-bye. Really? With all my pay going home? I know I wasn't great about sending messages myself, but I've been really steady with it over the last few months. You might think she'd have a little more to say." He leaned forward to grab the rum bottle.

Tromp peered carefully at van Walbeeck, who peered back. They exchanged dubious and worried looks over the up-timer's head.

As Leonora walked up the stairs to Danish House with Rik Bjelke at her side, she found it surprising that there was no sign of life in it. Or around it. "It is quite strange," she muttered. "The whole town seems to have come to a halt. And it shows no sign of starting up again. Just how long can all those people cheer and shout and make all that bothersome noise?"

Rik smiled as she took him by the hand and led him into what she had, at least in her own affairs, preserved as the sacrosanct domain of her own sex: the sitting room. His eyes widened a bit; whether it was because she had taken his hand or was inviting him into the house's equivalent of the Forbidden City, he could not discern. She pulled out two chairs from the table, arranged them so they faced each other, and sat in one of them.

Rik sank into the other. He was both smiling and frowning, the two expressions blended into one by the profound perplexity behind both.

"Rik Bjelke," she began, "I wish you to know, if it was not already quite plain, that I hold you in the very highest and fondest regard."

"As I do you. In extremely fond regard, dear Leonora."

She waved that aside; when he called her "dear Leonora" her otherwise reliably organized mind became quite disorganized. It was not a disagreeable sensation— not at all—but right now, she needed to retain all her focus. When she had quite composed herself, she announced, "After seeking Dr. Brandão's counsel, and giving the matter much thought, I have decided to become a physician. This would include seeking tutelage of up-time practitioners."

Rik nodded. Eagerly, Leonora thought. She pressed on. "I realize that this may seem a peculiar ambition, given my sex. So I must make this clear." She steeled herself. "I will not be what you, or any man, may think or want me to be. I must be myself, and I have discovered that to be so, I must do my best to achieve this goal. We, by which I mean women especially, need physicians whose art and practice of it is better suited to our true medical needs. It is crucial that medicine not only begins to embrace the more rigorous and provable scientific method brought by the up-timers, but also the presumption that listening carefully to the patient is as crucial a part of diagnosis and treatment as any other."

Rik nodded again. His expression, while not exactly puzzled, was quite singular. It was akin to what might be expected if a scholar had sat him down and, with great gravity, solemnly informed him that water was wet. Still nodding, he said, "I profess no expertise, but your purpose sounds wise, prudent, and overdue."

Leonora was happy and relieved that he was agreeing. Although he was doing it with an almost unsettling degree of ease. "It will mean travel," she continued. "I aspire to study with the finest. And that means—" She found herself unable to utter the words, despite having practiced this speech at least a dozen times. Worse yet, she felt her gaze falter, her traitorous eyes sinking away from his despite her best efforts.

"It means," he finished for her, "that you must

return to Europe. That is the proper, indeed the only, place where you may study under the American physicians. Of course; I understand this completely." From his tone, he might as well have said, *Yes, water is indeed wet.*

"And you have no reservations?"

"Only one." Now it was Rik's eyes that fell. "That you will find someone you prefer to me."

What? She stood instantly. *"That* will not happen."

"But . . . I—"

"Surely you must have learned, and seen further evidence in this decision I have taken, that I know my own mind, Rik Bjelke. You are the man for me; there is no other." She stared at him.

He stared back, perplexed.

Leonora fussed with the hem of her new dress, counted the seconds. She was in no rush. She could be patient. To help, she would start counting.

When she reached "three," her patience was quite gone. "Well, what are you waiting for?"

"I beg your pardon?"

"Well, are you going to formally propose or not? I am a modern woman; I do not insist that you take a knee to do so." She twinkled. "But it would be nice."

When Hugh O'Donnell's bark *Eire* came round the headland and saw Oranjestad Bay once again cluttered with ships, and some kind of celebration in full swing, he wondered if Oranjestad was now hosting quarterly trade markets. But no, the balance of new vessels were warships, including not two, but four steamships. Well, no great shock there.

But what did surprise him as the festivities began

shifting more into the town's streets, was the sight of a lone figure, waiting at the end of the wharf. A woman. *No, it couldn't be...*

But it was indeed Sophie Rantzau.

He belayed his earlier order to make fast halfway down the dock: *Berth* Eire *here, at the far end, and smartly, if you please!* Which didn't make the next nine minutes feel any less like nine hours.

When he finally jumped down to the wood planks, Sophie simply smiled and put out one hand. He took it; she nodded, turned, and walked, leading him off the wharf. He didn't need to know where they were going; that she had learned of his arrival and taken special pains to meet him as soon as he stepped off his ship left him so overjoyed that he was the slightest bit light-headed.

She headed south, not on the irregular and rocky shore, but on the embankment of long grass that followed along above it. When they got to a place where all they could see and hear was the ocean, the wind, and each other, she stopped and sat. She did it so suddenly, without hint or preamble, that for a moment, he didn't even know what to say.

She didn't give him the chance to find words; she had her own ready. "Hugh O'Donnell, I love you and we should live our lives together however we wish. Whatever that might mean, here in this truly New World. I no longer care what consequences may follow back in the Old World. What rights to property I might still possess in Denmark would likely be forfeit. I would not be surprised if I was exiled. Or if we were condemned in our respective churches. None of that matters. The only thing that matters is whether or not you still have the feelings in your heart that you professed in that poem."

"No," Hugh said, "they are not the same. They have grown stronger with each passing day, Sophie Rantzau. Yes, we shall live our lives together. And I have given much thought to that, as well."

He smiled. "I confess, it is hard to see what that means exactly, what shape it takes, when two people join in a union solely of their own making, rather than one sanctioned by a church." He leaned toward her. "But a woman who can lead me along a foreign shore without a word of invitation or explanation can certainly lead me into the uncharted territory of such a union. And I will follow. As gladly as I followed you here."

She smiled and leaned toward him and their lips met. It was a very long, and in some ways, very careful kiss. The passion he felt, and sensed in her, had to be contained, at least until the words that she had come to speak were all spoken. And then, there was the irony of the union to which they had just consented. He almost laughed at it.

She drew back, not offended or alarmed, but wondering and wry at the same time. "I was not aware my lips were so...deficient."

He laughed. "Now there's a statement fully at odds with reality. I have never encountered lips so very much *without* deficiency!"

"Then what amuses you?"

"Merely this: a few days ago, I received a telegram that shines a rather different light on the ostracization that you and I had both expected. It seems that the world is determined to defy human projection. Well, at least my projections."

Sophie looked neither happy nor worried at his comments, merely intrigued. "And what surprising reactions have you had?"

He produced an already well-worn and much-seamed flimsy from his pocket. "My godmother Isabella, the archduchess of the Spanish Lowlands, had this to say in response to our intentions as they existed, and related to her, just before I gave you the poem." He read from the paper. "'Dearest godson, I cannot fully express my delight that your heart has found its own measure and mate. And I am untroubled by the condemnation you wisely anticipate, because a marriage so at odds with convenience must surely be one of love. A stronger bond than this cannot be hoped for.'"

He managed not to smile at seeing Sophie's eyes so much wider than he had ever seen them before. Unable to resist a little waggish fun, he added, "She goes on to mention that she was set to fight tooth and nail to ensure that Fernando, King of the Lowlands, would grant me a title, but it seemed no persuasion was necessary. He was already contemplating what rank and estate he might confer—his words, now—'in appreciation for the earl of Tyrconnell's signal actions in securing and defending Our oil interests on Trinidad.'"

Hugh folded the paper. "Well, although someone obviously exaggerated my deeds and merit, I shan't look in this gift horse's mouth. Oh, and by the way, he was happy to give his official blessing to our marriage, and apparently convinced Pope Bedmar himself to go along. Although that's hardly necessary, now that we are relying upon ourselves as the basis of whatever union we shall have."

Sophie was still staring. "And . . . and with all that

laid at your—at our—feet, you are still satisfied with a union of our own design and making? There is much in what you just shared that speaks to a most promising future."

Hugh shrugged. "I often give quite a lot of thought to the future. But today, as far as what comes next... I'm resolved to think about that later. I can't even say when I will think on it, if at all. I have been a creature of duty all my life, and right now, there is no reason to worry about how these grand honors could affect my future, because the having of them will not hasten the one reason I might hold them dear: a concrete opportunity to address Ireland's many needs. Alas, that bright hope remains well beyond a horizon over which it may never rise."

Sophie sat silently and seemed to be considering his words in far greater depth than he had. "So," Hugh continued in a lighter tone, "since we have decided upon going forward together, what shall we do first?"

Sophie's expression had not changed, however. She nodded slowly, solemnly. "First and foremost, we must do the *right* thing."

"Which is?"

"This." She took his hand, but it was a serious, firm grasp. She breathed deeply. "We must acknowledge that for others, if not ourselves, it seems the best way to begin our union is, in fact, to be married. In a church that will marry us across our faiths."

"Sophie, darling; my head is spinning far more than when we danced, and it was like as a top, then. That was the shortest independent union a man and woman have ever known, I'll wager. So please, help me understand how the marital bonds we just agreed were wrong for our union are now 'the right thing to do'?"

She took his hand in both of his. "Because there is a country that may one day look to you. For the sake of those people, the life you make with me must not divide them in their willingness to rally behind you and to take up arms against their oppressors, should it come to that. If neither one of us had responsibilities beyond our personal happiness, then we might decide differently. But the strange lottery that decrees to whom and into what circumstance each one of us are born has decreed differently for you. And therefore, if we are to be together, I must share that duty with you." She sighed. "But I do not think my choice will be so blessed by those of my own country. I cannot foresee Christian IV being comfortable with one of his Lutheran nobles marrying so very far outside their faith and traditions."

"You mean, by marrying a papist from a country of bog-hoppers?"

"That is not how I think of it, but it may very well be how he does."

"Well, then," Hugh said lightly, slipping an arm around Sophie's surprisingly muscular shoulder, "we'll just have to convince him otherwise, won't we?"

Chapter 69

Outside Oranjestad, St. Eustatia

Hans Musen did not like going to what Jehan de Bruyne called his "villa."

However, he allowed, the building did warrant the label. It was the largest house on St. Eustatia, situated on the largest tract, was kept and maintained spotlessly, and was fitted with furnishings from all over the world. The food was always good, the drink was better. And because both Musen's wife and Jan Haet's were always invited along with them, it made the wives happy in the days leading up to the visit. Although afterwards, they complained for days about the comparative shabbiness of their own domiciles. Hans suspected that his wife even harbored amorous feelings for de Bruyne, who, for his part, gave no sign of having ever noticed.

But that wasn't the real reason Hans Musen did not like trips to the de Bruyne villa. It was because all such invitations were, in reality, a summons. Usually to be peremptorily told what to do, or castigated for having carried it out improperly. And today was shaping up to be no exception to that rule.

After a light meal that was too early to lunch, Jehan had asked them to join him for schnapps in the study. Which was another overly grand label, Musen thought, but de Bruyne did have a large desk in there and shelves of books.

However, Jan Haet was hardly in his seat before he had bolted back his schnapps and commenced ranting about conditions over the last several months. About how intolerable they had become, how the landowners who had converted their slaves into bondsmen were actually becoming more affluent than they were. "Our life here," he railed, "and all our plans to disgrace Tromp and keep our slaves are coming apart. The slaves we leased for labor are coming back having been trained for the militia. And not just with weapons. One of my foremen tried disciplining a recent returnee for sullenness and found himself thrown to the ground. Except he wasn't really thrown; it was some trick, some movement of the hips and legs that turned his charge into a fall. And the idiot did nothing! Didn't use the whip! I wouldn't have blamed him for using his machete or pistol, if it came to it. But instead he walked away, making threats. And now it is too late to make an example of the resentful creature without looking weak. Without looking like a husband who does not strike his harpy wife as soon as an insult comes out of her mouth." Haet stopped, almost panting with indignation.

De Bruyne, who drank from a glass, swirled his Spanish brandy around, letting the centrifugal force raise it halfway to the rim. He looked up at Haet. "Do you know," he said calmly, "that the townspeople now call it The Whipping Square? Hundreds—literally hundreds—saw what you did. Both of you. And with those hundreds telling and retelling the story and making it even worse than it was, no one is going to forget what went on there anytime soon." He tossed back the brandy. "We are done here, thanks to you two. The entire colony's opinion has sharpened against us. Those who had been undecided are so no longer."

Musen had fully intended on waiting until Haet had received the greater measure of de Bruyne's icy ire. "Right now, my worry is about the inspectors," he said. "They are all over us. And the *Politieke Raad*'s public tribunal will soon be convening to determine the damages we owe for holding our slaves back from fulfilling the labor contracts."

De Bruyne nodded. "You—just *you*, Musen—will approach van Walbeeck and negotiate for us. We want him and his inner circle to forgive the damages and cancel the tribunal. In exchange, we shall immediately convert our slaves into bondsmen, but only on the further condition that half of them will be hired at the highest rate for five-year labor contracts."

"And if they refuse?"

"They will not. They will take this bait without question. It frees all the slaves and puts half of ours in their hands, both to work on their projects and train as militia. And the government can worry about their productivity, and their sustenance, too, if they are not pleased with the minimum that we will provide.

"The half of our slaves who shall remain as our bondsmen must be the best workers and most docile. We shall reduce the price of their bond by one third, if they are able to pay it all off in two years' time. They will work like dogs, and we will have full advantage of selling their output without tariffs."

"And then?" asked Haet.

"And then we leave. If we have not already. Because by then, many things will have changed for the worse, if we stay here. Those changes have already begun, as I'm sure Hans has informed you. Our last means of maintaining surreptitious contact with potential allies—the seamstress—has disappeared. I suspect we would find it nearly impossible to recruit an adequate replacement. Besides, with the business that you shall be concluding soon, we will cease to have need of such services."

Haet shook his head. "I do not hear how this is anything but surrender. Once our slaves are bondsmen, it is only a matter of time until we become poor farmers again. Yes, there will be a nice flow of currency until they are all free, but there is no way to turn that into new land, new slaves, new profits."

"Ah," said de Bruyne, with a didactic lift of his index finger, "that is precisely where you are in error. Currency is the key, you see. It is the only thing we can take away from this disaster, and right now, we can convert our present weakness—the government's proven determination to take away our slaves, and so, our livelihood—into a strength. If we act quickly enough, that is. And if you are able to perceive the sudden surge of currency we will realize through our 'compliance' as seed funds for a new project that will bring us greater wealth than we ever dreamed."

"To start plantations someplace new, and on our own, we will need a lot more than money."

"I am not speaking of plantations, *mijn Heer* Haet. Oh, yes, we shall have those, too. But what I am really talking about is slaves. Not as labor, but as our commodity."

He leaned over to read a passage from a book laying open on his desk. "This is from an up-time book. 'In 1637, a Dutch fleet also captured the Portuguese fort at Elmina on Africa's west coast, known as the Gold Coast. From there, Africans were enslaved and transported to work on Brazil's sugar plantations.'"

Haet shrugged. "And what good does that do us, anymore?"

Musen and de Bruyne looked at each other. Hans tried a simpler approach. "Jan, the slaves aren't going to be the *source* of our commodities. They will *be* our commodities."

Haet blinked. "You mean, that we should become slavers? What do we know about that, other than how to control them? We are not sailors or soldiers!"

"No," de Bruyne almost purred, "we are much more important than that. We will be the source of funds and connections, including many within both the East and West India Companies, that will make it possible to create the first New World slave market that serves all buyers equally. We pass no judgments, ask no questions, because—again—our only concern is currency. And as the history in this book and others show, to make the New World pay immense dividends and quickly, slaves were essential. There will be buyers. And given the whispers I have heard about French interests on the mainland, I suspect those buyers will be arriving soon."

"So where would this market be, then?" Haet looked concerned. "Jamaica? If we can make it more productive and agree to lease our land there, the Spanish may give it to us."

Musen wondered how long it would take for Jan

to remember that he had to think like a slave trader now, not a slaveholder.

De Bruyne was shaking his head. "Jamaica is too close to Dutch territory and colonies. Having our operations near those could complicate and jeopardize some of our most important contacts. But no more of this. You gentlemen have a long voyage ahead of you."

"What?" Musen said, along with Haet.

"You will find a ship in the harbor," Jehan went on. "It is a heavily modified and armed Bermudan sloop. Its master will be flying no colors and his accent will be a strange mixture of Dutch and Spanish, I am told. He will take you to St. Maarten by early evening, assuming the wind holds."

"And once there, what are we to do? Where are we to go?"

"You will not need to go anywhere. The ship will deposit you exactly where you are supposed to be. As for what you will do? You will make arrangements."

"What kind?"

"For travel, first for these slaveholders who have been our loyal allies." He handed Musen a list. "Then for their foremen. Then for yourselves and all our foremen."

"And you? And our families?"

"I must stay here to make sure that the government is not delinquent in paying what it owes us and that van Walbeeck does not discover some legalistic obstruction to delay or deny fulfilling its obligations. Your families will come later. I shall follow soon after."

Haet looked nervously from Musen and back to de Bruyne. "Shouldn't you be there to work out the details of so sweeping a relocation?" Musen smiled and nodded supportively while he considered how long he was willing to wait before punishing Jan—perhaps mortally—for that implied slight.

De Bruyne's eyes looked as bored as his voice sounded. "You two are traveling all the time. To St. Christopher, Nevis, Montserrat, even Saba occasionally. Also, you lost men and slaves on St. Maarten. So no one will think twice if you are seen traveling yet again, or if you are seen in the vicinity of St. Maarten. However, if I were to journey there, it might invite all manner of questions and speculations. We do not want that. Do we?"

"No," the two muttered.

"Good. Thank you for visiting. Your wives may stay on if they wish, but you must not keep our new contact waiting. The boy will see you out."

Oranjestad, St. Eustatia

It took Eddie and Anne Cathrine almost an hour to get through the well-wishers and then the onrushing wave of people who were streaming down every street toward the docks, most in the hope of seeing the face of a loved one, a friend, a son, a father.

They walked to Danish House, arm in arm, Anne Cathrine's gait more relaxed than it had been in almost half a year, her body swaying easily against his the way it always had before.

As they went up its steps, she pointed out the new crop of windmills going up. She told him about how their mechanisms had come from Holland, the timber from St. Kitts, and the foremen from Nevis, where they had built so many before. She was talking about everything they saw, everything that had happened, and not all of it made sense, and he didn't care a bit, and didn't stop her. Because she was Cat, and he loved the sound of her voice, no matter what it was saying.

When they got inside, she listened, shushed him, took one step further in. That was when Eddie heard it: male murmuring in the kitchen, followed by a female giggle. "Leonora?" Eddie whispered, forgetting to remain silent. "She really *does* giggle?"

Anne Cathrine frowned, swatted his arm in playful remonstrance, and then pulled him by the hand toward the stairs.

When they got to their room she pulled him down to sit beside her and began firing nonstop questions about—well, about everything.

It had been a long time... a long, *long* time since Anne Cathrine had eagerly sought every detail of his travels. This time she even called them "adventures," which struck him as really weird since he didn't think of them that way at all. But she was particularly interested in the hurricane and what happened after. It was like she wanted to live the story—and the present, flesh-and-blood reality—of his survival. Of how he had come back to her, now, here, today. So he told her.

After three weeks of repairs and kedging their ships off the sands onto which they had been pushed, the fleet returned to sea. But rather than taking a slightly faster route home, they elected to remain north of the Greater Antilles and set course for Anguilla as the point at which to enter the Leeward Islands. In the wake of a hurricane, the pirates of Tortuga much reduced, and the Spanish in much the same condition, all the senior officers deemed that they were very unlikely to meet ships in those open waters.

Halfway into that homebound cruise, much slowed by *Neptunus* and *Omlandia*, they reached radio range of St. Eustatia and learned that the surrounding seas had been clear of the Spanish and pirates since the fleet had sailed for Santo Domingo. They also learned that while not given up for dead, the ferocity of the hurricane left many fearing for the fate of the entire fleet, and that after the New Year, those dire anticipations had grown more widespread and grim.

"But now, here we are! Ta-da!" Eddie cried.

"Yes! Here you are!" Her brows fell. "But there is something serious we must settle."

Okay, well I got here as quick as I could to talk about whatever was bothering her, so this is good. A little scary when she starts a relationship talk, but good. Better, even. "I'm ready. Tell me what we need to settle," he said, prepared for anything.

Except what she did next. She playacted deep thought. "Well, I'm not sure how we should arrange your titles."

"My . . . my what?"

"Well, there are all sorts of protocols when one is presented to a room, you see. I am just wondering if it is best that you are first presented as the duke of a little island in the Orkneys . . . or as the duke of St. Maarten."

"What?"

"What do you mean, 'what?' The guns have not deafened you yet, have they? Papa was so pleased to hear about all your exploits on the island, and that you remembered to claim it for Denmark, that he made you its hereditary duke!"

"My exploits? Look, Cat, I didn't perform any 'exploits.' In fact, I barely—" He forgot what he was saying; that look was in her eyes. Yeah, *that* look. The one that said, *stop talking. Now.*

She grabbed him and kissed him and pushed into him. Not hard and determined like most recently, but like she wasn't even thinking, like it was second nature, like it was something rising up out of her that was only about joy and want and lust and love and she wasn't about to break it down.

Just like it had always been before.

When Eddie woke up, it was dusk. He drew in a great breath, started letting it out, then controlled it, so it wouldn't wake his darling, darling wife. He turned, looked at her, discovered that she was sleeping half on her side, facing away from him. She did not move. She hardly seemed to be breathing.

He wanted to touch her, but he also just wanted to watch her for a moment. So he did, noticing and trying to make sure he would remember for all time, just how her shoulders moved, just how her hair fell, just how it shone so softly and so red and so gold when touched by the light of a sunset. And he took a moment to feel just how glad *he* was that she seemed so happy, so exuberant, so like the way he had always known her.

But whatever solemn focus and restraint had dominated her demeanor during the months leading up to St. Maarten wasn't something to be left unremarked. Something had really eaten at her and he would let her know, first thing tomorrow, that he was ready and even eager to talk about it. And there'd never be a better time because now, at last, there would be time enough to work it all out, to help her deal with any shadows that might still be lurking behind the return of the easy laughter and passionate joy. Yes, tomorrow. At last. He rolled over, shut his eyes, was asleep in a minute.

About a minute after that, Anne Cathrine turned, alert, eyes focused on the back of his head.

Tomorrow, she thought, *tomorrow, at last I can tell him.*

Chapter 70

Tintamarre Island, St. Maarten

"I don't like this," Jan Haet complained as they waded ashore on Tintamarre, a long island one mile off the northeast coast of St. Maarten. Its terrain was as much naked rock as it was moss and wiry vegetation.

Musen rolled his eyes. "Exactly what don't you like about it, Jan? That this island is remote? That no one lives or even visits here? That no one saw us arrive?"

"I don't like this place...and I don't like this business!" Haet said, voice rising above the soft creaks and rush of the sloop leaving to stand offshore. "I don't like selling all my slaves and other property. I don't like moving to a place I've never seen—twice in just five years, now! And I don't like having de Bruyne treat me like a child." They moved up off the sand and into the low, rolling mix of rocks, grass, and small cliffs.

"Or is it that you don't like that he's usually right?"

"And I don't like your constant criticism. You aren't so smart, either." Haet spat into the shadows that were growing darker as the sun sank behind the low peaks of St. Maarten to the west. "And another thing: I don't like—"

A new voice interrupted from the shadows. "And I don't like it when a man almost spits on me. Or is making so much noise that his Dutch countrymen are likely to come see what all the commotion is about."

A slightly darker patch in the shadows rose. "I have the pleasure of meeting *mijn Heeren* Haet and Musen, yes?"

Haet, annoyed that he had jumped at the sound of the new voice, barked, "How—how do you know?"

The voice's French accent did nothing to disguise the droll tone. "Your reputation for dazzling repartee precedes you. Now come, be seated. Yes, those rocks behind you will do admirably. I tested them myself earlier, just to make sure they did not conceal any unseen dangers."

Musen managed not to snicker. "It is rather barren, here. Didn't see you."

"That was manifestly obvious, yes. And as for it being a barren place? Well, that is part of what makes it eminently safe. Certainly more so than any spot we might have chosen over there." He waved a dark hand at the silhouette of St. Maarten, framed against a burning bronze sky. "The last few Spanish are no doubt hiding in whatever dens they may, with troops roving after them. And although Dutchmen such as yourselves may be presumed to journey here on legitimate business, you would still be questioned and quite probably have your presence reported. And lastly, I may assure you that after Admiral Tromp's allies destroyed Tortuga, there are no pirates anywhere within five hundred miles of here. Quite possibly further. So we are quite safe."

Haet grumbled. "Well, I guess. At least we won't

wind up like my foreman Claus and the workers and slaves who were with him."

"Ah, yes, that." The voice dipped toward what sounded like sympathy. "I regret that I had no more knowledge than you regarding the sudden Spanish interest in St. Maarten. Until this past fall, it had been a wonderful meeting place: a convenient way station made more useful by its almost unexceptioned history of benign neglect. Even so, the death of your employees and chattels was in fact a fortuitous tragedy."

"Fortuitous?" Musen echoed. "How so?"

"My dear Hans, imagine what would have happened if your foreman had returned with my details for a rendezvous. The timing was such that we would have been attempting to have this conversation in the midst of the battles which raged here late last year. It is impossible to foresee what losses might have been incurred by both of us, or the many ways in which it could have led to the discovery of the careful plans you are cultivating on St. Eustatia. So yes, I consider it good fortune that our original plans for this meeting were disrupted and delayed until now."

Haet squinted. "I don't trust talking to a man whose face I can't see."

"Well, I can understand that, I suppose." The shadow moved forward.

This time it was Musen who started. "You! You were the French governor on St. Christopher. I remember meeting you just after we landed on St. Eustatia."

Pierre Bélain d'Esnambuc stepped into the failing light. "In the flesh," he said.

Haet glared suspiciously. "What happened to your left eye?"

D'Esnambuc grinned. "The eye patch suits me, do not you think?"

"But they said you were dead!" Musen persisted. "Twice, now. First they said you were killed during or after the Kalinago raid. And then again earlier this year, off Guadeloupe."

The Frenchman sighed. "It is a strange tendency of otherwise intelligent men to presume, simply because a person has disappeared during battle, that they must, perforce, be dead. It is stranger still when some must surely have known that the missing man is a very strong swimmer."

Jan scowled. "Or maybe you just have more than your share of luck."

"Luck?" d'Esnambuc scoffed. "Luck is what superstitious men call outcomes for which they do not see ready, rational reasons."

"And what was the ready, rational reason that preserved you when your entire crew died or became the up-timer commodore's prisoners?"

"There is a trick to seeming lucky," d'Esnambuc mused with a small smile as he rubbed lightly at the eye patch. "That trick, which I learned at an early age, is to travel faster and farther than word of your deeds. So it was with me.

"I regained consciousness on a patch of land called Îlet Cochon: a strange name, since I saw no pigs there. I discovered that, besides the loss of this eye, my injuries were otherwise superficial." He indicated still-pink scars consistent with wounds far more grievous than his words suggested. "Fortunately, I was well fed and in excellent shape, and so, was able to hide and wait, recuperating and formulating plans.

"While I did, the natives came and went in great number and with great agitation. At first, I felt it might indicate that the young up-timer had misstepped. So easy to do with such temperamental savages! But soon enough, it became apparent that he had found some means of causing them to have a very high opinion of himself. The activity was therefore a celebration, not a crucifixion. Such revels are part of their penchant for collective witness: in short, that for the tribe to embrace a promising new ally, the mighty among them must satisfy a social and hierarchical requirement by coming to see this person for themselves.

"In so doing, they confer their inchoate imprimatur upon this new ally by partaking in a great deal of jabbering and no small amount of feasting. So they mark their great events, or at least that is how it seems to me.

"I had much opportunity to observe their comings and goings. More narrowly, I was able to observe and determine those among them who arrived by boat and were most incautious. One such never returned to the festivities, which persisted even after the victorious ships departed. I gather that the Kalinago presumed the missing fellow had celebrated too much and had been lost at sea with his boat.

"I paddled it to Martinique. It is not a hard journey, and it is one that I knew would reward me well."

"Why would the natives of Martinique have rewarded you with anything but death?" Musen wondered. "We heard that the Kalinago of that island spared none of your countrymen after the failed attack on St. Eustatia."

"You heard correctly. But I did not go to Martinique to find either allies or companions, but equipment and provisions I had hidden in a remote place against the possibility of being in a situation such as the one in which I now found myself.

"After burning away any flesh in my eye socket that threatened to become black with gangrene, I spent two days recuperating and then began my slow journey back north along the leeward side of the Lesser Antilles. And, because I knew how and where to look, I found a ship of adventurers with whom I had mutual acquaintances amongst others of their calling. And so, here I stand before you! Now come, we must be about our business...as soon as you satisfy my one requirement."

Haet almost snarled. "You'll not have our money until after we—"

"Blast you and your precious money, you gin-swilling pig! It is useful, but it is not my master. My interest is upon news."

Musen frowned. "What news?"

"My nephew: Jacques Dyel du Parque...Does he live?"

The two Dutchmen stared. "Yes, he was returned from Guadeloupe with many women and became the administrator among the French who risked remaining on St. Christopher after your attack."

"How many took that risk?"

"About half."

"And the rest?"

Musen shrugged. "They fled to Guadeloupe. In small boats. Not all made it. And those who did... well, you know."

D'Esnambuc's eyes dimmed. "How well I know, indeed. Ah, well: it was too much to hope for any other outcome. But . . . Jacques: the boy lives!" Musen tried not to stare: was there a tear at the corner of the ruthless adventurer's remaining eye?

Before it could be ascertained if the well-bred monster actually had human emotions, the Frenchman slapped his thigh. "So, let us plan to make the first voyage to this well-situated harbor, while the wind favors our journey." He unfurled a map, laid it out in the dim light.

The two Dutchmen squinted at it. "This is the same place that is labeled 'Charleston' on up-time maps, I believe?" Musen asked.

"You are well informed. It is the very same, *mijn Heer* Musen. The very same."

"And how will we get there safely?" Haet complained. "The seas are thick with the Spanish between here and there."

"Well, not so thick as they were, but thick enough. And that is happy news for us."

"In God's name, why?"

"Though I suspect God would not wish his name to be invoked in projects such as this one, it is happy news because it is the Spanish themselves who have a vested interest in ensuring that we reach our destination. And after that, they will protect us so long as they need the services I have arranged to provide for them."

Haet frowned. "And what 'services' would compel them to even conceive of doing such things?"

"Why, that they might have access to these." The Frenchman opened a small chest beside him, moved it into the failing light: four radios, copies of up-time-designed models currently being manufactured in the

United States of Europe. "At first, we shall arrange leases between ships of my adventurer friends and the Spanish. Each ship retained shall be at the Spaniards' disposal and shall include an operator for this equipment. Once we are firmly established in our new colony and well reinforced there, we shall be free to sell these devices to the Spanish, if they still want them. Which I rather presume they will."

Haet kept trying to find flaws. "And what surety will we have that they will not eliminate us once they have the radios themselves and have learned how to use them?"

D'Esnambuc seemed to gather his reserves of patience before responding. "Firstly, when I stipulated that our colony would be well reinforced before we sold any of the radios, I mean a level of defense that even the Spanish would find very costly to overcome."

Musen waited. "You said that point was your first. Is there another?"

The Frenchman nodded. "The Spanish will not be able to attack us without inciting sustained reprisals from our new adventurer friends."

"And how is it that you know they will flock to our defense?"

D'Esnambuc nodded, made a dismissive gesture. "Because this new colony shall be their new, but much safer, Tortuga. Some weeks from the seaways upon which they prefer to prey, yes, but that also puts it well beyond the reach of any great power. So they will return to the Caribbean and Bahamas to hunt, but retire to this Charleston to restore both their ships and themselves. And of course, to spend their hard-earned gains." He became contemplative.

"There is also the matter of the adventurers' personal regard. For me."

Again, Haet jumped in. "And what have you done to instill such love in their black hearts?"

He shrugged. "I correctly warned them what would become of their alliance with the Spanish. You see, since receiving their letters of marque, they have collaborated with their new sponsors three times over the past two years: at Trinidad, Vieques, and Curaçao. The first two were unmitigated disasters. The last was a success only because it was carried out without any regard for Spanish leadership or planning. Overall, my adventurer friends felt ill used and that the relationship was not profitable for them. At least not beyond the initial silver that they were paid and have since lost in lives and hulls. So now, they think me something of a savant."

Musen nodded. "Because of your warning."

"Yes, but I suspect it is also because I repeatedly urged them to be on their guard at Tortuga. But alas, their leaders were proud. They thought they knew better. Now they are dead. And through the very agency I predicted, no less."

Musen smiled. "So you are Nostradamus reborn, then?"

D'Esnambuc smiled back. "If only that were true. But in this case, prophesy was not required. Only clear sight.

"As the Spanish increasingly relied upon the pirates, the allies realized that by eliminating the latter, the former would have far fewer well-placed agents with ready eyes, fewer ships that could sail swiftly against prevailing currents, and almost no commanders with sufficient versatility and inventiveness to perceive and seize opportunities. But initially, Tromp and his lackeys despaired of eliminating the pirates since, whenever confronted strongly, they could simply fade away."

Musen nodded. "Until they began concentrating at Tortuga."

"Exactly. And not just concentrating. Once the Spanish gave them letters of marque, they began to become more predictable. Artisans converged on Tortuga for a share of that silver, as did captains—both known and aspirant—looking for crews. The buccaneers' great guarantee of invulnerability—no point of origin, so no point of weakness—slipped away from them without their realizing it.

"But the up-timers knew the greater history of the place, knew that Tortuga was already in the process of becoming a regular port and community. They saw or reasoned that once the buccaneers made a formal agreement with the Spanish, it would accelerate that transformation. And so, once enough of their organization was there, the allies struck. Unexpected and almost unopposed, until their troops went ashore."

"Were many of the pirates killed?"

"A good number, although I very much doubt that was the primary object of the attack. But the facilities are ruined and the allies have sent a clear message: do this again and we will hunt you again."

"And so . . . ?"

"And so, you and those now homeless gentlemen of fortune have common interests."

"Common interests?" Haet almost screamed. "With dogs such as those? Never! We—"

Musen waved him down. "Yes. I see. We are outlaws

too, now. As are you. As are all who will bring slaves into the New World. And your pirates need a safe harbor, far beyond the easy reach of either the Spanish or the allies."

"Precisely. This location, Charleston, is not a particularly difficult or long journey from here at the northern extent of the Leeward Islands. The winds are favorable all the way to, and then up along, the North American coast. Most of my new associates say it is about two and a half weeks.

"Once it is well established, adventurers throughout the region will see this colony—or perhaps, city-state?—as a safe harbor, a place to refit, and a thriving market which accepts them and their trade without prejudice. I suspect they would even welcome proposals for mutually profitable endeavors." His voice lowered. "For although the Spanish did not know how to make use of the skills and inventiveness of pirates, you, *mijn Heeren*, certainly will. That, too, is revealed in the histories the up-timers brought with them. Not all of you Dutchmen are so encumbered by the impossible and unrealistic moral niceties of Admiral Tromp and his new friends."

D'Esnambuc looked into Haet's face and then Musen's. "No further questions? Excellent! Then let us lay out a schedule for conveying the first of your number to the place we shall call Charleston, at least for now. The sooner we finish, the sooner you may return to your ravishing Dutch wives!"

Chapter 7

Oranjestad, St. Eustatia

Eddie flinched awake. Someone was knocking. At the front door. He sat up, rubbing his face. Low voices, then a heavy tread on the stairs. A pause, followed by a light tapping at the bedroom door. Cuthbert Pudsey's voice as an almost inaudible whisper: "Commodore, begging your pardon, your many pardons. But Don Michael is here. Says it's urgent."

What the—? "Tell him I'm coming." Eddie pulled on a pair of trousers and a nightshirt, slipped out the door, hoping that Cat hadn't awakened.

Cuthbert was there with a lamp, handed it over silently, and followed at a discreet distance as Eddie thumped down the stairs.

Mike was in the foyer, standing like a graven image. Eddie couldn't hold back a yawn. "It's two in the morning, Mike. What's—?" And then he saw the look on Mike's face, a face he'd known for as long as he could remember, and so could read like a book. He swallowed. "Priority from The Quill?"

Mike nodded. "'Need to know' only, Eddie. You

can't share the actual content, but we'll come up with a cover story." He handed Eddie a flimsy. "At the fort. Thirty minutes. Sorry, son."

The young up-timer was already reading the telegram as Mike jogged out the door and into the dark. Shortly after the door closed, Eddie exhaled a whispered, "My God." He went up the stairs as quickly as he could, slipped back into his room, grabbed his ready uniform—set aside for emergencies like this one—and then slipped out again.

Anne Cathrine lay facing the window so that her face was turned away from the door. So that Eddie would think she was still asleep and not see the tears running down her face.

Hadn't they done almost exactly this, half a year ago? Was it so much to expect, so much to ask, that she would have him back for long enough to sit down with him, with everything just right, and tell him the news *that* way? It wasn't fair; it just wasn't fair.

She refused to succumb to the sobs until she heard Danish House's front door close, for fear that Eddie might hear her.

It was dawn when Tromp and the others emerged into the small parade ground of Fort Oranje. Joost Banckert, who'd stormed out before the meeting was properly over, was already barking for the guards at the main gate to open that portal and get out of his way. Dirck Simonszoon glared after him.

"Well, I guess he's pretty pissed off," observed Eddie. "Not like that wasn't clear from the briefing."

Van Walbeeck shrugged. "Give him time. It is a

shock. And while this portends a serious challenge for you, it does for us as well."

Tromp looked at the still-lightening sky. "Yes, it will be a challenge. But most of our advantages remain. I suspect half of Joost's anger is about not being able to gripe about this with anyone. But he is professional; he understands the need for absolute secrecy."

Eddie sighed. "I sure hope he does, because if anyone lets this cat out of the bag, the USE's chief spook—Estuban Miro—will probably send assassins after *me*."

"Well, then he'd better hurry up about it," Mike McCarthy said, "because you're going to be pretty hard to find by this time tomorrow."

Eddie nodded wearily. "Isn't that the truth. And speaking of secrets, I've got to chase down Hugh and Rik and get them moving." He glanced at Maarten. "Are you sure you can spare Evertsen?"

"Yes, Eddie, but it is ironic, don't you think?"

"What do you mean?"

Tromp smiled. "Do you remember why I sent him to Antigua with you?"

Eddie's face was momentarily blank before a crooked grin grew at one corner of his mouth. "Yeah. You wanted to make sure you had a replacement for me."

"And now both of you will be gone. But it is just as I predicted: it is not God who is calling you from us, but John Simpson."

McCarthy frowned. "Except that Simpson *isn't* calling us."

Eddie shrugged. "He doesn't have to. There's only one possible response to this situation."

Mike sighed. "Wish I could disagree with you."

Tromp shook his head. "Let us not waste time with regret. We have made the only sensible decision. And Eddie, I will inform Kees. As it is, you already have too much running around to do before you depart." *To say nothing of bidding farewell to a wife you returned to less than twenty-four hours ago.*

Eddie nodded and headed for the outer gate.

Mike blew his cheeks out with a powerful exhalation. "Well, I guess we've got our work cut out for us. We've got to turn those ships around in a day. Finding the crewmen that are on liberty, and then telling them they've got to report immediately, is going to be a bitch in *all sorts* of ways. We may need to send two-man teams out on those details."

Van Walbeeck nodded. "There is also the matter of the cover story. I will need to go over that with you gentlemen. We must be certain it does not immediately or eventually become self-contradictory, and there are so many details to consider, no one of us can be trusted to see them all." He stared at the closing gate. "I hoped Joost would help us, as well. I just wish he had not had such a falling out with Eddie. I understand his resentment, of course—"

"I don't," said Simonszoon flatly. "It is as Maarten said: Eddie and Mike are doing the only thing they can do. We in the Caribbean may think we have the luxury to be unconcerned, being far away. But we are so distant only because we are at the end of a very long branch, and if the tree dies, it won't be too long before we do, too."

Mike patted the previously untouchable Dirck on the shoulder. "It'll be all right. Joost will come around. Now, what about some schnapps, everyone?"

Van Walbeeck started, glanced at Tromp. "Eh, the admiral never drinks before three in the afternoon." He glanced at his friend. "But perhaps he will make an exception and maybe have a drink with us? Just one?"

"No," Tromp said, trying to smile. "I will have two." *God knows I need them, now.*

Anne Cathrine leaned her head against the back of Danish House's front door. There were too many comings and goings today. Particularly goings.

It had started with Eddie's departure in the middle of the night, but when the sun came up, it got worse. Much worse.

First Eddie had come back. She had hoped that maybe the news that had called him away in the middle of the night would not ultimately call him away for longer. It had been a narrow hope, she'd known that, but when he walked in the front door, she knew. He was leaving. Immediately.

She gathered herself, asked where he had to go.

They had to catch up with the oil shipment that had left for the Netherlands just a week before. Why? Because intelligence indicated that the Spanish might have learned of it, with the intent of sinking it.

So he would be back soon? He couldn't say, but it wasn't just him going. Hugh and Rik were leaving, too. That had brought Sophie and Leonora to their feet.

Anne Cathrine tried not to grow desperate, tried to resist asking the questions that she knew would be deflected by the wall of lies he was having to put up, but she pushed anyway. She did not hate him, but she hated those lies, she hated not being able to know, to be frankly and plainly told, why he was really sailing on such bafflingly short notice. So she pressed him for answers. Would Eddie's squadron really be able to locate and catch up with the oil convoy someplace out in the middle of the Atlantic, and if so, how? He couldn't say. Are three out of the four remaining steam warships really required? Is the Spanish threat really so great? Again, Eddie could not say.

But she stopped short of asking the questions that were most urgent, most penetrating, which were spinning like a fiery potter's wheel, deep in her belly: *Do any of you actually think anyone who knows you, who lives with you, will actually believe this ridiculous story? Or that you are allowed to reveal where you are going and why, but nothing else? Can you truly believe that we will not immediately realize that if that was your actual mission, and your actual destination, you would not be allowed to tell us? And that therefore, you are lying and that when you leave, we will have no idea of where you are actually going and why? Do you think that we are all so stupid and unobservant as that?*

Because if she had asked those questions, she knew what Eddie's reply would—*had to*—be: he couldn't say.

So instead, she just nodded and the silence grew long and gray between them. He reached out and hugged her; she hugged him back, very tight. And then he was gone. And she had stood there, hating the world of armies and ships and spies that made this her reality, as long as she could foresee. It was a world that tore loved ones apart so often and so quickly that, by the time she learned about Leonora's engagement to Rik and Sophie's rather confusing semi-betrothal to Hugh, it was already too late to celebrate them. What should have been two wonderful announcements—and then, her own—had been swept aside by events that were apparently so dire that they could not even be revealed. Because he would not be heading across the Atlantic with almost all of the steamships if the situation there was not terribly dire.

She had still been standing by the door when, no more than two minutes after Eddie left, Sophie strode past her and was out and gone without a word. But she knew where her friend was going: to find Hugh. To learn, as soon as Eddie left, if he knew and could share what Eddie would not. But of course, she, too, already knew the answer to her questions: of course Hugh couldn't say, either.

Not long after, there was a knock at the door; it was Rik Bjelke, who bowed very low and, before Anne Cathrine could even speak, asked if he might have a word alone with Leonora. She waved him past. He took Leonora's hands in his, and led her back to the shelter of the pantry.

Anne Cathrine did not remember sitting down, but she evidently had, because she rose when Sophie rushed into the house, again without speaking. She ran up the stairs, and in two minutes, was running back down, in the dress she had worn to the market-fair dance.

On her way to the door, Sophie stopped and quickly relayed something that Hugh had remarked in passing. When she arrived, he had been busy sending two of his adjutants out trying to locate equipment for the Wild Geese that had been put in storage and needed to be added back to each soldier's kit: cold weather clothing. He was also concerned that many had arrived without any such apparel and if there was any more to be had. Which seemed unlikely given the local climate, a problem exacerbated by the fact that almost half of the mostly German ship's troops were being replaced by members of the Wild Geese.

She and Anne Cathrine exchanged long looks that were visual echoes of the doubts and thoughts they could read in each other's minds. Yes, the oil would arrive in Europe—probably the Netherlands—just as February was blowing into March, but would they *all* need cold winter gear? It was not uncommon for watch personnel to wear it on deck, but typically, both for reasons of expense and storage, such clothing tended to be shared, and so, maybe twenty sets of cold weather gear were required, at most. And why had almost half the regular ship's troops been replaced by members of the elite Wild Geese? And beyond that, why were their two most senior and seasoned commanders, Hugh and O'Rourke, traveling to oversee them during what was typically the least hazardous or challenging of all duties: deck security for a convoy isolated in the middle of the Atlantic?

The cold weather gear was still a mystery, but given recent news, the secret departure of three steam warships provided with the best boarding troops available indicated the expectation of close, sustained naval action. And the only place in the Old World where recent events made that not only possible but likely was in the Mediterranean. And specifically, wherever the Ottomans might be sending a battle fleet or supply convoy.

Anne Cathrine had still been puzzling through that when Rik bowed his way hastily past and ran into the street the way officers do when they are late for—well, whatever they were late for. And so, wondering when all the coming and going would stop, Anne Cathrine had leaned her heavy, whirling head against the door.

She heard movement behind her; Leonora had emerged from the pantry, was sinking into one of the seats at their table in the sitting room. As Anne Cathrine walked slowly toward her sister, she detected that the fourteen-year-old girl's shoulders were trembling.

"He is very clever," Leonora seemed to tell the far wall, without bothering to name Rik as her subject. "He is very skilled. He is very competent. He has been in many battles and has never even been wounded." She looked up furtively at Anne Cathrine; her eyes were red. "Tell me that it is logical for me to expect the same outcome. Please."

Anne Cathrine sought to find a comforting response that was not a lie, but she could not find any words to suit that purpose.

Leonora became very still, stopped quivering; the color drained out of her face as tears ran out of her eyes. "No. I am glad you did not say anything. Because I know better. This is war. The only rule is that the die is being cast at every horrible minute, so that no prior outcome bears upon the next. The only rule is uncertainty." She put her head down and wept harder than Anne Cathrine had ever heard, even when she had been a very little girl. Anne rested her hand on the back of her head and wished her sister's insights weren't so terribly, terribly accurate.

Like this one.

Anne Cathrine stood on the walls of Fort Oranje, watching as the three steamships weighed anchor, following two conventional vessels that were going ahead of them to Antigua, where they could be fully provisioned and readied for their voyage. Far off, well down the wharf, two female silhouettes, one tall and one of less than average height, were holding each other as the ships' sails unfurled into the wind and started moving away at increasing speed. Anne Cathrine wished she was on the wharf with Sophie and Leonora, but it hadn't been safe. They had gone to say final farewells to Hugh and Rik. And Eddie, too. Which was why Anne Cathrine had said her goodbyes to her husband in private at Danish House. Not because of any intimate exchange she envisioned, either conversational or conjugal, but because she feared that her resolve might fail and she would blurt out what she had been waiting to share with him on this very day. And so, by now keeping that secret, she was resolved to keep him safe.

Because she remembered all too well the misery in Sophie's voice as she lamented the way she had sent Hugh off to war: with his heart broken and thoughts elsewhere when all his attention had to be focused on surviving, on winning. Because it was axiomatic that those who triumphed were far more likely to return than those who lost; the side which flees usually dies in droves.

So now Eddie must have only that, only victory, on his mind if he was to have the best chance of coming home to her. And to the child he did not know she was carrying.

There was little doubt of her pregnancy, anymore. Brandão had followed the signs that had arisen just four weeks after the fleet had sailed to confront the

Spanish at St. Maarten. Indeed, although no one else would notice yet, she was starting to show. She had wanted to shout it out and dance around Danish House with Leonora and Sophie and, in so doing, chase away the fear that had plagued her for half a year: that she was barren. That despite almost infinite opportunities over the course of nearly two years of blissful and amorous marriage, she still had not conceived.

But in wanting to wait for just the right moment to tell Eddie, she had waited half a day too long. And it felt like shattered glass in her gullet that now, for all their sakes, it was best she kept it a secret. She had never kept anything from Eddie and, of all things, he would so very much want to know this.

But a voice within her kept shouting—whether out of fear or prudence, she could not tell: *but he* must *return to me. So he must have* all *his focus on the coming battles. I will not let him be distracted by worries about me, about this birth, about our child.*

And he might not understand my choice to keep that secret, when he learns. Maybe he never will. But it is better that we spend decades contending over a choice I made than it is that I should be made a widow and that Eddie—my good, darling, clever Eddie—should be cold in the ground or at the bottom of the sea.

No, not that, she had decided, and now affirmed once again as his ship sailed beyond the headland of the bay and faded from sight.

Anything but that.

Chapter 72

St. John's Harbor, Antigua

As soon as the squadron arrived in St. John's Harbor, Eddie summoned Hugh, Rik, Kees Evertsen, and Karl Klemm. They arrived almost simultaneously, so he was able to usher them into *Intrepid*'s decidedly compact "great cabin" all at once. He gestured them to seats, asked if they wanted anything other than the water in the pewter pitcher at the center of the table. They demurred, very much focused on him. Which was totally understandable. Called away from their lives with no warning, and an obviously bogus explanation, they had come expecting to finally be clued in to what was actually going on.

Eddie didn't waste any time doing exactly that. He turned to Klemm. "Karl, you have twenty-four hours to ask me and Lieutenant Evertsen everything that goes on here at Antigua and all the projects currently in process. You can interrupt whatever I'm doing to get the explanations you need."

"Yes, sir. Thank you, sir. But sir . . . may I ask why?"

"Because as of this moment, and until further notice, this is your duty station."

He frowned. "Very well."

"I don't think you understand. Starting sometime tomorrow, you are going to begin doing my job, but without the rank. Mostly, I suspect you'll be reporting to Mike McCarthy, but that may change. The folks back here are going to be calling those shots for the foreseeable future."

"What? Why? Where will you be?"

Eddie faced the room. "Heading across the Atlantic with all three ships. And with all three of the officers who are staring at me like owls, right now. Rik, you're going to be acting XO of *Relentless*. Kees, you'll be in the same role on *Harrier*. Lord O'Donnell—"

"You have a terrible memory, Eddie; my name is 'Hugh.'" But the Irishman's smile was rueful. "I've a glimmering now of why so many of the German ship's troops were given liberty this morning and their billets were filled with my lads."

Eddie smiled. With Rik and Hugh along, there was a decent chance he wouldn't wig out before this mission was all over. "Yes. Lor—Hugh, you are senior officer in charge of all infantry on board these three ships."

"And why, might I ask, is it that you felt it needful to bring so many of my Wild Geese along?"

"Because I suspect we will either be boarding enemy ships or being boarded by them."

"And just where might that be happening, do you suppose?"

Eddie looked at Karl. "Larry Quinn assured me that you can keep a secret better than anyone he knows. Including me. Is that true?"

"I have never revealed one yet, sir."

"Okay, then you can stay for this. Larry's going to have to bring you up to speed on the operational changes here, anyway." He looked at the others. "Although we will rendezvous with the oilers, the convoy protection mission is a cover story. Didn't fool our families, but it's legitimate enough that our enemies should buy it for a while. In actuality, we're heading into the Mediterranean."

"Ah," murmured Hugh, "the Turks. Only a matter of time, given the sad business about Vienna."

"But, sir . . ." Rik began.

"Rik, I'll brief you all on the details once we are underway. Part of the reason is OPSEC. We will also be traveling under strict radio silence, barring the need to send distress signals."

"Admiral Simpson's orders?" Kees wondered.

"Admiral Simpson doesn't know we're coming."

"What?" the three officers asked. Karl seemed entirely unsurprised.

"There's a saying John Simpson likes to repeat," Eddie explained, "that is now going to bite him in the butt. 'Better to ask forgiveness than to ask permission.' That's what's happening here. And for good reasons. Which, as I said, I'll explain when we are underway. From this point forward, all the information we get from the outside world will be gained by monitoring routine transatlantic traffic from home, *not* from Europe. We'll be scanning for embedded codes that will give us a basic picture of what's going on both ahead of us and behind us."

Rik frowned. "Why just basic codes? Why not more complete data?"

Karl coughed politely. "If I may, Lieutenant Bjelke, I suspect it is for the same reason we on *Courser* had

blind codes for narrowly defined conditions and operations, such as Contingency: Class Reunion. All those
codes told us was that we were needed back home and
to which of the one hundred grid blocks we were to
plot a course. Although imprecise, it obviates the need
for cyphers. Which is crucial, since the use of cyphers
increases the likelihood of decryption."

Kees leaned forward. "How so?"

"Cyphers are strings of different signals. The longer
the message, the more individual signals you send. The
more you send, the more opportunities there are to
decode the message they comprise. Patterns emerge,
even if they are buried.

"But with a blind code, particularly if it has a one-
to-one correspondence—that is, each signal is, in effect,
a whole message that will only be used once—then
there is no way for anyone else to know what it means."
He looked at Eddie. "I suspect this is what you have
arranged."

"Yes."

"And I suspect that you have employed this because
Admiral Simpson has either confirmed or strongly suspects that the security of his communications has been
compromised."

"Uh, correct."

"And that therefore, informing him of this mission
could lead to its interception or at least undercut its
potential to achieve tactically significant surprise."

How the heck—? "That is, uh . . . fundamentally
accurate."

"This further indicates why the blind codes must come
from The Quill Array rather than Europe. Obviously,
USE counterintelligence in Europe has not identified

the source or level at which its communications has been compromised. Consequently, its uncompromised New World personnel will be tasked to compile intelligence estimates from routine news and hints contained in personal and proprietary messages."

Wow! "Okay, Karl: stop. Right now." *My God, how does he do that?* Eddie leaned back. "I am neither going to confirm nor deny that string of conjectures. And you are going to forget you ever had *any* of those thoughts. Got it?"

"Perfectly clear, Commodore."

"Being a very simple man," Hugh said with a smile, "I have only a very simple question: why are we heading back, Eddie?"

Eddie felt his stomach grow cold. "Because the only reason Admiral Simpson would be moving the main fleet from the Baltic to the Med is because some big—*really* big—operation will be getting underway soon. That's pretty much what he sent in the message we received at 0130 this morning. And because his comms are compromised, he has no way of telling us and we have no way of learning exactly what's happening. But there's only one thing I can think of that makes sense."

"The Ottomans," said Hugh. "In some way, shape or form."

"Yup," Eddie sighed, "although I've got one hypothesis about the form." He leaned forward on his elbows. "Without breaching security, I can tell you that there was *no* lead-up to this. And the tone of Simpson's message was not of a man about to start a long-anticipated offensive. It sounded like a man who has to put out a fire. With whatever he has on hand."

"But then why wouldn't Simpson have summoned you?" asked Kees.

Eddie shrugged. "Well, Kees, until a few days ago, he'd have been in the same situation as Oranjestad: totally in the dark as to whether or not we survived that hurricane. Until eighteen hours ago, he still didn't have a report on whether we came home with all our hulls. And he doesn't have the report on ship readiness either, because it's still forty-eight hours away from being compiled."

Rik nodded slowly. "So since Admiral Simpson had no way of knowing how many ships were left, in what condition, or how long until they'd be ready, he had to consider the possibility that we were unable to help. Or that we were barely holding on, particularly after having lost *Resolve*."

Eddie shrugged. "That's what I'm thinking, and now, we can't update him, given the compromised comms."

"Still," O'Donnell observed with a nod, "he was wily enough to include all the information you need to create a logical progression of imperatives."

I keep forgetting Hugh went to college, killed it, and got a degree. Probably in classic rhetoric, from the sound of it. "That is correct. And while those of us who saw the message can't be certain about the situational dominos or how they'll fall, I don't think this model could be too far off.

"First, some of you have seen the classified traffic about the Ottoman attack, so I think we can be pretty sure who the enemy is going to be in the Med. Which means, in turn, that Admiral Simpson is going to need all the help he can get, particularly if he's rushing to put out a fire rather than mounting a planned operation. Either way, nobody in their right mind takes the Ottomans lightly. And let's not forget that—"

Eddie began counting off on his fingers. "One: if

the USE loses or is crippled in a war, that's probably the end of everything we've achieved here. Without that support, we're dead in eighteen months, tops.

"Two: Admiral Simpson's message is his necessarily oblique way of giving us a heads-up about the very real possibility of that happening.

"Three: the only meaningful assets we can get in theater quickly, and that are strong enough to be of significant help, are our steam warships.

"Four: three ships is not a lot, so we have to amplify their potential tactical impact. The only way we can do that is by preserving the element of surprise. Which means traveling silently and secretly so that no one—not even Simpson—knows we're coming."

There were nods all around the table.

"We need a name," Rik blurted out. "For this task force, I mean."

"I'm open to suggestions."

"In your up-time literature," Karl commented, "it seems that such code names are usually both enigmatic yet meaningful in retrospect. Is this true?"

Eddie shrugged. "Uh . . . I guess?"

"Well then, as you mean this formation to turn the tide, I suggest 'inflection point.'"

Spoken like a true math nerd. "That has a nice ring to it, Karl . . . but isn't it a bit *too* obvious?"

Klemm frowned, thinking.

Hugh smiled. "Now, there *is* the surprise aspect as well."

Rik nodded. "Ah! So something more like, Unexpected Inflection?"

Hugh shook his head, glanced at Eddie. "Actually, I was thinking how very surprised Admiral Simpson is going to be when his protégé shows up to lend a needed hand."

"Protégé?" Eddie scoffed. "Given that I'm probably doing the last thing he wanted me to do, I'm hardly going to be any kind of prize pupil or golden child. More like a prodigal son."

Hugh just grinned and nodded. Then Rik did as well. Even Kees joined in.

Karl was frowning even more deeply than before. "Commodore, why are they all smiling that way? It is most disturbing."

Eddie shrugged. "Beats me, Karl. Gentlemen?"

Hugh seemed ready to laugh. "And you didn't even hear yourself name your own task force, just then? Now an' it's sure there's no using anything else!"

Rik leaned forward. "Commodore: 'Prodigal Inflection.'"

"Oh," said Eddie. "Yeah, sure. I guess." Those cool-sounding code names always sounded a bit too melodramatic to him. "Rik, I'd like you to work as senior staff officer for uh, Task Force Prodigal Inflection. Kees, I want you to be his second. Under different circumstances, I'd make sure at least one of you was on my flagship, but I need one senior naval officer who's aware of our actual mission on every hull. So, first order of business is to get a schedule for the next twenty-four hours. That means we set preparation tasks, benchmarks, and target times for completion. We also need to plot a course, and no, Karl, you can't help; you've got to learn your new job here before we leave. Now: questions?"

"Just one," Evertsen replied. "Choosing a course in this situation may mean having to balance speed against other factors, such as prevailing storm paths and avoiding the places where we are more likely to encounter other ships. What is the priority, sir?"

Eddie didn't have to think. "Speed."

"I see. So when is the latest you feel it acceptable to enter the Mediterranean, Commodore?"

Eddie Cantrell sighed. "Yesterday, Kees. Yesterday. Now let's get to work."

Cast of Characters

Anne Cathrine – Oldest daughter of Christian IV; "king's daughter," not "princess," because she is not in the line of succession

Banckert, Adriaen – Dutch naval officer

Banckert, Joost – Vice admiral of the Dutch Fleet

Bjelke, Henrik – Lieutenant, Norwegian nobleman

Brandão, Ambrósio – Sephardic physician

Cantrell, Eddie – Commodore and senior officer presently of the USE Navy

Carpentiere, Servatius – Councilor of St. Eustatia

Chaffin, Mason – Up-timer, in charge of Jennings Oil Field, Louisiana

Christian IV – King of Denmark

Corselles, Pieter – Lieutenant governor of Oranjestad

d'Esnambuc, sieur Pierre Bélain – Adventurer, ex-governor of French St. Christopher

de Bruyne, Jehan – Councilor of St. Eustatia

de Castellar y Mantilla, Gregorio – Spanish captain

de Contreras, Alonso – Spanish captain

de Covilla, Eugenio – Spanish captain

de Curco y San Joan de Olacabal, Antonio – Spanish admiral of La Flota

de Irarraga, Juan – Spanish captain

de la Plaza Equiluz, Antonio – Spanish captain

de Murga y Ortiz de Orué, Francisco – Governor of Cartagena Berrio

de Ruyter (Adriaenszoon), Michiel – Dutch lieutenant

de Somovilla Tejada, Juan – Spanish lieutenant; field engineer

Álvarez De Toledo, Fadrique – Spanish admiral

de Viamonte y Navarra, Juan Bitrian – Captain-general of Hispaniola and Santo Domingo

Diego (de Los Reyes) – Ex-pirate

Evertsen, Cornelis ("Kees") – Dutch lieutenant

Floriszoon, Pieter – Dutch captain

Gallagher, Neal – Lieutenant, Wild Geese

Gallardo, Manrique – Spanish captain and engineer

Garrett, Jennifer – Up-timer, Louisiana oil surveyor

Haet, Jan – Councilor of St. Eustatia

Hargault, Marcel – French engineer; balloon designer

Hart, Morgan – Up-timer, Louisiana rig chief

Hyarima – Nepoia cacique

Jol, Cornelis ("Houtebeen Peg Leg") – Dutch admiral

Klemm, Karl – Technical expert and oil prospector, assistant to Larry Quinn

Koudsi, Ann – Oil drilling expert

Leonora – "King's daughter" of King Christian, sister of Anne Cathrine

McCarthy, Jr., Mike – Up-timer, technical instructor

Mulryan, Tearlach – Ensign, Wild Geese

Mund, Edel – Widow of Pros Mund

Musen, Hans – Councilor of St. Eustatia

O'Bannon, Kevin – Major, Wild Geese

O'Donnell, Hugh Albert – Earl of Tyrconnell, colonel of the Wild Geese

O'Rourke, Aodh – Aide-de-camp to Hugh O'Donnell; senior sergeant of the Wild Geese

Pudsey, Cuthbert – English mercenary in Dutch service

Quinn, Larry – Major, USE Army, CO of Louisiana special project forces

Rantzau, Sophie – Danish noblewoman

Rohrbach, Ulrich – Oil drilling foreman

Sehested, Hannibal – Danish nobleman; agent of King Christian

Serooskereken, Philip ("Phipps") – Councilor of St. Eustatia

Simonszoon, Dirck – Dutch captain

Stirke, Timothy – Bermudan ship captain

Svantner, Arne – Lieutenant, XO of *Intrepid*

Touman – Kalinago cacique

Tromp, Maarten – Admiral of the Dutch fleet

Tulak – Ishak chieftain

van Walbeeck, Jan – Governor of St. Eustatia

van Holst, Hjalmar – Dutch captain

Glossary of Terms

Ship types

Ship designs and designations were not standardized in the early seventeenth century. The definitions that follow are therefore approximations which are generally accurate but from which any particular ship might deviate to one extent or another.

By the period covered in this book (1636–7), up-time influence upon down-time naval architecture begins to complicate some of these terms further. For instance, the Spanish fragata *was originally a smaller square-rigged whip with the same overall lines as the galleon. However, in this book, just as the Dutch and the USE have begun to launch true "frigates" with much different lines and hull shapes, the Spanish (and other powers) have begun to make similar changes. This means that sometimes the correspondence between these terms in actual history, and what they mean when encountered here, may have begun to diverge significantly.*

Barca-longa: A two- and sometimes three-masted lugger, a vessel using a lugsail, which is a modified version of a square sail. Often used as fishing vessels.

Bark (Barque): A small vessel with three or more masts, the foremasts being square-rigged and the aftermast rigged fore-and-aft.

Fluyt: A Dutch cargo vessel, generally two to three hundred tons, about eighty feet long, and with a distinctive pear shape when viewed fore or aft.

Galleon: A three- or four-masted warship developed from the heavy Carrack cargo ships, but with a longer and lower design. Not usually more than six hundred tons. Typically, the mizzenmast was lateen-rigged.

Galleoncete: A smaller galleon, generally of one hundred to two hundred tons. Many were designed to be able to use oars. New models are more streamlined and do not have provisions for oars.

Jacht: An agile and fast vessel with very shallow draft, originally developed by the Dutch to hunt pirates in the shallow waters of the Low Countries.

Nao: A galleon adapted for cargo-hauling.

Patache:	A light two-masted vessel with a shallow draft, often favored by pirates and privateers.
Piragua:	A one- or two-masted native boat that was also adopted by the Spanish and pirates. It was narrow, often made from the trunk of a tree, and could be sailed or rowed. Commonly for a crew of six to thirty.

Gun Types

As with ship types, naval ordnance was not yet standardized in the early seventeenth century. It varied widely over time and between nations. The definitions reflect this extreme diversity.

As with ships, artillery, particularly as used aboard ships, have begun to diverge significantly from historical norms. Greater standardization is occurring, resulting in changes of terminology. Also, whereas guns encountered on ships during this historical period often had similar or identical carriages to their land-based counterparts, distinctions between naval and land versions of the same gun are becoming much more prevalent. However, the heterogeneity of guns among the same type, and of different bore/weight pieces in the same battery, persists.

Cannon:	A "true" cannon is a very large gun which fired a ball of 42 pounds. As naval carriages became more prevalent, however, the term *cannon*

was used for a variety of larger standardized weapons or "pieces," particularly those firing 32-pound and 24-pound balls. Also, as the distinction between naval and land-based guns of the same pedigree grew, it became common in some circles to refer to a naval piece as a "gun," and a land piece as a "cannon."

Carronade: A short-barreled gun firing shot that ranged from 6 to 68 pounds. They were much lighter than cannons firing an equivalent weight of shot, but had much shorter range. Predominantly used as a broadside weapon, it was originally designed specifically for naval combat.

Culverin: More lightly constructed than cannons, guns of this type fired shot from 16 to 22 pounds.

Demi-cannon: A gun-firing shot weighing from 22 to 32 pounds.

Demi-culverin: Slightly larger than a saker, this weapon fired shot from 9 to 16 pounds.

Peterero: Predominantly antipersonnel weapons, petereroes could be any of a number of weapons mounted on the rails or along the gunwales of ships and boats.

Saker: A small carriage-mounted gun, firing shot of eight pounds or less.

Rigging Terms

Fore-and-aft-rigged: A sailing rig consisting mainly of sails that are set along the line of the keel rather than perpendicular to it.

Foremast: The mast nearest the bow of a ship.

Lateen-rigged: A type of fore-and-aft rig in which a triangular sail is suspended on a long yard set at an angle to the mast.

Mainmast: The principal mast of a sailing vessel.

Mizzenmast: The mast aft or next aft of the mainmast.

Square-rigged: A sail and rigging design in which the main sails are carried on horizontal spars that are perpendicular, or square, to the keel of the vessel and to the masts.

Stay: A strong rope or wire supporting a mast.

Yards: The spars holding up sails.

Yardarms: The tips of the yards.

Afterword

Recommended reading order for the 1632 series (aka the Ring of Fire series)

by Eric Flint
June 20, 2019

Whenever someone asks me "what's the right order?" for reading the 1632 series, I'm always tempted to respond: "I have no idea. What's the right order for studying the Thirty Years' War? If you find it, apply that same method to the 1632 series."

However, that would be a bit churlish—and when it comes down to it, authors depend upon the goodwill of their readers. So, as best I can, here goes.

The first book in the series, obviously, is *1632*. That is the foundation novel for the entire series and the only one whose place in the sequence is definitely fixed.

Thereafter, you should read either the anthology titled *Ring of Fire* or the novel *1633*, which I co-authored with David Weber. It really doesn't matter that much which of these two volumes you read first, so long as you read them both before proceeding onward. That said, if I'm pinned against the wall and threatened with bodily harm, I'd recommend that you read *Ring of Fire* before you read *1633*.

That's because *1633* has a sequel which is so closely tied to it that the two volumes almost constitute one single huge novel. So, I suppose you'd do well to read them back-to-back. That sequel is *1634: The Baltic War*, which I also co-authored with David Weber.

Once you've read those four books—to recapitulate, the three novels (*1632*, *1633* and *1634: The Baltic War*) and the *Ring of Fire* anthology—you can now choose one of two major alternative ways of reading the series.

The first way, which I'll call "spinal," is to begin by reading all of the novels in what I will call the main line of the series. As of now, the main line consists of these seven novels:

> *1632*
> *1633* (with David Weber)
> *1634: The Baltic War* (with David Weber)
> *1635: The Eastern Front*
> *1636: The Saxon Uprising*
> *1636: The Ottoman Onslaught*
> *1637: The Polish Maelstrom*

All of these novels except the two I did with David Weber were written by me as the sole author. The next main line novel, whose working title is *1637: The Adriatic Decision*, I will be writing with Chuck Gannon (Dr. Charles E. Gannon, if you want to get formal about it). That novel probably won't come out for a while, however, because there is a novel that has to be written first, in order to lay the basis for it.

I call this the "main line" of the Ring of Fire series for two reasons. First, because it's in these seven novels that I depict most of the major political and military developments which have a tremendous impact on the entire complex of stories. Secondly, because these "main line" volumes focus on certain key characters in the series. Four of them, in particular: Mike Stearns and Rebecca Abrabanel, first and foremost, as well as Gretchen Richter and Jeff Higgins.

The other major alternative way to read the series is what I will call "comprehensive." This approach ignores the special place of the main line novels and simply reads the series as an integral whole—i.e., reading each novel and anthology more or less in chronological sequence. (I'm referring to the chronology of the series itself, not the order in which the books were published. The two are by no means identical.)

The advantage to following the spinal way of reading the series is that it's easier to follow since all of these novels are direct sequels to one another. You don't have to deal with the complexity of reading all the branching stories at the same time. Once you've finished the main line novels, assuming you're enjoying the series enough to want to continue, you can then go back and start reading the other books following the order I've laid out below.

The disadvantage to using the spinal method is that you're going to run into spoilers. Most of the major political and military developments are depicted in the main line novels, but by no means all of them. So if spoilers really bother you, I'd recommend using the comprehensive approach.

All right. From here on, I'll be laying out the

comprehensive approach to the series. If you've decided to follow the spinal method, you can follow this same order of reading by just skipping the books you've already read.

Once you've read *1632*, *Ring of Fire*, *1633*, and *1634: The Baltic War*, you will have a firm grasp of the basic framework of the series. From there, you can go in one of two directions: either read *1634: The Ram Rebellion* or *1634: The Galileo Affair*.

There are advantages and disadvantages either way. *1634: The Ram Rebellion* is an oddball volume, which has some of the characteristics of an anthology and some of the characteristics of a novel. It's perhaps a more challenging book to read than the *Galileo* volume, but it also has the virtue of being more closely tied to the main line books. *Ram Rebellion* is the first of several volumes which basically run parallel with the main line volumes but on what you might call a lower level of narrative. A more positive way of putting that is that these volumes depict the changes produced by the major developments in the main line novels, as those changes are seen by people who are much closer to the ground than the characters who figure so prominently in books like *1632*, *1633*, and *1634: The Baltic War*.

Of course, the distinction is only approximate. There are plenty of characters in the main line novels— Thorsten Engler and Eric Krenz spring immediately to mind—who are every bit as "close to the ground" as any of the characters in *1634: The Ram Rebellion*. And the major characters in the series will often appear in stories outside of the main line.

Whichever book you read first, I do recommend that

you read both of them before you move on to *1634: The Bavarian Crisis*. In a way, that's too bad, because *Bavarian Crisis* is something of a direct sequel to *1634: The Baltic War*. The problem with going immediately from *Baltic War* to *Bavarian Crisis*, however, is that there is a major political development portrayed at length and in great detail in *1634: The Galileo Affair* that antedates the events portrayed in the *Bavarian* story.

Still, you could read any one of those three volumes— to remind you, these are *1634: The Ram Rebellion*, *1634: The Galileo Affair* and *1634: The Bavarian Crisis*—in any order you choose. Just keep in mind that if you read the *Bavarian* book before the other two you will be getting at least one major development out of chronological sequence.

After those three books are read, you should read *1635: A Parcel of Rogues*, which I co-authored with Andrew Dennis. That's one of the two sequels to *1634: The Baltic War*, the other one being *1635: The Eastern Front*. The reason you should read *Parcel of Rogues* at this point is that most of it takes place in the year 1634.

Thereafter, again, it's something of a toss-up between three more volumes: the second *Ring of Fire* anthology and the two novels, *1635: The Cannon Law* and *1635: The Dreeson Incident*. On balance, though, I'd recommend reading them in this order because you'll get more in the way of a chronological sequence:

> *Ring of Fire II*
> *1635: The Cannon Law*
> *1635: The Dreeson Incident*

The time frame involved here is by no means rigidly sequential, and there are plenty of complexities involved. To name just one, my story in the second *Ring of Fire* anthology, the short novel *The Austro-Hungarian Connection*, is simultaneously a sequel to Virginia's story in the same anthology, several stories in various issues of the *Gazette*—as well as my short novel in the first *Ring of Fire* anthology, *The Wallenstein Gambit*.

What can I say? It's a messy world—as is the real one. Still and all, I think the reading order recommended above is certainly as good as any and probably the best.

We come now to Virginia DeMarce's *1635: The Tangled Web*. This collection of interrelated stories runs parallel to many of the episodes in *1635: The Dreeson Incident*. This volume is also where the character of Tata, who figures in *Eastern Front* and *Saxon Uprising*, is first introduced in the series.

You should then backtrack a little and read *1635: The Papal Stakes*, which is the direct sequel to *1635: The Cannon Law*. And you could also read Anette Pedersen's *1635: The Wars for the Rhine*.

You can then go back to the "main line" of the series and read *1635: The Eastern Front* and *1636: The Saxon Uprising*. I strongly recommend reading them back-to-back. These two books were originally intended to be a single novel, which I wound up breaking in half because the story got too long. They read better in tandem.

Then, read *Ring of Fire III*. My story in that volume is directly connected to *1636: The Saxon Uprising* and lays some of the basis for the sequel to that novel,

1636: The Ottoman Onslaught. After that, read *1636: The Kremlin Games*. That novel isn't closely related to any other novel in the series—with the exception of its own sequel—so you can read it almost any time after reading the first few volumes. While you're at it, you may as well read the sequel, *1637: The Volga Rules*. You'll be a little out of sequence with the rest of the series, but it doesn't matter because at this point the Russian story line still largely operates independently.

Thereafter, the series branches out even further and there are several books you should read. I'd recommend the following order, but in truth it doesn't really matter all that much which order you follow in this stretch of the series:

1636: Commander Cantrell in the West Indies picks up on the adventures of Eddie Cantrell following the events depicted in *1634: The Baltic War*.

1636: The Cardinal Virtues depicts the opening of the French Civil War which was also produced by the events related in *The Baltic War* and which has been foreshadowed in a number of stories following that novel. *1636: The Vatican Sanction* picks up the "Italian line" in the series, which follows the adventures of Sharon Nichols and Ruy Sanchez.

Iver Cooper's *1636: Seas of Fortune* takes place in the Far East and in the New World. The portion of it titled "Stretching Out" has a few spoilers to *Commander Cantrell in the West Indies* and vice versa, but nothing too important.

1636: The Devil's Opera takes place in Magdeburg and might have some spoilers if you haven't read *Saxon Uprising*. My co-author on this novel, David Carrico, also has an e-book available titled *1635: Music and*

Murder, which contains stories published in various anthologies that provide much of the background to *The Devil's Opera*.

1636: The Viennese Waltz comes after *Saxon Uprising* in the sense that nothing in it will be spoiled by anything in *Saxon Uprising*, but you might find out Mike's whereabouts early if you read it first. On the other hand, the e-book *1636: The Barbie Consortium* (the authors of which are Gorg Huff and Paula Goodlett) is a direct prequel to *Viennese Waltz* and should be read first if you want to be introduced to the young ladies dancing that very dance.

1636: The Viennese Waltz is also one of the three immediate prequels to the next main line novel in the series, which is *1636: The Ottoman Onslaught*. If you're wondering, the other two immediate prequels are *1636: The Saxon Uprising* and my short novel *Four Days on the Danube*, which was published in *Ring of Fire III*.

The next volumes you should look at are these:

Ring of Fire IV (May 2016). There are a number of stories in this volume written by different authors including David Brin. From the standpoint of the series' reading order, however, probably the most important is my own story *Scarface*. This short novel serves simultaneously as a sequel to *The Papal Stakes* and *The Dreeson Incident*, in that the story depicts the further adventures of Harry Lefferts after *Papal Stakes* and Ron Stone and Missy Jenkins following *The Dreeson Incident*.

Continue on to *1636: The Chronicles of Dr. Gribbleflotz*, by Kerryn Offord and Rick Boatright (August 2016). As with *The Devil's Opera*, this is a story set in the middle of the United States of Europe as it evolves—in this case, relating the adventures of a seventeenth-century scholar—a descendant of the great Paracelsus—who becomes wealthy by translating the fuzzy and erroneous American notions of "chemistry" into the scientific precision of alchemy.

Then you should return to the main line of the series by reading, back-to-back, my two novels *1636: The Ottoman Onslaught* (January 2017) and *1637: The Polish Maelstrom* (March 2019).

Following those two, read two novels that are "outliers," so to speak. Those are *1636: Mission to the Mughals* (April 2017) and *1636: The China Venture*. Keep in mind that the term "outliers" is always subject to modification in the Ring of Fire series. *Right now*, those stories taking place in (respectively) India and China don't have much direct connection to the rest of the series. But it's a small world in fiction just as it is in real life, so you never know what the future might bring.

Finally—using the term very provisionally—read two novels that take place in the New World. The first is *1636: The Atlantic Encounter*, which I wrote with Walter Hunt and which came out in August of this year. And the second is this one, *1637: No Peace Beyond the Line*.

This brings us full circle. You may recall that toward the beginning of this afterword I said that the next main line novel required that another novel be written first. Well, that's the novel you are holding in your hand. Chuck and I will start writing the next main line novel next year, which means it probably won't come out until 2022.

❖   ❖   ❖

That leaves the various issues of the *Gazette*, which are *really* hard to fit into any precise sequence. The truth is, you can read them pretty much any time you choose.

It would be well-nigh impossible for me to provide any usable framework for the ninety-two electronic issues of the magazine, so I will restrict myself simply to the eight volumes of the *Gazette* which have appeared in paper editions. With the caveat that there is plenty of latitude, I'd suggest reading them as follows:

Read *Gazette I* after you've read *1632* and alongside *Ring of Fire*. Read *Gazettes II* and *III* alongside *1633* and *1634: The Baltic War*, whenever you're in the mood for short fiction. Do the same for *Gazette IV*, alongside the next three books in the sequence, *1634: The Ram Rebellion*, *1634: The Galileo Affair* and *1634: The Bavarian Crisis*. Then read *Gazette V* after you've read *Ring of Fire II*, since my story in *Gazette V* is something of a direct sequel to my story in the *Ring of Fire* volume. You can read *Gazette V* alongside *1635: The Cannon Law* and *1635: The Dreeson Incident* whenever you're in the mood for short fiction. *Gazette VI* can be read thereafter, along with the next batch of novels recommended.

I'd recommend reading *Grantville Gazette VII* any time after you've read *1636: The Cardinal Virtues*. And you can read *Grantville Gazette VIII* any time thereafter as well.

And . . . that's it, as of now. There are a lot more volumes coming.

For those of you who dote on lists, here it is. But do keep in mind, when you examine this neatly ordered sequence, that the map is not the territory.